Seeking a Distant Shore

By A.L. Porter

APORTER PUBLISHING
Chicago, Illinois

Manuscript formatting by Kevin Theis, Fort Raphael Publishing Company
Cover graphics by Paul Stroili, Touchstone Graphic Design
Cover photo by A.L. Porter

ISBN (Print): 979-8-89282-142-1

ISBN (eBook): 979-8-89282-143-8

*To my wife, who bore with me through this project,
to my daughter, who was my faithful critic,
to Rev. Kunz, who was my reality check,
and to the Spirit that drove me to attempt this project.*

May I have rest, at last.

Contents

Seeking a Distant Shore

Prologue

It was the Renaissance, though no one knew it by that name. For most Englishmen life was built around old, familiar struggles for survival in the face of plagues, wars, and famine. They met these challenges with the ancient tools of faith, hope, and fortitude. But the world was, in fact, changing — even if the changes were not always welcome.

For the people in this story, it was simply "now." Now there were wars and rumors of wars. Now there were signs on Earth and in Heaven. Now there were plagues and pestilence, soon the end of the world would come . . . Now there was a whole new world to the west, just beyond the Atlantic horizon. Now the world was getting smaller, even as it grew larger. Now, the yoke of oppression could be shaken off. Now, the spirits of rebellion threatened chaos and catastrophe.

As the familiar structures of their world began to fade or crumble, people looked for new ones; as the traditional foundations of truth and faith were shaken, they tried and tested others. The old ways did not yield easily; the new ones were born into strife and bloodshed.

Throughout this turmoil, nearly everyone took it for granted that God was at work in the world and that the meaning of events could only be understood with that in mind. People disagreed — violently — about what God's purpose and will were, but none doubted that God was active in the world; they saw God's hand in every part of their experience.

A modern mind might dismiss such a belief with the observation that people tend to see what they expect to see. That may be true, but then it is also true that people tend to overlook things that they do not expect to see.

It was an age of splendor for the very few, adventure for those willing to risk it, and simmering dissent for those whose eyes were turned to heavenly realms. It was also an age of martyrs . . .

Volume 1: Facing the Fire

Part 1: The Preachers

Norwich, 1531: The Lollards Pit

The bells on the cathedral had just struck ten when the procession left the gate of the Norwich Guildhall. First the sheriff's guard, then the slight figure of Master Thomas Bilney and his friend Dr. Warner, followed by the bishop, the Lord Mayor, and by files of priests and brothers — Grey friars, Black friars, White friars, Austin friars, each in their habit. The guards marched in step, and Bilney, short as he was, matched his cadence to theirs, quite unconsciously. This might have been difficult, but the guard knew better than to inconvenience the bishop and the mayor by walking at a pace that would force them to hurry, or stumble on the cobblestones; they measured their steps accordingly.

People stood along the path of the procession as it turned onto the main street, passed the cathedral, and headed for the Bishops Bridge, just outside the city wall. Some were there for curiosity; a few to jeer or gloat; many more were there to bid farewell to a man they admired. "Little Bilney" they called him — a man who had earned a reputation for piety and kindness. It was said that he ate but one meal a day, so that money for the other meals could be used to feed the poor — and there were plenty of poor to feed. On this day, Bilney had arranged for his friend, Dr. Warner, to distribute alms to the poor among the crowd that lined the street.

Soon enough, they passed out of Norwich altogether, across the Bishop's bridge, to a hollow on the opposite bank of the river. It was an ancient stone quarry, and the sides of the pit formed a kind of amphitheater. Here another crowd had gathered, standing or sitting on the slopes of the hollow. At the bottom of the hollow, in the center of the pit, stood a large wooden post or stake. This was the end of Thomas Bilney's journey.

The hollow had been a place of execution for well over a century; not for hanging felons, or beheading nobles, but particularly for burning people to death. A century previous, a large number of heretic Lollards had met their ends in this place, thus the name — the Lollards Pit.

Bilney approached the stake and noted that the fire was not quite ready. He asked for, and received, permission to address the crowd. "Good people," he began, "I am come hither to die, and born I was to live under that condition, naturally to die again . . ." He recited the Apostle's Creed. He confessed to the crowd that he had once preached at Cambridge after his license had been revoked, an offense, he said, that he hoped that God would not judge him too harshly for.

Some were there expecting to hear a recantation from Bilney. He offered none. Some thought he might blame his impending death on the deeds of others. He did not. Turning to the stake, he knelt to pray on a ledge at the base, which he later would stand on, and prayed.

He stood and turned to the guards, asking if they were ready. They were. Bilney took off his outer garments and stepped up onto the ledge (so that the crowd would be able to see better), with his back to the stake. The guards passed a chain around his torso and stapled it to the backside of the stake, to hold him in place. His friend Dr. Warner approached him for a last few words, then left sobbing.

A delegation of friars and other churchmen approached him with a request. "The people," they said, were "persuaded" that they were the cause of his death, and might retaliate by withholding the alms on which the friars depended for their daily sustenance. Would Bilney do them "charity," so that "charity" would not be denied them? Bilney addressed the crowd one last time — ". . . never be the worse to these men for my sake as though they should be the authors of my death; it was not they."

The guards piled reeds and faggots — bundles of firewood — around Bilney, and set fire to the pile — the reeds would catch first, and then, when the fire was hot enough, the wood would catch also. The reeds flared up, and the flames crept closer and closer to Thomas Bilney . . .

Until a gust of wind blew into the pit, and the flames retreated. The wind faded, and the fire advanced. Another gust, and the flames retreated again. The wind faded again, and the flames advanced. Yet a third gust, and the flames retreated again. Finally, the wind calmed, and the flames advanced again. Some heard Bilney cry out, "Jesus!" Others said it was "Credo!"

When the guards were sure he was dead, one of them thrust his halberd into the back of the stake and pried loose the staple, so that the chain was loosened and Bilney's body fell forward into the flames. Then more wood was piled on to complete his immolation.

The crowd dispersed as the flames died down. The ashes would be thrown into the river — heretics are not buried in churchyards. Other burnings would be more famously remembered, but Bilney's was a spark that would spread and would consume many, many more.

Cambridge, 1510: A World of Possibility

Thomas Bilney was not burned for heresy because he had once preached a sermon without a preaching license. That offense might warrant a fine or even excommunication, but not a burning.

Thomas Bilney was a heretic. He came by his heresy honestly enough — he read his Bible, as so many heretics do; and this got him into trouble, as Bible reading will. Bilney's particular station in life made his heresy dangerous. As a scholar, his opinions carried weight and could influence many other minds, especially at Cambridge, a training ground for the nation's future leaders. As a licensed preacher, he could spread his opinions to broad audiences — people who might otherwise remain ignorant of biblical teaching, and thus, compliant and obedient to the religious authorities.

The conflict that Bilney got swept up in was more than a century old, in England. A priest named John Wycliffe had undertaken to translate the Latin Vulgate Bible into English. He attracted a large number of followers, who helped him make copies of his Bible, and disseminate them. Wycliffe also trained laymen as preachers and sent them out to spread his message. The message was unwelcome to the established church. "Lollards," as they came to be called, taught noxious ideas, such as insisting that the ecclesiastical authority must refrain from involvement in secular political affairs — no churchmen should participate in government, that practices such as confession, pilgrimages, and veneration of relics are blasphemous or idolatrous. They rejected the doctrine of transubstantiation, the requirement for clerical celibacy, prayers for the dead — the list of objections was long.

It did not take long for the established church to declare these views heretical.

Soon after, the government was enlisted to assist in suppressing the movement. In 1410, the first Lollard heretic was burned alive at a place called Smithfield, just outside the walls of the city of London. Soon, there were many more. The movement was never completely suppressed; it was forced to move "underground." The church of Bilney's day had to be ever vigilant against the threat of "Lollard" ideas, and the persistent appearance of new copies of their English Bible.

Bilney was born in 1495, just ten years after Richard III died at the battle of Bosworth field, and was supplanted by Henry Tudor, ending decades of civil war. Henry Tudor was crowned Henry VII and ruled throughout Bilney's youth. England was grateful for some decades of peace. A few years later, a Genoese navigator named Cristoforo Colombo persuaded the King of Spain to pay him to sail across the Atlantic to India, which he found to be populated by — Indians, what else? Henry VII sponsored an Italian navigator of his own, Giovanni Caboto, to make his own voyage across the Atlantic, in search of China, when Bilney was still just thirteen years old. Caboto did not find China, but he did find "new found land," and even better, an ocean teeming with cod fish, which turned into a vigorous and profitable industry for English, French, and Portuguese fishermen. (Some said that Bristol fishermen had been visiting these grounds for decades already and that Caboto had simply spilled a well-kept secret. Fishermen are known to tell stories about secret fishing spots and such — take it for what it's worth.)

It took several years for the Spanish to discover that some of the "Indians" were civilized, and a few decades for them to destroy those civilizations and subjugate their peoples. They also found gold and silver in large quantities, which made Spain, for a while, the wealthiest and most powerful kingdom in Europe.

Henry VII won his crown at Bosworth Field as a combatant — a full suit of armor, astride a war horse, with a sword in hand. He was to defend his claim at the battle of Stokes two years later in the same fashion, and after that, never again. Improvements in firearms and Spanish innovations in infantry tactics soon made knights in medieval armor better targets than combatants — other men might go into battle that way, but not a king.

In consequence, the power of the nobility began to wane. The titles still existed, and large landholdings were still a basis of wealth for the noble families, but there were other pathways to power and wealth. One was through the wealth of commerce, and another was through service to the king, particularly as lawyers or clerics. Both these paths ran through the universities. Many noble families recognized this and sent their sons to Cambridge and Oxford. Ambitious middle-class families did the same, and the sons of butchers, mercers, or blacksmiths could compete with the sons of knights and nobles in the academic world and hope, with luck, to rise to positions of wealth and power exceeding their aristocratic classmates.

Henry VII was king until 1509, Bilney's 14th year. Upon his death, he was succeeded by his son, known to history as Henry VIII. Henry VIII continued his father's policies in choosing and rewarding his advisors and administrators based on their competence rather than their bloodlines. There were still positions for aristocrats, of course, but men whose chief qualifications were in their pedigree might not be as loyal as those whose station depended entirely on their King's favor.

The Old-time Religion

The religion of Bilney's youth was the product of centuries of tradition and experience. The fundamental condition of mankind was sin, which led inevitably to an eternity in Hell. That condition, and its consequence, could be remedied only by the atoning death of Christ. Men and women who put their faith in Christ could be delivered from sin and earn an eternity in Heaven, instead of Hell. The Church was the means of this redemptive work, through the spiritual power of seven sacraments — Baptism, Confirmation, Eucharist, Penance, Anointing of the Sick, Holy Orders, and Matrimony. Sacraments were divided into three categories: initiation, healing, and service.

Baptism was the first sacrament that most people received, usually a few days after their birth. It started the new person on the path to salvation, and none of the other sacraments were available until a person had been baptized. So powerful was the grace received by this sacrament that it practically guaranteed an eternity in heaven, unless for some reason a person renounced their faith. Confirmation was administered after a person had been instructed in the Catechism — the basic doctrines of the Church. After Confirmation, a believer was entitled to receive the Eucharist — quite literally the body and blood of Jesus Christ, as the bread and wine were "transubstantiated" — miraculously changed from ordinary substances to holy ones. Eating these substances completed the initiation of a believer into the Kingdom of God. It also had power to cleanse the soul and prepare it for eternal life in Heaven.

Penance was the first of the "healing" sacraments. Believers could confess their sins to a priest, and, if truly repentant, could receive absolution. Ordinarily, some act of penance was required to complete the process, often involving repairing the injury done to others by the sin; it was also thought to deter repeat offenses.

Anointing of the Sick was a sacrament that could aid a person's physical recovery from illness, or when administered just before a person's death (called "Extreme Unction"), could prepare an individual for eternal life in Heaven. This was important because it was also believed that any unconfessed sins, any failure of contrition or penance, would require that the soul be "purged" before it could enter Heaven. The place for this process was called "Purgatory," and it was conceived to be a place of suffering for the soul. The worse condition the soul was in, the longer it stayed in Purgatory.

This last point was critical to the mission of the Church in Bilney's time. Just as many of the dead were believed to be in Purgatory at any time, it was possible for their sufferings to be eased (or the purification process accelerated) by acts of piety by living persons on their behalf. Relatives of the dead could pray for them, and employ others to pray for them; giving alms to the poor, or to the church on behalf of the poor, was considered to be effective. Paying for a mass to be conducted on the deceased's behalf was particularly effective, though not everyone could afford to do so. For the really wealthy, a bequest of land or money to the church was most effective of all. Over time, a significant portion of the Church's revenue, not to mention her large land holdings, came from providing these services.

Another asset that the Church was believed to have was a "treasury of merit," an accumulation of spiritual merit composed of the "infinite merits of Christ" and the "abundant merits" of the saints. Portions of this merit could be applied to reduce the severity of a penance for the living or the condition of souls in purgatory. Some church officials began to sell "indulgences" based on this treasury. They collected a great deal of money, but the practice was widely criticized for the appearance of corruption. There was a lot of trouble over it in Germany.

The supposed merit of the saints had much to do with the practice of praying to the saints for intercession with God, or even for supernatural assistance. Many believers needed more than words to feel a connection to the spiritual world. Images of saints were present in most places of worship. The ritual of praying before the Saint's image and lighting candles was widespread. Church officials were careful to insist that no worship of the images should ever take place, but it was difficult to know how fine a distinction the parishioners were making as they knelt before them. Some churches also had relics — mementos of a departed saint's life. They might be an item of clothing or even a body part. Educated people did not believe that the relics had any intrinsic spiritual power, but for many common people, they were another, possibly better, conduit to the blessings of God.

Indeed, there was a wide gap between the rhetoric of university scholars, discoursing the fine points of theology in Latin, and the typical English parishioner, whose only experience of the Latin language was in hearing the Mass each week. While Bibles could only be read in Latin, confession was in English.

Matrimony was a sacrament of service. It was the sacrament by which the majority of believers were to live their adult lives. The requirements for a valid marriage included that both parties be competent to take the vows, and do so of their free will (forced marriages were not considered valid). It was not merely a contract between two people or two families. The sacrament of marriage was said to be administered by a man and wife to each other — distinct from other sacraments. It was based on a lifelong vow, and was therefore indissoluble, while both parties were living.

Holy Orders was the other sacrament of service. It was reserved for the legions of monks, nuns, priests, deacons, friars, bishops, and other clergy. Matrimony was the sacrament denied to them, though it had not always been so. Parish priests had been permitted to marry through much of the history of the Church. Experience had shown that the twin obligations of Matrimony and Holy Orders led to conflicts of loyalty among the parish priests, and in 1139, a church Council declared that priests must be celibate. This was not universally embraced at first, and in most of Europe, there were priests who maintained secret families. As for mistresses? Bishops, cardinals, and even a few popes had maintained such relationships and fathered illegitimate children. For the laity, these relationships were scandalous, undermining the reputation of the Church. Soon, these sacraments would all come under attack, and the foundations of the ecclesiastical establishment would be shaken. Thomas Bilney was shaking them.

Cambridge 1524: Little Germany

Thomas Bilney was from a village in Norfolk and was admitted to Cambridge at the age of fifteen. At Cambridge, he earned a degree in Canon Law and was awarded a faculty fellowship. In 1519 he was ordained a priest.

At Cambridge, he met a generation of rising and influential churchmen. It was a time of ferment at the university. A torrent of controversial ideas was flooding the university from abroad, amplified by the printing presses that were springing up in every city. Books and tracts and confessions were more plentiful (and cheaper) than ever before. Martin Luther's call for reform had thrown Europe into turmoil, the stuff that scholars loved to discuss and debate — in their chambers, and especially in taverns like the White Horse Inn, where Bilney and others earned the name "Little Germany" for their preoccupation with Luther's ideas. It is said that the group included men like Thomas Cranmer (future archbishop of Canterbury), Nicholas Ridley (future bishop and martyr), Hugh Latimer (future bishop, royal chaplain, and martyr), William Tyndale (future Bible translator and martyr), Myles Coverdale (future Bible translator), Matthew Parker (future archbishop of Canterbury), Stephen Gardiner (future bishop and chancellor), John Rogers (Bible translator and martyr), Nicholas Shaxton (future bishop), Robert Barnes (martyr), John Frith (martyr), Richard Bayfield (martyr), Thomas Benet (martyr), and Thomas Arthur. These were the sort of men whose careers would be made in the new meritocracy.

It was they who called him "Little Bilney" — a man of small stature and, truthfully, limited prospects in a place that was grooming a generation of bishops, archbishops, and England's ruling elite. But his learning gave him expectations of stable employment and even prosperity, and there were men who had leveraged such learning into careers of fame, wealth, and power. At thirty-four years old, he was at the threshold of a career: respected by his colleagues, admired for his character. It was not enough for Little Bilney. He found the sophistication of the scholastic traditions at Cambridge abstract and disconnected from the world. As a priest, he found the actual behavior of his fellows and their superiors to be riddled with corruption, greed, and self-interest.

In 1520, he obtained a copy of Erasmus' recent translation of the New Testament. It was a "diglot" translation in both Latin and Greek. In his Latin translation, Erasmus had dared to point out some questionable translations in the standard Latin "vulgate" translation that was the only legal "Bible" allowed by English law. Erasmus' Latin translation was supported by the Greek text that was printed side-by-side with the Latin. Although the book was technically illegal to own, Bilney knew where to get a copy (books of all sorts were smuggled in from across the North Sea), and knew enough not to publicize his acquisition.

At first reading, Bilney was intrigued by the style of Erasmus' translation (the Vulgate was more than one thousand years old, and Latin had changed over the centuries, as all languages do). But then, the text began to touch him on a more intimate level. He began to read the book for how it made him *feel*. As he later recalled, he was reading the first epistle to Timothy, when *"immediately I felt a marvelous comfort and quietness, insomuch as my bruised bones lept for joy . . . After this, the Scripture began to be more pleasant unto me than the honey or the honeycomb; wherein I learned that all my labours, my fasting, and watching, all the redemption of masses and pardons, being done without truth in Christ, who alone saveth his people from their sins; these I say, I learned to be nothing else but even, as St. Augustine saith, a hasty and swift running out of the right way."*

Had Bilney contented himself with the newfound pleasure of reading his New Testament in private, his life could have been long and unremarkable. But he shared his experience with others, especially in "Little Germany." Many others were coming round to his emerging convictions that veneration of saints and relics and pilgrimages were not merely extraneous to the Christian faith; they were distractions to a believer who truly sought a life that was pleasing to God and should be actively discouraged. Within the walls of the university, such ideas could be vigorously presented and debated, without much interference from the outside world. Cambridge, like other universities, would jealously defend the ancient prerogatives of academic "freedom," and if any constraint were imposed, it would be most likely to come from the authorities of the colleges themselves.

And debates there were. Plenty of scholars were willing to defend the status quo and reject the Lutheran teachings, as well as the older Lollard ideas. One such was Hugh Latimer. Bilney dared to convert Latimer to his views by asking Latimer to hear his "confession." Bilney's risk of exposure was somewhat mitigated by this since the seal of confession would protect anything he said from disclosure to anyone else. The "confession" lasted long enough to change Latimer's mind completely, and he joined the ranks of the dissidents. Others, like Stephen Gardiner, would not be moved.

In 1525, Bilney was granted a license to preach in the Diocese of Ely, which included London. Most parish priests in England were prohibited by law from preaching to their congregations, unless licensed by their local bishop, as a means of suppressing "Lollard" preachers, and other dissident voices. The majority of English parishioners attended services that were conducted almost entirely in Latin; little, if any of it was in their native language. Licensed preachers, on the other hand, preached in English, and were much in demand, and a popular preacher could make his living in this way. Bilney and his friend Thomas Arthur were both licensed to preach in the Diocese of Ely. They began to draw crowds as they preached — sometimes indoors, sometimes outside. Bilney's message was influenced by his reading of the New Testament — he advised his listeners that praying to saints was useless, that no spiritual merit could be obtained from relics or pilgrimages, indeed that no acts of penance or charity could affect a soul's fate in Purgatory — because Purgatory did not exist(!) Indulgences and penances were enriching the church but were of no value to the believer at all. As he preached, Bilney sensed that his words were hitting home. The congregations hung on his words, and he felt the power of a crowd drawn together to one mind, one yearning. He was energized as he had never been before, and he knew that he had found a divine calling. God was speaking through him, he was certain. That certainty gave him a sense of purpose that he had never known.

The local religious authorities received complaints about his preaching but did not find that his ideas qualified as heretical, merely radical and annoying. When specifically questioned on his views of the Eucharist, or the authority of the Pope, he professed to be orthodox.

To make matters more complicated, Bilney acquired a reputation for virtuous character, through visitation to the sick, and generosity to the poor. His preaching was energetic and compelling, however eccentric. His deeds of piety gave him credibility since he insisted that he expected no spiritual advantage from performing them.

Hampton Court Palace, 1526: The Lord Chancellor

Thomas, Cardinal Wolsey was the most powerful man in England, apart from the king, and given Henry's willingness to let his chancellor take care of the daily details of running a kingdom, in many practical matters, he *was* the king. He had a palace in Hampton Court, near London, built for himself, and from there, he conducted diplomacy, negotiated with Emperors and Popes, financed armies and sent them to war, rewarded his friends, and thwarted his enemies. Enemies he had — aristocrats who resented the privilege acquired by this son of a butcher, as well as his wealth, his prestige, his arrogance, and ruthlessness. Other men of lesser birth envied him, even as they sought to emulate his successes. No matter. He had reached this pinnacle of power because he had outworked and outwitted such people.

His power rested on two pillars. One was the trust of the King, earned through faithful service and competence. Lesser men might gnaw away at the base of this pillar, but it might as well be made of stone or iron — he knew how to stifle their efforts, even, when necessary, to crush them. He was Lord Chancellor of England, outranked only by the king himself.

Wolsey was also a prince in his own right — a prince of the Church, a kingdom far greater in extent than England or any other temporal principality, This was the second pillar of his power. The Church was literally the source of daily bread for multitudes of the desperate poor, as well as steward of the sacraments that could bestow an eternity in heaven, deliver from purgatory, or condemn a soul to hell. It was also the guardian of the sacred truths of Holy Scripture and the main source of hope for the majority in every nation who would live short lives, under the constant threat of loss, suffering, and poverty. Wolsey was a ruler in two kingdoms, if you like (Wolsey certainly did), kingdoms which did not always share the same purposes or priorities. Awkward as that might be, he would rather sit near the top of those realms than at the bottom.

It had taken centuries of patient diplomacy and theological persuasion for the Church to gain enough influence and power to function as a check on the excesses that secular princes were naturally prone to, to channel their violence and aggression into crusades or other noble causes, to establish norms of justice wherever the Church was established. In time, the Church might be able to bring all the secular princes under her influence, to the point of eliminating warfare altogether. Wolsey spent much of his time and energy on diplomacy — resolving disputes through compromise when possible, through threats if necessary — working toward a great peace between the kingdoms of Catholic Europe, under the guidance of the Pope, united against external threats, like the Turks.

This future was under threat; heresies, like insatiable termites, were continually emerging from one place or another and would cripple the Church if left unchecked. Wolsey was determined to defeat them. When the Church was weakened, secular princes were quick to expand their own power, at her expense. Just now, the poisonous doctrines of Martin Luther were spreading across Europe. In Germany, whole kingdoms had fallen under the sway of these falsehoods, and revolts, wars, and turmoils were the natural result.

The attacks came through multiple paths. Luther published his ideas relentlessly, not only in Latin, but also in German, and translations were quickly made available in English. He found an eager audience. Luther compounded his rebellion by translating the Bible into German, and numerous copies were printed. Now every half-literate German could read the Holy Scriptures and felt entitled to interpret them for himself. Most dangerous was Luther's assertion that the scriptures alone were authoritative, and whatever the church taught that could not be supported by scripture could, and ought, to be rejected.

Wolsey was well aware that the Latin versions of Luther's publications had reached England and were read with interest in the universities. This was more an annoyance than a threat — the academics were always on about something. But English translations were also appearing. Imports of these were strictly forbidden, and anyone found to be in possession of them was subject to punishment. When found, these documents were burned — but they continued to be smuggled in.

England had faced this kind of challenge before, and it was only defeated with bloodshed and fire. John Wycliffe had translated the Latin scriptures into English almost a hundred-fifty years ago. It was fortunate that no printing presses existed, or copies would have flooded the country. As it was, Wycliffe's followers transcribed hundreds of copies by hand, and wandered all over the country as "Bible Men," preaching and teaching Wycliffe's pernicious doctrines. The infection spread over the whole land. The "Lollards," as they came to be called, were arrested, convicted of heresy, and either recanted or were burned at the stake. But they were not all caught. They went into hiding and continued to spread their message for many decades. There were places in England where they still preached, protected by stubborn and rebellious laymen, sometimes overlooked by sympathetic churchmen.

And now it was starting all over again. An expatriate academic named William Tyndale had taken it upon himself to make another English translation of the New Testament (from the Greek), and had it printed. Now the books were showing up in England. Hundreds were found, seized, and burned. Hundreds more were smuggled in. The volumes were small — about 9 1/2 inches by 6 1/2 inches, and could be concealed almost anywhere. It was believed that Tyndale was funded by wealthy merchants, but it was difficult to prove. And preachers were beginning to present the new ideas in pulpits across the country.

"It is Lollardry, under a different name, but Lollardry just the same," said Wolsey. "They deny transubstantiation. They condemn the veneration of saints. They reject the doctrine of purgatory. They teach that pilgrimages are of no spiritual merit. They reject the requirement of celibacy for the clergy. They say that every man is able to understand and interpret the scriptures. They reject the authority of the Pope!"

It was time to fight back.

The Cardinal had ample resources for this campaign: he employed agents and informants all over the kingdom, as well as the rest of Europe, to keep him informed on all matters of interest. It would not be difficult to identify the troublemakers. William Tyndale was at the top of the list. Putting a stop to the printing of his New Testaments would be more effective than trying to intercept them all, but it was not that easy. The title pages stated that they were printed by one Hans Lufft, in the city of Marburg, but no such printer existed in Marburg. Other false leads had to be tracked down, and Tyndale kept moving, now in Wittenberg, then Cologne, then Worms, Antwerp, or maybe Hamburg, hidden by his friends. This was going to take some time. Meanwhile, the New Testaments were turning up in Scotland.

Informants were assigned to follow preachers like Bilney and Arthur, looking for any taint of heresy. Agents of the chancellor bought up copies of the New Testament, to prevent them from falling into the wrong hands. Tyndale's New Testament was formally condemned by the bishop of London — all the old punishments for possessing the Lollard Bible would now apply to Tyndale's translation, as well.

London, 1526: A hearing

Cardinal Wolsey sat in a great chair, dressed in the red robe that was his official garb. The bishops were also in their vestments, the lawyers in simpler black, befitting their rank. A parade of suspects was presented for questioning. They had rounded up more men than he was expecting. Next on the docket was Thomas Bilney, preacher. A small man, respectful. His answers to the questions were spoken clearly but with an air of self-possession. Wolsey sensed that the little man was not intimidated by his accusers, nor by his judges. Perhaps his conscience was clear; that did not make him innocent. It proved difficult to pin him down. His answers were careful, sometimes with a touch of ironic humor.

Did he preach that people should rather pray in their own language, than in a "learned unknown tongue?"

"No, but Paul says in the First Epistle to the Corinthians that the congregation is more edified when they hear a word in a language they can understand."

Did he believe that the whole Scripture ought to be translated into English and that ordinary people should be able to own such?

"No, but I would rather that the people learn to recite the Lord's prayer in English, and that the Gospels and Epistles be read to them in English."

And so it went. The man was clever — he did not pretend that his preaching didn't challenge custom, but he was careful not to cross the line into what he supposed was heresy. He knew the scriptures better than most priests — but he was a scholar, after all, it really couldn't be held against him. Furthermore, he firmly denied that he had advocated for the teachings of Luther, whom he denounced as a heretic. The other bishops were inclined to view him as eccentric, but harmless.

Wolsey was alarmed at what he was hearing and exasperated that the other bishops were not. "Do you not see the peril that men like these represent? Preaching to the people in their own language — how is this different from Lollardry?"

The Bishop of Ely replied, "It is different because he is licensed to preach. Licensed by myself, as it happens. There is benefit in what he teaches the people. He exhorts them to righteous living, and corrects many superstitions."

"I have heard the same," chimed in another bishop, "The people are hungry for knowledge of the scriptures. Many attend Mass only three times a year. Those that can read a little Latin are vulnerable to error or confusion. Better they should hear the truth in English, from a man learned enough to dispel the confusion and avoid the error."

"No," replied Wolsey, "better that they should learn to trust the Church, and leave the parsing of scripture to those who are trained to handle it. Look at all the heresy that comes from exposing ordinary men to the scriptures — Cathars, Waldensians, Lollards, and now, Lutherans! Talking to laymen about the Scriptures is a waste of time. They must learn to trust the Church. Men are not saved by what they know or think they know. They are saved by where they place their trust!"

The Bishop looked at him in surprise. "Would you make a Lutheran of me?" Then he smiled.

Wolsey shook his head and had to chuckle. "I should have said that all of us will be judged by our deeds and that our deeds are determined by what we believe. More knowledge is useless unless it leads us to trust God more. The simplest belief is often the strongest — like that of a child."

"As, indeed, our Lord Christ has taught us," agreed the bishop. "But this man's preaching exhorts his hearers to the good deeds that you have mentioned. The complaints we have received are from some mendicant orders, who may feel that the fees he receives would better be collected by their own preachers — none of whom draw crowds as large as he does. I think this has more to do with jealousy than anything else."

In the end, Bilney's oath that he would not "preach, rehearse, or defend any of Luther's opinions" was sufficient to obtain his release. Wolsey was not entirely satisfied, but there were plenty of other troublemakers to deal with. Perhaps the little man would take heed from this hearing. Wolsey would ensure that one of his own informants would keep track of every sermon he preached.

At supper that evening, the Cardinal was in a reflective mood. Among his companions were a few of his proteges, men he had carefully chosen for their abilities, which he had nurtured while promoting their careers. Stephen Gardiner was the best canon lawyer he could find, probably the best in the kingdom. And Thomas More, well, brilliant did not do the man justice. He succeeded at everything he put his hand to — philosophy, politics, diplomacy. Wolsey had gotten both men appointed to the commission tasked with negotiating the military alliance with France, in support of the Pope, against the Holy Roman Empire. Both men were positioned for even greater things, and Wolsey gave himself a good deal of credit for this. In return, he counted on their loyalty.

"Sirs," he addressed them, "or may I call you friends?" Gardiner nodded with his usual somber expression. More smiled. "We live in perilous times. The Holy Church is under attack from princes and heretics alike. This is nothing new. It has taken centuries of strife, sprinkled with the blood of martyrs, for her to reach the place of influence that she now enjoys, and still the battle rages. We have far to go before it can be said that every knee has bowed to the lordship of our Christ. I shall not live to see that day, nor will you. But we must be faithful stewards of that which has been entrusted to us."

Both men nodded again.

"Imagine what would happen if we should fail. If every sovereign claimed a divine right to pursue the promptings of his ambition and avarice without restraint, if every half-literate half-wit could claim to speak God's truth or seek redemption on his own behalf, without the mediation of the church? Surely, it could only lead to chaos, to lawlessness, to endless war, and savagery!"

"The judgment of God would fall hard indeed, upon us all," offered Gardiner.

"It would not need the judgment of God; it would be hell on earth," added More.

"This is why we must be vigilant, and relentless," continued Wolsey. "The saints appeal to us, and the martyrs cry out for vindication. Their sacrifice must not be in vain."

Both his companions nodded. More spoke: "It has fallen upon men such as us to defend the Church from her enemies, at this day of testing. May we never slacken or weary of the battle, however long or bloody it may be. God help us."

The Cardinal slept well that night. With the loyalty of men like these, he could finish the work that God had called him to, and pass his legacy on to a younger generation. Kings would learn obedience to the rule of Christ, the poor would enter the Kingdom of Heaven, and justice and peace would possess the earth. Heretics would be ground to dust under the feet of the Church. His legacy would be secure, as long as men like these would stay loyal to him, and to his cause.

Westminster Hall, November 27, 1527: Examinations

I t did not take long for Wolsey's skepticism to be vindicated. Bilney and Arthur returned to their preaching, and the Cardinal's men took careful note of what they said. Their sermons became more strident, to the point that Bilney was forcibly removed from the pulpit on two occasions. When enough evidence was in hand, Wolsey had them arrested. He assembled a panel of examiners and included the lawyer, Sir Thomas More, now a close advisor to the King, and onetime Speaker of the House of Commons. More's presence was unusual in an Ecclesiastical court, but Wolsey had long been his patron and trusted him. Since the Ecclesiastical courts had very limited power to punish heretics, Wolsey needed the cooperation of the Civil authorities to actually execute a man like Bilney. Sir Thomas was well-positioned to bring the full force of government power to bear.

Wolsey led the questioning, and presented the accusations against Thomas Arthur:

- He had stated that all men were priests, and any who would restrain them from preaching were tyrants, and would be cursed for constraining the gospel;
- that no one should pray to saints because Christ is the only mediator, and that the adoration of saints and their images is idolatry;
- that the preaching of the gospel would continue even under the threat of death.

There were other sworn affidavits, but this was enough to satisfy the examiners. Arthur knew that they had enough evidence to condemn him as a heretic, and he promptly recanted, and submitted himself to the "judgment of the church."

Bilney's examination followed, and the list of accusations was longer. Among them:

- he said there had been no good pope for the previous five hundred years — "they have borne the keys of simony," not the keys of St. Peter, that they had "slandered the blood of Christ;"
- that many preachers had been "antichrists," and that his preaching was necessary to correct their errors;
- That "Jews and Saracens would have become Christian long ago, had it not been for the idolatry of Christian men, in offering of candles, wax, and money to stocks and stones," by which he meant the images of saints;

- That "kings and princes" should destroy those images, just as Hezekiah had destroyed the brass serpent;
- That pilgrimages were "foolish."

The list of accusations was longer, and Bilney took days to answer them all. Some he denied, others he defended. It was not until December 4 that the sentence was pronounced. Bilney was a heretic, the sentence was burning at the stake — unless Bilney would abjure (or recant) his words. Bilney asked to present other witnesses that could support his views; that request was denied. He asked for time to consider his situation. He was given three days. On December 7, at the urging of his friends, Bilney abjured.

For Wolsey, it was as good a result as he could get. Bilney had proved a tough nut to crack. Public recantation and humiliation were the most effective ways to repair the damage that Bilney's sermons had done. Bilney was required to lead a procession to St. Paul's cathedral the following Sunday, shouldering a large bundle of faggots (pieces of firewood, symbolizing his heresy), and stand before the whole congregation during the sermon. After that, he would be imprisoned in the Tower of London, until the Cardinal decided to release him.

If Bilney had hoped to be treated as gently as Thomas Arthur, he was disappointed. Wolsey was content to avoid burning him — burning can make martyrs, and martyrs can be more troublesome than living men. Better to contain the problem behind walls of stone. In the meantime, Wolsey had plenty of other problems to attend.

Hampton Court Palace, 1528: Divorce and Diplomacy

When church and temporal authority worked together, like a team of horses, a nation would know stability and prosperity. If they failed to do so, discord, rebellion, and heresy would result. Thomas Wolsey was the perfect realization of the former state and determined to avoid the latter. This ideal concord was not always easy to maintain. Sometimes a monarch needed to be guided away from excess and error. In exceptional cases, a prince could be excommunicated to force him into compliance. But the church could also be flexible when it was warranted. In situations where the temporal need seemed to conflict with the church's law, a third way could often be found to meet the pragmatic requirement while preserving the integrity of the church's authority. This was the sort of task that cardinals were called upon to take care of, and Wolsey was particularly good at doing so.

Just now, Wolsey was occupied with just such a problem. King Henry's wife, Catherine had borne him six children over eight years — four were stillborn. A son, also named Henry, lived less than two months. The only child to survive to adulthood was a girl, named Mary. Henry needed a male heir. Catherine was previously married to Henry's older brother Arthur, who had died when Henry was twelve years old. Under canon law, Henry was forbidden to marry his brother's widow, but in the interest of diplomatic necessity, the Pope was persuaded to issue a special dispensation to remove the "impediment" and allow the marriage to proceed.

Henry became convinced (or convinced himself) that God was punishing him and his family because his marriage to Catherine was, in God's eyes, incestuous — dispensation notwithstanding. Now, Henry had become enamored of one of Queen Catherine's "ladies in waiting" — awkward enough, but Henry had had mistresses before. Anne Boleyn was not willing to be Henry's mistress; she would be Queen or nothing. Henry was determined that she should be his queen. He expected Wolsey to make it happen.

It was an assignment that the Cardinal could not refuse. He was old enough to recall the carnage and turmoil that a kingdom without a secure succession could experience. If Henry died without a male heir, civil war was crouching at the door. It was also the sort of problem that he felt confident he could solve. It needed diplomacy, and lawyers — good lawyers. Henry's theory that his marriage was the result of a previous Pope's error would not be likely to gain a sympathetic hearing from the current pontiff. No doubt a lot of money would be involved, though there was no point in talking of specific sums until a deal was in hand.

The diplomatic effort was complicated. Catherine's family was well-positioned to oppose an annulment or divorce. Her nephew, Charles, was not only the King of Spain, but he was also, as Charles V, the Holy Roman Emperor — titular ruler of most of Germany. As King of Spain, he ruled Spain and her vast American colonies, as well as half of Italy. The German principalities were divided between Lutheran states in the north, and Catholic states in the south, with civil war just over the horizon. And then there were the Turks, advancing steadily from the east, threatening his frontier from Venice to Vienna. The only major kingdom not under Charles' direct control or influence was France — England's traditional foe.

Wolsey tried realignment. He had negotiated a treaty in 1525 with French ambassadors (Francis I, the King of France, was a prisoner in Madrid at the time). The English would attempt to get Francis released, and the French would try to help persuade the Pope to see Henry's marriage from the English point of view. Once Francis was released, nothing came of the alliance — Francis renounced the terms of his release, stating that he was under duress at the time.

But then a diplomatic opening appeared. In 1527, the Pope decided to go to war with Spain and allied himself with France and several major Italian cities. Perhaps the Pope would not hesitate to offend an Emperor that he was at war with, especially if it gained him another ally. Perhaps if England joined France as the Pope's allies, something could be worked out?

Wolsey sent Stephen Gardiner, his secretary, to present the case to the Pope directly. Gardiner was an eminent legal scholar, perhaps the best that England could produce. All Gardiner really needed was a decretal to permit the matter of Henry's marriage to be adjudicated in England, before English churchmen (Cardinal Wolsey could use his influence with his bishops to obtain the desired outcome). Gardiner arrived too late. The Pope was hunkered down in the fortress at Orvieto, south of Rome. Charles V's armies had sacked Rome and slaughtered the Pope's Swiss Guard. The Pope needed to make peace with the Emperor. He would not issue such a decretal — yet. He referred the question to a panel of Cardinals, and Gardiner. Their discussions produced no decision.

There were other approaches available. One lay in the ancient "Statute of Praemunire," by which Parliament had established the primacy of the English King over "foreign" (including papal) influence in ecclesiastical appointments. At a stretch, this might be taken to mean that the king's courts could overrule ecclesiastical court decisions. Some of the heretics that Wolsey was pursuing had expressed just such opinions, and when Henry became aware of this, he was pleased, never mind the source of the ideas. Wolsey could not pursue this theory to its logical conclusion without undermining his own ecclesiastical authority, but it might be used to support a larger case. The first task was to ensure that the decision would be made in England.

Finally, the Pope budged a little. In April of 1528, Wolsey was able to get an agreement to let the issue be decided in England by two papal legates, one of which would be Wolsey himself. This was the lifeline that Wolsey needed — Henry was impatient, and Anne Boleyn's influence at court was growing. Wolsey had to wait now for the Pope to appoint the other legate. Once the legate arrived in England, they would convene an ecclesiastical court, with full papal authority, to hear the King's case. Henry and Anne would just have to wait a little while longer.

London, May 1528: The Sweats and the Tower

While Wolsey waited, other events intervened. In late May, people in London began to fall ill with a mysterious disease. The symptoms began with a sense of foreboding, followed by severe chills and headache. Within hours, the chills were replaced with intense fever and sweating, delirium, chest pains, and heart palpitations. About half the victims died within the first twenty-four hours. It was known as "the sweats" or "the sweating disease." The disease spread quickly throughout the kingdom. Unlike other plagues, this disease seemed to prefer the wealthier and nobler citizens of the kingdom. King Henry left London altogether; it was said that he would not sleep in the same bed two nights in a row for fear of the disease. Anne Boleyn caught the disease and recovered.

The disease had struck England before. Most notably, it appeared for the first time in 1485, the year that Richard III was overthrown. At that time, some said that it was a punishment from God, upon all those who had supported the overthrow of Richard III by Henry VII. When Thomas Wolsey fell ill, there was murmuring that he had become the target of God's wrath — perhaps because of his arrogance, or his extravagant lifestyle, who knew?

Wolsey recovered, which was the best answer he could have offered to the murmurers. The papal legate, an Italian-born cardinal named Lorenzo Campeggio, was appointed in June but was in no particular hurry to arrive in England while the disease was raging. Campeggio had served as the Pope's legate to England for many years, though he did not often live there. The King had objected to the appointment of a "foreigner" to this post, but Wolsey had brought him around (and advanced his career in the process). Once again, Henry and Anne Boleyn would have to have patience.

The Tower of London had a variety of accommodations for those compelled to reside there. High-status individuals were kept in cells that were far larger than those reserved for humbler folk. Bilney's cell was far from large or comfortable — but ample, compared to the cells he had lived in as a young monk. The food was sufficient to sustain life, but not much more. The smell of the place was oppressive, but he got used to it. Ironically (or providentially), Bilney's isolation protected him from exposure to the sweating sickness outside the prison walls.

It was small comfort. He had saved his life by recanting his beliefs. But what had he saved? He could not preach if he was dead, but neither could he from within these walls. He was cut off from nearly all his friends and colleagues nearly as completely as if he *were* dead. So what is the purpose of a man's life, if he cannot or dare not speak the truth? Bilney had recanted his beliefs to save his life, and received the humiliation and imprisonment with equanimity — it was the price of survival. But his mind had not changed. He had acted the part expected of him by men who had the power to compel him. That did not mean that he agreed with them. Indeed, their coercive power confirmed his judgment that they were spiritually corrupt. Men of integrity would have been persuaded by his witness, but these were men who would protect their privilege and power at all costs, even to the point of taking his life, never mind holding a multitude of believers in bondage to ignorance and superstition to squeeze money from them with false hopes and promises. It occurred to Bilney that in acting the role assigned to him — the repentant heretic — he was now part of their whole corrupt regime. It was a bitter realization. Bilney was not a man given to bitterness, but this sense of helpless complicity gnawed at his mind through the many months of imprisonment in the Tower.

He realized, in a moment of insight, that all men spent their lives acting in some role or other. Freedom was a fancy that academics maintained; practical men had fewer illusions. Had he chosen to go to the stake, would he be any more free? Perhaps. Maybe death was the only true freedom that any man would know; perhaps choosing it was the only truly free choice any man could make. He was not flirting with suicide — that might well have served the purposes of his persecutors. But why would God reveal a truth, only to let it be ignored, or worse, be used to serve corrupt purposes? Bilney was in deeper waters than he had gone before. The theological answers that came readily to his mind failed to speak to his condition. Could it be the will of God that a man should receive the truth, and then remain silent? Or could it be the will of God that a man should receive the truth, and speak it until he is persecuted to the point of death by burning (or even crucifixion)? Did not Got have the power and the intention to protect his servants, and justify them? God had spoken to him, of this he was certain. Had God then failed him, or had he failed God? In either case, he doubted if God had any more use for him.

His old friend Dr. Warner was one of the few who dared risk a visit to his cell. Warner tried to cheer him up. "God has not asked you (or myself, thankfully,) to forfeit your life for the truth — surely God has some some further purpose for you, which shall appear in due time?"

"I fear I may have missed my purpose through cowardice or carelessness."

"If that is the case, God is able to set you back on the right path. Trust and hope."

Bilney was silent for a moment. "I do not know what I should hope for. If my failure is cowardice, how shall I be redeemed but by embracing the very fate that most terrifies me? Or, perhaps it is pride that has brought me to this place. Perhaps I treated the truth as a tool to advance my own reputation and fame, to draw attention to myself, to bask in the praise of other men, or to fancy myself some great hero of the faith."

Warner replied, "If the latter is true, you have succeeded in garnering some measure of fame. Not the sort that most men seek, but beggars cannot be choosers." There was a twinkle in his eye as he said this. Bilney realized he was being teased.

Warner continued. "What man can say that he has never used the gifts of God for selfish or prideful purposes? That every breath he draws, every meal he eats, every thought in his waking mind is dedicated purely to the worship of God? None of us can. We can do no better than to re-dedicate ourselves with each morning, to God's purpose; though none of us will ever succeed. I could name a multitude of men who shudder to imagine that their obedience to God might lead them to a cell like this one — and yet in their deepest hearts, they wonder if they would be better off as you are. They envy you, in their inner torment."

Bilney looked surprised. "Such men could join me if they truly wished to." His smile was ironic.

Warner nodded. "Perhaps some shall, ere long. Trust and hope must be our food until the purpose of God is revealed. Each must stumble along our own path."

"Stumbling I understand," Bilney replied. "I fear that I may have stumbled into a place from which I may never recover."

Warner shook his head. "No one travels the path on his own, nor moves under his own strength. God is powerful and faithful. He will bring you to the place that is prepared for you. Trust and hope."

Bilney smiled wryly. "It seems like a great deal of trouble — for both of us."

Warner chuckled. "For all of us, you mean!"

Bilney laughed. "I am grateful to you for coming to me. My spirits are lifted by this conversation."

"As are mine, though I cannot explain why."

After Warner had left, Bilney was left to reflect on his own. Nothing had changed, yet his heart was lightened, a little. He felt hopeful that God might have some greater purpose for him, after all. He realized (ruefully) that the desire to fulfill some greater purpose was in part a prideful one. Pride — always at the door, or just out of sight somewhere, looking for a little hospitality; a warm, comfortable place to rest by the fire . . . Bilney shook himself. Well, there was little hospitality in this small cell. Pride would have to wait outside. His belief in the power of God was fortified; his hope was stronger. He would indeed be led to his destination, even if it broke him. He did not trouble himself with worry about what that might entail.

London, 1529: Trials

Cardinal Campeggio arrived in London on October 5, 1528. Henry and Wolsey were eager to begin the trial immediately, but Campeggio would not be hurried. Throughout the fall and into the spring, there were innumerable meetings between the King, his lawyers, and the papal legates. Nothing ever seemed to get decided. Wolsey was worried that Campeggio was stalling — an impression that was amplified over time. What was Campeggio's game? In July of 1529, Campeggio suspended the trial until October (the sweating disease was back), and then it was revealed that the Pope had decided to hear the matter in Rome, instead. Campeggio soon left England. Wolsey was left to face the King's wrath alone.

It was clear enough now that the Pope had never intended to annul Henry's marriage. Campeggio's instructions all along had been to stall the process, and try to effect a reconciliation between Henry and Queen Catherine, unrealistic as that was. The King (and Wolsey) had been played for fools. Wolsey now owned a problem that he could not solve. He faced indictment from a furious king, for violating the law of praemunire — putting his loyalty to the Pope ahead of his loyalty to the King. Wolsey's enemies were closing in — accusing him of corruption, of spending the kingdom's money on his own luxurious lifestyle. In desperation, Wolsey "gifted" his palace at Hampton Court to the king — a clumsy attempt at placation that blew up in his face. When the King came to inspect his new palace, he was stunned at the splendor of the architecture and its furnishings. It was easy to believe that Wolsey had been helping himself to the royal treasury.

In October, Wolsey was indicted; he surrendered the Great Seal of England on November 19, 1529, ending his Chancellorship. Three days later, he signed a confession of praemunire and surrendered all his possessions to the King. He was able to avoid prison but was a ruined man. In the Spring, the King issued a general pardon but returned none of his wealth or position. He was banished from London, and forced to return to York, where he still held the title of Archbishop. Among his accusers were men he had mentored, like Thomas More and Stephen Gardiner, both of whom the King promoted. Thomas More was now the Lord Chancellor. Gardiner was now the King's personal secretary.

Wolsey took one more ill-advised gamble, by maintaining a correspondence with the Pope and other church officials. Perhaps he could redeem his position if he could somehow get Henry the annulment that he wanted. The correspondence was intercepted, and had the appearance of another attempt at praemunire; Wolsey was summoned to London to answer a charge of treason. Once pardoned, he could not expect mercy for a second offense. Wolsey died on the way to London, on November 29, 1530. Anne Boleyn, on hearing of his death, commissioned a musical play entitled *The Going to Hell of Cardinal Wolsey.* All of her courtiers agreed that it was a great success.

Thomas Bilney was released from the Tower in the general pardon following Wolsey's fall, a broken man. He had friends who would see to his material needs, but his greatest needs were not material. A sense of failure and hopelessness preoccupied him. It actually mattered little whether he was behind stone walls, or not. He was as much imprisoned by his fear of death, as by any prison cell. "Death makes all of us cowards," he remarked. He slept poorly and ate with little appetite. His friends worried that he might try to end his life. They took turns watching him. He sought relief in prayer and Bible reading, but the reading only sharpened his sense of failure.

London, 1531: The New Chancellor

Sir Thomas More was now the Lord Chancellor of England, and he took to his job with energy and a sense of purpose. More's brilliance had long been recognized. He had served with distinction in Parliament while in his twenties, then as the Master (judge) of the Court of Requests, which specialized in hearing cases from poor people, where his decisions were noted for their prompt (and less expensive) decisions. He was employed by Cardinal Wolsey as a diplomat on the King's behalf, then elected Speaker of the House of Commons. As Undersheriff of London, he led the effort to root out Lutherans and other heretics. He became a member of Henry's inner circle — the Privy Council. He was a vocal and prolific advocate for church reform. If all this were not enough, he was a celebrated author, most famous for writing *Utopia*, a book whose title entered into the English language as a political and literary convention. More's Utopia was a place of religious toleration, communal property, and education for women as well as men, and had no lawyers because the laws were few and simple. In practice, More insisted that his daughters be educated on a par with his sons; the rest of his lifestyle was decidedly non-utopian.

More was recognized as a man of unusual integrity. In the world of power politics, where survival depended on responding to every minor shift in the wind, More could be counted on to maintain any opinion or position when he believed it to be right — which was practically all the time.

As chancellor, More brought a new energy to the campaign against Lutheranism and other heresy. Heretics seemed to be multiplying, and there were new sorts appearing.

The campaign to stop the importation of Tyndale's New Testament was intensified. Agents were sent to Europe to buy as many copies as they could before they could be shipped to England.

They had some successes. In 1529, they had captured Thomas Hitton, an associate of Tyndale, in the process of organizing more channels for smuggling Tyndale's New Testaments into the country. More took satisfaction when "the devil's stinking martyr" was burned in February of 1530. But other men stepped into Hitton's place, and the smuggling continued. Men were constantly crossing the North Sea to Antwerp and back, where Tyndale was said to be working on an English translation of the rest of the Bible. They brought back New Testaments, and an array of other religious texts — too many to completely intercept. Tyndale and his colleagues kept up a relentless stream of other tracts and letters, which excoriated Catholics generally, English Catholics in particular, and men like Thomas More by name. More redoubled his efforts to silence him.

More's objections were not strictly on criminal grounds — he fiercely objected to many of Tyndale's translation choices. Tyndale had "elder" instead of "priest," which undermined the sacramental role of the priesthood; and "congregation" instead of "church," which elevated the authority of laymen, at the expense of clergy. Tyndale's translations included glosses, or marginal notes, that undermined the legitimacy of church hierarchy and clerical privilege. More vigorously attacked these ideas in writing, declaring Tyndale's translation to be the work of the "antichrist." As More pointed out errors in the text, Tyndale made revisions and reprinted his books.

1531: The road to Jerusalem

The news of Thomas Hitton's burning came as a shock to Thomas Bilney. It was a humiliating reminder of his own trial and condemnation. He tasted the fear again and was reminded of the helplessness of his current condition. Later, there was an odd sense of vindication — if Hitton knew the risks he was taking, and believed them worth perishing for, Bilney's own brush with the fire seemed less foolhardy. Bilney had chosen life, and Hitton had chosen — what, exactly?

It was said that Hitton had been tortured before his execution, to extract the names of his colleagues in the smuggling business. He did not give them up — there were no more arrests and executions for nearly a year.

The next heretic to be burned was Thomas Benet. Benet was nowhere near London or the Bible-smuggling conspiracies. He had moved his family to Devonshire, in England's far southwest, to avoid the pressures of persecution. He earned his living as a school teacher and met others who shared his beliefs. They corresponded or met surreptitiously. Yet there was something reckless about his behavior. He began by anonymously posting a written document to the door of Exeter cathedral (a la Martin Luther), proclaiming, among other things, that the Pope was "antichrist," and that veneration of saints was idolatry. The local bishop was alarmed, and ordered that sermons be preached to directly contradict these heretical ideas, and urgently sought their author's identity. It took some time for the authorities to identify the source of the document; the civil authorities did not see the urgency, and the bishop had to employ his own investigators. Benet did not flee the city even then. Instead, he continued to attend services in the cathedral and eluded capture for some time. The bishop called for a special service to excommunicate and curse him *in absentia*. Benet secretly attended the service and burst into loud laughter — resulting in his immediate arrest. He refused all entreaties to recant and was burned on January 15th, 1531.

Thomas More heard the news with little satisfaction. It was clear that the heresies of the "reformation" had now reached the remoter regions of the kingdom. The boldness of the heretics was also worrisome. It was unrealistic to suppose he could end the epidemic of heresy by simply burning men and women. The burnings served merely as deterrents to the masses of potential heretics. Recantations were the preferred result because the recanters became living witnesses to the truth of orthodoxy. Burning a few from time to time showed that the kingdom was serious, but if men would not be deterred, there was not enough firewood in the kingdom to cleanse it. Meanwhile, Tyndale's New Testaments continued to find their way into the country. Despite their best efforts, the Chancellor's men were losing their war against heresy.

The news of Benet's immolation hit Thomas Bilney very hard indeed. Benet was a personal friend, from his days at Cambridge, and later. Benet was married, had children; Bilney had met some of them. If any man had reason to hide his convictions from the authorities, it was Benet. He had given up a lucrative career as a preacher and sought obscurity in the countryside, but it was not enough to protect him. And at the last, he had abandoned obscurity altogether.

Bilney received a visit from his old friend, Nicholas Shaxton. Shaxton's career had taken a different path since their days at the White Horse — he was now a respected religious authority whose opinions were sought and valued by the King himself. He was a candidate for the doctorate of divinity. Bilney found no little irony in their situations.

"How is it, Nicholas, that two men born in the same year, in the same shire, educated at the same university, serving the same God, partakers of the same truth (unless your opinions have changed; mine have not), should find ourselves in such different circumstances?"

Shaxton looked at Bilney with sympathy, even sadness, and shook his head. "I am ashamed to say that it is because you spoke the truth more boldly than I. Too boldly, perhaps."

"Perhaps. But you were always better than I when it came to threading the needle in an argument. I always admired your ability to make a point, without giving away too much of your heart."

Shaxton nodded. "And I always admired your simplicity and sincerity. You could always see through sophistry and self-deception, like a candle in a dark room."

Bilney nodded. "The candle has burned me, I think."

"Do not say so! Many have been blessed by the light you have brought."

"And yet, I have recanted. What then of the light?"

"No one who knows you blames you for your recantation. It is what men like us must do, to preserve our lives, until the truth may safely be spoken again."

"You did not believe my recantation?"

Shaxton chuckled. "Of course not! I reckon that most of your examiners did not believe it, either. The law required that your life be spared if you recanted. When you did so, they followed the law, as they were required to do. The Cardinal clearly didn't believe you, else why send you to the tower? If your recantation was sincere, you would have been more use to him in public, confessing the error of your ways.'

Bilney shook his head at the thought. "Better the tower, than a career as the Cardinal's puppet. God has been merciful."

"Quite so. And now you are a free man. What will you do?"

Bilney shrugged. "That is the question that I wrestle with every day. I am not licensed to preach, even if I dared to. And I know myself to be a man that loves his own life, more than the truth."

"You are too harsh with yourself," said Shaxton reprovingly. "Nothing would be gained by going to the stake; not for you, nor for the people you preach to, nor for God himself."

"And nothing is gained by denying the truth, except for me, and the bishops," replied Bilney, "I find no satisfaction in that. I feel like a player on a theatrical stage — I appear, I speak the lines, and I pass from view, and all is just a performance out of some playwright's vain imagination. If I am not to speak the truth while I live, why speak at all?"

"All men, as you say, must perform the roles assigned to them, the King as much as a beggar. But surely each can also find God's purpose in the midst of their labors, and receive God's help and comfort, while they live. And this 'stage', if you like, is only our temporary condition. All men have hope of an eternity in Heaven, regardless of what role they are cast in this life."

Bilney bowed his head. "And yet, it grieves me to think that all my earthly life is merely a dramatic fiction. I have felt the Spirit of God move my soul, and I believed it to be real, more real than anything else in my experience. Am I now to think that this is just another device in the hands of a master playwright? It terrifies me to think that might be true, but there is one thing that terrifies me even more. What if the Spirit of God is the only real thing, the only thing of value, like a priceless pearl? What if, by choosing to go on playing my role, I am giving up the only real thing, in exchange for a sham? What if, as Jesus says, a man must lose his life, in order to preserve it?"

"Each of us must do the best we can," replied Shaxton. It sounded lame the moment he heard it. It was not an answer that satisfied him, nor one that satisfied Thomas Bilney.

Some days later, Bilney's friends noticed that his mood had improved. Most of them were still reeling from the news of Benet's death, but Bilney had the appearance of a man released from the weight of a heavy burden. "I must go to Jerusalem," he said. They understood his meaning and tried to talk him out of it, but he would not be persuaded. At last, they gave up and wished him blessings.

Bilney had a plan. He would revisit all the places that he had preached before his trial, and seek to undo the damage that his recantation had caused. He started near London preaching to people in private homes, or sometimes outdoors. He retracted his recantation; some of his views had become more radical over the years. Everywhere he went, he was greeted by people who somehow had word that he was coming, as he worked his way gradually northward, toward Norwich. He had a few of Tyndale's New Testaments with him, which he left with various people on his journey. In a way, it was a kind of pilgrimage, though not the kind that would accrue any of the spiritual credit that other pilgrims might expect. Everyone knew the consequences of his actions: a heretic might recant — once — but if that recantation was retracted, the consequence was death — a second recantation would not save his life.

He came at last to Norwich, and spoke to many there, indoors and out. He gave his last New Testament to a nun at a convent there. Shortly afterward, he was arrested. As fate (or providence) would have it, Bilney was a friend of the local sheriff, who made his incarceration as comfortable as he could. Bilney's friends were able to visit him, and he was held in the Guildhall, instead of the city jail.

He was also visited by a variety of local clergy and monks, whose hope was to persuade him to recant again. Everyone understood that this would make no difference whatsoever in his sentence, but there might be some satisfaction for the clerics in saying that they had turned him from his errors at the very last. Bilney tolerated their efforts, even as he pitied them, the forlorn citizens of a world that was passing away. (This would become more apparent sooner than anyone, including Thomas Bilney could have imagined.) But Bilney had "set his face" to "Jerusalem," and now that he was here, he would finish the journey. At ten o'clock on August 19th, 1531, Bilney stepped out of the Guildhall for the final leg of his pilgrimage. A friend approached him, and urged him to be firm: He replied that he was like a sailor in a storm at sea — he would be sustained by the hope of reaching a distant shore. "To face the executioner's fire is a fearsome thing," he admitted, "but there is another fire at work within me — a Spirit that I dare not disobey."

London, 1531: Complications

Chancellor Thomas More was informed of course, of the events in Norwich, and the news was not all good. In the first place, it seemed that the whole business had been rushed. No doubt Bilney was guilty, but the normal authorization for his execution should have come through London. The Bishop of Norwich had gotten ahead of himself. More troubling were reports of the mood of the crowds at Norwich. Many had openly sympathized with Bilney. The civil authorities were less than enthusiastic about performing their role. People were still talking about Bilney's humility, sincerity, and generosity as if that were relevant to his case. Worse, the wind that had suddenly blown the flames of his pyre away from him (three times!), was the source of superstitious speculation — was this a sign from God?

"First of all, it had been windy in Norwich the previous two days, had it not?"

"Yes, sir."

"And Bilney recanted at the last did he not?"

"Some say they saw him mumble something before he stood to the stake, but none agree on what he said."

"Well then, he must have recanted."

"Sir?"

"It is settled. Bilney recanted before he burned."

The necessary thing was to minimize the damage of superstition. By no means could Bilney be regarded as a martyr. Thomas More would insist, without evidence, that Bilney had recanted, to his dying day.

In December of that year, they arrested a book dealer named George Constantine, a one-time associate of William Tyndale, for disseminating the illegal books. With some persuasion, Constantine gave up the names of his co-conspirators. Constantine subsequently escaped to Antwerp, but More had the name of John Tewkesbury, and Richard Bayfield — both Cambridge men, both translators working for Tyndale. Bayfield was arrested and tortured for more names, before being burned on December 4, 1531, with More in attendance. The burning took place in Smithfield ("smooth field"), an open space just outside the ancient walls of London. The space was sometimes used for a livestock market, as well as the Bartholomew Fair, an annual event that drew large crowds. The southeast side of the field was dominated by St. Bartholomew's priory, a large monastic house with a prominent chapel, known informally as "Saint Bart's." The open space had also been used as a place of execution of Lollards and other heretics for centuries, and it was here that Richard Bayfield ended his life.

Bayfield's burning was clumsily handled — not enough wood was applied at first so that it took half an hour for him to die. One of his arms fell off his body before he was dead. More declared him "Well and worthily burned."

John Tewkesbury was also arrested and held for trial in More's house. Tewkesbury was another heretic who had recanted, and his subsequent association with Tyndale was enough to condemn him. He was burned on December 20, 1531, "burned as there was never (a) wretch I ween better worthy" — in More's words — also at Smithfield.

They burned two others that year, as well — one in Yorkshire, the other in Buckinghamshire. In 1532, they would burn four more — a lawyer in London (at Smithfield, again), two commoners in Wiltshire, another in Buckinghamshire. Clearly, the problem was just as severe in the countryside as in the capital. And if they had caught four, More knew that there must be many, many others out there.

Meanwhile, other matters had taken center stage. King Henry was still determined to get his marriage to Catherine annulled. He had made one last attempt in 1530 to get the Pope's cooperation. Thomas Cranmer and Stephen Gardiner, now the King's secretary, had taken refuge from the sweating sickness in Cambridge back in 1529. Cranmer had suggested that Henry could bypass the Pope altogether if he could get a consensus of English scholars to support his case. Henry wanted to try, so Gardiner was dispatched to Cambridge in 1530, to obtain an official opinion from the faculty that his marriage to Catherine was unlawful. Among the scholars who supported the King's case was Dr. Nicholas Shaxton, the old friend of Thomas Bilney. Shaxton's support was noted, and he was rewarded with a position in Anne Boleyn's household. With the favorable opinions of the scholars in hand, Henry compelled the leading churchmen and aristocrats of the kingdom to sign a letter to the Pope asking for an annulment. The Pope was not impressed.

By 1531, Henry had given up on getting the Pope to cooperate, instead, he issued a royal decree that required all the English clergy to take an oath recognizing him as the "Supreme Head of the Church of England." This was not mere rhetoric — refusal to take the oath could now be construed as treason, a capital offense. More had refused to sign the letter, and would not take the oath.

In the first place, More believed that the King's marriage to Catherine was valid, and could not be annulled. God's law must be respected, by the king and pope alike. Secondly, More recognized that making the King the supreme head of the church would eliminate the long-standing balance of power between church and state that had served Catholic Europe so well. Left to their own inclinations, secular princes tended to become tyrants. The church was the advocate for justice for the powerless, sometimes the only defender of the God-given rights of the poor. Removing that moral accountability meant going back centuries, to a dark barbaric past, and he would not be part of it.

In May of 1532, Thomas More resigned the chancellorship. Several high-ranking churchmen, including a cardinal, also refused to take the oath and were replaced by Henry with more malleable men, as he was now empowered to do.

Henry was finally able to marry Anne Boleyn. In 1533, she was crowned Queen of England. Sir Thomas More failed to attend the coronation, though he sent a letter to the King wishing them well. Anne did not take it well. More was now her enemy, as Wolsey had once been. The Pope responded to the marriage by excommunicating Henry, and his Archbishop, Thomas Cranmer.

In 1534 Parliament validated Henry's claims by passing an Act of Supremacy, specifying that the King was the only head of the church, an Act of Succession, which made Anne's daughter Elizabeth the presumed heir of Henry (and Catherine's daughter, Mary, a bastard,) and a Treasons Act, which made it a capital crime to disavow either the Act of Supremacy or the Act of Succession. More would not swear an oath to affirm any of them. Henry ordered him arrested and confined to the Tower of London.

His quarters in the Tower were relatively comfortable, as befit his social rank. He had time to write and reflect. He was visited several times by Thomas Cromwell, now Henry's leading advisor, who urged him to find a way to take the oath. After all, More was now a private citizen. The King was eager to pardon him and put the whole thing in the past. The King was going to do as he pleased, anyway. Was this really worth dying for? A good question. More thought of the heretics he had burned. If such men willingly died for heresy, should not an orthodox Christian hazard his life for the truth?

Others had faced the same question and answered affirmatively. All across the kingdom, monks. Priests and bishops denounced Henry's claim to supremacy and were paying the price. Beginning that year, the London Charterhouse of the Carthusian monks was targeted. The Carthusians were a cloistered order and had little or no contact with the general public. For this, they were considered less corrupt than many other orders. The respect they held in the public eye did not protect them; no less than eighteen refused to take the oath and were executed — some by hanging, others by starvation. In York, two were hung by chains from the city wall until dead.

Men Like Nicholas Shaxton and Hugh Latimer found royal favor and the preferments that came with it. Latimer was appointed Bishop of Worcester, in place of an Italian prelate who refused to take the oath. Shaxton was appointed to Cardinal Campeggio's position as Bishop of Salisbury. The heretical ideas that Thomas Bilney had been burned for just three years previously were now being promoted in their dioceses and others.

More's trial began on July 1st, 1535. He avoided all questions about his opinions on Henry's claim to supremacy — he would not dispute them, or affirm them. Thomas Cromwell led the prosecution on behalf of the King. The case turned on the testimony of Sir Richard Rich, the King's Solicitor General, who stated that he had heard More deny that Henry could be the legitimate head of the church. No one else could be found to corroborate Rich's account, and More attacked Rich's credibility. How likely was it that he would confide his secret thoughts to "a man I had so mean an opinion of, in reference to his truth and honesty?" Rich had already acquired a reputation as a man more of opportunity than integrity, but impeaching his testimony did not suffice. More was found guilty of treason, and sentenced to death. After all, how likely was it that the court would defy the clear wishes of Henry and his queen?

More was supposed to be hanged, drawn, and quartered, but the King commuted his sentence to beheading (a method of execution ordinarily reserved for men of noble birth). On the scaffold, he recited the 51st Psalm, and when asked, forgave his executioner before the axe fell.

Antwerp, 1535: The Fugitive at Bay

In Antwerp, William Tyndale had outlived his nemesis. His translation work continued, and he had help from a number of other Cambridge men, both in the translation and in the transport of his New Testaments into England. Soon, he would be finished translating the Old Testament books and be able to print an entire Bible in English. He was living in the English House, the home of Thomas Poyntz, an English merchant. The English House served as a refuge similar to that of a foreign embassy because foreign merchants enjoyed a measure of autonomy in Antwerp. Antwerp was part of the Hanseatic League, a trade association of cities that reached from England to Russia. The "Hansa," as it was called, was not a nation or an empire, but it did protect the interests of its member merchant communities to the point of occasionally fielding armies or navies within its sphere of influence. It was difficult for More's men, or any other agents to get at Tyndale as long as he was inside the English House — so he ventured outside infrequently. It was understood that he could be arrested if he ventured outside, so he stayed inside and worked. The printing of his New Testaments had turned out to be profitable; booksellers could sell as many as the printers could turn out. Some sellers did a substantial business by selling them directly to English agents, who bought and burned them in large numbers, thus financing the printing of more.

Friends came to see him; some assisted him in his translations. Among them were Myles Coverdale and John Rogers, both expatriates educated at Cambridge. Coverdale was working on his own translations of some Old Testament books; they collaborated on others.

Tyndale was finally seized in the street outside his home in 1535. He was led to his captors by a young English noble he had befriended, named Henry Phillips. Phillips needed money, and the bishops in England were willing to pay. Tyndale was held in a prison near Brussels, tried for heresy in 1536, and sentenced to burn. His execution occurred on October 6 of that year. Atypically, he was chained to the stake, then strangled before the fire was lit. This may have been merciful, or perhaps just literally overkill. In any case, More's campaign had succeeded, though he had not lived to see it.

Myles Coverdale in the meantime, had published his own English Bible. It included Tyndale's New Testament, Tyndale's translation of the Pentateuch and Jonah, and Coverdale's own translations of other Old

Testament books. In England, the official attitude toward such translations had changed after the death of Thomas More. Coverdale's Bible featured a frontispiece dedicating his edition to King Henry. The King was pleased to receive a copy. Through the efforts of Thomas Cranmer the Archbishop of Canterbury, a royal license was issued to sell Coverdale's translation in England. The door was now open to legalization of an English translation of the Bible. In particular, the Archbishop communicated an interest in a new translation, that might be legally printed in England. Thomas Cromwell, known to favor an English Bible, was using his influence with King Henry to prepare the way.

John Rogers prepared a "new" translation, which he presented as the work of one "Thomas Matthew," dedicated to King Henry. It became known as "Matthews Bible." There was very little "new" about it, apart from its printing; it was comprised of Tyndale's New Testament translations, plus some more of Tyndale's translations of Old Testament books, a little of Coverdale's work, and one translation of Rogers himself. Had Henry known that most of it was translated by a convicted heretic he would probably have rejected it. As it was, the translation was licensed, and the first fifteen hundred copies sold quickly.

So successful in fact was this promotion, that in 1538 Henry was persuaded to proclaim that every church in England must have its own copy of the Bible in English, "at some convenient place," to be available for reading to all his subjects. Thomas Cromwell commissioned Myles Coverdale to produce it. The "new" Bible was in fact, a combination of Coverdale's and Roger's previous work — and almost all of it was Tyndale's translations. Coverdale removed some glosses and margin notes that were deemed objectionable, It became known as the "Great Bible," because it was much larger than its predecessors — fourteen inches tall. It was often chained to the pulpits of churches to prevent theft. More than nine thousand copies were printed, which was not enough for every parish in the kingdom, so Matthew Bibles were supplied to make up the difference.

It was seven years since Thomas Bilney had been burned for, among other things, owning an English New Testament, and insisting that Bibles should be available in English, to other Englishmen. It was three years since William Tyndale had been burned for producing the very Bible translation that was now required to be publicly available in every parish church in the kingdom.

For Dr. Nicholas Shaxton, now Bishop of Salisbury, the change of circumstance was an affirmation of the careful path he had chosen in his career. It was both a vindication of his views, shared by so many of his friends, and a validation of his patience and caution. The winds of religion had changed so completely, and so quickly that it could be nothing other than the Spirit of God himself, coming to the aid of his servants with power to overrule even the Pope! When he thought of his old friend Thomas Bilney, it was with sadness that Bilney had not lived to see this day. If only Bilney had been a little more careful, or a little more patient, could he perhaps have been saved? Or was his death a part of some holy purpose that was hidden from men like Shaxton? The Bishop doubted that he would have shown such courage in Bilney's place. He felt with a little shame that a part of him was grateful not to have faced such a test. Perhaps God protected his servants from trials that they could not endure. Perhaps. Shaxton did not wish to think that hard testing might still be ahead of him.

Part 2: The Articles

1536: Ten Articles

Under the Act of Supremacy, the Church of England was Henry's to run as he saw fit. No one, including Henry, knew exactly what that meant. He had his annulment and a new wife. He could fend off any interference from the current or future popes. If any of his officials, laymen or clerics, proved cantankerous, he could fire them. What was left was an arena of uncertainty about what England's church would stand for. There were plenty of ambitious men eager to enter that arena, and the contest to define the new entity was joined.

Initially, Henry probably assumed that things would continue pretty much as they had done — just without the interference of pesky popes. He certainly did not consider himself anything but Catholic. His advisors had other ideas. Despite the decades of suppression, many of the heretical notions coming from Europe had made an impression on English churchmen. Many of the heretics that had been burned were priests, and many surviving priests shared some or all of their opinions. In the universities, the influence of Lutheran, and now Calvinist ideas, was widespread. And it was from those very universities that the next generation of Henry's advisors were recruited.

At first, few things changed. The mass was said in Latin. Priests were still priests, deacons and archdeacons, canons, bishops, and archbishops still held their positions unless specifically removed for disloyalty to the King. Priests were still required to be celibate (never mind that many bishops and cardinals had not-so-secret wives, children, and mistresses). One of the first changes was that "Peter's Pence," the penny-per-household tax that kings of England traditionally paid to the Pope each year, was abolished. So far, so good. Henry saw no reason to subsidize a papacy that he rejected, and tightening the Pope's budget a little sent a message that he knew would be heard.

Other men had bigger changes in mind. Thomas Cranmer, who had promoted the idea that Henry could bypass the Pope in his quest for an annulment, was now Archbishop of Canterbury. Hugh Latimer, Thomas

Bilney's old friend, was now a bishop as well. They envisioned the Church of England as a reformed institution, though not a Lutheran one.

Thomas Cromwell became the most influential of them all. A blacksmith's son, he was trained as a lawyer, not a churchman. He had traveled widely in his youth, served as a French mercenary in Italy, and worked for a banking family in Florence. He spent years living among expatriate English merchants in various cities on the mainland, learning the local languages and developing relationships that would serve him later. He was, if you like, a "Renaissance Man," in a sense that few men of his time actually were. He had first-hand experience of the forces that were shaping his world. Medieval traditions and noble bloodlines were declining in importance. Commerce and new ideas were taking center stage. Cromwell was uniquely prepared to thrive in such a world.

Cromwell's career in English politics had been advanced by the sponsorship of his mentor, Cardinal Wolsey. When Wolsey fell from power, he had found other allies. First, he allied himself with Anne Boleyn's faction in the struggle over Henry's marriage. The King began to entrust him with other problems, and he usually solved them. With each success, his influence increased, and he was rewarded with more offices and power.

Cromwell was often called upon to prosecute the King's enemies, and people feared to face him in a courtroom.

Cromwell had no appetite for burning heretics, indeed, little interest in theological crimes of any sort. The only capital offense he cared about was treason, which was his chief instrument in defending the King's interests. Theological sins were of interest only if they represented some threat to the throne or the prosperity of the nation. Sometimes they were or could be made to appear to be, in which case they were treasonous. Just that simple. In the new regime, treason could mean anything that the King did not like.

Thomas Cromwell had religious convictions, and they were decidedly reformist. He maintained contacts with men like William Tyndale and Myles Coverdale, even when the government was pursuing them. When Tyndale was arrested, Cromwell used his influence to try to obtain his release. Cromwell was particularly interested in seeing a "legitimate" English language Bible, and he began to look for ways to make that happen. From Cromwell's point of view, such a Bible had political advantages. He was convinced that England's future lay in asserting her autonomy from "foreign" influence. An English Bible could be instrumental in that process. When Englishmen could read the Bible in their own language, they would no longer look to Rome for their religious instruction. And the more widely it was read, the fewer would fall victim to superstition and manipulation by ecclesiastical elites. This served the King's interests, above all, by reducing the power of ecclesiastical institutions, just as the King's policy of elevating men of common birth reduced the power of the aristocratic families.

What was needed was a clear statement of what Henry's English church stood for. To that end, Cromwell called a convocation of church officials to address this need. They came up with "Ten Articles" that would define the doctrines of the Church of England. The list was a compromise that satisfied no one. The articles stated that:

1. The Bible and the three ecumenical creeds were "the basis and summary of true Christian faith." (this was an implicit rejection of Papal authority, but did not go as far as the Lutheran position. Thomas Bilney would have been comfortable with this formulation);
2. Baptism imparted remission of sins and regeneration and was necessary for salvation, even in the case of infants. (The Anabaptist teaching that baptism was for adults and that persons baptized as infants needed to be re-baptized was heresy. Bilney, on the other hand, would have approved);
3. The sacrament of penance, with confession and absolution, was necessary to salvation. (Many Protestants by this time were insisting that there were only two valid sacraments — baptism and communion, and rejected the role of the priesthood in hearing confession. This article placed the Church of England between the Lutheran and Catholic positions. Many were by now rejecting the notion that any kind of "absolution" could be offered by a priest — and Bilney would have agreed with them);
4. That the body and blood of Christ are really present in the Eucharist. ("Real presence" was a term that implicitly rejected the Catholic doctrine of transubstantiation, without committing to the Lutheran one of consubstantiation; it was a rejection of the "sacramentarian" view (held by Anabaptists and Calvinists), that Christ was "spiritually" present in communion elements, but not in any physical sense. Thomas Bilney could have been comfortable with this ambiguity);
5. Justification is by faith, but good works are necessary. (This tempered the Lutheran "justification (solely) by faith" teaching, but

stopped far short of endorsing the Catholic idea that anything can be "earned" through good works. Bilney would have agreed with this formulation);

6.   Images can be used as representations of virtue and good example and also to remind people of their sins but are not objects of worship. (Bilney could have lived with this statement, but would have preferred that the images be removed);

7.   Saints are to be honored as examples of life and as furthering the prayers of the faithful. (Bilney would have rejected the notion that saints could mediate in any sense between the believer and God, but would not have objected to treating the saints as examples of good behavior);

8.   Praying to saints is permitted, and holy days should be observed. (Bilney would have emphatically rejected the idea of praying to saints);

9.   The observance of various rites and ceremonies, such as clerical vestments, sprinkling of holy water, bearing of candles on Candlemas, and giving of ashes on Ash Wednesday, is good and laudable. However, none of these has power to forgive sin. (Bilney would have felt fully vindicated on this point);

10. It is a good and charitable deed to pray for the dead. However, the doctrine of purgatory is biblically uncertain. Abuses related to purgatory, such as the claim that papal indulgences or masses for the dead offered at certain localities (such as the *scala coeli* mass) can deliver immediately from purgatory, are to be rejected. (Bilney would have been pleased by this statement but would not have supported praying for the dead).

The Ten Articles were greeted with outrage in parts of England. The Catholic traditionalists were alarmed that only three of the seven sacraments were affirmed. Church officials recognized immediately that their revenues were in jeopardy if people would no longer pay for prayers to release the dead from purgatory, or bring cash offerings to the images of saints in their churches. These ideas were heretical — dissenters had been burned for promoting them. Why embrace them now?

The radical reformers liked it no better. The Ten Articles left in place the penances and pilgrimages that they considered to be superstitious, or even idolatrous. They still left the priesthood in a position of power that no man should ever wield over another.

Nonetheless, the King ordered that the articles be incorporated into a larger publication "The Bishops Book" that explained the doctrines in more detail and that parts of the book should be read from the pulpit each Sunday. Some people began to take it seriously. Some priests took wives or began conducting the Mass in English. There were instances of vandalism, where religious images were removed from churches and burned. The demand for English-language Bibles grew.

1536: The Dissolutions

The one part of the church establishment that Henry could not easily control was the network of monasteries, convents, priories, and friaries that spread across his kingdom. More than ten thousand monks, nuns, and friars inhabited these places, and no less than one hundred thousand laymen were financially dependent on them — some employed as tenants or servants on the large estates; a great many of the poorest folk were fed on any given day by the charity of the holy orders. They represented a core of resistance to the new ideas that were taking root in England. Some of the orders reported directly to the Pope, independently of the local bishops and archbishops. Not even the Supreme Head of the Church could demand their loyalty.

Furthermore, they were wealthy. No one was quite sure how wealthy, but they had been receiving gifts of land and treasure for several centuries, so it had to be a lot. Henry and his advisors were determined to find out. The late Cardinal Wolsey had set a precedent many years before when he ordered that thirty "decayed" monasteries be dissolved; these were places whose members were too old or too few to be economically viable: the monks and nuns were transferred to other, larger institutions, and their real estate was sold. Wolsey used the proceeds to found and endow other institutions, such as schools and university colleges.

Thomas Cromwell led the effort to inventory the ecclesiastical assets of the kingdom, beginning in 1534. It was an open secret that the government was looking for more revenue, and taxing the church lands was the goal. In the following year, an act of Parliament known as the "Suppression of Religious Houses Act" authorized Cromwell to "visit" all the monasteries and friaries in the kingdom, to evaluate the quality of their spiritual life, and suppress, or close, those found wanting or any so small that their yearly income was less than two hundred pounds. Cromwell delegated this task to a commission of "visitors," who reported back to him. The visitors reported a long list of "superstitious" practices that the houses had been encouraging, such as renting out "miraculous" pieces of clothing to the sick, or to pregnant women. Many of these objects were confiscated by the visitors and sent to London. The visitors also discovered that in many cases, monks and friars were receiving an annual income from houses that they no longer inhabited, preferring to supplement their income with jobs in the secular world. Other, more lurid, stories emerged, of monks engaged in sexual misconduct, or squandering the houses' assets on personal luxuries.

The result was that two hundred forty-three small houses were identified for dissolution, their assets to become the property of the King. Houses that cooperated with the process could avoid being closed, by paying large fines (assuming they had the resources); the rank and file were offered a choice between transfer to a larger house, or a lifetime pension. Many took the pension. The pensions were funded out of the resources of the houses themselves so that Henry did not immediately receive the full value of his appropriations. The process of managing these assets was given to a "Court of Augmentations" that Cromwell created for the purpose. Each house's case had to be decided before this court — how many pensioners, what assets were available, who would manage or purchase the properties, and at what price.

The Lord Chancellor of the Court of Augmentations was none other than Sir Richard Rich, the prosecutor who had sealed the fate of Sir Thomas More. Sir Richard was about to become a very wealthy man.

Henry's marriage to Anne Boleyn had not produced the heir that he was expecting. Anne had several miscarriages and bore one healthy child, a girl named Elizabeth.

Henry's disappointment turned to desperation, then a determination to be free of his marriage to Anne. He ordered his chancellor, Thomas Cromwell, who had been her ally, to find grounds for divorce. In the end, Cromwell found such grounds. Anne was tried for incest, adultery, and treason, for a supposed affair with her brother. The evidence was thin, but the verdict was favorable to the King. Anne Boleyn was executed on May 19th, 1536; Catherine, his first wife had died just four months earlier. Henry was now a widower — twice in the same year, by some accounts. He announced his betrothal to Jane Seymour the following day, and they were married ten days later. An outbreak of the plague started in London soon after, delaying her coronation.

The dissolution of the small houses and the publication of the Ten Articles met with resistance, particularly in the north of England. There was a rising in Lincolnshire in October 1536. Twenty-two thousand or more armed insurgents took control of the city of Lincoln, and demanded, among other things, the end of peacetime taxes, the Ten Articles, the dissolution of the monasteries, and a purging of "heretics" from Henry's government. Henry responded with a show of military force, and the rising collapsed. The leaders, including lawyers and monks, were arrested and executed.

The following October there was another, larger rising in Yorkshire. Forty thousand or more "Pilgrims" declared a "Pilgrimage of Grace," and took control of the city of York. Catholic religious practices were restored, religious houses were reopened, and monks and nuns were persuaded to return. The rebels singled out Thomas Cromwell and Richard Rich as the source of their problems, (men of low birth, unsuitable to govern), and urged their dismissal. So large was the revolt, that Henry's military commanders were forced to negotiate a truce, and offer a general pardon to the participants, promising them a new Parliament. Henry had not authorized such negotiation and felt bound to pardon no one, nor to call a Parliament.

The following February, there was a third rising in other parts of the North. This time Henry's army responded forcefully, and the rising collapsed; the leaders were arrested, along with leaders of the "Pilgrimage of Grace," and more than two hundred were executed: their heads were displayed on London Bridge.

Another burning took place in 1538, and it was an unusual one. John Forest was a friar who had served Catherine of Aragon as a chaplain while she lived. He had vocally opposed the annulment of her marriage to Henry and refused to take the Oath of Supremacy. He was a marked man and was confined to various friaries, as one by one, they were dissolved. He was convicted of treason under the Law of Supremacy, for denying that Henry could be head of the Church of England. He was also convicted of heresy, under the same law. Unlike the dozens of clerics who were similarly convicted and hanged, it was decided that he should burn. Forest was the first, and last, orthodox Catholic to be burned in England. The method chosen was particularly awkward — he was chained and dangled over the flames at Smithfield. It took two hours for him to die.

Henry was convinced more than ever that the religious houses were a threat, and he determined to be rid of them. The large houses now received the same treatment as the smaller ones just two years previously. Sir Richard Rich and his Court of Augmentations were very busy for the next few years.

Nearly all the lands of the great houses became the property of the King. In a few cases, families that had granted land to the houses in the distant past were able to reclaim them, but the King suddenly had a great deal of property to dispose of. The Court of Augmentations sold most of them to eager buyers. Sir Richard and his commissioners reviewed each property and assessed its value. The price was usually set at twenty years' worth of the revenue that the property could expect to generate. This number was always a bit negotiable, and Sir Richard picked up about one hundred properties for himself. This included the priory of St. Bartholomew the Great in Smithfield, London. The chapel was converted to a parish church, and Rich demolished the Prior's residence and replaced it with a new house which became his city residence, right next door to the church with a pleasant view of the open field beyond. The crowning jewel of his acquisitions was the monastery at Leigh's, in Essex, near the village of Felsted. Rich renamed the place "Leez Priory," though it was his personal country estate — a mansion, more precisely. He also acquired a hundred or so smaller manors in Essex, which provided a comfortable annual income for himself and his family (Lady Rich had fifteen children), for generations to come.

1539: Six Articles

Henry was ruthless in putting down rebellion, but he also realized that some accommodation might help avoid future risings. Things had gotten out of hand. Parish priests were getting married, and conducting services in English rather than Latin. Protestant extremists were removing religious images from local churches and destroying them. Worse, the upheavals in Europe were washing their dregs up on the shores of England. Refugees were finding their way across the channel and bringing new heresies with them. Among them were Anabaptists, the worst of the "Sacramentarians'". They were neither monks nor priests nor scholars. They were laymen, mostly, but insisted on preaching their heretical views to any who would listen. They insisted that baptism must follow an adult confession of faith, and re-baptized members who had been baptized as infants, thus dismissing the validity of the sacrament of baptism for nearly all Englishmen. They taught that the "true" church must be separate from the influence of government and that churches controlled by the government (like Henry's) were apostate. They denied transubstantiation, consubstantiation, and the "real presence." They rejected the sacrament of confession. They claimed that the Bible was the only valid ecclesiastical authority. Whenever they could, the English church arrested and burned them — ten in 1535 alone, two more in 1538, at Smithfield, in front of Sir Richard Rich's new house. Still, they kept coming. And they found Englishmen willing to listen. Thomas Cromwell, now Viceregent and Vicar General of the Church of England, ordered that every parish in England would begin keeping accurate records of every christening, marriage, and burial, to help identify Anabaptists, who would not present their children for baptism.

Henry had never really been happy with the Ten Articles. He tasked Parliament with producing something nearer to his own conservative views. Parliament came up with Six Articles, more to Henry's liking:

- Transubstantiation was endorsed as the Church of England's official position, and dissenters faced death by burning — without the opportunity to recant;
- Communion in "one kind" (bread only, no wine) was endorsed;
- Priestly celibacy was required;
- Vows of chastity (such as in religious orders) must be maintained;
- Private masses would continue;
- Confession was affirmed as "expedient and necessary," particularly for "the helping of souls in purgatory."

Refusal to affirm any of the above beliefs was punishable by hanging except the first, which required burning.

The Six Articles became known among the Protestants in England as "the bloody whip with six strings." Hugh Latimer and Nicholas Shaxton resigned as bishops in protest. Both were arrested and accused of treason. The King relented, and removed them from their offices, with the stipulation that they refrain from promoting their views.

Thomas Cranmer, Archbishop of Canterbury, quickly sent his wife and children out of England. Hundreds of Protestant scholars fled the country. Some found refuge in Geneva, Switzerland, others in the Lutheran cities of Germany. From there, they wrote and printed an avalanche of books, tracts, and statements critical of the Church of England and its Supreme Head.

Henry's third wife, Jane Seymour, gave birth to a son in 1537. Jane died of complications from the delivery just twelve days later. Henry was a widower once more. The boy, named Edward, was healthy. Henry had his heir at last.

Thomas Cromwell was now "Baron Cromwell of Wimbledon," a reward for faithful and effective service. His enemies were more determined than ever to bring him down; he was a usurper of power and prestige that properly belonged to the hereditary nobility. Ironically, after managing Henry's marriage problems so successfully, it was a royal marriage that caused his undoing, just as it had for Henry's two previous chancellors — Wolsey and More. With Jane Seymour dead, and the royal succession settled, Cromwell began to look for strategic political alliances that could be secured with another marriage for the King. Henry took some persuading — he had his heir, after all, and he mourned Jane Seymour as the only one of his wives who had not betrayed him.

Cromwell recommended that Henry marry a princess of Cleves, a small Lutheran principality in northwest Germany. Cleves was not a military power, but, as part of the Empire, it offered England diplomatic leverage in the emerging alliance between the Empire and France. Eventually, Henry agreed to the marriage, with Princess Anne.

The whole thing was a fiasco. Henry had never met Anne. His impression of her appearance was formed by a small painting, which turned out to be over-flattering, from Henry's perspective. He did not find her attractive and refused to consummate the union. Cromwell's enemies had a more attractive option. Catherine Howard was seventeen, vivacious and pretty — and, as it happened, a cousin of Henry's second wife, Anne Boleyn. She was placed among the Queen's "ladies in waiting," where the King was sure to notice her. Henry noticed and favored Catherine with gifts. Henry demanded that his marriage to Anne be annulled. Cromwell got the annulment, though it involved a large financial settlement for Anne, who retired to the countryside to live out her days. But Cromwell's favor with the King was irretrievably damaged. He was arrested in June of 1540, accused of a long list of treasonous offenses, including too much leniency in protecting Protestant heretics (and even Anabaptists) from enforcement of the Six Articles, and seeking personal gain from his office. Prominent among his accusers was his associate, Sir Richard Rich. He was convicted by act of Parliament of these offenses without trial and condemned to death.

On July 28, 1540, Thomas Cromwell was publicly beheaded. The King was out of town that day — he was attending his wedding in Surrey. Catherine Howard was now Queen.

The following month was a busy one in Smithfield. On July 7, a lawyer named William Collins was burned for heresy. On the 30th of July, three more were burned as Protestant heretics, including Robert Barnes — an associate of Thomas Bilney, William Tyndale, and Thomas Cromwell — and two clergymen. For good measure, three Catholic clergymen were executed the same day by hanging — for refusing to take the Oath of Supremacy.

By August the royal couple, and anyone else who could, had left London. It was another plague year.

1543: True Religion

Henry's fifth marriage lasted less than two years. At forty-nine, the King suffered from chronic painful ulcers on his legs. He became moody and depressed, given to outbursts of anger. He berated his advisors, accusing them of using "false accusations" and "pretexts" in contriving the death of Cromwell, "the most faithful servant" he ever had. This was bad news indeed for Cromwell's accusers. Worse, Catherine failed to play her part.

It was discovered that she had been seeing a younger man in private. Perhaps she did so out of boredom, but further investigations revealed that she had paid blackmailers for their silence about supposed indiscretions that occurred before her marriage to Henry. When faced with the coercive means available to Henry's investigators, the blackmailers were all too willing to abandon their silence. By November 23, 1541, she was a prisoner, awaiting trial. Her supposed lovers were executed for treason on December 10, their heads displayed on London Bridge.

Most of Catherine's close relatives were sent to the Tower of London, to await the outcome. They had staked their ambition on the discretion of a seventeen-year-old girl, and it was too much for her. In the end, she did what she could to protect them, asking for mercy for them, while accepting the "worthy and just" sentence that Parliament had (once again) imposed, just before she was beheaded on February 13, 1543. Henry was a widower again.

The religious turmoil in England did not abate with Cromwell's downfall, or the brief ascendancy of the conservative bishops and nobles. Too many refugees with heretical ideas, too many laymen with their own Bibles, too many monks and friars willing to face hanging for opposing the King's supremacy, too many Protestants willing to risk the fire. And too many noblemen who saw opportunity for advancement in the King's ill health and marital woes.

Parliament took the matter in hand in 1543. The "Act for the Advancement of True Religion and for the Abolishment of the Contrary" sought to alleviate the problem by restricting Bible reading, declaring that people of "the lower sort" did not benefit from reading the Bible in English. Clerics, nobles, gentry and wealthy merchants might read the Bible privately or publicly. Women of those classes were allowed to read the Bible, but only in private. Persons of Yeoman or lesser rank were forbidden to read the Bible in any circumstance. The Bible could not be read in English in a church service (too many low-class people might be present). Tyndale's translations were specifically condemned. (Parliament may not have been aware that the Bibles placed in every parish church were actually Tyndale's translations.) Pamphlets, books, and songs that referred to the Bible or to religious matters were also forbidden unless approved by the King. Printing of Bibles or religious books was illegal. Songs, rhymes, and dramatic plays which satirized the church, or its officials, or promoted heretical ideas were forbidden. Violation of this law was heresy, and the usual penalties applied.

This was a case of closing the barn door after the horses were out. Henry's government did not have the resources to search every house in the realm for contraband Bibles. Wolsey and More had tried and failed to shut off the supply of Bibles and other religious books that were smuggled into the country. They tried to suppress poems and songs that referred to the Bible or satirized religious authority because they were thought to be particularly responsible for corrupting the youth (this simply made those things irresistible to the young, who were looking for things that would scandalize their parents and must therefore be enjoyed in secret). Musicians now joined other heretics at the stake.

The King's health was clearly failing and there was a scramble to find Henry another wife among the various factions that contended for positions of power — never mind the King's propensity for beheading his closest advisors. The Protestant faction won the next round. Henry was introduced to Catherine Parr, a woman of thirty-two years, twice widowed. She was a niece of Thomas Cranmer, the Archbishop, and a member of the household of Henry's oldest daughter, Mary. She was also committed to Protestant beliefs, though not publicly. Henry and Catherine were married on July 12, 1543, at Hampton Court Palace, Cardinal Wolsey's luxurious old residence.

Queen Catherine devoted herself to Henry's care and earned his loyalty. She helped reconcile him with his two daughters, Mary and Elizabeth and grew close to his son Edward. For the first time in many years, Henry had something like an intact family. In 1544, Henry determined to go to war in France and left Catherine to rule as regent in his absence. She performed better than expected. Her enemies had difficulty finding something against her.

The only promising line of attack was her religion. Catherine was in the habit of reading her Bible in the company of her ladies and discussing it with them. Under the law, she was within her rights to read the Bible in private. If a charge of heresy was to be lodged, evidence would have to be produced. Henry's new Lord Chancellor, Lord Wriothesley, and Stephen Gardiner, now bishop of Winchester, persuaded Henry to issue a warrant for her arrest so that she could be examined, but Henry changed his mind. They would have to get at the Queen by indirect methods, through her associates. They could not attack through members of her inner circle, so they looked further afield.

Fortune seemed to favor them. In May of 1546, they arrested a woman named Anne Askew for "gospelling" (street preaching) in London. Askew had been arrested before and remanded to the custody of her Catholic husband, who finally expelled her from his house in frustration. She was well-educated, and one of the earliest known female poets in the English language. She was well connected in London; one of her brothers was cupbearer to the king, she had family connections to Archbishop Cranmer and members of the Privy Council. She was also an avid reader of the English Bible and had developed the scandalous habit of quoting the scriptures and explaining them to people in public places. Askew had been examined before, and the examiners were exasperated by her knowledge of scripture and her "plain" refutation of basic doctrine. How could she deny the "real presence" of Christ's body in the Eucharist? "It is a piece of bread. For more proof thereof… let it but lie in the box three months and it will be mouldy," she replied. This was Sacramentarianism — ample evidence to burn her for heresy. But it was also possible that she could name other Protestants in London, and lead them all the way to the Queen herself.

Askew refused to give up any names, even under threat of death. The only recourse was torture. As a point of law, women could not be tortured, but Gardiner, Wriothesley, and now Sir Richard Rich were determined to forge ahead. Anne Askew was put to the rack in the Tower of London. She was urged to name names. She would not. She was racked until her screams were heard in the courtyard outside and then passed out. She was revived, refused again to name names, and racked again, screaming until she passed out. At this point, the Constable of the Tower, Anthony Kingston, refused to continue with the torture. He excused himself, then sought the presence of the King, to beg pardon for failing his duty. Wriothesley and Rich took over and stretched Askew to the point that both her arms and legs were pulled from their sockets. Still, she refused to give names. The Lieutenant of the Tower, hearing her cries, intervened and returned her to her cell. She had to be carried since walking was now impossible.

Having failed to extract any names, Wriothesley and Rich were stymied. Their unlawful torture of a woman was an embarrassment. Still, an execution was in order. Best to brazen it out and wait for time to erase the disgrace.

Anne Askew was not the only heretic they found. Nicholas Shaxton was summoned to London from his parish in the countryside. Shaxton, now in his sixties, knew what the stakes were — he remarked to his wife that he must "either burn, or forsake the truth." He was convicted of heresy for preaching against the Six Articles, and sentenced to burn. It was the test he had been avoiding most of his adult life, certainly since Thomas Bilney's execution, fifteen years before. King Henry sent a delegation of bishops and chaplains to confer with him, and three days before his scheduled execution, he signed a statement of recantation. The first condition of his release was to visit Anne Askew in prison and persuade her to recant as well. Failing that, he would have to preach a sermon at her execution, refuting all her heresies, while confessing his own errors. Askew would not be persuaded.

July 12, 1546: Smithfield

A kind of reviewing stand was set up at Smithfield, in front of old Saint Bartholomew's, just a few yards from Sir Richard Rich's new house. Various dignitaries were seated there, including Sir Richard himself. A large crowd had gathered around the four stakes that were erected for the executions; so large, that the people crowded too close for their safety. The preacher for the event was Nicholas Shaxton, the old associate of Thomas Bilney. Shaxton was a friend of Anne Askew and would have had a place at the stake, but for his recantation of the heretical ideas they once had shared. Shaxton's penance for his recanted heresy involved the usual standing in the church square with a bundle of faggots on his back — plus preaching the sermon at the execution of his friend. Rich found the irony touching, almost profound.

Some of the dignitaries were not familiar with burnings. One of these was seated next to Rich.

"How long does a burning take?" Evidently, he had somewhere else to be. Or maybe he was squeamish.

"It varies," replied Rich, "though this one should not take too long — we're using gunpowder to hasten the end."

"Gunpowder?" the man looked around nervously as if looking for a safer place to sit.

"It is a method used on the mainland," he explained. "Not to worry, it is just a small bag of gunpowder hung around the neck of each heretic. When the fire reaches it, there is an explosion — usually it is enough to end their life."

"Can you be sure of it?"

"You can never be sure how it will explode. I have heard that some are decapitated by the blast — which is a quicker end than they deserve."

Rich's companion's eyes widened a little.

Don't worry, if that happens, *they* may get a surprise," he nodded to the crowd, "but it will not reach us."

Rich imagined a human head flying through the air and landing in his companion's lap. <u>That</u> would be a story to tell his children. No, too grisly. Undignified. Gallows humor.

Sir Richard was all too aware that he was being carefully watched by his companions in the reviewing stand. The scandal of his role in the torture of Anne Askew was still fresh. It remained to be seen whether it would damage his career, but any sign of weakness or wavering would surely make things worse. His choice to be here today was a show of confidence in himself. His rivals could stare all they liked. Besides, it was practically at his front door. Watching the procedure from inside his house would look as if he were hiding from something.

Some whispered that a man who could not wrest a confession from a woman on the rack was either incompetent or a fool. That stung. But perhaps Askew would make a good show of it. If she recanted at the last, he would be vindicated.

The condemned were brought to their respective stakes. Anne Askew had to be carried in because she could not walk. The three men were chained to their stakes standing, but, since Askew could not stand, a small shelf or seat had been attached to hers, and she was chained in a seated position.

Now it was time for the sermon. Nicholas Shaxton took his place and began to preach. Incredibly, Anne Askew began a running commentary on his sermon. Her voice was strong enough to carry across the crowd to the gallery. "Amen," she said when Shaxton made a point she agreed with. "There he misseth, and speaketh without the book," she proclaimed when she disagreed with him. Shaxton was clearly flummoxed by the whole performance. The crowd was captivated, as if they were hearing two sermons at once — which in a sense, they were. Rich felt grudging admiration for her brazenness, at the threshold of a painful death — no chance that she would recant, now. Shaxton finally made it to the end of his sermon and issued the obligatory appeal to the condemned to recant. None did. As the flames were lit, Anne Askew began to sing:

> "Like as the armed knight
> Appointed to the field,
> With this world will I fight
> And Faith shall be my shield.
>
> Faith is that weapon strong
> Which will not fail at need.
> My foes, therefore, among
> Therewith will I proceed.
>
> As it is had in strength
> And force of Christes way
> It will prevail at length

Though all the devils say nay.

Faith in the fathers old
Obtained rightwisness
Which make me very bold
To fear no world's distress.

I now rejoice in heart
And Hope bid me do so
For Christ will take my part
And ease me of my woe.

Thou saist, lord, who so knock,
To them wilt thou attend.
Undo, therefore, the lock
And thy strong power send.

More enmyes now I have
Than hairs upon my head.
Let them not me deprave
But fight thou in my stead.

On thee my care I cast.
For all their cruel spight
I set not by their haste
For thou art my delight.

I am not she that list
My anchor to let fall
For every drizzling mist
My ship substancial.

Not oft use I to wright
In prose nor yet in rime,
Yet will I shew one sight
That I saw in my time.

I saw a rial throne
Where Justice should have sit

> But in her stead was one
> Of moody cruel wit.
>
> Absorpt was rightwisness
> As of the raging flood
> Sathan in his excess
> Suct up the guiltless blood.
>
> Then thought I, Jesus lord,
> When thou shalt judge us all
> Hard is it to record
> On these men what will fall.
>
> Yet lord, I thee desire
> For that they do to me
> Let them not taste the hire
> Of their iniquity."

Or so it may have been. The lyrics were hers, composed during her imprisonment, and published after her death. That she sang them is likely enough, but she may not have had time to finish the ballad — there was, naturally, a lot of screaming before the gunpowder ignited.

The whole performance was stunning. Rich for his part, felt vindicated by Askew's steadfastness (or stubbornness) — how could the rack break a woman that stood to the fire as she had? He had shown himself ruthless in his service to the King, and above all, loyal. Henry would surely recognize that. And his rivals would think twice before attacking him. As the crowd dispersed, he walked back to his house, for supper. His mood was optimistic, his appetite hearty.

1549: Uniformity

King Henry died barely six months after Anne Askew and her three companions were burned and the government was too preoccupied to pursue heretics for a while. Henry was succeeded by his son, Edward VI, who was just nine years old. The kingdom was placed under the temporary rule of a council of regents. Edward Seymour (brother of Jane Seymour, Edward's mother) was appointed Lord Protector and effectively ruled the Kingdom. Seymour's religious views were Protestant, and during his brief rule, Parliament repealed the Six Articles, the Act for the Advancement of True Religion, and the ancient heresy laws. This did nothing to set aside the King's supremacy over the church, and charges of treason could still be brought against religious dissenters — which included any clergyman who showed loyalty to the Old Religion. It did however create an opening for reform-minded Protestants who were willing to accept the Act of Supremacy.

Thomas Cranmer, still the Archbishop of Canterbury, undertook to make England a Protestant kingdom. He published a Book of Common Prayer — a complete liturgy in English — which was to be used in every church service. No more Latin. The doctrines that the BCP taught included justification by faith alone: confession and penance (the Sacrament of Penance) were rejected because no human act or work could gain forgiveness. The sacrament of the Eucharist was also rejected — a spiritual communion with Christ as a rite of remembrance, no transubstantiation or "real presence." Prayers for the dead were rejected because there was no Purgatory. Veneration of Saints was denounced as idolatry.

Predictably, there was strong resistance to the reforms in the countryside. There were outright revolts in Cornwall, Devon, and Norfolk, which had to be forcibly suppressed. More than five thousand died in the mayhem. But there were also many clerics, no longer constrained by vows of celibacy, who married — not only parish priests but bishops and friars. Cranmer was able to bring his wife and children back from exile and acknowledge them publicly. The BCP was made mandatory by the Parliamentary "Act of Uniformity" passed in 1549.

Edward Seymour awarded himself the title Duke of Somerset, once he consolidated his political power. Among the council of regents were Sir Richard Rich and Lord Thomas Wriothesley, who together had racked Ann Askew. Wriothesley opposed Seymour's power grab and found himself alone. Sir Richard supported the Duke and was made "Baron Rich of Leez" for his display of loyalty. A month later he replaced Wriothesley as Lord Chancellor of England.

The Duke of Somerset's position was weakened after the turmoil surrounding the Act of Uniformity. This was enough to embolden his rivals, and Baron Rich was among those on the council who voted to depose the Duke, which led to his execution in 1552. Baron Rich resigned his chancellorship that year but kept his title.

1553: Forty-two Articles

eanwhile, King Edward had reached the age of fourteen and was beginning to make his opinions felt in the government. His opinions, more than anything were strongly Protestant. Young as he was, he was Supreme Head of the English church. He urged Cranmer to revise the Book of Common Prayer, including a list of forty-two doctrinal statements or articles. These laid out in more detail what English church members should believe. The forty-two articles were published in June of 1553 by royal mandate. Edward died, at the age of fifteen, the following month.

Edward had specified that his successor be neither of his half-sisters, Mary and Elizabeth, but his cousin, Lady Jane Grey. Baron Rich, always attentive in times of crisis, sided with the supporters of Lady Jane, but threw his support to Henry's oldest daughter, Mary, when it became clear that Mary's supporters had the upper hand. Not all the Baron's colleagues were as nimble.

Mary was Catholic in her convictions and determined that England be reunited with the Catholic traditions of her past. This was very bad news for men like Thomas Cranmer. The forty-two articles were the antithesis of that policy, and Cranmer could not disown his authorship of them.

Mary began her reign with a statement that she would not compel any Englishman to conform to her religion. Stephen Gardiner, secretary to Cardinal Wolsey, and Henry VIII, architect of the Act of Supremacy, was now Lord Chancellor. Shortly thereafter, Mary began arresting prominent Protestants. Thomas Cranmer was sent to the tower, along with bishops like Nicholas Ridley and John Hooper, Hugh Latimer (Bilney's old friend), and John Rogers (translator of the Matthew Bible). Mary convened a Parliament in October, which repealed the religious laws of Edward VI, and re-instated the Six Articles which required clerical celibacy. The following year, Parliament repealed Henry VIII's Act of Supremacy — the Pope was once again head of the English Church. Her attempt to return the lands and assets seized during the dissolutions failed — too many members of Parliament were in possession of those properties and saw no reason to give them back. Nonetheless, the Pope agreed to take England back and let the noblemen keep their property, and England was officially Catholic once again.

Baron Rich of Leez was out of a job since his Court of Augmentations was shut down. Once again, he must find ways to offer useful service to his sovereign. He had made such adjustments before and would do so again; to do less would risk losing all his property and position, quite possibly his life. Fortunately, he had an established reputation for prosecuting heretics should the need arise.

Parliament obliged Mary (and Baron Rich) by renewing the Heresy acts, and burning heretics was once again the policy of the government. More than eight hundred prominent Protestants fled the country. They found refuge in Lutheran parts of Germany, and in Geneva, a self-declared republic with a Protestant constitution. Geneva was dominated by the leadership of John Calvin, and the English refugees came under the influence of his teaching. Henceforth, English Protestantism would be Calvinist, not Lutheran. Among the refugees who fled to Geneva was Myles Coverdale, Bible translator.

In England, Mary was now married to Philip II, Crown Prince of Spain. It was the alliance that English diplomats had sought for generations. Henry VII had foreseen that Spain would be the rising power in Europe and a counterweight to French power, even before the treasures of the New World began streaming into her treasuries. Henry VIII had sought a Spanish alliance for the same strategic reasons — only to lose the chance when he determined to annul his marriage to Catherine, Mary's mother, and Philip's great-aunt. Parliament placed some restrictions on the terms of the marriage, including the proviso that Philip could never inherit the English throne, in the case of Mary's death. Philip disliked the idea but agreed because the alliance was worth it.

England's support would help Philip maintain his control of the Netherlands, which was looking more difficult each year. Philip was twenty-seven years old, and already a widower. His first wife, a princess of Portugal, had died just four days after giving birth to a son. Mary was thirty-eight. Philip's responsibilities kept him in various parts of the Spanish realm during most of his marriage to Mary. Mary needed to stay in England — her absence would make it too tempting for men of title to attempt her overthrow. Philip visited from time to time, and it was he who persuaded Parliament to restore the Heresy Acts. It was up to Mary to enforce them. In this effort, she had no more dedicated assistant than Baron Rich of Leez. His personal knowledge of the men at the highest levels of government made him invaluable at identifying heretical sympathies, or any taint of disloyalty to the new queen and her agenda.

Mary began in 1555. On February 4th of that year, they burned John Rogers, the Bible translator and pastor of St. Sepulchre church, at Smithfield. The following week, they burned bishop John Hooper and two other clergymen, each at a different location. In March, they burned ten more — two were clergymen, but the others included barbers, butchers, and fishermen. They burnt another prominent clergyman in April, another clergyman, an upholsterer, and two husbandmen in May. In June it was drapers, fullers, and weavers. Sixteen more burned in July — the busiest month yet. In August, it was eighteen — as many as six at a time, for efficiency.

The public mood was turning against the executions, in part because the middling classes were being so clearly targeted. Clearly, the Protestant infection was no longer a problem only among the academic elites, the politically ambitious, and a few extremist street preachers. It was embedded in the middle class of tradesmen and merchants. Burning was no longer a tactic of deterrence — the government appeared to believe that it could kill all the heretics, given enough time.

Mary's popular support plummeted. She had earned the nickname "Bloody Mary." Her advisors warned her of revolt unless she moderated her policies. This was not an argument likely to change her mind. She had endured a life of rejection by her father, and by extension, the English nation. She had been declared a bastard by act of Parliament, denied her legitimate rights until well after her 30th birthday, all because of these Protestants and their heresy. She was temperamentally like her father, who met rejection with redoubled aggression and nurtured grudges to the end of his life.

In October of 1555, it was the turn of Hugh Latimer, the King's chaplain, and Nicholas Ridley, Bishop of London. They were burned at Oxford University — a warning to the academic establishment, perhaps. Thomas Cranmer was compelled to witness the death of his friends after he had recanted. The recantation made no difference in the long run; Cranmer was sentenced to burn, anyway. Just prior to his execution on March 21st, 1556, Cranmer retracted his recantation and went to the stake an unrepentant heretic. By that time ninety others had preceded him.

Nicholas Shaxton, by contrast, was rehabilitated by the new regime. Shortly after the execution of Anne Askew, he separated from his wife and three children and resumed the celibate life required by the Six Articles. When Mary came to the throne, his policy of supporting the sovereign was rewarded with promotion — at seventy years of age. He received a pardon for his marriage from one of Mary's cardinals and led the prosecution and burning of heretics like John Hullier in Cambridge, his old alma mater. Hullier was burned in 1556, the same year that Shaxton's friend Thomas Cranmer was burned. Shaxton died in August of the same year. He had escaped the fire at the cost of his family and friends. Whether the cost was worth it, who can say? It is hard to place a value on a human life.

Over the next three years, no less than two hundred eight-four men and women would be executed for heresy in England, not counting more than thirty who died in prison, awaiting the fire. They included maids, glovers, hosiers, sawyers, tanners, wheelwrights, tallow chandlers, glaziers — every trade imaginable. Protestantism in England was a middle-class religion, now. At this rate, it would take many years to suppress it. And Mary did not have many years.

In 1556, Philip's father, Charles V died and Philip was crowned King of Spain, which came to include Portugal, half of Italy, the Netherlands, and Spain's vast empire in the Americas. He did not succeed his father as Holy Roman Emperor, but his realm was larger than any other European kingdom — more than enough to demand his full-time attention. In the Spanish view, the entire Pacific Ocean between South America and the Philippines (Philip's namesake islands) was "Mare Clausam" — closed to navigation by any but Spanish ships. Philip visited Mary briefly the following year, then returned to Spain. War was brewing with France, The Netherlands were restless, and Spanish Kings were no longer welcomed by the populace in England.

Mary died on November 17th, 1558. The last batch of heretics condemned to burn on the following day were reprieved — because Mary was no longer alive to sign the certificates of execution. Baron Rich was out of a job again.

1559: Thirty-nine Articles

There was really only one logical candidate to succeed Mary: her half-sister, Elizabeth, daughter of Henry and Anne Boleyn. In spite of all his wives, Henry had produced only three living descendants — and the other two were deceased. Elizabeth was twenty-five years old, and unmarried, despite efforts to find her a suitable husband. Philip, the King of Spain and Mary's widower expressed some interest in a match. Given the attitude of the country to all things Spanish, this did not seem feasible. Henry had a niece named Mary who could have been a candidate, but she was married to the Crown Prince of France — again, not what the English were looking for.

Elizabeth's coronation occurred on January 15th, 1559. Her religious leanings were Protestant, but she wished to avoid the civil strife that had plagued so much of Europe, as Catholic and Protestant factions vied for political supremacy in France, Germany, and the Low Countries. Parliament passed a new Act of Supremacy that year, which made Elizabeth the "Supreme Governor" of the Church of England ("Supreme Head" was rejected, because Parliament agreed that a woman should not be "head" of a man, even if she were the Queen). The Heresy Laws were also repealed, so burning was now out of fashion; hanging, torture, and exile would have to do. A new Act of Uniformity was passed, so Cranmer's Book of Common Prayer was mandatory again (with some minor editions). The Act required all Englishmen to attend church services. Failure to do so (whether by refusal or neglect) was punishable by fines, even imprisonment or death. Elizabeth remarked that she couldn't know, and didn't care what a man's secret beliefs were — she would not "make windows into men's hearts and secret thoughts." It was enough that they conform to the rites of her church. The standard of conformity was Cranmer's forty-two articles, minus four that the bishops thought unnecessary, plus one more addition stating that the wicked "do not eat the body of Christ" in the Eucharist (in other words, the real presence did not happen if an unworthy person partook of the elements), resulting in a total of thirty-nine articles. And thirty-nine articles it would be, for many years to come.

1565 — 1569: Legacies

Elizabeth's reign lasted nearly fifty years. This was unusual for any European monarch, the more so since her realm was surrounded by hostile ones. Philip II, King of Spain, declared that he was the rightful ruler of England, once it became clear that Elizabeth would not marry him. France had their own candidate in Elizabeth's cousin Mary, now Queen of Scots. The Pope's excommunication meant that a significant portion of her subjects were morally obligated to depose and execute her. Elizabeth survived by playing her enemies off against one another, by avoiding outright war when she could, and most of all, by gaining the loyalty of her subjects. Catholics might yearn for a more sympathetic religious environment, but when an actual revolt was staged, most would take up arms to defend her. Puritans would harp on the corruption of her church, but when invasion threatened, they rose to her defense with righteous, full-throated fury. And the majority of middling English churchmen and women had no reason to imagine that a Catholic monarch would treat them any better than Bloody Mary had done.

The resentment and outright hatred of things Spanish and Catholic would be a destabilizing feature of English society for centuries to come — thanks largely to Mary's legacy. The heretics she burned were celebrated as martyrs in a popular book written by one of the Swiss refugees, John Foxe. He published it in 1563 under the title "Actes and Monuments," though it soon became known as "Foxe's Book of Martyrs." Thomas Bilney was a heretic no longer, but a martyred prophet of the new religion.

Baron Richard Rich had seen his "three score years and ten" by the eighth year of Elizabeth's reign. He served the new queen in a variety of administrative roles, none as prominent as his Chancellorship for King Edward, or as lucrative as his service with the Court of Augmentations for King Henry. His service to Mary in prosecuting heretics would be remembered, thanks to John Foxe. This was not a flattering legacy, but the Baron had few regrets. He had lived his life at the apex of political power and influence and had survived. Few of his peers could say the same; most of them, in fact, could say nothing at all — the fire and the executioner's axe had taken them, one by one. For the Baron, the prosperity of his family was the most important legacy; he had positioned them to be influential and powerful in their own right for generations to come (unless they be fools). What more could a man do for his children? He was survived by fourteen legitimate children (four male, ten female), and at least one illegitimate son, Richard, who was acknowledged and provided for in his will.

He spent most of his last years in Essex, where he founded a school in the village of Felsted for the education of children born on his numerous manors. He died in 1567, a month short of his seventy-first birthday. He was buried in the church at Felsted. His eldest son, Robert, succeeded him as 2nd Baron Rich that year. His will specified that a chapel should be constructed at the Felsted church to house his tomb. The chapel was completed by his grandson, the 3rd Baron Rich, and stands to this day.

Myles Coverdale was a survivor, too. He was one of the very last of the associates of Thomas Bilney and "Little Germany," nearly fifty years prior. He had a knack for knowing when to run, and he had escaped arrest by the narrowest of margins, more than once. It was luck — or divine providence — that he was still alive: scores of his friends had perished. He returned to England in 1559 and found employment as a tutor to an aristocratic family, then a church rector for two more years. In 1566, he resigned his rectorship at the age of seventy-eight. He spent the last years as a popular "wandering priest"; he was often invited to preach at various parishes. In 1569, aged eighty-one, he died. Coverdale's will stated that he had no living descendants. He left no legacy, apart from his Bible translations, now in the hands of tens of thousands of English men and women.

Part 3: Gloriana

1562: The Dance of Diplomacy

From the beginning of her reign, Elizabeth's throne was in peril. Spain, now the superpower of Europe, was ruled by a man who insisted the English throne was rightfully his. The Catholic church had reorganized and reformed itself after the sack of Rome, and was going on the offensive against Protestant heretics, like Elizabeth. Catholic subjects were encouraged to depose and assassinate excommunicated rulers, and they did so with alarming frequency. In the early years, there were few potential allies for England and plenty of potential enemies. Spain controlled the Netherlands, directly across the North Sea. South of the Netherlands sat France, the traditional rival of England. To the north, Scotland was ruled by Elizabeth's cousin Mary, a Catholic queen with strong French support, as well as the Pope's endorsement as the legitimate queen of England, not to mention the affections of many of Elizabeth's Catholic subjects. England was not wealthy enough to challenge any of these rivals militarily. Sooner or later, an invasion was likely from one direction or another.

Elizabeth's political acumen was confirmed by the success of her religious compromise. She wanted, above all, to avoid a religious civil war, and in this she was successful. Not so France. In 1562, Elizabeth's third year, a Catholic noble attacked a Protestant assembly of five hundred or so meeting in a barn, killing fifty of them, and wounding many more. The "Massacre," as it came to be called, was widely and luridly publicized all over Europe. It was the first of many clashes between French Calvinists, or Huguenots, and the militant Catholics who contended for control of the French kingdom. The civil conflict would continue intermittently for thirty-five years. Nearly three million Frenchmen would die in these conflicts in battle, from mass execution, or the disease and famine that resulted from the conflict. Large numbers of religious refugees would flee the kingdom, seeking refuge in England, the Netherlands, and Germany. They brought with them the accounts of their brutal persecution, and Protestant fear and loathing for "Papists'" was reinforced, as was their loyalty to Elizabeth. For the duration of these wars, the French threat to Elizabeth would be eased. For good measure, Elizabeth offered limited military assistance to the French Huguenots from time to time. The assistance was rarely enough to gain the Huguenots a military advantage, but it prolonged the conflict, and prevented a unified France from threatening her throne, at the very least.

By 1566 the diplomatic situation had shifted a little further in England's favor. The Netherlands, directly across the Channel from England, erupted in revolt against Spanish rule. The revolt was not successful at first, but it tied down the Spanish armies, reducing the threat to England. The revolt continued, beginning what is now known as the Eighty Years War. Over the coming decades, Elizabeth would sporadically offer aid to the Dutch rebels, who established a republic in the northernmost provinces. From there, they launched an aggressive maritime campaign of trade, colonization, and naval warfare. Dutch "Sea Beggars" attacked Spanish ships in the English Channel, as well as throughout the Americas. The Channel would become a naval battleground, with English, Spanish, French, Dutch, and Portuguese navies all contending at one time or another with each other for control of the sea lanes. As the Dutch Republic became wealthier and more powerful, the Spanish presence would wane.

In 1567, Elizabeth's cousin Mary, Queen of Scots, was forced to abdicate her throne, in favor of her one-year-old son James, under the pressure of Calvinist nobles in Scotland. She fled to England, where Elizabeth offered her refuge, but kept her confined to various castles and strongholds, and eventually in the Tower of London so that Elizabeth's spies could watch her every move. The threat from Scotland was neutralized, and the threat from France was further mitigated.

There were setbacks as well. In 1571 a fleet of over two hundred Spanish and Italian warships met a Turkish fleet of similar size at Lepanto, off the coast of Greece. Most of the ships involved were galleys — gunships propelled by oarsmen. The Spanish added a few larger ships with heavier artillery. Most of these ships would not have been large enough to brave the Atlantic, but in Mediterranean waters, they were quick, maneuverable, and lethal. As many as thirty thousand sailors perished in the battle that followed, more than any land battle of the time. Lepanto was a victory for Spain and her allies, that stopped Turkish expansion in the Mediterranean permanently. The king of Spain could now turn his attention westward, to the Netherlands, France, and England.

For a time, Elizabeth allowed the Dutch "Sea Beggars" to use English ports as bases of supply, but in 1572, yielding to Spanish pressure, she closed the English ports to them. The Sea Beggars responded by seizing the small port city of Brielle on the Netherlands coast. In short order, several more Dutch ports were opened to them, then cities in the interior — a full-blown revolt was underway. Spain would pour resources into the effort to suppress the revolt, but would never quite succeed. The northeast provinces would maintain their *de facto* independence until the end of the Eighty Years War. Elizabeth, for her part, could insist that the whole business was the result of doing what Spanish diplomats had demanded.

In France, Calvinist Huguenots were still a strong and growing minority. Many influential aristocrats, particularly in the southern provinces, were pressing for toleration, if not dominance, in French religious affairs. Philip II of Spain led the Catholic reaction to these demands. In 1572, a rumored Huguenot coup attempt led to the assassination of several dozen Protestant aristocrats, and the massacre of thousands of other Huguenots, beginning in Paris, and spreading across France. The number of dead was so great that rivers in France were choked with corpses. In Arles, in the south, the citizens avoided contact with the river Rhone for three months, due to the stench and corruption.

The "Saint Bartholomew's Day Massacre" shocked both Protestants and Catholics with its ferocity. The Pope disowned the leaders of the massacre and declared it murder. Philip II was said to have laughed out loud when he heard the news (some said it was the first time in his adult life that he had laughed). More Huguenots fled France, comprising a sort of "brain drain" on the French middle class. They found refuge in England, Scotland, and the new Dutch Republic. They were among the best-educated and highly-skilled segments of French society, and they prospered in their new refuges, as they contributed to the prosperity of those places. Their plight also fed the antipathy to all things Catholic that had already taken root in their new homelands.

1572: The Jackpot

The same year as the massacre, a seaman named Francis Drake undertook a daring raid on the isthmus of Panama. Drake had been involved in trade with the New World for several years. He had tried his hand as a privateer on the west coast of Africa, raiding Portuguese colonies for slaves, which he transported to South America to sell to the Spanish. The raids were successful, but he couldn't sell enough slaves to make a profit. At least ninety of them were abandoned in South America before he returned to England. He did, however, identify the location in Panama where the gold and silver from the Spanish mines in Peru was hauled overland from the Pacific to the Atlantic Ocean, before loading onto ships bound for Spain. He resolved to attack the mule train and its treasure. The forests of Panama were populated by indigenous people, as well as "Cimmarons" — escaped African slaves who had established settlements in the backcountry. These people had no affection for the Spanish, and Drake recruited them to assist him in attacking the Spanish seaport at Nombre de Dios and then ambushing the treasure shipment. The total came to more than twenty tons of gold and silver. It was more than Drake and his crew could take back to England, so they took the gold and buried much of the silver. Drake's success could not be acknowledged publicly in England for diplomatic reasons, but the queen was entitled to claim fifty percent of the take, which went into the royal coffers. Officially, England and Spain were not at war — yet.

Elizabeth had found a source of revenue that did not require the cooperation of Parliament. She wanted more, and she devised a plan to get it. She sent Drake on a mission to break into the Pacific — Spain's "Mare Clausam" — and attack the treasure ships that regularly sailed from Peru to the Philippines. It was thought that these ships would not be heavily armed or escorted, since no ships of any other nation were permitted to sail those waters. In 1577, Drake led a flotilla of six ships across the Atlantic toward the tip of South America. It took a year to reach the Pacific, during which four of the ships had to be scuttled because so many sailors died in transit, and another was found to have a rotting hull. Once in the Pacific, however, he discovered it was just as expected — ports were not heavily fortified, and treasure ships were not protected by escorts.

Drake sailed north up the coast of South and North America, captured numerous prizes, and claimed the coasts of Oregon and Northern California as "New Albion" for his queen. Then, rather than return to South America, he turned west across the Pacific to the Portuguese Indies, then further west around Africa, and back into the Atlantic. He arrived in England in the autumn of 1580, laden with Spanish treasure and Asian spices. Most people had assumed that he and his crew were dead. The queen's share of the treasure was more than the entire royal budget for that year. She declared that all logs and diaries from the voyage were Secrets of the Realm. Drake and his surviving crew were sworn to secrecy about where they had been for the last three years.

On the European mainland, Spain consolidated her power. There was a crisis of succession when the young king of Portugal died without an heir, and Philip, King of Spain moved quickly to invade the country and declare himself the new King of Portugal. Philip's empire now included all of Central and South America, as well as colonies in Africa, India, China, and the Spice Islands; it completely encircled the globe, now — the first empire in history of which it could be said that the sun never set upon it.

1581: Private Warfare

Drake's success was a poorly kept secret. English seamen joined the race for a share of the wealth that the Spanish and Portuguese were extracting from their African and American colonies. It had started with trading voyages — slaves from the Portuguese colonies in West Africa could be sold in the Spanish colonies, for gold and silver. As hostilities among the European nations developed into full-blown war, it became more profitable to seize slave ships en route to America, and sell their human cargoes, than to purchase slaves directly. On the return trip, seizing trading vessels bound for European ports was a second chance at profit. Then there were the Spanish treasure fleets that transported tons of gold and silver each year from the mines of Mexico and Peru back to Spain. These fleets traveled in convoy and were heavily armed, but the payoff was too tempting to ignore.

Turkish pirates had long been raiding coastal towns all over Europe, including England, and even venturing as far as Iceland. They took slaves and anything else of value back to North Africa or the Levant. Sometimes the captives were ransomed, sometimes not. For cities like Tripoli, in Tunisia, piracy became the basis of their economy.

European seamen emulated the practice, sometimes taking slaves from Turkish lands, as well as West Africa and the New World. As the Ottoman Empire's westward push in the Mediterranean was stalled, Turkish ships became the target of Spanish and Italian privateers: Mediterranean trade was rich and tempting.

Spain, in her eighty-year-long struggle with the Dutch, established privateering havens at places like Dunkirk, on the Channel coast. "Dunkirker" became synonymous with "pirate" in the North Sea, and in places as distant as the Baltic and Mediterranean.

In times of war, sea captains were given royal authorization to attack other nation's ships as "privateers" — legalized piracy. When the war ended the seamen sometimes continued their business as "buccaneers," freelancing pirates, who could be called back into the service of a king if war broke out again. The North Sea and the Mediterranean were rife with them. The Caribbean, with its rich cargoes and island colonies from half a dozen different nations, would soon become a haven for these crews, as well.

Part 4: The Journeymen

April 6, 1580: Earthquake

It was Holy Wednesday, the day before Maundy Thursday, two days before Good Friday. It was the end of Lent, when men's hearts, minds, and prayers should be focused on repentance, and the awful price of their redemption. It was a time of portents and signs, of waiting for God to speak, to declare his power, to rebuke the forces of evil.

Just around suppertime, the earth began to shake. Men and women fell out of their chairs around their dinner tables; the quaking caused bells to ring in church towers all over the kingdom — not with the measured peals of human hands, but helter-skelter, a cacophony of clanging, as from a hand so powerful, that melody and measure were irrelevant.

Everyone agreed that God had sent a sign — how could it be otherwise, in the middle of Holy Week? No one agreed on what it meant. By the following day, broadsides and pamphlets appeared on the streets of London, proclaiming that God's judgment was about to fall on the world — for the righteous, good news; for the wicked, not so good.

It took several days for people to settle back into their familiar routines. After Easter, there were crops to plant, and businesses to conduct. Fire did not fall from heaven, as some had predicted, so what else was there to do? Work, eat, drink. Hope for a prosperous year. Beneath the surface, a sense that something had moved, and might move again.

1580: The Great Road

When the Romans ruled Britannia, they built roads, roads that lasted for more than a millennium. Many of these roads were still in use in the years that Elizabeth ruled England, indeed, they comprised a large portion of the kingdom's thoroughfares. Maintenance of the roads' routes was spotty — some had fallen into disuse and disappeared. But many were important enough to justify the expense of maintaining or even improving them.

Among these was the "Great Road" that ran North and East from Londinium (now London), through Caesaromagus (now Chelmsford), to Camulodum (now Ipswich), and beyond, to Venta Icenorum (Norwich).

Along this road, a steady stream of traffic would flow, from countryside to city, from city to countryside, carts, animals, people — whether on foot or the back of a donkey or a horse, occasionally even in a carriage. The Romans built on elevated roadbeds, to improve drainage, which helped with the mud. Nothing in the road's design could disguise the fact that the animals using the road defecated when and where they pleased. Anyone walking the road needed to keep an eye on where they placed their feet.

The roads had demographic consequences. For people in the countryside, they were the pathway to marketplaces, perhaps even to a more prosperous life. The government saw migration from rural villages to urban centers as a threat to the nation's health and undertook to minimize it. London was the largest city, and thus the most attractive to migrants. It was also the dumping ground for broken dreams and lost fortunes, a crowded accumulation of poor folk, packed into small spaces, each with its quota of rats, each on the threshold of another outbreak of some plague or other. When a plague broke out, the wealthier citizens would flee to their homes in the countryside; the poor stayed put and died. Within a few years, the lives lost to epidemic disease would be replaced with fresh immigrants from the countryside, and the whole cycle would begin again.

Parliament tried to address the problems when it passed a "Statute of Artificers" in 1563. Under this statute, every boy in the kingdom (aristocrats excepted) was required either to work on a farm or be apprenticed to a legally recognized trade. The apprenticeships began at around age thirteen (after finishing grammar school), and lasted for seven years. If everything went as planned, the apprentice became a journeyman after seven years and could earn wages for his work (although technically under the supervision of his "master," until becoming a "master" himself after a few more years). Under inheritance law, only the eldest son in a farming family could inherit the farm; the family was responsible for arranging apprenticeships for any younger sons. In years when the harvest was poor, apprentices could be required to suspend their apprenticeships and return home to bring in the crops — the nation's food supply took priority, whenever it was threatened.

John Porter was one such journeyman; a woodworker on the road from Braintree to Chelmsford, in the summer of 1580. He was twenty years old. He had served his apprenticeship in Braintree, a substantial town near the village of his birth. Braintree was not a large town, but there was plenty of work for carpenters, and John's Master had employed several apprentices. One of those apprentices was the Master's son, which meant that John was expected to find his own employment as a journeyman. He was well enough pleased with this situation; it gave him as much freedom as a young man could expect in his day and age, more than most workmen could hope for. He had to find work where he could, but carpentry paid five shillings a week for a journeyman, which came to ten pence a day, or thirteen pounds per year if he worked steadily. A plowman, by contrast, earned only one shilling a week. Food and lodging could be had in the local inns for five pence a week, including laundry.

His biggest personal expense was clothing. A coat could cost almost two weeks wages, boots or shoes even more. He typically wore a knee-length tunic over woolen trousers (called "hose"), and linen breeches, with a loose-fitting shirt, a plain doublet (if dressed for church), and a leather jerkin in cool weather for working. Anything fancier could have gotten him fined for dressing above his class. When working, he wore a leather apron over his clothes. The tools of his trade were presented to him by his Master upon completing his apprenticeship. They were made of wood, steel, and iron, and it was no small task to carry them with him. John solved this problem by fashioning a small wheeled cart, or barrow, which could carry a wooden chest of his personal belongings, and another chest for his tools, as he wheeled it from village to village to town. Not every village was large enough to support a full-time carpenter, so he often found small jobs for a week or so, then moved on. In winter, he tried to find indoor work in one of the larger towns or cities. It was a satisfying life for a young man — traveling, meeting new people, enough income to meet his needs, the freedom to quit a job if the employer was difficult and move on.

On this particular day, he was moving on. He expected to find work in one of the villages along the old Roman road to Chelmsford, or even in Chelmsford itself. It was about ten miles from Braintree to Chelmsford, a distance he could cover in a day, even with his barrow, but he would probably find something before he traveled that far. It was good that he was not in a hurry; there was a lot of traffic on the road this morning. When horse-drawn carriages or post riders appeared, the pedestrians, like John, were expected to yield the right of way. Then there were the teamsters and their wagons of farm produce and merchandise, some drawn by horses, others by oxen. Somewhere ahead, someone was driving a flock of sheep across the road, which halted everyone for a while. As he drew up to the back of the crowd that waited, he found himself alongside two other men, who were engaged in conversation.

The younger of the two men was dressed in black, like a clergyman of some sort. He had an air of confidence about him, as if he knew his place in the world, and was proud of it. The other man was older, and . . . it was difficult to place him by the way he was dressed — plainly enough, yet lacking the distinctive details that would identify him as a tradesman or . . . what, exactly. There was nothing particular about his clothes at all. If he had not been conversing with the younger man, you could miss him altogether in a crowd like this and never recall that he was there. Both men were on foot, and each carried a staff or walking stick, as well as a bundle that was surely their changes of clothing, and other personal items.

John could tell that they were talking about religion, and he really couldn't help overhearing their conversation. As he waited next to them, they noticed him and introduced themselves. The younger man identified himself as Edward Chase, recently graduated from Cambridge, currently employed as a "lecturer." The older man introduced himself as William Payne.

"John Porter, journeyman carpenter, at your service," he said.

Edward Chase was in effect, a traveling preacher who made his living preaching sermons outside the confines of the local Parish church services. The ancient laws prohibiting preachers from speaking without a license were still in effect, but he had such a license; it was unlawful for him to preach in any church during a regular Sunday service, but it was becoming more and more common for people to meet in private homes for teaching and discussions of "profitable questions." A "lecturer" might be invited to speak to such "conventicles." Sometimes he preached in private homes on Sunday afternoons, sometimes outdoors (weather permitting); occasionally a local parish priest would invite him to preach to the congregation on a Sunday morning (technically illegal; the priest was risking censure or worse, if his bishop found out), but, "Your Sunday morning service is always constrained by the liturgy — I am allowed to speak for barely an hour. It may take me an hour to lay the groundwork for a truly inspired message — it takes at least two hours to do it justice, sometimes even three. I actually prefer to preach with more freedom, and to listeners that will let me take my time." William Payne smiled at this last remark as if suppressing a chuckle. (Clearly, here was a man with much to say, and all of it profound!)

John had heard more than a few "lectures" himself and had to agree that two hours of preaching from an inspired and capable preacher was more edifying, and less tedious than the short homilies of many parish priests. Three hours was a little excessive, he thought and smiled just as William had.

Traffic had begun to move down the road again, and as John moved his barrow forward, the two men sidled up to him on either side, matching their pace to his. This was awkward for John because he wasn't sure of the social rank of his two companions and couldn't be certain to avoid offending one or both, for lack of manners. If Edward were a priest or a scholar, he would clearly be John's superior and would expect the deference due his rank, but John didn't really know where a "lecturer" fit on the social scale. Was "lecturer" even a social position, or merely a description of how the man earned his living? As for William, it was impossible to know his rank without more information, and William wasn't volunteering anything.

As the three walked along, John began to relax. Both his companions wanted to make conversation and include him in it. John was unaccustomed to conversing freely with men who might be his social betters, but if they wished to speak informally with a yeoman like himself, that was a prerogative that the better classes could exercise. Both of them were clearly better educated than he was, but if they wished to mix with their social inferiors, he saw no reason to refuse — and risked offending them if he did refuse.

Edward was from Norwich, a yeoman's family like John's, but somehow prosperous enough to send him to university. There, he studied for the priesthood but was not yet ordained. He was employed by various church officials on errands that took him from town to town in Norfolk, Suffolk, and Essex — occasionally even into London. Most likely, he would be assigned to serve a parish somewhere, eventually. For now, he said, "I am a man of many journeys — a journeyman, if you like," winking at his own witticism.

William hailed from Peterborough, a cathedral town to the north and west of Chelmsford. His destination was Ingatestone — a village eight miles or so beyond Chelmsford. He had some business there.

John described his own situation — eldest son of a second son of a yeoman freeholder in Felsted — a village five or six miles west of Braintree. He had the fortune to be born into the yeoman class, with no prospect of inheriting any land of his own, unless his uncle John Porter (eldest son of his grandfather John Porter), and his cousin (also named John Porter) somehow were unable to inherit the family freehold. He did not wish for anything so tragic to happen to any of his beloved relatives, so apprenticeship to a trade was the obvious choice. Other men in his situation might go to sea, or turn to soldiering, but he would make a life for himself as a carpenter.

"A carpenter, even as our Lord was employed!" remarked Edward. John supposed he was being mocked, but saw no malice in the man's eyes. "William, I believe this carpenter may be just the man to settle our dispute. What say you?

"He may indeed. At any rate, I would be glad to hear the wisdom of a *sensible* fellow on this matter. John, (if I may call you by your Christian name), will you hear our dispute, and judge which of us is in the right?"

John was curious now, even as he thought that both of them might be toying with him for their own amusement. "Willingly, Sir" he replied. (When in doubt, be deferential.)

William spoke first. "Our companion," he nodded at Edward, "maintains that there is a 'true church'; not the one that you or I know, but a body of 'elect' men and women known only to themselves (or perhaps not; he seems to waver on this point). The church that all of us know is, in fact, a false church ('Whore of Babylon', I think he might call it, or the church of Antichrist, perhaps), according to him. He would "purify" this false church, leaving only the 'elect' (what he would do with the non-elect, he does not say). His evidence for this bold assertion is the corruption of so many bishops and priests, the church's habit of aiding tyrants and oppressive governments, the cruelties with which this 'church' seeks to suppress any and all dissent from its pernicious and self-serving doctrines. Have I stated your case fairly?" he asked, looking at Edward.

"Not unfairly, but you have missed several weighty matters. I am well able to present my own case," Edward replied. He continued: "The corruption of the Queen's church is, I trust, apparent to everyone. You cannot make the case that the Catholic church is any better — consider only the hundreds martyred by Bloody Mary, or the thousands slaughtered in France upon Saint Bartholomew's day. The Church of England has martyred its share of Lollards, Anabaptists, and Catholics — all in the name of preserving the *government* of the realm. The true church is a spiritual church. It owes nothing to the temporal world, and less to any government!" He was getting carried away, his voice rising, and his cadence shifting to the rhythm of a street preacher. He lowered his voice a little.

He continued, "The true church cannot serve both God and the government. Government we must have, but let it leave the church alone. When government chooses the church's leaders, they owe their allegiance to that government — allegiance that belongs to God alone. We were better to let the congregations choose their pastors (though I do not think this the best policy) than to submit to bishops that serve only their bellies and the government's whims."

John was a little shocked at Edward's frankness. This was the sort of thing that you might hear in an alehouse after a man had passed the limits of strict sobriety, but saying such things in broad daylight, within the hearing of strangers, was risky.

Edward looked at William: "Now I will summarize my companion's argument. He says that the true church is composed of anyone who is baptized, in any parish, by any priest (regardless of character). He purports to believe that the purpose of the church is to "feed" the souls of these members, so that they may live in eternity. To that end, he welcomes the assistance of government in protecting them from heresy, correcting their sinful excesses, and defending their property (at least those who have property). He believes that the church should be the conscience of government — restraining tyrants, mitigating cruelty, and promoting justice (especially justice for the poor and weak). He argues that the church cannot fulfill this task unless its leaders have the trust and respect of the governing authorities and must therefore be a proper part of the government. He presents scant evidence that his church, for all its worldliness, is willing or capable of the mission he has assigned to it."

Throughout this monologue, William maintained his composure with a slight smile, until the last remark, at which his lower lip protruded, just a bit.

Edward continued: "He concedes that his church has been disgraced by the cruelties and injustice that governments have visited on their people in God's name, but he says the church is not to blame. The church merely points out the heretics and dissenters — it is the government that punishes. I say that the prosecutor who gains a conviction on false evidence is just as culpable as the executioner who carries out the sentence. Have I presented your case fairly?"

John was stirred a little by his words. Clearly, Edward Chase was a preacher who knew his business.

William replied, "You have not done my position full justice, but I will amend your omissions." Turning directly to John, he began, "I do concede that the church has often failed its duties and has been *used* to further the corrupt purposes of men and governments. But if there are rotten apples on the tree, I would pick them out and remove them, not throw away the entire harvest. A small church is a weak church. Only a large church can deter the powerful from the fulsome excesses that their wicked impulses urge upon them."

It was clear to John by now that both his companions were much better educated than he. Both must be university men. It was near noonday. They stopped at a suitable spot by the side of the road for refreshment. John had a loaf of bread he had purchased that morning for a penny in Braintree, and some cheese in his pack. He offered to share it with his fellow travelers. William produced more cheese and some dried beef from his pack, and Edward came up with a flask of wine and more bread. There was enough for all of them. As they ate, attention turned to John.

"So, carpenter, which of us do you agree with?" asked Edward.

John drew a breath. "I would not seem impertinent, but I cannot entirely agree with either of you," he replied.

At this, Edward's eyebrows raised, and William's body stiffened a little with attention. "There is no impertinence in giving an opinion," said William.

"I perceive that both of you are men of education, whilst I have only been to grammar school," John began. "All my opinions on these matters can only be based on what I have read in my Bible, or at least that is my hope. You will forgive me if my views seem simple, or unlearned?"

They both nodded; he had their full attention.

"On the first matter, I must agree in part with Master Chase. Our Lord says in Matthew's gospel that the road to destruction is broad, and traveled by the many," (He looked in the direction of the Great Road, still teeming with traffic) "while the road to life is a strait one (he nodded in the direction of a cowpath along the meadow where they sat). It stands to reason, then, that where the great crowd goes, we must doubt whether they are bound for eternal life."

Edward Chase could not help smiling: "Well said, carpenter," he murmured.

"But I am not persuaded that a man's destiny is set before he is born, for what is the use of urging men to repent, if it makes no difference in their eternal circumstance? I suppose it better that all men be baptized, and all be regarded as part of God's church, rather than any be excluded because someone decides that they are not "elected" to that destiny. God is able to judge, and will judge, on the Great Day."

William Payne nodded in agreement.

"I have heard it said that the church has a great store of saintly virtue that it can spend for the redemption of sinful souls, or that Purgatory is the place where the dead wait and suffer until they are pure enough for Heaven. I see nothing in my Bible to endorse such a notion. I believe Purgatory to be Popish nonsense, and I do not place my hope on the virtue of any man, including myself. Let God's grace and mercy suffice for me and for all men."

Both of his companions muttered "Amen!" at practically the same instance.

"As for the governments, I am well aware of the cruelty and oppression that they do. But a small church cannot hope to direct the deeds of any but a small nation. A large kingdom requires a large church for its spiritual guidance. And this kingdom nowadays is less oppressed than once it was, or others that I could name — may it always remain so. May God save England, and our Queen."

"Amen!" his companions replied, almost reflexively.

When John finished speaking, both his companions were silent for a while. He supposed that he had offended them both, in one way or another.

In fact, both of them had heard much more than they expected from a journeyman carpenter. Edward spoke first: "Carpenter, I perceive that you have read with diligence — and you have done well. But consider that God is surely sovereign, and all things must be as he determines them to be. How is it possible that God has not determined every man's fate before he is born, or that a mortal's choice could change the mind of God?"

"Do not mortal sovereigns change their minds all the time?" asked John. "What is sovereignty, if not the power to change one's mind? And did not Moses change God's mind about destroying the Children of Israel after they worshipped the golden calf?"

"Predestination and free will are matters of some difficult theology, which I could explain to you, but now is not the time," Edward replied. "Your argument will stand until then."

"John, you have made a clear case for the free will of mankind," said William, with a smile. "However this 'Puritan' (he nodded at Edward) may twist and shape it, the Holy Scripture is on your side. Men make choices, and will be held to account for them."

"Puritan" was a label that most men took as an insult, and was usually intended that way. Edward, however, dismissed it with a wave of his hand. "You do not need to resort to insults. If you suggest that I am trained in the reformed doctrines as expounded by John Calvin, you are right. And I would be happy to see the Church of England reformed as thoroughly as the churches in Geneva were in Calvin's day, or in Scotland when John Knox was living."

William turned to John: "Do you not agree that the Church should care for all men, as a mother hen protects her chicks, feeding their souls through the ministries of the Word, and Holy Communion? Surely this is the most important thing."

"Whatever I am, I am no chicken," John replied. "Better that all men should face their God with trembling and reverence, as God gives them understanding through the Holy scriptures. No priest or bishop need stand between a man and his God, no intercessor but Christ himself. Each of us must answer for our deeds on that day, and no saint or cleric will stand with us then. As the apostle says in the Epistle to Philippians, salvation is worked out in fear and trembling."

"Well spoken, Carpenter!" said Edward. "No sacraments or rites will save a man, only Faith. And let the idolatrous images be removed from our houses of worship, lest they lead men astray!"

"I know the figures of which you speak, and have seen some destroyed," said John, "but I will admit that I miss some of them. I have worked with enough wood in my life to recognize good workmanship, and I cannot help but admire the excellence of the work. I am not offended by them, in or out of the sanctuary."

Their conversation continued, as their meal was complete, and the remnants stowed away. As they got back on the road to Chelmsford, it occurred to John that these men, learned as they were, had not often spoken freely with men of his class in England. He knew his opinions to be quite common in alehouses and homes among men who earned their living by toil. Whether his choices were free, or predetermined, he would live with the consequences. A man who worked with his hands must believe in cause and effect, else it was folly to work at all. Let the scholars wrestle with the paradoxes of sovereignty and free will. He was not persuaded that the resolution of that debate would make any difference at all in this life, or the next.

As the three men continued on their way, they continued to talk of many things, not all religious. Though John had not resolved any of the dispute between Edward and William, it did not seem to matter. They had begun by intending to use him as a sounding board for their own ideas; now they seemed to find his ideas on a variety of topics interesting in their own right. He began to sense a feeling of comradeship with his companions and sensed that the feeling might be reciprocated. His two companions, by no means in agreement with each other on many topics, seemed nonetheless to enjoy each other's company and the banter that filled their conversation. Perhaps this was how men who earned their livings by their intellect amused themselves. At any rate, John no longer felt mocked by them, or patronized by them.

By late afternoon, the city of Chelmsford was in sight, and it was time for partings. William had the longest yet to travel, to reach Ingatestone, eight miles distant. "I fear I have slowed you down, with my barrow," John said to him.

"That is true, Carpenter," William replied. "But I have enjoyed your company, and I will make more speed on my own, now that we are parting. I know that you are looking for work here," he said, "but if you do not find work in the city, I recommend to you the village of Little Baddow, not four miles east of here. Their carpenter died earlier this year, and I do not think anyone has taken his place in the village. They may have work for you." He turned to Edward. "Master lecturer, it has been a pleasure to be your companion this day. Perhaps we shall meet again, on some road or byway."

"The pleasure is mine, Sir, and godspeed you," Edward replied.

William turned to his left and took a road that led round the outskirts of the city. John and Edward took the road that led to the center of town. As they passed through the city gate, Edward told John where he might find lodging for the night. A week's lodging would cost a tuppence; if his stay was less than a week, he would negotiate a daily rate. "I wish you health and prosperity, Carpenter," he said as they parted, and then added, "You seem an honest man, but I will offer you warning of a danger you may not be aware of. Our traveling companion is a Papist. I am quite certain he is also a Catholic priest, which means that the authorities are pursuing him."

"Are you going to report him?" John asked.

"No, and neither should you. I haven't the time to spend answering questions from the crown's inquisitors about what he said, what he looks like, where he's going (though I think I know his destination). Besides, I like the man, and I don't believe he means harm to anyone. But if the authorities question you, you must be careful what you say to them. Do not lie, but tell them only the verifiable facts (if the authorities question you, you must assume that others have been observing you, and reporting your movements). You met this man on the road, you walked together, you ate together. You separated just at the edge of town and went your separate ways. His name was William Payne (that almost certainly is not his real name), and you may mention that I was there, as well. If I am questioned, I will tell the same truthful story. It might be convenient if your memory is a little hazy about what we discussed. No reason you should give a detailed account of your own beliefs. Do you understand?"

John nodded. "Is there anything I can do to avoid questioning?" (He had heard that the examination methods of the crown could be harsh).

"No, do nothing different than what you would ordinarily do. Find lodging, look for work."

"I appreciate your advice," said John. Then his eyes narrowed "Whose idea was it for the two of you to join me on the road?"

Edward sighed. "I think it was his, as well as mine. When I realized he might be a Catholic priest, I thought that three would draw less attention than two, just as two may appear less suspicious than one man alone. If anyone noticed that the three were in disagreement on some matter, so much less likely that they were part of some conspiracy. I apologize if I have put you to any inconvenience or peril, but I don't think I have."

"In that case, I thank you for your warning."

"I bid you farewell, and a prosperous life, John Porter. I hope I have made a friend today." And with that, he bowed slightly (a deliberate flouting of proper manners; John should be bowing to him), and turned into an alleyway. John found that he was standing in a city square, with an inn just across the way. It looked as good as any place to spend the night.

When Edward Chase left John, it was nearly dusk. He had extra time to spend; his errand was best completed in the dark. He found an alehouse, and ate a leisurely meal, nursing his drink for as long as possible. He conversed freely with the patrons, flirted with the serving maids, and when at last he left the alehouse, it was full dark, and the streets nearly deserted. It had begun to rain lightly. Perfect. He pulled a cowl out of his pack and pulled it over his head and shoulders. Nothing to see here. His destination was some distance from the alehouse, a deliberate choice. He took a winding path across town, meeting virtually no one. When he was certain that he was not followed, he approached a substantial house and walked round to a rear doorway. He knocked. The door opened a crack — only dim light was visible.

"Who?"

"Edward. Edward Chase."

He was quickly ushered in. His cowl and cloak were taken by servants, and he was escorted into a windowless room and offered a large, upholstered chair. A fire was set in the fireplace. His host soon appeared and sat down opposite. "Welcome Edward. We have been expecting you. How went your journey?"

"Well enough. I met a Catholic priest on the road today."

The Host raised an eyebrow. "Are you certain?"

"Quite certain. He is a papist at least, and traveling to Ingatestone, under an assumed name."

"Ah. You took some risk, then." His host gave him a reproving look.

"Not as much as you might suppose. Any man traveling alone draws more attention these days, than two together. We attached ourselves to a third man, a journeyman carpenter from Felsted, on the way."

"So, you used the disguises of another man to conceal your own mission and drew in an ignorant bystander to boot. Clever. Do you have something for me?"

Edward rose to his feet. "Indeed I do, and news as well. Have you a pen knife?" The little knife was quickly produced, and Edward removed his doublet and picked at the seam of the lining until he could pull out the stitches. From within the lining, he drew three sealed letters. "Here you are. Letters from Braintree, Ipswich, and Norwich."

His host unsealed the letters and scanned them. "Well done! I shall have answers to these ready in a few days. In the meantime, you will stay with us. You should not be seen outdoors, but our cook is capable and we will furnish you with a comfortable bed."

"I shall be glad of it," Edward replied. "The soles of my shoes are getting worn. I have need of a cobbler."

"I know a good one. I have a servant about your size, who can pass your shoes off as his own, and have them re-soled at my expense. We shall re-sew the lining of your doublet when the return letters are ready. I must ask you to excuse me, I have much to do. The servants will show you to your room."

Thus dismissed, Edward bowed and excused himself. A good night's sleep would be welcome.

By the time William Payne reached the village of Ingatestone, it was dark, and the road was nearly deserted. He skirted the village on the West side, then turned East toward the great house of Ingatestone Hall. The hall was the principal residence of the late Sir William Petre, now survived by his widow, Anne.

William Petre was the son of a yeoman family, as were so many successful men of his generation. As the second son, he would not inherit the family holdings and was sent to Cambridge, where he excelled and rose rapidly in the King's service. He served as Secretary of State to no less than four English monarchs, from Henry VIII to each of his children, including Elizabeth. He had done so with adroitness — a survivor, like Baron Rich of Leez. (He was Rich's assistant in the dissolution of the monasteries, and acquired this estate, and others, during his service.)

William Petre differed from his contemporaries in one notable respect — he was openly Catholic, loyal to his traditional faith through all the changes that Henry and his children had mandated in the English church. This was an awkward stand to take during the reign of Edward VI when Catholic nobles and priests were executed for treason. It was scarcely less so in Bloody Mary's reign when the queen wanted to return all his lands to the religious orders that he had taken them from. Elizabeth's determination to find religious compromise made things a little easier, but the Petre family had to negotiate a careful balance between the Pope's demands for resistance to the heretic queen, and the suspicion of treason by the government. They were labeled "recusants," and it was not a compliment.

It was difficult for very personal reasons, as well. Catholic priests were extremely rare in England. This meant that the sacraments of baptism, confirmation, penance, matrimony, eucharist, and last rites were not available to most English Catholics. Ordination of course was plainly treasonous, as long as the Pope proclaimed it the duty of loyal Catholics to depose and execute their queen. The dearth of sacraments was more than a hardship for English Catholics. It threatened their very existence.

Without the sacraments, the soul could not be prepared for a life eternal. Without baptism, the soul could not begin its spiritual pilgrimage. Without the Eucharist, the soul could not be nourished. Without absolution, the soul could not be cleansed.

William Petre had continued to serve his government faithfully. As a nobleman, he enjoyed near-immunity from charges of treason due to his professed faith, unless it could be proved that he was somehow involved in a plot to overthrow the government. And he was not subject to arrest and examination unless someone of lesser rank could be induced to testify against him. Like many Catholics, he conformed outwardly to the Acts of Uniformity and privately worshipped in his own manner. After Petre died, his widow Anne continued to run the estate, according to her Catholic beliefs. Ingatestone Hall was known to be a refuge for like-minded Englishmen.

Men like William Payne (not his real name, as Edward Chase suspected) volunteered to provide the sacraments to the beleaguered English Catholics. Some would die in the attempt. Dozens of them slipped out of England in the early years of Elizabeth's reign. They were trained and ordained as missionary priests in places like the English College in Douai, France. From there, they found their way back into England, taking refuge with sympathetic "recusant" hosts.

By 1576, Payne had established himself in Ingatestone Hall, as the steward of the Petre household. It was a credible role for him to play; the steward of a great family had reason to travel to the various holdings and properties of the family, which included even some in London, so his travels did not seem particularly suspicious. He began by celebrating masses in the chapel at Ingatestone, for the family and its servants first. There were also a large number of children in the household awaiting baptism — no priest had been available for several years. He heard confessions and performed a few marriages. Soon there were requests for a visit from towns and villages all over Essex. Payne traveled as much as he could. He dared not take vestments with him on his travels, but there were sympathetic men in many towns and villages who had been Catholic priests themselves not so long ago, (some were still serving in the Church of England), and many had kept artifacts and mementos of that time in their lives. So, with borrowed vestments and vessels, he celebrated masses in countless secure places; mostly the private homes of the wealthy; sometimes in humbler places. Without exception, the worshippers welcomed him with gratitude and humble devotion. This was not so in other lands where Payne had served as a priest. He realized that the Englishmen he was serving were only the most pious and devoted — men and women of middling or lesser commitment did not risk their money, reputations, or safety for the sake of a mass.

Things had gone on this way for more than three years. He established a regular circuit of places in Essex and in London, where he traveled to serve his little flocks. He did not visit them in any predictable order or at any pre-determined date, but when he arrived he was always welcomed, and soon the faithful were gathered to receive the sacraments.

This year was different. There was news from various parts of the kingdom that the government had begun arresting Catholics in groups, imprisoning them on various dubious charges, or fining them for recusancy. Cynical men said that it was all a pretext for improving the Crown's revenue, making the English Catholics pay for the expense of suppressing a revolt in Ireland — a revolt encouraged by Jesuit Priests under the direction of the Pope — who had sent a Jesuit "mission" to Ireland, along with a small mercenary army. In any case, the Jesuit mission was blamed for the troubles, and English Catholics were paying a price. Payne had to be much more cautious in his movements.

Payne approached the manor slowly, in the darkness. The exemptions from prosecution that his host enjoyed did not extend to him; on the contrary, if he were found guilty of performing a mass, the best he could hope for was a quick execution. More than likely he would be tortured first. Once under the roof of Lady Petre, he would be relatively safe. He entered a rear garden and knocked at a servant's entrance. Soon the knock was answered "Who goes?"

"Master Payne," he answered. The door was opened, and he stepped inside.

"Welcome, Father!" He was greeted by an old servant. "Let me take your cloak and burden." This done, Payne stretched his arms and took a deep breath.

"The Lady Anne has been looking most anxiously for your arrival. She left instructions that she would speak with you as soon as you arrive."

Very well, a meal and bed would have to wait. He was led to an inner room of the great house and seated in a comfortable chair. He relaxed. It did not take long for the Lady to arrive.

"Father, it is a blessing to have you safe with us again."

"It is a blessing to enjoy your hospitality, as always," he replied. "I am always grateful for a rest, especially so after this journey."

"Your rest must be short. I received this letter for you three days ago. I took the liberty of reading it." It was the aristocrat's prerogative, he reflected — the house was hers, and any correspondence received was her business. She handed him the letter, opened. He began to read it.

"You have been summoned to London," she said. "It seems that great matters are afoot. The day of our deliverance may be closer than we imagine."

Payne stiffened a little at these words. The letter was a summons, true enough, and to London. It did not specify exactly what his business in London was to be. It appeared to be a request from a London merchant to meet him, to settle some account or other. A steward's task. Except the name of the merchant was a code name, used only by other priests, which indicated it was church business. Three days? He would have to leave in the morning.

"You must eat, of course," the lady said. "Then a good night's rest." The servants will have fresh clothes for you by tomorrow morning."

Edward Chase's stay in Chelmsford was not long. He rested the first day and took his meals in his room. The following day, his shoes were returned to him, with new, thick soles. Evidently, he was going to be walking a lot. The evening of the following day, he was invited back to the same windowless room he had visited the night of his arrival. This time the room was crowded with nearly a dozen other men, older, mostly, dressed in the sober black or brown clothes of churchmen or merchants.

"Come, be seated." His host pointed to a vacant chair. "I thought it proper that you be informed about these matters, as much as these worthy men, since you have carried out your part so capably. I will not introduce you or them by name, for discretion's sake, though I think you know some of them."

Edward looked at the "worthy" men around him. He did, indeed know most of them. All were from Chelmsford or its nearby villages. If any men deserved to be called "Puritan," it would be these men — some clerics, some men of wealth, none of them aristocrats, but none of them poor.

"The news that our messenger has brought us." began the host, "is of two kinds: large and small. There is to be a great conventicle in Norwich, later this year, of men who share our opinions and commitment to the purification of the Church of England. There will be men there who have the ear of Archbishop Grindal, and several other bishops will be sending representatives. We are invited to send a representative from among our number here in Chelmsford. It is a fair distance to travel, but I believe any one of us (he looked around the room) could find a credible reason to make the journey. The bishops who share our purpose will be in attendance, as well as scholars, and other notable men. The business of this convocation shall be to make plans to further efforts to complete the reformation of our Church, God be praised!

"Amen!" the Worthy Men intoned.

"Our message," continued the host, "continues to go forth, and is received with gladness by more of our countrymen. The number of books that are published with our message is increasing, and I am told that we now have our own printing press, right here in England. Soon, we will not have to import our literature from overseas."

A secret printing press? That was news to Edward. It would have to be operated in secret, of course, to avoid the censors. If the government ever found out about it, there would be trouble.

"I have also in these letters the names of young men just out of the universities, men whose soundness in doctrine is approved. We should be looking for opportunities to place them, not just in parish churches, but in other positions of influence, like business associations, or in local government. None of us in this room would be as prosperous as we are today, but that other men found opportunity for us. We must do the same for our next generation."

"Amen!" the Worthy Men agreed.

"Finally, I thought it might be well to hear from our courier, here," he nodded at Edward, "who has been walking the roads of our realm, and associates with the lower sorts of our countrymen. What news, sir?"

Edward was not expecting this. Before he could speak, he was interrupted.

"I have a question." A balding man spoke from across the room. "If we have our own printing press, will we not now speak with more boldness? Surely it is time to call out the corruptors of our Church for what they are? If, as you say, our message is received by the people, what are we waiting for? Let us rally the people to our side and put an end to this apostasy!"

Edward paused. No one else in the room spoke for a bit. "A good question," responded the host. "Perhaps that is a question for the convocation in Norwich? What say you, courier?" He gestured to Edward.

"It is certainly not a question that I have an answer for," began Edward, "but I can attest that some of our message has received acceptance from the common folk. Some — not all. I do not think they are ready yet to be rallied to challenge the Church hierarchy." He thought of the carpenter he spoke with on the road. "They will not be seduced by the errors of Popery, and they have none of the old reverence for bishops and priests, but they fear the power of the Queen and her Church. They read their Bibles, but they stubbornly resist any doctrine that they do not find plainly written in it, and they tolerate the nuances of our theology in the way that one might tolerate the incoherent mumblings of a drunken friend while dragging him home to his bed. We need time to fully instruct them in the way of truth."

"How much time?" asked the Balding Man. "It has been nigh twenty years that we have labored in this vineyard. Do you think it will take twenty more? or forty?"

"Perhaps," said Edward, "I cannot say. The Queen is known to oppose our efforts at reform. Even though Archbishop Grindal sympathizes with our views, he has been unable to change her mind on these matters. She has made him a virtual prisoner in his own house because he refuses to suppress our conventicles, our prophesying meetings, and our preaching. We have other bishops on our side as well. And we place more young preachers in parishes every month, men trained to preach and to teach sound doctrine. Time is on our side; eventually, we will prevail."

"In that case, you may live to see it, but I will not," said the Bald Man. "I am not content with that."

The Host responded. "None of us can know what God may do in the future. The Queen, God save her, is forty-seven years old. Our best hope may come when her successor is crowned. Patience has served us well, thus far. May God bless our patience with success!"

"Amen!" the Worthy Men replied.

Edward was left to wonder how long their patience would last. He prayed silently "God, give us the patience to wait for your deliverance, and the wisdom to know when it has come."

William Payne left Ingatestone the morning after he had arrived. It was probable that no one, apart from the Petre household, even knew he had been in the area. So much the better. He rejoined the old Roman Road south of the village and turned toward London. It was nearly forty miles, so it would take him most of two days. He was forty-eight years old, but the years of walking from village to town to city had kept him fit. There was a rhythm to his gait when he walked alone that ate up the miles and relaxed him. On this trip, it was risky to walk alone. The closer he got to London, the more likely he would cross paths with one of the Queen's agents and be questioned. He had papers with him that would explain his reasons for traveling, but you never knew what might raise suspicions. Joining a group would be safer, though it would slow him down. If he were fortunate, he might hitch a ride of some sort, for part of the journey. So, two days at least.

The business in London came as a surprise, though perhaps it shouldn't have. Upon making the appropriate visit to a certain merchant's shop, he was instructed to visit a large house in an old part of the city. When admitted, and identified, he was shown to a large interior room of the house. Others were there ahead of him. Some he knew; they were priests like himself. Among them was a man he had not seen for years — Edmund Campion. Campion's presence in England was not unexpected — even the Queen's agents had known he would try to enter the country. What astonished William Payne was that he and so many of England's Catholic priests had been assembled in one place, in the face of such palpable risk. Why summon them now? Why here?

Campion, and his companion, Robert Persons, soon began to explain. Members of the Society of Jesus — Jesuits — had been tasked by the Pope to undertake a mission to England. To that end, priests were recruited and trained for this noble purpose. Robert Persons was in charge of this mission; Robert Campion was his chief assistant. Payne and others had questions.

"Why the Jesuits?"

"A mission of this magnitude requires men of discipline and rigor. The Jesuits are particularly suited to this sort of task."

"Why now?"

"The condition of the Catholics in England is perilous. If no priests are available to serve them the sacrament of baptism, for instance, Catholics will become extinct in England in a matter of a generation or two. They are becoming fewer in number every day. If the Faith is to prosper here, we must make converts."

"Do you not realize that you, and everyone in this room, are hunted men?"

"Yes, of course. We have stated clearly that this mission has nothing to do with politics, only with serving the needs of English Catholics. We affirm our allegiance to Queen Elizabeth, there is nothing treasonous whatsoever in our purpose. Father Campion has prepared a 'Challenge to the Privy Council', in which he offers to present our positions to them personally and debate any Protestant scholars they might choose, on their doctrines and ours, given their promise of his safety. He has also requested an audience with the Queen."

Payne was struck by the boldness of the man, and the improbability of his challenge. "Do you really think it likely that you could win such a debate, assuming that it was agreed to?"

"I will quote the challenge in part . . 'because I know perfectly that no one Protestant, nor all the Protestants living, nor any sect of our adversaries . . . can maintain their doctrine in disputation. I am to sue most humbly and instantly for combat with all and every one of them . . .'"

No question that the man had confidence in himself. Payne reflected that the Privy Council was unlikely to meet this challenge, much less grant him a promise of safety under any circumstances. And the judge tasked with choosing the winner of such a debate would not be a Catholic. "Do you think it likely that they will accept the challenge?"

"Probably not. But who can say? Imagine if we won our debate, in front of the Queen and her Council, and converted all of them to the True Faith. Surely the whole nation could be redeemed? We cannot rule out a great miracle. Even if they do not, we have thrown down the gauntlet. If they do not pick it up, it will show them as the cowards that they are."

Payne did not wish to spend time debating a moot point. He thought of the carpenter he had walked with less than a week ago. That man would not change his religion over who won a debate in London, nor would most Englishmen. Most of them still thought "Bloody Mary" when the words "Catholic" or "Pope" were mentioned. In any case, he was sure that no such debate would happen. In the meantime, this "challenge," once it was published, would give the government all the excuse it needed to arrest Edmund Campion. "Combat" was a word of war, and if it was a war, Elizabeth's instinct was to take no prisoners — or at least not keep them alive for very long.

"We have undertaken to bring our own printing press into the country," said William Persons. "Soon, we will be able to distribute our message more easily, and we intend to redouble our efforts to publish the tenets of the True Faith in this land."

Payne realized that the situation was now out of his control. Any chance that the Mission to England would be received with toleration had ended when the Mission to Ireland was accompanied by an invasion of Papal mercenaries. Printing more polemical religious literature (on a clandestine printing press!?) would only make the Mission more visible, and more threatening to the government. The persecution of England's Catholics was going to intensify. His own life was in more jeopardy than ever.

Payne lingered in London for a few days. It was not difficult to fade into the crowds of a large city and find safety in anonymity. Besides, he was still officially the steward of Ingatestone Hall. No reason he should not be doing business for his patron.

***

Edward Chase left Chelmsford on the same day that William Payne arrived in London. Edward's path lay northward — back in the direction he had come days earlier. Braintree, Ipswich, then Norwich. More letters to deliver, more to pick up. He did not have to hurry, and his travel expenses were provided. He also had a chance to preach on a Sunday afternoon in a village barn (it was raining a little), and his hearers professed themselves edified by his message. They took up a small offering, so his purse was a little heavier.

In Norwich, three days later, he was entrusted with another letter, this one for London, to be delivered with haste. He was glad that it was Summer; everything slowed down in Winter. It was arranged for him to ride on top of a coach for the first leg of his journey. The ride was bumpy, but not wearying to his legs. When the coach stopped for the night, he ate a meal, then continued through the night on foot. This was not without risks from highwaymen and other ruffians, but the staff he carried was not merely to help him walk, and he also had a long knife concealed under his doublet. By morning, he was back in Braintree; tired, but halfway to his destination. He rested for a few hours, then pushed on. The new soles on his shoes served him well, and he made Chelmsford by afternoon. There he rented a room at an inn, ate, and slept 'til morning. Early on the third day he set out for London.

Two days later he arrived, late in the day. He planned to rent a room in an Inn and eat. He would not deliver his letter until after dark. The city was abuzz with the latest news, as it often was. A Catholic priest named Edmund Campion had issued a challenge to no less than the Queen and her Privy Council, to allow him to debate with any Protestant spokesmen of their choosing, the relative merits of their doctrines and his. Campion was sought, but not found. So much for the debate. Still, a cheeky thing for him to do.

"It is like Elijah and the prophets of Baal," some said. "And Campion thinks he is Elijah!"

"Aye, but he will end up as Jezebel if he is not already out of the realm."

Edward entered an alehouse. When his eyes adjusted to the dark, he spotted a familiar figure seated on a bench against the far wall. It was William Payne, looking glum, or bored. He approached him with caution. "Sir, may I join you?" Payne looked up, recognized him, and nodded. "Will you join me for a drink?" asked Chase. Payne nodded again. Chase caught the attention of a serving maid and ordered them each a mug of ale. "Have you heard the news?

"You mean about Campions's Brag, as they call it?" Chase nodded.

"Yes, everyone is talking about Campion's Brag," said Payne.

"You will admit he is bold," said Chase.

"Yes, bold, and arrogant; perhaps not wise."

"No, certainly not wise. I wonder what he was thinking." If anyone in the alehouse knew anything of Campion, it would be this recusant priest.

Payne did not take the bait. "Who can know the mind of a Jesuit?"

"I believe that Campion lived here during the reign of Queen Mary, did he not?" Probing again.

"Yes, and since then. He has met Queen Elizabeth on at least one occasion."

Chase looked at him in surprise. "When? How?"

"After Mary died when Elizabeth visited Oxford, he was selected to welcome her, and they became friends. He is also befriended by Baron Burghley and the Earl of Leicester, who sit on the Queen's Privy Council."

"So when he asks to debate in front of the Queen and her Council . . ."

"He supposes that he will be standing before friends that may support him, or at least protect him."

"So, bold, but not mad."

"Bold, but not mad; brilliant, but perhaps a fool."

Chase felt a pang of sympathy for his companion. Both of them knew that Campion would never win his debate and that English Catholics would suffer for it. And men like Payne would be swept up in the peril, perhaps to the point of losing their lives. Campion, in his own words, had thrown down a gauntlet. His enemies had picked it up, but they would choose the weapons, and the weapons would not be logic, reason, or eloquence.

"I am sorry to say that I am sure he will never see the Queen or her Council, nor a debate. Sorry, I say, because I had some professors at Cambridge that would make short work of him in a debate," he laughed. More seriously, he leaned closer to Payne: "William, I think I know how and why this troubles you." Payne looked startled. "Do not worry. I think of you as a friend. I would no more betray you than I would my own family. But please be careful. Hard times are coming."

Payne nodded. He was afraid for his own life, but more afraid for his various little flocks, scattered around Essex and London. Who would care for them when he was gone? He sighed and felt an urge to return to Ingatestone and Essex, and his flocks of faithful ones. However much time remained, he wanted to be with them, to nurture them, to protect them, as a mother hen protects her chicks.

1580: Prophesying

Edward Chase's letter was delivered that same evening, at Lambeth Palace, the residence of the Archbishop of Canterbury. The palace was on the south side of the river, across from Westminster, where Parliament met. There was only one bridge across the Thames in those days, and London Bridge was far to the east. Edward could have hired a ferry to cross over but decided to take the long walk around. A ferryman might remember him if anyone was asking questions. He was confident that he could detect anyone following him on foot over a long distance, and confident also that he could elude them, when the time came, to conceal his destination.

This errand was particularly ticklish because the message he carried was for Edmund Grindal, the Archbishop of Canterbury himself. Ticklish, because Grindal's administration was under intense scrutiny from Queen Elizabeth's agents. The Queen was unhappy with Grindal's apparent sympathy for Puritan reformers in his church, or, as Elizabeth preferred to think of it, her church. He had arrested Protestant preachers from time to time, but they were usually released after a short sentence, and most returned to their troublesome ways. There were no complaints about his treatment of Catholic priests and recusants — he had tried and condemned his fair share.

The Queen was particularly insistent that Grindal suppress the "conventicles," assemblies of scholars and clerics who met at various times and places outside of the supervision of the official church, to worship, pray (extemporaneously!), study the Bible, and "prophesy," or expound on the meaning of some text. Worse, the conventicles had begun operating as a shadow church. The conclusions of their "prophesies" carried more weight with their members than the official positions of the Church of England. They shared the conclusions of their "prophesies" with other conventicles so that a demand for reform originating in one parish or diocese would soon appear in the sermons preached in parishes all over the kingdom. Many of their ideas, frankly, were indistinguishable from the teachings of the Lollards, or heretics like Thomas Bilney. The one thing that shielded them from accusations of treason was their effusive praise of the Queen, and their strident defense of her legitimacy; Elizabeth needed their support. If only she could force them to fall in line with her religion.

Elizabeth was all too familiar with the mistakes her sister Mary had made, and was determined to avoid them; She was not demanding that anyone be burned for their beliefs. Only three heretics had gone to the fire in the previous twenty years of her reign — two of those were Dutch emigres, members of a conventicle connected to their own "strangers church" (Anabaptists, probably), the other was a man who denied the divinity of Jesus, and the authority of scripture — probably just a madman, or maybe a Unitarian; the bishop of Norwich had probably been overreaching, since he had failed so far to suppress the reformers, and hoped to make an impression by burning the man.

Catholic priests, of course, were a different matter. Elizabeth saw them as primarily a political threat and used the power of the secular government to imprison and execute them as traitors. She preferred that Protestant dissenters be disciplined by the Ecclesiastical authorities. It was a kind of separation of Church and State, and it worked well, as long as everyone recognized that the Queen was the supreme authority over both. All she wanted was for Archbishop Grindal to do the job to which she had appointed him.

This Grindal refused to do. He wrote a six thousand-word defense of the right of the dissenters to meet for "prophesying," including the statement that "I choose rather to offend your earthly Majesty than to offend the heavenly majesty of God." The Queen may or may not have read the entire letter, but she certainly understood the last part. Grindal was deprived of his jurisdictional powers — those related to the discipline of the clergymen under his supervision — and confined to the palace at Lambeth.

Edward Chase was familiar with conventicles and prophesyings; he had been invited to speak at more than one and had attended many more. His primary occupation, after all, was to attend such gatherings and spread the conclusions and prophetic words from them as widely as he could. It was an exciting, if perilous, occupation for a young man. Someday, he supposed, he would be too old for all this hustling from town to town. Someone, like the archbishop, perhaps, would find him a vicarage somewhere, or maybe even a faculty position in a university. 'Til then, he was in the center of a titanic spiritual contest between the forces of tradition and corruption, and a renewed and purified Church that was struggling to be born. He had a front-row seat to the contest, and his side was winning, at least for the moment.

He had all of this in mind as he approached the palace from the rear, on its East side. There were several servant's entrances here, and it took a moment to find the right one, dark as it was. He knocked, and identified himself, then was admitted. The archbishop was expecting him.

Chase was led through narrow passageways adjoining the palace kitchen, then up some narrow stairs to a library, where the archbishop was seated at a small table or desk. Edmund Grindal looked weary. "Ah! Mr. Chase! Please take a seat." Chase bowed, "Yes, Your Grace," and found a chair.

"You have a letter for me, I presume?"

"Indeed, I do." Chase removed his doublet and began to pick at the threads of a seam in the lining. He removed a letter, still sealed, and handed it to the Archbishop.

Grindal opened the letter, and scanned it, then reread a section. "My colleague, Bishop Freke, has been busy."

Chase nodded. "Too busy, I think. All our conventicles in Norwich must be conducted in secret, now. Meetings in the countryside have been raided, and people arrested. We still have most of the magistrates on our side, but the bishop is making things difficult. Last year, as you know, he burned that plow wright — a heretic, no doubt, but the burning was intended to intimidate us — of that I am sure."

Grindal nodded. "I quite agree. But none of our people have been tortured?"

"None, yet. As I said, the local magistrates are sympathetic to our cause. Many of the gentry of the region are protecting our vicars in the countryside, as well. Still, I won't deny that Bishop Freke has dealt our cause a setback. Patience has been our policy and discretion. But, patience is wearing thin. There are stirrings of rebellion, and there are men prepared to stir more vigorously."

"Men? What men?"

There is a preacher named Robert Browne, who has been preaching in the countryside, to groups of one hundred or more. His message will not surprise you — he demands that the church be purified, and soon. He regards the bishop of Norwich as the enemy of the true faith. Now he appears to be gathering a congregation in the city, of men and women who are willing to "covenant" with him to form a purified church."

"Bishop Freke will certainly put him out of his pulpit if he hasn't already done so," said Grindal.

"Browne is not the rector of any parish. He preaches where he will, and does not recognize the authority of Freke."

"How is this possible?"

"His uncle just happens to be Lord Burghley, the Queen's Lord High Treasurer, and chief advisor. Browne has been jailed often enough, but he is protected from sterner measures."

Grindal chuckled. "I can only imagine how displeased Bishop Freke is with that situation."

"I think Browne is more a threat to our efforts than Freke's attempts to suppress our conventicles and prophesyings. If preachers like Browne continue to form their own "covenants" with the people, the Queen's supremacy over the church will be weakened, and this at a time when the threat from the Pope and his Jesuits is increasing. I cannot imagine our

Queen will accept this; she will turn to Bishop Freke and his ilk to protect her throne, and we will suffer for it.”

Grindal nodded. “You understand the Queen’s disposition well, I think. It would be a cruel irony if our efforts at reform through persuasion were overturned by some careless hothead. Still, if he is protected by Lord Burghley, I’m not sure we can do anything about it. Lord Burghley is one of our strongest allies. We can’t afford to offend him. I wonder if all this is some project of Burghley, some political maneuver that has nothing to do with reform at all? Best to stay as far away from it as we can.”

Chase sighed. “Browne is not the only one, only the most notorious. Many men of my generation chafe at the slow progress of our mission. Young men, you might say, men who long for a better church.”

Grindal nodded and smiled. “I was young once, myself. I spent years in Zurich, waiting for that wicked Queen Mary to pass on to her just reward. It was difficult. But my patience, and the patience of others was rewarded, and when we had a new Queen, we were able to come home. Hundreds of other men like myself returned, and many hold positions of influence in the kingdom, some in government, some in the Church. Our patience has borne fruit.”

“Yet, you have not succeeded in reforming the Church. The Gospel is not yet truly preached in every parish; indeed, there is no preaching at all in half the parishes in England. Papist superstitions are still practiced, and the forces of tradition are gaining strength. I fear that if we do not move forward, we will inevitably slide backward. Can you assure me that your policy of patience will succeed?”

Grindal sighed again. “Young man, I can assure you of nothing. You see how I am living — comfortably enough, but practically a prisoner in this palace. Nothing is assured, nothing is certain. I believe that God is with our cause, and therefore we must eventually prevail, however long it may take. I do not expect to see the Church purified in my lifetime; I am the Lord’s vessel, privileged to be just a part of his work. Perhaps the men of your generation will see the success we all yearn for, perhaps it is for men yet unborn to see it.”

“And if the future belongs to men like Freke, or like Browne, will your soul rest content with it?”

“*The Lord hath given, and he hath taken it. Blessed be the Name of the Lord,*” murmured Grindal. “I fear a future like Freke’s; I cannot imagine that Robert Browne’s teaching would ever amount to more than a crowing rooster.”

"Let me imagine for you. Our position is that the Pope and his hierarchy are not only corrupt (as the Lutherans say), but that the sacraments they profess to manage are a lie intended to enslave the hearts, minds, and especially the financial assets of men — do you agree?"

"That is a harsh way of saying it, but I will not dispute that description."

"Also, we reject the superstitious paraphernalia, and the trappings that they have devised to cloud men's minds, and hide the truth from them?"

Grindal nodded.

"We teach that the Church would be better governed by presbyteries, selected by the congregations of true believers (like in Scotland, or Geneva), than ruled from above, do we not?"

"I must caution you and remind you that you are speaking to your Archbishop," said Grindal. "You will understand if I do not follow your argument to the point that my own position is put in jeopardy."

"Alright, I will speak for myself, and the men of my generation. We recognize the prerogatives of the Crown and accept the supremacy of the Queen in matters of church government. It is a compromise; we think the church would be better governed by a hierarchy of presbyteries and convocations, but we are grateful to be ruled by a Queen who will protect us, in the face of so many enemies. I do not say we would be grateful for a sovereign that persecuted us (as her late sister did), or that the compromise would hold in such a situation."

Grindal raised his eyebrows.

"Your Grace, I speak freely, because I rely on your discretion. If the words of this conversation ever reach the ears of the authorities, I trust it will fall harder on you, than on me." He smiled a little, then wondered if he had crossed a line with that implied threat. Grindal gave him a stern look, then smiled.

Grindal laughed. "Go on, then. Do your worst."

"See what follows. If the church is better governed when its leaders are chosen (however indirectly) from the laity, it is a short step to speculate whether it needs any governance at all, apart from the laity. And if laymen are competent to choose the leaders of the church, who is to say that they are not competent to select their secular leaders, as well?"

Grindal stiffened and sat upright. "Take care, Mr. Chase, lest you cross the line into seditious speculations."

"Other men have already done so. Geneva, as you know, is a republic, Zurich may as well be, and the Netherlands will be if they win their war with Spain. Many of our scholars, including Calvin himself, have postulated that a republic is the preferred form of government for a Christian nation, and for the True Church."

Grindal shook his head. "Those scholars ignore the fact that governments and Princes rule by the ordinance of God himself, as the apostle Paul says in his epistle to the Romans, '*The powers that be are ordered of God*'. Christians must submit to the authorities, even if they do not please us."

"Fifty years ago, (had I been born that long ago) we both would have applied that teaching to the Pope, would we not?"

"But the Bible knows nothing of Popes. The papacy is a failed attempt to govern the Church as if it were just another earthly kingdom. The corruption of the church is the inevitable result. Rejecting the Pope is the only godly way to correct the error. Our church is better ruled by a just and benevolent sovereign like our Queen, than by any ecclesiastical prince."

"I agree that we are better off. But corruption in the Church persists. We believe that the Bible is a better authority than any Pope could be, and we preach it, and teach it tirelessly, even as the government tries to prevent us from doing so. But men like Robert Browne will say that our bishops and archbishops (I do not wish to offend Your Grace), are just little Popes when they rule as bishop Freke has. We who would defend the episcopacy are left to explain why the reasons for rejecting the Pope would not apply as well to the Bishop of Norwich. Bishop Freke does not help our argument."

Chase continued, "Once you promote the idea that a God-ordained ecclesiastical ruler ought to be ignored by his subjects when his rule is corrupt or tyrannical, you open the door to letting every man choose his own spiritual authority. That is the practical effect of separating ourselves from the Catholic communion — if the Pope's authority can be rejected, any other leader's can be, as well. The only authority that must be obeyed is the government. The ultimate spiritual authority is the Queen herself.

"That is the law of the land," Grindal nodded. As long as men like Robert Browne remember this, they are not in serious danger. At present, it is the Pope and his Jesuit minions who threaten our realm. As long as that threat remains, Browne and his ilk are just a sideshow."

Chase nodded. "I am sure you are right. But before you dismiss these views as the babbling of heretics or madmen, consider this: Do you not suppose that there are at least a dozen noblemen in this kingdom who believe they would make better rulers than our Queen (if they were to admit the truth)? And would not any of these men seize the throne for themselves, given the opportunity? I am not talking about recusants — they hide their personal ambition behind the mask of the Pope's support. I am talking about good, solid, Protestants, men whom you know, or their ambitious sons. Remember that our Queen's grandfather came to the throne in just that way."

Grindal nodded, "You are right. I can think of six or seven living right here in London. But what of it? This is the way of worldly politics."

"We have taught that the government of the church should be overthrown when it is found to be corrupt or tyrannical. It is a short step from there to the proposition that a corrupt or tyrannical prince could be rejected by his subjects, and replaced by another (chosen by those same subjects). And if it can happen once, you leave the door open to removing that chosen one and replacing him with yet another, and so on. Once men are accustomed to choosing the church of their preference, they will try their hand at choosing their government."

"If the Queen or her agents heard you speaking like this, you would be in danger!"

"Quite so. I hope that my words do not leave this room. But you can be sure that there are others in this kingdom who are thinking in that way. Books are in circulation that are full of such ideas. It is out of our control. One day, they will be on the lips of men everywhere."

"I hope I do not live to see that day."

"So do I. But we must understand what has been unleashed in our own time. Young men are impatient; some older ones, as well. The future portends conflict and violence. Men like Browne and Freke will be in the midst of it."

"I will pray then, like King Hezekiah, that there will be peace in my time," said Grindal. *An old man's prayer* thought Edward Chase, but a worthy one. *Pray for peace, old man.*

Grindal had other business that evening, and Chase excused himself. It was a long walk, back across the bridge, to this lodging. On the way, he wondered if he had been too free with his opinions. Somewhere along the way, he realized he was being followed. Nothing new, there.

The archbishop reflected on his conversation with Edward Chase and decided he needed to find out more about Robert Browne.

1580: Little Baddow

John Porter found some work in Chelmsford, enough to pay his room and board, but the work wasn't the sort that would keep him through the winter. Chelmsford was a prosperous and lively town, and plenty of other tradesmen, including carpenters, had taken up residence there. In a town the size of Chelmsford, craftsmen could become quite specialized, and their workshops could employ the Master, and his apprentices, and sometimes take on a journeyman or two for a specific job. Some specialized in cabinetry and household furniture, others in the construction or repair of buildings. John's apprenticeship was served in a smaller town, and his training included a variety of disciplines so that he was able to offer his skills to a variety of workshops, though only for as long as the workload was more than the shop could handle with its regular staff.

John was glad for the work but needed a situation where he could work inside for the coming winter. He remembered William Payne's suggestion about the village of Little Baddow. In late August, he was on the road eastward. There were two villages in the area named "Baddow," which some said was derived from "Beadwan," an ancient name for the river that flowed through them. Others said it came from the old Saxon for "Bad Water." In any case, Great Baddow was the larger of the two villages, and nearer to Chelmsford. Little Baddow was smaller, and farther from town.

As John walked through the village, he looked for signs of buildings in need of repair, or other employment opportunities. He spotted several possibilities. There were several large houses, timbered and plastered, two stories with gables and glass windows, with tiled roofs. Most buildings had the traditional thatched roofs, fewer glass windows, and lower profiles. One cottage on the edge of town caught his attention. It was situated near a smallish barn, which was noticeably leaning. The cottage itself appeared to be sagging a bit at one corner.

A woman was at work in a garden at the western side of the cottage. She was plainly dressed, as befit a woman of her status — long brown homespun kirtle, an apron, an open-collared white blouse with long sleeves, a grey fitted bodice. A white cloth cap covered her hair, which was topped with a broad-brimmed straw hat. She had a wicker basket, which she was filling with vegetables from her garden. John recognized turnips and cabbages.

"Goodwife," he addressed her. "I am a journeyman carpenter. I believe I can do you service."

The woman rose and turned to him. "I do not know you sir, nor you me. If you did, you would not call me 'wife,' and perhaps not 'good,' either."

John realized that she was younger than he had supposed and apparently unmarried. He looked at her more closely. Grey eyes. An expression that bordered on impertinence (though she had no reason to believe that she owed him any deference). Dark hair, perspiring a little in the August heat. A little sunburn on her cheeks, some freckles across her nose, standing like she owned the ground she stood on. Well, it <u>was</u> her garden. Still, a man was accustomed to a little *respect* from a woman of his own age and class. Maybe he had chosen the wrong house.

"And what service do you propose to do me?"

"I beg your pardon, I thought I was addressing the goodman's wife. Is she about? Or better, could I speak with the goodman himself?"

"The goodman has no wife," she replied. "And since he is not here, I can speak for him. What is your business?"

John realized that she was no older than he was. Probably the farmer's daughter. Oh, well, might as well see it through. "I see that your barn leans a bit to the West. I am a carpenter by trade, and I might be able to rectify that. Also, I think the floor in a corner of your house may be sagging a bit."

She turned to the barn, then the house. "Quite right. We knew that." She gave him a careful looking over. Average height, looked sturdy enough. Large hands, thick forearms. "How long to make the barn right, and how much will it cost?"

"I would have to see inside the barn, to tell you that," he replied.

"Come and see," she tossed her head in the direction of the barn and began walking toward it. John followed her to the barn.

It took a while for his eyes to adjust to the light. Several stalls on each side of the barn, a milking stanchion; evidently they had milk cows somewhere. Also, some old harness hanging from pegs in the far wall, a pitchfork and other hand tools, a moldboard plow, a harrow. Standard farm equipment; he was familiar with all of it.

The barn was old, and none too sturdy. The outer walls were constructed of large posts, tied together at the top with cross beams. There was a single large beam spanning the space between the two side walls at each end of the barn, which was the source of the problem. There should have been diagonal braces tying each vertical post to its connecting horizontal beam, to prevent any movement. The braces within each wall were in place, but one brace across the end of the leaning corner was broken (How?), and the one on the opposite end was missing altogether. So, the side walls were sound, but there was no bracing to keep them from leaning in the wind. Evidently, the strong winds in this place came from the East — off the North Sea. Thus, the westward lean.

There was a hayloft above the barn floor, under a thatched roof. The only thing keeping the walls from falling flat was the floorboards of the hayloft, which rested on joists that spanned the space between the side walls.

John found a ladder in the barn and climbed up to where the diagonal braces should have been. Sure enough, there was evidence that they had been there at some time in the past — he could see the broken-off stubs of the oak pegs that had once secured them.

He came down the ladder and faced the woman. "You are missing the braces that would keep the walls perpendicular. If we pull the walls back to true vertical, I can put the braces back in place, and that will hold the walls in position."

"You do not look strong enough to pull the walls back upright, to me," she observed.

"No, it would take a team of oxen, or a least a couple of horses to do that," he admitted. He was thinking about how to stabilize the walls, once they were vertical, while he installed the bracing. Block and tackle, maybe. Or a couple of stout farmers, and a lot of rope . . .

"How much would you charge for a job like this?" she interrupted his thoughts.

"I get ten pence a day," he replied. "Plus, there will be a cost for materials, and the use of the oxen."

"Don't worry about the oxen. Where are you lodging?"

"I have just arrived here. I don't have lodging. Perhaps you could recommend someplace?"

"Perhaps I could. How much are you prepared to pay?"

"I usually stay in an inn for two pence a week. I take my meals, there, as well."

"You won't find an inn worthy of the name in this village, and not many have homes large enough to take on boarders. You'll most likely have to sleep in someone's house."

"I have done so before, when necessary," he said. This must be a poor village indeed if it had no inn.

"I can put you up for a few nights," she said, "and feed you as well as I feed my own family. I will take the cost out of your fee. My name is Sybil. Sybil Vessey." She extended her right hand.

"John. John Porter." He surprised himself by shaking her hand. Business of this sort should be conducted between men and sealed with a handshake. But with a woman, and such a young one? "Is there no man in the house?"

"My father, Thomas, is master of the house. He is in the field at present. I am his eldest daughter, and I am authorized to act on his behalf. Do we have a deal?"

The handshake made it a deal, and John realized that he didn't know exactly what the terms were. But the job should take a day, at most. This could be his introduction to the entire village. Offending his first customer wasn't good business. He nodded.

"Tell me, mistress Vessey, is there a place in the village where I can purchase the wood for this job?"

"I am not a mistress," she replied, "as you surely know. Nor am I a ' good wife'; you may address me as 'Sybil', for that I am called by everyone I know."

Fair enough. "Mistress" was a term ordinarily reserved for women of higher status than her, or any of his kin. Addressing her as "mistress" could be flattery or irony, but "Sybil" it would be.

"Then you must call me John," he said.

"If you continue down the road to the East, you will see an alehouse. Across the street is the workshop of a carpenter who once lived here. His widow still lives above the shop. I believe that she will sell you whatever you need."

"Alehouse? I thought you said there was no inn in the village?"

"I said there was no inn worthy of the name. The ale is good enough, but I would not rent a room from them, if I were you, nor eat any food that they serve. I know the cook."

It occurred to John that he had entered into a bargain without knowing all the pertinent facts. He wondered if this job would actually be a profitable one. Never mind; if he did good work here, it could lead to other, more profitable jobs.

"If I may, I will leave my tools with you, and wheel my barrow into town," he suggested.

She nodded, and he unloaded his two chests, then started toward the village center. It was pretty much as she had described it. The road became a street lined with shops and houses. The Alehouse was identifiable by a sign hung over the door, and across the street, he saw what must have been the carpenter's workshop. He walked up to the door and knocked. Shortly, a window opened in the living quarters above the shop, and a voice demanded "Who's there, and what's your business?"

"My name is John Porter, and I hope to buy some lumber from you."

"Wait there. I'll come down."

Shortly, the door to the shop opened. A woman stood in the entrance, clad in the usual kirtle, bodice, and cap. Her hair was grey, but her blue eyes were clear, and she stood erect. "You may call me Widow Smith," she said, "though how a carpenter gets the name 'Smith' is still a mystery to me." She chuckled at her own joke. "Follow me, John Porter."

He followed her through the shop to the rear, where the carpenter's inventory lay. "Where are ye from, and where would ye be working?" the Widow Smith asked.

"I arrived today from Chelmsford. I am a journeyman looking for work. I need wood for a job at the Vessey farm."

"Vessey?" the Widow raised both eyebrows. "You'll have been dealing with Sybil, is my guess. What's the job?"

"I'm going to stabilize their barn before it falls down flat."

"And she agreed to pay you?"

"Yes, she did." The tone of the question made John wonder if he had made such a good deal, after all.

"Well, if Sybil agreed to pay, then you'll get paid. Old Thomas would let that old barn fall down before paying to fix it, and his agreements are not always honored in the manner expected, so to speak."

John was convinced, now, that his first job in Little Baddow was going to be complicated. He looked around the shop. As he hoped, there were several lengths of heavy timber and a stock of stout oak pegs. This was all the wood he needed for the job, and he selected what he needed. He paid the Widow Smith from his purse and loaded the wood onto his barrow. The Widow smiled as she took the payment, "a pleasure to deal with a man who pays in advance," she said. "Where are you lodging?"

"I'll be staying at the Vesseys until I finish the job."

"Ah, most likely in the barn, then. If you get tired of that, you can rent a room from me."

The barn? John realized that Sybil had not agreed that he would sleep in any particular place (nor had they agreed on a price, for that matter). Careless of him; he wouldn't have made that mistake dealing with a man. This was going to be complicated. He would have to negotiate the specifics as soon as he got back to the farm. His negotiating position was weaker, now that he had just paid for all this wood. He sighed as he turned back up the street with his load.

The Widow watched him leave. *Not at all bad-looking*, she thought. Sybil would have to watch herself with that one.

1580: Sybil

Sybil Vessey was eighteen years old when John Porter appeared at her gate. She had been running the household for nearly a decade. Her life was divided into two periods — before and after. Before her mother died, she was the third child in a family of seven children, and the oldest girl. After her mother died, when she was eight, everyone looked to her to somehow keep the household running. Some neighbors came by the house to guide her, of course, but after a few years of teaching her to cook, sew, and clean, she was on her own. She had two older brothers, Samuel and John, and then Thomas, Susan, Mary, and Francis — born just before their mother died. Sybil had cared for Mary and Francis through their infancy, while Thomas and Susan were old enough to get into trouble, but not able to help much with the work. The two older boys helped their father with the farm work when they were not in school, so at least Sybil didn't have to do the milking those first few years.

Samuel was the scholar of the family; everyone agreed that he was destined to be a clergyman. The local priest found a patron for him, and at age thirteen he was off to university. Two years later, John (not a scholar) was apprenticed to a butcher in Great Baddow, nearer Chelmsford. This very nearly did not happen, as Old Thomas resisted paying the apprenticeship fees that the butcher demanded. Finally, some anonymous help was found, and John Vessey was off to his career. That left Sybil in charge of the house and four younger siblings. Thomas and Francis helped their father on the farm; Sybil kept Susan and Mary busy around the house. As time passed, it was Young Thomas's turn to find his way in the world, with an apprenticeship to a blacksmith in Braintree, a village several miles distant. Soon it would be Francis's turn, though the family's financial resources were nearly exhausted — thus the leaning barn and the sagging house. Susan was now fourteen, and Mary was twelve. They were old enough to ease Sybil's workload a bit — if she could keep their minds on their work. There were fewer mouths to feed, and a really good harvest this year could ease the financial strain that they faced.

Hope for a good harvest was what prompted Sybil to engage the carpenter. There would be no place to store the harvest if the barn fell down. They needed to fill the hayloft to feed the livestock through the winter. The grain could be sold for cash in Chelmsford, but buying hay was a losing enterprise. She knew that her father would complain that they could not afford a carpenter, and he was probably right. But they wouldn't make it through the winter without hay. Besides, she had kept the family going this long by seizing opportunities when they presented themselves, by driving hard bargains, and by being smarter than the people she dealt with most of the time. She would do the best she could with the carpenter.

It was late afternoon when she spotted him on the road, trundling his barrow with the wood he had collected. She opened the gate as he approached so that he could haul his load directly to the barn. When he had stacked it near the barn, he stood and spoke to her. "We have not agreed to where I will lodge, nor how much you intend to charge me," he began.

"Haven't we? I thought it was clear enough. You wouldn't be trying to change our terms, would you? Because if you are, you're wasting your time. I am not a wealthy woman. You cannot expect to wring blood from a turnip."

John was surprised by this change in tone. "I am not trying to change the terms. I do not think the terms have been set. I . . ."

"Here now, what's all this?" Sybil turned to see her father, standing at the corner of the barn, by the pile of wood.

"Papa! This is John Porter, a carpenter. I have hired him to repair the barn."

"But what is <u>this</u> ?" He gestured to the pile of wood.

"Why Papa! It is a pile of wood."

"I can see that it is a pile of wood. Why is it here?"

"The carpenter is going to repair the barn with it."

"Is that so?" Thomas Vessey replied. "Well, Carpenter, suppose you show me how you propose to repair my barn." He turned into the open doorway, and John followed him.

"I must see about supper," said Sybil, and quickly headed into the house.

John followed the farmer into the barn, pointed out the problems he had identified, and described how he could fix them. The farmer nodded. "Oxen, you say?"

"Yes. Syb —" (too familiar) "I mean your daughter, said she would arrange for them."

"No doubt she will. I expect you'll have some preparation before you need them?"

"Yes, I can cut the braces to size ahead of time, and drill the holes for the pegs, as well. I should be ready for the oxen by midday tomorrow."

"Very well, you might as well get started." He turned away and shouted "Francis! Time for the milking! Shortly a cow entered the barn from the opposite end, then another. A young man — Francis, apparently, — guided them into the milking stanchions. A couple of cats appeared and sat down nearby. This was a very familiar sight to John, who had milked plenty of cows in his boyhood, right down to the cats who were hoping for a taste of the dairyman's labors.

John fetched his chest of tools from the front of the house. He moved the ladder to one of the braces that was still in place and took measurements. With these, he cut two identical-sized braces from the section of beam that he had purchased. It was sweaty work — the beam was made of oak. Before he was done, Francis had finished milking three cows and herded them, plus a pair of oxen into their stalls. He whistled out the opposite doorway, and John was surprised to see a large draft horse enter the barn. So, the family was poor, perhaps, but not destitute. Once the animals were in their stalls, Francis climbed into the hayloft, and pitched hay down to them. The horse got a nosebag with some grain to boot.

It was dusk. John packed up his tools and headed back toward the house. Time to find his bed for the night. Before he got to the front door, he heard shouting.

"Papa! Samuel is back! Papa! Come see!" A man about his own age was standing at the gate, dressed in clerical black — hot for a day like this one. Evidently, he was a member of the family — there was a clear resemblance to Sybil, her father, and Francis. Three young women bolted from the house and embraced him. One of them was Sybil, the other two had to be her sisters — the family resemblance was unmistakable. He stood back a bit, while the rest of the family greeted the man they called Samuel. Then, Sybil turned to John, her face radiant and smiling. "Come, meet my wayward brother! Samuel, this is John, John, greet my brother Samuel!" She said it with such delight, that John nearly forgot to extend his hand.

"Everyone, wash up!" said Sybil, "Dinner is ready!" and she rushed back into the house.

The house was typical for a farmhouse — the main room, called the Hall, was where meals were taken. There was a table with benches on either side and a chair at each end, and a large fireplace along one wall, which functioned as the kitchen. There was at least one room through a doorway opposite, which would be called the Hall Chamber. A narrow stairway led to a loft, where most of the family slept.

They sat down, with Old Thomas in one chair, and Samuel at the other. John sat on one bench, next to Francis. The three young women sat opposite. Old Thomas prayed over the meal at some length — He invoked God's blessing on the food, the Queen, the members of his family, and even John, their guest. By the time he finished, the youngsters were fidgeting. Supper was some sort of pottage, or vegetable stew — lots of carrots, rutabagas, cabbages, and turnips. There was a chicken in there somewhere. There was also dark bread and ale. John, as was customary, brought his own set of utensils to the table — a spoon and a table knife. The pottage came with a ladle, and Sybil served him his portion into a wooden bowl. Samuel brought news. Now that his studies were complete, he had a position — in Great Dunmow, a village to the Northwest, not far from Braintree. He was to be curate (assistant) to the parish priest there. Assuming he did well, he might well be rector of his own parish in a number of years.

The rest of the siblings were full of news of their own teased each other, and laughed freely. Old Thomas sat back and gazed at his brood — proudly, it appeared, but with a hint of sadness. John ate and took it all in. The sincerity of this family's enjoyment of each other, modest though their meal might be, was touching.

"Oh, how I wish that we had something special to serve on this occasion," Sybil sighed.

"Is there no more cheese in the pantry?" asked Old Thomas.

"No," Sybil looked downcast. "We ate the last of it last week." There was an awkward silence.

"Perhaps I can come up with something," said John, rising from his seat. He stepped outside into the darkness, where his pack was still sitting, and came back to the table with a small round of cheese, that he had purchased that morning in Chelmsford. "Will this do?"

Sybil looked at the cheese with evident delight and smiled broadly. "Yes!" She took the cheese to the back of the house where there was a small work table. She returned shortly with a platter, on which small slices of the cheese were arranged — one slice for each.

The mood was festive again. So much pleasure from a small piece of cheese! Sybil and her sisters cleared the table and began to wash the bowls and utensils at the rear of the Hall, in a tub of water. The pottage and the bread were put away in a wooden hutch; there was no sign of the cheese. No doubt Sybil had it safe somewhere.

John was beginning to get the feel of the family. Samuel was clearly the great hope of the family legacy, the one with the best chance of rising above his humble beginnings. His brothers would do well enough as craftsmen. For Sybil and her sisters, the best hope was a good marriage, though their dowries would not be large. It was probable that they would marry men no more prosperous than their father.

John rose from his seat and moved toward the door. Time to get his belongings inside and find out where he would be sleeping tonight. Sybil followed him to the door. "I must speak to thee, John" (she used the familiar "thee" pronoun as if he were family). "Thank you for your gift." She was referring to the cheese, which, he realized, was now entirely hers, as far as she was concerned. "I fear I must apologize to you." (*For what? The pottage wasn't that bad, he'd eaten much worse in his travels*) "About your lodging." (*Wait. What now?*) "I haven't the room to offer you, now that my brother has arrived, I'm afraid we'll have to put you up elsewhere." (*Ah, now he got it*). "I have asked Francis to bring you some bedding, you must sleep in the barn tonight." John was beginning to feel that he was getting a good deal less than he had bargained for with Sybil and her family. He didn't want to spoil the mood, so he held his tongue; he had slept in barns before. No doubt she'd charge him less for sleeping in the barn, than for a room in the house. Not that they had actually agreed on what he would pay . . . Oh, well. The barn it would be. Assuming that it didn't collapse on him overnight, he would finish the job tomorrow and settle accounts with Sybil.

John put his chest of personal belongings on the barrow and wheeled it back to the barn. The heat of the day had faded; it should be comfortable enough in the hayloft. Soon, he heard footsteps approaching. It was Francis, with a pallet, and a set of sheets. Well, could be worse. Behind him came Samuel, carrying a pillow, and a light blanket. Better than sleeping on a pile of straw. John was a little mollified. Francis carried the mattress up the ladder, to the hayloft, Samuel followed with the rest of the bedding. John followed them up.

"You don't have to do all that," he told them, "I can make my own bed."

"Nonsense! It's the least we can do, for a paying boarder," said Samuel. Apparently, everyone knew what this arrangement was going to cost him, except John himself.

The barn remained standing for another night. John fell asleep to the sounds of the animals below and once heard a faint fluttering — barn owls, no doubt. He fell asleep quickly.

He awoke in the twilight before dawn, to the sound of animals stirring below. Of course. Milking time. Francis had the cows back in the stanchions, and the cats were at their stations. John dressed, descended the ladder, and wondered about breakfast. He'd wait until Francis was finished with the milking, and go into the house with him, rather than catch the rest of the family unprepared.

"Do you enjoy farming?" He was trying to make conversation.

"It's alright. Been doing it all my life."

More footsteps. It was Samuel, carrying a wooden plate, with some slices of bread and cheese, an egg, probably hard-boiled, and a stein of ale. "Here's your breakfast," he said. I'm to help you with the barn, today."

John ate his breakfast and considered the offer. "I'm not sure I can afford to pay you."

Samuel laughed. "No, I'll be helping you for free. Charging you for my time is something Sybil would have thought up. I'm guessing an extra pair of hands would be welcome?"

Good guess. "You'll want to get all of the livestock out of the barn before we start."

Samuel led the horse out into a nearby pasture. By then, Francis had finished the milking, and the cows followed.

John began by drilling the peg holes in the braces he had cut yesterday. He used a brace-and-bit, one of his most prized tools. His master had spent a tidy sum on this tool, and it was worth every penny. It consisted of a long, crooked handle, and a set of steel bits of various sizes. The bits fit into the lower end of the brace, and he could crank the handle to turn the bit to drill a neat, cylindrical hole in any type of wood. The top of the handle had a smooth wooden knob, which he could put his full weight on while turning the shaft as vigorously as his strength would allow. He drilled three holes in each end of both braces — twelve holes in all.

Next, he walked to the East of the barn about twenty yards, and drove two large posts into the ground, aligned with the section that was leaning. He needed a sledgehammer to do it, but one was available — every farm needed a sledgehammer. It took time to drive the posts, but he put Samuel to work on them. He did well enough — scholar or not, he was a farmer's son before he went to the university; some things the muscles do not forget.

With the posts in place, it was time to rig the harnesses. There was a convenient gap in the siding of the barn, through which he could thread a rope tied 'round the leaning upright just below where it met the cross beam. He found enough stout rope — barely — to reach from there to the posts in the ground, with enough left over to rig to a team of oxen. From his tool chest, he pulled another prized possession — a block and tackle. It consisted of two pairs of wooden pulleys tied together with rope. One pair would be tied to the posts, and the other pair was tied to the top of the leaning post. The main rope would be threaded through the pulleys. The power of the oxen could be doubled or quadrupled with this rig. The key was that the distance the barn frame needed to be moved — about six feet, in this case, was in proportion to the length of rope that was pulled through the pulleys. Pulling the pulleys twenty-four feet would move the post six feet with only 1/4 the force. There was just one catch. The cross-beam across the end of the barn was fastened to the vertical members of each side wall with long oak pegs. If the lean was so severe as to shear off those pegs, then straightening one wall without the other would leave the cross-beam hanging in the air. This would make things much worse. He would have to move the wall a little at a time until he was sure about the pegs.

By the time he had the pulleys rigged, it was almost time for supper, the mid-day meal. A dozen or so strangers were standing around the barn, now. Neighbors, come to gawk. Good for business, if he succeeded; disastrous if anything went wrong. Just at noon, more people gathered, including some women who were apparently bringing food. Another farmer showed up with his own team of oxen, pulling a wagon with several more people aboard. There were now close to thirty people in the farmyard.

Some planks were set up to make a rough table, and food was spread across it. Some rude benches were assembled, and everyone was summoned to eat. Samuel Vessey, the new curate, gave the blessing, and everyone dug in. Everyone had brought their own utensils and plates. It was a little bewildering to John, but there was plenty to eat — some roast chicken, some mutton, plenty of root vegetables and bread. It soon became apparent that Sybil Vessey had arranged this — she was directing people to seats, pouring ale, and just generally supervising. The men ate first, as was customary at an occasion like this, then the women and children.

He was getting comfortable, until Samuel announced "Friends, it is time to see what we came to see. Carpenter, tell us what to do." John was flattered to have his work so prominently featured, and more than a little anxious about the possibility of failure.

Nothing to gain by delay. He had Francis and Samuel hitch the oxen to the rope near the pulleys on the two posts he had driven into the ground East of the barn. "I want the team to move forward three feet, no more," he instructed them. He drew a line in the dirt where he wanted them to stop. Three feet of movement from the team should move the wall nine inches — enough to tell whether the oak pegs were damaged, but not enough to pull the post completely from under the cross beam. He moved the ladder to the front of the barn, near where the pulleys were attached.

The oxen pulled forward on command. At first, the rope simply grew taut. Then, there came a groaning sound from the barn. The wall was moving. "Stop!" cried John. He climbed the ladder and looked at the intersection of the cross-beam and the post. So far, so good — no apparent slippage at the intersection. He came down the ladder and moved it to the opposite wall. There might be some daylight on that side, hard to say. Nothing major, though. Time to move some more.

The Oxen pulled again, and there was more groaning from the barn. This time, John was sure that the oak pegs at the top of the cross-beam were holding. He checked the wall with his plumb bob. Definitely straighter. Less than five feet to go. "Give me four more feet!" he shouted.

Another pull, more groans, though it seemed less noisy. The top of the cross-beam was firmly seated on both posts. "Four more feet!" he cried, again. By this time the top of the barn was more than halfway to plumb, and the building seemed to sigh with relief. The plumb bob said it was less than three feet out of line. "Give me four more!" At this pull, the building shifted as if on its own accord, settling back to an approximation of its original shape. The rope behind the oxen went slack. John told Francis and Samuel to unhitch the oxen and tie off the rope around the two posts with the pulleys attached. He checked for plumb. Nearly perfect on the west side, only inches off on the east. That would do; now to hold it in position. Francis and Samuel were smiling. Everyone was smiling, even Old Thomas, just a little. He caught a glimpse of Sybil — hard to read her expression. Pleased, maybe, but something was on her mind. People began to drift away; the spectacle was over and had lasted only minutes.

Placing the diagonal braces at the corners where the cross-beam met the posts, was difficult, only because they were heavy, and had to be held in place while he drilled into the beams with the brace-and-bit. Samuel and Francis wheeled a farm cart next to the west side wall, and with a combination of rope and brute force, held one of the diagonals in place, while John drilled into the cross-beam and the post. They stood on the bed of the cart, but it was still tiring overhead work. Once John had a hole drilled, he drove one of the oak pegs into the hole with a heavy mallet. When one hole was pegged in each end, the diagonal would stay put; the ropes could be removed, and no one needed to hold it in place. After the first six holes were pegged, John needed to rest and stretch his muscles. Samuel brought him some ale, and they chatted.

"So, you'll be heading to Great Dunmow?"

"Yes. Do you know of the place?"

"Indeed. I was born in Felsted, just four miles or so from there. My family is still there."

"Felsted? Isn't that near Leez Priory?"

"Yes, it is. My grandfather rents some acreage from Baron Rich each year."

"Baron Rich. That's a famous name."

"Or infamous. This baron is the son of the man whom you have heard of, I think. Chancellor for old King Henry, and Bloody Mary, as well."

"Yes, that one. Is the family recusant?"

"I'd say not. They attend church regularly at my family's parish — Holy Cross, in Felsted."

"You know him then?"

"Not really. I know what he looks like, but he would not recognize me. I was apprenticed in Braintree when I was twelve years old."

"Still, sitting in church with a baron . . ."

"His pew was in front. Ours was in the back."

"Of course," Samuel chuckled. "You've done good work today. It has been a pleasure assisting you. You have met most of my family; tell me about yours."

"Well, you know my name. My father's name is Thomas, like yours. My mother is Ann, I have one sister, Ellen. My father has a brother named John, which is also the name of my grandfather, and my cousin. If you look for John Porter in Felsted, you will certainly find at least one, perhaps not the one you want. My father is a second son, like yours, so my uncle John will inherit the family freehold. Meanwhile, my father farms some of our lands and rents others. He will inherit none of it of course, which is why I am a carpenter."

"Our families are not that different, I think. We also must rent our land. We own the house, the barn, and the rest of the buildings you see. Everything else is rented. Which is why my three brothers are to be apprenticed to tradesmen. I would have been as well, except for sponsors who paid my way to school."

"Yet, you may have some inheritance here."

"I have three sisters, with little dowry, and an aging father. Whatever this estate is worth, it must provide my father a place to live until he passes, and afterward, my sisters should be the beneficiaries, whatever the law and my father's will says."

John nodded. A man of Samuel's station, or his, would do better to marry a craftsman's daughter, or a merchant's — someone with a substantial dowry. He should live in a town where his sons could hope to prosper, and daughters could be provided with dowries of their own. Farming was a hard life, and a discouraging one, unless a man owned his own land.

It took the rest of the afternoon to finish the work and clean up. John went back to the house to settle accounts with Sybil. He was tired but pleased with his work. He had plenty of witnesses to his skill and success. With any luck, everyone in the village was talking about his work.

Sybil met him at the door. "Finished?" she asked.

"All but the payment," he replied. "If we can settle our account now, I will be moving on."

"Surely, you're staying for dinner?"

"Yes, I'd like to. But …"

"Then you might as well stay the night. It's late, and you won't easily find a place to stay this evening. You won't get work tomorrow, either. It's Sunday. Stay and go to church with us in the morning."

John had forgotten what day of the week it was. True, no one in a small village like this would do business on a "Sabbath." He might as well stay over. "But about my pay . . ."

"We'll talk of it tomorrow. You should get washed up for supper." She smiled as she turned and went into the house. John was sure that she was putting him off, for some reason. But confronting a woman, and possibly insulting her, just before she served your dinner was foolhardy. Going to church with the family was a good idea: it would get him introductions to people in the village and remind them of his success with the barn.

John said little during the meal. There was mutton in the pottage, this evening. There was the usual bread and ale, and Sybil produced a pie that she had baked that afternoon, the early apples were now ready to harvest. The pie was a bit tart. Sugar was an expensive luxury, and honey wasn't much less so. John liked pie whatever the filling, and it put him in a better mood. He was tired. He went to bed early.

In the morning, he was awakened by the milking again. He rose, got dressed in his best shirt, doublet, and hose, with some clean stockings. He tried to clean up his only pair of shoes a little. He dusted off his hat. Breakfast was bread, cheese, and ale, with another hard-boiled egg.

The bells in the church tower rang, and they all walked down the road into the village. The Vessey women wore sober dresses, with simple white collars folder over the necklines. Samuel wore black, as befit his profession, Thomas and Francis were dressed no better than John, but no worse.

The church of Saint Mary the Virgin looked very much like the church of the Holy Cross in his native Felsted. The service conformed to the litany of the Book of Common Prayer; it was all very familiar. The sermon, if anything was better than average, though not long. Probably not long enough for people to fall asleep in the warm August morning; at least no one did.

His hopes for finding some work were more than realized when over a dozen parishioners approached him on his way out of the church. They all had jobs that they wanted him to look at. He noted their names, and their locations in the village, and promised to call on them the following day. He was greeted by the Widow Smith, as well. "I hear that you have had great success," she remarked.

John nodded with a modest shrug. "I am looking for lodging for the next several days. Do you still have a room to rent?"

"Indeed, I do. Call on me tomorrow." Evidently, the man was going to be in the village for a while, perhaps longer than he had planned. Odd that he wasn't going to stay on with the Vesseys. Sybil wasn't the sort to let a paying boarder get away. No mind, the Widow thought, a little more income would be welcome. Who knows? It might develop into something more profitable . . . She asked around, caught up with the gossip. Seems that Sybil was making the carpenter pay for sleeping in her barn. The Widow chuckled at this news — no wonder the poor fellow was looking for another place to stay!

They walked back to the farm, for supper. Sybil served the usual bread and ale with some roasted vegetables and cheese. John wondered how many meals she could get out of that one cheese — his cheese. There was another apple pie, which pleased him very well. In the afternoon, they walked back to church. There was to be a lecture for those interested in "spiritual edification." Samuel, it turned out, was the lecturer. He was on friendly terms with the parish priest, who had helped find the sponsor who paid for Samuel's education. The priest was curious to hear some of what all that learning had effected in his protege. Evidently, others shared his curiosity — the sanctuary was full that afternoon. Samuel began the lecture with a prayer and then began to speak. He had chosen a passage from the prophet Isaiah for his text — Isaiah chapter 48, verses 18 and following:

"Oh that thou haddest hearkened to my commandments! Then had thy prosperity been as the flood, and thy righteousness as the waves of the sea."

"Thy seed also had been as the sand, and fruit of thy body like the gravel thereof: his name should not have been cut off, nor destroyed before me."

"Go ye out of Babylon, flee ye from the Chaldeans, with a voice of joy: tell and declare this: show it forth to the end of the earth: say ye, the Lord hath redeemed his servant Jacob."

"And they were not thirsty: he led them out through the wilderness: he caused waters to flow out of the rock for them; for he clave the rock, and the water gushed out."

Samuel began to speak. He explained how true Christians were like the ancient Israelites, captives to rulers who served false gods. This was the consequence of their own past disobedience. But deliverance was promised, and liberation was coming. When the time was right, they would see God's mighty hand, and the church would be renewed, just as ancient Israel had been delivered and renewed.

John was not unfamiliar with these ideas. Ordinarily, "Babylon" was to be identified with Rome and the Pope; "Israel," of course was the Church of England. But Samuel did not make that explicit connection. Instead, he described in lurid detail the disobedience that had produced their bondage — superstitious Catholic doctrines were among them, but not everything he denounced was distinctively Catholic. He spent more of his time describing the corruption and debauchery that could be found in London, or, God forbid, even in Chelmsford. (The villagers could comfort themselves with the knowledge that they did not live in any of those places.) The Church of England (and particularly its bishops) received rougher handling than the Pope. They lived in luxury and splendor while the poor starved. Judgment was coming. Babylon would surely fall. God's people must separate themselves from the wickedness all around them and wait for God's deliverance. When the time was right, God himself would restore them, and lead them. Though the desert might seem dry, there would be water to quench their thirst when they most needed it. While they waited, faith, hope, and love must be the fabric of their lives. Renounce selfishness, greed, cruelty, and dishonesty. Show generosity to the poor, honor the Queen, and love your neighbor as you love yourself.

Samuel's listeners sat spellbound. When he finished, John was surprised to realize that hours had passed. He felt energized, inspired. He felt that he understood his life's purpose; he was part of events much, much larger than himself. Others must have felt the same way. They gathered around Samuel, congratulating him on this eloquence, professing their inspiration at his message. The parish priest was smiling, too, though he took Samuel aside for a few minutes to talk of some matter.

After the crowd dispersed, John and the Vesseys walked home through the village. "A fine message," John said to Samuel.

Samuel nodded, "I hope it has edified you. I have not often spoken to so large a gathering, but it is my fortune to be trained by some very fine preachers, I fear I did not speak long enough to meet their standard; they say that a really good preacher should take at least three hours."

"I heard a man say as much, not more than a month ago, though he did not convince me. I think your message was exactly the right length."

"Who was this man?"

"Said his name was Chase. He spoke well enough, though I did not listen to him for three hours."

"Edward Chase? You know Edward Chase, the great preacher?"

"I met a man of that name on the road to Chelmsford. A learned man, I think. Claimed he needed at least two hours to deliver a complete message and would rather have three. I cannot say I know him well, but he was my traveling companion for a day, and I believe he did me a good turn." (This last remark he added, because Samuel so clearly admired Chase. Chase's warning was welcome, but wouldn't have been necessary if Chase had not used John's companionship for . . . whatever he was using it for. No reason to acquaint Samuel with his ambiguous feelings about Edward Chase).

"That could be no other man, than the one who has been my mentor. I believe that my position in Great Dunmow was due largely to his influence."

So. Whatever Edward Chase was doing, it had something to do with placing particular young men in particular positions in particular parishes. Interesting.

"Next time you see him, tell him that John, the carpenter on the road, greets him."

As they neared the house, John asked Sybil for a few words. "Is not my brother an inspiring speaker?" she asked.

"He is, indeed. I was hoping we might settle accounts this afternoon."

"On a sabbath? That hardly seems a godly activity for the Lord's Day. We can settle in the morning." She turned and walked into the house. John stood speechless for a moment, then walked back to the barn, changed out of his church clothes, and waited for dinner.

In the morning, he rose with the milking, loaded his tool chest and personal things onto the barrow, and wheeled it to the front of the house. He was about to knock, when Samuel opened the door, holding a wooden plate, and a mug of ale. "Here's your breakfast," he said. There was bread, cheese (the same cheese?), an egg, and a slice of apple pie. "Sybil was particular that you should have pie for breakfast," Samuel said, "She would speak with you when you have been fed."

John took the food. He *was* fond of pie. When he finished, he knocked at the door, and Sybil stepped outside. "Please meet me at the rear of the house," she said, "and we will settle accounts." She took the plate and the mug back inside.

John did as she asked. She emerged from the rear of the house and invited him to sit on a small bench near the back door. "First, let me say that we appreciate the work you have done. We need the barn to survive the winter, and I believe it will stand for many winters to come. Now, I believe you said that you charge five shillings per week, or ten pence for a day's work. Saturday was the only day you actually worked, so we owe you ten pence for the labor." John had to agree; he hadn't worked on Sunday. "We gave you lodging for three nights, with meals. I think a penny per night for lodging, and a penny a day for the meals was what we agreed on?"

"We agreed to no such thing! When I remind you of this, you put me off. No inn would charge so much as a penny a day for lodging!"

"But you weren't staying in an inn."

"I was sleeping in a <u>barn</u>!"

"And a fine barn it is, as I already said," she replied. "Alright, a penny per day for both lodging and meals. You ate meals on four days, including today, but I will only count three days, which comes to three pence. If I subtract that from what I owe you, it comes to seven pence. Agreed?"

"You have forgotten the cost of materials."

"How much did you pay for the wood?"

"Five pence."

Sybil looked surprised. "So much? Don't you think you were overcharged?"

John felt overcharged, but not for the wood. Three pence to sleep in a barn for three nights and eat eight meals was outrageous. "No, I paid a fair price for the wood. You, of course, are entitled to all of the scrap wood left over after the job — since you are paying for it."

Sybil looked distressed and was silent for a moment. She sighed. "John Porter, I will speak truthfully and plainly. I do not have twelve pence to give you now." John had a sinking feeling, and it must have shown on his face. "You have seen how my family lives, and you surely understand that we are not affluent. We are but a poor harvest away from being destitute. But the harvest is coming, and if it is a good one, we will be on better footing. I promise you that we will pay our debt to you. We need more time."

She looked like she might cry. She was embarrassed, ashamed. "I can offer you only this." She held out a small coin, a ha'penny.

John choked down the inclination to scoff at her offer. He should have guessed that something like this would happen — the way she kept avoiding him when he wanted to set the terms. And she had kept him in her barn for three nights, just to whittle down what she owed him. Ruthless woman. Yet, he respected her frankness, even if was late in coming, and he felt a grudging admiration for her resourcefulness. "I'll take no ha'penny from you, Sybil Vessey. I will hold you to your promise to pay me when you can. Good day to you." He stood and began wheeling his way into the village. He was annoyed and disappointed, but he had appointments to keep.

His first stop was at the shop of the Widow Smith. She showed him a small, private room at the back of the shop with a bed in it and a small window. They agreed that he would pay her two pence a week for the room, including laundry. The widow herself lived upstairs, over the shop. She employed one servant, who lived with her upstairs and cooked as well as cleaned for her. John left his tool chest in the shop and put his clothing and personal items in his room, then began making calls on all his new customers.

By late afternoon, he had a month's work lined up and still had six more visits to make. He was careful to set the terms for his wages and insisted that the customers pay for the materials in advance. The first few customers seemed surprised by the latter requirement, but none turned him down. By noon, the customers he saw simply nodded and smiled when he mentioned it. News traveled fast in the village; since he charged everyone the same wage, everyone was expecting the same arrangements. Though John didn't know it, everyone knew about the "deal" he had made with Sybil Vessey. This might have inspired some of them to try to drive a harder bargain, but in fact, it burnished his reputation. Everyone knew the Vessey family's situation, and John was credited for compassion by not raising a fuss about it. The smiles were smiles of understanding and suppressed chuckles: the carpenter had been misled by Sybil, but had learned his lesson. Besides, plenty of people had witnessed his work on the barn and were favorably impressed with his skill.

He made his last stop just before dinner, and the family invited him to eat with them. These folks were prosperous, and had a whole roast chicken on their table, along with the usual bread, ale, and root vegetables. A very satisfying meal. He returned to his lodgings at dusk, to discover that the clothes in his personal chest had all been washed and sat folded on the bed in his room. The widow's servant offered him a nightshirt, and an invitation to have breakfast upstairs in the morning; she would call him when it was time. All in all, a good day.

Sybil's embarrassment and shame about not paying the carpenter was genuine, but should not have troubled her as much as it did for the rest of that day. She had spent the bulk of her life scuffling and struggling to keep her family housed and fed, cutting corners when she could, presuming upon the tolerance of others, turning every conceivable ambiguity to her advantage. She didn't enjoy it, but it had to be done, and she usually shrugged it off. Not this time: it nagged at her all day. Her brother Samuel saw her distracted look during dinner and took her aside. "What is troubling you?"

"Nothing in particular, I'm just weary."

"Is it the carpenter?"

She nodded and began to cry. "He did good work. He did not deserve to be sent away without his pay."

Samuel nodded. "True, but we will pay him in due time. Now that I am employed, I will try to send you a little money. Things will be easier, now."

"Samuel, you don't know. Papa is getting weaker, less interested in . . . well, in living. I fear for him, and I don't know what we will do if he dies."

Actually, Samuel reflected, their father had never recovered from the loss of his wife, their mother. He got himself up every day and dragged himself through his work. But time had only made him withdrawn and bitter. Too much of the weight of the family was borne by the children, most of it rested on Sybil. They had survived, mostly through her efforts.

"Sybil, remember how when Mama died, you stayed home while I went to school?" She nodded. "And you made me teach you what I had learned every evening?"

"I could not keep up with you," she mourned.

"But you did learn to read, and you taught our sisters to read, and they all can read the Bible, and write their names, and do Arithmetic. All this is your legacy. All of us are your legacy. God knows your heart and has seen your faithfulness. Trust Him to sustain you, and all of us."

"I will, Samuel. Thank you." She rose and finished washing the dishes. Her brother was right, God had indeed sustained her and her family. All four of her brothers were positioned for prosperous lives. Her sisters would grow into attractive women, so might hope to marry well, even if there would be no dowry. As for her, she would care for Papa as long as he needed her. There was no shame in that. Nor did she feel bitter. Life was a blessing, regardless of the circumstance.

Samuel rose the next morning and packed his belongings for the journey to Great Dunmow. After breakfast, he hugged his family goodbye (even his father), and bid them farewell. When he stepped onto the road, he turned east, toward the village. He had one more farewell to make.

John Porter was summoned to breakfast the same morning. He dressed quickly and went upstairs to find an ample room with a dining table in the center with eight chairs around it. More chairs were backed to the outer walls of the room. Breakfast was already set out — a poached egg, bread with butter and cherry preserves, a stein of good beer, and some bacon. It was a better breakfast than he had enjoyed for a good while. He sat opposite the Widow, who wanted news of his previous day. He told her that he had found enough work for several months, perhaps enough to last through the winter. She said she'd be pleased to rent him a room for as long as he had work.

In truth, she was glad to have a man staying in the house. It had been only her and her servant since her husband died. She felt financially secure, but she had a workshop full of lumber that wasn't going anywhere. If the carpenter stayed a while, he would likely buy it from her, liquidating the inventory, and putting money in her purse.

John for his part was glad to be settled for a while. He felt sure that there would be enough work to keep him employed until Spring, and two customers had already advanced him money for materials. More money in his purse felt good. After breakfast, they went down to the workshop, and he paid her for the lumber he would need for that day's work. He discovered that the previous craftsman had a lathe. John had worked with lathes during his apprenticeship, but it was much too large to take on the road. Having access to a lathe would mean he could take on more kinds of work, especially in the Winter. "Mistress Smith? This is a lathe. How much would you charge me to use it, if I get a job that requires it?"

"I know what a lathe is, and I know what it is used for. Do you know how to operate it?"

"Indeed, I do. How much to use it?"

"Let's say a penny a week, for any week you actually use it. How do you propose to use a machine that takes two men to operate?"

"If I do use it, I'll have to hire some stout fellow to keep it spinning. But this will open up more opportunities for me." True enough. He could not take an apprentice as a Journeyman — only Master Carpenters were allowed to do so. But nothing prevented him from hiring a little extra help from time to time.

He was on his way to his first job when he met Samuel Vessey, who had evidently been looking for him. "I am on my way to Great Dunmow, and I wanted to speak with you," he said. "I want to thank you for your forbearance on the matter of your wages," he said in a voice loud enough to be overheard, then in a lower voice, "and I hope you do not think ill of my family because of our financial straits. My sister Sybil is particularly pained to think that you should harbor some hard feeling toward us."

"I do not think ill of you, or your sister," John replied,

"I am relieved to hear it. It would ease her mind considerably, I think, if you would greet her cordially sometime — not today, but sometime when you are passing by the house — just bid her good day, or some such courtesy."

"I shall do so," John said. "And Godspeed you on your journey. Remember to greet our friend Chase, if you see him." What a strange family, the Vesseys.

With that, Samuel turned back the way he had come. Great Dunmow was to the west. He congratulated himself for a deed well done.

Part 5: The Weight of Friendship

1581: Recusants

Through September and into early October, John was busy. It seemed that each time he completed one job, another one or two became available. He was gaining a reputation for quality work in a short time — which meant lower prices. He had ample commitments to see him to March, or possibly even May. September and October are harvest months: his meals got more interesting as pumpkins, apples, and squash were now plentifully available. Sometimes he ate at the alehouse, (and he had to admit that the cook was nothing special) but he was often invited to dine with the households where he was working. The food was generally tasty, and none of them expected him to pay for the meal. He often breakfasted with the Widow Smith, who seemed to enjoy his company.

Every Sunday, he was in church and saw the various families that he had worked for, including the Vesseys. They were friendly enough, though Sybil was polite, at best. He was beginning to feel part of a community.

On one particularly fine day, he was passing the Vessey farm and saw Sybil in her garden. He walked up to her and said, "Good Afternoon!"

Sybil stood up and looked at him with surprise, then frowned. "I suppose you're after your money. Well, I don't have it, yet."

"No, I was just passing, and wanted to wish you a good afternoon." Under the circumstances, it would seem self-interested to ask how the harvest was going.

"And Good Afternoon to you, John Porter," she replied, then turned back to her work. A bad time to call, perhaps.

At the end of the day, he was back in the shop, preparing for the next day's work. He left the door open, because the weather was mild but crisp, and the air was fresh, when a shadow appeared in the doorway. John went to the door and saw — William Payne. "John, the carpenter!" said Payne. "So, you took my advice about work in Little Baddow?"

"I did, indeed," John replied. "And I am in your debt. I have found plenty of work here, and a comfortable situation, as you see."

Payne smiled. "Is the Widow Smith at home?"

"I believe she is. Do you want me to call her for you?"

"Never mind. I know the way," Payne said, as he headed toward the stairs.

John was surprised at this familiarity, then realized the obvious: If Payne had known that Smith the carpenter had died, he must know the widow as well. No great coincidence.

Soon after, the Widow's servant hurried down the stairs, and out into the street, on some errand or other. A while later, she was back and hurried upstairs. John finished his preparations and thought about dinner. He would be eating in the alehouse across the street this evening. Perhaps the cook would outdo herself.

When he returned from dinner (which was marginally better than usual), the Widow's servant was waiting for him at the bottom of the stairs. "Mistress said to tell you that she is entertaining guests this evening, and you should not be alarmed if you hear them coming or going on the stairs." Alarmed? More likely annoyed — he imagined a parade of loud, half-drunk, dinner guests staggering down the stairs above his room late that night. He probably wouldn't be getting a good night's sleep, but it wouldn't be alarming.

It was not as he imagined. There was continuous creaking on the stairs through most of the night, as people came and went, but only one or two at a time. None said anything that he could hear, and he fell asleep soon enough. It wasn't until the following morning that he began to make sense of it all. William-not-his-real-name Payne was, according to Edward Chase, almost certainly a Catholic priest, which made the Widow Smith a recusant, which meant John was living in a recusant house! The realization shocked him, for a bit. Why were people coming and going in ones and twos? Because they were going to confession. Why at night? The better to avoid being identified.

John assessed the risk to himself. The Widow had given him no reason to suspect her of recusancy — she attended the Parish church, just as he did. No doubt all of last night's visitors attended the Parish services, too. Which meant that all of them were people he knew, people he worked for, people he liked — yet he never suspected them!

How likely was it that the authorities would have reason to suspect them?

John knew very well that his civic duty was to denounce them all. He decided almost immediately that he would have no part in any denunciations. The news, when it reached Little Baddow, was full of accounts of how Edmund Campion and an unknown horde of Jesuit priests were at large in the kingdom. The government's pursuit of them was widely publicized; indeed, it took on the atmosphere of a fox hunt or other sporting event. Some people were thrilled by the hunt; some people rooted for the fox. Most regarded the whole thing with detachment. It all seemed so far removed from life in a village like Little Baddow. No doubt the Londoners followed it with excitement, but in the countryside questions about the harvest this year got much more attention.

John decided he would avoid any contact with the visitors that might allow him to identify them or make him appear to be complicit with them in any way. He wasn't a practiced liar, but ignorance was as good a defense as any in situations like this one. His resolution was tested almost immediately. The Widow's servant came downstairs and invited him to breakfast with the Widow Smith "as soon as it is convenient." John sighed inwardly and collected his thoughts.

The room upstairs was furnished just as it had been many times before. Widow Smith was already seated, and another guest was present: William Payne sat across from her. John seated himself, and breakfast was served.

"John, I think you know my guest." Payne smiled and nodded at him. John nodded back. "I am sure that you noted the number of guests I entertained last night . . ."

John interrupted her "In truth, I slept very soundly last night, I did not see any of the guests that you said you would be entertaining, and that is for the best, I think." She looked at him with some surprise. "And before either of you explain anything to me, I would caution you to refrain from informing me of anything that I do not absolutely need to know. I think that my ignorance may serve you as well as me." The Widow sat back in her seat, a bit, and William nodded and smiled.

"I am in debt to both of you," John continued, "in more ways than one. This breakfast I am eating would not be set before me, but that both of you have shown me kindness and generosity. I consider both of you my friends. You can be confident that I will never return your favor with any slanders based on idle speculation." There, he had said it. He hoped they understood him.

"In that case," said the Widow, "I will inform you merely that I will be entertaining more visitors today."

"As well you should. A woman like yourself cannot have too many friends. I am sure that many people value your generosity, and enjoy your company."

William Payne could not suppress a chuckle. Once again, the carpenter had surprised him with his cleverness and tact; he could say so much while saying nothing at all. He thought himself a good judge of character, and this man confirmed his judgment — no worries here.

John finished his breakfast and went to work at a job site in the village — it was another bright, crisp Autumn day. He was invited to dinner at the farmstead where he was working. He got back to the shop late and went to bed early — no need to meet any of the "guests" that the Widow was hosting. When they came, it was all at once, or so the creaking of the stairs suggested. There must have been two dozen sets of feet on the stairs, all going up. Then, no more creaking for at least an hour, followed by a flurry of footsteps going down. John satisfied himself with the knowledge that he had seen nothing and slept soundly the rest of the night.

In the morning, just as John was ready to leave the shop for work, Willam Payne appeared, dressed for travel. "I am leaving," said Payne, "and I wanted to bid you farewell. I think our meeting on the road last summer was due to the grace of God: you have found a place where you are needed and respected, the Widow has a paying tenant to support her finances, and I have made a friend. May God prosper you in your work." It was a blessing, and John could not help recalling that he was being blessed by a Catholic priest. A blessing is a blessing, he supposed and could do him no harm, whatever the source. "Godspeed to you, William," he nodded.

Payne left the shop and headed East. The rules for safe travel had changed, since the Summer. Edmund Campion's "brag" had stirred the government to action. Once, the matter of recusancy had been focused on the loyalty or disloyalty of a few aristocratic families; now everyone was suspect. The highways and alehouses were full of spies and informants, hoping to collect the cash bounties that were more available than ever. Payne did not attach himself to groups of strangers on the road anymore. It was all too likely that a stranger could be his betrayer. He now kept to himself, used back roads when he could, and sometimes traveled at night. He no longer presented himself as the steward of the Petre family at Ingatestone Hall. It was risky to be associated with a family whose sympathies were known to be Catholic, and, if he were detained, it could only be more dangerous for them, as well. He continued to make his rounds, ministering to his flock. He would continue to do so, as long as he was able. As he walked, he prayed: "Lord God, protect these you have placed in my care. Give me the courage to care for them, and may it please you to protect me, until my work is finished."

John Porter had plenty of work through the winter, as he had expected. When the weather was foul, he worked indoors; he had opportunities to use the lathe in the shop, with the help of a strong local farmhand who would have otherwise been idle in the inclement weather outside. He paid the Widow regularly for his lodging, as well as for her inventory of lumber, which was gradually shrinking as he used it up. The Widow was well pleased with the arrangement, and so was John.

He continued to attend the Sunday services at St. Mary the Virgin (as required by law). He resisted the urge to guess which of his fellows were recusants; he preferred to enjoy the fellowship of a community where he felt accepted and respected, without complications. He saw the Vesseys there, of course — Thomas, Francis, Sybil, and her two sisters, Susan (now fifteen years old) and Mary (thirteen). They greeted him with cordial smiles — Except for Thomas, who seldom smiled at all. Some smiles were more than merely cordial. Several young women, and their mothers, made a point of greeting him every Sunday and enquiring about his business affairs, his health, and his preferences in food. He got several invitations to Sunday supper and noticed that an item he had expressed a taste for on one Sunday was often featured on someone's table the following week. John appreciated their thoughtfulness but avoided eating too often at any particular house or seeming to prefer the company of any particular family. Always at the back of his mind was the fact that he was lodging in the house of a recusant and that he, and anyone thought to be close to him, might be at risk of denunciation.

⸻ ◇ ⸻

Sybil Vessey saw things quite differently. Seeing John Porter every Sunday reminded her of the debt her family owed him, and it gnawed at her. She liked and respected him, but seeing him mix so freely with others, who had employed him and been able to pay him irked her, somehow. The debt felt like a barrier, that blocked her path — to what, exactly, she could not say. And she was annoyed with the way that so many young women in the village were *openly* flirting with him. She kept this to herself, usually, but sometimes would blurt out to her sisters: "Did you see young Rachel Carter after church this morning? Hanging around John Porter with that silly grin!"

"She's set her cap for him, I reckon," said Susan with the hint of a smile. She gave a sidelong glance at Mary, who was grinning.

"I hope I never see either of you act like such *hussies* around some young man. We are a poor family, but we can conduct ourselves with self-respect." Both girls nodded soberly as if they had received an important life lesson.

The harvest had been good last Autumn, and Samuel, true to his word, had sent some money home. Things were easier this winter. After paying the rent, and the apprentice fees for her brothers, Sybil actually had a little money left over. She resolved to pay off the debt to John Porter, just to get it over with. After calculating her resources, and setting some aside for emergencies, she realized she did not have quite enough. She could only offer him six pence — half of what she owed. Well, half a debt paid would be half a burden lifted. She considered how to pay him. Offering it to him in public risked the possibility that he might refuse it, as he had refused the ha'penny the previous year — that still stung. Better to do it in private. She would invite him to dinner. She could make something he liked (apple pie, wasn't it?) to sweeten the deal. And she didn't have to wait for Sunday to invite him, any day of the week would do. On second thought, if she did invite him for next Sunday, and he accepted, he would have to turn down any other invitations from those other scheming mothers, and their half-wit daughters. There was something appealing about that idea.

John was a little surprised at the invitation to supper with the Vesseys; his last encounter with Sybil had been civil, but hardly friendly. He walked back from church the next Sunday with the whole Vessey family. It was a fine Spring day. There was news to share — Samuel seemed to be prospering in his new position; the milk cows had delivered calves (one of them delivered twins), the spring planting was well underway. John, for his part, had pretty much caught up with the backlog of jobs over the winter. He planned to look further afield for work, in villages further east.

There was news from London and the greater world, as well. Edmund Campion's "brag" was talked about even in a small place like Little Baddow. Parliament had responded to the "brag" by passing "An Act to retain the Queen's Majesty's Subjects in their due Obedience." The fine for failing to attend the Church of England's services was now twenty pounds per month and could include imprisonment. Attending a mass or celebrating a mass was punishable by fines and imprisonment, as well. The government prosecuted the new law energetically. Only the very wealthy could afford to pay the fines, so many were simply imprisoned. Always there was questioning — what, if anything did they know about the fugitive priests? The tiniest hint of incriminating evidence was used to justify torture. Confessions, once extracted, could lead to more arrests, and more imprisonments. Always, the justification was the pursuit of treasonous priests, especially Edmund Campion. The Pope did his part by declaring that assassinating the Queen was no sin, but rather "gains merit." None of this had reached Little Baddow, yet. John looked at his companions and wondered how they would fare when it did come.

Supper was pleasant enough. There was some sort of green vegetable that Sybil called "asparagus," besides the usual pottage of root vegetables, with sausage. The seasoning was a bit more complex, and to John's palate, tastier. The usual bread and ale, of course, but also some honey. There was pie for dessert. It was sweeter than he remembered; evidently, Sybil had got her hands on some sugar. All in all, a satisfying meal.

Afterward, Sybil invited him to join her just outside the front door. "John, I am in your debt, and I will not rest easy until it is paid. We had a good harvest last Autumn, and I promised to pay you when I could." She offered him a sixpence. "This is only half what I owe, but please accept this as a downpayment."

John now understood the reason for his invitation to supper, as well as for her cool politeness at their previous encounter. The woman had an accountant's sensibility in matters of money, and a sense of honor that only a wealthy man could afford (though few wealthy men, in his experience, actually practiced such). If she were a man, she could be a moneylender. He admired her determination to defend her family's honor. He smiled and took the coin from her hand. "Thank you. Let's hope for another good harvest."

Sybil sighed audibly. The feeling of relief was so strong, that she had an urge to embrace him, which she suppressed. Her eyes were tearing, a little. "Yes! Another good harvest!"

They stepped back inside the house. Both of Sybil's sisters were just inside the door, with odd expressions on their faces. John thanked the family for their hospitality, praised the meal, and bid farewell.

Sybil watched as his figure receded down the road to the village. When she turned into the house, her eyes were still a little moist, and she felt flushed. "Are you feeling ill, sister?" asked Mary.

"No, not all," she replied, "Why do you ask?" wondering if they could see how flustered she was feeling, not sure she understood her feelings, herself.

"She's thinking of another good harvest," said Susan, and both sisters giggled.

John returned to the shop half a shilling richer, with a full stomach. It was a good day. He reflected on his conversation with Sybil, and what it revealed about her character. She would make someone a good wife, he thought. Pretty, in her own way; too bad that she wouldn't bring much of a dowry. Matrimony was something that John rarely allowed himself to think about. He was by no means immune to the charms of a pretty face, or a feminine figure, but he had other priorities. A man in his position had to focus on his future. Marriage was out of the question until he was in a solid financial position. For now, he had to make a living — that much he had achieved in Little Baddow, but for how long? His next step had to be finishing out his stint as a journeyman and obtaining his Mastership in carpentry. It would soon be time to find a project that he could submit to the guild masters for their approval. Then, if he could establish his own workshop, and take on some paying apprentices, then and only then would he be in a position to court someone. Women with dowries had fathers, and fathers were not inclined to give away their daughters (and those dowries) to a man without financial means, or prospects. In time, God willing, he would have the means and the prospects to woo and win his own wife.

By the time he had hashed this out in his mind, he was at the door to the Widow's shop, which reminded him sharply of the principal threat to his plans for the future. How long before the Queen's agents came to Little Baddow, and began asking questions? How long before someone in the village volunteered some tidbit of information that would lead to the arrest of one of their fellows? If the Widow Smith were discovered, John himself might be accused. Even if he avoided that peril, all her property would likely be seized, and John would be out of a workshop and a home. He thought of his friend William Payne, who must surely be living in fear. He found himself hoping that William would never return to Little Baddow.

1582: End of a Journey

William Payne had continued his travels through the Winter and into the Spring, nonetheless. Several of the aristocratic houses at which he stayed had constructed secret rooms or chambers where he could hide, colloquially known as "priest holes." He used them more often, now, and had several narrow escapes. He continued to celebrate masses and hear confessions when and where he could. On more than one occasion, he was warned in the nick of time to avoid traveling to this town or that village, because his hosts had been arrested and imprisoned. Gradually, the number of places that still had viable groups of recusants declined. He did not dare to make contact with any new groups. For all his caution, he was arrested in July of 1581 at an estate belonging to the Petre family and imprisoned in the Tower of London.

Later the same month, they caught Edmund Campion. He was arrested at the home of the Yates family, known recusants, in Oxfordshire, then taken to London, and imprisoned in the Tower. He was questioned first by high-ranking officials of the Privy Council, including his old friend and patron the Earl of Leicester. Campion insisted that he considered Elizabeth to be the legitimate Queen of England (the Pope's proclamations notwithstanding), and was offered his freedom, and even a prominent role in the Church of England, if he would affirm her place as the sole and "supreme governor" of the English church, in effect renouncing his Catholicism. This he refused to do, and under the Act of Supremacy, was charged with treason. Neither the Queen nor any of his other powerful friends were able or willing to grant him an exception to the law of the land. There followed several months of imprisonment, including two or three sessions on the rack, before he was brought to trial. His challenge to a debate with Protestant scholars was granted, though not under the safe conduct that he had requested. Observers reported that he presented his positions eloquently and persuasively, but this was a moot point — he was indicted and tried that November, and only one of his theological positions was pertinent: his view that the Pope was the only true and rightful head of the Church.

Campion and two other priests were sentenced to death: "You must go to the place from whence you came, there to remain until ye shall be drawn through the open city of London upon hurdles to the place of execution, and there be hanged and let down alive, and your privy parts cut off, and your entrails taken out and burnt in your sight; then your heads to be cut off and your bodies divided into four parts, to be disposed of at Her Majesty's pleasure. And God have mercy on your souls." The sentence was carried out on December 1st, 1581.

Robert Persons, Campion's companion, was now the senior leader of the Mission in England. He prudently fled to France soon after Campion's arrest. Over the years, he would recruit and send more missionaries to England. Over the years, more would be arrested. No less than forty of them would be executed for treason. Persons became a vocal advocate for the overthrow of Elizabeth by military means and was involved in multiple attempts to replace her with Mary, the titular "Queen of Scots" as the legitimate, Catholic Queen of England. None of those attempts would be successful.

The clandestine printing press was found soon after Campion's arrest, and the printers were arrested. One was executed, the other, surprisingly was released and fled to France, where he joined Robert Persons. The printing would continue, but not on English soil.

William Payne had languished all these months in the Tower. It was discovered that he had been arrested previously, under the name John Payne, in 1577, and deported to France. (He had returned to England two years later.) Payne and his companion received similar treatment to Campion: imprisonment in the Tower, sessions on the rack. Throughout, he maintained that his ministry was solely to bring pastoral care to English Catholics and that he recognized Elizabeth as the legitimate Queen of England. He learned of Campion's conviction and execution while still in the Tower.

In March of 1582, he was abruptly transferred to the jail in Chelmsford, to face charges of treason. The government had decided to send the recusants in Essex a message, and the spectacle of his execution would serve that purpose. The responsibility for conducting his trial, and imposing his subsequent sentence would fall upon Robert Rich, 3rd Baron of Leez.

1582: Chelmsford

Robert Rich had inherited his title only the year before, when his father, the 2nd Baron had died. His lands and estates were inherited from his grandfather, Richard Rich, the 1st Baron, who had obtained them during the dissolution of the monasteries during the reign of King Henry. The 1st Baron was an ambitious man, who had served no less than four Tudor sovereigns in his career, changing his religious loyalties from Catholic to Protestant, back to Catholic, and finally back to Protestant, as circumstances required. His son, the 2nd Baron, had the luxury of needing only one religion during his lifetime, and was firmly and reliably Protestant, as was Robert, the 3rd Baron.

The 3rd Baron did not welcome the news that a recusant priest was to be tried in his domain. There was no mistaking that London considered the trial to be a mere formality preceding the expected execution; the charge was treason, and the sentence would be deliberately gruesome. This would have been of no particular concern to Rich if the business had been kept in London, but his grandfather's reputation for burning heretics had not worn well over the decades since, either in the popular mood or, for that matter, among his descendants. All of that was in the past, and he preferred that it stay there. Also, he thought that London's decision to send a message to the hinterlands was heavy-handed and would likely backfire. As much (or as little) as he knew about the attitudes of the common folk in his domain, he believed them all to be loyal to the Queen, though they had no great affection for her representatives. To propose that they were hatching plots for her overthrow was laughable — except London seemed to be taking it seriously. If they wanted to find plotters, they should look to the Catholic aristocracy — who might think they had something to gain from sedition.

No doubt a public execution would draw a crowd. Some would attend just for the gory thrill of the thing; others to assuage their fear of a Catholic resurgence. But crowds could change their mood in unpredictable ways. He had heard that the crowd at Edmund Campion's execution had turned against the execution and that it had required troops to prevent a riot. Perhaps that was it: The government was afraid to have another execution so near to London, so they just changed the venue. For that matter, maybe someone thought his presence at the scene — given his family's history — would send a few shivers down some recusant spines.

Or maybe this was a test of his loyalty; you could never tell what the government was thinking. Ruling by fear was a risky proposition — you could only frighten people into submission for so long; better to earn their respect than terrorize them with threats of torture.

He was annoyed with the whole situation. At minimum, he would demand that London send some armed reinforcements; at least he could ensure that things would go smoothly.

John Payne was surprised by the articles of his indictment. He was accused of plotting to murder the Queen and place her cousin Mary, ("Queen of Scots"), on the throne of England. It was a laughable accusation. Who would believe such a thing? The court did. The source of the accusations was revealed at his trial. A man named George Eliot had been employed by the Petre family and testified that Payne had confided the details of the plot to him. Eliot had also been involved in the arrest of Edmund Campion and his associates and thus was a kind of expert on these matters. Payne pointed out that Eliot stood to gain financially from his testimony, by collecting a bounty, and denounced the accusations as a ridiculous pack of lies. The court took mere minutes to find him guilty. His execution was scheduled for April 2, 1582. He would be drawn and quartered, just as Campion and his companions were.

Payne was not a stranger to Chelmsford; he had a brother who had lived in the town for years. His jailers knew his family and treated him with some consideration. Nonetheless, he was surprised to receive a visitor, just days before his execution. It was Edward Chase.

Chase had heard of course, of Payne's arrest months before. He did not immediately make the connection between the man he knew as William Payne, and the John Payne who was convicted of treason. However, Chase traveled a lot, and knew a lot of people, and it was surprising how many details of the condemned man's life were circulating in the channels of gossip, details that would have led to his arrest much earlier if the authorities had been paying attention. When he heard that Payne was being held in Chelmsford, he resolved to speak with him. It was a bit risky to associate with a condemned traitor, but Chase was confident that no one could sustain an accusation of recusancy against him, and he knew the officer in charge of the jail personally. He visited Payne after dark when he wouldn't be easily identified on the street.

"So, William, we meet again!" he tried to sound cheery.

"You may call me John," Payne replied. "I am surprised to see you in this place." Chase looked him over. Pale, from months in prison. Thin — meager meals probably. Sunken cheeks, lined more deeply than he remembered. Humiliation and torture left their marks on a man's face.

"I wish I could say the same about you," he looked at Payne with sympathy.

"I should like you to hear it directly from me. These charges against me are complete falsehoods. I have never in my life expressed anything but loyalty to our Queen."

Chase nodded. "I doubted the charges when I first heard them. You never struck me as an assassin."

"Do you remember our conversation on the road, the day we met?"

"I do, indeed. A lively discussion. I suspected that you were a recusant priest, even then. I recall that you spoke in favor of a church powerful enough to stand up to governments, to protect the people from tyranny and injustice. I argued that the government would always win any contest with the church, and would ultimately corrupt the church if it could; better that the government leave the church alone."

"Or something like that, I suppose. So, which of us was right? Am I to die because our government has corrupted and weakened the church, or because the church has abandoned its duty to call the government to account?"

Careful there, thought Chase. A statement implying that government control of the church was a problem could be taken as a treasonous attack on the Queen's authority. "I think the government has failed you. They are so frightened of their enemies that they are willing to terrorize their citizens — and use perjury and slander to do it. Justice is the least you should expect from a good government, and you have not received it. The Church of England is complicit in this tyranny."

He continued, "Your church has done you no better. It is run by men who would risk your life to gain some temporal advantage; men who spin plots with no chance of success, because they believe their cause has the support of multitudes that will rise when summoned. There are no such multitudes in England — only believers that yearn for the old ways, and ambitious aristocrats who imagine themselves on the throne, and seek money from the King of Spain, or the Pope to make it possible . . ." He stopped to catch his breath, then continued:

". . . The same Pope, by the way, that sealed your fate, when he urged English Catholics to assassinate their Queen. As if justice could be served by assassination, or righteousness by force of arms. Any chance you had of receiving leniency was lost with that proclamation."

Payne sighed and nodded. He had doubted the wisdom of the Jesuit Mission from the beginning. But for them, he might still be serving his scattered flocks; discreetly, so that local officials could look the other way, while the government in London would be concerned with greater matters. Now, he was the symbol of some great threat to the kingdom, an example for all men to abjure, a pawn, really, of a government that did not trust the people that it ruled and would use fear and manipulation to control them. Whatever the men in Rome had intended, the result was more hardship for his little flocks of believers, not deliverance.

"Is there any service that I can do for you?" Chase asked.

Payne thought for a moment. "There is one thing. Can you deliver a letter for me?"

Chase looked troubled. "You know that anything you give to me must be read by your jailers before they will let me take it out of here?"

Payne chuckled. "Do not fear. I'll not be sending any messages to my fellow Catholics from this place. Doing so would only serve to identify them to the authorities. Nor would I put you in any danger by asking you to deliver some secret message. There is someone I should like to bid farewell to — a firm Protestant, like yourself. He lives not far from here — a few hour's walk. He is a carpenter, living in Little Baddow. Do you know the place? '

"I know of it. As you say, it is only a few hour's walk from here. I can deliver your letter if it would ease your mind."

Payne turned to a small desk in the corner of his cell. "They have provided me with writing materials. They read anything I write, hoping to find some evidence to accuse others. There will be nothing in this to help that effort." He wrote briefly on a piece of paper, then folded it. He did not bother to seal the note but handed it to Chase.

"The village has only one carpenter's shop; it is across the road from the only inn. The carpenter that resides there is someone I believe you will recognize. He has shown me hospitality in the past, and I wish to thank him and offer my blessing since I have no other means to repay him for his kindness. The letter is not sealed, you may read it for yourself."

Chase folded the note again and tucked it into his belt. "Farewell, William Payne. This is a sad parting for me. In a different world, I think we could have been close friends."

Payne nodded. "In a different world, perhaps we shall be."

Chase called to be let out of the cell and left the jail. On the way out, he surrendered the note that Payne had written. A guard looked at it, then held it up to the light of a lamp. No evidence of secret writing. He shrugged and gave it back to Chase. "Pretty much like the others," he commented.

"Others?"

"Yes, the traitor has been settling personal accounts with several of our citizens, all good Protestants, of course. We wouldn't allow him to conspire with recusants right under our noses. It goes to show how devious these priests are, befriending loyal Englishmen while consorting secretly with recusants. Still, I guess all of us will want to tie up the loose ends, so to speak, before we die."

Chase nodded and tucked the note back under his belt. He wondered about the other letters. The guard's nonchalance suggested a simpleton's mind unless the whole conversation was a performance intended to lull him into carelessness. No mind, there was nothing for him to betray, since he had no idea what the message might mean. He left the jail and walked back to his inn. In the morning, he would walk to Little Baddow.

<hr>

Edward Chase left for Little Baddow early the next morning. It was a breezy, showery April morning, the air smelled fresh and bracing. The fields he passed were green with the first flush of a promising harvest; flowers bloomed at the roadside. He was halfway to his destination when he realized he was not alone on the road. There was a figure behind him, who seemed to follow him, getting no closer, nor falling behind. He stepped off the road to relieve himself behind some shrubbery. When he looked back down the road, he saw that the figure behind him had stopped, as well. He was startled. This must have something to do with his visit to John Payne! What had he done? What had Payne written? He thought of destroying the note, then and there, but he paused. He took the note out and read it. Nothing but a thanks for some favors done, a blessing for a long and prosperous life, and eternity in heaven. Payne did not even mention that he was due to be executed tomorrow, and had not signed it. Curious. Why didn't he sign it?

Chase got back on the road and continued on his way. Sure enough, the figure behind him began moving, also. A mile or so farther on, he stopped and squatted by the side of the road, as if inspecting something on the ground. He glanced behind him, and the figure had stopped, as well. No question he was being followed. He considered his options: he could continue through the village, then try to lose his shadow and double back; he could wait for a bend in the road that would temporarily conceal him, and then cut across country (if there was enough foliage to conceal him), or he could turn back now, and confront his pursuer, or at least get a good look at him. The last option was attractive but risky. He reminded himself that other people's safety might depend on what he did. There was a chance that his follower did not yet realize that his presence was known. Better to avoid contact. When he got to the village, he could look for a way to lose his pursuer; first, he needed to know the layout of the place.

He approached the village from the southwest. As he entered, there was a crossroads; the majority of the business appeared to lay along the intersecting road, to his left. He quickly turned, moving northwest, now. The shops and houses on the road put him temporarily out of sight of his pursuer. He quickened his pace and stepped into an alleyway to his right before his pursuer made it around the corner. He ducked down behind a large barrel, with a view of the street.

Sure enough, a man appeared, walking quickly to the northwest. A large broad-brimmed hat concealed most of his face, a grey cloak obscured most of his clothing. He appeared to be confused. Good. Now what?

What had Payne said? There was only one carpenter and only one inn. He didn't remember any more specifics than that, and it hadn't seemed important at the time; he expected he would ask for directions when he reached the village. There were other people on the street, going about their business, but now it seemed risky to speak to any of them or be seen by anyone who might remember his face, or describe his clothing.

His pursuer had passed down the street, and he stood to get a better look at the place. There was the inn, across the street, and several buildings down to the right. That would mean that the carpenter's shop was on his side of the street. He turned back down the alley, and cut to his left, across the rear lots of the houses. Sure enough, the third lot had the unmistakable signs of a carpentry shop — lumber, sawdust, scraps. There was a large double door at the back of the building — large enough for a wagon to pass through. It was partially open. Chase took a breath and stepped inside.

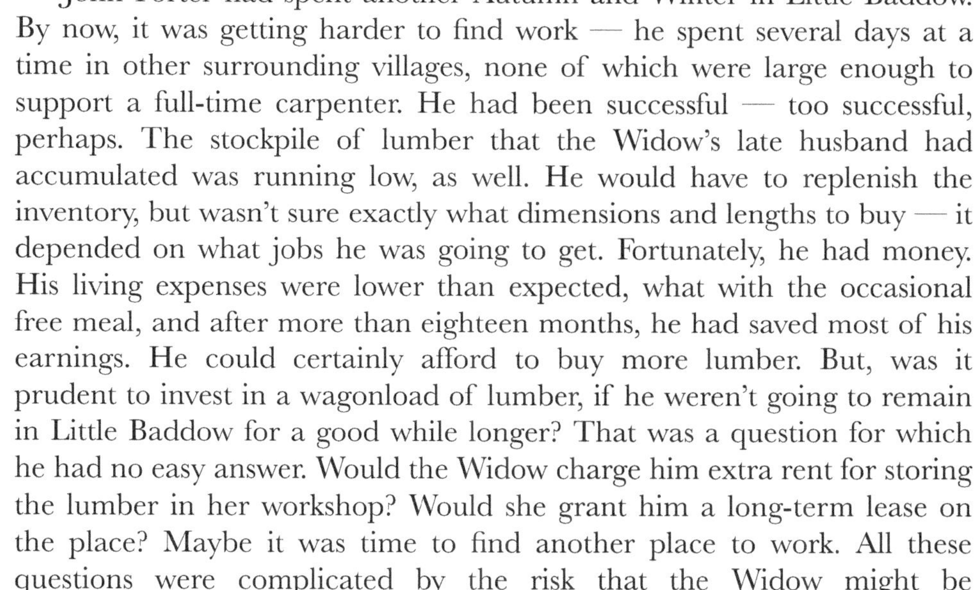

John Porter had spent another Autumn and Winter in Little Baddow. By now, it was getting harder to find work — he spent several days at a time in other surrounding villages, none of which were large enough to support a full-time carpenter. He had been successful — too successful, perhaps. The stockpile of lumber that the Widow's late husband had accumulated was running low, as well. He would have to replenish the inventory, but wasn't sure exactly what dimensions and lengths to buy — it depended on what jobs he was going to get. Fortunately, he had money. His living expenses were lower than expected, what with the occasional free meal, and after more than eighteen months, he had saved most of his earnings. He could certainly afford to buy more lumber. But, was it prudent to invest in a wagonload of lumber, if he weren't going to remain in Little Baddow for a good while longer? That was a question for which he had no easy answer. Would the Widow charge him extra rent for storing the lumber in her workshop? Would she grant him a long-term lease on the place? Maybe it was time to find another place to work. All these questions were complicated by the risk that the Widow might be denounced as a recusant and arrested. He would be under suspicion as well, of course. But assuming that he could exonerate himself, the Widow's property, including the workshop and its contents would be seized by the Queen's agents. It would do him no good to explain that some of the inventory was hers, but the rest was his. They could take it all, including his tools and other personal property. He was beginning to feel trapped in the village, and it was not a feeling he liked.

He was working in the shop that morning, preparing for another trip to one of the nearby villages. He had left the backdoor open, to let in some fresh air, and some sunlight. Suddenly, the light was interrupted. A shadow at the door, the sound of footsteps, a man's figure, silhouetted against the light. "Who comes?"

Edward Chase did not answer immediately. It was dark inside the shop, and he couldn't see clearly at first. Then he recognized the carpenter, and his mind flooded with answers to his questions. The letter wasn't signed because it didn't need to be signed. Chase himself was the only one who could identify both the source of the note and its intended recipient. If the note had fallen into anyone else's hands, it could never be delivered, unless Chase himself had turned it in to the authorities, and if any of the Queen's agents tried to deliver it, the carpenter would truthfully state that he had no idea who the note was from. "Good day, John Porter," he said at last.

John did not recognize him, still just a silhouette against the sunlit doorway. "Who comes?"

"I am Edward Chase, whom you met on the road to Chelmsford, nigh two years ago," he replied, stepping forward.

John recognized him now and greeted him with a handshake. "Welcome to Little Baddow."

Edward looked around. "You've done well for yourself, carpenter!"

"The shop is not mine. I am renting the space. But I have no complaints about my situation. I have prospered here. I am curious as to what business of yours brings you to this place."

Edward nodded; might as well get straight to the point. "I was asked to bring you a note from a condemned man. His name is John Payne, and he is to be executed tomorrow." He handed John the note.

John read the note, then read it again. "I do not understand. I know no man named John Payne." He had, of course, heard of the arrest of the recusant priest, and the execution was widely publicized — the government wanted the largest possible turnout for the event. John had no interest in such public spectacles, squeamish, perhaps. Pointless cruelty, the cheapest form of entertainment.

"You and I knew him as William Payne. I did not know his real name until yesterday when I visited him in the Chelmsford Jail."

John's face showed a brief flash of surprise, then recognition. "It was he that told me about this opportunity, that day on the road," he said with a nod.

A quick recovery, Edward thought. The statement was doubtless truthful, but Payne would not assume that John had actually settled in Little Baddow unless he had seen him since that day on the road. The carpenter would not acknowledge that fact, if he had his wits about him.

He did. "I see that the note is not signed. No one but you or I know the author?" Chase nodded. The guard at the jail didn't count, surely.

John leaned back against a bench, looking worried. He needed to think, and think clearly. At length, he asked, "Did you bring this note directly from Chelmsford?"

"I received it yesterday. I left Chelmsford this morning, and no, I did not discuss my purpose with anyone else."

"Were you followed?" Edward hesitated. John repeated the question more forcefully, "Were you followed?"

"I believe so, yes. I managed to lose him before I came here. That's why I used your back door."

"What did he look like?" Edward described the man. "Wait here," said John. He walked to the front door, stepped outside, stretched, and yawned, while he scanned the street. He came back inside, and closed the door. "The man you described is outside, strolling up and down the street. He appears to be speaking with the villagers. No doubt he is asking for your whereabouts."

First things first. He walked to the small fireplace near the back of the shop, where some embers were still glowing. He touched the note to the embers, it burst into flame and was ashes in a moment.

John turned to Edward. "I think it best if you leave without being seen." Edward agreed. "You may leave the way you came. Do you intend to return to Chelmsford?"

"I thought I would," said Edward, "but now I am not so sure."

"Now that you have been followed here, you need an excuse for making the trip, that has nothing to do with our friend William Payne."

"John Payne," Edward corrected him.

"He is William, as far as I know." Edward conceded the point with a nod.

"I can provide you with a reason, though it must have nothing to do with me. Do you understand?"

Edward nodded. The man was full of surprises.

"I will go to the lot back of this shop, and when no one is within sight of the lot, I will signal you to come outside. You will have to cut across some fields to avoid being seen from the road, but you can circle 'round to the southwest. Do not return to Chelmsford today. There is a farm just outside the village, on the road to Chelmsford. The cottage is near the road and has a vegetable garden in the front. The family name is Vessey. The mistress of the house (John could not suppress a chuckle, at the term), will invite you to supper, if you tell her that you are a friend of her brother, Samuel Vessey, who is presently the Curate in the parish of Great Dunmow. You can tell her that you simply want any news she may have about her brother. "

Edward was speechless. He knew Samuel Vessey of course, and knew very well where he was serving. But how in the world could this carpenter know these things?

"What if I go to the wrong house?"

"So much the better, just don't be seen in the village. If you have to ask for directions, that will make one more witness to support your story. Once you have found the place, wait until I arrive. I have some business with the family today. It may be that we will both spend the night there. The accommodations are . . . rustic." He chuckled again, to himself.

"You are going to a great deal of trouble for my sake, and to conceal the purpose of my trip. If things go as you have planned, I will be grateful," said Edward.

"It is more trouble than you know," replied John, "but it is more for my sake, and the sake of this village, than yours." He walked to the back lot. One of the neighbors was using the privy. He pretended to be busy with something, until the neighbor went back inside, then signaled to Edward, who slipped out the back and cut across the fields to the southeast.

With Edward safely away, he returned to the shop. He went to the front door, opened it, and looked down the street. The stranger was still visible, speaking with the passers-by, asking about a man that none of them had ever seen. He stepped back inside, and locked the door, then ascended the staircase, and knocked at the Widow Smith's door. Her servant appeared. "I would speak to the Widow Smith, on an urgent matter," he said. The servant disappeared briefly, then reappeared, and ushered him into the room where he had breakfasted with William — no, John Payne, less than a year before. The Widow Smith invited him to sit down.

"Good Day, John. What is this urgent matter?"

"I received a note this morning, from our mutual friend, William Payne." The Widow appeared surprised. "I believe the message was intended to be shared with you, after a fashion."

"Where is the note?"

"I thought it prudent to destroy the note. It came from a condemned man, who expects to die soon. He is in the Chelmsford Jail, awaiting execution for High Treason. The man who delivered the note to me was followed here from Chelmsford. The fewer of these details that you know, the safer it will be for you, and your friends." The Widow stared at him, and paled, a little.

"Your safety is the only reason that I am speaking to you at all," he continued. I am resolved to leave Little Baddow today. I shall seek work elsewhere."

She gasped a little. "Do you not think it rash, to leave so soon?"

"I think it prudent. I am the only known link between John Payne and this village, and I would not have my friends in this place subjected to the questions that might be put to them by the Queen's agents. The sorts of questions they would ask might well lead to pain and death."

"What was the message?" she asked.

"It was not signed. It merely thanked me for a favor I did him once and wishes for my prosperity and eternal happiness."

"I see. Your leaving will be a loss to us. You are well-liked and respected in this place. Is there anything I can do to help you on your way?"

"No, I think it would be best if you keep no recollection of this conversation at all, and maintain sincere surprise at my sudden disappearance."

"Quite so. Consider your rent paid in full. I will give you one keepsake, for our friendship." She stood, left the room, and returned with a large, broad-brimmed hat, such as fashionable tradesmen wore. "This was my husband's. He has no use for it, now. Godspeed, John Porter."

John stood and went back downstairs. He packed up his tools (how he hated to leave that lathe!), and all his personal belongings, tied them securely to his barrow and prepared to leave. The Widow's servant appeared, and gave him a bundle with cheese, bread, and a small jug of ale, then disappeared.

It was not yet noon when he emerged from the shop with his loaded barrow and started down the road to the southeast. Anyone watching him would have seen an ordinary workman, on his way to some job or other. Even to his friends, there was nothing unusual about the way he was dressed, or the direction he took. At the crossroads on the edge of town, he turned southwest, towards Chelmsford, and was soon out of sight.

<hr>

Edward Chase found the house he was looking for without much difficulty. A woman was working in the garden in front, near the road. He greeted her. "Good day, Mistress! Is the the Vessey farm?"

The woman straightened up and looked at him. "Sir, you have the advantage of me. You seem to know my name, if not my station, but I have never seen you before in my life."

"My name is Edward Chase. If your name is Vessey, I am a friend of Samuel Vessey, a member of your family, I think."

The woman (younger than he had first supposed) looked at him intently, then turned to face a barn behind the house. "Samuel!" she shouted. "Are you there?"

Shortly, a man he recognized emerged from the barn. "What is the matter?" Then he recognized Edward and strode forward to greet him. Both men embraced and laughed, clearly pleased to see each other.

"What brings you to Little Baddow?" asked Samuel.

"I am not at liberty to say, but I did not expect to see you here. I thought you were in Great Dunmow."

"I am only here for a short visit. A family matter to settle. I am due back in Great Dunmow in three days. Oh, let me introduce my sister. This is Sybil Vessey, the rock of our family. Sybil, this is my friend and mentor, Edward Chase."

Sybil greeted him with a nod and curtsey. "Pleased to meet you, Mr. Chase. Samuel speaks very well of you."

"You must sup with us today. How did you find us? Did you ask for us in the village?"

"Yes, I got instructions from a mutual acquaintance, a carpenter — John Porter, I believe is his name. He asked me to meet him here." At this, Chase noticed that Sybil had tensed a little.

"Will he be expecting supper when he comes?"

"I cannot say for certain. He did not say when we should meet.

Sybil turned to the house. "It sounds like I need to get busy, then." She went inside.

Edward turned to Samuel. "Have I offended? Was it something I said?"

"The name John Porter strikes her oddly, sometimes. A complicated matter, never mind. But you must tell me something about your work and your travels since we were at university!" Edward followed Samuel back to the barn. Just as well to be out of sight of anyone on the road.

John Porter arrived at the Vessey farm just before suppertime and wheeled his barrow directly into the barn. He checked beforehand that there was no one on the road, to see where he went. He was surprised to find both Edward Chase and Samuel Vessey in the barn; they had been expecting him.

Samuel explained that he had returned home briefly to arrange an apprenticeship for his youngest brother, Francis. Now that he was working, the family had just enough money to pay a master craftsman to take Francis on and also hire a farmhand to help Old Thomas in the fields. Once that was arranged, he would return to Great Dunmow. A fortuitous coincidence that John had sent Edward here just at the time that Samuel was visiting. The question of why either Edward or John was in this barn on this day hung in the air. Neither man seemed inclined to answer it.

"I need to ask your favor," said John. "I would like to leave my barrow in your barn for a few days."

"You know our family well enough to know that that favor is not mine to grant," replied Samuel. "You will have to ask Sybil."

John nodded. "Is she in the house?"

"Yes, but she is busy, just now. She did not expect to have two such distinguished guests for supper." He laughed.

So, they waited in the barn until Sybil called them in. Old Thomas and Francis came in from the fields, and the table was crowded. Samuel and Edward regaled them with reminiscences of their university days, John said very little. Sybil wondered what was really going on, but no one gave her any clue. After the meal, Thomas and Francis went back to work. John approached Sybil.

"Sybil, I have a favor to ask," he began.

"I think I have done you one already today. You are welcome at our table, but arrangements should be made in advance, at our invitation!"

"Then please accept my apology. Let me say it differently. If you would allow me to store my barrow in your barn for a few nights, I would consider it partial payment for your debt to me."

"How much partial payment?" This she could understand.

"I am thinking a penny per night, beginning tonight."

"Done!" she said. He thanked her and went outside. Just like that; rude man, no manners, no warmth. Not that she was looking for any warmth from the likes of him. Still, what would a little friendliness cost him? Why not stay long enough for some light conversation?

John met Edward in the barn. Both of them understood implicitly that they should be seen by as few people as possible. John placed his barrow where it could not be seen from the road, even with the barn doors wide open. "So, what do you have in mind?" asked Edward.

"I think you can return to Chelmsford this evening, or tomorrow morning, with a credible explanation of where you have been, and why," said John. "For my part, I am leaving Little Baddow. If asked, you can answer truthfully that you delivered a note to me and visited your friends in Little Baddow. I will not be found in Little Baddow, if anyone bothers to look for me, so I hope my friends here will not be subjected to the harsh questioning of the Queen's inquisitors. None of them (with one exception) will know that I am gone until I am far away from here."

Edward found the man's logic compelling. He seemed to have thought of every connection between this place and John Payne and contrived to sever them all. "It is a high price you are paying, to protect these people."

"I am protecting myself, as well. None of us knows how we would hold up under torture, but I doubt my own steadfastness would prove stronger than the rack. In any case, I would be leaving Little Baddow sooner rather than later. There simply isn't enough work in a village of this size, to take on apprentices and prosper, even if I were a Master carpenter, which I am not. I am seizing the opportunity of the moment."

The last remark seemed doubtful to Edward. "I suppose I should have refused to deliver the message," he said. "It would have avoided all these complications. It can hardly matter much to a condemned man whether anyone actually receives such a message."

"I will disagree with you, there. It matters to more people than you know, and may save someone's life."

"Don't you think it is time the two of you told me what is going on?" Samuel spoke from behind them. How long had he been eavesdropping?

"The less you know, the better," said John.

"I already know more than I probably should, and could guess even more," Samuel said. "And after all this *is* my barn!"

John and Edward looked at each other. Samuel's imagination could only make things worse if left to ramble.

Edward spoke first. "I will briefly explain our situation, though you will not thank me, I suspect, when you know the facts. John and I have a mutual friend, named William Payne (not his real name). It turns out that he is the notorious Catholic priest John Payne, who will be drawn and quartered in Chelmsford tomorrow. I visited him in prison yesterday, and he asked me to deliver a message to someone in Little Baddow for him. He did not tell me who the message was for, but it turns out to be John, here." He nodded in John's direction.

"John, you are a recusant?" exclaimed Samuel.

"No, I am not a recusant. Payne sent the message to me precisely because he knows I am not a recusant — he did not want to put any of his own flock at risk. He trusted me to make sure that the message would reach them, and I have done so. It is not safe for me, nor anyone in the village, for me to remain here. I am leaving Little Baddow.

"There are recusants in Little Baddow?"

"I have reason to think there are, though only a handful. I do not know their names, but I see no reason to put them in peril. If the Queen's inquisitors come here, there will be questions and threats. There may be denunciations, whether truthful or not, and lives may be ruined, or even ended. I want no part of it."

Do you really believe it would be as bad as that?"

"If you were the Queen's agent, and I told you that I believed there were recusants in Little Baddow, but I had no idea who they were, would you take my word for it, or would you torture me before believing my story, just to be sure? That alone is reason enough for *me* to leave."

Edward spoke to Samuel. "I warned you that you would not thank us for the truth."

"Where will you go?" asked Samuel.

"That I will not tell you, and you may thank me for that. I have permission from Sybil to leave my barrow in your barn. I have business in Chelmsford tomorrow. When I return, I will disappear,"

"You have told this to Sybil?"

"Certainly not! We agreed that I could rent a space in this barn for my possessions, against the sixpence that she owes me, nothing more. The rest can be no concern of hers."

No concern? For all his cleverness, the man could be clueless, thought Samuel. He sighed, "The less she knows, the better, I suppose. What is your business in Chelmsford?"

John was silent for a moment. "I am going to attend the execution. Yesterday, I had no interest in seeing it at all — such things are senselessly cruel to the condemned, as well as to the spectators, (however much pleasure they derive from it). But knowing that the man who will be dying is a friend compels me to be there. I can do nothing to help him, other than stand witness to his suffering and death. So, that much I will do."

"I shall go with you," said Edward. "He is my friend, too."

"We should not travel together." John shook his head, "You are already under suspicion, and If I am seen with you, it will undo all the trouble I have undergone to keep our connection secret."

Edward nodded. A good point. He needed to be mindful of the likelihood that there would be more than one stranger watching his movements. "I am headed that way myself," said Samuel, "back to Great Dunmow in the morning. I will accompany you as far as Chelmsford."

Edward demurred. Much safer for everyone if he walked alone. Besides, he had thought of one more favor he could do for John Payne, but it was far too risky to invite anyone to join him. "Well, we have a busy day tomorrow. Can you show me to a place where I may sleep tonight?"

John laughed. "I can. You're already here."

April 2, 1582: Chelmsford

The morning of April 2 was showery, but the skies were clearing, and it looked to be a pleasant day. Robert Rich, 3rd Baron of Leez, rose early to inspect the place of execution. He had donned the robes suitable to his duties of the morning and walked to the city plaza. There was no scaffold as such, but seating for the Baron and a handful of other officials had been set up. Two dozen mounted soldiers had been sent from London, at his request. The local constabulary would be out in force, as well.

The hanging would be accomplished by the simple manner of forcing the traitor to stand on a ladder, which was already leaning against the stone wall of a building facing the square. The hangman's rope was tied to a projecting beam on the second story of the building. When the time came, the noose would be placed around the condemned man's neck and the ladder would be pulled away — simple.

The purpose, however, was not to kill the man by hanging. He was to hang until nearly suffocated, then revived. This meant that the executioner would have to put the ladder back, climb it to where the man was hanging, and release him from the noose, while he was unconscious but not yet dead. The timing of the thing was ticklish, but the terms of the sentence were quite specific on this point. London had sent Simon Bull, royal executioner, to take charge. The Baron had been assured that he knew his business and would have no trouble on this point.

After the hanging, the court had directed that the condemned man must be revived. Then while he watched, his "private parts" were to be cut off, and he was to be disemboweled, and his intestines burned "before his eyes." Once that was done, he would be beheaded. Once dead, his body was to be quartered — divided into four more or less equal pieces and disposed of. Sometimes the body was tied to four horses and pulled apart, sometimes other methods could be used; it made no difference of course, to the condemned man — who was already dead. It could be a crowd-pleaser, though. And engaging the crowd was the major purpose of the whole exercise.

Baron Rich reflected that the whole ritual actually required a variety of skills from the executioner. He hoped the man was up to the task. The last thing they needed was sloppiness or inefficiency.

Before long, a crowd was gathering in the square. Baron Rich had the soldiers dismount and form a cordon around the executioner's block, in the center of the square. He stationed some local guards around the ladder. Crowd control was vital, here. The condemned man was to be dragged from the jail behind a horse. In the past, the condemned had sometimes died on their way to the place of execution, which made all the rest of the process seem pointless. Nowadays, men were tied to a "hurdle" — a sort of wickerwork sled, before they were "drawn," which meant they would be bruised and battered when they arrived, but nearly always alive. Rich signaled that the prisoner should be fetched, and soon you could hear the iron horseshoes on the cobblestones, and the scratching of the hurdle, growing closer and closer until they entered the square. John Payne was untied from the hurdle and pulled to his feet before the crowd. He was unkempt, thin, clad in a dirty shift that hung to his knees. Pale, his face haggard; his eyes had the look of a man facing a mortal threat that he lacks the strength to oppose. Still, a certain composure — no doubt he had ample time to prepare himself for this moment, thought Rich. It was hard not to feel pity for the wretch; best to finish this quickly.

First, of course, there must be a sermon (short, hopefully), and prayers, then a recitation of the crimes of which Payne had been convicted. There was an interruption when a local minister proclaimed that Payne's brother, a local man, had told him that Payne was treasonous. A murmur went through the crowd. Payne himself spoke. His brother was a Protestant, said Payne, but would never have made such a false accusation against him. Let his brother be summoned, he said, and this falsehood exposed. There were calls from the crowd: "Let his brother be summoned! Yes! Let him be summoned!" Soon there was shouting from all around the square.

This was not at all what the Baron wanted to hear. Getting the crowd involved in the execution was the goal, but he could not allow the case to be retried in the public mind. The statement of the minister was irrelevant to the case and probably self-serving. Why couldn't the man hold his tongue? Proceeding with the execution without at least looking for Payne's brother, would seem hasty, as if the government's case was weaker than it claimed to be. Reluctantly, he dispatched some constables to seek out Payne's brother. It was going to take longer than he hoped to finish this business.

Edward Chase had squeezed himself to the front of the crowd, not far from the ladder, in full sight of John Payne. It seemed that Payne had glanced his way once, perhaps recognized him, but did nothing to acknowledge his presence. Chase's eyes scanned the crowd, which now filled the square, and was gradually pushing forward. He recognized a figure in the crowd, directly opposite. It was John Porter, looking uncomfortable in the press of people beside and behind him.

It took at least half an hour for the constables to return. They had not been able to find John Payne's brother anywhere, they said. There was audible protest from the crowd, that the constables were incompetent, or perhaps merely feigning a desire to find the brother.

Baron Rich had no choice but to proceed with the execution, even though the mood of the crowd had clearly changed. He signaled the executioner to proceed.

John Payne mounted the ladder, the rope was placed about his neck, and with a push, the ladder was gone, and Payne was hanging from his neck, his legs flailing and twitching.

Just then the crowd surged forward. The soldiers around the executioner's block were engulfed. The constables at the base of the ladder moved forward, to fend off the crowd. It was a mistake — the farther they moved from the ladder, the wider the space between each man and the next; the crowd easily slipped through and grabbed John Payne's legs and feet.

Edward Chase was among the first to surge forward, and when the constables stepped toward him, he simply tripped the man in front of him and seized one of John Payne's legs. Soon, others were piling around behind and on top of him, pulling, pulling. He looked directly ahead to see John Porter, pulling down on the other leg of their friend, a look of grim determination on his face, then a smile of recognition.

Baron Rich was caught by surprise at what he was seeing. He thought, at first, that the crowd was trying to lift Payne, to ease the pressure on his throat. But, no, by all appearances they were trying to pull him *down!* Was the man so hated that they wished to hasten his death? . . . No, not hated . . . loved? Rich shouted orders to the soldiers to leave their posts at the block and take control of Payne's body. He must be revived, if at all possible. By the time that they understood his orders, and forced their way through the crowd, the Baron knew that Payne must be dead; it was a wonder that his head was still attached to his body.

They dragged Payne's body to the block, and the executioner waited, to see if he might revive. After a ridiculously long wait, his remains were castrated, disemboweled, and beheaded — to the letter of the law. The quartering was gratuitous, and hardly anyone stayed to watch it. Simon Bull was embarrassed by the whole situation, but it was not really his fault. It was not his job to manage crowds, merely to fulfill the terms of the sentence. He would be returning to London soon, where things were handled in a more professional way.

Baron Rich was embarrassed, too. But this was not really the sort of thing he had much experience with. If only that minister had kept his mouth shut, things might have turned out differently. No doubt there would be snickers and eye-rolling when news of this fiasco reached London. On a brighter note, perhaps they would hesitate before asking him to supervise any more executions.

Edward Chase slipped away from the square in the tumult and was headed to a house where he knew he could lie low for a few days when he spotted Samuel Vessey on the street. He could tell from Samuel's face, that he had also been at the execution.

"You should have told me what the two of you were planning," he complained. "I would have joined you."

"We planned nothing. We never spoke to each other about it," replied Edward. Come to think of it, it was an unlikely coincidence.

John Porter left the square long before the executioner had given up on reviving Payne. The execution, for him, was not the end of anything, only the beginning. Surely, the government would redouble its efforts to identify any of Payne's friends and associates, now. Best to get as far away from Chelmsford and Little Baddow as possible, and quickly.

By late afternoon, he was back in the Vessey's barn. He would wait there until dusk, then travel several miles before finding someplace to sleep. He had in mind to go East, to one of the port cities on the North Sea. Lots of ships there, and ships were made of wood.

Sybil was just finishing dinner, that evening, when Francis came in the back door, and said, "Did you know John Porter was in the barn?"

"No, what is he doing there?"

"Trying to stay out of sight, is my guess."

"Why would he be doing that?"

"There was a big fuss in Chelmsford, today. The crowd interfered with the execution. Lots of soldiers everywhere. Looking to arrest people."

"Here. Take him some dinner. Tell him I'll be out later, to settle accounts."

It was dusk by the time she had cleared the dishes. She walked to the barn and found John, just inside the barn door. "Good evening. Did you find the meal satisfactory?"

"Indeed, I did," said John with a smile. "Are you here to settle accounts?"

"Yes, I am." The sleeves of her blouse were rolled up to the elbows; she had just finished washing dishes; some strands of hair showed damply from under her cap. John found the contrast between her businesslike attitude and her end-of-a-long-day disarray comically ironic, and appealing at the same time. He felt an unaccustomed warmth toward her.

"We agreed that I would pay a penny a night for storing my barrow. I will be leaving soon, so that's one penny. You fed me for two days, so that is certainly worth a penny each day. Also, I owe you for a night's lodging, in your comfortable hay loft." He smiled again. "That adds up to four pence, I believe."

Sybil nodded. "Fair enough. That means I owe you two pence, and if the harvest is a good one, I will pay the rest in October, or November. Will you come to collect it then?"

He shook his head. "No, I cannot come then. You will have to hold it for me, for a while."

"Where will you be in October, that you cannot come? Or is a tuppence too modest a sum to be worth your while?" She was annoyed at the prospect of having a two-penny debt hanging over her head. She was more annoyed that the man did not seem to understand why this was important to her, or care.

"I do not know where I will be in October, but it will not be anywhere near Little Baddow. I must leave this place, and I am leaving tonight."

"Why, are you in some sort of trouble? Does this have anything with the events in Chelmsford, today?"

"The less you know of Chelmsford, or of my whereabouts, the safer you will be. I would say nothing to put you or your family in harm's way, and I fear I have said too much already."

Sybil was exasperated. "When can I be rid of my debt to you?"

"If you will be patient with me, I promise I will return, to free you from this debt, but I dare not say when. If God wills that I live long enough, I will keep my promise." This was ridiculous. He had just bound himself to the repayment of the debt *she* owed *him*! If only she could let it go, both of them would be free. He looked at her eyes. Resolution was there, no promise of release for either of them. Lives entangled over a two-penny debt.

"You cannot leave without some explanation!" she insisted.

"If you would know more, you should ask your brother Samuel," he replied. "I will leave to his discretion what you should be told."

"Samuel! Is he involved in all this?"

"I will speak no more about it. It is time for me to leave." He realized that it must seem like he was teasing her, though that was far from his intention.

"I believe you are right," she said, indignantly. She felt like he must be teasing her, somehow.

"I do want to thank you for your hospitality. I am pleased that we have met. Please know that I hold you in high regard, and I pray for your prosperity." John was surprised to feel a surge of sentimentality, but this was probably the closest he would come to bidding farewell to any of his friends in Little Baddow. He felt he wanted to embrace her, but hesitated. Then . . . why not? He put his arms around her and squeezed. He held her for longer than was really necessary or proper, then released her.

Sybil looked stunned, then horrified. She turned and ran into the house.

Apparently, John reflected, he had mishandled the moment; she was offended, frightened, or both. He sighed . . . no way to recover from such a social blunder now, and no time to do it, even if he knew how. He wheeled his barrow out into the dusk. He turned toward Chelmsford until he came to a crossroads, that led around the village to the northeast. He would skirt Little Baddow and head for the seacoast.

<hr>

John Porter's estimation of the efficiency of the Queen's agents was exaggerated. There was, of course, an uproar in London over the botched execution in Chelmsford. But they didn't hear of it for a day or two, and, though they certainly were alarmed at the idea that a large portion of the crowd sympathized with the priest, there were lots of other things to be alarmed about. It took more than a week to send investigators to Chelmsford, and the more witnesses to the execution that they interviewed, the more contradictions they recorded. The crowd was led by a thin man, or a husky one; the crowd had acted spontaneously, or maybe the whole thing had been a conspiracy; Someone had incited them —

perhaps the accusation from the nameless Protestant minister was a tactic to delay the execution; the crowd was so indignant at the treason of the papist that they really didn't know what they were doing. Reports were sent back to London, to be buried under piles of more reports, from across the kingdom. John Porter's name never came up. The disappearance of a carpenter from a village in Essex was noted, but no search was conducted for his whereabouts.

Edward Chase had been the subject of surveillance for quite some time, though never in connection with recusants, or Catholic priests. The jailer at Chelmsford was not the simpleton he pretended to be: he had memorized the content of John Payne's note perfectly — which shed no light at all on the intended recipient of the note, or upon its meaning. There might have been some sort of coded message in the note, but if so, it was a mystery. Investigations in Little Baddow were undertaken, but absolutely no one in the village could recall ever seeing such a man, much less speaking with him. Perhaps Chase had merely been passing through Little Baddow on his way to some other village when his pursuer lost track of him.

The widow Smith was indeed the intended recipient of John Payne's innocuous message. They had agreed some years ago that if she received such a message, it would be an indication of his arrest and probable execution. Over the next several days, she relayed similarly innocuous messages to a network of people, mostly local. It was to notify them that a friend and pastor was gone, that they should avoid assembling anywhere for the indefinite future, and that any stranger who presented himself as a priest should be regarded as an agent of the crown.

Part 6: Seaworthy

1583: Careening

It took John Porter a full day to reach the town of Colchester because he used backroads and lanes to approach the city from the south. He dared not be found on the old Roman road, so close to Chelmsford. He did not look for work in Colchester — too close to Chelmsford for comfort. The following day, He left Colchester, eastbound, to the seacoast. He used backroads until he was well east of town. By noon, he was back on the main highway to the seaport of Harwich.

Harwich was everything he was hoping it would be — a bustling port, with busy shipyards, and a busier harbor. First, he needed lodging, which he found amid a string of inns, alehouses, and brothels near the waterfront. He considered looking for a room in a quieter part of town, but he reasoned that his best chance of finding work would be among the crowds of sailors, longshoremen, and dockworkers near the harbor. He was immediately struck by the exotic smells of the place and the appearances of the men walking the streets near the docks. There was the smell of the sea, to begin with — somehow light and heavy at the same time, light with the hint of distant shores, heavy with the overpowering strength of the sea. As he passed an inn, there were other unfamiliar smells — food was cooking, but with seasonings that his nose had not encountered before.

The men he passed in the street were remarkable for their appearance as well. Many of them, he decided, were not Englishmen, but foreigners of one sort or another. There were men with tawny faces and heavy black beards (Berbers?), men with curly beards and strange-looking hats on their heads (Turks?), one man with no hair on his head at all, skin like dark-stained walnut, and a gold ring in one ear (must be a blackamoor, John decided).

He chose one establishment that looked promising and stopped just inside the door, blinking to adjust his eyes to the darkness within. The room was large, and filled with more men, many looking very exotic indeed. They were drinking; some were eating, and a few in the far corner were singing. There was a bar in the corner, and behind that, a stack of kegs — beverages, no doubt.

He found the proprietor of the place, a man named Danny Cornwall, behind the bar. Danny was tall and lean, with a long scar that ran from above his left ear, down and across his face. He had one bright blue eye; the other was covered by a black leather patch tied around his forehead. Danny had a room, for the going rate of two pence a week, laundry included.

"What's ye'r business in Harwich, then?" he asked.

"Looking for work," John replied.

"Going to sea, then?"

"No, no. I'm a carpenter. I'm hoping to find work in the shipyards."

"No doubt you will. There's plenty of work these days. I don't know how ye'll do without tools, though."

"I left my tools outside," said John.

"Outside in the street? Why would ye do such a careless thing?"

John was startled, at a loss for words.

"Come with me!" said Danny, and headed quickly through the crowd, to the door. John followed him with a sinking feeling in the pit of his stomach. There was no trace of his barrow, or his belongings where he had left them.

"What did you leave here?" demanded Danny.

John described the barrow, and the two chests, one for his tools, one for his personal effects. Danny turned to a scrawny boy who loitered near the front door of the inn. "Roger!" he exclaimed, "Did ye see this man leave a barrow with two chests in front of my door? Roger nodded. "And did ye perhaps, just perhaps, notice who took it?" Roger shrugged and cocked his head.

Danny turned to John, and said, "Give the boy a penny." John gave him a questioning look. "I said, give the boy a penny!" John complied. Roger took the coin and smiled.

"Now Roger," said Danny, "This here's Mr. Porter. He lodges with me. Do ye understand?" Roger nodded and smiled.

"Now that Mr. Porter has paid ye, ye'll be working for him, won't you?" Roger nodded and smiled again.

"So," Danny continued, "You must go to whoever took this man's property, and tell them to return it — all of it — immediately, or they'll be answering to Danny Cornwall. Do ye understand?" Roger nodded again. "Off with ye, then!" Roger disappeared down the street at a run.

"We'll wait here," said Danny, "Shouldn't take long." Sure enough, in a matter of minutes, Roger came in sight. He and another boy not much larger than himself were struggling to push the barrow toward them. John started to walk in their direction, but Danny put a hand on his arm. "Wait. Let the boy earn his pay."

When they finally reached him, John saw that both chests were firmly lashed to the barrow, just as he had left them.

"Ye will want to check the contents, but I'm sure ye will find that nothing is missing," said Danny. "There is a storage room in the back, where ye can keep this barrow secured. Both your chests will go into your room."

Danny showed him the storage room, which had ample space for the barrow, then to his room, which was on the second floor, and had a window facing west, across the estuary. "Thank you for your help," said John. "Without it, I would have had to find a constable."

"Constable? That sort of thing doesn't go well around here. The constable might recover some of your property, but not all, and in the process, there would be arrests, and punishments — maybe even a hanging, if your possessions were valued highly enough. Around here, we've seen more hangings that we like. We have our own ways of solving problems like yours. Ye'll be better off paying young Roger a penny a week to look after your affairs."

"A penny a week seems like a lot."

"Ye'll find him well worth it. Roger sees things and knows things that most people don't. He can find people and opportunities that you would never find on your own. And if you have enemies, Roger's the one that will watch your back."

John reflected that contact with the local constabulary was probably not desirable, given his recent experiences in Chelmsford. A penny a week might be a prudent investment.

After he had stowed his belongings in his room, he went downstairs. It wasn't time for supper yet, so he stepped outside and found Roger nearby. "Roger, they tell me you are a man of wide knowledge." Roger looked surprised, but straightened himself a bit, at the supposed compliment. "I am a carpenter, looking for employment in the shipyards," John continued. "Can you direct me to someone who might hire me?"

"That depends," replied Roger. "What are you skilled at? You don't talk like a seaman, so I don't imagine you've worked on ships before. Have you built houses or barns, roofs or floors, stairways or doorways?"

John was taken aback at the kinds of questions an employer might ask — coming from the mouth of a child. "Houses and barns, roofs and floors, stairways and doors, also furniture and decorative work, new construction or repair."

"In that case, I know of a shipwright who can use you. For a penny, I will take you to him and introduce you."

Another penny. John considered the offer. "I'll pay the penny, if and when I am hired."

"Come, then." Roger turned and started down the street. John followed him.

Roger was as good as his word. They soon stood at the water's edge, looking up at the nearly finished hull of a great ship. She was at least eighty feet long and loomed at least twenty feet above the keel amidships, nearly thirty at her stern castle. This was substantially larger than any house he had worked on, as big as a large barn.

Roger led him to a man who appeared to be directing the efforts of half a dozen workmen, apparently the shipwright. The man looked up as they approached. "Here now, young Roger, have ye brought me another man of skill?"

Roger introduced John to the shipwright, who subjected John to a quick series of questions about his skills, and the tools he owned. There were a few trick questions about technical matters. Evidently, his answers were satisfactory; the shipwright ended them with, "We start at daybreak. I pay five shillings a week; if I like your work, I pay six shillings. I need to get this ship launched soon, no more than two weeks. After she's afloat, we'll finish and outfit her in the harbor, about three weeks. He spat into the palm of his hand and extended it to him. Agreed?"

John nodded, spat into his own palm, and shook the shipwright's hand. So, five shillings or maybe even six shillings for the next five weeks. A better beginning than he had hoped. Roger was looking at him expectantly. Of course — he had earned his penny. John dug into his purse and gave Roger his payment. Roger smiled and turned to the shipwright, who also pressed a coin into his outstretched hand.

John returned to the Inn where he was lodging. It was time for supper. He ate that evening in the inn. Supper was a kind of fish stew, with the usual bread and ale. He was not accustomed to eating fish, and this was seasoned in an unfamiliar manner. It was tasty enough, though, and filling.

He was up before dawn and carried his tool chest down to the main floor. Danny Cornwall was there. "Breakfast is served every morning," said

Danny, "and we can pack you a dinner to take to the shipyards, if you like, for just a penny per day." John thought that a fair enough price and agreed. Danny also told him where the local Carpenter's Guildhall was — John would stop there on the way home from the job, to introduce himself (and pay his dues).

There was plenty to learn on the job site. It turned out most of the techniques were the same as putting up a building: a deck was pretty much like a floor, and the ribs and trusses of a ship's hull were a lot like the roof of a large building. Many of the smaller features of a ship were similar, as well — ladders, railings, and windows. There were, of course, some important features unique to the ship. A leaky roof on a building could be repaired with a few well-placed shingles; a leaky hull required a more robust solution. Indeed, while you could imagine turning a ship's hull upside down on land to make a kind of house, doing the opposite — putting a house upside down in the sea — would clearly not work.

John was introduced to certain terms immediately: the front of the ship was the "bow," the back was the "stern." The pole that turned the rudder was the "helm." When you moved toward the bow, you were going "forward," or "fore"; if you moved in the opposite direction, you were going "aft." If you were facing the bow, the left side of the ship was the "port" side (even when a seaport was visible on the opposite side of the ship), the right-hand side was "starboard" (whether stars were actually visible, or not).

John's first days on the job involved finishing the lowest decks of the ship, the Orlop Deck. This meant he had to climb a ladder from the slip to get to the top of the hull and then go down a second ladder into the hull itself. The Orlop Deck was wider than the upper decks would be and was where most of the cargo would be stored. There were a couple of small hatchways leading down below the Orlop, to the bilges below. Most of the bilge was filled with ballast — stones or other heavy materials, which served to hold the ship upright when it was afloat. It was also where the masts were stepped, or attached to the keel. This meant that all the decks were pierced by the three masts that this particular ship would have. It was relatively easy to "step" the masts during construction; replacing a broken mast after the ship was afloat was a ticklish business.

Here, some of the differences in ship construction became apparent. The floor of a house could simply be laid perpendicularly across the supporting floor joists. They contributed to the stability of the house by tying the joists together, as well as supporting the weight of the house's occupants and furniture. But no one expected the floor to hold up the walls of the house above the level of the floor — the ceiling joists and the rafters were expected to perform that task. On a ship, the "walls" were the hull — and the hull had to withstand a beating, whether from waves or hostile artillery. Therefore, the decking was braced and reinforced in a way to add strength and rigidity to the hull — the extra weight of the material was justified only if it contributed to the seaworthiness of the whole vessel. And the lowest parts of the hull needed to be the strongest.

Depending on the size of the ship, and the depth of the hull, called its "draft," the water pressure below decks could be tremendous. The hull had to be strong enough to withstand that pressure — not only when the ship was at anchor, but when it was maneuvering. If the ship were sailing in any direction other than directly before the wind, the pressure on the hull would be different on one side of the ship than the other. That difference was "steerage"- the ship moved through the water in response to the pressure difference. If the ship was not moving, the pressure would be equal everywhere, and steering the ship would be impossible. When the ship moved, the pressure on any part of the hull could increase or decrease as it turned. If that change in pressure were sufficient to cause the hull to flex or shift even a little, water might leak through the seams, into the hold. A little of this was expected; a lot could be disastrous.

It took a few days to adjust to the new terminology. With the Orlop Deck complete, they installed the next one, the Gun Deck, bracing and reinforcing as they went. A large hatch was located in the center of the deck so that cargo could be lowered into the hold from the decks above. Smaller hatches, with stairways, allowed the crew to move between the Gun Deck and the Orlop.

The Gun Deck had to be particularly strong for different reasons. It was above the waterline, so water pressure against the hull was not a primary concern. A ship this size might be outfitted with ten large guns on each side of the ship, and numerous smaller ones up on the main deck. A full-sized cannon was nine feet long and weighed up to twenty-five hundred pounds — too large for most ships. A smaller gun, like a demi-culverin, weighed nearly fifteen hundred pounds, and was eight feet long — still a tight fit below decks. The guns were mounted on wooden carriages, which allowed them to be rolled forward when firing (so that most of the smoke would be outside the ship), and withdrawn into the ship for reloading (which could only be done from the gun's muzzle). The recoil from such a gun when it was fired was enough to hurl it backward across the gun deck and crush anyone unfortunate enough to be in its path. Firing all the guns on one side of the ship — a "broadside" — unleashed enough recoil to shake the whole ship. The recoil was managed by tying each gun carriage to the ribs of the hull with ropes, to limit the distance that the carriage could move. This meant that the ribs needed to be very strong indeed. Pulleys and tackle allowed each gun's crew to reposition the gun for the next firing. Even so, it was a job for three or four strong men to handle just one gun and its carriage.

There wasn't a lot of headroom on the gun deck — less than six feet. A tall man had to stoop while moving about, and duck to pass under the beams that supported the main deck above. The main deck was narrower than the gun deck because the hull was built with "tumblehome" — it sloped a bit toward the center of the ship at its highest point. The main deck had a large cargo hatch in the center, which aligned with the cargo hatch opening on the gun deck, to form a kind of well directly down to the orlop deck in the hold. Other, smaller hatches and stairs connected the main deck to the gun deck.

Above the main deck, shorter decks were constructed at the bow and the stern. These were referred to as "castles." The "castle" at the bow was called the forecastle, or foc'sle. It provided an elevated platform at the bow, for defense, and for observation of the waters immediately in front of the ship. At the rear was the aftercastle, or "aft castle," which was larger and higher than the foc'sle, and on this ship, was built of two short decks, on on top of the other. The first of these decks was called the quarter-deck; the rear of this deck was topped by a small "poop deck." The ship's whipstaff, or helm was located on the quarterdeck. The whipstaff was a pole attached to the rudder at the stern. A helmsman on the quarterdeck had a good view of the entire ship, and the waters in front of it. The area under the quarterdeck housed the captain's cabin and any other officer's accommodations. The poop deck covered part of the rear of the quarterdeck and provided a small cabin area beneath it, as well as an elevated platform for the navigator or captain to view the whole ship and direct the ship's movement.

The hull and decks were finished in the slip two days short of the two-week deadline; John and his coworkers had earned their extra shilling per week. Once she was launched, the finishing touches were applied while the ship floated in the harbor, moored to a pier; the slip from which it had been launched was already busy with a crew laying the keel for another ship. John and a crew of carpenters and other workmen finished up the hatches, cabins, magazines, and other details essential to the ship's operation. They were not alone; a small army of painters, riggers, and other craftsmen were busy on the hull as well. The spars and rigging were added and then sails. Ballast — stones, usually, had to be placed in the bottom of the ship, near the keel. Inevitably, some water seeped into the lowest regions of the hull — the "bilges." Over time, the planks of the hull swelled a bit, and the seepage was less, but bilge pumps were a necessity.

John discovered that the block and tackle of which he was so proud was actually quite primitive by nautical standards. All sorts of ingenious applications of pulleys and levers went into the operation of a modern ship. Another notable difference in shipbuilding was the availability of iron nails — always expensive and used sparingly in land-bound construction, but worth the cost in a shipyard. They were used liberally in both new construction and repairs.

By the time the ship was ready for her maiden voyage, John had learned a great deal about ships and shipbuilding. He felt more than a little pride the day that she sailed out of the harbor. She was built as a galleon, an armed merchantman in times of peace, convertible to a warship in times of war — "broad in the beam," or wide, in proportion to her length, or "carlin," to maximize stability and cargo capacity. This meant that she would not be as fast as narrower hulls, other things being equal. But the investors who had paid for her construction were expecting to make money from trade; her armaments were merely an insurance against unnecessary loss.

As the months and then years went by, John worked on other ships. Some were new, but there was also a lot of repair work in the shipyard. Shipworms bored holes in the planks of the hull, and they had to be replaced. Sometimes, the hulls were damaged by storms, other times because the ships ran aground on some shoal. Sometimes, the damage was from other, hostile vessels. The North Sea had its fair share of Dunkirkers, Barbary Pirates, and privateers. Often, a merchantman was captured by these smaller, faster ships, but sometimes, the merchantman escaped — though often with some significant battle damage. More than one limped into Harwich, her bilge pumps working full-out, with a leaky hull damaged by cannonballs.

Repairing such damage was not simple. Particularly if there was damage below the waterline (such as from shipworms), the vessel had to be taken out of the water. There were two methods for achieving this. One was to use a dry dock — a water-filled basin that the ship could sail into, and then, by closing the basin and pumping out the water, the ship's hull could be exposed. Dry docks were expensive and usually reserved for naval vessels. For everyone else, the solution was "careening." Careening involved grounding the ship on a beach, for as long as it took to repair and clean the hull. The ship had to be lightened as much as possible, by removing all her cargo and armaments — everything possible, and running her aground at high tide. From there, if the equipment were available, she could be dragged far enough above the high-tide line to prevent her floating away on the next high tide. Typically, the ship would be leaning on one side or the other; only a flat-bottomed ship could be balanced on its keel.

Once the damage was exposed, the weakened planking was removed, replaced, and caulked. The hull would be scraped to remove barnacles and other sea life that had attached itself, since the last cleaning. These small life forms could slow a ship down considerably — a newly careened ship was a lot faster and nimbler.

Getting a large ship in and out of the water in this way involved a lot of planning and plenty of tackle. Once she was afloat, her cargo and armament had to be reloaded. In a port like Harwich, there were wharves to make the loading and unloading easier, before moving the empty ship to a nearby beach.

John had the opportunity to repair several careened ships and got familiar with different types of vessels. No two were exactly alike — each was the creation of a Master Shipwright, who directed the construction without detailed blueprints, or standard plans. There were general principles of size and proportion, but much of the final product was figured out as the construction went forward. Symmetry was desirable, but seldom perfectly achieved. If the ship had idiosyncrasies in its handling, the crew would discover that once she was on the water and make adjustments to ballast and cargo as necessary.

The purpose of the ship guided its construction. Fighting ships needed to be fast and maneuverable, which would argue for a narrow beam. But stability was also needed if the ship was to serve as a stable platform for guns. The recoil from a broadside could "rock the boat," quite literally. The slimmest and fastest warships of the age were war galleys. They were used extensively in the Mediterranean, and sometimes appeared in the North Sea, as well. They could be eight times longer than they were wide (their beam), and they were propelled by oarsmen. In a sea battle, they were quick and maneuverable and carried enough artillery to be dangerous. They also could carry soldiers to board opposing ships, and once they grappled with an opponent, the armed oarsmen could join the fight. Spain and Venice had scored major sea victories in the Mediterranean with ships like these. They did not, however, fare well in the Atlantic. Their shallow draft and narrow beam could capsize in heavy waves.

A large merchant ship, by contrast, might have a length only twice her beam. She was slower but could carry more cargo. Sails were the means of propulsion, and such ships would have multiple masts, each outfitted with various types of sails, to improve maneuverability. She didn't need oarsmen, which left more room for cargo — or, in time of war, room for soldiers and munitions. The broadest of these vessels were called carracks and could have as many as four decks.

The most modern ships of the time were called galleons. They were narrower than the carracks — about three times as long as they were wide — and therefore faster and more maneuverable, while still offering ample room for cargo. The first ship John had worked on was a galleon. Galleons were the queens of the seas — the Spanish used them as treasure ships in the Pacific, the Atlantic, and the Mediterranean. They were usually heavily armed, and proved their superiority to Turkish galleys in sea battles, even when heavily outnumbered.

The English navy was beginning to build a new version of the galleon, called a "race-built" galleon. These ships were five times longer than their beam, which made them faster and more nimble than the Spanish galleons. Innovations in gun carriages made them more stable as gun platforms. Francis Drake had sailed around the world in a race-built galleon, the *Golden Hind*, in 1580, and defeated several Spanish galleons while doing so. The new designs were the talk of shipwrights and other craftsmen in the port — speed and maneuverability were desirable traits in any ship, but the money was in cargo, and cargo capacity was a premium consideration. The navy might well sacrifice cargo space for combat effectiveness, but the government could only afford a few dozen ships for dedicated military use; most shipbuilding would continue to be for maritime trade . . . so the debates went.

July 6, 1583: Another Archbishop

Edward Chase was sitting in a public house in London when the death of Edmund Grindal, Archbishop of Canterbury was announced. He and two companions were in the midst of a conversation about other news when the word came. All of them greeted the news with some trepidation.

"Well, I never felt that Grindal was completely on our side, but at least he stood up for us against the Queen, in the matter of the conventicles," said a tall man.

"More than likely, his successor will be worse," said the other man, short, with a round face. "I wonder who it will be?"

Chase shook his head. "It will almost certainly be a bishop hostile to our cause. The Queen is still determined to crush us, by any means short of exile or execution. Grindal bought us some reprieve, while he lived. Now, we will be tested. Pray God that the seed we have sown these last few years may still ripen to a godly harvest."

"Robert Browne is in Scotland you know," said the short man.

Chase had not heard. His heart sank. "Why? Why does he trouble us so? Why does he not stay in the Netherlands, with his separatists?"

"I am told that his followers are here in London, members of a secret church, with as many as a thousand members."

"What church? Where?" Chase was exasperated.

"No church you've heard of. An 'underground' church, they call it, though you won't find it under the ground. They meet in secret locations; they choose their own elders and preachers — like in his book."

Ah, yes, thought Chase. Browne's book. *A Treatise of Reformation Without Tarying for Anie*. Browne's case for complete separation of the "True Church" from the Church of England — no government control, no bishops, just congregations running their little church as they see fit. Silly. Except that the book was being read everywhere, and little "Brownist" groups were popping up all over the place. A thousand members in London? Ridiculous! No, not merely ridiculous. Dangerous. It gave the government all the excuse it needed to intensify the pressure on reformers like himself and his friends.

Browne had written a second book, *A Booke which sheweth the life and manners of all True Christians*, a blueprint, really, for setting up independent congregations. Also, an indictment of all other congregations in the realm for not conducting themselves as "True Christians." The man's arrogance would be comical if so many were not eating up his every word.

He had seen it coming; no comfort in that. Powerless to stop it. "Could things get any worse for us?"

"They already have," replied the tall man. "In Bury St. Edmonds, there is more trouble. Someone has defaced the image of the Queen's arms in St. Mary's church. They have painted a text from the Apocalypse of John, 2 and 19 over it.

"*I know thy works and thy love, and service, and faith, and thy patience, and thy works, and that they are more at the last, than at the first.*" That one?

The Tall man nodded. "That one."

Chase sat back in his seat, bewildered. "It is an encouraging message, for men of our persuasion, I suppose. We have indeed been faithful and patient, and our works are better now than they once were. But why paint such a message in the church? And why, of all places, over the Queen's coat of arms?"

"I suppose it is a reference to the verse that follows. A way of making a statement, without actually saying anything seditious."

"Seditious? How is it seditious?"

The tall man quoted, ". . . *thou sufferest the woman Jezebel, which calleth herself a prophetess, to teach and deceive my servants . . .*" He cleared his throat, "That verse."

Chase was shocked, then angry. "What idiots would do such a thing? Anabaptists?"

"I believe they are followers of Robert Browne and his associates. They have adopted some Anabaptist ideas, but they are no pacifists. This is a direct challenge to the Queen's supremacy over the church."

"How long did it take for the rector to remove this libel?"

"The rector refuses to remove it or paint it over. It is still there, above the entrance to the nave."

"Bury is a cathedral town. Surely the local bishop will summon the civil magistrates to repair this insult to the Queen!"

"The bishop is powerless; the civil authorities refuse to do his bidding in this matter. It appears that many of the local nobility are covertly supporting them, as well."

Chase went through a list of hot-headed men that he knew, trying to decide if any of them might do such a reckless thing. Young men, who might imagine that their knowledge of scripture was so much more sophisticated than that of their rivals, that they could use an indirect reference to insult the Queen, without her realizing what they were doing? No, this was not some juvenile prank. Juvenile, yes, but no prank.

The message made no sense unless it was intended that the whole congregation would understand it. They must have expected that the Queen's agents would understand it, too. He decided that he knew one or two who might try such a thing, if influenced by willing companions, and maybe some extra ale. But the deed could not truly be the act of drunken youth. Someone else must be involved, someone calculating, deliberate, and sober. Chase felt his heart sink. There would be blood from this, and quite possibly fire.

Summer, 1583: Bury St. Edmunds

Edward Chase's prediction was fulfilled quite soon. Richard Bancroft, a trusted cleric, was dispatched to Bury St. Edmunds by Bishop Freke, to get the matter in hand. By the time his investigation was finished, eight parish priests, forty or more laymen, and a handful of the local nobility had been indicted for treason or sedition in the shire of Suffolk. Many of them were known to Edward Chase, who had visited Ipswich, the principal town of the shire many times. Ultimate responsibility was laid on the writings of Robert Browne, whose books were now banned and burned wherever they were found. Two men, John Copping, and Elias Thacker, were convicted of distributing Browne's books and sentenced to death. Curiously, no one was held directly responsible for vandalizing the Queen's coat of arms — no one would admit doing so, nor point the finger at anyone else. One of the condemned men had been in prison at the time of the vandalism; their possession and sale of Browne's books were enough to secure their conviction. They were duly hanged.

Richard Bancroft's success in the matter burnished his reputation and advanced his career. He would, in time, serve the church as the Archbishop of Canterbury.

1585: Expedition

John Porter sat eating his supper in Danny Cornwall's alehouse — now upgraded to a Public House, or pub, by royal license. Cornwall called the place "The Galleon," now. John still rented a room in the place, and usually took his meals there, as well. The food was generally tastier than most similar places on the waterfront, and it was convenient. He had fallen into a familiar routine over the last two years: he had his breakfast in the morning, took a dinner (midday meal) with him to the shipyards, and ate supper at The Galleon in the evening. Roger showed up once a week, to collect his weekly fee, which he had earned on more than one occasion — he had kept John steadily employed for more than two years. Often, Roger found work that paid a little more than the standard rate, which more than paid for the penny per week that John gave him. Roger always seemed to know where a new pair of breeches or shoes could be had at a bargain, or who in town needed a carpenter for a small side job, which could be done in an evening, for a little extra income.

John, in short, was comfortable. The years of work in the shipyards had made him stronger, physically and financially. His only regret was that he was still a journeyman. If he were ever to become a Master craftsman, he had to present some piece of work to the local guild that demonstrated his "mastery" of his craft. Work done on part of a ship, under the supervision of a shipwright, didn't qualify. As of today, he had finished restoring an old merchantman. He didn't have his next job, yet. No doubt Roger would come up with something in a few days.

On this particular evening, he was in a reflective mood. He thought of his family, in Felsted, wondered how they fared. He thought also of Little Baddow, of the Widow Smith, and also of Sybil Vessey, and the rest of her family. From time to time, he heard news of the arrests of more Catholic priests and recusants in various places, but nothing about a village named Little Baddow. He supposed that the people of the village had evaded discovery. He took some satisfaction in the idea that his efforts to protect them had been successful.

Much of the news passing in conversations in The Galleon were rumors about Greater Matters.

In June of 1584, the heir to the throne of France died. The next in line of succession was a Huguenot, known as Henry of Navarre. France was in the throes of civil war. Henri III, King of France, tried to head off the conflict by excluding Navarre from the succession, but it was not enough to satisfy the militant Catholic faction, led by the Duke of Guise, who aspired to make his own man next in line to the throne. Guise and his allies from the Catholic League promised to eliminate the Huguenots once and for all. Philip II, King of Spain agreed to finance the armies of the Catholic League in their continuing civil war with the Huguenots. The secret Treaty of Joinville, so-called, specified that France would become an entirely Catholic kingdom and that Protestants would be exterminated (in line with Philip's policies for Spain). Philip would choose the next French King (the Duke of Guise, quite naturally, expected to be that choice), and France would stop its policy of aiding the Dutch rebels.

The secret treaty, of course, was soon made public all over Europe. For Protestants, it looked like Spain was leading a "crusade" that would eliminate their faith in all of Europe. Philip's plans were not so ambitious — he saw an opportunity to put an end to the long rivalry between France and Spain and eliminate some heretics in the bargain.

But for England, and the rest of Protestant Europe, the threat was existential. Elizabeth signed a treaty with the Dutch rebels in 1585, at her Nonsuch Palace. The Treaty of Nonsuch, so-called, committed England to provide garrison troops for several Dutch ports, as well as a small army, to fight alongside the rebels, and money for the rebels to hire mercenary soldiers of their own.

Upon hearing of the treaty, Philip promptly declared war and began preparation for an invasion of England. The preparation would take time; nothing so ambitious had ever been attempted in Europe before. Sailors and ships would have to be transferred from the Mediterranean and the Americas, concentrated and outfitted before the invasion could be undertaken. A large portion of the Spanish army was tied down in Italy and the Netherlands. Transporting such a large force would be expensive and time-consuming. Elizabeth was able to move much more quickly. She was expanding her small navy with privately financed warships and preparing to strike before the Spanish were ready.

With Spanish money financing the Catholic armies, it appeared that the Huguenots would finally be defeated. Once that happened, those armies would be turned against the Dutch rebels in the Netherlands, and ultimately, against England. Philip had announced his intention as nothing less than the eradication of Protestantism in France and the Netherlands and had long insisted that he was the rightful King of England, through his marriage to "Bloody" Mary.

In July of that same year, William the Silent, leader of the Dutch revolt had been assassinated by a man who claimed to be an agent of Phillip (or at least hoped to collect the bounty of twenty-five thousand crowns that Phillip had pledged to anyone who could kill William). Leadership of the revolt passed to William's fourteen-year-old son, Maurice. The Dutch cause seemed lost.

In England, the Queen's policies seemed headed for failure. Her privy council drew up a "Bond of Association"; a pledge, basically, that all the noblemen in the kingdom were pressured to sign. Under this "Bond," the signatories were pledged to resist any attempt to overthrow the Queen and execute any Englishman who was party to such an attempt. This was largely a response to yet another plot that was uncovered to assassinate Elizabeth and place her cousin Mary on the throne. The "Bond" further stated that in the event Elizabeth died without an heir (a strong possibility, since Elizabeth was now fifty-one years old, and unmarried), Parliament would choose her successor and that any successor would have to be a Protestant. At first glance, this was just another way of declaring that Mary would never sit on the throne of England. In the case of a successful Spanish invasion, the Bond would be moot. However, the precedent that Parliament could determine the religious affiliation of their sovereign would be applied in years to come in unforeseen ways.

No one doubted that a full-scale war with Spain was imminent. The consequence of this was debatable. In the short term, the government was spending liberally on the construction of more warships, as well as the purchase of merchant ships, and their conversion to military use. Business was booming in the shipyards. There was also an increase in the import of war materials, which was good for commerce in general. The prospect of a Spanish conquest was not pleasing, but even this had a bright side: if Philip succeeded in bringing France, England, and the Netherlands under his sway, it would almost certainly put an end to the Dunkirkers, and severely reduce the depredations of the Barbary and Turkish pirates. Behind the bravado, few people who had been abroad thought that England could win a war with Spain, and few imagined that a Spanish government would be anything but ruthlessly cruel, harsher than the rule of Mary had been. Still, there might be opportunities for trade with Spain's New World colonies. A man could prosper in such circumstances if he were enterprising and flexible.

There was singing again, in a far corner of the pub. They had finished with "Greensleeves," and begun on "The Maid of Amsterdam," both favorites:

> In Amsterdam there lived a maid,
> Mark well what I do say,
> In Amsterdam there lived a maid,
> Who was always pinchin' the sailor's trade
> I'll go no more a roving with you fair maid!
>
> A rovin', a rovin',
> Since rovin's been my ru-i-in,
> I'll go no more a roving,
> With you fair maid!

A typical sailor's story; An exotic location, a willing woman, a financial setback.

John's reverie was interrupted when Roger stepped up to his table, accompanied by a stranger. The man was of average height, with a red beard, and a receding hairline, a weatherbeaten face — maybe fifty years old, John guessed. The man spoke first:

"Foxe, Captain Billy Foxe," he announced. "I'm told you're the man who can help me with my ship."

"John Porter, at your service," John stood and bowed a little, acknowledging the captain's social rank. "What is wrong with your ship?"

"Careened, down the coast. Hull damage. Got to get her fit for service."

"Who's the shipwright?" asked John.

"Don't have a shipwright, can't get a shipwright. All of them say they're too busy to help me. Some of them say you're the best man they know for this sort of work."

John thought that this last remark was a bit of flattery. Perhaps one of the shipwrights knew he would be looking for work, and mentioned his name, just to get the man out of his hair. "How much damage are we talking about?" he asked.

"That, you should see for yourself. If you're as good as they say, I'll be counting on you to tell me how bad it is."

Flattery, again. Well, what did he have to lose? "All right, I'll take a look at your ship. When can I see her?"

"Right now. She's just a mile or so down the bay."

"It's dark outside. I'll need to look her over in daylight."

"In the morning, then. I'll be here at Sunup." The Captain turned and stalked out of the pub.

John turned to Roger with a questioning look. "He has lots of money," said Roger. "He has wealthy backers and an old ship that they want to convert to a warship. The government is commissioning merchantmen to convert to privateers, and his backers have government connections, so . . ." Roger shrugged.

"So, I'll go take a look in the morning." Roger looked at him as if expecting something. "And there'll be a penny for you, if and when I take on the job," John smiled. Roger nodded and was gone.

Captain Billy Foxe was a man of his word. John barely had time for breakfast before he pulled up in a horse-drawn cart in front of The Galleon and called for him. Roger was there, too, and the three rode back up the estuary. It was a bit more than a mile to the beach where the ship lay, beached on its port side. Or was it the starboard side? What exactly, was he looking at?

A great hull lay across the beach, at least one hundred twenty feet long, and thirty feet at the beam. She was larger than anything John had ever worked on before. Her draft was shallow, considering her size — no more than eight feet, he guessed. He walked down to the beach and looked at the hull on the starboard — yes, it must be the starboard side. There was visible damage at first glance — planking at the waterline was splintered — probably battle damage. Could be shipworms below the waterline as well. A crew of men were scraping her hull clean of barnacles.

He turned to Captain Foxe. "What do you call this?"

"I call her the Egyptian Queen," Foxe replied with a tone of pride.

"But what kind of vessel is this?"

"This," Foxe waved his arm dramatically, "is called a galleass. A great warship of the Venetian navy. She fought the Turks at Lepanto and was used by the Venetians for 10 years before she was boarded by Barbary Pirates, and taken. After that, she was recaptured by the Spanish, who used her to supply their armies in the Low Countries, until she was overtaken by the Sea Beggars in the North Sea, whence the damage you see here" — he pointed to the splintered hull. Most of her crew was sick with the scurvy when the Dutch boarded her. She's a little large for the Sea Beggars, so they sold her to me."

John looked at him, amazed. So, this was a galleass — a mongrel among ships, combining features of ancient galleys with more modern galleons. He had heard of them, never seen one."How many oarsmen will it take to sail her?"

"No more oarsmen for this lady. We're converting her for modern war. Just imagine how many guns you can mount on a deck like this!" By now they had walked round to the other side, where the broad deck was visible. Only there was no deck, in the usual sense of the word. They were looking at a vast hollow cavity, where a hundred fifty or more rowers had strained to propel the ship into battle. No doubt she was fast, in her day. Without the rowers, there was indeed room for a lot of guns — big ones. Her broad beam and shallow draft would be a stable platform. But she would need new masts, and larger sails to keep up with smaller vessels. And there was no telling how her hull would hold up in a North Sea tempest.

John turned to Billy. "Converting a ship of this size will be costly."

"My investors have deep purses. Cost will not be a problem. Will you help me?"

John thought a moment. "I can repair the splintered hull for you. I will have to inspect all the rest for shipworm damage. Depending on what I find, it will take a few days."

"I will pay you six shillings for a week's work. Eight shillings if she's ready to float in three days."

John was impressed. A week's pay for three day's work? The purses must be deep indeed. "I can get started today, if you will fetch my tools from the pub. Take Roger along to vouch for you; Danny knows and trusts him. Also, I will need some oak planking and some caulking to repair the hull. He spat into his palm and held out his hand. Captain Foxe reciprocated; they shook hands. Deal done.

John was able to get a good view of the condition of the hull from the inside, as well as out. He found a little shipworm damage, but nothing major. That left the port side of the ship, which was resting on the beach. Given her shallow draft and broad beam, most of the port side hull was visible as well. The hold of the ship was empty, and he could see the inside of all the hull planks, except those in the bilges. There was good light in the hull because the deck side faced the morning sun. From the inside, everything on the port side looked good.

By midmorning, Captain Billy Foxe and Roger were back with his tool chest, and John was able to measure the dimensions of the starboard planks he would be replacing. He gave the measurements to Foxe, who sent someone off to fetch the wood. John found it unexpectedly difficult to pry off the damaged planking — it was thicker than it looked, and the builders had used plenty of nails. The spaces left were a little irregular, but not bad — he could shape pieces to fit easily enough. Everywhere he looked, he saw evidence that the shipwright had overbuilt — planks and ribs were surprisingly thick, with lots of nails. There was enough wood in this ship to build two good-sized merchant galleons — surprising that no one had thought of that.

By late afternoon, he had planed and cut the short sections of planking he needed and nailed them in place on the starboard side. Almost immediately, a team of caulkers and painters appeared to seal the hull and apply a protective layer of tar. Clearly, the captain was in a hurry.

"That's all we can do today," John said to Foxe. "Tomorrow, we can careen her over on the starboard side and get a good look at the port side. Then we have to inspect the bilges."

"If she floats tomorrow, there's another two shillings for you." Foxe gave John and Roger a ride back to town for the evening.

The next morning, Captain Billy Foxe was waiting for him with the cart. He got started on the port hull early. There was shipworm damage on a few planks, but he had them replaced by midmorning. By noon, the entire port side of the hull had been caulked and tarred. Now for the nasty work. The outside of the hull all the way down to the keel was now sound, which left only the bilges inside the ship to inspect. Ship worms could conceivably have gotten through the bottom of the hull into the bilges, which were always underwater, and weakened the keel, or the ribs where they met the keel.

All of this was under the orlop deck. Access was through a small hatch in the orlop deck, or in this ship, two such hatches — one fore and one aft, since it was so large. The clearance was only a few feet since the bottom of the bilge was filled with ballast — heavy stones that helped keep the ship upright. Someone needed to crawl into the bilges and inspect the condition of the keel and the ribs under the ballast, John was not looking forward to the job, but his apprehension proved unfounded. Captain Billy had recruited a dozen or more ragged-looking boys for the task. "There's a tuppence for each of ye that goes down into the bilges," he told them. "And a shilling for any worms or rot ye find, once you have showed it to the carpenter, here." Somewhere, he had acquired more than a dozen candle holders, each with a candle in it. The boys seemed willing, even eager to make their fortunes in the dark, slimy, and fetid world of the bilges.

After an hour or so, A call was raised that someone had found something, and John was called upon to crawl down into the bilges, himself. He chose the aft hatchway. What he found was astonishing. Everywhere he looked, the ballast stones were piled up on one side or the other. The boys had lifted every one from its position, all the way down to the keel, looking for any evidence of damage. The "find" was near the center of the ship, as luck would have it — the smell of the place was nauseating, and he had to creep forward in a stoop, to reach the place. There was good news and bad news. The damage, as it turned out was rot. This made sense, he reflected, since the water in the bilges — if it could be called water — was so foul that no shipworm could live in it for very long. But wood submerged in salty water did not rot quickly — rot was usually a problem for wood that was wet, but not continually under water. So it was in this case. The rot was in the bottom end of the mainmast, right in the center of the ship. John could tell in the dim light that the other end of the bilges had received the same treatment — ballast stones were piled everywhere, as far as he could see. Just to be sure, he crept all the way to the forward hatch. From there, he could tell that the boys had checked under all the ballast, all the way to the bow.

He emerged from the forward hatch, gasping from the stench, not caring that anyone he got close to would know his misery first-hand. He approached Captain Billy, who barely flinched. "Well?"

"The ribs and keel are sound. You're going to need a new mainmast."

"A new mainmast?" Captain Billy Foxe laughed. "Indeed, I will!" He seemed very pleased. "I'll call the boys out and pay them off!"

"You should know," said John, as his stomach settled a little, "That all of your ballast has been moved around. Can't say how she'll ride, once she's afloat."

"Aye, that's a good point," said the Captain. He called to the boys, who emerged, one by one from the bilge hatches. They scrambled off the ship onto the beach, "Who's the man who found the rot?" Two of the boys insisted the find was theirs. "Well, now, that's a problem," the Captain stroked his chin as if in deep thought. "I reckon there's only one fair way to do this." He handed a silver shilling to each of the claimants and smiled. Then he told the boys to line up and gave each the promised tuppence.

"Now, boys, would any of you fancy a cruise on my ship?" Their response was unanimous and positive. "Then you'll have to help me get the ballast right. There's a Spring Tide this evening, and we'll float her then. Someone has to get into the bilges and shift the ballast, so she floats level." All the boys shot their hands into the air. "It's settled, then," said the Captain. "Come back at sunset, and ye'll earn your cruise!"

John was impressed by the way Captain Foxe had acquired so much help so soon, and with such enthusiasm — of course, the money had something to do with the enthusiasm. "Will ye be coming back this evening, to help us float her?" he asked.

"I wouldn't miss it for a shilling," John replied.

At sunset, a crowd of men had gathered on the beach. Some of them John recognized from the previous two day's work, others he had seen in town. He realized that this must be the crew of the Egyptian Queen. A dozen boys were there, as well. The tide had risen to the point that waves were lapping all along the length of the hull, and anchors were tied to her stern and dropped into deeper water. With a combination of ropes, tackle, and brute force, the ship was dragged back into deeper water by the anchor ropes. As she moved deeper, she gradually righted herself, until the keel was grounded on the beach, but both sides of the hull were floating. Suddenly, a high wave pushed toward shore, and she bobbed a little, her keel barely touching. As the wave receded, so did the ship, until she was bobbing gently in the shallows. Men in longboats tied to her stern were pulling at the oars to move her to deeper water. Captain Foxe had been aboard during the whole process, shouting encouragement. Once the Queen was anchored in the channel, the longboats came ashore and ferried the crew and the boys out to the ship, along with John.

It was the boy's turn to get to work. Once again into the bilges, they crawled, with their little candles. Captain Foxe stood on the forecastle and faced the longboats, one on either side. From the boats, an observer could see whether the ship was listing either to starboard or to port, and by how much. The list was to starboard, and Foxe shouted instructions down to the boys in the bilges to begin shifting ballast stone from the starboard to the port side. As they did so, the ship listed less and less. When she was right, Foxe ordered the boys to stop. The longboats then moved to opposite sides of the ship, where they could see whether she was low at either the bow or the stern. If anything, it looked like the bow was riding a little high, but the sailors deemed it close enough.

Then it was time to board the ship, tie off the longboats, and raise a large, triangular sail at the mainmast. The ship began to move, and the helmsman turned her slowly down the estuary, toward the harbor. A full moon rose to the east as they drifted on, and finally docked at a pier at the southernmost end of the harbor. The boys all cheered. They were in no hurry to disembark, but the crew rounded them up and herded them onto the dock. They drifted off toward town, to whatever homes they had. John wondered how many would return to their mothers stinking like bilges, but with money to show for it. Would they be praised, or scolded? How many had no mothers at all to praise or scold them?

John turned to the Captain. "We got her in the water in three days. I believe that comes to eight shillings, plus the two you promised me yesterday." Foxe stroked his chin. "Ye've certainly earned the eight, but we didn't actually get her into the water *today*. It's well past nightfall."

John started to protest. Foxe raised a hand to interrupt him. "I'll give you one extra shilling for the good work you did, and another for your best judgment on a matter of concern to me. Come, walk the deck with me." He grabbed a lantern from one of the crewmen who stood on the dock and walked up the gangplank onto the deck of the ship. John followed him. They stood amidships, where they had a view of the entire vessel. The moon had risen just enough to spill some light into the hold.

"Now, if you were a shipwright," Foxe began, "How would you alter this fine vessel to ready her for war?"

John looked her up and down. He had gotten a good look at the Egyptian Queen during the day, especially since she carried no cargo, and the hold of the ship was open to the air down to the orlop deck. "Your forecastle is not as high as most warships, but it's broad, and has four gun ports. The newest galleons have low forecastles, anyway. I'd change nothing there unless the foredeck needs reinforcing to support the guns." He turned aft. "Your Stern castle isn't high, either, but that seems to be the fashion. The quarter deck is ample, and the poop deck is bigger than most. I suppose you've got more than the usual cabin space back there." Foxe nodded, with a smile.

John turned his attention amidships. "Down here is where most of the work would have to be done. You can see that the broadside batteries were located just below us, above the rowing benches. Better to remove the rowing benches and move your main batteries nearer to the waterline — much more stable. You'll probably have to install a new gun deck down there and bridge the gap between the port and starboard side with new decking. As wide as her beam is, you'll still have ample space between the batteries, even allowing for recoil. It depends, of course, on how big your guns are. Where are they, by the way?"

Foxe cleared his throat. "Can't say for sure. The Sea Beggars stripped all her guns before they sold me the ship."

John raised both eyebrows. "I believe I mentioned that you need a new mainmast. I'd replace the other two masts as well, if I were you, and rig her with all the sail you can. A warship without guns is going to have to do a lot of running."

Foxe smiled laconically. "We have guns coming. Just haven't seen them, yet. How many guns do ye think she could mount?"

So it was "we," John thought to himself. "We" would need deep purses indeed, to fully arm this ship. A culverin that could fire a 5-inch, eighteen-pound cannon ball could cost up to three hundred pounds, or more; a 4-inch, twelve-pound demi-culverin, at least two hundred. "Apart from the four guns in the bow, and as many in the stern, you could easily fit ten to twelve demi-culverins in each broadside battery, plus some lesser guns on the deck above — minions, maybe, or sakers, plus a dozen or so swivel guns."

Foxe did not flinch at this. He nodded, as if in agreement.

"You've got ample space in the hold," John continued, "for your munitions. I'd have to look at the powder magazines to see if they're large enough. With that many guns, you'll need at least a hundred men to man them in a sea battle. There's enough room below to sleep them all, I can't say how much room you'll need for the galley."

"Aye, the Beggars stripped the galley, as well," Foxe admitted. "How long do ye think it would take to get her shipshape, as ye described?"

"Depends on the size of the crew," said John. "Four carpenters and eight helpers could get it done in a month, I think, assuming," he paused for emphasis, "that you had all the lumber and nails for the job ready to go. You should replace the masts first before you do anything else. Then you can have crews work the rigging, while the carpenters work on your hull."

"Exactly!" Foxe exclaimed with satisfaction, "You and I think along the same lines!" He gave John 10 shillings and thanked him for his help. John stood on the deck for a moment, but Foxe had turned away, and his mind was clearly elsewhere. John bowed and excused himself.

He returned to the pub. It was late, but the place was nearly full. He realized that the stench of the bilges was still on him, so he went up to his room to change before supper.

When he came down, he walked to the bar, where Danny Cornwall was standing. "I hear ye've had a productive day," Cornwall said with a smile. Evidently, the story about the bilges was already in circulation.

"Profitable, surely, if not pleasant," John smiled back. He reflected that it wasn't every day that he could take credit for launching a hundred-twenty-foot ship; there was some satisfaction in that. "Do you know Captain Foxe?"

"Aye. He's well known hereabouts."

"I'm surprised he had so much trouble finding a shipwright the other day."

"Well, that's the thing about Billy Foxe. Always in a hurry, always got some newfangled project going on."

"But he paid me what he promised, and promptly. He seems to have plenty of good, hard money, and he's willing to spend it. I'd think that would count for something."

"No one would deny that Billy pays his debts — when he has the money. And he's a pleasant enough fellow. There's many a sailor will tell you he's a good captain — not harsh like some, looks after his crews like they were his own blood. Not so many will sail with him more than once, though."

"Why?"

"It's a matter of luck. Billy's seems to be bad, too often. Don't get me wrong — Billy's had his successes. Brought a lot of cargoes to port through foul weather, with ships that other men would have lost, to his backer's profit. Sailed the Baltic, the North Sea, even the Caribbean with Drake, according to some. Knows the sea as well as any man, I'd guess. But sailors are a superstitious lot, and most of them reckon that sailing with Billy Foxe is just too risky. He's the sort of man who looks to try things that others don't dare to, or just never thought of. Sometimes, his schemes make money, sometimes not. Most men know that going to sea is dangerous, without looking for trouble. Billy would gamble with the Devil if he thought the odds were favorable."

"Well, he's got a project, now," said John. "Wants to turn that galleass into a warship. Not sure who he's going to war with, or where he'll get the guns to do it."

"A galleass, ye say? Like one of those flimsy Venetian rowboats?" Cornwall's prejudices were showing.

"Not flimsy. Solid, overbuilt. A floating fortress, if he can find some guns, a crew, and enough sail to move her."

"If Billy is looking for guns, he'll find them. And in case ye hadn't noticed, England is at war with Spain, now."

"Is it official?"

"Might as well be. The Queen can either sit in London and wait for the King of Spain to come calling, or she can slap him first. My guess is she'll make the first move. Her agents were in here today, recruiting private ships to join her navy."

"That must be what Captain Foxe is planning, get the Royal Navy to pay him for a ship, then use the money to arm her."

"It doesn't work that way. The navy won't pay in advance. But Billy has backers — I hear the Rich's are financing him."

You mean the 3rd Baron Rich? From over Felsted way?"

"More likely his bastard uncle Richard. Same family."

John felt a pang of nostalgia to think that a man from his home parish could be right here in Harwich. Then he remembered where he had last seen the 3rd Baron, and where, possibly, the 3rd Baron had seen him. Not the stuff of hail-fellow-and-well-met.

"So ye think Billy's ship could be seaworthy?"

"Certainly. And she's broad-beamed enough to carry plenty of cargo. Not sure how fast she'll be, though."

"Speed isn't everything on the sea. Seamanship is the necessary thing, and Billy Foxe is a seaman, sure enough."

When John came down for his breakfast in the morning, he was surprised to see Captain Billy Foxe standing at the bar, speaking to Danny Cornwall. "There's my carpenter!" he cried as John approached. "I was talking about you to your landlord, just now. He told me you'd be along soon. I have a proposition for ye."

"A proposition?"

"Aye. I've discussed yer proposal with a few shipwrights I know, and all of them agree that yer ideas could work. Wouldn't ye know, every one of them has his hands full with getting some ship or other ready to join the Queen's navy? I'm back where I started a few days ago, except that thanks to you, I have a plan. And who better to bring that plan to being than the man who made the plan?"

His meaning was clear. It wasn't really a plan, just a . . . what, exactly? All of the recommendations he had made were within his skills. The ship was already built, and certainly didn't need a shipwright to complete the work — it was all carpentry, rigging, painting, and such. With a couple of journeymen like himself, plus a few laborers, the carpentry could be managed. "You should know that I am no master carpenter, only a journeyman. A work crew like the one I described should be supervised by a master craftsman."

"Wouldn't ye know, I thought of that? But there's not a master carpenter in Harwich that hasn't been contracted to someone else. Like I said, everyone's working for the navy, now. I have to be the supervisor; I just need men of skill to do my bidding."

John recalled how the ragged boys and the crewmen had all showed up at the careening beach just when they were needed. Evidently, Captain Foxe understood how to coordinate men and resources. "In that case, you can surely find men of skill to do your bidding," he replied.

Foxe sighed and nodded. "The truth is, men of skill are in short supply, just now — that is, men that are looking for work. What inducement would persuade you to work for me? "

John reflected. "I could demand an exorbitant wage, but soon enough, I would draw the attention of the guild. Apart from legal problems I could have, I'd probably lose any chance of ever being recognized as a Master Carpenter, if the Masters of the guild think I'm taking advantage of you. In the long run, I'll be better off waiting to complete a masterwork that the guild declares worthy of a Master."

"Why, couldn't the Egyptian Queen serve as your masterwork?" asked Foxe.

"I don't know. That would be up to the guild."

"If the guild agrees that rebuilding the Queen is a worthy masterwork, will you work for me?"

"In that event, yes, I will. But the wages must be at the standard rate; everything must be aboveboard." John was pretty sure the Masters of the guild would reject the Queen as a "masterwork"; not the usual sort of thing, for them. But it seemed a shame to give Captain Billy Foxe a firm refusal. More comfortable to make someone else the bearer of bad news.

Foxe smiled and left the pub briskly. Cornwall smiled at John, and said, "You drive a hard bargain, carpenter. But you may have underestimated Billy Foxe."

In less than an hour, Foxe was back at the pub with three dignified-looking companions. Master Carpenters, it turned out, all in good standing with the guild, and all friends of Captain Billy Foxe. Foxe led them, including John, down to the pier where the Queen of Egypt was moored. John explained to the carpenters what he had proposed to do with the Queen, and they asked a lot of questions. They wanted to tour the ship and expressed interest in some of the construction techniques that the Venetians had used in building her, all of which were visible since there was nothing in the hold. At length, the three conferred briefly, and one of them spoke to John: "This is an unusual project for us to consider, but if you do the work that you have described to us, or supervise others in doing it, the guild will evaluate your work as a masterwork. If the quality is good, you may expect to be recognized as a Master Carpenter."

John's feelings were mixed. This was the opportunity he had been waiting for. But he couldn't help feeling he had somehow been outmaneuvered by Captain Foxe. He took a breath and nodded. "I shall do my best," he replied, not knowing how much help he would get, or how they would respond to his supervision.

"We'll get started today," exclaimed Foxe, with enthusiasm. Turning to John, he said, "Take all the measurements you need, to determine how much lumber this is going to take." He signaled to two of the crewmen who were working nearby. "These are your servants until I find some more skilled help. They will do whatever you tell them to do." He looked at the men, and they nodded. "As soon as ye can, I need to know how much lumber to order. I've got two masts that should be arriving today, to replace the mainmast and the foremast. If they want someone to sign for delivery, you can do so in my stead. We'll keep the mizzenmast just as it is. Ye can use any crewmen on the ship to help you remove the old masts and prepare the new ones. Riggers are coming tomorrow to raise and secure the new masts and rig them for sails."

John was dizzied by the rapid-fire delivery of so many instructions. Captain Foxe was certainly not wasting any time. He started to walk back to town. "Where are ye going, now?" Foxe demanded

"I'll need my tool chest to get started here."

"Nay, ye are the foreman here, now. Send a servant to fetch yer tools. Davy, here, is a stout lad," — he pointed to one of the sailors — "he'll get yer tools. I need ye here to keep an eye on things — I have business elsewhere." With that, Foxe was off, striding quickly toward town.

John told Davy where his tools were, and sent him off to the Pub, with a note to Danny Cornwall, who had a key to his room. While he waited, he went back on board and refined his plan. The powder magazines were on the orlop deck, at the stern. They were located below the waterline, for safety, but there was no evidence of any leakage that would require repairs. The magazines were ample in size — evidently, the Queen had been built to carry and supply a lot of guns. In his mind's eye, he located where the galley (or kitchen) would be located, and the bilge pumps. The most obvious alteration would be the elimination of the rowing deck. As originally built, the hull had numerous small portholes on either side, to accommodate the long oars that propelled the ship. Now, guns instead of oars would be located at that level. This required larger ports, but fewer. He would remove the hull planks for that whole section and replace them. The deck above the rowing deck was where the guns used to be and was cantilevered out from the sides of the hull about three feet. Placing large guns there was impractical. He would turn that into the main deck, but leave the cantilevers, which overhung the gun deck and would make boarding the ship more difficult. The existing top deck was just a narrow band along the perimeter of the hull, with a railing to keep sailors from falling overboard. Most of that level was open all the way to the hold, with a few bridgeways connecting the port and starboard sides. He planned to close that opening, with the exception of a few hatches, by extending the new gun deck all the way across the open space below. This would require stout beams to connect the port and starboard ribs, which would add strength and rigidity to the whole ship. Adding more wood to the upper decks would make her more top-heavy, but placing the guns lower would more than compensate for that. He had no idea how all this would affect the handling of the ship. The existing top deck he would remove, and replace with a lower and narrower platform along both sides of the main deck, which meant that the top of the hull would become a thwart, or sidewall, high enough for a man to stand behind, while firing an arquebus or a swivel gun, and duck down behind if someone was firing back at him. The space between the platform and the main deck would be less than four feet high but could be used to stow equipment that needed to be available on the main deck.

Davy returned with his tool chest, and he put his crew to work measuring the dimensions of the ship. He came up with a surprisingly large order. He wondered how Captain Foxe was going to find it all, considering that every other shipwright in the harbor was looking for the same materials.

He had barely finished his calculations, when he was hailed from the dock. The new masts had arrived, just as Foxe had predicted. They were too long for any cart, wagon, or even a barge, so they were towed in, floating. Captain Foxe was on the boat that towed them in. He greeted John, and took the lumber order, in his usual ebullient mood: "I brought ye a crew to step the masts," he said, indicating a half dozen sailors that disembarked behind him. Evidently, he expected to do it promptly.

John had never done anything like this before. Fortunately, Foxe's crew was familiar with the routine. They started with the old foremast. They tied it to the mainmast and loosened all the other stays (ropes) that held it in place, then lowered it forward as far as it would go by gradually feeding the stay connected to the mainmast. Once lowered, the mast was detached from the keel and lifted out of the way. The mainmast was removed with the same method, using the mizzenmast (the mast nearest the stern) to control the process of lowering it. With both the old masts lying on the dock, it was apparent that the new masts were considerably taller. John gave them a closer look and realized that the new masts were constructed of several sections, closely joined together. He was impressed at the workmanship but wondered how they would stand up to the force of a wind strong enough to move a ship of this size. The answer, he realized, must be in the stays that held the masts up — each section had to have its own set of stays, and the tension on all the stays must be balanced so that no section experienced more force than the others. He began to think that sailing a ship was more complicated than he imagined.

It became apparent that the opening in the orlop deck through which the mast must pass was smaller than needed to fit the new mainmast, which was quite a bit larger. John was sent down to open up a larger opening in the orlop deck. He was followed by a blacksmith, who had replaced the old mast step — a frame attached to the keel that helps keep the base of the mast in place — with one of the proper size. This took more than an hour, then the new mainmast was stepped and raised. Foxe's crew swarmed all over the ship, fastening the stays, and adjusting the tension. Foxe insisted that the mast be raked — slanted slightly to the stern, rather than standing perfectly vertical. The new foremast was raised using the same method. John went back down to repair the orlop deck, where the mainmast passed through.

By this time, it was late in the day. Captain Foxe had disappeared, again. John realized he had missed his supper, and it was almost time for dinner. The rigging crew was gone, but several of the crew were still about, looking at John as if waiting for instructions. He looked at the two old masts. The foremast was sound enough, just shorter than the new one. He could salvage most of the old mainmast, as well, if he cut off the two or three feet that were rotting at the base. "Let's see if there's room for these in the hold," he suggested. The men responded immediately; they rigged some tackle to the spar on the mizzenmast, and lifted the old foremast into the hold, while John sawed two feet off the old mainmast, and shaped it to fit the old step. Then they lifted the old mast into the hold, as well.

John knew he should have something to keep the men busy, but there wasn't much to work with. As if on cue, Captain Billy Foxe appeared. This time, he was in the first of a train of flatbed wagons, loaded with lumber. Either the man was a magician, or he had been planning this day for some time. Either way, John had what he needed. He set the men to work unloading the wagons, sorting the lumber by dimension and type, into piles on the dock. There were also kegs of nails, and a few tools on the wagons, not to mention three or four new men that Foxe had hired. "Carpenters, like yourself," said Foxe.

One of them, Ned, was old, and nearly toothless. He professed to have experience in the shipyards. Another, Frank, was missing a hand — though he had a hook at the end of his arm that looked handy; he actually was a Master carpenter. The third man, Willy, stood about four and a half feet tall and had crossed eyes — possibly a disadvantage when it came to carpentry, but he had bought his own tool chest. John led them around the ship and described what the work would entail. None of them objected or tried to quit. So far, so good.

"Well, what do ye think?" asked Foxe.

"Each of these men will need a full-time assistant," John replied. "But I think they can help us."

Foxe nodded with satisfaction. "Got more men coming in the morning. We'll have our guns by the end of the week."

"Will the guns have carriages?"

"Nay, we'll have to build 'em. Need to see the guns, before we know how to size the carriages."

John realized that Foxe was serious. He must have reasons to be in such a hurry. What did he know that made this so urgent? "When do you plan to sail the *Queen*?"

"We need to be at sea no later than September the first of this year."

Six weeks, then. John wanted to ask what was so special about that date but decided he would ask around, before approaching Foxe directly.

That evening, John ate more than usual at the pub. He resolved to get back to the job site early, to give him time to plan how best to use the men that Foxe had hired. He questioned Danny Cornwall before he went back to his room. "Have you heard anything that would make September first a particularly auspicious date to go to sea?"

"September first?" Cornwall looked thoughtful "Favorable tides, I suppose. It's a good time to be sailing west if that's your fancy. The trade winds get stronger in September."

West. Why would Captain Foxe be sailing west? Unless of course, he was privateering; the Spanish treasure fleet would be using the same trade winds on their eastward journey. A long, low ship with a large crew and lots of guns. Yes, a privateer; that had to be it. Joining the Royal Navy was a pretext; Captain Billy Foxe would sail under his own flag. John was tired and went to bed early.

He got back to the dock at sunup, to find the watchmen that Captain Foxe had placed, as well as half a dozen new men. So much for planning out the day. He put several men to work tearing the rowing benches out and prying the hull planks off from around the oar ports. As soon as the three carpenters showed up, he assigned them each an assistant or two. Ned had brought tools but no longer had the stamina to cut all day. John gave him two men who would cut wherever he scribed a line. Frank had a saw, as well, but he needed help handling wood. Willy? John gave him helpers to double-check all the measurements before cutting. He focused on measuring the timbers for the new gun deck and relaying the measurements to the other three teams. Other men were available to anchor the cross beams to the ribs. He had them cut the longest one first — if it came up short, it could still be used where the hull was narrower. After a few miscues, they got into a rhythm, and things began to come together.

It took the rest of the week to frame the gun deck. From that point, they could lay down the decking as fast as the sawyers could cut it. They left two large hatches in the gun deck down to the hold, for cargo, and four smaller ones with stairs for the crew to use. They built latticed hatch covers for the cargo hatches, to prevent workmen from falling into the hold. Foxe specified that they must leave at least thirty feet between the cargo hatches — "for the longboat." The guns had arrived, as promised, at the end of the first week, but they sat on the dock until the deck was finished. Little risk that anyone would run off with them; they each weighed from half a ton to fifteen hundred pounds.

By the third week, the gun deck was complete, and John could measure the guns, to construct carriages for them. They were not of uniform size or caliber. The best of them were cast of bronze, which the sailors insisted on calling "brass." The others were iron, which was heavier for a given caliber, but still serviceable. Each large gun was seven to eight feet long. Each had a prominent metal knob at the breech end, called a cascable. Near the middle of the barrel were two solid cylindrical protrusions known as trunnions. The gun would rest on its trunnions when placed on its wheeled carriage, so each carriage had to have a semicircular groove on each side to accommodate the trunions. When mounted, an iron clamp would be installed over the top of the trunnions, locking them to the carriage — lest a gun fly completely off the carriage from the recoil.

Most of the large guns had a 4-inch caliber. There were four iron Culverins that had a 6-inch bore, which meant that separate ammunition had to be kept in stock. It could have been worse; some warships had to carry six or more calibers of shot. The caliber, of course, was nominal — no two guns had precisely the same muzzle diameter. The difference between the actual diameter of a 4-inch cannonball and the gun's bore was called "windage." Wadding was used to close that gap when firing the gun.

The gun carriages were assembled on the dock, while work continued on the main deck of the ship. All the while, wagonloads and small boatloads of supplies were arriving, and being stowed in the hold. Captain Foxe supervised the stowing with some particularity. He wanted the cargo to be balanced, of course but also insisted that certain items be placed where they could quickly be retrieved from the hold.

By the end of the fourth week, the main deck was finished. It also had two large cargo hatches, aligned with the ones on the gun deck, and four smaller ones for the crew. The large hatches had latticed covers like the ones below, plus solid ones to prevent waves on the deck from spilling into the hold in foul weather. A twenty-three—foot longboat was mounted on the main deck, between the two cargo hatches. All of these hatches had to be removed when cargo was being loaded, an added hazard to the men working on deck.

During the fifth week, the guns and their carriages were placed on the gun deck. There were ten 4-inch demi-culverins on each side of the ship.

John tried to balance the load by making his best guess at how much each gun weighed. Two of the 6-inch culverins would be mounted in the bow, two more at the rear of the quarterdeck at the stern. Captain Foxe intervened, insisting that he supervise the placement of the guns himself. "If the crew sees that she lists the wrong way, they'll be expecting bad luck. It's a superstition, but we'll make sure she lists the right way."

As September approached, news from abroad trickled in. Queen Elizabeth had signed a treaty in August with the Dutch rebels. England was officially at war with Spain, and her allies. The Queen had resisted the alliance for years — she feared that a successful rebellion in the Low Countries would feed her own subject's seditious inclinations — but the situation was desperate. If both France and the Low Countries fell under Philip's power, her throne was lost. She was not wholly without resources, and she would use what she had.

Billy Foxe's determination to build a warship was based on more than a lucky guess: rumors about the negotiations had been in circulation in the higher levels of society for some time. It was known, for example, that many of Elizabeth's most influential advisors had been arguing in favor of war for years.

Elizabeth's diplomatic game of hampering Spanish interests in Europe without resorting to open warfare had become more difficult to play. The military assistance that she was able to offer to French Huguenots or Dutch rebels was rarely large enough to be decisive — merely to prolong the conflicts. Her privateers were having more success at sea than her small armies could achieve on the Continent, but neither were numerous enough to prevail in a head-to-head confrontation with Spain.

And Spain was closing in.

Foxe's main investor, Richard Rich, was connected to the channels of influence in London, his illegitimacy notwithstanding. Richard Rich was, in fact on good terms with his half-siblings and their families. He had not inherited as much as they from his father's estate, but he was no pauper, and without large land holdings of his own, it was only logical to look for opportunities overseas. Privateering was just one of his business interests. Captain Billy Foxe was just the sort of risk-taker that Richard Rich liked to invest in.

With September just a week away, John was scrambling to meet his deadline. The large-scale work was done. At Foxe's insistence, he and his crew were remodeling the spacious captain's cabin at the rear of the quarterdeck. In its original state, it had been carpeted and lavishly furnished. The previous owners had helped themselves to the furnishings, except, improbably, a large Italian tapestry that covered one wall. Foxe wanted the space divided into multiple smaller cabins. The largest remaining space would serve as the officer's mess and a chart room; he would not say what the others were for. Each of the smaller cabins would have four bunkbeds; that was all he would say. The space under the poop deck would now serve as the captain's cabin.

There were more sleeping accommodations to be installed "before the mast" (forward of the mainmast), which was where the crew were expected to sleep. The carpenters installed pegs and hooks on the ceiling of the gun deck — this is where most of the sailors would sleep, in hammocks hung from the hooks. A typical gun crew consisted of four sailors, so the hammocks would be hung so that each crew would sleep near its gun. Twenty-four large guns required at least ninety-six gunners. Add in the officers to coordinate the firing of the guns, and a dozen or so gunners on the upper decks, and it would take well over one hundred men to take the *Egyptian Queen* into battle. More would be needed in the rigging as the ship maneuvered, so everyone else on the ship would be expected to participate — "all hands on deck" meant that cooks, carpenters, blacksmiths, and other skilled tradesmen would be trained in some other job, and be expected to perform it competently.

Foxe directed that more cabin space be created under the foredeck, and hooks for another hundred hammocks, some on the gun deck near the center, others on the main deck under the eaves of the walkway that John and his crew had constructed. It looked as if he were expecting more passengers.

September 1st fell on a Sunday. After church, John toured the ship one last time. He found a few details unfinished, but the ship was as ready as he could make her — fresh paint and varnish were still not quite dry, and he could smell the fresh tar on the ratlines. With her sails furled, and flags at the mast, she looked like a well-dressed lady, he thought. There was a figurehead at the bow, a woman who looked like a queen of Egypt, as far as anyone knew. "Beautiful, is she not?" The voice of Captain Foxe came from behind him. "Yes," John replied. "Beautiful!"

"We'll be needin' a ship's carpenter on this voyage," said Foxe. "Why don't ye sail with us?"

John shook his head. "I am no seaman, nor a fighting man. I'd be no use to you on a voyage like the one I believe you are undertaking. Why not ask one of the other carpenters on my crew?"

"Ye mean Ned? A fine old gentleman, to be sure, but less fit for battle than you. Or Frank? I've always admired a man with a hook — gives him a certain swagger, I think. But we need a carpenter with two hands, at least. And Willy? Some on this crew would likely bully him mercilessly. He'd disappear one day, and we'd find him stuffed into the bilges. Nay, ye are the one these sea dogs respect; your work has not gone unnoticed. They will follow your lead in a pinch, which is where we'll be if this ship is badly damaged in a storm or a battle. Did I mention that I'll pay you a master's wage, and you'll get an officer's share of any booty? There's a bunk in the stern castle for you if you want it."

John laughed. "Speaking of a master's wage, when will the guild masters review my "masterwork?""

"We can do it first thing in the morning," Foxe replied. "But what about my offer?"

"I'll give it some thought," said John, putting him off. If he was accepted by the guild as a Master Carpenter, he could go anywhere he liked. But not to sea. Never to sea.

In the morning, Foxe had the guild members on the dock, true to his word. They toured the ship with John, amid the bustle of sailors boarding, and stowing their gear. They asked questions, and nodded when his answers seemed to satisfy them. "We will meet with the guild masters in a few days, to make our decision. If it is favorable, your name will be enrolled as a master in good standing of our guild. You will receive a letter to that effect. The work looks good to us." They left, still talking among themselves. John took a deep breath. Grounds for optimism. John left the dock before Foxe could corner him. If he was admitted as a master, the next problem would be to collect his last week's pay from Foxe, before he sailed.

The *Egyptian Queen* did not sail the following day, nor the day after. John did not approach the ship, because he didn't want to finish his business with Billy Foxe until he had his letter from the guild in hand. It was apparent that Foxe had influence with the guild; if he were offended, he might possibly block John's application. Better to wait him out.

On the fifth day, Friday, there was a commotion on the waterfront, as a troop of eighty soldiers marched down to the dock where the *Queen* was moored and began boarding her. They brought wagonloads of provisions with them, which took some time to load. This had to be what Foxe had been waiting for. The ship now had a complement of more than two hundred forty men. John decided he had to speak to the captain if only to get his last pay. He found Foxe in his cabin and was greeted warmly. "So, carpenter, ready for the adventure of yer life, are ye?"

John shook his head. "I am sorry to disappoint you, not least because I know you to be a man of influence, and I hesitate to offend you, with my mastership hanging in the balance. But I have not come here to join your crew, I merely want the last five shillings you owe me for last week's work."

Foxe looked at him as if in pain. "The last five shillings, is it? Ye shall have them; they are well earned. But I am pained to the heart at the suggestion that I would ever do anything to hinder your livelihood. I have only the greatest respect for *you*, John Porter, a man of skill and noble character. It pains me to think ye think less of *me*. I invited ye on this adventure because ye are the kind of man I want at my side in danger, or good fortune, a man trusted because he has proven himself trustworthy."

John felt ashamed that he had spoken so bluntly. The Captain was showing a sentimental side that he had not seen before — had he been drinking? Probably the remark about the mastership was more than he should have said. He wanted to be honest, but maybe there was such a thing as too much honesty. "Captain, I'm sure you'll find the man you need. When do you sail?"

"We would have sailed last Monday, if the soldiers had arrived when ordered to. Can't sail today, the crew thinks it's bad luck to sail on a Friday. Superstitious lot." Foxe frowned "Is there nothing I can do to persuade ye to come with us? This is going to be a lucky cruise; I can feel it. There's fortune for the man bold enough to seize it!" John shook his head firmly. "Right. Here's yer five shillings, then, plus one to show there's no hard feelings." John bowed slightly and left the cabin. He greeted several of the crew on his way off the boat, men he had worked with for the last six weeks. He would remember them with fondness. He hoped they would find the fortune that they were seeking. If his mastership was approved, he thought he might go home to Felsted for a while, returning to his family with his badge of success. Maybe he would stop in Little Baddow again, to let Sybil Vessey repay him that last tuppence. Maybe he would even embrace her again, when their account was settled. Maybe.

When he got back to *The Galleon*, he told Danny Cornwall about his plans. He paid his account with the pub off, and thought of relaxing until the guild's decision was made. How long could it be? Surely, by the beginning of next week, he would have their decision. He went up to his room, and began to pack.

Part 7: Pressed

September 1585: Surprised

John took his time over supper that evening. He listened to the singing in the far corner of the pub and even sang along with them. He had the feeling that a certain chapter of his life was coming to an end, and a new one, full of hope and promise, was beginning. He felt, in short, like a successful man.

It was after dark when he walked to the privy behind the pub. As he returned, he was met by a silhouetted figure. "This the way to the privy?" asked the man. Before John could answer, he was in the grasp of someone behind him, his arms pinioned. Something — a rag? — was stuffed into his mouth, and some sort of bag was pulled over his head. It happened so quickly, that he didn't really struggle until everything had gone dark. By that time, it was too late. His feet and arms were tied, and he was lifted off his feet. He heard some shouting, then more sounds of struggle, then quiet. He was being carried, and whoever was carrying him was in a hurry — he heard them breathing heavily. It was not many minutes until he heard the sound of footfalls on a wooden dock, and shortly thereafter, he was dumped onto a wooden floor. He heard the thud of another burden being dropped, and then a door closed, and the footfalls receded. He was aware of a rocking motion where he lay. So, the floor was afloat and could only be the deck of a ship. He had been abducted, but by who, and why? Turkish pirates, perhaps — maybe he would be held for ransom. No one would pay a ransom for him; maybe he would be sold as a galley slave. Not Turks; Dunkirkers, maybe. Could mean the same fate. Clearly, they had picked the wrong victim; he was of no great value to anyone, except . . . he knew someone who wanted a carpenter desperately. How much would he be willing to pay? Would it be enough to satisfy his captors? A bell rang six times. He knew that meant something on board a ship, but he wasn't sure exactly what. Some time later, the bell rang again — he counted seven times. Later still, the bell rang eight times. He supposed that the bells were keeping time in some fashion.

Shortly after the eighth bell, he heard distant shouts that sounded like commands, and there was a change in the movement of the floor beneath him. It could only mean that the boat was moving. The pressure on his bladder told him that it had been at least three hours since his last visit to the privy. After what might have been another hour, footfalls approached; he heard a door open and heard a familiar voice.

"Here now, what's this? Untie these two!" His bonds were loosed, and the bag pulled off his head. He was looking at the face of none other than Captain Billy Foxe. Foxe was holding a lamp close to John's face. Other men stood behind him, in the dark.

"I told ye to fetch the carpenter, and I clearly said there was to be no cuttin' or bruisin'. I told you to be persuasive, and compel him if necessary. I said nothin' about a bag over his head, or a gag in his mouth" — with this, Foxe pulled a wad of rags out of John's mouth. "And who's this other one?" Foxe turned to the other prisoner, whom John immediately recognized as Roger.

"The little one raised such a ruckus, that we had to bring him along, too," said a deep voice in the background. "And this big one wouldn't have come along willingly. There could have been trouble in the street, if we let him holler."

Foxe helped John to his feet. "I am truly sorry it has been so inconvenient for ye to join my crew."

"I have not joined your crew! I have been forced here against my will! You have no right to bring me here or hold me! This is a crime!"

"Actually, I do have the right. Ye've been pressed, Carpenter. Yer name is on the roster, and the purser has an account for you. Ye are entitled to a fair share of any plunder we take, and you'll earn a carpenter's pay in the bargain. I should point out that as Captain, my word is law aboard this ship. Refusal to serve could be considered mutiny, and the penalties for mutiny are harsh."

"Pressed?" spluttered John.

"An ancient law of the realm. In times of war, or dire emergency, the navy is entitled to seize such men as are needed to defend the nation. We are at war with Spain, and men like yourself are needed. I have great respect for you, but do not imagine that I will spare ye at the peril of your country, or that I will overlook insubordination for the sake of friendship."

Friendship, was it? John's head was spinning, he needed to clear his thoughts.

"Do you know this one?" Foxe nodded at Roger.

"I work for him," said Roger.

"So, when you saw your master in trouble, you came to his aid?"

"Something like that," replied Roger.

Foxe laughed, "Brave boy! You'll do well at sea!"

Roger looked like he might enjoy doing well at sea.

"I have no tools," said John.

"Those are in your cabin, along with your personal items. I sent Davy for them. You'll recall that you authorized Davy to fetch your tools from the pub a few weeks ago. Danny Cornwall was happy to oblige when he learned that ye were going to sea with me, after all."

John took a deep breath. Clearly Foxe had carefully planned the whole thing — except for Roger, of course. "What about my barrow?"

"Cornwall has agreed to keep it safe for you at no cost, provided he can use it from time to time, in your absence."

John shook his head slowly. Foxe had thought of everything. "What if I just leave the ship?"

"That would be desertion, which is a very serious matter, punishable by flogging or even death. I doubt it would come to that, unless ye are a very strong swimmer. We're ten miles out to sea by now, I reckon."

John's shoulders sagged. He could swim, but not that far. The next time they made landfall, it wouldn't be in England. "Wait . . . you told me it was bad luck to sail on a Friday."

"So I did, but it's Saturday, now. A few hours past midnight. A splendid day to sail!"

John sighed. "I'm tired. Where can I sleep?"

"Davy, here, will show you to your berth."

The berth in question was a bunk in a small cabin under the quarterdeck. Snug, as he well knew, since he had planned and built it. There were three other bunks in the small room, each with a snoring occupant. John fell asleep quickly. He would have to deal with things tomorrow.

He was roused only a few hours later, along with his cabin mates. The sun was barely up. He stumbled out to the main deck, where the rest of the crew, including the soldiers were assembling. There was a high-pitched whistle, and all the sailors fell into ranks on the port side or the foredeck. An officer shouted an order, and the soldiers lined up on the starboard side. John found a place in line with about a dozen others on either side of the quarterdeck. Then Captain Billy Foxe emerged from his cabin behind them and climbed the stairs to the poop deck astern, where he could overlook the entire ship's complement. He began to speak, in a loud voice.

"Seamen and soldiers! We are embarked on a Great Expedition, in the name of England, and our Queen! Glory and fortune lie ahead for the valiant, shame and disgrace for those who are faint of heart, in our country's time of need. This ship is your home, now, and with her I intend to strike fear into the heart of the king of Spain. We shall fight, we shall plunder, and by God's grace, we shall triumph!" He paused dramatically, which was the cue for all the sailors to shout "Hurrah!" three times. The soldiers were a little slow on the uptake but joined in on the second and third hurrahs.

Foxe continued, "I am not at liberty to tell you our destination, at present. But as long as you are on my ship," (he glanced at John, and then the soldiers) "you are under my command. Remember that always! I can tell you that we will soon be joined by other ships, and together we will strike a blow that our enemies will not soon forget. God save the Queen!

Three more "Hurrahs," this time in unison. John joined in because — well, because that was what any loyal Englishman did when someone said, "God save the Queen." Foxe stepped down to the quarterdeck and disappeared into his cabin. The sailors returned to their stations, the soldiers to their duties. John found himself standing with Roger on the quarterdeck. The sun was rising to port, so they must be sailing south. There was no sight of land, just the endless sea. He looked starboard — no land in sight there, either. Roger said, "I'm hungry. Let's find something to eat."

1585: Little Baddow

The years that followed John Porter's disappearance from Little Baddow had not been unusual. Soon after the priest's execution, there had been more than the usual number of curious strangers in the village, but in a month or so, they had moved on. As luck would have it, a journeyman carpenter appeared in the village less than a month after John's disappearance. He took up residence in the Widow Smith's shop in the village. The villagers were pleased to have a carpenter in the village again, and the new man was very friendly. Unfortunately, his work was not up to the standard that people had come to expect. He seemed unfamiliar with some of the tools and techniques of the carpenter's trade. As time passed, fewer people were willing to hire him, and he was often idle. After four months, he moved on — hoping, it was supposed, for employment elsewhere.

For the Vessey family, these matters were of only passing interest. More important was the fact that that the harvest was good that year, and the next year as well. Samuel was still sending money home, which helped pay for a laborer to help Old Thomas in the fields. Samuel's younger brother John, finished his apprenticeship the second year and was able to send money home, as well. This was just barely enough to continue paying the apprenticeship fees for young Thomas, and now Francis, who was apprenticed to the village's only tailor. Even with the help of a farmhand, Old Thomas couldn't quite keep up with the work. He was by this time fifty-five years old, and the years of hard labor were beginning to tell. Added to this was the cloud of brooding sadness that seemed to hover over him on most days.

Sybil was forced to take on some of the farm work, herself — milking, feeding the livestock, moving the cattle and the horse to new pastures, plus the gardening that she had already been taking care of. She got behind the plow a few times during planting season and could handle a team of oxen well enough. At harvest, she helped with the threshing. She drew the line at the haying.

Fortunately, her younger sisters were older and more able. Sybil turned the cooking and housekeeping over to them. Susan was now seventeen, and a passable cook. Mary, now fifteen, could help her with just about anything around the house and had a particular aptitude for sewing.

"Just one more good harvest," Sybil kept telling herself, knowing full well that a bad harvest would surely come later, if not sooner. Still, she could imagine a future for herself and her siblings that did not always teeter on the precipice of poverty. Samuel, it seemed, was doing well. No doubt he would marry and have a family of his own. The same with John — the butcher's trade was a prosperous one. Young Thomas would be a journeyman blacksmith by next year, and Francis — well, Francis. He was clever, witty, restless, given to sarcasm at times, but she supposed he would settle down in time. He would probably find employment in the city — who knows, he might become a tailor to wealthy and influential men. Yes, the city life would suit Francis, better than any of the rest of her family.

That left Sybil and her sisters. She had done her best to teach them the skills they would need to run their own homes. They were pretty enough, she thought — maybe that would be enough to cause a suitor to overlook the lack of a dowry. They were both inclined to be witty, clever, and irreverent — not necessarily endearing traits to the sorts of men who might be willing to marry them. Sybil worried about this — perhaps, if their mother had lived long enough, she would have raised them to be more sensible young women. Perhaps they would learn to be sensible only after they were married. Sybil was all too aware of how the responsibilities of a woman's life could squeeze the laughter and frivolity out of the long days. Their lightness had been a comfort to her, in the years that she had struggled to hold her family together. She would miss the laughter when they were gone.

As for Sybil, the only future she imagined for herself was here, in Little Baddow, on this farm, with her father, Thomas. She may have had other dreams for her life, once, but she could not recall them. Her family was her life's work, and it seemed that she might just finish it with honor — "just one more good harvest."

It was more than three years before Samuel came to visit again. Right after harvest, he appeared at her door along with his friend and mentor, Edward Chase. Now that Francis was away, there was room enough in the house for both of them to sleep. They sat together after supper, discussing something or other in low tones. Sometimes they laughed, sometimes they shook their heads as if relating some folly.

Sybil felt within her rights to demand some explanation and approached them. "You know that you are always welcome here, brother," she began. "But you have been away a very long time (longer than necessary, and with too few letters), and now that you are here, I sense some business is afoot. Tell me what is going on, and why Mr. Chase is with you."

Samuel sat back in his chair and drew a breath. He looked at Chase. and spoke: "What I tell you must be confidential." Sybil nodded.

"Our local priest is being considered for promotion to a larger parish, which means that Little Baddow will need a new priest. Edward," he nodded at Chase, "thinks that I would make a good replacement."

"You're coming home to stay?", Sybil exclaimed with delight.

Samuel raised his hands slightly and shook his head. "It hasn't been decided yet, and it must be confidential until the decision is final. Edward has the ear of the bishop, and thinks my chances are very good."

Ear of the bishop? Sybil was puzzled. Who exactly, was this man? How did he have the ear of the bishop?

Both men noticed her puzzlement but said nothing. There was an awkward silence.

Sybil looked thoughtful. "I have one other matter that you may illuminate me about. It concerns that carpenter, John Porter. When I last spoke to him, it was just out there, in the barn. He refused to say where or why he was leaving. He said it was up to you," she looked Samuel in the eye, "to explain his business."

Samuel sat back in his chair again. "That was three years ago. I'm not sure I remember anything that would answer your question."

"I remember the day very well; it was the day they executed that priest in Chelmsford. The same day that both of you disappeared. The carpenter came back that evening to collect his barrow. None of you have been seen around here since that day. Do you expect me to believe that all of this is purely a matter of chance?"

Samuel exhaled and glanced at Chase. "You are right, it is not merely a matter of chance. John Porter disappeared to protect you and our family; indeed, the whole village." Chase nodded.

"Protect our family from what?" Sybil demanded.

"No doubt you have heard of how the priest died that day, how his torture was interrupted by the crowd, how he died before his mutilation?" asked Chase.

Sybil nodded. "John Porter was among the crowd that hung on his legs until he was dead," Chase explained.

"Why would he do that? Was it not enough that the man was to be gutted and castrated?"

"Too much, I reckon. The crowd was determined to shorten his suffering."

"And why was that any of John Porter's business?"

"They were friends. John owed the priest a favor, I'm thinking."

"You're telling me John Porter is a recusant?"

"No," said Edward, "not a recusant, just a friend determined to repay a debt in the only way he knew how."

"How do you know this?"

"It was I who introduced John to the priest, nearly five years ago. And it was the priest who suggested that John come to Little Baddow for work. John was grateful and wished to spare his friend needless suffering if he could, that is all."

Sybil was silent for a moment, thinking. Then she spoke: "The crowd was large, so I have been told; you would not have been able to see who was pulling on the priest's legs unless you were in the middle of the crowd yourself." It was a statement and an accusation.

Edward smiled faintly, and said, "I can neither affirm nor deny your allegation, and I would not admit it to you, even if it were true."

Sybil shot him an exasperated look. Then she turned to her brother. "And what is your role in all this?"

Samuel replied carefully. "I was there for the execution. I did not join the crowd that hastened the priest's death, though I admit I admired them for what they did. I was just an observer. But I did recognize a face or two in the crowd, and it seemed best to me not to put them at risk by submitting to an interrogation. I reckoned that Great Dunmow was far enough away to put me beyond the investigators, and I was headed that way, in any case. As for the frequency of my letters to you, I apologize. I have been very busy."

Sybil sat with her arms folded, reflecting on what they had said. "There is more to this story than you have told me. How did John Porter find out that his friend was going to be executed?"

"I told him," said Edward. "I visited the priest in the Chelmsford jail two days before the execution. He was my friend, too. I agreed to carry a message to John for him."

"You carried a message to John from the Chelmsford Jail? Did it not occur to you that the authorities might follow you here?"

"A man in my business is accustomed to being followed. And yes, I was followed to Little Baddow. It was John who came up with a credible reason for me to be here on that day, without revealing his connection to me, or the priest."

What business accustoms a man to being followed, she wondered, "So, your appearance at my door was a pretense? How did you know that Samuel was here?"

"That part was pure luck. It gave me a good reason to be in Little Baddow, since Samuel and I went to school together, and did not connect me with anyone else in the village." The two men looked at each other with expressions of satisfaction, as if they had succeeded in some clever maneuver, or some noble quest, known only to them — and now to Sybil, of course.

"I underestimated that carpenter, as do many, I reckon. He managed the whole deception masterfully and helped his friend, and did so without placing his other friends in peril. We should toast his memory."

"Agreed," said Samuel, there was still a bit of ale in his mug, and he clinked it against Edward's. "To John Porter!" Sybil thought they were really toasting each other, as much as anything. Men — just like boys!

Sybil was not entirely satisfied with their story. "If the deception was, as you say, masterful, why was it necessary for him to leave?"

"There was still the matter at Chelmsford. Others from Little Baddow were present at the execution. The whole thing could have unraveled if his name was mentioned to the authorities. They might have turned the village upside down looking for him. He did what he thought was necessary to protect the people he cared about" — here Samuel caught Sybil's eye — "and we are safe. That is all you need to know."

It was not all she wanted to know, but these men would not have answers to the questions most urgently on her mind. Those questions she did not articulate, even to herself, not least because she wasn't prepared to deal with the answers. She had more news than she could digest.

In her prayers, she asked God's blessing and protection for her brother and his friend. She also prayed for John Porter.

1585: The Way of War

Sybil's prayers for John Porter could not have been timelier. He stood at a railing on the quarterdeck and watched as the *Egyptian Queen* traversed the Dover Straits — Dover to the west, France to the east, they told him. He was trapped on a world of wood, floating on an immense sea, without a clue of how he could reach land. He was angry that a man he had trusted had betrayed him, angry at himself for ignoring the clues that he was in peril. For years, he was accustomed to choosing where he worked, where he lived, how he spent his time. If his choices did not always bring him success, they were still his choices, and he would own the consequences, without complaint. In this situation, complaint was all that was left to him — every other aspect of his life was directed by someone else — when and where he slept, when and what he ate, where and how he worked. And Captain Billy Foxe was most to blame.

He was not the only man on the ship in this situation. He met his cabin mates the first morning, one of whom was the "surgeon." The surgeon was hungover and confused; he could not explain how he arrived on the *Queen* — his last clear memory was an alehouse in Harwich. His name was Benedict Harrington; of that much he was sure. Somehow, his bag of medical instruments had made it onto the ship with him. He kept asking if someone had something for him to drink — rum, brandy, anything to clear his head. No one had any to offer him, which disappointed him greatly. On board ship, it turned out, alcoholic beverages were strictly rationed — a ration of rum for every man once a day, ale with meals. For Dr. Harrington, it was going to be a long, dry voyage.

Another of his mates was a blacksmith, named Robert — sober and cheerful, which only increased John's sense of irritation.

The fourth companion was Reuben Cox, the boatswain. John would report directly to Reuben on most matters since the boatswain was chiefly responsible for the maintenance of the ship.

Other cabins off the quarterdeck housed the first and second mates, the helmsman, the navigator, and the gunnery officer. The lieutenant in command of the soldiers was an officer named Cooper, and his aide slept aft as well. A unit of this size would ordinarily be commanded by a Captain, but the senior officer failed to make it to Harwich in time for their departure: the rest of their command slept "before the mast," with the crew.

The ship generated a constant hum of noises, punctuated by bells, or shouts all day, and all night. Most of the creaks and groans of the ship faded into the background, but any time there was a change in course or speed, there was also an audible change in the ship's "song." John learned to sleep through the ordinary noise, and even the ringing of the ship's bell; he still woke, briefly, when the weather or the course changed.

John was surprised to discover that he would eat his meals with the other officers in the mess at the stern, rather than with the rest of the crew. The food may have been a bit tastier than what the sailors were eating (he hoped so), and the conversation was interesting. Everyone appeared to accept as fact that he was the ship's carpenter, regardless of his view on the topic. Evidently, the job was a respected one on board ship; he learned a bit about each of them the first few days.

John was not prepared for the exotic origins of his fellow seamen. The gunnery officer was clearly from somewhere in Africa, as was the navigator. The first mate looked English enough but spoke with a Dutch accent. The Second Mate looked Italian or some such; he was also the purser — the man who kept the crew's roster and would be responsible for paying them at the end of the voyage. The rest of the crew was more English-looking, though at least a third of them appeared foreign to John's eyes, men with shaved heads, or hair in braids, large earrings, prominent tattoos. Brown skin, olive skin, skin that was nearly black. They appeared to work together efficiently enough but spoke a dialect of English (if it was English) that he couldn't always understand.

The gunnery officer was a large, dark man called "Dick Benby," born it was said, in Angola. The Navigator was "Homer," though his birth name was Omar — from Senegal. Piet Van Doorn was the First Mate, from Amsterdam. The Second Mate went by Paul, though his mother had named him Paolo.

The second day out, John was summoned to the captain's cabin. Roger stood just outside the door to Foxe's cabin; evidently he was now a cabin boy. He found Captain Foxe seated at a wide table covered with nautical charts. Foxe greeted him heartily, "Well, carpenter! How do ye like yer berth? Is the food to yer liking? Are yer mates congenial enough?"

"I have no complaints about the berth, or the food, or the crew. My complaint is that I am here against my will. I have no desire to sail to wherever this ship is bound, in any berth, with any 'mates', under any captain, least of all a man that I trusted, and has betrayed me to injury or even death on the high seas!"

At this, Foxe gave him a somber, even hurt look. "It grieves me that yer regard for me is so low. I have always regarded ye highly. Ye say that I have betrayed you? That is over harsh, I think. I have done what I have done to fulfill my duty to our queen and homeland. In times like these, all men must be prepared to sacrifice their comfort and safety for the sake of the nation. Ye might be grateful that God has seen fit to place you in the front ranks of this noble effort."

So, now it was God's fault that he had been abducted. A convenient way for Foxe to look at it, thought John.

Foxe continued. "I promised you a master's wage, and an officer's share of the booty on this voyage, and I will stand by that promise. If we return to England safely, you'll be a fair sight more prosperous than you are now. If we take a rich prize, you'll be a wealthy man, as well. I cannot guarantee that you will survive this voyage, any more than I can guarantee any man's safety. But, as your captain, I will do everything in my power to bring this ship and all its crew safely home, as is my duty. I expect you to do your duty, as well."

John stood with his arms folded and scowled. Duty? He had no answer for "duty."

"There will be danger, as always, in any war. And I think your fear is reasonable, given your lack of fighting skill. I will remedy that as best I can. I have ordered combat training for men like you, so that ye will be more able to defend yourself, and this ship when needed. You will have to learn other men's skills, so that you can fill the ranks, when they need filling. The gunnery officer will teach you how to work a culverin, and will also instruct you on the use of smaller firearms. The Lieutenant will drill you in infantry tactics — though they are of little use on board this ship. It will be important for you to gain some skill with the cutlass — might save your life. We'll get to that in a few weeks. I've informed the bosun that you will need to be excused from your other duties for an hour or so each day for your training."

John's shoulders sagged, and he nodded in grudging consent. As long as he was trapped on this ship, he would do what he could to improve his odds of survival.

"One more point. As carpenter of the ship, you are an officer. You are subject to the chain of command that starts with those who command me, and you must obey orders, even as I must. This ship is now part of her majesty's navy, and so are you. By the same token, you also must give orders, and those orders must be obeyed. If the ship is in a crisis that requires your skills, every man on board is at your command, in order to save the ship. You would do well to carry yourself as an officer, in a manner that will command the respect and trust of your mates. Our lives may depend on it. Good day, Sir!"

John realized that he had been dismissed. It took him a moment to collect himself and leave the cabin. "Sir" was not a form of address he was accustomed to. Roger was still standing just outside the cabin door, smiling broadly. Evidently he had overheard the conversation. He stood erect, as if at attention. John spoke to him: "Roger, I am sorry that you were pulled into this situation on my behalf. It was brave of you to come to my aid, but I fear that that you will pay a great price for your valor."

Roger smiled more widely, "Do not feel sorry for me, Sir! I count myself fortunate to be at sea with you! This is the chance of a lifetime!"

John gave him a quizzical look. "Would you not rather be at home in Harwich?"

"No Sir! I have a comfortable berth here, the food is good, and someone does my laundry for me. The pay is better than anything I could hope for in Harwich." He stood even taller, "I am the cabin boy on this vessel, and I report directly to the Captain. He gives me orders to deliver, and when I do, I am respected as if the the Captain himself were speaking. What better life could a man of my station hope for?"

Man? "Roger, how old are you?" John realized he had never asked this question. He noted that Roger was a good deal taller than when they first met three years ago. It occurred to him that he knew nothing at all about Roger's family, or if he even had a family. They must be poor indeed, if they could not afford some sort of apprenticeship for him. A career at sea might be the best apprenticeship a boy like Roger could hope for.

"I am nearly thirteen. "

So, a man indeed, small as he was. Just then, Captain Foxe called for Roger from within his cabin, and Roger was off to another assignment. There were half a dozen other boys among the crew, but Roger's proximity to the Captain gave him a sense of seniority over them. The other boys served in a variety of ways, but were trained as "powder monkeys." In a battle, their job would be to transport gunpowder from the magazines to the gun crews on the main deck and the gun deck. Speed and agility was required; short stature was an advantage in the cramped spaces below deck.

John considered his own situation. He was an officer, now, on a ship of war. That felt oddly like a promotion from where he was just three days ago. Like Roger, he had a berth, free meals, and someone to do his laundry. Then there was the matter of pay — a master's pay, according to the Captain. Considering that his berth and meals were provided, the Captain was correct in predicting that the voyage could make him a prosperous man. It was flattering to think of himself as a man of authority. Of course — chilling thought — if he failed in a moment of crisis, the ship and all the lives on it could be lost . . . He determined that he would survive this voyage, whatever it took. He would begin by applying himself to learn everything he could about seamanship. He resolved to pay more attention to his spiritual condition, as well. He set aside some time every day to read his Bible and pray.

September 1585: Dead Reckoning

That very day he learned about the bells. The boatswain called him to the quarterdeck just before midday. Piet, the, first mate, was there, alongside the helmsman, who held the ship's whipstaff with both hands. A sailor stood behind them, with a sandglass looped around his neck — an hourglass, basically, encased in a wooden stand. Piet told him to stand by, and relieve the sailor of the glass, as soon as the sand finished running to the bottom. When it did so, the sailor called out, and the ship's bell was rung eight times — it was the end of the third, or forenoon watch, and the beginning of the fourth, or afternoon watch. "You must do as he did." John was instructed. "As soon as the sand runs out, you must turn the glass upside down. Then you ring the bell — once on the first turning, twice on the second, and so on. When you ring eight bells, your watch is over, and you will be relieved. Do not do this either too early, or too late."

The system was simple. The sandglass held enough sand for exactly half an hour. Each turning of the glass was announced by the ringing of the bell — one bell for the first turning, two for the second, and so on. When eight bells rang, it was the end of a four-hour watch, which meant there were six watches in a day.

At each turning, the first mate looked at the compass in the binnacle — a cabinet in front of the helm and recorded the ship's heading at that moment. At the end of the watch, those headings could be used to calculate the probable course that the ship had sailed during the watch. The navigator could then estimate the ship's position and choose the headings for the next watch. John watched all this with some interest for a while, but by the time he rang eight bells, he was bored. The navigator noticed this and summoned one of the ship's boys to take the glass from John. "Are you bored?" asked Homer. "Perhaps you do not grasp why the time must be measured so carefully?"

John shrugged and nodded, in agreement."Perhaps you can explain it to me."

"Aye, those are the Captain's orders. Report to me on the third watch, tomorrow."

The *Egyptian Queen* sailed west all that day, and the next — more or less. The winds were from the north, or westerly for most of the time. Sailing directly into the wind was not an option, so the *Queen* had to tack — sail a zigzag course at an angle to the wind. She could make six knots with a good following breeze, but progress to the West was slower than Captain Foxe wished — he was on the quarterdeck a good deal of the time, looking for a faster tack, or hoping for a shift in the wind. They were sailing more or less parallel to a coastline — John supposed it must be England, since he believed that France was in the opposite direction. The second day, the wind shifted to the northeast, and the *Queen* was trimmed to a "broad reach" — the wind was not directly behind the ship, but mostly from the stern. With the proper trim, her speed increased noticeably. Captain Foxe went to the poop deck, to measure the speed himself."That's ten knots!" he cried in satisfaction. But before long, the wind shifted again, and it was back to tacking.

Foxe was clearly frustrated with their slow progress. He paced the quarterdeck, was in and out of his cabin. John knew enough about geography to understand that if they continued westward, they would eventually reach the coast of Cornwall and then pass into the open Atlantic. This was a little confusing, because he was pretty sure that Spain was to the south. Perhaps the Navigator could explain it to him.

John found the Navigator on the quarter deck at eight bells — beginning of the third watch. Homer took him into the chartroom, off the quarterdeck, and spread out a map of the Atlantic Ocean. John looked at it, and was able to find England, France (to the East, just as he thought), and Spain (he was right about Spain, too).

"So, Master Carpenter," said Homer. "If you wanted to sail from England to, say, Portugal, how would you set your course?"

John traced his finger from England southward "I'd sail due south, until I hit Spain, and then sail west along the coast, until I could go south to Portugal."

Homer nodded. "And if you wanted to reach Brazil?"

John traced his finger South and West across the Atlantic to South America.

Homer nodded again. "And if you sail westward, and strike land, how do you know you have reached Brazil, instead of Panama, or Cuba, or Virginia?" he indicated all four locations with his own finger.

John was stumped for a moment. "I suppose I could land, and ask someone where I was, but that assumes that they will be able to speak English. I really hadn't thought about it, before."

Homer chuckled. "You have put your finger on the problem, carpenter. Here is how we must do it. See the lines running from West to East on the map?" John nodded.

"Those are called lines of *latitude*. They measure the North or South distance from any spot on the map from the equator. You will see that the latitude of Brazil is not the same as any of those other locations. If I know my latitude, I can tell the difference between Brazil and Panama, without having to ask anyone."

"But how do you know your latitude?" asked John.

"We have instruments, like this sextant. If we measure the height of the sun above the horizon exactly at noon, the angle of elevation can be used to calculate our latitude, to within a few nautical miles. At night, we use the North Star in the same way.

"Doesn't the sun's height change with the seasons?"

"It does, indeed, but we have a book that we use to correct for the seasonal changes. Latitude can be accurately measured — as long as we take the measurement at the same time every day. If we are five minutes late with the sextant, our calculation will be wrong."

John understood, "So you have to know the correct time, every time you take a reading!"

Homer nodded again. "Knowing the time is also used to track our progress along our course. You have observed that we do not always sail a straight course. Depending on the wind, we must take different headings, at different speeds. After a day sailing on the open sea, how do we know our position?"

"I was going to ask about that," John said. "I thought we were headed to Spain, but I think we have been sailing west for the past two days. Even I can see that that course will not get us to Spain." John pointed to the map.

Homer chuckled. "You are quite right. We are not headed for Spain, at present." He pulled out another chart; this one appeared to show the coast of England. Various ports were indicated, with names familiar to John.

"We are approximately here." Homer indicated a spot on the map.

"How do you know? The whole coast looks like it has the same latitude."

Homer nodded. "You are beginning to think like a navigator. We use a method called 'dead reckoning'. We start with a known location and track our headings and speed to estimate how far we've sailed, to plot our course. Look. Here is where we left the Dover Straits and turned west. He pointed to the extreme southeast corner of England on the map, a place labeled 'Dungeness'. The Second Mate was on watch when we passed it two days ago, and noted the time, and the heading. From there, by tracking our heading and speed, I can plot our approximate course." He traced a zigzag line westward and slightly southward, from Dungeness. "Two days later, we are approximately here," he pointed to the chart again.

"I am a carpenter," said John, "and I know from experience that every measurement has some error. A series of measurements, each based on a previous one, simply increases the error. You have to be able to compare your measurements to the actual structure, or you'll waste a lot of wood."

Homer looked at him. "You are correct. That is why we check our latitude at least twice a day and reset the sandglass every day when the sun is due south — at noon. All of our instruments are subject to error, so we have to check our plots against any landmarks when we can. We check our speed and heading every half hour. And then we correct our calculations as best we can. Here is an example. Look at the chart. If we continue due west from where I think we are, what will happen to the ship?

"She'll run aground on this large island," said John, leaning over the map, and pointing to a feature labeled 'Isle of Wight'.

"Very Good. So, unless we are far off course, we should sight the Isle of Wight by this evening. If we do not sight it by dawn tomorrow, we will know that we are far to the south of where I think we are. If we do sight it, the time and heading will allow us to correct our position, and we will begin our dead reckoning again once we can no longer see land."

"Can you tell me where we are headed?"

"This is not general knowledge. But, as you are an officer, I can tell you that we are due in Plymouth" — he pointed to a spot on the map at the extreme southwest — "two days from now. The Captain fears that we may not make it in time, which is why he paces the deck so."

"How far is it?"

"Well over a hundred miles. With a following wind and a broad reach, we could make it in less than a day. As long as we have to tack into the wind, our progress will be slower."

John left the chartroom with a fresh appreciation for the sailor's craft. Not that different from carpentry, in some ways. Careful measurement, and constant double checking.

It was at the beginning of the sixth watch that John heard the lookout cry "Land, Ho!" It was the Isle of Wight, just as predicted. They sailed well south of the Island since their destination was both west and south. They were still tacking into a westerly breeze.

Later that night, during the first watch, John was awakened by a change in the creaking rhythm of the ship. He could tell that they were moving faster — hopefully in the right direction. He was back on deck at four bells of the second watch. The sun was rising in the East, and the *Queen* was humming along on a broad reach, before a northeast wind — nine knots, according to the helmsman. The waves had whitecaps, and spray was splashing at the bow. The surgeon, back in his cabin, was seasick, but John, on the quarterdeck, felt invigorated. What a way to travel!

By noon, the wind had shifted again, and they were back to tacking. The Captain paced the deck impatiently. They still made progress all that day — the officers were still learning how to handle this particular vessel, which practically speaking, was on her maiden voyage. Minor changes to the sails and the tack headings began to squeeze out just a little bit more speed and distance.

They were completely out of sight of land, now. The navigator had gambled that a more direct heading would save them time, might even find a more favorable wind. "There is a headland at Start Point, that reaches far to the south," explained the navigator. "If we strike it directly, we can save 10 miles. Plymouth is actually northwest of the point."

All that day, there was little to see except seabirds. At dusk, the lookout spotted land, and they passed Start Point in the dark. From then, they were tacking directly into a northwest wind, toward Plymouth. They sailed into the harbor at the end of the morning watch. John was already up, curious to see what their destination was all about.

The harbor was full of ships. Men who could, crowded the rails to see the sight. Two dozen ships, at least, he thought, were anchored together. Five or six large galleons, plus smaller brigantines and caravels, some carracks. The *Egyptian Queen* anchored near them, and Captain Foxe and the First Mate boarded a longboat: which was rowed to one of the galleons. It was a while before he returned, and he was smiling. "We made it, Lads!" he addressed the crew. "We will be leaving with the tide."

Within hours, the tide had turned, and the fleet eased out of the harbor to the open sea. All the captains seemed to know their new destination and formed into a more-or-less orderly assembly of ships, all headed in the same direction — south. John felt vindicated. Spain, after all!

Just before nightfall, the crew and soldiers were assembled on the main deck. Captain Foxe addressed them from the quarterdeck. "Seamen and Soldiers! Brothers! We are on our way at last! No doubt some of you have deduced that we are bound for Spain. You see that we are part of a mighty fleet, and we number in the thousands. Our commander is none other than Sir Francis Drake!" At this, there was a great buzz: Drake, who had raided Panama, and captured forty tons of silver, so much that he could not carry it away! Drake, who had sailed around the world and brought back treasure worth 600,000 pounds! The men were excited and began to cheer. Foxe waited until they got quiet. "Each of us must know his duty and do it. God willing, we will triumph. Long live the Queen!"

John joined the hurrahs almost reflexively. "*And long live the Egyptian Queen*, he thought to himself. *May we all be protected*," though he knew that was most unlikely. It was bracing to be part of such an enterprise, at such a time as this. He sobered himself with the reminder that this was war.

At dinner, with the other officers, the sense of excitement persisted. There were questions for Captain Foxe, most of which he answered evasively, if at all. Inevitably, the questions focused on their prospects for plunder and riches. "That will depend on circumstances that I cannot control," said Foxe. "If we happen to catch the treasure fleet, then we will have a fight on our hands, but we could be home in just a few months. If we do not, then we shall have to seek our fortunes farther afield. Remember that half of any cargo we take belongs to the crown, and our investors will claim at least half of what's left. After we divide our portion among the crew, there may well be some grumbling. You can count on your wages; any more than that will be a bonus."

The infantry lieutenant, Alexander Cooper, was younger than John had first supposed. His family were coopers — barrel makers, as his surname suggested. They had enough money and influence to obtain an officer's commission for their second son, which might well lead to a career if he survived long enough. He had no actual experience in battle, nor did most of the recruits under his command. The presumption was that he would learn his trade under the watchful mentorship of his commander, an experienced soldier. Somehow, at the last moment, his commander and twenty of the most experienced soldiers in the unit had not shown up for the muster, and Cooper had led the rest to their rendezvous with the *Egyptian Queen*. Thus, the delay that Captain Foxe had been so annoyed by. "I know I owe you an apology for our tardiness," he said, "but I am still learning this business of warfare."

"Still learning? What have ye learned thus far?"

"Well not very much. I know how to drill the men, and I have heard something of tactics. I shall have to rely on my commander's orders for the rest, I suppose."

Foxe snorted, "Let us hope that 'something of tactics' will be enough!"

Cooper ignored the sarcasm. "I confess that I am inexperienced in the arts of war. I hope and trust that my courage will overcome whatever I lack in that regard, in the heat of battle. I have heard that Englishmen can outfight any army in the world."

Foxe looked at him hard, with a hint of pity. Then his expression softened, and he nodded, "I have heard the same."

"My only fear," added Cooper, "is that my courage may fail me on the battlefield, in front of my men, and that I shall disgrace myself and my family. Better death, I think than dishonor."

This was more than John or any of the officers were prepared to hear. John looked across the table at Benby, who merely gazed back at him.

"Noble sentiments!" said Foxe. "I hope it will be neither." Later, he confided to John, "It seems a shame to send such a tender calf to the lion's den. His captain should have a guilty conscience, for abandoning him and his recruits to their fate."

"Why do you say abandoned? Do you know why the commander failed to show up?"

"I am not certain, but most likely our missing commander got a more lucrative offer and took his most experienced soldiers with him. They could be fighting in the Netherlands now, for the Dutch, or the Spanish; a mercenary soldier follows the money."

How do you know that Englishmen can outfight any other army?"

"I don't know anything of the sort. I merely said that I have heard others say so. In Antwerp, you could hear the same thing said — about Dutchmen, and in Madrid, the same about Spaniards."

"But you have fought in battles yourself, have you not?"

Foxe sighed. "That is something that I do not dwell on." He looked at John with a clouded gaze. "I will say only that I have seen many things that I do not care to recall and learned that most men's talk about fighting prowess is puffery. Boasting cheapens the cost of war, and only a fool would predict the outcome of a battle."

They sailed south by dead reckoning. Sixteen days later, Drake's fleet attacked Vigo, a port city on Spain's northwest coast. The city was not heavily defended, but neither was there much loot to plunder. John stayed aboard the *Queen* for the 10 days it took to resupply the fleet. Then they were off to sea, again, bearing west, then south.

Volume 2: The Way of the Sea

Part 8: Casualties of War

October 1585: Arms and Men

They were out of sight of land for nearly a month. The weather was generally pleasant, and their progress was limited to the speed of the slowest vessel in the fleet. The *Egyptian Queen* was among the faster ships, a fact that Captain Billy Foxe mentioned more than once. No one said what their destination was, but after two weeks, it was clear that Spain was behind them. John's military training began in earnest.

It started with the artillery. John reported to Dick Benby, the gunnery officer, at the bow of the *Queen*, next to one of the large cast iron culverins. Benby was born to the name Ndikwe Mbembe in a land he called Ndongo, an African kingdom that the Portuguese called "Angola." A thousand or so of London's residents were ex-slaves of his sort; smaller numbers could be found in various port cities. For Dick, employment was hard to find. Going to sea again meant regular meals (usually) and a place to sleep. Over several voyages, he learned the skills of a sailor, then mastered them. And he had a knack for gunnery; his crews loaded guns faster and shot more accurately than most. His English was not fluent enough to get him an officer's berth on very many other ships, but Captain Billy Foxe needed a gunnery officer when the most experienced men were already hired for another ship. For Dick, this was an opportunity for advancement in his new profession. Foxe's reputation for risky decisions did not deter him.

"So, Carpenter! They tell me you built these gun carriages?" Benby's accent was somehow rounded, and smooth, but intelligible.

"Yes, I did."

"Good work, I think." He smiled. "I show you how to work this gun." He signaled to a crew of four men. At his command, they hauled on the tackle to pull the gun fully inside the hull. This was no mean feat — the gun and its carriage weighed nearly a ton. Extensive use of block and tackle gear made it feel more like five hundred pounds, but it was still more than one or two men could easily move, even with the wheels on the carriage. Then one man shoved a "swab" (a pole with a wet rag on the end) down the muzzle; as soon as the swab was pulled out, a crewman on the opposite side of the muzzle shoved an imaginary powder charge down the barrel and tamped it with another pole-like tool. A third man fitted a fuse (twisted rope with embedded gunpowder) into a small hole at the butt end. Next, a "cannonball" was shoved down the muzzle. It was slightly smaller than the bore of the gun, so the gap, called "windage," had to be filled with more material. Then, the gun had to be "run out" — rolled forward so that the muzzle protruded out the gun port of the hull — work for three or four men. The gun and its carriage had to be tied off so that the gun could not fly backward with the recoil when it was fired. Lastly, the fuse was lit, and if everything worked, the gun would fire a 6-inch iron ball with enough force to shatter the wooden hull of another ship. Benby ran the men through the drill twice and then replaced one of them with John. John got to practice each of the operations several times until he began to feel the rhythm. It took most crews, he was told, about four minutes from firing such a gun, to retrieving, swabbing, loading, running out, and firing it again. Benby wanted his crews to do it in three minutes. Loosing and tying the tackle, at the right time, and in the right order when you were in a hurry, was the complicated part. Moving the gun was just brute force unless someone forgot to untie it — in which case it was impossible. Similarly, failing to tie the gun off before firing it could be disastrous. Men had been crushed to death that way.

John came away with the hope that he would not be called upon to man such a gun in a real battle — not least because that would mean that the regular gun crew was wounded or dead, but also because he didn't know whether he might commit a fatal error in the process — fatal to himself, perhaps.

The following day, Benby called him to the foredeck and introduced him to the swivel guns on the upper deck. The basic principles of a large gun applied — fire, swab, charge, load, fuse, and fire. These guns had a bore of about one inch and were loaded with a handful of small projectiles — the effect was like a shotgun. Their range was not long, and they were intended to be fired at the crew of a nearby ship. "A very personal weapon," Benby observed. In this case, John was actually able to fire the weapon — in a direction that no other ships in the fleet were occupying — and reload it. It was loud. There was a great cloud of smoke, and the barrel was hot to the touch after it had been fired. The smoke was a blessing, John supposed. It would obscure his view of the damage that the weapon had done to someone.

The last firearm he had to learn was a caliver — a gun carried by infantrymen into battle. It was loaded from the muzzle, much like the other guns, but it was portable. It had a wooden stock and a trigger mechanism. Like larger guns, a lit fuse was used to ignite the powder in the bore, but it was fired by pulling the trigger. It was really a version of a personal firearm called an "arquebus" — it was different in that it was constructed for a uniform "caliver," or caliber of ammunition. All the arquebusiers in an infantry company could use the same standard ammunition, which solved a lot of logistical headaches for the army. The cleaning and loading of the caliver was much like any other firearm, except that a single ramrod was used for all the operations. Trained men could reload and fire within just one minute, some claimed to be able to do so in just twenty seconds.

Since the company of soldiers on the *Queen* included forty arquebusiers, John was instructed to drill with them. Drilling consisted mainly of marching and countermarching to the officer's orders and rehearsing the cleaning and loading of the caliver. For the forty or so pikemen in the company, it was much more awkward, even hazardous. The sixteen-foot pikes could only barely be maneuvered on the main deck. Turning the formation around was a delicate business. Captain Foxe observed them from the quarterdeck and snorted: "It's a good thing we'll not have much use for pikes on this voyage. These lads will skewer each other before the enemy is sighted." John was exempt from these drills, as were the other arquebusiers. The pikemen were equipped with steel helmets, armored breastplates, and leg protectors, which John envied until it occurred to him what would happen if one of them fell into the sea.

Every man in the company carried a straight sword, which was the preferred weapon for close-range combat. Sword drills involved everyone in the company. John was given a training sword and taught to parry, thrust, and slash. The results were not impressive, apparently. After a few days, Dick Benby called him aside. "Captain says you have had enough of that infantry training. Better you should fight like a seaman." Benby took him to the foredeck, where he had a pair of shorter, curved swords. "On ship, you fight with a cutlass!" The cutlass was sharpened on only one edge — the other was blunt. Unlike the infantry sword, the hilt was protected by a steel "bell" — once his hand was on the hilt, the steel wrapped almost all the way around his hand — which was needful, since cutlass fighting involved more slashing than thrusting, and chopping off an opponent's sword hand was an obvious tactic. A proper stance held the other arm behind the body, well out of reach.

Benby walked him through a series of drills, emphasizing footwork and agility. This went on for several days; eventually, he insisted that John spar with him. John was reluctant at first, but he soon realized that Benby was skilled enough to defend himself against any of John's flailing attacks. Over time, John learned to control his blade and keep his balance, and the sparring took on the character of a dance. John began to feel confident with the cutlass until Benby showed him just how easy it was to get his legs crossed and fall to the deck. It was discouraging. "You getting the way of it; don't have to be as good as me, just good enough to survive," said Benby. "In a real fight, the deck will be slick with blood and cluttered with the wounded. You don't have to dance, just keep your feet under you and that blade in front of you." John did not feel as encouraged by Benby's advice as he supposed he should.

Day by day, the weather grew warmer, and the sun was a little higher each noon. It was like changing the season by changing latitude, John realized. The color of the sea also changed — not the deep blue or gray of the North Sea, but brighter, sometimes even turquoise. It also occurred to him that he was much farther from home than he had ever imagined he could be. He was careful to find some time each day to read his Bible — something he had been neglecting in recent years. He was drawn to the Psalms, and found new relevance in passages such as Psalm 29: "*. . . The voice of the LORD is upon the waters: the God of glory thundereth: the LORD is upon many waters . . . The voice of the LORD divideth the flames of fire . . . The LORD sitteth upon the flood, yea, the LORD sitteth King forever.*" He found an unexpected comfort in passages such as these; he began to think that God himself was speaking to his situation. Perhaps this whole misadventure might be serving some greater purpose of God. His resentment began to subside. During the warmer days, he noticed that the other officers were no longer wearing their doublets, and the wool stockings he had known all his life were uncomfortable. Soon, he adopted their dress when he was on watch — a loose-fitting shirt, loose breeches, and the broad-brimmed hat that the Widow Smith had given him. On a night watch, he wore a doublet for the chill.

John's life on board developed a rhythm. There was not a great deal of carpentry work aboard the *Queen* — most of her was newly built. He was assigned to a regular rotation of watches and inspections. He was not always on duty at the same time of day; watch assignments were rotated so that none of the officers had to work all night, every night. He found time to sleep when he was off duty. When he did draw a night watch, he walked the deck and gazed at the starry skies; most of the constellations were familiar, but as they sailed farther south, new stars appeared across the southern horizon at the ship's bow. In the distance, the lamps of the various vessels could be dimly seen. Otherwise, the night was completely dark unless the moon was visible. On a moonless night, the stars shone brighter. On one such night, Homer the navigator joined him on the quarterdeck. "Have you seen these stars before?" John pointed to the south.

"Indeed. These are the stars of my childhood," replied Homer. "They are only visible here, and places farther south."

"Your homeland is near here?"

Homer sighed and nodded. "A few days sailing, with a favorable wind. But we are not going that way."

"How long since you have been there? Do you have family in that place?"

Homer sighed again. "It has been many years. I once had a family, but no more." He looked at the sea. "In my youth, I lived on the banks of the great river they call Senegal. There was a war. The Portuguese were trading guns for slaves, and all my village were traded for firearms. Our kingdom was at war with another, and they raided our village when I was still only sixteen years old. Our king did the same to their villages because no kingdom can survive without the weapons to defend itself. All of us were taken to the ships, and then to Brazil, to labor in the sugar fields."

"Perhaps your family is still living, in Brazil?" John suggested.

Homer shook his head. "If you had ever made that crossing, you would know that most do not survive it. Those that do are put to work in the fields. Some few have escaped into the forest; most succumb to the fever after a few years. I watched as most of my family died on that ship and were thrown into the sea. That should have been my fate as well, but Allah had other plans for me."

"I did not know you were a Saracen."

"That is what you call me. I have served God by many names; Allah is the one I knew from my youth."

Uncomfortable, John changed the subject: "If we continue southwards, will we see more new stars? How many could there be?"

Homer nodded. "Though I have never been so far south that all the stars are unfamiliar, I believe that there must be places where even the Pole Star cannot be seen. Nonetheless, the sky is full of stars. Portuguese seamen have said so."

John was surprised to think this was possible. That there should be stars that no one in England had ever seen! If there were a place on the earth where the sky was completely different, how could the earth itself not be alien as well? What bizarre beasts and peoples might inhabit such a place? There was something that stirred him about the possibilities but also troubled him. Something was lost when the familiar was left behind. It left a void that the new and exotic could not fill.

On another morning, just before sunup, John was on the quarter-deck again, when Dick Benby emerged from a cabin below him and walked across the main deck. Benby had a wooden bucket and a length of rope. He walked to the rail and lowered the bucket into the sea. Then he took off his shirt and breeches, and dumped the sea water over his head, so that the water ran down his body, and off the deck, back into the sea. He repeated this with three more buckets. He shook the droplets off his body and stood at the rail for several minutes. Then he appeared to rub something over his body, before dressing again.

John turned to the helmsman: "What is he doing?"

"I think it has something to do with his religion."

"Does he do this often?"

The helmsman nodded "Most days, I think. It appears to be a habit."

As Benby turned toward the quarterdeck, he greeted John, "Good day, Sir!"

John was still not accustomed to being addressed as "Sir" but he returned the greeting. "and to you, Sir. But I must ask what you have been doing at the rail this morning?"

Benby smiled. "Bathing."

"But I am told that you do this nearly every day. Is it a religious ritual?"

Benby chuckled. "No. In my homeland, a man who neglects to bathe and groom himself is — how you say — a failed man? I do not know the English term for it — not meeting his obligations to his people. Not civilized."

"I can't remember the last time I bathed. Englishmen hardly ever bathe, except if they are babies!"

"I have noticed."

"But with seawater? Doesn't that make your skin itch?"

"Fresh water is better if it is clean. But this ship does not carry enough fresh water for bathing. I use a little olive oil after I bathe, to keep my skin from getting too dry. You should try it sometime." Benby smiled.

The helmsman, all this time, had been silent, focused on his task, his eyes on the sea ahead. His belief that the customs of foreigners were not only bizarre but possibly health-threatening, was confirmed by everything he was hearing. As Benby returned to his cabin, John caught the helmsman's eye with a look of astonishment. The helmsman merely shook his head and shrugged.

November 1585: Santiago

It was early in November before they made another landfall. When they did, they were already at twenty degrees north latitude; Drake had chosen the Cape Verde islands as his next target. Santiago was the largest of these islands. It was an important center of the trade in African slaves. Otherwise, it was not particularly wealthy. When Drake's fleet appeared, the port was found to be protected by two small forts at the harbor mouth. More than 1000 soldiers, including Lt Cooper and his men, were landed by night to the east of the port. They left their pikes on board the *Queen*. In the morning they attacked the fortifications from the land side, while the ships bombarded them from the sea. John got to witness firsthand the efficiency of the *Queen's* gun crews. With all the smoke and noise, it was impossible to say exactly which guns hit which targets, but the *Queen* gave a good account of herself, he thought.

When the soldiers entered the town, they discovered that the inhabitants had fled to the countryside, except a few dozen slaves who lay sick with fever in the local hospital. The amount of loot they plundered was disappointing. In the harbor were seven Portuguese slave ships, one of which was added to the fleet; the rest were stripped of guns and anything else of value. Raids were launched against some smaller towns on the island, but once again, the wealthy inhabitants escaped with their personal treasures. They did find some goods worth taking in the warehouses and replenished their casks of drinking water.

Captain Foxe sent some crewmen ashore with orders to harvest any fruit they could find in the local orchards — "helps with the scurvy," he said. Most of his crewmen stayed on the *Queen*, except to replenish water, and seize some livestock, which added variety to their diet. He ordered them to avoid the town, and especially the hospital — "Don't want the fever on my ship," was his reason.

Drake tried to extract a ransom from the governor of the island but without success. In frustration, or perhaps for some strategic reason, he demolished nearly all the buildings in the towns he captured. At the end of November, Lieutenant Cooper and his soldiers re-boarded the *Queen*, and the fleet prepared to leave. Some of the soldiers looked sickly, and Foxe wanted to leave them ashore, but he was overruled — Drake needed all the soldiers he could get, for the next stage of his expedition. Foxe was furious — "Bringing sickness aboard a ship is madness!" — he tried to make arrangements to separate the sick men from the rest of his crew, but there simply wasn't room on the *Queen* to do so. "We'll lose men before this disease has run its course," Foxe confided gloomily to his officers.

It was November 30, 1585. The fleet, now strengthened with the addition of more ships, stood to sea and headed west. When it was apparent that this was now their course, John sought out Homer. "We are headed west," John said. "This can only mean the Americas." It was a statement, not a question.

Homer nodded. "I'll make a navigator of you, yet."

"But how will you correct the errors of your dead reckoning, on such a long voyage, with no landmarks?"

Homer smiled. "It is not by chance that we stopped in Santiago. The latitude of that place is almost the same as our destination. We only need to correct our latitude each day, to be sure of reaching our destination, no matter how many days it takes. And we will have favorable winds — the westbound trade winds are strongest this time of year."

"Still, how will you know how close we are, with nothing but open sea?"

"We cannot know, for sure," he replied. "We can calculate our speed, but there are currents in the ocean that may help or hinder us on our way."

Captain Foxe's first impulse was validated when one of the sickly soldiers died two days later. Soon, the fever was spreading to everyone who lived before the mast. Some men took to sleeping on the main deck at night, just to avoid the sweltering, crowded gun deck, with its growing numbers of sick men. Captain Foxe tried to separate the sick from the healthy and ordered that the main deck and the gun deck be washed every day. Dr. Harrington was a busy man but admitted he knew next to nothing about what caused the fever, or how to treat it. More men were sickened; several died.

It was only then that they noticed one glaring omission in the crew that Billy Foxe had "recruited." They had no chaplain or priest. This was not surprising; priests were exempt from impressment; and the church still had the power to protect its own. Simply abducting one was too risky, even for Captain Billy Foxe. Naval vessels, of course, had such chaplains assigned to them. Privateers were in no position to demand that the Church supply chaplains for them, even if the notion of providing spiritual sanction for legalized piracy did not seem a contradiction in terms.

John was summoned to Foxe's cabin the day that the first soldier died. "Carpenter, I have an assignment for ye. We have a man that needs buryin', and someone needs to say the right words before we commit him to the sea."

Plainly, Foxe thought John was the man to say the "right words." John protested, "I am hardly qualified to serve as a chaplain!"

"Ye're more qualified than most. You own a Bible, and you have been seen to read it. I'm sure you've been to funerals before. How difficult can it be? Here!" Foxe handed him a book. It was entitled "<u>The Booke of common praier, and Administration of the Sacraments, and other rites and Ceremonies in the Church of England</u>."

John was shocked. "You cannot imagine that I am qualified to administer the sacraments to a dead man, or anyone else!?"

"No, no, no sacraments. Perish the thought. I am surprised you would say such a silly thing! But there are prayers in this book, for various occasions. I am only asking you to read some of the words when we put the man into the sea. It would be a great comfort to his companions if something dignified was said."

"You could read them, as well as I."

"I could, but the crew holds you in high regard in religious matters. They believe you to be a man of spiritual . . . integrity. They are more likely to believe that God hears a prayer from your mouth than one from mine (for reasons that you may deduce)."

The last argument had some merit. John was not the only member of the crew to have been "pressed," or otherwise coerced aboard the *Egyptian*

Queen. Now that men were sick and dying, some might blame Foxe for their situation. Of course, Foxe was trying to flatter him, but he had a point.

John was caught on the horns of a dilemma. He knew that words of comfort were needed in times of loss and peril. It seemed callous to refuse such comfort if it were in his power to offer it. On the other hand, acting the part of a priest without the cover of an ordination was illegal, quite possibly treasonous. John did not put much stock in sacraments; he doubted that prayers for the dead were of any use at all. But he knew that others, particularly those who most wanted the prayers to be said, believed, and it would be disrespectful to them (and perhaps even to God), to pretend he was offering a spiritual benefit that he himself doubted.

"What words would you have me say?"

"Ye can pick out whatever you like. There is a whole section of prayers for funerals and visiting the sick. Just pick something dignified, and cheerful."

John took the book. He knew some of the liturgy by heart, after listening to it every Sunday for years. He could certainly find something "dignified"; "cheerful" was another matter.

He began with a reading from his Bible, the 139th Psalm: *Whither shall I goe from thy Spirite? or whither shall I flee from thy presence? If I ascende into heauen, thou art there: if I lye downe in hell, thou art there. Let mee take the winges of the morning, and dwell in the vttermost parts of the sea: Yet thither shall thine hand leade me, and thy right hand holde me."*

When it came time to read the prayers, John found the words moving. The crewmen did, as well. They stood with hats off, and heads bowed, some were weeping. When the canvas-wrapped body sank out of sight, the men looked solemn, but somehow satisfied, as if a necessary task had been completed. John felt he had done a good thing.

Of course, that was not the end of it. There was another death, then another, and John was called on to read prayers again. Soon, he was asked to visit the sick and pray with them, as well. Some actually recovered. Among those who did not was a soldier from Lt. Cooper's company, who asked John to hear his confession. "I am no priest, I can offer you no absolution," said John.

"Just listen, then. It will ease my conscience," whispered the man. So John listened. When the man had finished, he whispered a question: "Is there forgiveness for a man such as I?"

"I am certain of it," replied John. "There is forgiveness for all who repent."

"I repent." whispered the man weakly. "What about Purgatory?"

"I do not believe such a place exists. The dead in Christ must go to Heaven, or so my Bible tells me."

"Ah, good." the man smiled. A moment later, he was gone. John found himself praying, without words, for repentance, and grace, and an end to suffering. When he stood, he saw Lt. Cooper, who was looking at him intently. "Priest or not, you have helped a soul to heaven, today," said Cooper.

John shook his head. "That is not up to me."

"No, but you have done what you could. What is the purpose of any of these rites and prayers, but to help men trust their maker? To repent, and receive the grace that is offered them? To face the unknown with confidence? The rest is up to God."

John had no answer to this. It seemed too easy and at the same time too difficult.

In the course of a week, John detected a change in the attitude of the crewmen toward him, a certain deference; a kind of respect, or maybe fear. For some, his appearance below decks was a harbinger of illness or death. For others, it was a sign of mercy. Either way, he sensed that he was becoming an object of superstition, which was the last thing that he wanted. It seemed almost blasphemous to let the situation continue on those terms, but he was at a loss to do anything about it. In the meantime, there were more sick and dying to pray for.

Occasionally, they were close enough to other ships in the flotilla to see that they were also burying their crews and passengers at sea. Some said they saw sharks following the ships, waiting for luck to smile on them. By the end of the second week, ten of the *Queen's* crewmen were dead, along with eight of Lieutenant Cooper's men. Other ships suffered greater losses.

Mercifully, Homer's knowledge of the trade winds was accurate. The fleet made the crossing in less than three weeks. By the time the fleet landed on St. Kitts, hundreds of men were ill. They were able to get fresh water and some fruit. Men began to recover. But the fighting strength of the expedition was seriously weakened; at least three hundred had died on the crossing.

The lack of a priest on board the *Egyptian Queen* became known, and a priest from one of the great galleons was ferried on board. When Father Chambers heard that no priest had officiated the burials of eighteen men, he was aghast. His reproaches fell on John: "It is sacrilege for a layman like yourself to perform the sacraments!"

"I have performed no sacraments. I was asked to read from the Book of Common Prayer, and I did so."

"What parts did you read?"

"I read from the <u>Order for the Buriall of the Dead</u> and also from the Psalms. I read only the Collect from the Book and read the other passages from my Bible — John, Job, and Timothy."

Father Chambers appeared to be a little mollified. "Where is your priest?"

"As far as I know, my priest is in Harwich."

"I mean, the priest for this vessel?"

"We have no priest aboard this ship."

"How is this possible? What sort of men undertake a dangerous sea voyage without the company of a priest?"

"Men like me. Men who are pressed into service against their will. Men who would rather be sitting in their parish church on a Sunday."

"Pressed? Are others of this crew pressed?"

"I am certain that many are, though I could not tell you how many." Father Chambers thought a moment. "I think I may have judged you too harshly. I did not know that you were pressed aboard this ship. What services have been performed while this ship is at sea?"

"No services. Only a reading and a prayer for the burials."

Chambers sighed, "It is long time past for these men to receive the sacrament of communion, then."

John nodded. "I know that I would welcome it; others would also."

"It is settled then. I will fetch my vestments, and we shall have church right here, on the deck. I will need your assistance."

John shook his head. "I have no qualification to assist a priest in his duties."

"Necessity confers qualification. I shall say that you are a lay deacon, so that you may help me with the bread and wine."

It was as the priest said. A short service was conducted on the main deck, which was attended by most of the crew. Father Chambers led the service from the quarterdeck, and John assisted him with lighting some candles and handing him the various elements at the proper time. It was Christmas Eve. After the service, they sang some carols. John was homesick.

Drake sent some ships ahead to scout their next target, while the bulk of his fleet rested. By the end of December, they were ready to move on.

January 1586: Santo Domingo

Drake's attack on Santo Domingo commenced on January 1, 1586. The strategy was similar to the assault on Santiago. Troops landed 10 miles to the west of the harbor. This time, the pikemen brought their pikes — the Spanish were believed to have cavalry in the area. The soldiers attacked the fortifications from the land, while the ships bombarded them from the sea. Things did not go as easily as they had at Santiago. There were thirty or so warships in the harbor, and they put up a fight. On land, the Spanish did indeed have cavalry, and the pikemen had to fend them off. The infantry was finally able to force the city gates, and occupy the city, except for the citadel. Bombardment of the citadel continued until nightfall. In the morning, it was discovered that the garrison had escaped.

The *Queen* waited outside the harbor until the English flag was raised over the fortifications, and the guns were silenced. Then, she followed the large galleons into the harbor, where the enemy fleet waited. The Spanish ships outnumbered Drake's, but none were as large as the six war galleons, nor as heavily armed. Foxe took the *Queen* into the thick of the fight. John was stationed on the poop deck, manning a swivel gun. He watched as the *Queen* approached a smaller vessel, flying a Spanish flag. There was a lot of smoke and a strange whooshing noise in the air above his head. It took him some time to get his bearings. He was jolted to attention when a cannonball struck the *Queen*, splintering his hard work. It struck the gunwale on the starboard side, above the gun deck, and two men went down. When the *Queen* replied with a broadside, the whole ship trembled. John could see the impact of the *Queen*'s broadside on the Spanish ship — a cloud of splinters and smoke flew up, all along the length of the ship. He could dimly hear the voice of Dick Benby, roaring from the deck below. Then, before the other ship could fire again, a second broadside from the *Queen* tore through her hull. Then he heard Foxe shouting from the quarterdeck: "Hurrah, lads! She's striking her colors!" It was true, the Spanish ship was lowering her flag, signaling surrender.

So ended the *Queen*'s first sea battle. It was John's first battle, as well. He realized belatedly that amid the smoke and noise, he had not fired his swivel gun, nor taken any part in the battle at all — as far as he could recall. Foxe pulled the *Queen* alongside the smaller ship and sent a boarding party over to accept the surrender. Shortly, he joined them. John looked around the harbor. Similar battles were playing out elsewhere. A few

Spanish ships had decided to run for the open sea, as soon as the last of the English fleet was inside the harbor. They escaped. The rest of the Spanish fleet was already surrendering to the larger English warships. There would be no more fighting for the *Queen* today.

The two sailors lying on the deck were still alive — most of their injury was from splinters embedded in every imaginable part of their bodies. Casualties aboard the Spanish ship were more serious — both broadsides from the *Queen* had torn straight through her gun deck: maiming or killing most of the gun crews. Most of the gun carriages were damaged, which prevented the ship from returning fire, and fires were burning below decks. If any flames reached her powder magazines, the whole ship would be blown to splinters. Surrender was the only sensible option. By the time a boarding party from the *Queen* arrived, the survivors of the Spanish crew were desperately working to put the fires out. John briefly viewed the carnage on the gun deck. The sights were shocking, and he felt faint. He climbed to the main deck and clung to the rail for several minutes. By the time the fires had been extinguished, he felt stronger.

Foxe and his crew scoured their prize for anything of value. The Captain was pleased to note that while many gun carriages were damaged, the guns were all in good condition. These were transferred to the hold of the *Queen*, along with all the gunpowder and shot they could find. Under English law, the crew of a privateer could keep any personal property that they took from the crew of a prize — and take they did, right down to the gold earrings that some of the Spanish crew displayed. Foxe, for his part, ransacked the captain's cabin, took all the charts, the Captain's sword, and other weapons, the money for the crew's payroll, anything at all of value. John was sent below to look for anything that might pertain to carpentry. He found nails, some useful pieces of lumber, a tool or two that was of better quality than his own. The Spanish ship was an armed merchantman — sadly, she had already unloaded whatever cargo she had brought to Santo Domingo, and not yet loaded a cargo for the return voyage. That return cargo was, no doubt, in a warehouse near the harbor, but the soldiers had first claim on that, and in any case, the crown was entitled to half of such plunder.

The *Queen*'s surgeon, Dr. Harrington was summoned to attend to the wounded. Fortunately, he ministered to the *Queen*'s crew first, because the injuries to the Spanish were more gruesome. He persuaded the Spanish surgeon to find him some rum — "just to calm the nerves" — and shortly thereafter, was unable to speak intelligibly in English or Spanish. Captain

Foxe had him locked in his cabin. "No more rum for him!" The surgeon for the Spanish ship was more efficient. In a few hours, he had treated the seamen whose wounds were treatable and done what he could for the rest. Several had died during the fight, more died in the next several hours.

After John had arranged to stow the nails and lumber aboard the *Queen*, he was summoned to the Captain's cabin on the Spanish ship. Foxe was waiting for him there. "Carpenter, I need yer help," he said. He swept his arm around the Spanish cabin. "Ye see that nothing in this room is what ye'd call symmetrical," he said. John looked around and had to agree. "Either the carpenter who built this was out of his wits, or he had some other purpose, like building some hidden spaces where a man might keep his most valuable things, I'm thinkin'. What do ye say?"

John was intrigued. "You could be right."

"I need you to make a thorough search, and I need discretion."

John nodded. "Can I have Roger's help? Do you trust him?"

"Like my own son," said Foxe. He went to the door and shouted, "Roger! Where's Roger?"

Roger appeared in just moments. John closed the door to the cabin and explained what the task was. "We're looking for a hidden compartment, that might be built into the walls, floor, or ceiling of this cabin. It might be small, so we'll have to be thorough. All of this is a secret. Understand?"

Roger smiled and nodded. They rolled up the rugs on the floor and looked for loose boards. They took down some tapestries to look behind them. They tapped on the paneling, listening for a hollow sound. They found storage spaces under the bench beneath the stern window — full of clothing. There were also two storage closets hidden behind the wall paneling, which accounted for the asymmetry of the cabin's floor plan. More clothes, shoes, a cutlass, a steel helmet, and a pair of sea boots. Finally, Roger said, "What's that?" and pointed to the ceiling. The beams that supported the deck above formed a decorative gridwork. The space within each grid was, in turn, covered with carved wooden panels, also decorated. John had to admire the craftsmanship of the work — except one panel seemed to be out of alignment. On closer inspection, it was loose and had shifted slightly — probably due to the two broadsides that had struck the ship just hours before. The ceiling was low enough that John could hoist Roger up to it, and sure enough, it moved aside, to reveal a cavity. Roger could get one arm and shoulder into the space and felt around. "Something here. It's heavy."

"Well, fetch it down, lad!" Foxe exclaimed. With some effort, Roger pulled the object to where the end of it was visible below. It was a small chest, perhaps twenty inches long, half as wide, and twelve inches tall, bound in brass, with hinges and a hasp. Foxe was excited. "That's more like it!" It took two of them to get it down and set it on the floor. It was heavy — sixty pounds or more, John guessed. "Check for more," Foxe said.

John stood on the chest and reached into the space. There was more. First, a smaller wooden case, about five inches deep and twenty inches long. It turned out to be a pair of odd-looking pistols, richly decorated — for dueling, perhaps. He reached in again, and pulled down a long, arquebus, or caliver — except something was wrong with the firing mechanism; there was no place for a fuse. John looked at this with some puzzlement when there was a knock on the cabin door. "Captain!" Foxe threw one of the tapestries on the chest, before opening the door. "Aye, what is it?"

Two crewmen entered. "You're wanted aboard the *Queen*," one of them reported, looking round the cabin. "The boatswain."

"Tell him to meet me in my cabin in five minutes, or so, and bring the Captain of this vessel with him."

The two crewmen took in the open space in the ceiling. "Find anything?"

"Aye, so we did. Look here." Foxe picked up the pistol case, and displayed its contents, then pointed to the long gun that John was still holding. "Ever see the like?

"It's called a snaphance. Don't need to light a fuse, uses flint and steel to strike a spark." The sailors looked at it with interest. "Reckon it's the carpenter's share since he found it," said Foxe. The crewmen nodded.

"I need to secure this cabin until I have finished my search. You two guard the entrance, until I get back. The carpenter and Roger will take what I've found so far to my cabin."

The seamen nodded and went outside. Foxe winked at John and Roger. "I leave it to you to get this" (he pointed to the tapestry) to my cabin, without anyone else seeing it." Then he was gone.

John was at a loss, for a moment. Then he said to Roger, "Take the guns to my cabin, along with the cutlass. Then empty my tool chest and bring it back here." Roger grinned and complied. When he returned, they put the Spanish chest, still wrapped in the tapestry, into the tool chest. John put the sea boots and the steel helmet on top. Now to get it off this ship, and into Captain Foxe's cabin. There were handles on both ends of the toolbox, so John and Roger could carry it together. "The trick," said John, "is to carry this as if it is just some tools. It must look as if it is lighter than it actually is." Roger nodded, and off they went. The ticklish moment came when they had to cross back to the *Queen* on a footbridge of planks, without seeming to worry about their footing, or — God forbid — dropping their burden into the sea. Once across, John breathed easier. They entered Foxe's cabin, where he and the Spanish Captain were seated at a table. John and Roger set the toolbox on the floor.

"Captain Gomez," began Foxe," This is our ship's carpenter and my cabin boy. We found something interesting in your cabin, just now." He nodded to John, who took the boots off the tool chest, and lifted the corner of the tapestry so that Gomez could see what lay beneath. "I need the key to that chest, Captain Gomez, and unless I am mistaken ye have it on your person, probably around your neck," said Foxe pleasantly. "I could take it from you by force, but I would prefer to have your cooperation. I am a discreet man, and I am prepared to share the contents of that chest with you, in return for your discretion."

Gomez recovered from his surprise. "Share? How much?"

"A tithe for you, the rest for me."

"That is too little," replied Gomez.

"If I take the key from you by force, you will get none of it. If you don't actually have the key, I'll have the carpenter here smash it open — a shame, it is a pretty box — and you will get none of it. I think I am being generous, to offer you so much for just a key!"

Gomez thought briefly, then sighed, and pulled a small key from under his shirt, tied to a cord that hung round his neck.

John and Roger lifted the chest onto the table, and Foxe used the key to open it. Everything inside appeared to be gold — which explained why a small chest could be so heavy. There were handfuls of gold coins, plus a few items of jewelry, which included gemstones. John had never seen anything like it.

"I will allow you to choose your share, since some of these items may have sentimental value," said Foxe. "We shall have to consider the safest way for you to leave with your share. You may have to stay aboard this ship, for a few days, until we can put you ashore somewhere outside the city." Gomez nodded.

"Also, in the spirit of our business partnership, I will return this to you." Foxe stood and retrieved the sword that Captain Gomez had surrendered to him just hours before, and placed it on the table. It was long and straight and gorgeous — a rapier — with an etched design on the blade, and some sort of jewel on the hilt.

Gomez smiled in surprise. "Gracias, Señor! The sword has been in my family for many years." He reached for it, but Foxe placed his hand on it first. "It won't do for ye to walk the deck of my ship with a weapon like that! One of those seamen might think ye were looking for a fight or might just take a fancy to it. I'll hold this until it is time for you to leave. In the meantime, you and your officers will be confined below decks. It won't be pleasant, but ye'll eat what we eat until I can find a safe way to put ye ashore." Foxe hid the chest and called some crewmen outside to escort Gomez back to his confinement.

When Gomez was gone, Foxe turned to John "Well, carpenter, you're about to earn your pay. Your first task is to repair the damage to the *Queen*. Next, I want you to build me a new table for my charts. I should be at least four feet square, and heavy — heavy enough that it can't be moved by less than two men. There needs to be a hidden cavity under the table large enough to hide something of value if you take my meaning?"

John nodded. They would hide the chest in plain sight, inside a piece of furniture.

"This find of ours," Foxe continued, "is the personal property of Captain Gomez, as far as I am concerned. There is no reason that the crown's assessors should claim half of it for Her Majesty, so we won't mention it to them. The crew may be entitled to a share when we get home, but in the meantime, it is nothing but a temptation to mutiny for some of our mates. Do ye understand?" John and Roger both nodded.

"Why did you offer a share to Captain Gomez?"

"The thing about a secret is, it doesn't keep unless everyone in the know stands to lose something by spilling it. If Gomez tells anyone about this treasure, he'll lose the share I've promised him. I'm hoping that will ensure his discretion."

"What about the rest of his crew?"

"I don't think the rest of his crew knows about his treasure, and he'd be a fool to tell them."

"I mean, what are we going to do with them?"

"What, indeed. Winning a sea battle is more inconvenient than most think. We can't just turn them loose until we're ready to leave. Keeping them will be a lot of trouble and expense. What, indeed. I imagine that Commander Drake will have a plan."

"Should we go back to finish searching Captain Gomez's cabin?"

"Aye, though I doubt ye'll find much. The two I left to guard the door probably started their own search as soon as you and Roger left." John discovered that Foxe's prediction was true. No one was guarding Gomez's cabin when he returned — both men were inside, ransacking the place.

It was late in the afternoon when John got back to his own cabin. Roger had piled the snaphance, the cutlass, and the two pistols on his bunk. Dr. Harrington lay on his bunk, snoring. John stowed the items under his bunk and went to inspect the damage from the battle. The gunwale, he decided, could be easily repaired — no damage to the ribs that he could see. He went below to the gun deck and found Dick Benby. No damage was apparent here, either. "It's because of our low decks," said Benby. "Their guns were ranged for a taller ship, like a galleon, Everything they shot at us passed overhead." John continued down into the hold. No damage, as far as he could see. He would use some of the nails and planking he had taken off the Spanish ship since it was handy.

It was four bells into the sixth watch before John made it back to his cabin. As he fell into his bunk, he realized that he had survived his first sea battle — and without firing a shot. He had done nothing, in fact, other than stand on the quarterdeck next to a swivel gun, and watched the machines of war kill and maim other men. He felt a little ashamed of that, considering the crew mates that had been wounded. He reminded himself that he was not on this ship by choice and had never imagined himself to be a man of war, but something about the randomness of the violence — some killed, some spared — seemed unfair. A sense of guilt crept around the back of his mind. Why should he be spared, while others perished? As he lay there, the jumble of memories overwhelmed him — blood-soaked decks, dead and dying men, a hidden chest of treasure, victory, and agony. He would sort it out in the morning.

Twenty-three Spanish ships were captured or sunk in the harbor that day. Drake's men began a systematic looting of the public buildings in Santo Domingo. They emptied the vaults of the local bank of sixteen thousand ducats — a large sum, but less than they had hoped for. Drake established his headquarters in the governor's mansion and demanded a ransom of one million ducats before he would leave the city. In the meantime, the cathedral was looted for anything made of precious metals — the bronze bells, the crucifixes, altar hardware, vestments.

By noon on the day after the battle, John had replaced the broken planks on the starboard gunwale. He was cleaning up when the ship's longboat pulled alongside. Captain Foxe was aboard. He inspected the repairs carefully, then nodded his approval. "Come to my cabin," he said, then, "Fetch Dick Benby, and the First Mate, tell them to meet me here!"

When they reached the cabin, Foxe turned to him and said, "There is another matter I need you to attend. I have just been in conference with Drake and the other captains. Some of our ships took heavier damage than we did, yesterday. Some have lost more men to the fever than we have. There is to be a *reapportioning* of our crews. One of the great galleons lost their surgeon in the battle, and I have been ordered to send a replacement. I cannot refuse, so Dr. Harrington will be leaving us."

At that moment, Dick Benby and Piet VanDoorn entered the cabin. "I have an urgent task for the three of ye. We have been granted the right to recruit some local men to replace our lost crewmen, from among the prisoners in the local jail. I do not expect ye'll find many prizewinners among them, but we will have first pick if we are the first on the scene. The three of you must take the longboat to the docks, find the jail, and bring back a dozen or so of the best you can find. Arm yourselves and take along a couple of trustworthy seamen — I'm told that things are unsettled ashore. Take this with ye" — he pulled a paper from inside his jerkin and handed it to John — "it is signed by Drake himself and gives you the authority to take such men as you like out of the jail. And hurry; it is best you get there ahead of any other ship's crewmen. Take some money, in case you need to bribe someone."

It occurred to John that Foxe had probably obtained the document from Drake in return for giving up his surgeon. It seemed unlikely that Drake knew anything of Dr. Harrington's drinking habits; Foxe had unburdened himself of one problem and was about to mitigate another. Drake had been out-bargained, or (John smiled to himself), "outfoxed." John felt a grudging admiration for his captain (easier when he was not the one being "outfoxed"). He was still grinning when he left the Captain's cabin and went to his own.

Dr. Harrington was nowhere to be seen. John took one of the pistols, and the cutlass from under his bunk, and met Dick Benby on the quarterdeck. "Can you show me how to use this?" he asked.

Benby took the pistol and looked at it. "This is a fine piece! How did you come by it?"

"Found it in the Spanish captain's cabin. Captain Foxe told me to look after it."

Benby shook his head and smiled. "This is a gentleman's weapon. I can show you how to fire it. Do you have any ammunition for it?" John beckoned him into his cabin and showed him the case. Benby laughed. "You have two of these!? Look here!" he lifted the second pistol out of the case, then lifted the lining to reveal a small powder case, and a dozen lead balls, cloth patches, and some small tools. "Put these in your pocket," he said, handing John the flask of powder, six of the balls, and a few patches. "You'll notice there is no fuse on this gun. It doesn't need one. You load it like this." Benby poured some powder down the barrel of the pistol. "You don't need to measure the amount, the powder flask measures it for you. There is a ramrod built into the pistol stock, like so," He pulled the ramrod out, rolled a patch around one of the balls, and forced it down the barrel. "Then, you sprinkle a little powder on this little pan, and pull this cover down on top of it, like so. When the cover is down, the powder won't fall out. When you want to fire, you cock this back and pull the trigger. The flint will strike the edge of the cover, which will pop open, and the sparks from the flint on the steel will ignite the powder in the little pan, which fires the gun. See?"

John nodded.

"A gun like this will fire, even in a rainstorm," said Benby. "Here, tuck it into your belt."

He took a step back and looked at John. He nodded "A right fine buccaneer!" he laughed. "You need a scabbard for that cutlass. We'll find one in the armory."

Soon, John, Benby, and VanDoorn were ready to go ashore. They had six oarsmen with them, all armed. They left two of the seamen in the longboat and took the other four with them. The streets were full of soldiers; most civilians were hiding indoors. It took a while to locate the jail, which was guarded by a sergeant and four arquebusiers. Their paperwork got them inside the jail, and the Spanish jailer was still at his post, along with a few of his guards.

Many prisoners were held in a series of long, underground corridors, behind iron bars. Others were milling about in a large courtyard, surrounded by a wall. They were a ragged, sickly looking group. Where to begin?

"Let's eliminate the common felons, and look for men that speak our language," suggested John. Benby and VanDoorn agreed. It was not as easy as it sounded. Most of the prisoners were employed as slave laborers during the day, and locked up at night, regardless of their crime; they needed the cooperation of the jailer to determine what crimes they had committed. Piet and Benby both spoke a little Spanish and with some effort, were able to exclude an arsonist and some rapists. Still, there were hundreds of them.

Finally, John shouted, "Is there an Englishman here?" and sixty or so men approached him. These, at least, he could interview for himself. Most of the sixty were the crew of an English ship that had been captured by the Spanish while trying to conduct some illegal commerce with the local population, or possibly some outright piracy. Good prospects, these — seamen. The physical condition of many of them was very poor — old, malnourished, or diseased. He selected five of the youngest and healthiest-looking and asked about their skills and experience. One of them was named Wilkes, evidently the captain of the ill-fated vessel: "You must take all of my men out of here, not just the healthy ones!"

John was touched by the man's concern for the crew. "I am sorry, but I can't take you all. There will be other crews along shortly. They will also be looking to fill their ranks with Englishmen." John found a couple of men that said they were experienced gunners, a cook, and a navigator among them. Along with the captain, he thought he had what he needed.

Dick Benby, meanwhile, had been shouting at the crowd in a language that John could not identify. Three men stepped out of the crowd and began conversing excitedly with him. "These men are from my homeland," said Benby. "They don't speak much English, but I can make gunners of them." John looked them over. All were as dark-skinned as Benby, one nearly as large, one slender and tall, one older. Benby had a look that said there was no point in arguing with him, and John had no reason to: they would be gunners.

Piet VanDoorn had done the same thing, addressing the crowd in Dutch. There were two crews of Dutch privateers in the crowd, or what was left of them. Piet identified three men out of forty or so, that he said could help the *Queen*.

They left the jail and headed for the docks. "Wait," said Benby, "If these men come on board dressed as they are, it will shame them. We should make them look respectable to their new mates."

They found a barber in the city, and pounded on the door, until the barber appeared, looking scared. When they explained what they wanted, and that they were willing to pay, he was relieved and agreed to trim the whole shaggy lot of them. While this went on, Piet located a tailor who had an inventory of shirts and breeches. Benby insisted that all the "recruits" should submit to a cursory shower before putting on their new clothes, something that the English and Dutch treated as an indignity. The Africans seemed pleased with the whole business.

It was late afternoon before the whole party made it back to the dock, where the longboat waited. It was a tight squeeze to get all eighteen of them into the longboat. By now, it was clear that the other ships in the fleet had been finding replacements in the jail, as groups of ragged men were traipsing down to the waterfront. *Well*, thought John, *at least we got first pick.*

Captain Foxe interviewed the recruits the following day and expressed general approval of their choices. John had supposed that he might be displeased with the Africans, because of their limited English, but it was not so. "Dick Benby will train them quickly, and if they are as loyal as he is, we'll have no trouble with them." His reservations, surprisingly, were with the English recruits: "A ship with two captains will always sail a crooked course," he said.

"But surely, another captain's experience could be valuable?" asked John.

"That's as may be," conceded Foxe. "but do not forget this man is an adventurer. If the day comes that we capture a rich prize, he'll be looking to command his own ship, or maybe this one. Failing that, he'll be thinking he's entitled to a captain's share. Mutinies have begun for less."

The crew of the *Queen* was still without a surgeon. John wondered if they should return to the jail to look for one when he remembered the surgeon on the Spanish prize. She was still tied to the *Queen* — the officers were confined in the *Queen*'s hold, the sailors in the hold of the prize ship. John found the surgeon on the prize, still treating the wounded seamen. Four had died of their injuries, but one of them had undergone the amputation of an arm and seemed to be recovering. Another had a deep wound on his leg, that had been sutured, and looked to John like it would heal. He was no surgeon, but John thought the Spaniard had shown his competency. The man's name was Antonio Lopez. He spoke some English. John asked if he would consider serving the crew of the *Queen*. "Si Senor, just as soon as I finish here." He inspected the wounds of a few more men, then stood, and picked up his medical bag. When they got across the plank bridge, he turned to John, and asked "Señor, where is the . . . *hombres infermo ?* . . . the sick?

John shook his head "No, no *infermo,* we need a surgeon for the ship." Lopez was confused. "The ship? I cannot help you with the ship."

John spotted Homer on the quarterdeck and waved him over. "This is Dr. Lopez, a surgeon. I think he could be a replacement for Dr. Harrington."

Homer spoke to Lopez in Spanish, and Lopez replied in kind. Their conversation was rapid-fire and unintelligible to John. After some time, Homer turned to John: "He is willing to serve on this ship if we promise to return him to Amsterdam. He has family there. He is a trained physician. He could be of great use to us."

John arranged for Lopez to meet Captain Foxe that morning. Homer was invited in to help translate. Lopez was fluent in several languages — Spanish, Portuguese, Greek, Arabic, and Dutch, and a smattering of French and English. His medical training was extensive — steeped in the classical traditions (hence the Greek and Arabic). He was a *converso* — a descendant of Spanish Jews who had fled Spain to Portugal at the beginning of the Inquisition, then been forced to "convert" when the Portuguese government abandoned its policy of religious toleration. His family was nonetheless treated with mistrust in Portugal, vulnerable to accusations of secretly following their Jewish faith, while publicly practicing Catholic Christianity. John was reminded of the recusants in Little Baddow. There were limited opportunities for such people in Spain or Portugal, so his ancestors had found their way to Amsterdam when the city was still ruled by the King of Spain. They had the means to afford their sons an education, preferably in professions whose skills or knowledge was portable — you never knew when a change of government would force you to flee. Banking was a good choice, or Law, or Medicine. Lopez's family had chosen medicine for him. He had been schooled in Antwerp and Naples, places where the ancient Greek and Arabic traditions were still taught. When the Dutch revolt began, things got more complicated for people whose religious loyalties were suspect, and employment became difficult to find, even for an educated man like himself. Lopez was not Catholic enough to be completely trusted by the Spanish, and certainly not Protestant enough to be trusted by the Dutch. He had signed on as a ship's surgeon in desperation.

Foxe seemed pleased with what the Doctor had to say; Lopez was just the sort of misfit that Foxe liked to employ. He nodded a compliment to John, for finding them a surgeon: "Good thinking, Sir! Surprised it didn't occur to me, first!"

Over the next few days, John built Captain Foxe the map table that he had ordered. "It has these large, blocky legs," he pointed out to Foxe, "a lot thicker than needed, but the size of the legs will make the weight of the table seem less suspicious. Just to be safe, I'll nail the table to the floor, so no one will wonder why they can't move it."

"Good thinking, Sir. Ye're beginning to learn to think like a seaman!" Foxe smiled broadly and nodded.

In the end, Drake was only able to extort a ransom of twenty-five thousand ducats from the citizens of Santo Domingo. The city simply wasn't as prosperous as it had been decades before when Santo Domingo was the launching port for the conquest of Mexico, Peru, and Cuba. It took a lot of arm-twisting to get that much: Drake's men burned a large portion of the homes and warehouses to the ground before the citizens came up with the ransom. Drake decided to keep three of the largest and most seaworthy ships they had captured, the rest were stripped of their guns, ammunition, and anything else of value, then scuttled. The oddest prize was a war galley, manned by more than a hundred oarsmen, all slaves, mostly Turks. Drake took them aboard. The Turks were at war with Spain; perhaps they could be considered allies.

The process of loading all the loot onto the ships was slow. By the end of January, it was clear that departure from Santo Domingo was imminent. Captain Foxe ordered John, Homer, and Dick Benby to the longboat, with orders to put Captain Gomez and his officers ashore just outside the city walls. Gomez was given a hefty rucksack with some of his personal items, like clothing, that he was permitted to select from his cabin. Lopez took the rucksack to Captain Foxe's cabin, when he came back, it was noticeably heavier. Once Gomez was ashore, Homer handed him the sword, as promised.

Drake's fleet left Santo Domingo on February 1st, 1586, a month to the day from his arrival. In addition to the three ships that he added to his fleet, he took twelve hundred prisoners and slaves with him from Santo Domingo; some were intended to replace his losses from disease and battle, others to crew his new ships. He also had seized enough weapons and ammunition from the city and the ships in the harbor to arm them. His next target would be a tougher conquest.

February 1586: Cartagena

It took nine days for the fleet to sail the seven hundred or so miles from Santo Domingo to Cartagena des Indias, the major Spanish port on the north coast of South America. Cartagena was the collection point for the gold and silver mines of Colombia, as well as a transit port for the silver treasures of Peru. Treasure fleets assembled at Cartagena and sailed to Spain via Havana and the Florida straits, because the westerly trade winds to Europe were found to the north, off the coast of North America. If Drake managed to catch a treasure fleet at Cartagena, everyone in the expedition would be a wealthy man. If not, there was still the city itself to plunder.

Once the *Egyptian Queen* was at sea, the familiar routines were re-established. Lt. Cooper had some new recruits to train, and Captain Foxe had some new seamen. Fortunately, all the men they had taken from the jail in Santo Domingo had at least some experience at sea; it was just a matter of establishing their berths and duties.

Dr. Lopez was assigned to John's cabin, replacing the unfortunate Dr. Harrington. Foxe made room in the stern cabins for the English buccaneer captain, whose name was Wilkes. This was not merely to show respect for Captain Wilke's experience, as Foxe confided to John; "Best to keep that one near me, the better to watch him. Berthing him with the rest of his old mates might invite trouble."

The second day out, John was summoned to Foxe's cabin. Foxe was in a sober mood. "I've something for ye. Ashamed I did not think of it sooner." He held up a dull-colored garment, like a doublet. "Here. Try this on."

The garment was sleeveless and fit around his torso, with a high collar that stood up around his neck. The hem extended down below his waistline. It was surprisingly heavy. "Jack of Plates," said Foxe. "Lighter than the body armor that the infantry wears, but it will stop an arrow or a bullet. Next time we go into battle, I want you wearing this!"

John nodded. The garment was of canvas, with a felt lining. Sewn between the fabric layers were hundreds of small iron plates, that overlapped like fish scales. It weighed about seventeen pounds, he estimated. It would certainly stop arrows, and saber cuts; bullets . . . maybe not — depending on the caliber. Still, the collar would protect his neck, and he would still be able to move around. He remembered the helmet he still had in his cabin. Time to try that on, too.

He excused himself and went to his cabin. The helmet was made of steel. It featured a vertical crest, or comb that ran down the middle from forehead to nape, and a steel brim that curved along both sides, pointing up at either end. The helmet fit a bit tight, but there was a lining that he could trim back for a more comfortable fit. It was called a "cockscomb morion," because of the crest, or comb that was its most noticeable feature. Most of the pikemen in Lt. Cooper's company wore similar helmets.

The next day, John was directed to drill with the rest of Lt. Cooper's company. He appeared dressed in the Jack of Plates, with his helmet, his saber, and his snaphance. The Lieutenant looked at him with raised eyebrows, then inspected his kit. "That will do," he said with a nod. The drill was familiar, and Lt. Cooper pronounced himself satisfied after only an hour or so.

The fourth day out, the weather turned muggy. Clouds began to form overhead, though the wind dropped to nearly nothing. Soon, the whole fleet was becalmed. Most of the crew turned out on the main deck to escape the sweltering hold. Still, there was no wind. John and Homer scanned the sea in every direction, looking for some evidence of movement. The sea was glassy, scattered with the other ships of the fleet. It was lovely to look at, thought John. If only it weren't so unbearably hot.

Then, the rhythmic thump of a belaying pin on the ship's rail, soon joined by another rhythm, intricate, not simple, pulsing. John turned to the main deck. There, in the space between the longboat and the starboard rail, he saw the Ndongans, stripped to the waist, and dancing. Dick Benby and the oldest of his countrymen were beating the time on the railing, while two of the men he had taken out of the jail at Santo Domingo were — dancing, or fighting? Each man threw kicks and punches at the other. Each man dodged, and kicked or punched back, all in time to the rhythm. They circled, they leaped, sometimes they kicked so high that they landed on their hands. The rest of the crew began clapping in time to the beat, cheering their encouragements. John had never seen anything like it. He turned to Homer, who was bobbing his head and shifting his feet to the rhythm. "Are they fighting, or dancing?"

Homer chuckled. "Both. They are competing, but they are collaborating. It is a way of fighting in their homeland, but what you see is a demonstration of their training. These men are warriors." Then Benby and his companion began to sing, in a language that was incomprehensible, yet somehow familiar. The tempo of the drumming increased, and the two fighters picked up the pace until they were shiny with sweat. Captain Foxe emerged from his cabin, to watch the performance. The rest of the crew cheered their support. The performance was mesmerizing. It might have gone on for a long while, but suddenly, there was a clap of thunder, followed by a deluge of warm rain. Some of the crew sought shelter below decks, some took cover under the overhang of the gunwales. Foxe retreated to his cabin. A few, including the Ndongans, simply stood on the slippery deck, and let the rain wash over them. In a matter of minutes, the wind was up, and John and Homer were scrambling to find steerage for the *Egyptian Queen*. The other ships around them were doing the same. By the time they had set the heading, John was soaked to the skin, water running down his beard.

As the storm waned, a steady wind blew the clouds off to the south. They had steerage again, and a following breeze. The whole fleet was underway once more.

At supper, Benby appeared fully dressed, and smiling. "Carpenter! You had your bath today, eh?"

John, in dry clothing, nodded and smiled. "We all did, I think." Benby laughed. "We will all sleep better tonight, yes?"

"Tell me about this way of fighting," John asked.

"It is called Engolo, and it is the way that warriors are trained in my homeland. It is not just about fighting. It is about self-control and spirit, and, how do you say — stamina?"

John nodded. "But why don't they use weapons?"

"We do use weapons. But with Engolo, an unarmed man may disarm an opponent armed with a spear or a sword, and a small man may defeat a larger one. It is the spirit that matters, not the weapons."

"We? Are you trained in the way of Engolo?" Benby nodded.

"I am indeed. In my day, I was — how do you say, a master, or a teacher, of the ways of war."

"Then how did you come to be here?"

Benby sighed and lowered his eyes for a moment. Then, "My name is Ndikwe Mbembe. I was an officer in the army of my ruler, the King of Ndongo. We fought against the King of Kongo, years ago. It was my misfortune to be captured and sold to the Portuguese. I was put on a ship bound for the land they call Brazil, but the ship did not arrive in that land — it was blown off course and seized by a Spanish ship. I was still a slave, but some of the men and I were sent to row in a galley. The galley slaves do not live long, and I would have died, except that an Englishman — a privateer, like this ship, attacked the galley, and took the rowers as prisoners. The privateer would have sold us back to the Portuguese, except for this" — he opened his shirt to reveal the scar of a brand on his right pectoral muscle. "This brand identified me and my companions as the property of the King of Portugal. If the Englishman tried to sell us in Brazil, the Portuguese would accuse him of selling stolen property. He couldn't sell us to the Spanish, either, for fear that they might discover that we had been stolen from a Spanish galley. Poor fellow! What to do? He brought us back to England with him and tried to sell us as servants or laborers. But the sale of men is not legal in England. We were still the 'property' of the Englishman, but he couldn't afford to feed and clothe us, so we were hired out to any who would take us. The first of us to run away discovered that our employer had no legal way to compel us to work; we demanded to be paid as the law requires. Some of us had the skills to demand better wages, some of us have learned skills, and some have died from sickness. Many have discovered that the life of a seaman is easier than living in the poorest parts of your English cities and scrapping for every meal. I went to sea and learned the ways of seamen. Now, I am an officer again, and still a warrior."

John struggled to pronounce the name, "indeekway . . ?"

"You should call me Dick Benby. It is a name I have chosen for myself since the English are so poor at speaking any language but their own."

John decided not to take offense at this insult to his countrymen. Besides, it was true. Foreign languages were ridiculously difficult to pronounce.

On the seventh day, they reached the coast of South America. The fleet navigator's dead reckoning was calculated to ensure that they did not sight land west of Cartagena so that the entire fleet could sail west along the coast until they reached their destination. Another navigator's trick that Homer explained to John: "Since he cannot know our exact longitude, he sets a course that he knows will put him somewhere east of his destination; it does not matter how far east, just as long as he can be certain that the destination is to his west when he reaches the coast. That way, he can be sure that Cartagena is west of us, and not to the east."

John understood. "Better to cut a little long, than too short. You can always adjust a timber that is too long by trimming it. If it's too short, you have to throw it away and start over."

Homer smiled and nodded. "And, in fact, we are about a hundred fifty miles from Cartagena, even now. Another two days, and we shall be there."

It took less than two days for the fleet to arrive at Cartagena. News of their attack on Santo Domingo had preceded them, and Cartagena was ready. The city faced the open sea directly to its north, on an inhospitable shore that was defended by artillery — unsuitable for a landing. The harbor was "behind" the city, to the south, and accessible to ships only through two channels to the southwest. Once in the outer harbor, the fleet turned northeast, toward the city proper. The inner harbor was accessible only through a narrow channel, defended by a fort with large artillery. Within the inner harbor were heavily armed Spanish galleys, and a galleass, anchored as a kind of floating fortress.

Drake's fleet entered the outer harbor without difficulty. When they turned northeast toward the inner harbor, they came under fire from the fortifications on the east side of the channel.

John stood on the quarterdeck and watched as a handful of smaller craft sailed into the channel, testing the defenses. Puffs of smoke from the fortress were clearly visible, and plumes of water shot into the air where the cannonballs landed in the sea. The small boats retreated out of range of the guns. "See the splash?" Foxe was standing next to him, "Big guns, those; maybe forty-two pounders. There's no way we can land the infantry in range of guns that size."

Foxe's assessment was apparently shared by Drake. Orders came for a night landing in the outer channel behind them, out of sight of the Spanish fortress. At nightfall, the *Egyptian Queen* and most of the rest of the fleet moved back into the outer channel and began loading troops into longboats. Lieutenant Cooper was in the first boat, when he spotted John, in his Jack of Plates and comb morion. He shouted to John: "You can come with us, Carpenter, and share the glory!"

"Nay, he cannot," replied Foxe, looking sternly at the Lieutenant.

Cooper shrugged, smiled, and clambered over the gunwale into the boat below. It took several trips to transfer all eighty men to the beach. The forty pikemen wore armor, which was a little unwieldy for climbing down the ropes into the longboat, the more since a fall into the sea would mean drowning — no one could swim with that much steel on their bodies. Once in the boat, they had to handle their sixteen-foot pikes vertically — but not in a position to impale the next man coming down. The arquebusiers had an easier time of it, but the whole process took hours.

As his men came ashore, Lieutenant Cooper formed them up for marching — ten arquebusiers in front, in two ranks, then the pikemen, in eight ranks, five abreast, followed by six ranks of arquebusiers. Under ordinary conditions, some of the arquebusiers would have been deployed on either flank of the pikemen, as a "sleeve." In battle, the firepower came from the guns of the arquebusiers. The pikemen stood in rectangular formation with their pikes held upright, until contact was made with the enemy. When attacked, the arquebusiers retreated into the formation of the pikemen, whose job was to shield them from enemy cavalry or pikemen. Drilling trained the pikemen to turn their formation in the direction from which an attack came quickly, without breaking ranks. In a cavalry charge, the butt of the pike was planted in the earth, and the shaft pointed toward the enemy's horse, just high enough to impale a rider. The arquebusier's job was to keep firing, from within the formation, without hitting any of his own pikemen. In the worst case, two opposing formations of pikemen would come into direct contact. This was known as "push of pike" — masses of men shoving at each other with long spears. The Italians called it *"Brutta Guerra"* or "Bad War" — neither side was able to break through without suffering high casualties. Pikemen of every nation preferred to avoid "push of pike" — better to let the arquebusiers fire away until the other side retreated.

Shortly after midnight, the troops were on the move. They had landed on the south end of a spit of land that extended south of the city proper, about two miles to the north. Just outside the city, the spit narrowed to a width of about five hundred feet. Across this "neck" was a shallow moat, backed by an earthen wall, with trenches, and artillery. Within the trenches were the city's defenders — hundreds of them.

Lt. Cooper's men were assigned to the extreme right of the formation, with the water of the inner harbor on their right. He had time to reflect that this battle was not going to be as easy as Santo Domingo, where the Spanish retreated before his men were engaged. In some ways, this was going to be his first real test. "The first real test for them, as well," he thought as he looked at his command. He placed half of his arquebusiers in front, and the rest he held back, ready to charge if an opening appeared in the enemy defenses.

They were spotted, of course, even before the sun came up. They held back out of range of the enemies' small firearms, but still within range of their artillery. Cooper looked to his right and saw two Spanish galleys approaching from the harbor. When they got close enough, they would turn and deliver broadsides on the English flank — which was where he and his men now were. The first shots from the artillery passed overhead; no doubt the Spanish gunners would make corrections when the light was better. Cooper's pulse was racing, and he realized that he was having difficulty breathing. He had a vision of the artillery tearing through his formation, men screaming and dying. His men. Retreating was not an option; for lack of any other idea, he ordered the pikemen to turn to face the harbor and kneel. *Better to face the enemy's fire than stand and wait for it to come from the blind side*, he thought. The men evidently thought so, too, at least the kneeling part. The shots from the ships continued to pass overhead.

Orders came down the line to advance on the Spanish earthworks. There were trumpets and shouts, and the English line surged forward. Cooper ordered his pikemen to turn back to the north, and advance. At least they were moving, and a moving target was harder to hit, wasn't it? Not hard enough. A shot from the harbor tore down the line of arquebusiers. One man fell, and screamed; another said nothing, just lay there, dead. He urged his men forward as if nothing remarkable had happened.

He realized that he had gotten ahead of them, or that they were lagging behind. They were in range of small arms fire from the Spanish lines, now. He turned to rally them, to urge them more speed — *"better to close with the enemy than dally out here in the open while they take potshots at us,"* he thought. What he saw was a shock — one of the galleys had grounded and was spilling cavalry into the surf from some sort of ramp. The horses and men were wading through the shallows and onto the shore behind them. He froze for a moment, then caught the attention of the officer commanding the formation to his left. He pointed to the rear, where the Spanish cavalry was forming for a charge.

Cooper thought of his own men, next. He rushed toward the pikemen, ordered them to halt, and then wheel to face the rear. Upon his command, they planted their pikes and pointed them toward the advancing cavalry. Each man crouched, with his left foot forward, his left hand on the shaft of his pike, and his right foot behind the pike, to prevent it from slipping on impact. Every man's right hand was on the hilt of his sword — just the way that they had drilled. What about the arquebusiers? Some of them were hanging in the rear, as ordered, unaware of the threat that was bearing down on them. Cooper ran out in front of the pike formation, to order them to safety. At first, they didn't seem to understand his orders, then some looked behind, and most began to run. The last to catch on were excruciatingly slow, the cavalry was closing . . . "Lieutenant! Get down!" Cooper turned to face his men and saw a rank of his arquebusiers, ready to fire on the advancing Spanish. He realized he was in the line of fire, and dove to the ground. He heard a volley whiz over his head. He looked up. A couple of horses with empty saddles were running at him; the last two of his arquebusiers were still running, too. It looked like they might make it to the relative safety of the pikemen. The Spanish cavalry was still charging — lancers, he noticed, then realized that he was more exposed than any of his men. He stood to run — too late: his left leg gave way, he hit the ground, he felt the pain — "I'm shot!" he realized, "How ridiculous! How pathetic!" He saw the hooves of a horse. It got dark.

The Spanish galley's attack on the English infantry was visible from the quarterdeck of the *Egyptian Queen*, now back at the entrance to the inner harbor with the rest of the fleet. The *Queen* was ordered to engage them, along with the other large warships, regardless of the fire from the fort at the channel mouth. Foxe had the *Queen* ready, and she was one of the first into the channel. Foxe did not bother to return fire from the fort, as they passed. Fortunately, the enormous cannon balls passed overhead. Not all of Drake's ships were so lucky.

John stood to the starboard side of the quarterdeck, next to a swivel gun, with his morion, his snaphance, and his Jack of Plates. Captain Foxe stood behind him, within earshot of the helmsman. Foxe concentrated on a Spanish galleass, anchored in the harbor, a floating gun platform. He maneuvered the *Queen* to cross the other ship's bow and deliver a broadside straight at her bow. Benby's gunners on the starboard side fired in sequence, just as the other ship's bow passed in front of each broadside gun. John noticed with satisfaction that every shot hit its target. After the first pass, the bow guns on the Spanish ship must have been disabled, because when the *Queen* came about, and raked her with a broadside from her port guns, she did not return fire. Smoke was pouring from her midships as well, now.

"We'll keep pounding her bow until she sinks," said Foxe. "Whatever you do, don't pass her on either side, she could still rake us with a broadside!" The helmsman nodded.

The *Queen* came about again and prepared to deliver another starboard broadside. "What now?" exclaimed Foxe, as a new ship appeared at the *Queen's* bow, cutting across her path, straight toward the Spanish ship. "That's Captain Wilson. He intends to claim her as his prize," offered Piet VanDoorn. Foxe shook his head. "Not much of a prize, that. He'll pay a price for his 'prize' though!"

As the new ship passed them, and pulled up alongside the galleass, the Spanish ship fired a broadside, just as Foxe had predicted. Smoke and flames obscured the result, but it was clear that the English ship had been hit.

By now, the *Queen* was drawing across the galleass's bow, and Benby's gunners delivered another starboard broadside, like the first. This time, one of the shots apparently passed the length of the ship, because there was an explosion all the way back at the stern. Men were seen jumping from the ship into the sea. "Benby hit their powder magazine, all the way from stem to stern!" exclaimed Foxe. "That's one to tell your grandchildren about!" He laughed. "Well, she's done for, now. Captain Wilson is welcome to his prize." He laughed again.

The English captain was not deterred. He was joined by other ships, which surrounded the galleass, and boarded her.

"I thought a direct hit on the powder magazine would blow that ship to splinters," said John.

"Aye, it would. It would probably sink Wilson's ship, as well. Would have served him right, but I was exaggerating a little. Still a good shot, though."

"How many men do you think Captain Wilson lost, just to claim that prize?" John asked. "Why take such a gamble?"

Foxe sighed. "Hard to say. I won't ask, because I don't want to know. Sometimes a captain is pushed to take a foolhardy risk by his crew. They want prize money, you see, and plunder, and riches. If they wanted safety, they wouldn't take the voyage in the first place."

Like me, John thought. *I'd never have taken this voyage, given a choice.*

The two other Spanish ships were engaged and destroyed by the English fleet. Meanwhile, the infantry had broken through the Spanish defenses on the extreme left of their line, and "rolled up" the entire defensive position. The Spanish fled, and the city was now in the hands of the English.

The city was strangely quiet. It became apparent that it was almost deserted. The governor of the city had ordered all the civilians to evacuate when the English fleet first appeared. The troops, expecting to seize loot from Cartagena's citizens, were disappointed, then outraged, and then went on a spree of pillage and destruction. It took a day before the officers could get them under control.

John was summoned to the Captain's cabin at midday on February 11. "All the carpenters are ordered to report for shore duty. Take a couple of crewmen with you and bring your tools."

John found the rest of the fleet's carpenters, waiting in front of the house that Drake now made his headquarters. It turned out that more than sixty large guns had been captured from the Spanish, and Drake was determined to use them to defend the city from a Spanish counterattack. Some had been stripped from the galleys, and the galleass in the harbor, others were part of the land fortifications. The carpenters were to fit them with gun carriages suitable for use on land — similar to a naval carriage, but with much larger wheels, and a "tail" that could be used to tow the gun from place to place. It took a while to find the lumber they needed, but once they got started, It didn't take that long for thirty or so carpenters to build sixty carriages. They did require the assistance of some blacksmiths and wheelwrights, but they took wheels from any heavy wagon that they could find. They were finished in three days.

On the last day, he was on his way back to the harbor, when he was greeted by a soldier: "Carpenter, Sir, good day!" John recognized him from the drills on the ship — one of Lt. Cooper's men.

"How fare you, soldier? And your comrades?"

"I am well enough. Two of our comrades died in the battle. And our commander is sorely wounded."

"Wounded? Where is he?"

"I can take you to him."

John followed the soldier to a large public building, that had been turned into a kind of hospital. The doctors had been busy — there was a pile of severed limbs near the door, and the stench of decay permeated the place. Men lay on cots, or on the floor, groaning, or unconscious. They found Lt. Cooper on a cot, his leg bandaged. He looked pale, feverish. He was awake and glad to see John. "How are things aboard the *Queen*?"

"Well, very well. How are things with you?"

"Not so good, I fear. The doctor says he'll have to take my leg."

"What doctor?"

Our old friend, Dr. Harrington. You remember him?"

Indeed, he did. John was certain that if he were facing an amputation, he would choose anyone other than Dr. Harrington to do the job. "Is he here?"

"Somewhere nearby."

John talked with Cooper a while longer and excused himself. On the way out, he sought out Dr. Harrington.

"Doctor Harrington! Hello!" Harrington smiled when he recognized John. "Carpenter! I am pleased to see that you have survived this voyage!" In a softer voice, he murmured, "I don't suppose you brought anything to drink with you?"

"Sorry, I did not."

"Too bad." Harrington licked his lips. "This is thirsty work."

John nodded. "I have a friend under your care. Lt Cooper, from the *Queen*."

Harrington nodded. "A shame, that one. The wound was clean; I had hope he might recover. But the infection has set in — you can smell it. There's dead tissue all around the wound now, and it's putrefying. The infection will kill him, if we don't take the leg off."

"That is sad news, indeed."

Harrington shrugged. "Like I said, thirsty work."

John said farewell and returned to the *Queen*. On the way, his mind was restless. Losing a leg might not save the Lieutenant's life; it would certainly end his military career. He didn't trust Harrington's judgment.

He approached Captain Foxe in his cabin. "We're finished with the gun carriages," he reported. Foxe nodded. John drew a breath. "I have seen Lt. Cooper. He was wounded in the battle, and the doctor says his leg must be amputated."

"That is sad news. You should thank me for not letting you go ashore with him."

John nodded. "The doctor's name is Harrington."

"Harrington! I wouldn't let that man treat me for a headache!"

"I thought you might see it that way," said John. I'm wondering if you would let me take Dr. Lopez ashore tomorrow, to look at the Lieutenant's leg."

"I don't care to have any of my crew ashore in this place. There's fever in the city." Foxe paused. "But I will make an exception for our Lieutenant. Take the longboat tomorrow morning."

"Thank you, Sir." John bowed slightly and left the cabin.

John realized that he needed someone who could speak fluently with Dr. Lopez. He explained his mission to Homer, who agreed to come with them.

In the morning, John got four oarsmen for the longboat, and rowed into the city, with Homer and Dr. Lopez. He left the oarsmen with the boat and warned them about the fever in the city — hopefully, that would discourage them from venturing ashore on their own.

When they reached the makeshift hospital, John noticed that the pile of limbs was a bit taller — evidently, the doctors were busy. John introduced Dr. Lopez to Dr. Harrington and asked for permission to see the Lieutenant's wounds. Harrington shrugged and nodded. "You'll have to take the bandages off carefully."

Lopez was indeed careful in removing the bandages, to expose an oozing hole in the Lieutenant's leg. The stench was overpowering, and John nearly gagged. Lopez looked carefully at the wound and then spent some time inspecting the Lieutenant's lower leg, down to the foot. He said something in Spanish to Homer, who replied. "He says he would prefer to treat the Lieutenant aboard the *Queen*, said Homer. "If you and I can get Lt. Cooper back to the dock, he will meet us there in about half an hour."

John had no difficulty persuading Dr. Harrington to release Cooper to their care — it was just one less patient for him to worry about. On their way out, Lopez stopped at the pile of severed limbs and looked them over. He waved them on their way to the dock. When John looked back, Lopez was still bent over the pile, as if looking for something.

True to his word, Lopez joined them at the longboat in just about half an hour. He was carrying a lidded jar with him that he had probably looted from some shop in the city — perhaps an apothecary?

Once aboard the ship, they took Cooper to his cabin. Lopez spoke to Homer at length, in Spanish. "He says that he thinks the Lieutenant's leg may be saved. He says that it will stink at first, but the smell will get better if the treatment is successful. He says that this will be painful," Here Homer looked directly at Cooper, "but you must endure it if you wish to keep your leg." Cooper nodded, comprehending.

They boiled some clean dressings for the wound. While this was going on, Lopez removed the old bandages and began to clean the wound. Cooper gritted his teeth, and at one point, passed out. Lopez grunted with satisfaction and began to cut away as much dead tissue from the wound as he could. He spoke again to Homer, who translated: "The Dr. says that you can see the thigh bone down there, but that the bone is not broken. That is good. Also, you can tell that the leg below the wound is healthy and that the bleeding is not too severe. Those are both good." The doctor straightened and then opened the lidded jar he had obtained ashore, then spoke some more. "These," Homer translated, "are very helpful in wounds of this kind. They remove the diseased tissue and leave the healthy tissue alone."

Lopez spilled the contents of the jar into the wound. It was maggots, small and pale, wiggling. John went pale, too. Homer translated again, "These are not ordinary maggots. The Dr. has chosen them carefully, for their therapeutic abilities. By tomorrow, we will know whether the treatment is working." Lopez wrapped the wound in clean bandages and smiled.

By late the following day, Lt. Cooper was awake and said he was feeling better. His fever had subsided. Lopez inspected the wound and smiled, then applied clean bandages.

In a week, Cooper was alert and talkative. John was encouraged to note that the putrid smell was nearly gone. One day, when Dr. Lopez took off the old bandages, a pair of shiny green flies flew out of the wound before Lopez could cover it with a new bandage. Lopez chuckled. Cooper was shocked.

Within two weeks, the maggots had all turned to pupae or adult flies, but they had done their work. There was nothing left in the wound for the next generation of green flies to eat. Scar tissue had now formed in the wound, and the Dr. began directing Cooper to attempt to walk on it, just a little.

Word of Cooper's recovery had reached his men ashore, and they passed back the story of how he got the wound — heroically, as they told it, facing the Spanish cavalry alone, in front of his entire unit, while the last of his men ran to the safety of the pikemen. When Cooper heard the story as they told it, he protested, but Captain Foxe took him aside. "Do not be in a hurry to discount their telling. They believe it to be true, and that belief may help them follow you into danger when it is most needful — for you, as well as them."

"But I do not have the courage to face a cavalry charge on foot. I was only out there to get my arquebusiers to safety."

"Only a fool would have the 'courage' to face cavalry on foot, and alone. Men of that sort do not live long. You did the courageous thing when you thought of your men and forgot about yourself for the moment. Your men recognize this. Whatever they imagine about your state of mind is unimportant. They believe that you will do the necessary thing when the need arises. None of us can hope for more courage than that."

Cooper sighed. "It still does not sit well with me."

Foxe nodded. "Indeed. Nothing sits well when other men's lives depend on your leadership. You are fortunate to have learned this lesson. You were tested, and you passed the test. Thanks to Dr. Lopez and the carpenter, you still have both your legs. You are blessed, indeed."

The Lieutenant's discomfort only increased when he was ordered ashore the next week, to answer to his superior officers for his conduct. Foxe sent him ashore in the longboat, and John went along — the Lieutenant was still a little shaky on his feet and still needed a cane to steady him. Cooper's men were assembled in formation on the city square in front of the cathedral — pikemen in the middle, five ranks deep, eight abreast. The arquebusiers stood on either wing, also five ranks deep; two men were missing in the rearmost rank. Cooper called them to attention and looked them over. A sergeant stepped forward and handed him his morion helmet. "I wondered what had happened to this."

"Horse kicked it, sir, like a football." Sure enough, there was a dent in the side of the helmet. Evidently, he had been trampled, after he was shot, and a horse had kicked the morion off his head altogether. "Probably saved your life, Sir," the sergeant added helpfully.

"Lieutenant Cooper!" He turned to see several officers approaching him. Among them, he recognized Lieutenant General Carleil, followed by his staff. Cooper bowed, "Yes Sir?"

"What's wrong with your helmet?"

"Just a dent, sir. From a horse's hoof."

"I heard you had been shot?"

"I was, sir. The horse kicked me after I had fallen."

"Insult to injury, eh?" Carleil turned to his aides, who laughed at his wit. "I also heard that you were the first to give the alarm about that cavalry attack and that your men acquitted themselves courageously when it came?"

"I did give the alarm; I did not see the rest of the battle, because of this"- he held up the morion.

"Is this true? Your pikemen held their ground, without an officer to command them?" Can anyone confirm this?"

A sergeant stepped forward. "I can, sir. We stood where the Lieutenant ordered us and did what we were trained to do. We offered them our pikes, but those Spaniards decided pretty quickly that they didn't want to become any more familiar with them. We unhorsed a few, and the rest retreated."

"So, your men were well trained, Lieutenant, and they held their ground as ordered. You are commended."

The sergeant could not resist one more remark. "We had to hold, sir. We were determined to retrieve the Lieutenant, or at least his body. For the honor of the company."

This was news to Lt. Cooper. Carleil raised both eyebrows. "You *have* trained them well, Lieutenant. Or should I say, Captain Cooper? In the absence of your superior, who failed to make this voyage, you are breveted to the rank of Captain." There was a hoarse cheer from the ranks, Cooper was feeling lightheaded. He bowed, as deeply as he could, on his bad leg.

Captain Cooper did not return to the *Egyptian Queen*. From now on, he would bivouac with his men, ashore.

The thirty or so Englishmen who died on the day of the battle, and the dozens more who died of their wounds in the following week were buried ashore. There were plenty of priests available to perform the burial rites, and John was not called upon to participate — a relief, really. He'd had enough of death and commemoration.

Among the dead were several soldiers who had been struck by poisoned arrows — the Spanish had employed some indigenous archers in the defense of Cartagena. The remarkable thing was that a mere scratch from such an arrow was sufficient to kill a man — first, he experienced muscle cramping and paralysis, which spread through his body, until he stopped breathing. Once the threat was recognized, the soldiers became wary and nervous. The expected counterattack never materialized, but the English remained on edge. By the end of the second week, another threat was recognized. Men were falling ill with a fever, cause unknown. Some recovered, more than three hundred died. Efforts to quarantine the sick were only partially effective. Foxe insisted that his crew stay aboard the *Egyptian* Queen, and avoid contact with the rest of the expedition when it was necessary for them to go ashore for supplies. Other crews were not as careful, and the fever spread to the ships, as well.

The *Queen* needed to replenish her water supplies and find enough food for the next leg of their journey. Foxe reluctantly sent some small foraging parties ashore. The crew was eager to get a share of the loot in the city, but Foxe ordered them to avoid the city itself and forage outside it. Men grumbled. Foxe emphasized the threat of the fever, and moved the *Queen* to the outer harbor, as far as possible from the city docks.

The foragers had no difficulty finding livestock in the surrounding farms and supplied the crew of the *Egyptian Queen* with plenty of fresh meat. The galley aboard the *Queen* was of limited size, so the shore parties would slaughter and roast goats, hogs, and even cattle over a smoky open fire, or in a pit covered with leaves, on the shore — a technique called "barbacoa." This could be done within sight of the ship, and the cooked carcasses were cut up and delivered to the ship, where the galley crew served it. There were also fresh fruits and vegetables available. Generally, they ate very well, while they were at Cartagena.

Foxe was approached by Homer, with a request from Dr. Lopez to go ashore. Foxe was reluctant to let them go: "Now that I have a good doctor, I'm not willing to lose him to the fever. I need you alive, as much as I need him!"

"Dr. Lopez does not want to go into the city, he wants to look for some medicinal supplies in the countryside," explained Homer. Foxe relented. "See you go armed and take the Carpenter with you. I'll send along a foraging party."

The longboat was full, and they landed at the far southern end of the outer harbor. From there, they walked another two miles to the south, until they reached a small cluster of huts, well inland. The local population eyed them with suspicion — they had already lost some livestock to English foraging parties. Dr. Lopez approached a house and began conversing with a woman standing in the doorway — John did not understand the language, but the woman replied in kind and smiled when Dr. Lopez reached into his purse and displayed a few silver coins. The woman led Lopez to another hut and called out to whoever was inside. An older woman emerged and engaged the Dr. in a lengthy conversation. Some bargain was struck; the old woman went inside and emerged with several coarse cloth bags. The bags contained some dried leaves, some odd-looking roots, and some other materials that could have been animal, vegetable, or mineral. Dr. Lopez smiled and nodded, evidently pleased with what she was offering. Lopez handed her some money and took the bags. He turned to John and said, "Help, please." which was clear enough. John took the bags. A mysterious variety of unfamiliar aromas met his nose.

Lopez was not finished, yet. He reached into his purse and produced more money. He began talking to the younger woman, who nodded and left. When she returned, she was carrying a large basket on her head, which appeared to be fairly heavy. It was full of some sort of rounded, reddish fruits or roots. John did not recognize them — smaller than apples, larger than radishes. Dull red, with numerous dimples or creases in their skins. Dr Lopez appeared to be delighted. Money changed hands, and John handed his bags to Homer so that he could hoist the basket onto his shoulder. The woman looked at him and laughed. Lopez said something to Homer, who translated: "The woman is laughing because you are carrying the patatas all wrong."

They returned to the ship, and Dr. Lopez explained the value of his purchases to Captain Foxe, with Homer to translate. "These leaves are called *coca*. Chewing on them can ease a man's pain and give him strength and energy when he is weary. These roots are good for indigestion," and so on. When he came to the basket of *patatas*, he explained that the Spanish ships fed them to their crews, to prevent the scurvy. Foxe's attention was suddenly focused. "How many do they have to eat, and how often? How do you cook them? How long will they store?"

Homer translated: "One a day for each man is sufficient, though many Spaniards think they are very tasty. They can be boiled, roasted, fried, or even eaten raw, with a little salt. They can be stored in a dark, cool place for at least a year. If they are exposed to light, they will begin to sprout, so you have to cut the sprouts off before cooking them, or risk being poisoned."

"Say no more about poisoning. Is this all we have?"

Lopez nodded.

"Where can we get more? We need enough for the whole crew, for several months."

Homer translated: "We will find more. It will be easiest if we say that we are willing to pay for them."

Foxe agreed. "Not a word about 'poison'. Say as little as possible about these *patatas*, or why you are buying them, as possible."

In a few days, the longboat returned from shore laden with sacks of *patatas*. Homer and the Dr. arranged for them to be stored on the orlop deck, near the powder magazines, in the dark.

Over the next several weeks, Drake negotiated with the Spanish over a ransom for Cartagena. Some of his commanders recommended that the expedition occupy Cartagena permanently and turn it into an English colony in the heart of the Spanish Caribbean, a base for raids on the treasure fleets, and a thorn in the side of the King of Spain. Realistically, they did not have the resources to do so — the fever was taking men every day, and the expense of fortifying the place was more than the Queen's treasury could afford. The longer they stayed, the more likely that a Spanish fleet would appear outside the harbor, with troops enough to take the city back. The local authorities seemed to be stalling, in hope of just such an event. In desperation, Drake began burning buildings throughout the city, to compel a larger ransom.

In the end, Drake was offered a ransom of 107,000 pesos, to leave Cartagena. He and his men also extorted another 350,000 or so pesos from private citizens, along with church bells, slaves, and all the artillery they could strip from the ships and fortifications they had captured — in all, about 500,000 pesos in loot. The fleet prepared to leave.

The *Egyptian Queen* was ordered back to the inner harbor, to load a share of the loot — several captured artillery pieces. Among them were two large "brasses" — 8-inch culverins cast in bronze. Dick Benby got excited when he saw them:
"Captain! We must have these in the bow!"

Foxe agreed. It was an upgrade from the iron 6-inch guns that were mounted in Harwich, and the brasses were no heavier than the smaller iron guns. It took a while to locate ammunition of the right size, but the two brasses were installed in the bow of the *Queen*, much to Benby's delight. "I shall call them Mary and Martha," he said with a grin. John was called on to make some adjustments to the gun carriages, and the old iron culverins found a home in the hold, along with the other captured guns.

Captain Foxe was summoned to a commander's conference aboard Drake's flagship, and he was gone for several hours. When the longboat returned, Foxe climbed aboard with a subdued look on his face. He summoned all his officers to his cabin. "Sirs," he began, "I have just spoken with Admiral Drake. The expedition will be leaving Cartagena within days. We will be taking on some soldiers later today, and we must finish loading whatever we need for the next few months before nightfall tomorrow. You know that I have tried to keep the fever away from the *Queen* these past several weeks. I am sorry to report that some of the soldiers we will bring on board are ill."

There was murmuring from the officers.

Foxe raised his hand to quiet them. "Dr. Lopez, what can we do to avoid further infection?"

Lopez listened while Homer translated the question, then replied, at some length. Homer translated: "The Dr. recommends that we quarantine any sick men in the forecastle, and place strict limitations on the crew's movements. He has some herbs that may help them recover. Getting away from Cartagena may be the best remedy of all."

Foxe nodded. "I have volunteered us for a special task, at Drake's request. When we leave this harbor, we will separate from the rest of the fleet, for a few months, possibly until we reach an English port. I consider it an honor for us to be offered this assignment."

"Does this mean we are going home?" asked John.

"Not directly, but in good time."

Piet Vandoorn had a question: "If we are to separate, will we get our share of the booty now, or do we have to rejoin the fleet in England?"

Foxe sighed. "There'll be no share until we reach England if indeed we arrive there, and if the rest of the expedition arrives safely." He sighed again. "I will be frank with you on this matter. The booty is not as great as we had hoped. We took twenty-five thousand ducats of ransom from Santo Domingo and 500,000 pesos from Cartagena. Altogether, that comes to about 530,000 pesos or 106,000 pounds. We also took several dozen pieces of artillery, and some other valuables, but much of that will be treated as the personal loot of the men who seized it. Since this is a naval expedition, the Queen's agents will claim half of whatever we bring home. If you divide the remainder among all the crews, none of us should expect to live out our days in luxury, on the proceeds of this adventure."

A disappointed silence.

"Has our toil and sacrifice been for nothing, then, or nearly nothing?" Vandoorn again.

"I do not say so. We hoped to capture a treasure fleet; we did not. We also intended to harry the Spanish, and that we have done. We attacked in Spain first, at Vigo, to confuse the Spanish navy, and then at Santiago. The fact that we have seen no Spanish fleet is evidence that they are confused. We attacked and occupied four Spanish seaports, all told. The King of Spain will have to send ships to all those places, instead of England. That is something we can boast about."

"The crew will not be pleased at this news."

"Then do not tell the crew, until we are at sea. They will be paid their wages, and many of them got some personal loot from the ship we captured in Santo Domingo. In any case, our voyage is not over, yet. There may be prizes yet to capture."

There: a note of optimism. With that, Foxe dismissed his officers. John stayed behind. "Captain, how exactly is the booty divided?"

"Well, half for the crown, as I said . . ."

"Which would leave 53,000 pounds in coins and ingots, plus whatever the other stuff can be sold for. That could come to 10 pounds per man."

Foxe nodded. "Our investors will demand half of this ship's share . . . "

"Half!?"

". . . out of which they will pay the wages of the crew, including yourself."

"So, five pounds per man?"

"Plus wages if each man gets an equal share. As an officer, you are entitled to slightly more, the ordinary seamen should get less."

"I think the crew is expecting a lot more than that."

Foxe nodded. "Of course. Men go to war dreaming of uncountable riches. The reality is usually a rude awakening. I will address them all when we are at sea."

"Why not now?"

Foxe chuckled. "Because some of these lads would jump ship today, and search for loot ashore, where they might catch the fever, or disappear altogether. Most of them do not know arithmetic as well as you; they imagine that their share of 530,000 pesos will be a large sum. If their arithmetic was better, they might not have signed on for the voyage at all."

"Ye could be thinking," Foxe continued, "that fewer sailors on our voyage home would mean a larger share for you and those who stayed with us. But we need every man we have to make it home, and with the fever coming aboard, it's likely enough that some of us won't make it home, anyway. You can encourage yourself with that thought if you like."

John didn't like. He liked being part of the crew and was loathe to wish any of them harm. He reminded himself that he had not begun this voyage with any hope of riches — he was only here by accident — no, not by accident, by coercion. Had he signed on voluntarily, would his attitude be different? Would he see the death of a shipmate as a financial bonus? Were there other crewmen who would regard the possibility of his death, whether from disease or mischance, as a financial opportunity?

Foxe read the expression on John's face. "Aye, ye are beginning to understand that men's hearts are deep and devious. None of us is righteous, and none of us can be completely trusted. That is why we have laws and rules. That is why we have discipline aboard ship. If we had a captured treasure in our hold, it would be no different. It might be worse — men have mutinied for nothing more than a bigger share of the booty even if taking it meant killing their officers, and never seeing their homeland again."

John was jarred at the thought. He had accepted the privileges of an officer as a kind of compensation for his abduction. Now, he realized that it came with risks that he had not considered. And maintaining discipline aboard the *Queen* was a matter of preserving his own life, as well as those of his fellow crewmen — even when it involved withholding information from them. He was less a victim than he had supposed, and more a part of Billy Foxe's schemes than he wanted to be.

The rest of that day was spent loading whatever was sent their way. Two more "brasses" were delivered — 6-inchers. Dick Benby chortled with delight, and named them "Jacob" and "Esau." He installed them in the stern, replacing two cast-iron culverins, which found their place in the hold. In spite of himself, John calculated what his share of the sale of the two iron guns might come to — perhaps a shilling or two? In an idle moment, he thought of how he might spend an extra shilling or two. Silly, but it kept popping into his thoughts.

In the afternoon, the longboat began ferrying soldiers from the docks to the *Queen*. It was Captain Cooper's company, and they were welcomed aboard by nearly all the crew. In addition to the two men killed on the first day of battle, three more had died of the fever, but only three others were sick. Cooper himself walked with a slight limp but was stronger than when John had last seen him. He was particularly glad to greet John and Dr. Lopez, with a strong handshake, and a slap on the back.

The following evening, April 12, Drake's fleet slipped out of the harbor with the tide, and into the open sea — all except for the *Egyptian Queen*. She lingered in the outer harbor, while the rest of the expedition assembled in full view of the city. Anyone who watched them from shore would have noticed that they turned southwest, toward Panama.

On the 13th, the *Queen* remained in the outer harbor. That day, the officer's mess was served some roasted *patatas*, which the captain declared to be tasty. He ate three of them, with a little salt, and said he preferred them to rutabagas. The rest of the officers agreed that the novel food was palatable.

Midmorning on the 14th, the *Queen* sailed out of the outer harbor, to the sea, and sailed first to the northeast, in sight of the city, before turning southwest. It appeared that she was waiting for some reason. At midday, as if expected, sails appeared on the horizon to the north. A Spanish fleet had arrived — too late to intercept Drake, and not quick enough to catch the *Egyptian Queen*, who made her escape in plain sight of the Spanish ships, heading west and then southward.

Once the Spanish fleet was out of sight to the east, Captain Foxe assembled the crew on the main deck. He stood on the quarterdeck and addressed them: "Mates, I have news for ye. Ye'll have noticed that we are separated from the rest of our expedition. That is on purpose, according to the orders I received from our Admiral. From now on, we will be on our own for several months. The purpose of our voyage is to confuse the Spanish as to the location and destination of our fleet. To that end, we will be appearing at various ports in this region, to mislead them about our intentions."

"What about the booty?" The question came from Wilkes, the captain they had rescued from the jail in Santo Domingo.

"The booty will be shared among any of us who survive this voyage and reach England safely. That includes you, and any who have joined our crew along the way.

"Where is it?"

"It is in the hold of every ship of this expedition, including this one. No doubt you have seen the cannons in our hold. They will be sold when we reach England, and the proceeds will be shared, as with all the other cargoes that manage to get home."

"How can we be sure to get our fair share?" Wilkes was pushing a bit too hard, thought John. His tone was . . . not combative, not exactly sarcastic, but calculated to nurture the idea that somehow this crew could be cheated out of their rightful share. *If only they knew how small that share may turn out to be*, he thought to himself.

Foxe was not surprised by Wilkes' tone, nor unprepared for the moment. "All the cargoes that reach a home port will be inventoried and valued by the crown's agents. The Queen is entitled to half of our cargo, the rest will be apportioned to each ship, according to the number of crewmen who arrive safely. In our case, our investors are entitled to half the shares we receive and the rest will be divided among the crew of the *Egyptian Queen*."

Wilkes shook his head, "But we have no recourse, but to trust that the division will be a fair one, especially if we do not know how many ships actually return, and with how many men. We are at a disadvantage, unless we stay with the rest of the fleet, all the way home!" There was some murmuring among the men standing on the deck. Wilkes was making headway, John realized.

"Mr. Wilkes," Foxe began, but was interrupted . . .

"<u>Captain </u>Wilkes, if you please, sir!" There. Wilkes had shown his hand.

And Foxe was ready to slap it. "There is only one <u>Captain</u> aboard this ship, and that <u>I</u> am. Captain Cooper," here he nodded to the soldiers, "is a Captain of his company only. He has no other command than his men. You were a Captain yourself, once, or so you say. But on this ship, I and I alone am Captain." There was a general rumble of agreement from the men. They recognized that Wilkes had just been put in his place and they approved.

Wilkes forced a smile and nodded. Still, he pressed: "Can you at least tell us where we are bound?"

"I can, indeed." Foxe smiled broadly, as a benevolent parent might overlook a child's ill manners as if Wilkes' challenge was forgiven and forgotten. Small chance of that, thought John. Foxe was no fool.

Foxe continued, "We are headed for Panama. Nombre de Dios, to be precise. We are to make an appearance before the fortifications there." *Nombre de Dios!* There was a buzz of excitement among the crew. Drake himself had raided Nombre de Dios, just thirteen years before, and captured so much silver that he could not carry it all away. Legend was that it was still buried there, somewhere in the jungle.

Foxe had the crew on his side now, at least as far as Panama. That would have to do. He dismissed the crew and stepped back into his cabin.

Part 9: Freebooters

April 1586: Nombre de Dios

The voyage to Nombre de Dios took just three days. The latitude of the port was nearly the same as Cartagena, so the navigation was straightforward — reach the coast of Panama just slightly north of Nombre de Dios' latitude, then follow the coast southwards. The weather was fair, and the winds were mostly favorable. After weeks at anchor, John found it satisfying to be on the open sea again. The crew was in high spirits — rumors were circulating about Drake's treasure, lying somewhere in the jungle — surely Captain Foxe would try to find it, and if he did, well, they would all be rich!

John visited Foxe in his cabin on the second day. "Captain, I think you should know that the crew talks of little else but the treasure of Nombre de Dios. Do you think we might actually find it?"

"I am certain that we will not find it. First, because it does not exist. Second, because we will not be looking for it. Our orders are to conduct a demonstration before the fortifications at the harbor, then disappear."

"Disappear?"

"Disappear, until we reappear at some other Spanish port, and make our presence known. The whole purpose of our voyage is to overwhelm the Spanish with contradictory reports of the location of Drake's fleet until they are paralyzed into inaction, or a rash mistake."

"Will the rest of the fleet be doing the same? Where are they now?"

"I cannot say where they are now, but it is nowhere near where we are going. I think Drake will keep his ships together, and head for home with his cargo. Our task is to lead the Spanish fleet out of his path so that he will not be bothered by them."

"How is it we were chosen for this task? Are we regarded as expendable?"

"On the contrary. The Admiral has seen this ship fight. He has few ships with the speed and number of guns that the *Egyptian Queen* has, apart from his race-built galleons. We are well suited to this task."

"You volunteered us, didn't you?" John knew he was onto something when Foxe let a smile cross his face briefly. "What did you get in return?"

Foxe smiled more broadly, "Aye, Carpenter, ye have learned the way of me. Drake proposed to load us up with some slaves he had acquired, including some women. Taking this assignment made that impractical, since the value of such cargo declines, the longer they are at sea."

"The men will think you made a bad bargain!"

Foxe shook his head. "You would do well not to tell them that I turned down women, for the chance to lead the Spaniards on a merry chase. Women are a source of every kind of trouble, especially on a ship at sea. I'll have no women aboard the *Egyptian Queen!*"

John had nothing to say.

"Look," Foxe continued. "The facts are these: Drake's force is spent, from so many fever deaths. He's not strong enough to attack any major port. He might as well get away with as much loot as he can. The amount we have captured thus far is not enough to make any seaman rich, though Her Majesty will do well enough, and our investors will be taken care of. The rest will have to be satisfied with their wages, plus a small stipend. If this becomes widely known, there could be mutinies aboard any of Drake's ships, including this one — men will reason that they might as well seize a ship, and become buccaneers, as go home with so little to show for it."

John was sobered at the thought of mutiny. "If it comes to that, you can be sure that many will stand with you."

"Eh? How many, would you think?"

"I will, for one. I've wanted nothing but to get back home, since you dragged me aboard. The rest of your officers will back you too — Piet, Paolo, Homer, Dick Benby. And a lot of Benby's men will follow him. Then there's Captain Cooper, and all his men will follow him — him being their hero and all."

Foxe raised an eyebrow. "Ye've thought this over, have ye?"

"Indeed, I have. We all saw what Wilkes was trying to do the other day. I wonder that you don't already have him in the brig!"

Foxe chuckled. "I'd rather hang him, or maybe just shoot him. But it won't do to move too soon. Unless I miss my guess, he'll make another attempt, and soon. Then we may have a showdown. Given the rumors about treasure hunts, I will have to speak with the crew within the next few days, unless Wilkes makes his move first."

Foxe looked at John with a steady gaze: "I pegged you for a man of honor, Carpenter, when we first met. And you have confirmed my judgment of your character many times. I made a good choice when I picked you for my crew. Do not worry. I will get you safely home, if I live long enough, and see you prosper."

John felt a little embarrassed and excused himself. Praise of his character from a man so self-interested and devious seemed off-key, somehow.

Foxe had guessed correctly, as he was so often wont to do. The next challenge would come from an unexpected direction.

When the Panama coast was sighted, Captain Foxe ordered a surprising change. The English flag was run down the mainmast, and replaced with a Spanish one, which Foxe had somehow acquired. Now, to a casual observer, the *Egyptian Queen* was a Spanish warship. John reflected that the two flags were surprisingly similar; the English flag was white, with one red vertical stripe, and one horizontal one — the "Cross of St. George." The Spanish flag was also white, but the two red stripes crossed diagonally. John wondered if anyone ever mistook one for the other, especially in the smoke of battle.

The "demonstration" at Nombre de Dios was exciting, especially for the Spanish, but not as risky as it looked. The *Queen's* false flag allowed her to approach the fort at the harbor entrance without being challenged. By the time the defenders fired a warning shot, the *Queen* had already come about and was headed out of the harbor. She gave the fort a broadside, just as a parting gesture, and was out of range before any of the Spanish guns could find her.

Once they were out of sight of the port, Foxe ordered the *Queen* to heave to. He summoned John and the rest of his officers to his cabin. "Carpenter, it's time to let the crew know more about our plans. Fetch those two pistols and that snaphance from your cabin."

"How about the cutlass?"

Foxe shook his head. "No, won't need that. Tuck one of the pistols into your belt, give the other to Homer, and the snaphance to Piet. Dick, I want you near the swivel gun, on the starboard side of the quarterdeck." John did as he was told and returned with the guns. Foxe had meantime assembled the crew on the deck. He took his position on the quarterdeck, to the starboard side, directly at the top of the stairs down to the main deck. John, Piet, and Homer stood slightly behind him.

Foxe spoke first: "Mates, it has come to my attention that some troublesome reports are circulating about a treasure in the jungle hereabouts."

The crew was silent, hopeful, eager to hear what he had to say.

"Contrary to what you may have been told, we will not be scouring the jungle for buried treasure. Our orders take us elsewhere, and besides, the jungle is large, and we have no idea where such a treasure might be buried, even if it existed."

There was murmuring from the crew, sounds of disappointment.

"Captain?" It was one of Wilkes' men. "The accounts are clear enough. The treasure was buried in a river near Nombre de Dios, and on its banks. And we are here — near Nombre de Dios. Why wouldn't we a least take a look?"

"Which accounts do you believe, and how would you find the right river? In the jungle, all rivers look much the same. In any case, we are under orders, we have a task to complete, and I am not willing to fail my duty to Her Majesty, the Queen, for a diversion in the jungle."

'It need not be so difficult." Wilkes stepped to the front of the crowd on the main deck. *Here it comes*, thought John. Just as Foxe had anticipated.

"There is a man among us, who knows where the treasure is buried. He has been there before. With his guidance, we might well find it." *Bold*, John thought. *Outrageously bold.* What was his game? Unless there really was someone who knew where the treasure was . . .

Foxe had frozen, apparently caught off guard by this development. "Where is this man?"

"He is here." Wilkes turned. A crewman shuffled out from the crowd and nodded deferentially in Foxe's direction.

"Toby?"

"Yes sir!' Toby bowed a little. "At your service, sir."

Foxe relaxed, then descended the stairway until he could sit at the bottom. "Come here, Toby." He spoke in a softer tone, still loud enough to be heard by everyone on the main deck.

Toby approached him, followed closely by Wilkes.

"Toby, you and I have known each other for years, haven't we?"

"Yes, sir!"

"It seems to me we've had more than a few drinks together, all over Harwich?"

"Oh, yes sir! More than a few!" Toby chuckled. Wilkes shifted his feet uneasily. *Evidently, he didn't know that Toby and Foxe had a history*, thought John.

"We've swapped a few stories, you and I. I'd guess that you've heard all my tales of adventure on the sea, and you've told me plenty of your own."

Toby nodded. "Heard most of yours more than once, I'd say." He laughed, and Foxe laughed, and then the crewmen joined them.

"Then tell me, Toby, how is it that you never told me about this treasure?"

"Well, sir, to tell the truth, I must have forgotten it, over the years. My memory is not as clear as it once was."

"How clear is it now?"

"Captain, you know I'm old. It just isn't like it used to be."

"I know what you mean, Toby. Sometimes I feel like my memories are hiding from me, just to make a fool of me. I even remembered something, once, that never actually happened. Anything like that ever happen to you?"

Wilkes's face wore a peculiar expression, but before he could say anything, Toby replied, "Oh, I know what you mean Captain, it's just that we're both getting old."

"Tell us what you do remember, Toby."

Toby sighed. "I remember the jungle and a river. They told us that Nombre de Dios was just a mile or so away, so we had to be quiet. There was a particular tree there, that leaned over the river. It was a landmark, so to speak. The treasure must be buried near there." He looked at Wilkes, who was nodding, and smiling encouragement.

"Do ye remember the Captain on that voyage, Toby? Oxenham, wasn't it?"

"Yes! That's right! Funny how I couldn't recall his name! That's an old man's memory for ye! Captain Oxenham! Fine man!" Wilkes' face looked puzzled, or maybe panicky, John couldn't decide which. The situation was out of his control. And he was trying to calculate his next move.

"And do ye remember the galleys, Toby?"

Toby stiffened. A look of pain washed over his face. "I shall never forget the galleys. I may forget many things, but never that." He crumpled a little and began to weep. "I am sorry Captain. Sometimes it overwhelms me. Sometimes even drinking is not enough."

Foxe nodded, "I know lad, I know. It's surprising you remembered about the buried treasure, after all that happened to you on the galleys."

"To tell the truth, I had quite forgotten it, until Captain Wilkes, here, helped me recall it. He's been a good friend to an old man, has Captain Wilkes."

Foxe gave Wilkes a hard look; Wilkes did not meet his gaze. The rest of the crew saw and murmured.

Foxe was ready to strike, now. "You are lucky to have a friend in your old age. Does he ever share his rum ration with you?"

"How did you know that?" Toby asked, looking concerned.

"Hush, Toby, a Captain knows many things. Do not trouble yourself. I am not the sort to begrudge an old seaman a little extra rum."

Toby relaxed. "Thank ye, Captain, for understanding. It's an honor to serve under ye."

Foxe rose to his feet. John could no longer see his face, but he could imagine what was on it, just by looking at the crewmen in front of him. He spoke: "Mates, I will acquaint ye with some facts about the treasure that ye have heard so much about. Admiral Drake, who is still our <u>commander</u>," he paused for dramatic effect, "captured this treasure from a Spanish mule train in the year 1573, near Nombre de Dios, as ye have heard. There were nearly twenty tons of silver; more than his men could transport, so they buried most of it in the jungle. They had to flee with what they could carry, which was enough to make them wealthy men, with the Spanish in pursuit. Others have tried to locate it in the years since, men like Captain John Oxenham, who visited this place in 1577. Our mate Toby sailed with Oxenham, not with Drake. Oxenham's men were captured, the officers executed, and the seamen sent to the galleys. Our comrade Toby was one of very few to be rescued, before being worked to death at the oars. I believe some among us have been using Toby's painful memories to stimulate their own imaginings about buried treasure." Here he looked directly at Wilkes.

"We will not be diverted from our duty to the Admiral and our Queen, on a futile search for a treasure that does not exist. We will get home when we have fulfilled our orders." Foxe turned and mounted the stairs to the quarterdeck. The expression on his face was a mixture of triumph and anger — triumph at "outfoxing" his rival, anger at — what? The brazenness of Wilkes's manipulation, perhaps?

Incredibly, Wilkes had one more bid to throw down. "But, Captain, you do admit that the treasure could still be there?"

Foxe turned. "I admit nothing of the sort. The treasure was there, to be sure. But the men who buried it buried it in haste. The Spanish arrived at the site the following day and easily found the places of concealment, even those in the river. By their own account, they recovered nearly twenty tons of silver and sent it on to Spain. They had to beg the King's forgiveness for losing so much of his wealth. It is a matter of record."

"How can we be sure that this story is any more true than Toby's?"

"How? How indeed!" Foxe was visibly angry now. "I know because I was there. I sailed with Drake in '72. I attacked the mule train in '73. I buried the silver near the river. And when I returned to the place a week later with some others, we discovered that the Spanish had found nearly all of it. We got away with a few hundred pounds that they missed. It is not there anymore."

Wilkes looked pale, ready to faint. John suppressed a feeling of glee. This was a performance that he would not soon forget.

"<u>Mister</u> Wilkes, I will see you in my cabin." Foxe turned and strode into his quarters.

"Captain! I apologize for being deceived by the tales of an old sailor! It was a mistake, and I am sorry!" Wilkes knew he was in trouble and made a desperate attempt to save himself. Most of the men on deck laughed at his crude effort.

"Wilkes!" It was Piet Vandoorn. "In the Captain's cabin. Now!"

Wilkes had no choice but to obey.

In the few moments it took for Wilkes to climb to the quarterdeck, Foxe's cabin filled up with his other officers; Captain Cooper was invited to join them. Captain Foxe took a seat behind a small desk, the officers stood in a circle around the perimeter, with Wilkes standing in the center. John thought perhaps some sort of trial was imminent — Wilkes may have thought the same, because he looked frightened.

"Captain Foxe, it was a misunderstanding. The old man kept muttering about Drake's treasure. I talked with him, and I thought I could make sense of his story. I'm sorry I took him seriously." Was this Wilkes's best defense? *It is patently false*, thought John, anyone who overheard the conversation with Foxe and Toby could see that.

"Mister Wilkes, I have known Toby for years. He has never told any story about Drake's treasure before. I do not believe that he has remembered anything new from his past — any such memories are the planting of other men. I hold you responsible for undermining the morale of this crew, by encouraging them to dwell in vain imaginings of buried treasure. Such imaginings have made fools of many men and been the ruin of many good ships."

Wilkes interrupted: "If I have been such a fool as you describe, I am truly ashamed. I admit my error. I can do no more." Was this a plea for mercy? Who could believe such blatantly false posturing, John wondered.

Foxe stood and turned to John. "Sir, your weapon!" It took John a moment to understand that the Captain was asking for the pistol tucked into his belt. Then he handed it to him. Foxe cocked the pistol and pointed at Wilkes' face. "You, Sir, have sought to undermine my authority on this ship one time too many. You have forced me to recall events that I would prefer remain forgotten. Worst of all, you just forced me to humiliate one of my crewmen, in front of his mates. Toby has not much in this world to call his own, and little time left to enjoy it. You have contrived to take the little respect left to him, purely for the sake of greed and ambition. It would be best for this ship if you were fed to the sharks . . ."

"Captain, you cannot shoot him," John interjected hoarsely. Foxe held the pistol up to Wilkes' face for what seemed a long time, then carefully uncocked the hammer.

"Consider this your final warning," he said to Wilkes. If you give me cause to doubt your loyalty again, I will not hesitate to hang you by your neck until you are dead. Do you understand?"

Wilkes nodded. John saw sweat running down the sides of his face and hanging from the end of his nose. "You are dismissed. I could have you flogged for what you have done, but I don't think It would be to my advantage to do so. Get out of my cabin!"

Wilkes was gone in a flash. Foxe handed the pistol back to John. "I suppose ye think I should thank ye for stopping me from doing something I would later feel guilty about, by preventing me from shooting that man on the spot. I am not inclined to thank you, just yet."

"Actually," said John, "I couldn't think of another way to tell you that the gun wasn't loaded."

"Not loaded? I clearly ordered ye to fetch those guns from your cabin. Why wouldn't they be loaded?"

"You didn't order me to load the guns, just to fetch them," John offered lamely.

Piet Vandoorn was making a strange snorting sound as if suppressing a sneeze, or something. Then Dick Benby burst into loud laughter and was joined by the other officers until Foxe broke down and laughed with them.

"Captain," said Vandoorn, "imagine what would have happened if you had actually pulled the trigger!" then guffawed again.

When everyone had their laugh, Foxe turned to John. "Well, you saved me an embarrassment, that much I grant you." Then he laughed some more until he had to wipe tears from his eyes.

"Sirs, we must remain vigilant. Some men are like scorpions. Scorpions sting; it is in their nature. That man will be a danger to us all, as long as he is aboard this ship." With that, he sent them back to their duties.

From Nombre de Dios, the *Queen* set a course northward into the western Caribbean. Foxe kept the Spanish flag on the mainmast, in case they encountered any other ships. They saw a few sails of distant vessels but passed by them at such a distance that the flag would not have been identifiable, in any case — presumably they were Spanish ships.

The weather was pleasant, and the winds favorable. John persuaded Homer to show him the charts and asked for details about their destination. "Look for yourself," said Homer. "Here is the Caribbean — continents to our south and west, islands to our north and east. Here is our approximate position."

John looked. It was as Homer said — a zigzag of land to their west and a long, curving chain of large and small islands ahead to the north. He was able to locate Santo Domingo, Cartagena, and even Nombre de Dios without difficulty. Ahead of them more or less, was the coast of Mexico and the island of Cuba. "Where are we headed?"

"Where would you be heading, if you were the Captain?"

John looked at the map. "If I wished to be seen by the Spanish, I would head to a port, like Veracruz, or Havana. Aren't both those places visited by treasure fleets?"

Homer chuckled. "So they are. And both ports are fortified, for that reason. As you say, if we want to be noticed, both of those places would serve. We might perform another demonstration like the one at Nombre de Dios."

Captain Foxe entered the chart room. "What's this? Planning a raid on some rich seaport?" He walked up to the chart table and stood on the other side of Homer.

"I was trying to guess where we're headed next," John said.

"Aye, and I hope the Spanish are guessing, too. I have not entirely made up my mind on our next course, nor would I tell you if I had. Where would you go, Carpenter?"

John looked again. "It depends on where Drake's fleet is. If our task is to lead the Spanish away from him, we would want to make an appearance somewhere that he isn't, and never will be."

Foxe raised an eyebrow and nodded. "Ye've a subtil mind, Carpenter. I say it to your credit." He thought for a moment, and said, "Well, I'll give you this much. Drake was supposed to sail directly north from Cartagena just a week or so ago."He pointed to Cartagena on the map. "Drake intends to attack Havana if he is strong enough to do so," he pointed to Cuba."In any case, he will have to pass through this narrow channel between the western end of Cuba, and the Yucatan. It's almost eighty miles wide, but if the Spanish are going to intercept him, that would be the place to do it. Beyond that channel is the Gulf of Mexico, and Veracruz, and Havana, and the Floridas, and the trade winds that will take him back to England. Our main task is to be sure that the Spanish fleet is elsewhere until Drake passes through that channel. If we succeed at that, we are free to find our own way home. So, again, where would you go, Carpenter?"

John leaned over the chart. "Unless we know where the Spanish fleet is, we can't be sure of the best course. I can only guess where they might be, but if I put myself in the shoes of the Spanish admiral, I wouldn't be looking for Drake to the East, since that is the direction they came from. Looking South is impossible so that leaves North and West. Our attack on Nombre de Dios two days ago must have been calculated to draw them West, wasn't it?" Foxe nodded and gave a sidelong glance at Homer.

John continued, "If Nombre de Dios sent a report of the attack to Cartagena, that might draw them west. If the report was not sent, or if the Spanish left Cartagena before it arrived, they would be as likely to sail north as to sail west. If they sail west, well and good. If they sail north, they would very likely head for the same channel that you pointed out. If I were the Spanish admiral, that is what I would do. I would hope to get news of Drake's movements to the north, knowing that if Drake is really to the west of Cartagena, he is trapped in the seas near Panama, as long as I stay to his north and east. If I get to the channel before Drake, I can reverse course and still have a chance to catch him before he disappears into the open sea."

"A subtil mind, as I have said," replied Foxe. "But you still haven't answered my question about where the *Queen* should go."

"We should try to intercept the Spanish fleet somewhere to the North of Cartagena, if that is the direction they have taken, and lead them astray if that is our task. If the Spanish are bound for Panama, it is no matter — they will never catch up with Drake. If they are following his actual course, we should delay them for another week or so, until he passes into the Gulf of Mexico."

Foxe stared hard at John. "*The serpent was more subtil than any beast of the fielde,*" he quoted. Then he smiled. "I had not thought the answer as obvious as you make it seem, however devious your reasoning. What if the Spanish admiral thinks as you suppose, and we intercept him on his way north? Will not our appearance confirm to him that he is on Drake's trail?"

"It might," John admitted. "But such a confirmation does not make Drake's position any worse if the Spanish are already in hot pursuit."

Foxe nodded. "Right, you are, Carpenter. We are headed into harm's way. If we find the Spanish, we must engage them, whatever the risk. If we do not, it means that the Spanish are on the wrong course, or that we have simply missed them, in the vastness of the sea."

"Roger, call Captain Cooper and Dick Benby to join me here." Roger returned with Cooper and Benby in just minutes. "Captain Cooper, we may be engaging the enemy on the sea in just a few days. The greatest threat to our ship will be from a Spanish boarding party. I want you to begin training your men to repel boarders. The pikes won't be very useful; swordsmanship and firearms will decide the outcome. Mr. Benby will show you what a boarding attack looks like, and how best to repel it. Dick will drill the seamen for the same purpose. With the number of men we have on board, we will probably outnumber any such attack, unless we are boarded by more than one ship."

"Should we not train our own men for boarding an enemy vessel?", asked Benby.

Foxe shook his head. "I do not intend to capture any prizes, and I do not intend to let any ships get near enough to board us. Our goal is to harass and distract. However, we must be prepared for the unexpected."

"Still," said Benby, "it might improve the men's morale if they thought that the capture of a prize was at least a possibility."

"All right then, train them for boarding as well. Just don't raise their expectations too highly."

"And one more thing," Foxe continued. "For the last week or so, you both know that the officers have been eating a ration of *patata* with every dinner." Both men nodded. "It's a root that the Spanish feed their crews to prevent the scurvy. I want the whole crew to begin eating it, once a day."

"The Spanish, as you say, feed it to their crews. They also feed it to their slaves and animals. I do not object to such food, but some of the crew fear it — they call it 'the Devil's Apples'. They will throw it out, rather than eat it," said Benby.

"Why did you not tell me this, when we first ate it in the officer's mess?"

Benby shrugged. "I find it tasty enough. I ate it every day on the Spanish galley. I never got the scurvy, during all my enslavement. I didn't even know what the scurvy was until I was aboard an English ship."

Homer agreed. "I have noticed the same."

Foxe sighed. "Sirs, we need to prevent disease aboard this ship, we dare not seek battle with a scurvy crew."

Cooper spoke, "My men will eat the *patata*, if I order them to, as long as I am eating it also. In time, if some of the seamen get the scurvy, and mine do not, it will be obvious that the best way to avoid disease is to eat the *patata*."

"It will be most persuasive if we announce this experiment ahead of time," said Benby.

"I will ask for some volunteers among the crew to eat *patata*, also. Everyone will be watching to see which men get sick, and which do not. If *patata* prevents sickness, the crew will begin demanding a daily ration."

Foxe nodded and smiled. "So be it, then."

The news of the *patata* diet received a mixed response from the crew. Benby was able to get only a few volunteers from the seamen, at first. The Ndongans, who had already eaten *patata* during their enslavement, and declared it more palatable than most of what they had been given to eat, were among the first to agree. Cooper's soldiers did as they were told. There was quite a bit of resistance to eating "animal feed" among the rest of the crew. It didn't help that one of the cooks — a man that John had rescued from the jail at Santo Domingo, and part of Wilkes' crew, objected so loudly to cooking and serving a food that he insisted was poisonous.

The boarding drills were more popular. It was proof, in many seamen's eyes, that Captain Foxe was intending to capture a rich prize, or maybe more than one, before returning to England.

May, 1586: The Floridas

The *Egyptian Queen* made her way due north for a week, tacking most of the way since the winds were variable. During that time, sails were sighted only twice — and they were solitary vessels, not a fleet. The *Queen* did not get close enough to identify the nationality of any of these ships, though they were most likely to be sailing under a Spanish flag, as was the *Queen*. There was disappointment among the crew, as the potential prizes passed by unmolested. More experienced seamen counseled patience; "The captain knows what he is doing; the richest prizes are yet to be found."

Foxe did not inform the crew that he wasn't looking for prizes at all. After a week of working northward, with no Spanish fleet in sight, he began to hope that maybe the Spanish fleet was in Panama, or perhaps even still in the harbor at Cartagena. The uncertainty was unsettling — the sea was large enough to hide a dozen fleets. Maybe the Spanish were still coming his way, maybe they had already slipped past him and were on their way to Havana.

The best chance of intercepting the fleet now (if indeed it was northward bound) was to sail further north and west and wait for them in the channel between Cuba and the Yucatan. It would not give the *Queen* much room to maneuver or to lead the Spanish away from Drake's path, but there was at least a chance that they could harass them a little. It felt like failure, but that was all that was left to try. Foxe gave Homer the headings for their new course.

The *Queen* made good speed on the new course; the winds were a little off her starboard, but to the stern — not quite a following wind, but close enough that she could make a speed of six knots. John stood on the quarterdeck during the fourth watch, with the wind behind him, whitecaps on the sea on either side. It was exhilarating. He had grown accustomed to the rhythms and creaking of the ship under sail, no longer fearing that a groan or a thump was a warning of imminent disaster. The smells of the ship — especially below decks — was something he would probably not get used to, but the advantage of the quarterdeck was that he was upwind of most of that. His cabin was upwind, as well — it was good to be an officer.

It was May by the time the *Queen* took up her position in the channel. Foxe sailed east, then west, for two days, waiting for sight of the Spanish fleet. They made landfall briefly on the west side of the channel to replenish their fresh water supplies, then headed eastward again. On the third day, sails were spotted — but it was just a single ship, and it was headed southward. On the fourth day, the weather changed, and a stiff wind began to blow from the north. "It looks like a big one," said Homer. Foxe agreed, "With a headwind like that, they won't be coming northward until the storm passes."

It was time to look for shelter. Foxe turned the *Queen* westward, and they found a sheltered cove on the Mexican shore, to wait out the storm.

The storm lasted two days. By the time the *Egyptian Queen* put back to sea, Foxe was content that she had delayed long enough. The Spanish weren't coming, at least not in time to catch Drake. He was free to make his own way home.

Unbeknownst to Foxe, Drake had crossed into the Gulf of Mexico only a few days before the *Queen* arrived. He, too, had made landfall (on

Cuba), to replenish his supplies of fresh water. Drake had reached the North coast of Cuba just in time to catch the full force of the storm, which drove his ships first East, and then North. Havana was no longer a realistic target, so Drake collected his ships and headed for the Floridas. He would attack the small Spanish settlement of San Augustin at the end of May, and then visit the English settlement at Roanoke, Virginia on his way back to England.

The *Egyptian Queen* had weathered the storm better than some of Drake's other ships. There were some minor carpentry repairs that John had to make, but nothing that he couldn't mend while they were still afloat. The biggest casualty was a tear in the mainsail on the mainmast — the largest sail on the *Queen* but by no means necessary to her progress. The sail was taken down, to be repaired, and she could still make good speed if the winds were favorable.

The biggest threat was the cargo itself — all those cannons and culverins in the hold. "It is well we found shelter," observed the boatswain. "She's riding mighty low in the water. A really big wave could be trouble."

Captain Foxe called another conference with his officers. "Sirs, we have done our duty, as far as I can tell. We're homeward bound. We won't be looking to engage in any sea fights, so I think we can suspend the boarding drills."

"Pardon, Sir," Homer spoke, "I think we might want to continue the drills for a while. As long as the men think we have a chance to capture a prize, their morale will be better. If we're really going home with no more plunder than we have in our hold, I'd rather we were on the open Atlantic, with the trade winds at our back, before the rest of the crew is aware of it."

Foxe nodded. "Aye, that's prudent. Ye must realize that with Drake in the area, all the treasure ships will be moored in some fortified harbor until they think the coast is clear. No need to point that out to the crew."

"There is a man come down with the scurvy, Sir." That was Piet Vandoorn's news. "He specifically asked the surgeon if he could have some *patata* with his next meal."

"That's good then," said Foxe. "If he recovers, more will come around. Make sure everyone knows of his recovery — after you are sure of it." Vandoorn nodded.

Foxe turned to John. "Carpenter, have ye loaded those pistols?"

"Er, no sir."

"Have you ever fired them?"

"No, sir."

"See that ye do both — load and fire them. That snaphance, too. The men will see and think that some sort of action is afoot. Like Homer says, good for morale."

"Yes, sir."

"In fact, I want all the officers, except the surgeon, to be seen loading and firing a weapon. Mr. Benby, have you fired any of our new brasses — Mary, Martha, Esau, and Jacob?"

"No, indeed."

See that you do so. Drill the gunners, too. As far as anyone knows, the *Egyptian Queen* is looking for a fight. Am I clear?"

All the officers replied that he was clear. Foxe dismissed them.

John approached Dick Benby on the quarterdeck. "Mr. Benby, I could use your help with these guns."

Benby chuckled. "Yes, I think you could."

Benby and John went to the poop deck, where Benby drilled him on the process of loading, firing, and reloading the guns. "Take the time to learn it, until you can see it with your eyes closed. Missing a step could cost you your life."

"Do you really think we'll see a battle?"

"Hard to say. Best to be ready."

Firing the weapons was simple enough, but there were no obvious targets to aim at on the water — difficult to know whether your aim was good, or not.

"If we are boarded," said Benby, "the fighting will be close — hard to miss; just be sure it isn't pointed at me," he smiled.

"What if it's really close, too close for the pistol, or even too close for the cutlass?"

"You mean grappling with a man?"

"Yes, I guess it would be grappling."

Benby sighed. "I do not think you would do well, grappling. Best to keep your distance, I think."

"I have seen you at Engola. I think you would do well at grappling."

Benby nodded.

"So teach me something that I can use, if I have to grapple."

Benby sighed. "Engola requires years of training. It is a discipline of the mind, as much as the body." John looked disappointed. "I can teach you how to throw a man," said Benby at last. "That might make a difference."

The training began the next day. Benby showed John how to move his feet to keep his balance, while putting an opponent off balance, how to block a blow, how to sweep a man's legs from under him, how to hook a man's heel with his own, and put him on the deck. Naturally, this involved Benby putting him on his back multiple times, so he had to learn to fall in such a way that his wind was not knocked out of him. The first time he put Benby on the deck, he felt triumphant. Then Benby said, "All right, now you have to learn to do that at full speed." A lot of the crew watched the training and seemed to enjoy it very much — mostly, John thought, at his expense. A few approached him later and offered to teach him a trick or two that they were familiar with.

The crew were more convinced than ever that a sea battle was forthcoming, and morale was high. Foxe reflected that a disappointment might imperil their journey home, but he would enjoy the mood aboard ship while he could.

They were north of Cuba, now, and skirting a chain of small islands that curved from southwest to northeast. "These islands," Homer explained, "lead directly to the south end of the Floridas. If we keep them on our port side, they will guide us directly to the Florida straits, and then home."

It was the following afternoon when the 2nd mate reported to Foxe: "Captain, I believe we have a shadow."

"What's that?"

"A sail appears from time to time from between these islands on our port side. They are screened from our view by the islands, most of the time, but the lookout has spotted them at least three times today."

"Are you sure it isn't three different ships?"

"Pretty sure. The rigging is distinctive. Too far away to tell what flag she's sailing under, but she appears to be a small, quick craft, like one of those Spanish frigates."

"Or maybe a buccaneer?"

"Maybe."

Foxe summoned the boatswain. "Mr. Cox!"

"Sir?"

"Ye are repairing the mainsail on the main deck, I see."

"Yes sir. It's the easiest place to spread it out and find the tears. We're nearly finished."

"I think you should spread it out further, let it drape over the gunwales on the port side."

"Sir?"

"You heard me. Make sure it hangs down far enough to cover the gun ports on the port side." Then rig some lines to the yard arms so that it can be raised quickly, if necessary."

"So, you want to conceal our armament from anyone approaching from the port side, to make us look like a . . . merchantman?"

"Aye, you're a clever fellow. Do it quickly." Foxe remained on the quarterdeck, hoping to catch a glimpse of their shadow companion. At length, he spotted her, when they passed a particularly large channel between two islands. Too far away to tell what flag she was flying, just as the lookout said. He ordered a change of course, to the East, away from the islands, then waited to see how the other ship would react. "Run down the Spanish flag, and run up the St. George," he ordered. It would be night soon, and he didn't want to start a fight with another English vessel if it came to that.

The wind was from the east, which meant they had to tack to make any progress in that direction. The smaller vessel could sail closer to the wind than the *Queen* could, which would give her the advantage in a chase. If Foxe was going to outrun his pursuer, he would have to choose a different heading.

He ordered a change of course, to the north, which would eventually mean crossing the island chain somewhere. He was betting that they would do so before sundown, after which the shallows around the islands would be hazardous. No doubt the smaller ship had a shallower draft and knew these waters better than he did . . . better to have it out in the open sea than run aground on some sandbank. He set a course that would slow the *Queen* down and waited to see what the other ship would do.

"Roger! Tell Captain Cooper to prepare his men to repel boarders. I want them on deck in five minutes!" Unlikely that it would come to a fight, once the other ship saw how heavily armed the *Queen* was. Assuming that the other ship was a buccaneer, he might be able to lure her close enough to deliver a couple of broadsides, and then the tables would be turned — maybe there would be a prize, after all. Hard to say what sort of cargo a buccaneer would be carrying in these waters. Best to have his swordsmen on deck, just in case.

The other ship seemed to be closing. Yes, definitely closing. Foxe couldn't quite make out the flag, but it wasn't English or Spanish. French, maybe?

The soldiers were assembling on deck. The pikemen were in their armor but armed with their swords — the pikes were stowed below. The arquebusiers formed two ranks in front of the quarterdeck. As rehearsed, the men knelt down below the level of the gunwales on the starboard side — out of sight to any ship that approached.

"Mr. Porter! It is time you armed yourself! And make sure your guns are loaded!" Someone on the quarterdeck laughed, as John ran to his cabin, and loaded the pistols and the snaphance. He put on the Jack of Plates, and the Morion, and sheathed the saber in a belt around his middle. The pistols he tucked into his belt. He grabbed the snaphance and ran out onto the quarterdeck. Foxe looked him over, and said, "Terrifying. Truly terrifying," then smiled. Elsewhere, the other officers were appearing armed, as well. Everyone had a cutlass, some had helmets, and most had either some steel armor or a Jack of Plates like his. John's pulse was racing.

Foxe ordered a change of course: "Give me five points to the port, helmsman," he ordered. John gave Homer a questioning look. "This will force the other ship to change course, or close with us, but it will keep her downwind of us. It's called the weather gauge; if we are going to fight, that is the position we want to maintain. If she cuts across our stern to the starboard, to gain the weather gauge, it's a sign that she intends to fight."

"Unless she's a Frenchman," said Piet. "The French like to fight leeward."

"Unless she's a Frenchman," Homer agreed.

By now, the other ship was close enough that they could see that she was, indeed, flying a French flag. Surely by now, her crew could see that the *Queen* was flying an English one? She kept coming.

John took a position on the poop deck, next to a swivel gun. From there, he could look astern at the Frenchman, who was closing fast. He could make out the figures of men on the other vessel. She was smaller than the *Queen*, and her main deck was lower, too. Any attempt to board the *Queen* from that ship would involve climbing up and over the cantilevered half-deck and the gunwales. The one advantage that she enjoyed was that she was converging from the west — the lowering sun would be in the eyes of the *Queen's* defenders.

The Frenchman was close enough to be a little to the port side now. There was a puff of smoke, and a splash in the ocean, just ahead of the *Queen*, followed by the boom of a cannon.

"Mr. Cox!" Foxe roared, "get that sail off my main deck! Roger! Tell Mr. Benby to open his gun ports and run out his guns!" The boatswain and six seamen began rolling the sail up and hoisted it above the deck, where it hung like a dirty, old carpet. By now, it was clear that the Frenchman was going to pass on the leeward side. Foxe ordered a turn to the starboard, intending to train Jacob and Esau on her as she passed, but it was too late. He swung the *Queen* back to port, and Benby's gunners raked the Frenchman with a broadside, as she passed on the port side.

"Bonjour, mon Capitaine!" roared Foxe. John heard the rest of the crew cheering. As the *Queen* fell behind the Frenchman, Mary and Martha spoke from the bow. Splinters flew from the stern of the Frenchman, and smoke began to puff as well. Foxe ordered the helmsman to cross her wake, intending to deliver another broadside from the starboard batteries, if he could. He could see that the other ship was damaged. By now, the captain of the Frenchman had to know that she had bitten off more than she could chew. There was nothing left for her but to run. Unless she surrendered.

"She's striking her colors!" Piet exclaimed. So, surrender, then. She must be too damaged to flee. Indeed, Foxe could see that the French flag was being lowered. The *Queen* was now leeward of the Frenchman, as she turned into the east wind, and hove to. It took some maneuvering to sidle up to her port side. Smoke was still pouring from her hold, obscuring his view.

John, still on the poop deck, had a better view than anyone. Something odd was happening aboard the Frenchman — men were crowded on the port side of the deck, but no one seemed to be fighting the fires below. "Captain! It looks like they are preparing to abandon ship — they're all gathered on the port gunwales, and no one is fighting the fires!"

Foxe stiffened as if slapped in the face by an invisible hand. Then he roared, "Captain Cooper! Prepare to repel boarders on the starboard side! Mr. Vandoorn! Get the gun crews on the main deck, and quickly!" No sooner had he said so, than grappling hooks began soaring from the Frenchman, and fastening onto the gunwales of the *Queen*. "We have uninvited guests," said Homer. A rumble from below told John that Benby's crew had fired a starboard broadside into the Frenchman, tethered though she was to the *Queen*, before leaving their guns to rush on deck.

It was the drilling that saved them — that and the cantilevers at the gunwales. The buccaneers aboard the Frenchman had to sheathe their cutlasses and pull themselves upward from the main deck of their ship by their arms, which took time, and when they did so, they were face to face with Cooper's pikemen — without the pikes, but armored, and swords ready. The buccaneers were trapped between the ranks of pikemen and the gunwales, and as more and more of their mates scrambled aboard the *Queen*, they had no place to stand, except practically on top of the first men over. Cooper's arquebusiers were in position behind the pikemen, and on the foredeck and the quarter deck, firing into the mass of buccaneers backed up against the starboard gunwale. It was a slaughter. Buccaneers who tried to retreat to their ship ran directly into the mass of men who were still trying to board the *Queen*, and the arquebusiers just kept firing. John stood numbly on the poop deck, watching the whole gory business.

Three or four of the buccaneers broke from the mass, and charged the quarterdeck, to their left. John realized that Captain Foxe was not armed, and without thinking, drew both pistols from his belt, and fired on them. One man went down — a hit, or was he just dodging? The others came on, and John could think of nothing else but to draw his cutlass and rush them. To his left, he saw that Captain Foxe had a cutlass in his hand, after all, and then he was face to face with his opponent — a man smaller than himself, sickly looking, he thought. He parried the first few slashes from the buccaneer's cutlass and was parried in return. Somehow, the buccaneer seized John's right hand at the wrist, and John seized his. Now they were — grappling, John realized, grappling. What had he learned about grappling? Shift his weight, throw his opponent off balance, then what? A twist, a pull, and John was falling, over the starboard rail, still clutching his cutlass, and his opponent's wrist. John braced himself for the inevitable splash.

They landed hard. John was on top, and his opponent lost his breath with a whoosh!

John rolled to his knees, still clutching his cutlass. His opponent lay on the deck, gasping. John tried to figure out where he was. He looked up at the astonished faces of three men he had never seen before. One of them had a cutlass and lunged at him. His parry was a little late, and the cutlass struck a glancing blow along his ribs. He made it to his feet, as he parried the next blow.

Am I wounded? He glanced at his ribs. No blood. How am I not wounded? Of course! The Jack of Plates! The other two men had cutlasses, now, and began to circle around him. He saw the cutlass that his first opponent, still gasping on the deck, had dropped, and managed to pick it up with his left hand. His back was to the gunwale. Still outnumbered. *This is where I am going to die*, thought John, *on the deck of this*

Pirate ship. There was a noise to his left and another to his right. John turned to meet the new challenge and recognized Captain Cooper.

More of Cooper's men dropped to the deck beside him. The three buccaneers backed away then threw down their weapons. *"j'abandonne,"* muttered one of them. "I accept your surrender," replied Cooper. "Captain Foxe! The Frenchman has surrendered his ship!"

It took a few moments before the fighting aboard the *Queen* stopped. When it did, John saw the face of Captain Foxe peering over the railing on the *Queen's* quarterdeck to where John stood, in a daze, realizing that his ribs were beginning to hurt. "Carpenter! Where did you get that other cutlass?" There was something in his tone that suggested he was amused.

"It was his," John pointed to the man who lay gasping on the deck.

"So, you boarded an enemy vessel on your own initiative, and disarmed one pirate, all by yourself?" Definitely a tone, mocking him, maybe.

"It wasn't like that. He . . . dropped it and . . ."

Cooper interrupted, "Not only did he board the ship alone, and singlehandedly disarm a pirate, he held three others at bay, including the ship's Captain! I saw it with my own eyes!" There was a light in Cooper's eyes that John could not quite describe. The excitement of battle? Relief to have survived it? Did he think it was funny?

"I'd expect nothing less, from the carpenter of the *Eqyptian Queen!*" Foxe laughed with a roar, and Cooper and his men joined in. John was a little embarrassed but realized that their mockery was good-natured and that it was part of the excitement, and relief that the battle was over. No doubt they realized that he had fallen onto the Frenchman's deck by accident and was alive only because Cooper and his men had come to his rescue — as he recalled that series of events, he realized just how lucky he was to be alive. A chill washed over his mind, and he felt wobbly in his knees; he looked for a place to sit down.

In moments, Foxe himself came aboard to officially accept the surrender and began issuing orders. Men were sent below to put out the fires — before the magazines exploded — which were soon put out. Others went below to secure any plunder that might be aboard. They found disappointingly little. What they did find was a scene of disorder and disease — ten of the buccaneers lay in the gun deck, too sick to stand. The stench of the place was overwhelming. Sailors from the *Queen* identified their disease as scurvy — teeth had fallen from their swollen gums, their skin was covered in large, dark patches, some of which were oozing fluid, some were gasping for breath. Overwhelmed, John headed back to the *Queen*. He was missing his pistols — maybe they were on the poop deck. A gangplank was set up between the quarterdeck of the Frenchman, and the gunwales of the *Queen*. There was a steady stream of traffic going back and forth. Fewer than a dozen of the buccaneers were able to walk, and they were escorted to the *Queen's* brig. Aboard the *Queen*, there was more carnage to see. A pile of dead and wounded men lay against the starboard gunwale — fallen where the bullets and swords had found them. Blood was all over the deck. Dr Lopez was there, with a half dozen crewmen, separating the dead from the dying from the few that might possibly survive. There were clear signs of scurvy on the bodies of most of them. The dead were carried across the gangplank to the Frenchman, where they laid out on the main deck, in neat rows. The dying were carried to the port side, where Lopez knelt, looking at their wounds. He was not smiling. He looked up and spotted John "Señor Carpenter, what do you think of Purgatory?"

John felt numb, but responded, "Purgatory is a Papist invention, designed to extract money from the superstitious."

Dr. Lopez stood, and gestured with his arm, "Then welcome to Hell!"

John turned and mounted the steps to the quarterdeck. He found one of his pistols there; must have dropped it in the fight. He could see a bloodstain on the deck where the man he shot at had fallen — apparently, he had hit him. Either the man was wounded, and moved away under his own power, or he was among the dead that had already been removed to the Frenchman. He found the other pistol on the poop deck. He was surprised to notice that he still held a second cutlass in his left hand. It occurred to him that the pistols needed cleaning. Maybe he should go to his cabin and clean them? No. He shook his head and took a deep breath of the comparatively fresh air on the poop deck. No, there was work to do, carpenter's work. He turned his attention to the two ships, still tied together with grappling lines. By now, the dead buccaneers had been transferred to the Frenchman. A couple of sailors were swabbing the deck near the starboard gunwale, washing away most of the blood. John could see a few bullet holes in the gunwale, but nothing that needed immediate attention. In fact, there wasn't much damage to be seen on the *Queen* at all. He decided to cross back to the Frenchman and see what had happened to her.

There was a great deal of damage below decks and no cargo to speak of — just some food stores and ship's supplies. The ship mounted four small culverins on each side, plus a smaller gun in the bow — not enough armament for a fight with a warship like the *Egyptian Queen*. Her only tactic against a large ship was to get close enough to board and overwhelm the crew by sheer numbers — thus eighty men packed into the hold of a small, fast ship. Against a merchantman, they might have succeeded, but they didn't have a chance against a fully crewed warship.

There was ample evidence of the effectiveness of the *Queen's* broadsides — broken gun carriages, and mangled bodies. But there was also damage that the battle could not explain. The bilge pumps were damaged, and the orlop deck was under six inches of water. John went to the stern, where the powder magazine should have been located. He found the magazine and powder kegs standing in the water inside it. Most of the powder kegs inside showed clear evidence of water stains — the contents were almost certainly ruined. So, few guns, and wet powder — boarding was the only way that the Frenchman could attack anybody. John summoned some crewmen to help him salvage any kegs that looked dry — the rest he would dump overboard. At the back of the magazine, they found something else — a good-sized wooden chest, under a canvas tarp. It was heavy. "Go fetch Captain Foxe," ordered John, before realizing that the men were not accustomed to taking orders from him. Perhaps it was his matter-of-fact tone, but they smiled, nodded, and fetched the Captain.

Foxe appeared in a few minutes, accompanied by Homer and the blacksmith. "Ye might have chosen a fresher-smelling place for this little meeting," observed Foxe, "What is it?"

"I think you will be interested in this," said John pointing to the chest.

"Why, what's in it?"

"I haven't opened it, but it will take at least four strong men to move it. I thought it better we have plenty of witnesses before it's opened."

Foxe's eyebrows raised, and he smiled. "Right, you are, Carpenter. You four, take this up to the quarterdeck on the *Queen*. Leave the canvas over it, and if anyone tries to get inside, tell them they'll answer to me. I'll be right behind you."

Foxe looked around the orlop deck. "Seven inches of water?"

"It was six inches half an hour ago. If we're going to claim this ship as a prize, we need to get the bilge pumps working again."

Foxe nodded. "See to it. I'll order her guns transferred to the *Queen's* hold. That will lighten her a bit — might keep her afloat. Throw anything that can't be salvaged overboard." With that, he was gone. John recruited half a dozen crewmen to take turns manning the bilge pumps and began identifying items that could be thrown overboard. In an hour or so, the water level in the hold had receded almost to the level of the orlop deck. John emerged from the hold to discover that night had fallen. He was relieved by the boatswain for two watches — he would be back on the quarterdeck for the second watch. New crews would rotate to man the bilge pumps through the night. He ate a quick, cold dinner, and collapsed onto his bunk.

Captain Foxe was still busy. The captain's cabin on the Frenchman was a shambles; the *Queen*'s bow guns, Mary and Martha, had both scored direct hits on the stern. After clearing away some of the splintered mess, he found the Frenchman's charts — possibly the most valuable things in the entire cabin. He was a little surprised to discover that all the text on the charts was in Spanish. No matter — Homer was fluent in Spanish — but it suggested what he should have suspected; the "Frenchman" was, in fact, a Spanish ship, captured by these buccaneers some while ago. From the condition of the crew, they had not had much success recently. He would learn what he could from the buccaneer captain about the history of his ship.

John Porter was roused from troubled dreams at the beginning of the second watch, and stumbled onto the quarterdeck, still dressed as he had been the previous day. The helmsman greeted him with a nod, and he stood by while Homer recorded the heading and speed. It was a warm night, and the stars were blazing all around him; though there was already a hint of dawn in the east. The *Queen* was still headed northeast, but slowly, since the Frenchman was still lashed firmly to her starboard side. Without a crew to man the sails on the Frenchman, she was just dead weight, even if she was still afloat. The *Queen*'s helmsman had to fight the tendency to sail the two ships in a wide, clockwise circle. Still, it was a lovely night and looked to be an even lovelier day.

The chest from the hold of the prize was still on the quarterdeck with its four guards, who had just relieved four others from the previous watch. John wondered why Foxe was leaving it out in plain view, and guarding it so publicly as if daring someone to sneak a peek at what was under the tarp.

At three bells, the sun began to appear above the horizon. Dick Benby emerged from his cabin, with his rope and bucket, and greeted John on his way down to the main deck. He was joined there by several other men. It was the bathing ritual. The men stripped down and took turns dousing each other with seawater. John could hear them laughing and talking but couldn't make out exactly what they were saying. He was suddenly aware that he hadn't changed clothes since yesterday, with its smoke, sweat, and blood. "I'll be on the deck, just there," he informed the helmsman. He descended to the main deck and approached the bathers.

"So, Carpenter, you ready to join the ranks of the civilized?" Benby smiled with a chuckle.

"Today, I think I am," said John, and took off his clothes. "How does this work?"

"All you have to do is stand still," said Benby, as he dumped a bucket of sea water over John's head. It felt surprisingly warm, and John felt that the grime of the previous day was running down his body, and onto the deck. Then there was another bucket and another. Apparently, the whole group wanted a chance to dump on him. He laughed, not sure why, and the others laughed as well.

"That's enough!" said Benby. To John, he said, "One or two buckets will usually do the job, but in your case, we thought it best to be thorough."

John laughed as he got dressed again. "I am at least fully awake, now. Thank you."

"You will feel cleaner when you have fresh clothing," said Benby, as he headed back to his cabin. "I can fetch some for you if you like."

John nodded. Yes, clean clothes would be welcome. He had not slept well and had woken with a feeling that the previous day's events had somehow accompanied him in his dreams. A fresh day and fresh clothes would help him put it all behind him.

Benby returned with fresh clothes from John's cabin, as well as the two pistols, and the cutlasses. "These must be cleaned as well," he said, "not only because a dirty weapon may rust or misfire, but because cleaning your weapons after the battle is how you make an end of it, and prepare for the next one."

John stepped back from his position next to the helmsman and changed his clothes, then began cleaning the pistols.

Something in his eyes must have caught Benby's attention, since he looked intently at John and said, "You leave a little piece of yourself behind with every man you fight, every man you kill. You must come to terms with it. The battles of your past will haunt you like ghosts, unless you can finish them — in here," He pointed to his chest, "and face the next battle. The man who carries all the ghosts of his past into tomorrow's battle is a man who perishes."

John gazed back at him. Benby knew more about what was going on "in here," than John was willing to admit to himself. He nodded, and said, "Thank you."

At the end of his watch, John went to the officer's mess for breakfast. He had barely time for a bite before he was summoned to Foxe's cabin. The rest of the officers had gotten there ahead of him.

"Sirs," began Foxe, "we have decisions to make today, and I thought to include all of you since all will share in the consequences of what we decide. I have summoned the captain of this ship, and after I have questioned him, we will decide what our next course shall be."

As if on cue, the buccaneer captain was escorted into the cabin. "Sirs," Foxe began, "allow me to introduce Gerard Picot, lately captain of the *Vengeur.* Captain Picot is going to answer some questions for us, about the local waters, and about the circumstances of his attack on our vessel yesterday." He turned to Picot," Do you speak English?"

"*Oui*, a little."

"A little should be enough. The vessel you call the *Vengeur* is taking on water. If she is to be repaired, we need to find a sheltered anchorage, where we can inspect her hull below the waterline. Do you know of such a place?"

Picot seemed to relax a little at the question, "*Oui*, I know a place near here, sheltered, with fresh water, out of sight of most passing ships. It is not far."

Foxe stood and spread out a chart. "Show me where."

Picot looked at the chart and pointed to an island, one of the chain of islands to their west. Homer approached the table, looked, nodded, and then excused himself. Soon, John could feel the *Queen* changing her course. No time to waste, apparently.

"Thank you, Captain. We found a heavy chest in the powder magazine of the *Vengeur.* Can I assume that you placed it there?" Picot flinched just a little, John thought. It was definitely his chest. Picot did not deny it but nodded his head.

"And is it filled with the plunder you have taken in these waters?"

Picot nodded again.

"Do you have a key to unlock it?"

Picot shook his head. "*Non*, the key is kept by the gunner's mate. The contents of the chest are the property of the whole crew, each man entitled to an equal share — we agreed that it would be so when we started on this venture."

Foxe sat down. "Tell us about this 'venture'."

Picot took a breath. "We sailed from Le Havre last Spring, eighty strong, in a Portuguese caravel. We reached the Americas safely and established ourselves in the islands to the west of here. You probably know that all the Spanish treasure fleets sail these waters on their way back to Spain."

Foxe nodded. "Please continue."

"We could not hope to capture a treasure galleon with a ship so small, but there were plenty of lesser ships to choose from. We flew a Spanish flag, to help us get close to other Spanish ships so that we could board them. My men became practiced at seizing the lesser vessels, and we found enough gold and silver aboard them to fulfill our dreams of fortune. That is until our luck turned."

"Go on," said Foxe, as he leaned forward.

We ran aground on a sandbar, not many miles to the south and west of here. We could have gotten her off with the rising tide, but before it turned, a Spanish galleon appeared in the channel. We dared not ask for assistance, as you well know how the Spanish treat Frenchmen that they find in the Floridas."

Foxe nodded. Execution for the officers, slavery for the rest.

"Instead, they used us for target practice. By the time they were finished, our ship was just a broken hulk. I got as many men as I could into the longboat, along with my charts, instruments, and a few weapons, and others were able to cling to the flotsam of our wreckage. Twenty-two of my men drowned that day. We got the rest to shore on one of the small islands, but we had only the longboat to put to sea. The following night, we saw a small Spanish ship approaching up the channel. I put my best men into the longboat and approached her in the dark. She didn't see us until it was too late. We renamed her the *Vengeur* because we swore to avenge ourselves on the Spanish who had shown us no mercy."

Foxe shook his head. "From plunder to revenge? Have you found satisfaction?"

"A little. The contents of the chest you found contains what we have taken since that day. We offered the Spanish crew the chance to join us, and a dozen or so did. The rest we committed to the sea, like our comrades." Picot was standing erect now, with a steely expression on his face. *A brave face*, thought John, *for a man whose conscience harries him at night, and in his dreams.*

"The *Vengeur*, as you see, did not have as many guns as our first ship. It was more difficult to find prizes to attack. And when we did capture one, the crew spoke of *El Draque*. Over and over again, it was *draque, draque, draque.* Eventually, we figured out that the English buccaneer, Drake, was operating in the Caribbean, and the Spanish were terrified of him. Ships stopped navigating these waters — they are all waiting in some fortified port or other for *El Draque* to go home. We did not see a ship in the straits for two months until a fleet of ships flying English flags passed this way two weeks ago. Then, nothing more, until you passed us yesterday."

"And yet you attacked us. Why?" asked Foxe.

"You were sailing under a Spanish flag. We did not know how heavily armed you were until you showed us your broadside guns. We certainly did not know that you had soldiers aboard."

"Yet, after the broadside, you must have seen our English flag, and you knew that you were outgunned. Why did you not try to escape?"

"You have seen the condition of my men. We were desperate for food and medicine. Simply running away would not have given us much chance of survival."

"And if you had succeeded, would you have put us all into the sea, like the Spaniards?"

"With a ship as large as this one, I would have hoped to recruit most of your crew to our venture. With a ship like this, we could take on any ship in the Spanish fleet!"

"With yourself as Captain, I suppose."

Picot shrugged a little and smiled sheepishly. "You suppose correctly."

"And if I refused to yield to your authority, it would be to the sea with me, just like the Spaniards?"

"Oh, *non*, Captain. Any who would not join us would be marooned on one of these islands hereabouts. Many of them have springs of fresh water and food that you could gather, to live for years. The climate here is very pleasant all year long."

Foxe looked hard at Picot. "You have been more frank with me than most men would be, in the same circumstance. I give you credit for that." Foxe looked at the escort "Please take Captain Picot to join his men in the brig. And see if you can locate the gunnery mate from the *Vengeur.*" They took Picot out.

Foxe turned to his officers. "As you know, the law reserves half of any cargo we capture to the crown, and we are obligated to return half of what is left to our investors. The personal property of the prize's crew, however, belongs entirely to the crew of this ship. Do you agree?

"Aye," said each of them.

"Based on what Captain Picot has just said, I consider the contents of that chest on the quarterdeck to be the personal property of the crew of the *Vengeur*, not cargo, and therefore now the property of the crew of the *Egyptian Queen*. Does any man fault my reasoning?" No one spoke, some shook their heads, and many smiled.

"Under the circumstances, I propose that each man on this ship receive an equal share. I am aware that by tradition, officers, including myself, receive more shares than ordinary seamen, but that rule is applied to shares of cargo, not to personal property."

"What circumstances do you refer to? How is that to our advantage, or yours, for that matter?" asked Piet Vandoorn.

"I have discovered that when treasure is involved, seamen may come to resent it if another's share is greater than their own. Such a man might imagine that he could increase his share by telling his story to the crown's agents or joining a mutiny."

"But if the crown gets involved, they will seize all the plunder as evidence of fraud, and the seamen would wind up with nothing. Simple arithmetic would prove the folly of that. And a mutiny might well fail, and lead to a quick trial and execution. Who would be persuaded to pursue such folly?"

Foxe nodded. "Simple arithmetic is beyond the grasp of some of our men. And we have persuaders aboard, who would certainly lead a mutiny if the opportunity arose. I am willing to be satisfied with the same share as a cook if it means that I get home with my share and my head. When everyone gets the same share, each one recognizes that his mate's share can only get larger at the expense of his own. Most men will prefer the status quo to risking a loss and will be committed to our safe return."

Vandoorn nodded. Point taken.

The escort returned. "It appears that the gunner's mate was killed in the fight. He is not in the brig."

"Then find the body and search it. Look for a key. Probably tied around his neck! Carpenter, go with him!"

The ghoulishness of the task made John shiver a little. By now, there were three dozen corpses laid out on the deck of the *Vengeur*, each wrapped in a shroud, and each bloating in the tropic heat. The smell was sickening. They had only the vaguest description of what the gunner's mate had looked like, so there was nothing to do but search each body in turn. Flies were buzzing around. *How do flies find a corpse so far from shore,* John wondered.

One corpse looked strikingly familiar. Even with the features bloated, John was pretty sure it was the man he had shot at on the quarterdeck. So, he must have hit his target. Or had he? There was no key around the man's neck, but no obvious wound on his upper body either. Perhaps he had missed, and the man had died at some other hand?

"Sir!" his thoughts were interrupted by his companion. "Could this be it?" He held up a large, iron key.

"Yes, that's probably it." John was relieved at the excuse to get away from the piles of death and decay. He hoped it was the right key; he didn't want to have to come back and search some more if it wasn't, but the only way to be sure was to try it. They took the key back to Foxe's cabin.

"Summon the crew to the main deck!" ordered Foxe, "And tell the foursome guarding that chest to move it down there, in front of them. Also, fetch a heavy tool of some sort, that will open the chest, in case this key doesn't work."

By now, it was mid-morning. John could see land to the west, not far away. The *Queen* hove to, and Captain Foxe emerged from his cabin to address the assembled crewmen. The chest, still covered by the tarp, was placed just below where he stood, still surrounded by four armed guards.

"Seamen!" Foxe addressed them with a flourish of his arm, "We have been through much together, and we have stood side by side in the face of the enemy. We have triumphed in battle, and some have paid with their lives. The reward for our sacrifice has not been all we could have hoped for, but we do not return empty-handed."

There was some murmuring from the men on deck. John hoped Foxe knew where he was going with this line of oratory.

"Yesterday, we were attacked by a foe that hoped to take the little we have from us. They made a grave mistake, and their ship is now ours."

Men cheered at this last remark. John felt more at ease.

"Three of our mates died yesterday. It is a high price to pay, and I am grieved at the loss."

Silence and nods.

"But our foes paid a higher price!" here the men nodded vigorously, and some cheered. "And this . . ." — at Foxe's signal the tarp was pulled away to reveal the chest- "is what we found in her hold. It is the only thing aboard that ship that may have great value."

There was a buzz from the men on deck. Now John understood the point of Foxe's arrangements. Everyone on the ship knew where the chest had come from, and that no one had had an opportunity to help themselves to its contents — yet. A mystery, a way to focus the men's attention on something other than their losses, and the grim business of cleaning up after a battle.

"This key," Foxe held it above his head, "should reveal what is inside. I have met with the officers, and we have agreed that every man of this crew is entitled to an equal share of whatever is in this chest."

"What about the Crown's share?" A voice from the back, possibly Wilkes's.

"I am reliably informed that the contents of this chest are the personal property of the crew of the Frenchman and therefore belong to us — all of it."

There was excited laughter, and some clapping and whistling.

"So, let's see what we have!" A different voice, again from the back, hard to place.

"Very well. Carpenter, open the chest!" With this, Foxe tossed the key to John, who wasn't expecting it. He barely caught it before it hit the deck. There were a few gasps from the crew as he struggled to catch it, and a cheer when he held it up. Showmanship, realized John. Foxe would give them a show; regardless of what was in the chest. John was hoping the final act would be worth the price of admission.

John approached the chest, bent, and put the key in the lock. It fit. He turned it and met resistance. Well, he could always break it open, if he had to . . . he jiggled the key and felt it turn. There was an audible click — the men behind him were holding their breath. John felt a slight shift in the lid, then tugged at it, and lifted it open.

He stood back. He was looking at a gown — a woman's gown. Silk, probably, expensive — but hardly a treasure that could be divided among some two hundred seamen.

"Look under it!" urged a sailor in the front of the crowd. John carefully gathered the gown in his arms and lifted it out of the chest. There was a cheer from the men. John thought they were poking fun at his awkwardness, arms full of a woman's gown, but no, they were not looking at him, at all. He turned to the chest and saw — gold, lots of gold. Gold coins, gold chains, gold objects of every sort, There was some silver, too, but the glow of gold outshone everything else. He felt short of breath.

Then he dropped the gown back on top of the chest, and the cheering died down.

Foxe was now down on the deck beside him and gave him a wink. "Well played, Carpenter," he murmured. Then turning to the crew, he said, "You see what we have won. Now we have to get home with it."

"Why not divide it up, now, so that every man knows he is getting his full and fair share?" A voice from the back again. Definitely Wilkes.

"Now, that's an idea, but I couldn't recommend it. I heard of a crew that did that once. Problem is, the men had trouble holding on to their share. Some lost it gambling, some insisted that their mates had stolen some while they slept. Led to hard feeling and fighting. The worst part was that after one man was killed in a fight, and his opponent had to be hanged, the rest of the crew couldn't agree on how to divide the dead men's shares. Cursed the ship, let me tell ye."

"But we can't be sure that what's in the chest now, will still be there when we get home, can we?"

"I catch your drift, and I can't say I am pleased with it," Foxe scowled visibly, then brightened, "but there is a way to ensure that every man's share is equal, and the full amount of the treasure is divided."

The men looked at him intently. "How?" the same voice in the back, but less aggressive.

"I propose that we weigh the contents of this chest, now, in the presence of the crew. We will separate the gold from the silver since everyone knows that the gold is more valuable by weight. We will divide the weight of each metal by the number of men in the crew. Whatever that comes to, will be payable to each man, out of this chest, when we reach an English port." There was general nodding, though some men appeared to be uncertain about what Foxe was proposing. Would they have to cut up the large pieces? It occurred to John that "dividing," in the arithmetic sense, was a foreign concept to some of them.

"What if someone dies, before we reach England?"

Foxed sighed and stroked his chin. "Well, that is a problem. If the share of a dead man is divided among the survivors, that could encourage one of his mates to help him on his way to heaven, so to speak, just so he could get a larger share. That is exactly the problem I want to avoid." Some of the men chuckled; some looked worried.

"I suggest that we agree that the share of any man who dies between here and England be delivered to his family at home, or anyone else he designates, when — and if . . ." he paused for effect, "we are safely in England. "

"How would we know who should get his share?" An honest question, to John's ears.

"Each man should write it down. We have paper and pens. The carpenter, here," he turned to John, "will write it down for you, if you ask him to." John was caught completely off guard by this suggestion but composed himself enough to nod, soberly. What was Foxe thinking?

There were murmurs of agreement from the crew. At Foxe's signal, Paolo the purser stepped forward and placed a low table on the deck. Another sailor brought him a chair, and he sat down and produced a ledger, which he opened. Two large pieces of canvas were laid out on either side of the chest, and Piet Vandoorn began emptying its contents — the gold on his right, the silver on his left. A set of scales was produced, and Piet began weighing the treasure a bit at a time. When each bit was weighed, he called out the weight, and the purser wrote something in the ledger. Each bit was placed back into the chest, and the next was weighed. After the gold had been weighed, Vandoorn did the same thing with the silver. That done, he closed the lid, and took the key from John, to lock it again.

Paolo, meantime, was doing some calculation. "It comes to two hundred forty pounds, five ounces of gold, and fifty-five pounds, seven ounces of silver." Men murmured with some excitement.

"What would my share come to?" The question came from Toby. The others looked at Paolo with a questioning look.

"That depends on how many of us there are."

"Call out the roster!" said Foxe.

Paolo read the names from the roster, one by one. "Did I fail to call anyone's name?"

No one spoke. "In that case, we have two hundred fourteen men on board, available for service. Each man's share of the gold will be approximately one pound of gold and a little more than four shillings of silver."

"Only one pound, four shillings?" Sounds of disappointment.

"A pound of gold is worth more than silver. Depending on the rate of exchange, it would come to about twenty-four pounds sterling and fourteen shillings, for each man."

"Ahh." Murmurs of satisfaction. John realized that the whole event was calculated to head off any rumors of fraud or deception on the part of

Captain Foxe and prevent any attempt to steal from the chest while they were at sea. Everyone had seen the weighing of the treasure with their own eyes and seen the chest emptied and refilled, then locked. As long as every man received as much as he had been promised at the end of the voyage, there would be little grumbling. As long as every man considered that the contents of the chest was his, each of them would be vigilant to prevent anyone else getting into the chest until they were home. Give them a low number at first, then revise it upward. End the song on a sweet note.

"I will keep this safe in the chart room," said Foxe, "and it will remain under guard until we reach England. We will be making landfall on one of these islands, to repair the Frenchman if we can. As soon as that work is finished, we sail for home."

At this, the crew cheered. They were already thinking about how they would spend their share of the plunder. Morale was high.

John took his seat at the table as Paolo returned his ledgers to his cabin. Paolo left him a quill pen and ink, and a small book with blank pages. Men lined up to tell him who should get their share, in the event of their untimely demise.

Part 10: The Trouble With Treasure

May 1586: Careened Again

By late afternoon, they anchored in a small cove on one of the islands to the west. As Captain Picot had stated, there were freshwater springs on the island and a small creek that flowed into the sea at one end of a white, sandy beach. The waters of the cove were a bright turquoise, the weather fair. John thought he would try swimming when he got the chance.

The first order of business was to offload the corpses of the buccaneers and bury them ashore. The three men of the *Queen* were buried separately and with more care. John was asked to say some words. The prisoners were transferred to shore as well. Sails from the *Vengeur* were taken ashore and fashioned into a complex of large tents, where the prisoners and the scurvy victims were placed. The accommodations were rustic, but more comfortable than the hold of the *Vengeur*. Once emptied, the *Vengeur* was careened on the beach, so that Reuben Cox and John could inspect her hull below the waterline.

Dr. Lopez had done what he could for the wounded, but "men with scurvy do not heal easily," he explained. Another five of the wounded buccaneers died ashore on the first day. Those who had been too sick to fight were getting weaker. Lopez directed that all the prisoners receive a ration of *patata* each day, which they ate without complaint — the crew of the *Vengeur* had been perilously close to outright starvation.

Patata was now eaten by nearly everyone in the crew of the *Queen*, as well. The sight of men with scurvy was enough to bring most of the skeptics around. Foxe was pleased at the news: "I hope we have enough to get us home."

Careening the *Vengeur* was accomplished in the same way as with the *Queen*, but it was easier because the Frenchman was only a quarter the length and half the beam. It was readily apparent that the ship was old. John found worm damage all along the bottom of her hull. He wasn't sure she could be made seaworthy. He could replace some hull planks, but if the damage was in the keel or the ribs, it wouldn't matter. That meant getting into the bilges. He felt weary — his nose had suffered so many assaults in the last few days, that his stomach was threatening to mutiny at the prospect. He would need light in the bilges. He swam back to the *Queen*, just for the feel of the clean, warm water — he would be slimy again soon enough. He explained the situation to Captain Foxe, while he got some candles from the ship's stores.

"Why not take Roger with you?", suggested Foxe. Roger, surprisingly, seemed willing enough. They took the longboat back to shore. Looking down into the bilge hatches, John realized that Roger had been growing — or were the hatches on this ship just smaller?

As he crawled into the bilge, he decided it was a little of both — the hatch was tight, and there was barely enough clearance between the ballast and the orlop deck above for him to crawl the length of the ship. On the bright side, it was not nearly as odious as he remembered. Then it came to him — just as seawater was seeping into the bilges, the bilge water must have been leaking into the ocean. It was fresher in the bilges of the *Vengeur*, just because her hull was so porous. Well, small mercies were mercies, nonetheless.

He bumped his head on the overhead deck twice, and banged a knee on a ballast stone before it occurred to him that hurrying the job was unnecessary — Foxe wasn't offering him an extra shilling to finish by sundown. "Roger, we're doing this wrong. We have time enough to take the ballast out of the bilges this time." Roger agreed. They started at one hatch, and pulled the stones out, one at a time, and laid them on the orlop deck. Once they had cleared the area under the hatch, there was more room to move, and they pulled out the stones farther down the bilge. The stones were oblong, most bigger than bricks, and heavy; they were dark and slimy, a little slippery to handle. Roger was able to get into the bilges more easily and hand the stones up to John. It was still a tight squeeze — Roger was growing, John decided. Roger was out of sight, now, except for his hand, which handed a slimy, dark stone to John. It slipped out of John's hands, and dropped to the deck, where it bounced off the other stones with a metallic clink! "What was <u>that</u>?" Roger's voice came from below.

"Nothing. I just dropped the slimy thing on the deck."

"It didn't sound slimy. It sounded like metal."

Roger was right. It didn't sound slimy. What kind of stone was this?

"Roger, do you have a knife?"

"Just a small one, Sir."

"Bring it here." Roger emerged from the hatch, offering John a small knife.

John scraped the surface of the stone he had just dropped. Under the dark encrustation was an unmistakable gleam of metal. "Is it Iron, Sir?"

"No, not iron. Softer than iron." John turned to another ballast stone and scraped it. Once again, the gleam of metal. Silver. Had to be silver. How was it possible?"

Roger, we have to see the Captain immediately. Do not show these stones to anyone or mention them. We can finish inspecting the bilges later. Come with me."

John picked up one of the smaller stones, and together they climbed out onto the beach. A longboat was beached nearby, and they were rowed out to the *Queen.* John tried not to appear excited; the oarsmen looked at him oddly, but he realized it was probably the bilge slime on his clothing, or maybe just the stench.

Once aboard, John said, "Roger, find the Captain, and tell him that I need to report on the condition of the *Vengeur.*" Roger did so and signaled that Foxe was available in his cabin. Roger stood by the door, but John pulled him inside and closed it firmly. Foxe looked up from his desk inquisitively.

"Captain, I have something to report on the condition of the *Vengeur.*"

Foxe nodded. "So Roger has told me. What is it?"

"This." John placed the ballast stone on the Captain's desk.

"It stinks. I suppose this came from the bilges?" Foxe wrinkled his nose a bit.

"Yes, but it is an unusual ballast stone. The like I have never seen before."

Foxe gave him a curious look. "How so?"

John took Roger's knife and scraped away some of the dark coating. "Do you see how silvery it looks?"

Foxe stood and bent over the stone. "Are there others like this?"

"Yes, several at least. Maybe all the ballast in the bilges."

Foxe sat down. "How many know of this?"

"Only Roger, and myself. And now you."

"Roger, come here." Foxe looked at him. "Roger, what's that under your chin?"

"My beard, Sir." Roger stood erect. Yes, he was definitely growing something, thought John.

"That makes you a man now, Roger. A man must know how to keep a secret. Are you ready to be such a man?"

"Yes Sir!"

"Very well. Carpenter, you may have stumbled upon something important, but it will only bring trouble if the matter is known. Do ye understand?"

John nodded. "I understand. This could upset all your efforts to keep the crew in harmony. What I don't understand, is why the buccaneers would use silver ingots as ballast on an old ship like this. Surely, they would have done better to simply return to France, with such a treasure."

"I doubt very much if the buccaneers had any idea of what their ballast was. Ye recall that this ship was a Spanish vessel?"

"But what sort of Spaniard would use silver for ballast? Is it so plentiful in this part of the world that they could pave the streets with it?"

"What sort? The sort that could bribe the local officials to divert some silver away from the Royal mines and bypass the King's accountants. The sort that would not dare to send it back to Spain as part of any ordinary cargo. The sort that could hope to fetch it out of the bilges after the King's agents had exhausted themselves searching the ship for contraband."

"So, it is not cargo?"

"No, not cargo."

"And the crown does not have a claim on it?"

"I think the crown's agents will claim it if they can. They might insist that it is treasure trove."

"How can that be? The law of treasure trove applies to treasure found in England. We are not in England, or anywhere near!"

"True enough, but it was found on a ship — an English ship if ye like since we captured her. It would make an interesting legal case, to be sure, but the Queen has many lawyers, and the case might take years to resolve."

"How is it any different from the treasure that we divided among the men yesterday?"

"That treasure was the property of the crew. Their captain said so. The law is clearly on our side."

"So, if we cannot share it among the crew, and the crown will claim it all, is it worth taking back to England?"

"A fair question. I can think of ways we might put it to use, if we can get it home, so long as no one outside this room knows of its existence. None of us can expect to profit from it directly. Do ye understand?"

John had no idea what Foxe was thinking of, but he nodded. In any case, it was a shame to leave such wealth on a rotting ship. He wanted to get it back to England, somehow. "We need to get it out of the bilges, to finish inspecting the hull. I don't know how we can get it aboard the *Queen*, without raising suspicion, though."

"I shall inspect the ballast on the *Queen*, personally," said Foxe. "I think we may discover that our ballast needs to be shifted or reduced a bit, because of all that heavy artillery in our hold. Of course, we may reduce it more than necessary, but that can be remedied by putting some of the ballast back. You should continue with your inspection."

That afternoon, John and Roger finished pulling all of the ballast out of the bilges of the *Vengeur*. It was not all silver, some were just ordinary stones. Still, there was close to a ton of material that John thought was contraband silver.

The news from the bilges was not good. There was damage and rot on the ribs and even the keel. The *Vengeur* was not going to cross the Atlantic again. She might have a few years of local voyages in her, but John and Reuben would not put any of their shipmates on such a vessel to hazard a voyage on the open sea.

Before going to sleep that night, John decided to take another swim in the cove, just to get the odors of the orlop and the bilges off. Afterward, he felt relaxed. He didn't have duty on the quarterdeck until the fourth watch. It would be a good night for sleeping. Sometime during the night, he found himself back on the quarterdeck. It was foggy, and he could barely make out the mizzenmast before him, much less any more of the *Queen*. It was quiet, just the sound of water lapping against the hull. Then he heard footsteps on the stairs and could make out the blurry silhouette of someone approaching. "Who goes there?"

"No one that you care about." The voice was gruff; he couldn't place the accent, though he felt that he should, somehow.

"State your business!"

"I have no business. Not anymore." The figure approached him, the face was familiar . . .

He knew that face, bloated though it was. It was the buccaneer he had shot. In the dim light, he saw that the man's face was rigid, the whites of his eyes showing. Worst of all, there was a hole in the middle of the man's forehead. Flies, small green flies, were swarming around him, and maggots — lots of maggots — began spilling from the wound. "No business for me, thanks to you."

John awoke with a start, sweating. His pulse was racing. He could not get back to sleep that night.

Over the next five days, John and Roger replaced some of the hull planks on the *Vengeur*. There was a great deal of coming and going between the *Vengeur*, the *Queen*, and the beach. From time to time, ballast stones were piled on the shore and then moved again. Captain Foxe spent a good deal of time shifting cargo in the hold, removing ballast, and then replacing it, until the ship was in "perfect trim," as he called it. Most of the rest of the crew spent time ashore, or swimming in the shallow cove. Dr Lopez ventured inland and came back with a basketful of little limes that he had found. He insisted the sick men in his care drink some of the sour juice, to aid their healing. By the end of the week, the men with scurvy showed marked improvement. The credit went to Dr. Lopez, for his marvelous skill. Two more of the wounded buccaneers died and were buried alongside their mates. All of the wounded crewmen from the *Egyptian Queen* were recovering.

John was grateful to be busy since he was not sleeping well. He continued to have nightmares, in which the dead buccaneer played a prominent role. He made a point of visiting the captive buccaneers and felt some relief when he recognized the man he had grappled with, still alive. One less death on his conscience, at least.

Curiously, the buccaneers asked him if he would say a few words over the graves of their dead comrades — since they had observed him doing the same for the crewmen of the *Queen*. John was willing to do so, even though he spoke no French. Many of the buccaneers were Huguenots, it turned out, from Normandy or Brittany. Most of them spoke at least a little English. It was just a formality, anyway, since John made clear to them that he was not a priest or churchman of any kind. "God understands all languages," said Captain Picot.

After that, John was bothered less by his dreams — perhaps the prayers he offered were as much for himself, as for any of the dead men.

It did not help that the crew of the *Queen* began to regard him as a man of heroic deeds. Captain Cooper enjoyed telling the story of how he and his men had seen the carpenter throw a buccaneer off the railing, and leap onto the Frenchman with a cutlass, how they had followed him over the side and found him holding off three buccaneers by himself, a cutlass in each hand. The story grew with the telling. He was at risk of becoming a legend, a tale told over and over again in the alehouses of Harwich. The treasure he had discovered in the powder magazine only added to the saga: "He could have claimed it all for himself, you know, by law. But he shared it with the whole crew, and every man an equal share! A right seaman, that."

And then there was his spiritual side: "A very pious man. Never heard him curse. You never heard a priest who could pray like he could. A holy man. He has a healing touch, you know."

It was all ridiculous, but all his attempts to explain what had really happened were treated as a kind of false modesty — more proof of his piety and humility. He gave up trying to explain himself.

On the eighth day, Foxe proclaimed the *Queen* fit and ready for the final leg of her voyage. One problem remained: What to do with the buccaneers? "I'll not have the like back on my ship," said Foxe. "They would be nothing but trouble, and we're running short of rations as it is. If we take them back to England, they might decide to say inconvenient things to the authorities."

"Do you mean to maroon them here?" asked John.

"It's no worse than they would have done to us; ye heard Picot say so. They have food and water here, and the climate is pleasant enough."

"How about their ship?"

"Might as well leave them the ship. Can't take her home, or so you said. They'll have no guns, but they can get her seaworthy enough to reach the mainland somewhere hereabouts if that's what they want."

The rest of the officers nodded. It was generous, really to let them go. Who knew? Maybe the buccaneers would succeed in boarding another Spanish ship in the straits. Maybe it would help, just a little, in the war with Spain.

Captain Foxe's decision was not well received by the seventeen surviving buccaneers, but there was little they could do about it. Dr. Lopez was reluctant to leave patients who were still recovering from scurvy or battle wounds, or both, but Foxe was determined to get home. Lopez advised them to keep gathering the little limes in the forest, to sustain their health. Foxe left them some fishnets (plenty of fish in the cove), two pistols, and some powder and shot. He also left them a skiff, a small boat that had been aboard the *Vengeur*, which was still careened on the beach. John made a point of finding the man he had grappled with and giving back the cutlass he had taken — it eased his conscience, just a bit, somehow, to give up the spoils of his so-called victory.

They were prepared to sail with the first fair breeze. The watch reported that the skiff had put out from the beach and was approaching the Queen. A lone figure stood in the skiff and asked to come aboard. It was Captain Picot, and they lowered a rope ladder to him. He begged to speak with Foxe.

"I have already told ye, that I won't be taking any of you back to England. That decision is final!"

"But I am a dead man if I stay with them!" Picot pleaded.

"Eh? How's that?"

"The men blame me for their predicament, and intend to hang me, in full sight of your ship!"

Foxe looked shoreward. "Under the circumstances, I might find that entertaining. What would you have me do about it?"

"Put me ashore on some other island, where they can't find me. Give me a chance to live!"

"Where would ye have me leave you?"

Any place is better than this. If you take me to a French port, I can pay you. Enough," he turned to be sure that crewmen on the deck could hear him, "enough for everyone on your ship to share in the reward."

It was clever of the man, John thought, to appeal to the crew with the promise of money. The harmony that Foxe had so carefully nurtured was now at risk. Picot was hoping that Foxe would agree, rather than risk disappointing his crew.

"How much are you willing to pay?"

"A hundred ducats."

"And where would you find this money?"

"It is hidden at a place near here."

"A hundred ducats is not enough. We will require two hundred fourteen ducats." John overheard one of the crewmen behind him mutter in agreement.

Picot hesitated. *Maybe he doesn't have two hundred fourteen ducats*, thought John. *Maybe he doesn't have any at all. Maybe he's lying, to save his life.*

Picot agreed. "*Oui*, two hundred fourteen ducats."

"When will you pay us?"

"Tonight. I will have to go ashore and return when the rest of the crew is not watching me. I will return to shore with the skiff now and tell them that I was negotiating with you for more supplies. Give me something to take back with me, to show that I was successful."

Foxe looked him over carefully. "Mr. Cox, fetch some rope. It is hard to hang a man without rope."

Picot blanched.

"Also," Foxe added with a smile, "Half a dozen of the cutlasses we captured, some shot, and a basket of those *patatas*."

Picot exhaled, "Your sense of humor is harsh, Captain."

"That is not all that ye will find harsh about me, if ye try to board my ship again, without the money ye have promised."

The supplies were transferred to the skiff, and Picot rowed back to shore. He was met by the other buccaneers. They did not hang him, not just yet.

"We will be delayed another night," said Foxe to John. "It grieves me sore, but I don't want to sail with a crew that believes they were cheated out of a fortune amounting to a whole ducat!" He said it loudly enough that some of the crewmen could hear him; soon everyone aboard would know why they were waiting another day, and how the Captain felt about the delay. If Picot didn't return, Captain Foxe could reasonably insist that he had tried his best to get each of them that last ducat.

John was on duty on the quarterdeck through the first watch, when a hail from the seaward side of the *Queen* announced the return of Picot. He had rowed the skiff out of sight of the other buccaneers and was pulled aboard. He had two dirty-looking bags with him — one appeared to be clothing; the other landed on the deck with a metallic clink. Captain Foxe was notified, and he emerged from his cabin looking a little annoyed.

"Shall we go to your cabin, to count the payment? " asked Picot.

"Nay, we'll count it right here on the deck, with John Porter as a witness, and"—he looked around — "someone fetch Captain Cooper."

It took a few moments for Cooper to be roused, and he did not appear any more pleased to be standing on the deck in the wee hours of the morning than Foxe did. Foxe explained that he wanted Cooper and John to count Picot's payment together and verify the amount. A lantern was fetched, and they spilled the contents of one of Picot's bags. It came to exactly two hundred fourteen ducats — they counted it twice to be sure. "Cut the skiff adrift in the cove," ordered Foxe. "The buccaneers can swim out to fetch it in the morning."

"Captain Cooper, take this money, and the Carpenter, to the map room. Explain to the guard that this is being added to the crew's plunder in the chest that we put there last week and allow the guard to watch you carefully. Then return the key to me," Foxe said, handing the old key to Cooper. John and Cooper did as instructed then returned the key to Foxe.

Foxe, in the meantime, had ordered the few crewmen on duty to raise anchor, and took his place on the quarterdeck, next to the helmsman. He guided the *Queen* out of the cove and onto the open sea. Once she was well out into the channel, he gave the order to put on more sail, and the *Queen* began to run fair out — a following wind, a course for home. The moon went down in the west, just as it grew light in the east. Homer came on deck at the end of the watch and took a few sightings to establish their latitude and speed. "Twenty-five degrees north, six knots," he reported. Foxe grunted with satisfaction. "This is what sailing should be," he said, "a swift ship, a stout crew, and home just beyond the horizon."

At the end of his watch, John did not return to his bunk; the sun would be up soon, and the events of the night had left him wide awake. Now that he was finally heading home, something inside him began to relax. He tried to imagine what his life would be like in England. He would try to get the letter from the Carpenter's Guild that proclaimed him a Master Carpenter, of course, then he could go where he liked. Not to sea — he would find someplace well inland. And then, he would have twenty-four pounds! With money like that, he might buy a workshop somewhere, and take on apprentices. He recalled that this was more or less what Foxe had promised him when the voyage began. Not that he was ready to thank the Captain for pressing him into service, but it was looking like he might survive this adventure after all, and Foxe, with all his devious and self-interested maneuvering, was due most of the credit for that.

John reminded himself that he wasn't home yet. Dick Benby and the bathers appeared on the main deck, and John joined them. The sea water was warm, and it felt to him a little like a ceremony, a washing away of the bloody and bitter past, an embrace of the possibilities of the future. Benby looked him in the eyes and said, "I see that you have ended some things, Carpenter. That is wise. You have not finished, though."

It was true, John felt. His heart was easier, but not yet at ease. The events of the last nine months would be with him for some time, yet — probably to the end of his life. But it appeared that he would have a life, and he was happy to think so.

June 15, 1586: Hurricano

They had several days of good sailing. Winds were westerly, but the *Queen* was headed west and north anyway. A broad reach was all she needed to make five or six knots. Homer was busy with his sextant and seemed dissatisfied with his readings. John noticed this, and asked him, "Is anything wrong ?"

Homer shook his head. "I don't know. My readings don't make sense. Let me show you." Homer led him into the Chart Room. Homer pointed to where he had been marking each estimated position on their northwestward course. "Here is where we were yesterday, and here is where we most likely are today. What do you see?"

"It looks like we are making good speed," said John. "I think I heard you say we were making six knots."

"Yes, very good speed. If you calculate the distance we have traveled in the last twenty-four hours, it comes to nearly two hundred sixty miles, based on our latitude."

"That's a lot!"

"Indeed, it is. If you calculate the speed necessary to go that distance, we would have to be traveling at eleven knots per hour, not six."

"That doesn't seem likely. Maybe the chart is wrong."

"The chart probably is wrong, but that doesn't explain the speed. It's based on the latitude I have calculated, not the chart."

John looked at the chart again. "See here," he said, "The chart says the coastline runs southwest to northeast. If it actually ran due north, you would gain more latitude in fewer miles, wouldn't you?"

Homer nodded. "You're right, we would. I tried calculating it that way, and it still comes out to nine knots, not six. And that doesn't explain why the compass readings say that our actual course is to the northeast. I have taken more than the usual number of sightings of the sun and the stars. I am confident that the latitude I have calculated is correct. I can't explain this."

"Can't explain what?" Captain Foxe stepped into the chart room. Homer showed him the chart with the calculated positions and explained the problem.

Foxe nodded. "I have heard of this. Others have reported the same sort of thing in these waters. Some say there is something about the place that befuddles the instruments or makes the sun and stars appear out of place. Some call the waters bewitched. One bright fellow even tried to convince me that there is a river in the ocean hereabouts."

"A river in the ocean? How would you be able to prove such a thing"?

"I don't suppose you could," said Homer. "If such a thing existed, you couldn't detect it with any of our instruments."

"I think you could," said John.

"And how would you do it then, Carpenter?" asked Foxe.

If two ships sail in opposite directions between two fixed points, the one sailing with the "river" would arrive at its destination before the one sailing against the "river," wouldn't it ?"

"Aye, but you've no way to keep the points fixed on the open sea."

John thought a minute and had to agree. "But if we turn about and sail the same course we have been on in the opposite direction, the latitude readings would make it appear that we were going slower than our calculated speed, wouldn't they? If there really is a river in the sea, that is?"

Homer nodded thoughtfully.

"Ye can put such a thought entirely out of your mind," said Foxe, "We are headed in only one direction, and that is homeward! If we are making as much speed as Homer's calculations say we are, we'll be home that much sooner. And do not mention any of this to the crew. If they hear a rumor that our ship has been carried off course by some invisible force that defies nature, it could lead to mutiny. They are superstitious enough, as it is."

Mutiny again, thought John. Foxe seemed preoccupied with the threat. Why? Where was the bold, aggressive commander of Santo Domingo? Was there something particularly perilous about these waters that Foxe wasn't willing to talk about?

That night, John had the dream again, of the dead buccaneer. He awoke with a start and heard eight bells. What was it — end of the first watch, maybe, or the sixth? He didn't want to return to his dreams, so he dressed and went out onto the quarterdeck. It was more crowded than usual, with one watch going off duty, and another just coming on. It turned out to be the beginning of the first watch — midnight, more or less. John stood along the starboard rail and breathed the night air. Clouds were forming ahead of them, stars were blazing to the stern.

"Trouble sleeping, Carpenter?" Foxe's voice came from behind him on the poop deck. John nodded and climbed the stairs to join him.

"Yes, trouble. And the same for you, I suppose?"

Foxe didn't answer immediately, but gazed astern at the brilliant stars, and then forward to the bank of clouds that lay ahead of them. At length, he spoke: "This part of a voyage tests a captain and his crew severely. Men bear the terror of battle, and the privation of a long voyage, only to fail just as success is in their grasp. Even in sight of a safe haven, their discipline may waver, or their luck may turn against them."

This was a side of the man John had not seen before. Had he been drinking? Was he obsessed with the fear of mutiny? Why now, when things were looking so promising? "Are you still worried about mutiny?"

Foxe turned to him. "This is not a conversation for the poop deck. Join me in my cabin."

John followed him down to the quarterdeck, and into Foxe's cabin. Foxe sighed as he lowered himself into a chair. John noted an open bottle of some beverage or other on the captain's desk — wine maybe, or something stronger.

"I speak from experience," Foxe began. "Often the end of a voyage is the most perilous part. And yes, I fear a mutiny, but there are other dangers ahead of us that I have no name for. I fear we are yet to be tested; I can feel it."

Or find it in a bottle? Thought John.

Foxe caught his glance at the bottle. "Nay, I know what ye're thinking. I'm not drunk, just looking for something to help me sleep." He corked the bottle.

"Surely, it's good news, if Homer's navigation is correct. The less time it takes us to get home, the less opportunity for a mutiny, or some other misfortune?"

Foxe nodded. "Unless this is an omen of trouble ahead. Unless some invisible power is propelling us into the teeth of some disaster. The sea can be a treacherous mistress, never forget that!"

The man was in a melancholy mood, whether the bottle was to blame or not. John had no idea how to improve the Captain's attitude, but it wouldn't help if the crew saw him in this state.

"Whatever we are to face, I trust that you will be able to lead us through it and bring us home." This was not entirely true, but it seemed like the right thing to say.

Foxe looked at him with a weak smile. "Thank ye for your kind words, Carpenter, but ye do not know the sea like I do."

"True enough," replied John. "But what I do know I have learned from you. I have seen your prudence, your care for the welfare of your crew, your coolness in battle. I have also observed how your deviousness and calculation have worked to the benefit of all, even though it has not always been to my personal advantage. I cannot think of a decision you have made that should have been done differently — unless it has to do with that bottle."

Foxe chuckled and put the bottle away. "Ah, Carpenter, you've a way with words, and that's a fact. Tell me, what is it keeps you up at night?"

"I am not suited to this seaman's life. There is too much death and peril. It does not help that I am an officer on this ship — it simply means that I share responsibility for all that goes on here."

Foxe nodded, "Aye, and ye have done well to shoulder the responsibility. Ye have shown yourself worthy of my trust, and the respect of everyone here. I chose well when I selected ye for my crew."

"That selection, as you call it, was no choice of mine. And the duties you assign to me are not my choice, either. You use me, as you use every one of the crew, for your purposes. I will not deny that your purpose is to assure our survival and success, but I am not suited to this life. Why should I be the one to vouch for the security of each seaman's share of the plunder?"

"I gave you that task because the men trust you. You have acquired a reputation among them — for honesty, for piety, and now, for valor."

"I strive to be honest with all men," John replied. "If I appear pious, it is only because we have no clergymen among us. As for my supposed valor, it is all the work of other men's imagination. I grappled with a man. I fell off the ship. That is all. If Captain Cooper and his men had not come to my rescue, I would be dead."

"And yet Cooper and his men believe that they were following your lead when they boarded the *Vengeur*. It resulted in the capture of Captain Picot, and the end of the battle. It saved a few lives in the bargain. Cooper praises your fearlessness to any who will listen."

"I think Captain Cooper burnishes his own reputation by telling the story that way."

Foxe nodded. "So he does. So all men do when they tell war stories. It helps to celebrate the valor of others when a man reflects on his own fear of death. Captain Cooper has his own war story to tell, of valor appearing when it was not expected. Why should this trouble you?"

"I think I may have killed a man, but that does not make me courageous. If I had acted with intention, I might claim credit, but this might as well have been an accident. A man has lost his life, and others praise me. I am uneasy with the thought."

"Uneasy? Why should it be otherwise? Men who become easy with the taking of another's life have traveled far on the road to perdition."

"I fought to defend my own life and the lives of my shipmates. I cannot recall enough of the battle to decide whether any died by my hand, or not. I would prefer to think that the men I fought with were only wounded or died of some other cause. The uncertainty nags at me."

"If it eases your conscience to think you can wash the blood from your hands only so long as you did not do the deed yourself, take such ease as you can. You may also tell yourself that you did not volunteer to be in this place, or that the fight was forced upon you by another man's greed or desperation. Some men find comfort in such thoughts. But you cannot deny that your actions have contributed to the death of some men and the survival of others. That is true regardless of whether any shot you fired or blow you struck, actually killed someone. It is madness to pretend otherwise."

"So, as long as I am aboard this ship, I am complicit in a world of bloodshed and death? Small wonder that I long to be in England!"

Foxe appeared to be completely sober, now. "Suppose that you could pay another man to be here in your place, facing the same enemy, with the same resources. Would it absolve you from responsibility for his deeds? Before you answer, consider that sending another man in your place to face the battle is precisely what princes and clergymen, and the wealthy have been doing from times long past. Are they free of blood guilt because of that?"

John shook his head. "No, they have a share, like everyone else."

Foxe continued, "It is war. Wars are the work of princes and the nations that do their bidding — from the lowest-ranking soldier to the banker who finances them, to the farmer who reaps a harvest to feed them all, and the pretty maids who send them off to war with a kiss and a smile. How can anyone's hands be clean?"

John said nothing. Foxe continued," The truth is, any man who would cleanse himself utterly from blood guilt must be prepared to pay with his own blood. Such men are called traitors — and treason is punished with a particularly cruel death. They may be remembered as martyrs, but memory is all that remains of them."

He continued, "Do not despise the men who would follow you, because they think your courage is greater than their own and would borrow some of yours, so to speak, to sustain them in their moment of crisis."

John shook his head again. "I did not seek their trust or admiration; it burdens me."

"As well it should. When men look to you for their welfare, you are obligated to serve them to the best of your ability. Anything less is tyranny. A good King understands this, as does a good ship's Captain, or the Master of any household in England. We could do with more good men and fewer tyrants."

Foxe added, "These men are not fools to admire you, or to trust you, or to follow you," he continued. "They know the difference between an honorable man and a rascal, even if they are willing to follow a rascal when there seems to be advantage in it. The esteem they hold for you is not because of the way that Captain Cooper tells the story of your battle with the buccaneers. They enjoy the story because it is the thing they would like most to remember of that day. What other story should they tell — that they trapped the buccaneers against a gunwale and mowed them down like so much wheat? Even a hardened seaman would find *that* story lying heavy on his conscience; many of these lads are younger than you."

"Cling to your recollection of the battle for as long as it pleases you," said Foxe in a gentler tone. "There is virtue in keeping the truth — your truth — alive in your memory for as long as you can bear the burden of it. Most men discover that over time their recollection of past events differs from what others recall. The more the story is told, the less recognizable it will seem. One day, they will tell the story, and the name of the fearless carpenter will not be yours. When that day comes, you will be free of your own legend."

John sighed. "I wish I could be free of it now."

"Nay, we are not safely home. Yer legend may yet be of use to me."

"Is that what a sea captain does? Use the legends told by other men, to achieve his purposes?"

Foxe was silent for a moment. "I knew ye to be a perceptive man, Carpenter, but ye have outdone yourself; that's a very astute observation. Yes, ye could say that that is what every successful Captain must do. He recruits his crew based on his reputation — the stories men tell about him. He maintains discipline aboard his ship, through a mixture of admiration and fear — either of which may be based on exaggeration in the stories men tell about him; no matter, just as long as discipline is maintained.

Investors who know nothing about seafaring will finance a voyage or not, depending on the stories that men tell."

"But how does this legend about me help you?"

"In the first case, it burnishes my reputation just to be associated with a man that others admire and respect, as you noted. If some in the crew should flirt with mutiny, your loyalty to me could tip the balance in my favor."

"You are staking a lot on my loyalty, considering how you got me aboard this vessel."

"I know how eager you are to get home. I do not believe you would trade that hope for the life of an outlaw. I know that you will not be seduced by the promise of greater riches, as so many men could be. Nay, do not shake your head. Honest men often imagine that all men have as much integrity as they do. It is a dangerous delusion. At least half the sailors on this vessel could be persuaded to throw me into the sea for nothing more than the promise of a handful of gold coins if they thought they could get away with it. That is why I had to take Picot aboard."

"Do you really think a mutiny is likely?"

"Right now, it is the likeliest thing that could make this voyage a failure, however likely or unlikely. If it happens, Picot will be behind it, or Wilkes, or both. We must be vigilant."

"Why not just lock them up?"

"If I did that, it would be an admission that they are a threat and that I fear them. That could prove more dangerous to this ship than letting them remain free. If the crew senses that I am acting out of fear, their courage will waver, and any little crisis become our undoing. We must put on a brave face, until the hour of crisis. Who knows? If we are strong, it may deter the trouble altogether. It is easier to face the danger when it appears than to worry over it, not knowing whence it will come."

There was a loud rapping on the cabin door. "Captain! You are wanted on deck!"

When they reached the quarterdeck, it was clear what the fuss was about. The wind had picked up, and heavy clouds filled the sky ahead. Flashes of lightning were visible all across the northern horizon. Astern, the clouds were thinner, but few stars could be seen. The helmsman struggled to hold a northeast course, with a northwest wind coming off the port side.

Foxe sized the situation up quickly. "We're in for a blow, lads!" he exclaimed. He ordered the sails on the foremast and the mainmast furled, and the hatch covers battened down. He called for the officers, and began firing orders: "Mr. Benby, secure all the guns on the main deck with doubled lashings; do the same for the gun deck. Mr. Vandoorn, secure the looted artillery in the hold — can't have it rolling around down there . . ."

So it went. Foxe was a man in his element, now; no more waiting for an unnamed disaster, the present one would suffice. He was everything that he needed to be at the moment — a Captain, a man in command . . .

A man, John realized, who needs a crisis to draw the best out of him. Without the crisis, he is something less . . . a man at the mercy of his talents and his ambition . . . A man who inhabits a world of his own creation but knows that he cannot control it. A man who knows in his heart that nothing he creates can endure. A man who knows his creation is born with the seeds of its own destruction, that he has populated his world with the agents of his downfall. A man who knows his cleverness and courage will never be enough to ensure his success.

As the westerly winds intensified, the *Egyptian Queen* changed her course to put the winds astern. "We'll let her run," said Foxe. "Just the one sail on the mizzenmast, to give us steerage. There will be waves, but we won't be crossing them — less water over the gunwales."

They were well into the second watch now, but there was no light from the stars. Lightning flared in every direction, and the waves grew taller. The wind tore at the whitecaps, and the spray flew across the decks from stern to bow. The waves were high enough that seawater spilled over the gunwales on either side whenever the Queen crested a wave — John hoped the hatch covers were tight. The bilge pumps were working nonstop, in any case. The only light was from the lightning which flickered almost continuously. Most of the crew was below decks, but John stood on the quarterdeck with Foxe, the helmsman, and Homer, who was trying to record the *Queen*'s speed, for his navigation. There were also watchmen on the bow and stern, though Foxe said it was unlikely they would see anything but waves and lightning — they were on the open sea, and no land was known to be in the vicinity.

The alarm came from the watchman at the stern, on the poop deck. He screamed something about a "sea devil," and Foxe climbed to get a view, followed by John.

The watchman pointed astern, where John could see three or four long, pointed clouds hanging down to the sea — "The Devil's teeth," said the watchman, as if he knew what he was talking about. There were more of them visible in the distance to port or starboard, as the lightning flashes illuminated them briefly, then they disappeared in the darkness. The watchman was clearly terrified, and it was hard to blame him. Then John felt a tingling sensation, and the darkness receded a bit. The watchman looked at him with wide eyes and blurted out "St. Elmo's fire!" John turned to Foxe, who was looking back at him with some surprise. "So it is," he said. "The saint is protecting us." John realized that a bluish glow was shining from the brim of his hat. He reached to touch it, but Foxe said, "Nay, touch it not! It is a holy thing!" John was too astonished by the whole scene to move, so he just stood there, which was evidently what Foxe wanted. "Look!" he said. "At the top of the mainmast!"

There was a brilliant blue aura at the top of the mainmast, now, that illuminated the whole deck. John looked back to sea, where the "teeth" appeared to be drawn back into the clouds, one by one. The light on the mast persisted for several minutes more, then faded.

By the next turning of the sandglass the winds had eased. There were still whitecaps on the waves but the lightning was farther away, now. John thought it must be near daybreak — four bells into the second watch. He was soaked to the skin, but somehow warm, his mind spinning with the excitement of the past hour. In another turning of the sandglass it was getting light in the east, and the rain had eased to a slow drizzle, which soon faded away. John went back to his cabin to change into dry clothing. He began to think of breakfast.

Before the mast, the crew of the *Queen* had had a rough night, but no one was seriously injured. Some of the Spanish cannons had rolled around in the hold, but the sailors were wise enough to stay out of the way. Men were short on sleep, but the story of the "Devil's teeth" and "St. Elmo" spread rapidly, and most were relieved and even cheerful to have avoided some grim fate. Several seamen approached John and asked to look at his hat.

Some damage was reported to the starboard gunwale, and John went to inspect it after breakfast. He found a crack in one of the starboard planks, where the wood had been weakened by a cluster of bullet holes. It would not be difficult to repair, thought John, as he recalled the reason for all those holes at just that spot, and the men who had died there — their graves on some nameless island in the Floridas. He sighed and turned his mind to other things. He didn't need to replace the plank; he could just cut another piece to fit the space between the ribs at either end of the damaged section. He went below decks with the Boatswain, and they found no other serious problems; the *Queen* had weathered the storm very well.

John fetched some wood from the hold and went to his cabin to get his tools. He met Foxe on the quarterdeck, who was in a very good mood. "I think I shall call you 'Elmo' from now on," Foxe laughed at his own joke. John reported the damage to the gunwale and the results of his inspection with the Boatswain. Foxe expressed satisfaction with his plan to repair the damage.

"Captain, the winds are shifting to the south. What is our heading?" Homer was on the quarterdeck, ready to make his calculations at the next turning of the sandglass.

"Keep the wind astern of us," replied Foxe. "Unless I miss my guess, the winds will gradually turn more southerly, as the day progresses. By nightfall, we could be sailing due north."

"How do you know this"? Asked John.

Foxe looked at Homer. "Can you explain it to him?"

Homer nodded. "We didn't pass through a storm last night; we barely grazed it. Storms like this occur in these waters — the Spanish call them *hurricano*. These storms move in a great circle, with the strongest winds near their center. I have heard that at the very center of a *hurricano*, there is a place of calm and sunlight, which moves wherever the storm goes. I have not seen such a thing, and I do not wish to. Last night. We sailed along the southern edge of the *hurricano*, and we were pushed far to the east. As the storm passes us, we will encounter the winds at its Eastern edge, which will be from the south, or so the captain expects."

"So, we're off course? By how much?"

"That is difficult to say until I can take some sightings of the sun or stars. That may not happen until tomorrow, or the next day. As long as the *hurricano* moves west, we will try to steer behind it to the east, until we are well away from it. However, we do know that England is both north and east of where we were, so we cannot be too far out of our way. Before long we will be at the proper latitude to catch the westerly trade winds, which will take us home."

"But we still don't know our longitude?"

Homer shook his head. "No, and we won't, until we sight land."

John took his tools to the main deck and began cutting his lumber to size. Crewmen passed him from time to time and greeted him. Some merely nodded and gave him a queer look. He supposed that the legend they would tell about him had gained another tale — of a man who glowed in the darkness of a storm; a man "tetched" by the supernatural, a holy man, perhaps, or maybe a sorcerer. He was not far wrong, though some of the speculations were even wilder than that — some thought he had been struck by lightning and survived. Others believed that he had received magical powers, and had employed them to deliver the *Queen* and its crew from the "Devil's Teeth"(There was at least one eyewitness to this event, and he was emphatic about what he had seen).

John was not surprised, then, when Wilkes approached him and asked to speak privately. "Mr. Porter," he was nearly whispering, "There is a matter Captain Picot and I would like to discuss with you, in private. A matter that could be to your great benefit, and the benefit of the entire crew."

So, here it was, just as Foxe had feared. John kept his eyes on his work. "There are not many private places on the ship. Where do you suggest we meet?"

"The foredeck is downwind of the rest of the ship; our voices will be carried away on the wind if we are quiet about it. Will you come?"

"You see that I am busy, now. I cannot drop everything and walk to the foredeck with you without it being noticed. I can meet you there in half an hour."

"Very good, Sir." With that, Wilkes was gone.

John focused on finishing the repairs, while he considered what to do. He needed to know exactly what Picot and Wilkes were cooking up. He also needed to avoid implicating himself in any mutiny or appearing to support such a thing. When finished, he collected his tools and took them back to the cabin. He found Roger on the quarterdeck and briefly whispered something in his ear. Roger nodded.

John left his tools in his cabin, then headed back to the main deck. He stopped to pick up several scraps of wood near the gunwale and took them below. Moments later, he emerged from the forward hatch and climbed the stairs to the foredeck, where Picot and Wilkes were leaning casually against the railing. They were at the bow, with a good view of the ocean in front of them. The great bow cannons — including Mary and Martha — were on the deck immediately under their feet.

John took his place between them as if admiring the view. "What is this matter that you would speak of?"

"The matter is delicate. Captain Picot has a suggestion that might profit all of us, but Captain Foxe must be persuaded to go along, and we think he is unlikely to give either of us a fair hearing on the matter," Wilkes explained.

"We know that he respects you, as indeed the entire crew does. We think that Captain Foxe might listen, if the suggestion came from your mouth, rather than ours," added Picot.

Or more likely, thought John, *If the suggestion is rejected, the captain's wrath would fall on me, rather than the two of you.* "What is the suggestion?"

"Before we tell you, we need to know that you are dealing fairly with us. What was it that you spoke to the cabin boy about, just moments ago?"

So. They had been watching him, ever since Wilkes had approached him. "Roger owes me a favor. If Captain Foxe summons me to his cabin sometime in the next half hour, I asked Roger to make some excuse for my absence, until our conversation is finished. Best we not tarry too long."

They seemed satisfied with this explanation. "In any case, our conversation must be confidential, as between three gentlemen, do you agree?"

Gentlemen did not properly describe the social rank of any of them, least of all John, but he nodded. "Go on, then."

"The bulk of our plunder from this expedition is in the form of the captured artillery in our hold, as you know," began Wilkes. "Of course, I do not include the treasure that we captured from Captain Picot and his men, which Captain Foxe has properly declared to be the property of the whole crew."

John glanced at Picot when the treasure was mentioned, and noticed a tightening of his neck muscles; otherwise, he appeared to be unfazed.

Wilkes continued: "But the crew's share of the cargo will only be what is left after the crown's agents take half of them, and then the investors take half of the remainder. Three-quarters of them will be taken before the crew sees any profit at all! But it doesn't have to be that way. If we sell the cargo outright, before the royal revenue knows about it, the crew's share would be four times larger."

"I can hardly believe that we could sell that many cannons in any English port, without the government finding out about it. Smuggling small items is one thing, but artillery is not the sort of thing that is bought and sold every day in the market. If we were caught, the penalties for such an attempt would be harsh!"

"We would not try to sell them in England. We would sell them in France." Picot's voice was calm and matter-of-fact. "There is war in

France, and the demand for weapons is high. We could get a very good price for them in France."

"And do you know where to find buyers, in France?" John directed the question to Picot.

Picot nodded.

"So, are you willing to help us?" Wilkes again.

"What exactly do you want me to do?"

"We want you to bring the suggestion to Captain Foxe. As I said, we don't think he would welcome any suggestions from the two of us. In fact, it would be best if you do not mention our names at all. You could just ask the question of whether he had thought of selling the artillery in France; he has promised to deliver Captain Picot to France on our way home anyway, so it wouldn't have to be out of our way. When we get back to England, we could say that the guns had to be thrown overboard in a storm, or something."

Wilkes was getting ahead of himself, thought John. It was one thing to plant a suggestion in Foxe's mind, but Wilkes was several steps ahead, to the point of creating an explanation for why the guns would never make it to England. No doubt the two of them had already made plans to bring their "suggestion" to fruition, with or without Captain Foxe.

As yet, however, they had not suggested anything like mutiny. That might well come, if Foxe refused their suggestion, or even if John refused to relay it to them. He decided to agree to their request. "All right, I will sound the Captain out. You must understand, though, that if any of this discussion reaches the crew, your suggestion will be rejected out of hand — Captain Foxe is not a man who will have his hand forced by popular demand."

Wilkes flinched, with a moment of recollection, and nodded. Picot was more discreet in his expression, but nodded, as well.

"I think it best if each of you leave our little gathering separately, and me last of all, lest it appear to anyone watching that you summoned me here and then dismissed me." Picot's expression said that he understood John's reasoning all too well; Wilkes's expression said he had forgotten that they were almost certainly being observed during the whole conversation.

"A fine tale, Carpenter," said Picot loudly enough to be heard, "A tale to tell your grandchildren, may you live so long!" Picot leaned away from the railing and wandered back to the main deck.

"Wait," said John as Wilkes started to pull away. "Wait awhile longer. Tell me something funny. Make me laugh."

Wilkes swallowed, at a loss for any words, much less funny ones. John almost felt sorry for him. Picot was cleverer, even ruthless, focused on his own interests. Wilkes was in over his head, searching desperately for some financial advantage, and thus a tool in Picot's plans.

Finally, John let Wilkes go, with a laugh loud enough to be heard on the main deck, and a slap on the back. John stayed at the bow railing a few minutes longer. "Mr. Benby?" he bent over the forward rail.

"Right here, Carpenter." Benby's voice came from the gun deck below, where Mary and Martha sat, waiting for some target to appear.

"Did you hear enough?"

"Aye, I heard it all."

John decided it was time to visit Captain Foxe.

June 17, 1586: Secrets

J ohn did not go directly to Foxe's cabin. He was assigned to the quarterdeck for the next watch and just had time to grab a little supper first. The wind did, indeed, turn gradually southward as the watch progressed. Foxe ordered the sails on the foremast and the mainmast unfurled, and the *Queen* began to pick up speed — "7 knots!" Homer reported with some satisfaction. The waves were white-capped, but not high enough to spill over the gunwales. As each swell overtook the *Egyptian Queen,* her stern rose a little, then lowered as the passing wave lifted her amidships, and finally her bow, before the next one lifted her stern again. A lively ride, a steady rhythm, pushing the ship forward, forward across a grey, trackless ocean, not knowing where they were, nor how long it might be before they sighted land, not caring, really. John reflected that nine months ago, this situation would have been alarming, but now he found himself enjoying it.

The skies were still grey, and the sea mirrored their color. Something in the way that the *Queen* rode the waves felt like a validation of his labors, and the seamanship of his companions. They had met what the sea and the weather had to offer and survived. The clouds thinned as they bore east, then north — nothing for Homer's instruments to sight on. Still, it was clear that they were making good speed.

At the end of the watch, John found Captain Foxe on the poop deck and asked for a private meeting. Foxe was in an ebullient mood, after the previous night's excitement, and was enjoying the waves as much as John had. Reluctantly, he led John down to his cabin. John felt some reluctance to be the bearer of bad news.

"So, what's yer business, Elmo?" He chuckled again at his witticism.

"I have become aware of some talk among the crew that might lead to discord or even mutiny. I thought best to make you aware of it."

"Eh? What talk?"

"Someone has suggested that the crew of the *Queen* would be better off if our cargo of artillery were sold, and the profits split among us, without surrendering a half share to the crown's agents."

"Aye, so they would. The arithmetic is easy enough to grasp. How do they propose to sell the guns without the government finding out, and hanging the lot of us?"

"They propose to sell the guns in France."

"France! That'd be Picot, then. How many others are in on this?"

"Only one that I know of. They asked me to present the suggestion to you, to see if you were receptive."

"By 'they' you mean that Wilkes and Picot are together, as I suspected they might be. If Wilkes is in it, the others from his old crew are probably in on it too . . . have you shared this with anyone else?"

"Only Mr. Benby. I arranged to have him eavesdrop on our conversation so that it would not be a matter of my word against theirs."

"That was clever." Foxe walked to the door, opened it, and said, "Roger! Ask Mr. Benby to come to my cabin. And quickly."

Benby showed up just moments later. He confirmed what John had told Foxe about his meeting on the foredeck. Benby stated that he had not shared what he overheard with anyone else. "Good!" said Foxe.

"They haven't actually talked of mutiny," John pointed out, "just offered a suggestion. I suppose that you could lock them up for the rest of the voyage, but you'd hardly have cause to hang them."

"Aye," said Foxe. "Hanging them is out of the question. This is just the first move in a chess game, though I think I know what their endgame is. Locking them up would make it look like I'm playing a weak hand. Men in the brig can still speak to the crew and still make trouble. We must find another way to neutralize them."

Foxe turned to John. "They asked you to suggest the change did they? Did you agree to bring the suggestion to me?"

"I did, and I have," John replied.

"Then take a message to them for me. Tell them I want to hear more about their suggestion. Tell them that no one else must know what we will be discussing."

John was surprised that Foxe seemed open to the idea, surprised also that Foxe seemed so amenable to meeting with men whose clear intent was to take his ship from him. Foxe, of course, had some plan of his own in mind, John realized. Wilkes was no match for Foxe in a game of this sort; he doubted that Picot understood what he had gotten himself into. He smiled to himself. He was going to enjoy this.

John found Picot and Wilkes below decks and separately informed them that the Captain wanted to hear more about their idea. Wilkes took the news with apparent excitement; Picot seemed surprised. *Not the response he was expecting*, thought John.

They met in Foxe's cabin after dinner, during the fifth watch. "Sirs, I am informed that ye have a notion of how our voyage might be made more profitable. I would hear you say more," began Foxe. *A good opening move* thought John. *Don't tell them more than necessary about what you know, make them come up with the details.*

Wilkes spoke first. "Most of the plunder in our hold is in the form of the Spanish artillery that we captured. At two hundred pounds sterling each, there's more than seven thousand pounds down there, maybe more. If everyone on the ship got an equal share, it would come to almost thirty pounds per man!"

"I see that your arithmetic is sound, but how do you propose to sell these guns in England, without the government finding out about it?"

"That's the beauty of Captain Picot's inspiration. We don't sell them in England, we sell them in France!"

"In France? I see it now. And does Captain Picot have a buyer in mind?"

"I know of several men in France, who would buy them," said Picot.

"And every man to get an equal share?"

"Not necessarily. It is common practice for the officers of a ship to get a larger share than the ordinary crewmen. We would have to ensure that every crewman was treated fairly, with enough at stake to guarantee his discretion."

"That's a good point," said Foxe. "If any one of them breathed a word of such a thing in England, every man in this room would be bound for the gallows. With the possible exception of Captain Picot, of course, assuming he stays in France." Ah, thought John, there's the fly in the ointment. Who would believe that two hundred fourteen men would keep a secret like that?

Evidently, Wilkes would believe it. "I think we could count on their discretion, for the thirty pounds!" he exclaimed.

"That's as may be," replied Foxe. "Tell me Mr. Wilkes, what are your feelings about the Spanish Navy?"

"I have nothing but hatred for them, after the way they treated my men in Santo Domingo. If I ever get the chance to pay them back, I will do it with relish."

"Captain Picot has reason to hate them as well, I think. But if we sold the guns in France, so that they wound up in the hands of the Spanish and were used against this ship, or any English ship, or, God forbid, to invade our homeland, you would rue the day we sold them, would you not?"

"I would never let such a thing happen. I would rather the crown's agents have all the guns, and give us nothing for them, than to let the Spaniards have them, at any price!"

Picot said nothing but looked uncomfortable. *There it is*, thought John. *Foxe has driven a wedge between the two. Wilkes, for all his greed and naïveté, is a patriot. Picot owes nothing to our cause, and might well side with the Spanish, as so many Frenchmen have. Picot's hold over Wilkes is weakened; yet he needs Wilkes because Wilkes can command the loyalty of the four men from his crew that we rescued from the jail in Santo Domingo.*

Picot's face looked as if he had just tasted something sour.

Foxe turned his gaze to Picot. "I think you will agree that once a thing is sold, there is no telling who may own it in the future?"

Picot nodded. Then, Foxe surprised John: "Still, thirty pounds is thirty pounds." Wilkes' face took on a hopeful expression, Picot's face showed surprise. Foxe continued "I think both of you would agree that a project like this requires total secrecy?"

Both men nodded, waiting for what he would say next.

"I cannot consider this further unless I have your assurance that no one outside this room has heard anything of this, nor will they, until I have made up my mind. Do you understand?"

They nodded again.

"If I hear the whisper of a rumor from the crew that something like this is afoot, the whole idea must be rejected, and I may be forced to hang someone for treason. Do you understand?"

Wilkes looked excited, Picot brooding. *That's it*, John thought, *he has trapped them. The two cannot bring any more men into their conspiracy, without jeopardizing the whole. Their best hope of pulling it off is if Foxe himself leads it. He has kidnapped their plan, and they have to wait for him to decide whether he adopts it or not, in his own time. If they knew Foxe at all, they would realize how unlikely it was that he would risk his career, his investors, and his ship for just thirty pounds.*

John reflected that Picot had probably intended this gambit as merely the first move in a long, complicated game that would end with him in command of the *Egyptian Queen*. But Foxe had created a split between Picot and Wilkes. Wilkes would insist on no further action, until it became clear what Foxe's intentions were, and Foxe would not be in a hurry to show his hand. Picot was now isolated — checked, if not checkmated.

Foxe stood up. "You have given me much to think about, and I thank you for your time." He was cordial, but both of them recognized that they had been dismissed.

Just before noon the following day, the sun came out. The winds were directly from the south, now, just as Captain Foxe had predicted. Homer got a reading at high noon, "33 degrees north latitude," he reported. "Either the storm pushed us farther than I thought possible, or my instruments are still unreliable." He shook his head.

"If the storm has indeed helped us," asked John, "how long would it take us to get home?"

"If we catch the westerly trade winds, it's about three weeks. The Atlantic Ocean is narrower at the northern latitudes. Of course, we still don't know our longitude. Four weeks, at most. I am confident of our speed — we've been making six knots steadily for the past three days — or more if you believe the instruments."

As the winds began to lessen, the *Queen* put on more sail. The heading was now north by northeast, even as the winds shifted from due south to a bit west of south. By the next morning, the skies were clear, and the *hurricano* was a memory. A brisk southwest wind began to blow, and Homer was elated: "We've found the trades," he said, "this is our way home!"

So it went, for two weeks. Fair weather, and steady winds. When they reached forty degrees north latitude, the heading was adjusted to east of northeast. "We are now at the latitude of Portugal," explained Homer. "There's no point in sailing to the north of 50 degrees, we'll wind up in Ireland. We'll be sailing due east when we reach 50 degrees, which should put us in sight of the English coast, once we've sailed far enough to eastward."

"And if we miss the English coast?"

"Then we hit France," Homer replied. "Once we know our longitude, we will find our way home easily enough."

The next day was stormy, though nothing like the *hurricano*. The storm came from the West, and if anything, the gusts pushed the *Queen* farther to the east, nearer her destination. Homer found that as her course became more easterly, the discrepancies in his latitude readings grew much less. Superficially, this eased his mind, a little, but he recognized that an eastward course changed his latitude not at all, and he had no way to tell if his speed and distance calculations were accurate, if his latitude didn't change.

It was about this time that Wilkes approached John again. "I must speak with you in private. It is a delicate matter," he said.

"Is Captain Picot a part of this conversation?"

"No, and I do not wish him to know of it."

Interesting. "Then let us go to the foredeck. You should act as if you are showing me some defect you have discovered, that might require carpentry to repair."

Wilkes did as suggested. He led John to the bow and leaned over it as if pointing to some problem. As luck would have it, John could see some sort of jetsam clinging to the hull below the gunports, seaweed, or some such. They looked at it together, as if it were interesting. "What is it you wish to speak of?"

"It is the matter that we spoke with Captain Foxe about a few weeks back."

No surprise, there; thought John. Wilkes and Picot were probably getting impatient. "And what about that matter needs discussing?"

Wilkes stood and turned his back to the railing, so he could see the whole ship. "I have been considering the matter, and I think it would be unwise to follow our suggestion."

This was a surprise. What were Wilkes and Picot playing at, now? "What has changed your mind?"

"It is Picot. I do not trust him. I believe he would sell the guns to the Spanish, and all of us as well, if he got the chance. If we try to do business in France, we could well lose the ship, and all our hard-won plunder."

"How did you come to this conclusion?"

"We have been talking, Picot and I. It is clear that he has ambitions, and he will pursue them at any cost. They are not ambitions for our prosperity or for England's. He thinks only of himself. I should have seen it when he so willingly abandoned the remnant of his crew in the Floridas."

"The crew that wanted to hang him, you mean?"

"We only have his word on that. I suspect that he invented that story to gain our sympathy then returned with the supplies that we gave him, to gain the trust of his men, and then betrayed them all while they slept. Where did the two hundred fourteen ducats come from, if not from a cache of treasure buried on that island? Most likely, it was treasure that all the crew had hidden there, and he helped himself to it when it served his purpose."

Could it be that Wilkes was catching on? Better late than never. John nodded. "You may be right about Picot. He has given us no reason to trust him, apart from the promise of money."

"My point, exactly," said Wilkes. "Each of us is better off with the twenty-four pounds in the chart room than with an empty promise of more, somewhere in France."

"All except Picot," John corrected him.

"Yes, all except Picot. Don't you see, the only way he profits from this voyage, is if he receives a portion of the sale of our cargo — it stands to reason that he would want us to sell it in France, where he could act as the intermediary."

"You think he is motivated by greed, then?"

"I am certain of it. He is no Englishman. He owes no allegiance to our nation or our queen. It is only the money he cares about."

"Why are you telling me this, now?" John was still not sure that Wilkes was speaking truthfully, but he couldn't see how this conversation might be part of some gambit that Wilkes and Picot had cooked up together.

"I think the Captain should know of this. I fear to approach him directly. Would you accompany me to his cabin?"

John nodded. This was getting interesting. Turning to the stern he said, loud enough to be heard by others, "Thank you for bringing this to my attention. It may be nothing, but I agree that the Captain should know of it." He then headed down to the main deckhand across to the quarterdeck, with Wilkes close behind him.

Foxe, as it happened, was in the chartroom. John introduced the topic of his conversation with Wilkes, and let Wilkes supply the details.

"So, ye're saying that we should not try to sell the guns in France, under any circumstances?"

"Yes. The farther we stay from France, the better. I fear that Picot might find compatriots there who would conspire with him to do us some harm."

John resisted the urge to snicker at the irony of Wilkes's words. Not two weeks ago, he was conspiring with Picot to do the very same. Or was Wilkes unaware of what he had been doing? Was it possible that he was oblivious to the meaning of his own actions?

More likely, thought John, *that Wilkes has concluded that the odds of success with Picot are too long, and that he would be better off ingratiating himself to Foxe, by throwing Picot overboard, so to speak.*

Foxe thanked Wilkes for his "opinion," and said he would give it serious consideration. "We should keep this conversation between ourselves," said Foxe, "Better that Picot not get wind of it. Do you agree?"

Wilkes agreed, with an expression of relief on his face.

"If anyone asks," volunteered John, "we will say that we were informing you of the condition of the bow of the *Egyptian Queen* and that Mr. Wilke's opinion (based on his experience at sea), and mine are the same."

"What? What's the condition of the bow?" Foxe was suddenly keen.

"The condition of the bow is fine. Both of us agree that there is only a bit of flotsam hung up below the figurehead, nothing more."

Foxe relaxed. "Thank you, Mr. Wilkes. Carpenter, I would speak with you on another matter." Wilkes excused himself.

"So, Carpenter, has Mr. Wilkes found a sense of honor?"

"I don't know. I have been trying to imagine how this could be part of some deep conspiracy between Wilkes and Picot, but I can't think of anything. I think it more likely that Wilkes has decided to side with you against whatever Picot is planning. If they are divided, they are much less a threat."

Foxe nodded. "I agree. I am tempted to disclose this conversation to Picot, somehow. It might nip the whole thing in the bud. Or it might force Picot to try something really desperate. If I could convince Picot that we are headed for France, while convincing Wilkes that we are not, I would have them both where I want them. But I cannot simply summon Picot here, and lie to him, however treacherous he may be."

"You have been content to deceive him, by letting him believe that you agree with him. Isn't that the same as telling an outright lie?"

"That is a question for the philosophers," Foxe replied. "Even if maintaining a deception through silence is the same as a spoken lie, the consequences are not the same. Anything that I say to Picot might still be confided to Wilkes, especially if what Wilkes just said to us remains a secret. If the two of them discover that I am saying different things to each, neither of them will believe anything I say, and my advantage over them is compromised. On the other hand, if Wilkes' story is a plan that both of them devised to sound out what my true intentions are, I give all my advantage away for nothing, by telling them what I intend to do. What do you think?"

"I think that all we need is to forestall them for another week or so. Once we sight England, the crew will be thinking of how they will spend their twenty-four pounds ashore. The sight of home will make them impervious to the appeal of mutiny. Nothing those two can say will matter."

"Right, you are, Carpenter. We need just a week or so." Homer came into the map room; it was the end of the watch. Foxe said," Homer, I need the best estimate you can give me of our position, right now."

Homer consulted a book and then did some calculation. "We are at 48 degrees, 30 minutes north latitude." That is all I can tell you for certain. He spread a chart out on the table and showed them where the line of latitude lay, in relation to the south coast of England, and the north coast of France. "We could be anywhere along this line," he said. Our heading is east by northeast, more or less. When we reach 50 degrees north latitude, I propose to sail due east, until we see land, either here," he pointed to the extreme southeastern coast of England, a place labeled 'the Lizard', "or here," he pointed to the coast of France.

Foxe frowned. "It appears that 50 degrees could run us aground, in either place."

"True enough. That is why we have lookouts."

"How long before we know our position?"

"At least a week, maybe two. Say, ten days, most likely."

"How can we be sure that we aren't already east of the Lizard?" asked John.

"We can't. But if that is true, we will sight the French coast in less than a week. That would be somewhere near Brest."

"Doesn't it make more sense to get to 50 degrees north, as soon as possible, so that whenever we sight land, we'll be closer to our destination?"

Foxe looked at the chart and nodded. "That's a point. If we're farther east than your estimate, Homer, it is to our advantage to be as far north as possible."

"I'll set our heading for north by northeast, then. It might make the voyage a little longer, but if we are farther east than I think we are, you'll see land sooner, and we'll know exactly where we are."

Foxe nodded. "No need to tell anyone at all about our change, of course, Homer. Not anyone."

Homer looked a little surprised but nodded.

Foxe turned to John. "Carpenter, I think that's the best we can do, for now."

John nodded and returned to his duties.

Foxe kept the crew busy for the next few days, scrubbing, inspecting, inventorying everything aboard the *Queen*. It was clear that he was preparing the ship for the end of her voyage. Particular attention was paid to the plunder — the guns in the hold were measured for their length and the size of their muzzles, and the metal they were cast from. John's duties involved a thorough inspection of the ship's hull and decks — after ten months at sea, the *Queen* was showing a little wear, but nothing serious. A good paint job would restore her. No telling what the condition of the hull below the water line was; "We'll careen her again, and scrape her hull, in Harwich," said Foxe.

By the end of the week, Homer announced that they had reached 50 degrees north latitude, at last. From now on, their course was due east. The winds were from the northeast, so they had to tack north or south of due east to make any headway. Although Homer was careful to guard his estimates of their position, the helmsmen recognized the change, and soon the whole crew knew that they were nearing England. The rumor was confirmed when a lookout reported land off the port bow one afternoon, just as the *Queen* was tacking back to the southeast. There was a discernible shift in the mood aboard the *Queen* — the men began singing more loudly, and laughter was heard from below decks.

The sight of land didn't tell them exactly where they were, and Homer wanted to turn north to make a more precise identification, but the wind was out of the north, and Foxe ordered him to proceed eastward. Overnight, the winds shifted westerly, and by morning, the *Queen* was making seven knots eastward. Only then did Foxe set her course a little north of due east: "If we're going to approach land, I want it to be in broad daylight — we won't be able to tell where we are in the dark, anyway, and there are shoals in these waters."

By the time Homer had a sighting, he was pretty sure they were somewhere south of Weymouth, at 50 degrees, thirty minutes north latitude, "or maybe closer to Bournemouth," he said.

"We'll steer clear of the coast, then, until tomorrow morning," Foxe declared. "There's weather coming our way, and it will probably rain tonight." Foxe was right, again. The wind picked up near evening, and visibility from the quarterdeck dropped dramatically. The ship rode out heavy seas and blowing spray, until the beginning of the second watch. By sunup, the sky was still overcast and rainy, but the wind was turning southerly, and the lookouts could see a few miles in every direction. The *Queen* eased back to the northeast. Just before noon, the coast came into view, and the skies cleared. Homer took another sighting of the sun, but it wasn't necessary — he recognized the Isle of Wight off their port side.

It occurred to John that this was the first landmark he had seen twice — ten months before on their outward voyage, and now on the return one. Full circle (though not exactly a circle), he was back in a world that was part of a previous life. It felt a little odd to think that the life he had known for the past ten months would soon be a memory (he was determined never to go to sea again!), and he would be picking up his old one, the way he might pick up an old garment, once laid aside because it was out of season, but now the very thing he needed to put back on.

Later that afternoon, Wilkes and Picot approached John. Picot looked pessimistic. Wilkes seemed a little embarrassed. They asked John whether Foxe was considering their idea about selling the artillery in France. "The Captain does not confide in me," said John, "you should ask him yourself."

Picot looked hard at Wilkes, who swallowed, and said, "Would you go with us to speak to him?"

So, this is it, thought John. Why not go with them? It might be an interesting conversation.

They found Foxe in the chart room, with Homer and Vandoorn. Foxe looked up at them and smiled. "Ah, I can guess why you men are here. You've seen the homeland, haven't you? So have the lads, I reckon. Home at last!"

Picot had the look of a man who realizes he has lost an argument before he even got the chance to speak. Wilkes appeared relieved.

"Of course," Foxe continued, "there is no way I could divert this ship to France now, even if I wanted to. The crew would be most disappointed. We'll make for Harwich; two days if the winds favor us."

Picot looked ready to speak, but Foxe cut him off. "Yes, Captain, I promised to deliver you to France, and I will. I can pay your fare on a pinnace from Harwich to almost any French port on the channel that pleases you. I think it would be prudent for you to find out the lay of the land, as they say, in France, before you choose your destination. Things may have changed there since you left. We can get news in Harwich about which ports are controlled by which sides in their civil war. It wouldn't do for you to fall into the hands of the Spanish, would it?"

That last remark probably stung, John thought. By his own account, Picot had reason to fear and detest the Spanish. No doubt Foxe had intended the jab. Now, Foxe was playing the part of a benevolent colleague, who wished to spare Picot the peril of a nasty surprise in some French port. The idea of sailing the *Queen* into any French port was out of the question now, and Picot could like it or not — the message was clear.

Wilkes probably missed the point of Foxe's remarks, John thought but nodded as if he understood it all. Plainly, the prospect of landing in England with twenty-four pounds to his name was looking like a happy end to his voyage. And why not? He was rotting in a Spanish prison just months ago.

Foxe, for his part, was anxiously anticipating some setback or other, just as their voyage was nearing its end. But luck did not turn against him, this time. Three days later, the *Egyptian Queen* was docked in Harwich, on the same long pier they had sailed from ten and a half months before.

Part 11: Picking up the Pieces

July 1586: Harwich

John Porter was expecting that the return of the *Eqyptian Queen* would be the occasion for a rush of seamen off the ship, and into the town. He was surprised that this did not happen. The first morning, Captain Foxe sent Roger and a few other men ashore, but everyone else stayed aboard.

"It is a tradition," Homer explained, "the seamen do not leave the ship until they have been paid."

"How long must we stay aboard? I am itching for a good meal."

"Sometimes, the sailors stay aboard for months." He chuckled at John's expression, "Be patient. Captain Foxe will not allow us to wait that long. I expect we will be ashore by tonight."

It was late morning, when Roger returned to the *Queen*, accompanied by several well-dressed men. They came aboard and were ushered into Foxes's cabin. When they emerged, it turned out that one of the men, Grimes, was an agent of the crown, authorized to assess the value of the *Queen's* cargo. The other, Fairchild, represented the Rich family, who had funded the purchase, refitting, and supply of the *Queen*. The two agents were taken down to the orlop deck, where most of the plunder was stored. They agreed that the most sensible thing was to lift all the captured artillery out of the hold, and onto the dock, where they could haggle over dividing the spoil. Foxe ordered some crewmen to begin moving the guns immediately.

The Rich's agent announced that he would be paying the crew that afternoon, and left with Paolo, the purser, to get the money, while the hold was unloaded. When he returned, there were more than forty guns lying on the dock — everything they had captured from the Spanish ship in Santo Domingo, or taken from the *Vengeur*, plus several more from Cartagena. There were also some chests of spices and hogsheads of rum, also from Cartagena. Foxe explained that neither of the ships that they had captured was carrying any valuable cargo. This was technically true since the treasure they took from the *Vengeur* was not actually cargo; none of the crew mentioned anything about it at all.

Just before noon, another of the shore party appeared, driving a wagon with a team of horses. Foxe greeted the sight with a shout, "Here, lads! I got ye some supper!" It was true. The wagon was loaded with bread — real bread, not the hardtack they had been eating for most of ten months, also a keg of ale, some wine, rounds of cheese, and enough hams to feed the crew. They brought it aboard and ate it on the main deck. John enjoyed it as he had not enjoyed eating anything since they left Cartagena. Things were looking up — staying on board for a few more days didn't sound so bad.

Grimes and Fairchild agreed that the artillery was the most valuable part of the plunder — around ten thousand pounds sterling — and agreed on how to divide them. By late afternoon, more wagons drew up on the dock and the Crown's share of the guns — twenty-two of them — were loaded and taken away. "They'll be stored in some royal warehouse, then put to use," explained Homer.

That left another twenty guns and the rest of the plunder. The Rich's were entitled to claim half, as the private investors who had financed the voyage. The rest could be sold and shared with the crew. Foxe addressed the crew and explained the situation: "Unless ye're thinkin' of taking a culverin home with ye, it's easiest to sell them right here on the dock, to our investors, and divide the money today." The crew agreed; getting paid today, even at a slight discount, was more appealing than waiting to find a buyer somewhere else.

Fairchild agreed to pay just over two thousand pounds for the crew's share of the guns; they voted to keep one hogshead of rum as their share of the rest. John calculated that every member of the crew would get about ten pounds as his share. It was not that simple. The rules of plunder specified that the Captain and the officers were entitled to a larger share than the crewmen — the captain's share was the largest, the powder monkey's the least. Fairchild and Paolo put their heads together and began paying off the crew with the proceeds. The men lined up in order of rank. Roger's share came to one pound, three shillings, which appeared to please him. By the time they got to John and the other officers, his share was ten pounds, five shillings — not bad at all, he thought.

At this point, Foxe addressed the men on the main deck again and explained that Captain Cooper's soldiers would be paid their wages ashore, where their company had been mustered. They were welcome to stay a while longer (here he winked at Captain Cooper), but he wanted the seamen to be paid their wages that afternoon. The crew cheered their approval. Fairchild agreed.

Once again, there was a lineup of men by rank. In this case, no calculation was required, since the wages for each man on the ship had been set before the *Queen* sailed. John's pay for the voyage was twelve pounds. A bit more than a pound per month, a master carpenter's wage. Foxe had kept that part of the bargain, after all.

When everyone had been paid, Fairchild disembarked. Foxe joined him on the dock for a brief conversation, voices low. More wagons had arrived, and the Rich's twenty guns were loaded and driven off. It was late in the afternoon, by now, and the *Queen*, unburdened of her cargo, floated higher in the water than she had for months. Foxe strode to the mainmast and addressed the crew: "Lads, we have just one matter of unfinished business. But first, I want to say that I am proud to have sailed with all of ye, and would do so again, on any ship, on any sea!"

The men gave a hearty and heartfelt, (or so John thought) cheer. "Now, to the business at hand," cried Foxe. "Bring out the treasure!" Cheers again.

John looked to port. No one on the dock. The gunwales of the *Queen* were too high to see over from that side, anyway. To starboard, only the harbor. He supposed that the sound of the cheers could carry across the water, but no one would know exactly what the cheers were about. Foxe had chosen their anchorage well.

The chest from the *Vengeur* was placed on the main deck, at the main mast. Foxe produced the key and dramatically handed it to Cooper, who opened it. Paolo sat nearby at a small table, with a set of scales. One by one, the names of sailors were called out, each to receive his share. Paolo had been ashore long enough to determine that the proper exchange rate for silver to gold was twenty-four to one, which everyone seemed to accept. The weighing was not difficult, but part of the treasure was in the form of objects, not coins. A gold plate or a necklace could not be easily valued, since the decoration made it more valuable than its mere weight. Some horse trading was necessary — Paolo bought back some of the larger objects with gold or silver coins from the officer's shares of the wages, just so that a fair distribution could take place. John exchanged some of his wages for a delicate gold necklace with a small cameo — it took a fair bit of his cash but was a lot easier to carry than three pounds of silver.

Thankfully, it all came out almost even; when the last man was paid, the chest was practically empty. There were just a few gold coins left; Foxe offered them to Picot.

"Speaking of Picot, where are those ducats?" Cooper asked.

Foxe snapped his fingers "Right you are! I nearly forgot!" (John doubted that was true; Foxe hadn't missed a trick yet.) "Roger, fetch that dirty bag from underneath my bunk!"

Underneath his bunk? Those ducats were placed in the treasure chest, the night Cooper and I counted them! How did they travel from the chart room to the Captain's cabin? John caught Cooper's eye. Cooper simply shrugged.

Roger returned with the bag, and every man lined up for his ducat. Picot looked distressed, John thought.

"Lads! This concludes our business," declared Foxe. "I trust that men such as yourselves know how to be discreet. Don't spend it all on women in the first pub ye visit!" Another cheer, and laughter from the crew.

Cooper got his men off the *Queen* first. It wasn't evening yet, and some of the soldiers had homes in the surrounding area. They formed up into ranks on the dock, before they marched into town, sixty-one strong. Sixty-one, out of the eighty that had begun just months ago. Two had died at Cartagena, and two more when they fought the *Vengeur*; the rest had died of disease on the voyage. It was a common thing for a third of the men on a long voyage to die of one disease or another; Cooper's command had been lucky. He ordered them to muster in a few days, to receive their pay, but until then, they were on leave.

The sailors followed after, a few at a time. John noticed Wilkes and his four crew-mates leave together; they seemed cheerful enough. Picot left on his own — Foxe had given him some money and recommendations for transport to France. It occurred to John that there might not be enough beds to rent in the town tonight, for two hundred or more men just back from the sea. Plenty of ale, though. He went back to his cabin, where Dr. Lopez was packing up his instruments and personal belongings. "Where now, doctor?" asked John.

"Amsterdam, as the Captain promised. He has paid my berth on a packet that sails this evening. I owe you a debt, Carpenter. If not for you, I might still be in Santo Domingo. *Gracias!*"

John nodded. "I am glad we met; there are men on this ship that might be dead, if not for you. I am sure that Captain Cooper thinks of you every time he stands on two legs."

Lopez nodded in return. Then, with a twinkle in his eye, he said, "Tell Captain Cooper not to worry if he hears a buzzing sound in that leg. Healing takes time." It took a moment for John to realize that Lopez was joking. Then both laughed. Captain Foxe stuck his head in the cabin door.

"Carpenter, I shall need yer assistance for some hours, yet. I will make it worth yer while."

John sighed. What now? Then he remembered the bilges and the ballast that lay there. His curiosity was piqued. What else was Foxe up to? "Very well," he agreed. Dr. Lopez left the cabin with a smile and a handshake.

"I need ye to go into town and fetch yer barrow from Danny Cornwall's place. While ye're there, tell Danny I'll be needin' to have dinner for three in my cabin tonight."

John walked into town (with a "rolling gait"), and paused at *The Galleon* to have an ale, before returning to the *Queen* with his barrow, which had been well cared for. As he expected, Danny Cornwall's rooms were all spoken for — even at three men to a bed. Cornwall had plenty of rooms for the following night — most of the *Queen*'s crew would be leaving town in the morning; hungover but headed for reunions with families that lived somewhere inland. When John returned, Foxe greeted him with a hint of impatience: "That took longer than I expected. Now I need ye to load up the barrow with yer personal belongings, and yer tool chest — only leave me a mallet and a pry bar, or something like that."

John was tired, and hungry, but loaded his personal chest, and the tool chest, plus the morion, the jack of plates, the cutlass, the sea boots, the snaphance, and his pistols. "Anything else?"

"Aye, take those things to Danny Cornwall's, and lock them in his storage room, then bring the barrow back here. Oh, and bring our dinner back with ye."

"Our dinner?"

"Aye, I ordered dinner for three — you, Roger, and myself."

So. Dinner for three. A sentimental farewell, perhaps? No, it had to be the silver in the bilges. Foxe, Roger, and John were the only people that knew about it. Maybe this really would be worth his while.

John did as requested. He made an interesting sight in the twilight, with his barrow and all the weapons tied on top. He remembered to wheel directly into the *Galleon*; Danny Cornwall seemed to have expected him. There were several crewmen from the *Queen* in the place, and they greeted him heartily, then turned to their table-mates and pointed at him, as he navigated to the back of the pub. They were telling tales, he supposed, probably about the voyage, maybe even about him. *So, the legend begins*, he thought, with a feeling of resignation.

It took only moments to secure his things, and when he emerged, Danny Cornwall had the dinner packed up, and ready to stow into his barrow. There was wine, and bread, and cheese, and — he sniffed it — roast beef! Also, a pie and some sort of stew. A finer meal than he had eaten in a long, long time. Worth his while indeed!

It was dark by the time he got back to the dock. Roger had been waiting for him and helped him take their meal into the officer's mess. There were just enough candles on the table, to see the meal that was set out. The stew was not hot, only lukewarm, at best. Still, John savored every bite. The wine was good, too: unaccustomed as he was to drinking wine, he began to feel a little tipsy. It appeared that Foxe was in worse shape than he was.

Roger did not drink as much. He ate heartily enough, and John realized that the ship's fare had agreed with him — he was no longer the gangly kid that had sailed with him from Harwich. Roger had grown at least two inches since then and put on muscle. It occurred to John that he probably ate better on board the *Queen* than at any other time in his life.

"Tell us, Roger, what will ye do with yer newfound wealth?" Foxe began.

"I'll be using it to help out me mum. I have five brothers and sisters at home. The money will make things easier."

Foxe nodded. "What of yer father?"

"Gone to sea and never returned. Could be anywhere, I guess . . . maybe dead."

Foxe was at a loss for words at the directness of Roger's answer.

"When I was young," Roger continued, I would imagine where he might be. They say I look a lot like him. I imagined a man who looks like me in a dungeon somewhere, or at the oars of a galley, or maybe as a buccaneer. Now that I have seen the seaman's life, I think he most likely died. But you never know, men sometimes return after ten years at sea . . ."

There was a tone of forlorn hope in his voice, Foxe was visibly moved and struggled for words. "There, lad," he said finally, "There, lad."

"How does your mother get by, then?" John asked and immediately regretted the question. Clearly, with five children at home, and a fourteen-year-old son who had grown up undernourished, she was desperately poor.

"She's a seamstress," Roger replied. "My older sister helps her, and my next sister looks after the other three little ones. I visited her yesterday while I was running errands. She had no idea I was at sea; she assumed I was dead these past months. The wages I have earned will pay off her debts; as long as no one gets sick, this will be a good year for our family."

John imagined a ragged, overworked woman — no, not ragged — patched (she was a seamstress after all), bereaved of her husband, and forced to send her oldest son to sea in his father's footsteps. And five more mouths to feed. He began to sober up.

"It is a hard life, but we have survived. I used to think that my father had the easier life, apart from his family, away at sea . . ."

"Nay, Lad, Do not say that!" Foxe interjected, "The men who go to sea suffer, apart from their families. It is only desperation that turns them that way."

John was startled to hear Foxe speak of family. "Captain, do you have a wife or children?"

Foxe's expression became morose, like an old dog's. "Aye, I had both once. My Nell — there was a woman for ye. Strong, saucy, and honest to the point of her own disadvantage. Clever, but sweet. Soft, but hard as iron. We had three little ones, Frances, Lizzie, and little Will . . ."

"Had? What became of them?"

"Plague. Carried them all off in the space of a week." Foxe was on the verge of tears.

"It is a hard thing, to watch your loved ones pass away like that," ventured John.

"I did not watch. I wish I had. I was at sea when the plague took them." Foxe took a ragged, sobbing breath, then composed himself.

Suddenly, John saw Foxe the man, as if a book had been opened. When he was ashore, burdened with the guilt and pain of loss, he wanted only to be at sea again. But there was no relief to be found at sea, only danger, the fickleness of fortune, and the same guilt and pain. At sea, he had the companionship of other men, men who knew loss, and desperation. But as their captain, he bore the burden of responsibility for their welfare. So he yearned for every voyage to end, to be home, yet home would not be found anywhere.

Foxe was composed, now, and turned to John, "And you carpenter, what will ye do with yer purse newly filled?"

"I will go back to work in my trade. First thing in the morning, I will visit the Carpenter's Guildhall . . ."

"What for?"

"I never found out whether they agreed to accept me as a Master of the guild. I only hope my application hasn't lapsed in my absence."

"I'll save ye the trouble," mumbled Foxe, and began rummaging inside his doublet. He pulled out a sealed letter. "Here!"

John opened the letter. It was from the Harwich Carpenter's Guild, welcoming him into their brotherhood as a Master Carpenter. John was stunned.

"How did you get this?"

"I picked it up three days before we sailed. Told them I'd deliver it to ye, as I have."

"Why didn't you give it to me before?"

"What, before we sailed? Ye might have left town with it!"

That much was true, John admitted. "But why not give it to me while we were at sea?"

"It was safer with me, than with you. Ye could have died on the voyage or lost it somehow."

That last excuse made no sense at all, but John knew that the point would be lost on Foxe.

"Look here, ye're none the worse for this. I paid ye a Master Carpenter's wage, even though ye thought yourself a journeyman. I've been more than fair, I think."

John sighed and shook his head. He tucked the letter into his own doublet.

"There will be dues to pay."

"Already covered it, paid three years in advance."

"So you read the letter, even though it was sealed?"

"Not as such. I have friends in the guild, you know."

Friends. Yes, Captain Billy Foxe had friends everywhere.

"None of them as dear to me as the two of you though, "Foxed added, "which is why I wanted this meal for just us three. We have some more business to attend,"

Ah. The silver in the bilges. John's curiosity was piqued. How did Foxe propose to cash in that pile of stones?

Foxe stood and invited them to his cabin. There in the center of the room, on top of the chart table — ugly, bulky thing — was the mallet and pry-bar Foxe had borrowed. Then it hit John. It must have hit Roger at the same time because he grinned broadly. "Carpenter, will ye do the honors?" Foxe gestured to the table.

It took only a few strikes of the mallet to open the cavity inside the table, and there was the chest from the Spanish prize, just where it had been left. "The trick," said Foxe, "is how to move this to a secure place, and how to turn it into money we can actually use. We dare not appear in public with a treasure like this. We will have to be patient — perhaps for years — before we can spend any of it. Agreed?"

Roger nodded, and John conceded the point. He had quite forgotten about the chest and had no plans to spend any of its contents. Still, what was Foxe planning?

"I have arranged a safe place for this. We have only to get it there without being discovered. Roger, go to the armory, and get me two cutlasses, and a *loaded* (here he glanced at John) pistol. Also get yourself a belaying pin, on your way back here. John, go out on the quarterdeck, and make sure no one is watching us."

It was dark on the quarterdeck. John let his eyes adjust to the dark as he scanned the dock. No place for anyone to hide there, really. The streets and alleys of the city beyond were a different matter.

Roger was back from below deck, with the weapons. "Now, Lads," said Foxe, as he covered the chest with the tapestry, "We have to move quick and quiet. You two put this in the Carpenter's barrow, and keep it covered." Foxe stood at the port gunwale, looking for any sign of life below.

It was not as tricky to get it onto the dock and into the barrow as John expected. Roger was a lot stronger than he had been, maybe John as well. Certainly, they were both more surefooted.

"Alright then. Slow and steady, eyes open." Foxe led them the length of the dock and into the city. Their path was slightly uphill, away from the waterfront. They tuned several corners until John had no idea how he would retrace his footsteps, given the need. Foxe stopped them at the entrance to an alley, which ran behind an imposing stone building of some sort. "Wait for me here," he said, then disappeared into the darkness.

Several minutes later, he stepped out of the dark alley and beckoned them to follow. They stopped at a servant's entrance behind the house. "Your barrow will be safe enough here," said Foxe. John and Roger lifted the chest off the barrow and carried it inside. Steps led down to a cellar, amply lit, and into a comfortably furnished room. A man was seated behind a large table. A large pair of scales was prominently in view on a side table, there were three more chairs. Roger and John set their burden on the floor and seated themselves.

"This here's Signor Scarlatti," said Foxe, as he made introductions. "You may call him Mr. Scarlatti if you prefer. He is as they say in Holland, a <u>banker.</u> His name is Italian, but his employer resides in Germany. Mr

Scarlatti's profession allows him to do some amazing things; ye might consider it sorcery. Men like him can make money disappear from one place and appear in another. They can change the form of a treasure from say, gold to silver, and back again. And all of these *transactions* can be done in secret, without the government's knowledge. We have a problem — a treasure that is too heavy to carry about with us, not to mention too dangerous. Mr. Scarlatti can help us, for a modest share of our wealth."

Scarlatti sat with his hands slightly folded, grinned through most of Foxe's introduction, and nodded at the mention of his "modest share."

"Sirs, let me see what you have for me," said Scarlatti.

They lifted the chest onto the table, took off the tapestry, and opened it. Scarlatti's eyebrows rose, and he sucked in his breath.

They emptied the contents onto the table in front of Mr. Scarlatti, and he scanned it carefully. He picked up a few gold cups and looked for maker's marks. There were a few pieces of jewelry, which he examined very carefully. Then he separated the relatively few pieces of silver and weighed them. He wrote something in a ledger and then began weighing the gold. When he was finished, he turned to Foxe and said. "Do you want this credited to just one account?"

"Nay," said Foxe, "each is to have his own account. Each is to have an equal share."

Scarlatti nodded. "As far as I can see, none of this can be identified as stolen property, at least not stolen in England."

"Nor should they be. They were taken from a Spanish ship, in the New World."

Scarlatti nodded. "That is to your advantage. My fee would be higher if the provenance was in doubt. By weight, the value of your property is a little more than twelve hundred pounds sterling. That's about four hundred pounds for each of you."

John's ears were ringing, he wasn't sure what he was hearing.

"There are a few pieces here that should have a value greater than their mere weight, such as the jewelry and the vessels. But they are not as easy to pass on, for that very reason. There are two ways we could value this hoard. One would be to add up the denominations of the coins and haggle over the value of the finished pieces. Then I would claim a percentage of that value, and we could haggle some more over which pieces should comprise my commission.

Or, I can simply credit you with the total value of the hoard by weight, and consider that the extra value in the finished pieces would be my commission. Your choice."

"I like the simple approach," said Foxe.

Scarlatti nodded and smiled. "How about the others?"

Roger nodded. John said, "I need to understand more about this 'credit'."

"Quite so. If you agree to this deal, you will never see any of this treasure again." He gestured to the table. "What you will receive in return is the right to withdraw an equal value of money from this bank, or any other bank in cities all over Europe, whenever you want it. That is what credit means."

"What will happen to the treasure, then?" asked Roger.

"It will be loaned to others, or sold for money, it might be withdrawn from one of our banks by someone else who has credit with us."

"How do I take this credit with me?" John again.

"We keep an account in our ledgers, that states how much credit you have. If you come to this bank to withdraw money, we will give you money and reduce your credit in our ledger by that amount. If you wish to withdraw money at some other location, we can give you a letter that will direct the other bank to give you the money when you arrive there. Some of our wealthier clients buy and sell these letters, as if they were money, even though they are made of paper. When we loan a large amount to the Queen, for instance, most of the transaction is in paper form. They use the paper to get smaller amounts of coins to pay soldiers, or sailors, whatever."

"It is easier to carry paper, than four hundred pounds of silver coins," agreed John, "but how do you know that a letter like the one you describe has not been stolen from its rightful owner?"

"Gold and silver can be stolen also," said Scarlatti. "But we will require you to sign the letter when we issue it, and your signature is also kept in a ledger here. That will be compared to the signature of anyone trying to withdraw money with it. Whatever you do, do not sign such a letter twice, unless you are selling it — that would make it too easy to steal from you."

John nodded. He wouldn't be withdrawing any of this money for years, anyway. "But what if I deposit money with you, and leave town? What if I come back in ten years, and want my money then?"

"If you deposit money with us, your credit will still be honored, after ten years. If you authorize us to loan it out to others at interest, your balance will grow."

"That sounds like usury," said John.

"In England, it is usury. But not in Germany, or the Low Countries. That is the advantage of a bank like ours, for our wealthier accounts. They can see their money grow, without breaking the law."

John shook his head. No wonder the rich prospered, while the poor starved.

"What'll it be, Lads?" Foxe spoke.

"I'll take the simple way," said John. Roger agreed. "Simple it is, then," said Foxe.

It took a while for the arrangements to be completed. Scarlatti showed them the ledger entries, and their signatures were noted. Each man got a letter stating his balance, with Scarlatti's signature as well as their own. John was not entirely satisfied with the whole business, but carrying his share of the treasure around England was clearly impractical, not to mention dangerous. If he was confident about anything, it was that no one would be able to trace any of the treasure back to him or his companions — the bank would make sure of that. He was oddly unburdened at the thought. At the very least, he had what was it? — The wages, the share of the buccaneers' booty, and the ducat — nearly thirty-eight pounds — more than three year's wages in his purse. He gave the treasure one last look, and something caught his eye, "Signor Scarlatti? Will you sell me that necklace?"

It was a small silver chain, with a dark red polished stone — a garnet, probably. "Take it. Consider it a token of friendship."

John put it in his pocket, and they left the way they had come. By the time they were back at the *Egyptian Queen*, it was midnight. Roger was left to clear away the dishes from their supper. John went to his old berth and fell asleep.

His sleep was disturbed by distant shouting. He roused himself and stepped out onto the quarterdeck. Sunshine — it was morning already. Someone was calling from the dock: "Ahoy the ship!"

John peered over the side. A dozen men were standing there, looking up at him. "State your business!"

"We would speak with Captain Billy Foxe," said one. "We hear he's hiring."

"Aye, so he is," Foxe's voice came from behind John. "Introduce yerselves!"

John was bewildered. Was Foxe taking on a new crew, and putting to sea again? He decided that it would be a good idea to get off the ship, as soon as possible. He headed for the gangplank. "Wait," said Foxe, there are just a few things left to do. Dr. Lopez left something in the chart room for ye. Give me ten minutes, and I'll walk into town with ye."

John waited. Foxe hired ten of the men, but just for the day. One was set to watch the ship while he was gone, the others he set to work unloading the *Queen*'s guns, and their carriages, lining them up on the dock. "Still got to careen her," he explained. "These lads can sail her down the estuary to the beach and kedge her up from there. Then we'll give her hull a good scraping."

In the chart room, Foxe handed John a basket of *patatas*, the last of the ones from Cartagena. "Dr. Lopez wanted you to have these. Look here. See these little green buds? He said they were 'eyes'. You can cut these into pieces and plant them. Each eye will grow to a full-sized plant, with plenty of *patatas* underground. If you can't get anyone to eat 'em, they're good for animal feed. Don't feed the leaves or stems to man or beast — they be poisonous. And don't eat the patatas if they're green — same problem."

John lugged the basket down to the dock and loaded it onto his barrow. He wasn't sure what he would do with the *patatas*, but he remembered that the Dr. had said they were good for scurvy. Might be useful; they hadn't had much trouble with scurvy on board ship.

Soon, Foxe joined him on the dock, along with Roger, rubbing sleep from his eyes. They walked to town together. John put his barrow in the *Galleon*'s storage room, and they had breakfast together. While they ate, a few hungover sailors from the *Egyptian Queen* emerged from the rooms upstairs and greeted them. No doubt more were still asleep, thought John. It was early yet.

"Roger, we need to pay a visit to yer mum," said Foxe. Roger looked surprised but agreed to guide them to his mother's lodging. It wasn't much, just a couple of rooms: a workplace in front, a sleeping space in the back. A crude kitchen off to the side, a window, which let in some natural light to the work area. Roger's mother was introduced as Harriet Frye. She was not as old as she looked, thought John. Lines of care and privation showed on her face. Roger's oldest sister might have been thirteen, the next twelve or so, the youngest of the lot were twin boys, seven. Lots of mouths to feed, but not many able to work, yet. There were some garments hanging up opposite the kitchen area, that appeared to be new, so Harriet was at least finding work. She saw him looking at them, and asked "Sir, is there some item of clothing you would be needin'?"

John realized that his garments were a bit worn from his days at sea. "I suppose I could use a new shirt," he said. "And what is that? A coat of some sort?"

"Aye, the coat was ordered for a gentleman, who changed his mind and would not pay for it. It's good quality kersey, but I'd alter it for you and sell it for four shillings. For another six shillings, I can make you two good shirts to go with it."

"How soon could I have them?"

"I can alter the coat today; the shirts will be ready next week."

"Show me the material for the shirts."

"Of course, Sir. Here, good English cotton."

John looked at the cloth. "Good enough. I will pay you ten shillings for the coat and two shirts."

"Try the coat on first," she suggested. He did so, and she walked around him. "I will let it out just a little in the shoulders, the length of the sleeves is fine, and it will hang to your knees. It will keep you warm on a chilly day. He took off his jerkin, and Harriet took measurements for the shirts.

Foxe, meanwhile, was engaged in some sort of banter with Roger's two younger brothers. They were laughing about something, which must be very funny, indeed. It occurred to John that this was a side of Billy Foxe he hadn't seen before — no longer in command, but relaxed, easy. It made him look younger, somehow.

When John left the seamstresses, Foxe and Roger stayed behind. It was a fine morning, with the wind off the sea. He took a deep breath. Now what? He had made general plans to leave Harwich and visit his family back in Felsted. No particular hurry, though. He had envisioned himself plodding down the roads with his barrow, arriving at home as the long-lost son, the tools of his trade with him. Now, he had the means to travel differently, if he chose to, and he had just committed himself to stay until next week, when the shirts would be ready. He was ashore, with time on his hands; no reason to look for work. What then?

He decided to look for a barber. Men of his class did not wear their beards as long as the gentry, and some sailors had told him it was bad luck to cut his hair while at sea — he realized he was shaggy. Time to do something about that.

For a tuppence, he got his beard trimmed, and his hair shortened just enough to allow him to tie it into a small knot in the back. The barber sprinkled him with something scented, for good measure. He found himself on the outskirts of town, near a stable. He walked into the place more out of curiosity, than anything. The smell of hay and horse manure was familiar enough — his youth on the farm had acquainted him with the care of horses, and the duties of cleanup. Now, it touched him with nostalgia for a moment.

"A horse, sir?"

"What's that?"

"Are you here to buy a horse?" An elderly man with a grey beard stood before him, questioning.

"Ah . . . no, I was just enjoying the aroma of the place." He chuckled.

"Home from the sea, are ye?"

"Yes, yes I am."

"A lot of men come here fresh from the sea and say that they enjoy the company of horses. Can't imagine why. Must be lonely at sea, or maybe it just smells bad." The old man chuckled.

"It smells like home, here."

"Ah. A farm boy. Most seamen grow up on farms. Are ye headed homeward, then?"

John nodded. "Yes, over Braintree way."

"Braintree? That's a fair walk."

John nodded again. "I've walked it before."

"Why walk, when ye can ride? Let me show you some horses."

Looking at horses seemed like a good way to pass the morning. The old man didn't seem too busy; he wouldn't be wasting the man's time. "Show me," he said.

The old man, whose name was Hector, had more than a dozen horses for sale, not counting nine or ten that he was boarding for their owners. The prizes of his herd were two fine-looking steeds, a large chestnut stallion, and a bay mare. "You won't find many handsomer mounts than these in Harwich," said Hector. John had to agree.

There were other, less glamorous horses, including a pair of large draft animals, with shaggy fetlocks. "Time was, a knight in full armor would ride horses like these," said Hector. "Those days are past, but these fellas will pull any load you hitch 'em to."

At the far end of the barn, John spotted a gray animal — sturdy like a plow horse, as far as he could see by looking at the horse's dappled gray rear. "What's that?"

"That'll be Gordon. Good natured as a horse can be, strong enough. It's a shame about the face."

"What about his face?"

"Gordon!" called Hector, "Oats!"

Gordon turned around to face them, his ears pricked up. Gordon was the ugliest horse John had ever seen. One of his eyelids was pink, the other black. It gave him a crazed look, or a foolish one perhaps. A broad nose, with a very distinct "roman" curve — it looked like Gordon was stupid, as well.

"I know what yer thinkin'. Any man would be embarrassed to be seen in public with a horse like this. That's why I can't sell 'im."

John stepped into the stall and looked Gordon over. Strong, well-muscled. Needs new shoes. He looked in the horse's mouth, no cups on teeth, or barely any. Nine years old? Perhaps eight. A little lean, maybe. "How much does he eat?"

Well, that's the thing. I really can't afford to feed him like the others. I keep him for sentimental reasons, you might say. My grandkids like to ride him. Gentle, he is."

John smelled a bargain. A horse like this could serve well on a farm, out of the public eye. "I'd like to try him in harness."

The old man looked surprised (or feigned it, more likely, thought John). "I'll hitch him up, if you like, Sir."

Hector had told the truth about Gordon's disposition. When he was hitched to a seven-hundred-pound sledge, Hector cried "Now, Gordon!" and he pulled it with a steady, determined attitude. When John halted him, he looked back as if to say, "Is that all?"

"I think I could use a horse like this," said John. "What are you asking?"

Hector rubbed his chin. "I really hadn't thought to sell him. The grandkids, you know. Almost a pet, really,"

"If he were a pet, he'd be better fed than he appears to be. I would take good care of him."

"You'll need a saddle if you're riding him all the way to Braintree."

"I don't intend to ride him at all. I'll need some harness, though. And a carriage, or something."

Hector brightened. "I can help ye there. Come back behind the barn. I've got a carriage I could sell ye."

There were several vehicles behind the barn, including a four-wheeled carriage with seating for four, not counting the driver, a sturdy haywain, and a two-person gig. Not what John was looking for. He spotted something at the far end of the lot. "What's that?"

"Broken, I'm afraid. Haven't got time to repair it."

"" It" was a two-wheeled, flatbed cart, that much was clear. The axle and wheels looked sound enough, but the shafts were broken, and the bed needed work. "How much would you take for this?"

"In its present condition, I'd let it go for five shillings."

"Five?"

"Four, then. But there's no warranty on how long it will last."

"If I take Gordon, the harness, and this cart, I'm willing to pay fifteen shillings."

"I'll let you have them for a pound, and I'll throw in a bit and bridle."

"The horse is ugly and needs new shoes. He's also underfed. For a pound, I'll pick him up next week, provided you allow me to repair this cart on your premises and see that he gets plenty of oats and hay, and include the harness and bridle. I'll take him to the farrier at my own expense. I also will want to have the cart painted, before I take possession."

Hector spat into his hand and extended it. "Sold!" he said.

So, now John had a horse, and a cart, and new clothes. It was an odd feeling to spend money so freely, but he enjoyed it. He walked back to town, to find a lumber yard.

John had his supper back at the *Galleon* that evening. A few of the crew from the *Egyptian Queen* were still around. Danny Cornwall joined him at his table. "You have made a name for yourself, Carpenter. A hero among seamen!"

John shook his head. "Don't believe everything you hear. I am glad to be home in one piece, and I never intend to go to sea again."

"Still, you're a richer man than you thought you'd be when you signed up, are you not?"

"I never signed up. I was 'pressed', or so Captain Foxe called it. I cannot deny that I have profited from his impressment, but I could as easily have died at sea. I know a lot of men who did."

"They say the *Egyptian Queen* will be putting to sea soon. Billy Foxe asked me to look out for you and tell you he'd like to make you an offer."

"If that's a warning, I thank you. What sort of offer?"

He didn't say, but I understand the *Queen* has been careened again, down the estuary south of town. He's bound to be somewhere near there if you're looking for him."

"I'm not looking for him, sounds as if he's looking for me."

Cornwall looked at him with his one good eye. "Do not judge the man harshly. He takes good care of the men under his command. He takes any advantage that he can, but within the law (as far as anyone knows), and he is generous to his friends."

John looked back at him. He wondered what Cornwall would say if he knew what he and Foxe had been up to not twenty-four hours earlier, or what was in the *Queen*'s ballast. Well, it probably was all within the law, and John could not deny that Foxe could be generous. "Taking any advantage he can," aptly described Billy Foxe. John wondered what stories Cornwall might tell about Foxe if he were in the mood.

"I do not have harsh feelings toward Captain Foxe. I have only respect for his seamanship and yes, generosity. But I am determined not to become entangled in any more of his schemes, however profitable they might be. The man surrounds himself with danger, like flies around honey."

Cornwall laughed. "Aye, that's the man. What will you do, if you do not sail again?"

"I have not seen my family for more than six years. It is past time that I see about them. I have the means to set myself up in business, now, somewhere far from the sea. Perhaps I shall marry and have children of my own."

"You have a lady in mind, then?"

John thought. Was it surprising that he had no prospects, at his age? "No. I will take care of one task at a time. I need to move my things out of your storeroom, for the night. I have a small carpentry job in the morning."

"I took the liberty of movin' your things into your room," said Cornwall."It's the same room you used to rent. The barrow is still in the storeroom."

John slept soundly that night, without the rocking of the sea, for the first time in many months. He awoke refreshed and remembered that he had work to do. He dressed in his leather apron and went downstairs for breakfast. Danny Cornwall was up, too. "Where today then, Carpenter?"

"As I said, I have a small job to do. I will be back this evening for supper."

It was August, and the morning was mild. He took his barrow and had his materials in hand before most of the town was up and about. Hector was up, looking after his horses, and John was able to see that Gordon got an ample portion of oats with his hay.

"Ye're a carpenter!" exclaimed Hector.

"That I am," replied John. Replacing the shafts was easy enough, and then he repaired and modified the rest of the cart to suit his purpose. He extended and reinforced the bed so that it was long enough to haul lengths of lumber. He put sides up about 2 1/2 feet, to hold the load in place (his tools and personal items, for instance), with hooks that would allow him to fasten a canvas tarp over the whole load. In a pinch, he could sleep under such a tarp, if the weather was not too cold. It was all designed to serve as a portable workspace. He imagined that one day he might attach a vise to one side of the wagon, to make it easier to work away from town. He was pleased with the work when it was done, not least because it was *his.*

Hector admired the work as well: "I see what yer doin', Carpenter. A traveling workshop. Ye'll get plenty of work with this rig."

John stayed long enough to see that Gordon got another generous feeding, then headed back to the Galleon with his barrow. Tomorrow was Sunday, no work then. Monday he would take Gordon to a farrier.

Once back at the *Galleon*, he remembered the coat that he had agreed to buy. He found his way to Roger's home before dinner. Harriet greeted him with relief, "I thought you might have forgotten us!"

John shook his head. "No chance of that. Just busy." He took off his apron and tried the coat on. It felt good — enough space to move around. "It's a little warm, for August," he said, but it will serve me well in September, and thereafter." He paid her the four shillings and prepared to leave for supper. "I shall have the shirts ready by Tuesday, and Roger and the Captain have been looking for you," said Harriet.

"Here?"

"They were here this morning and asked me to tell you that you should meet them tonight where the *Queen* is careened. Does that make sense to you?"

"Yes. Yes, it does. Thank you for relaying the message."

John walked back to the *Galleon* with a sense of annoyance. He would have preferred to avoid entanglement with whatever Foxe, and now Roger, were up to, but he was stuck in town for at least another few days. First, he would have his dinner. Then, he would meet them at the beach. And he would have one of his pistols with him, just in case.

Supper was not as relaxed as he hoped. His mind was in turmoil. Foxe was doing something tonight on the beach, probably involving the ballast in the *Queen*. Why did John have to get sucked into this? He had enough money. Yes, that was it. If he did not have the extra forty or so pounds in his purse, or the four hundred pounds in the bank (still not certain about that, but the imaginary wealth was already affecting his attitude), he would probably be hoping for another windfall. But now, he wanted only to avoid any dubious or risky situation imaginable. And dubious or risky described Captain Billy Foxe precisely.

After dinner, he went to his room and changed. More than likely, he would be grubbing around in the stinking bilges tonight — no reason to soil his best clothing. He waited till the sun was down, and exited the pub at the rear, by the privy. He stopped to consider how much the course of his life was set by events at this particular spot — a privy, of all places.

The *Queen* was careened well up the estuary, farther from town than the first time. It took him more than an hour to get there, which was fine — it was completely dark now, and whatever was going to happen, the fewer people knew of it, the better.

He heard voices before he saw anyone. He recognized Foxe's voice, but there were others. There was a candlelight on the far side of the hull, and John walked toward it.

"And here's the very man!" exclaimed Foxe as John stepped into the light. "John here is from Felsted — you've met before, I'm told, Sir Richard!"

Even in the dim light, John recognized Sir Richard Rich, and his nephew Robert, the third baron. The Rich's looked at him with curiosity. "Have we met?" asked Sir Richard.

"Not exactly. My family attends Holy Cross, as does yours. I remember seeing you there when I was a youngster."

"Ah," said Sir Richard. "Your family name?"

"Porter. John Porter, at your service." He bowed.

Sir Richard nodded. "I know the Porters. Quite a few named John. Stout yeoman folk. I hear you did your family proud, on the Spanish Main."

John bowed again. There were at least four other men with the Rich's that John did not recognize — probably retainers. He noticed two freight wagons, each with a team of horses nearby, out of sight of the road. He began to see what was about to take place.

"It was the carpenter, here, who discovered the secret of the Frenchman, so I thought it right he should be here for the transfer," explained Foxe.

"Transfer." Of course! Foxe couldn't cash the silver in — too obvious. But he could please his investors by giving them some profit that was off the books, so to speak. Whether the crown had any claim to the silver was debatable — but that debate was between the queen's agents and the Rich family, so long as Foxe did not profit in any material way. John relaxed. This should not take long.

It didn't. And John didn't have to crawl into the bilges, after all — the Rich's retainers got that job. Roger stood by — grinning. They loaded everything into the wagons and tied tarps over the loads. They were gone in less than two hours. Sir Richard and his nephew the Baron had a carriage nearby.

"John Porter!," called the Baron.

"Yes, My Lord?"

"I am told that you are schooled in the ways of war, and I am inclined to believe it, seeing you came armed to this meeting."

"Can't be too careful, Your Lordship. I was nearly kidnapped on the streets of Harwich, just last year."

"Quite so." The Baron nodded. "Dangerous times we live in. However, we must be prepared to defend our persons and our nation. If you come back to Felsted, you should seek audience with me. We have need of battle-seasoned men among our local militia. A man with your experience could be an officer."

"Thank you, My Lord." John bowed. *Officer of militia?* Not if he could help it.

The carriage pulled away. John turned to Foxe, "Is this why you were looking for me?"

"Aye, I wanted ye to be here, to witness what happened, just in case."

"Just in case what?"

"Just in case the queen's agents hear of this, through some indiscretion in the Rich family. All three of us will attest that the silver was turned over to the Rich's, with the understanding that they would take responsibility for any portion that the crown is entitled to. Our hands are clean in this matter."

John nodded. "Meanwhile, the Rich's may think they owe you a favor, which may make it easier to fund your next voyage."

"That's true enough. And they may think they owe you a favor, as well. The day may come when your discretion in this matter will be worth something to them."

"Like an officer's commission in the local militia?"

"Exactly. Something like that. Something that will guarantee your loyalty to them. This is how aristocrats work, John. Every favor they bestow benefits *them* in some way. But that doesn't mean ye should refuse them. They have the power to harm ye, if they think they cannot trust ye."

John knew he was right. In a way, the "favor" gave him some leverage, too. If Baron Robert ever recalled that he had seen John at William Payne's execution, John's knowledge of tonight's events might be enough to move him to protect John from the Queen's examiners. Ironic.

The three of them walked back into town together. It was almost midnight. John hoped that he was finished with the last remnant of his voyage with the *Egyptian Queen* and that he could begin a new chapter of his life. Foxe insisted on escorting Roger back to his mother's house. John went back to the *Galleon* on his own.

August 1586: Partings

The next day was Sunday, and John attended services at the nearest parish church. There were lots of seamen there, quite a few had been on the *Egyptian Queen*. Some admitted that they were fulfilling a vow, made in the heat of battle or the heart of the tempest, to be more faithful in their religion — if only they survived the voyage. Some were whispering and pointing in his direction when he sat down at the beginning of the service. The service followed the Book of Common Prayer, and the familiarity of it was a comfort to John, a reminder that he truly was at home again. At the end of the service, John filed out with the rest of the congregation to greet the vicar, who had evidently heard some talk of John's voyage — the vicar shook his hand vigorously and thanked him for attending. John decided that he would be well out of Harwich as soon as he could.

In the afternoon, he went to see his horse. He brought a small, early apple with him. "We're going to be spending some time together," he said to Gordon, "We might as well get off on the right foot." Gordon seemed agreeable.

On Monday morning, John was back in time to see that Gordon was getting his oats, and then put a bridle on him, and led him to the farrier. It was apparent that Gordon's hooves had not been trimmed in a while, but once he was trimmed and reshod, his gait was lighter, and his step livelier. Hector noticed this when John and Gordon returned; "Never seen Gordon look so spry. I think ye agree with him."

Hector continued. "I'll be paintin' yer wagon today. Paint will be dry by tomorrow. Will you pick it up then?"

"Wednesday would be more convenient."

"Wednesday it is, then."

John had nothing particular to do for the rest of the day. He grew a little restless; idleness was not his habit. He walked the streets of Harwich. Maybe Harriet was finished with at least one of his shirts?

He found the seamstress's house easily enough. There was a great deal of bustle. "Oh, Mr. Porter! How fortunate that you are here. We are moving today, and I wanted to tell you of our new location."

"Moving?"

"Yes! Roger and the Captain have bought us a larger place — an investment, they call it. It has a shop in the front, with bed chambers upstairs. The Captain will rent one of the rooms, so that he will have a place to stay when he is in port, and Roger is to serve as his aide on board the ship! When the younger boys are a little older, the Captain says they can earn a wage on board, as well!"

John refrained from explaining that having two or more sons aboard the same ship was to risk losing all of them at the same time, to disease or war. Clearly, for Harriet, this plan eased her fears for her children's future. At least the boys would all eat better if they were at sea.

He was surprised that Foxe had taken such an interest in Roger's family, yet why should he be surprised? Foxe looked happier than John had ever seen him when he was with Harriet's sons. Maybe this was a turn for the better for Captain Billy Foxe, as well as Harriet, Roger, and the rest.

"Your shirts are nearly finished. Come see us tomorrow at our new address!" She was off, down the street, carrying some burden, or other.

"Wait! Where is Roger?"

"In the shop, packing."

"Tell Roger that he can use my barrow from Danny Cornwall's, to help you move your things."

"That is very kind of ye, Sir," said Harriet. "Roger, come here!"

Roger emerged, and John gave him his permission to use the barrow. Roger was off in a hurry and returned after several minutes with the barrow.

"Oh, this will make it ever so much easier!" said Harriet. John found himself helping them load it and then wheeling the load to their new home — at least he would know where to pick up his shirts, tomorrow. The family didn't own that much — two trips were all it took to move all their earthly possessions. Billy Foxe appeared, just as they finished unloading the last of it.

"I hear you're an investor, now," remarked John.

"Aye, I wanted to put our windfall to some good use."

Aside, John said, "I suppose you pity Roger's mother, too."

"Pity? No, I do not pity. Courage I admire, and steadfastness in the face of desperation, and persisting in kindness and civility when your life has fallen apart. These things I understand, and I admire them. There is no cause for pity."

He was talking about Harriet, of course, John realized. Well, admiration might be the beginning of something durable, something to ease a man's heart. *Good for you, Billy Foxe.*

Tuesday, John had a leisurely breakfast at the *Galleon* and paid Gordon a visit. He brought an apple again, and it seemed that Gordon was glad to see him. The cart had been painted a dull blue, a good color for a craftsman. John visited a sailmaker and bought a large piece of canvas, and enough rope to tie it securely over the wagon bed. He was ready for departure, now, and still had most of the day ahead of him. He crossed over to the estuary and saw that the *Egyptian Queen* was afloat again. He could see the longboats as well, Foxe must have found new ballast, and his men were shifting it around in the bilges, to balance her. By afternoon, Foxe would have her back at the dock.

He turned to the east. The sea was fairly calm. He thought of Dr. Lopez, on his way to Amsterdam. Then of Picot — where might he be? He thought of the men whose bones rested beneath the sea. Somewhere out there was a Spanish Army, waiting to land on this shore, to kill Queen Elizabeth, and replace her with her cousin Mary. How long before they appeared? Maybe not this year, but surely by next. He turned his face landward, again. That is where his future must lie. He thought of his father, his mother, and his sister. All of his cousins, all in Felsted. He felt a pang of homesickness. For some reason, Sybil Vessey came to mind. Perhaps he would visit Little Baddow on his way home. Maybe the Widow Smith was still living, as well.

Later that afternoon, he dropped into Harriet Frye's new shop and picked up his two new shirts. That evening he intended to dine alone, but he had the company of mates and total strangers, interested in the tales he might tell of his adventures. It was flattering, but he would have preferred solitude. Just as he finished eating, Captain Foxe swept into the pub with a loud greeting and sat down next to John.

"I hoped I'd find ye here!"; he was in an ebullient mood; must be some good news. "I hear that ye are leaving Harwich, and soon," explained Foxe. "I must wish ye farewell and thank ye for serving me so well."

"I don't know what you've heard, or from whom. I am indeed leaving, to visit my family."

"Aye, so I've heard. Yer spending about town is talked of — a horse, a cart, new clothes. It's been a great help to me."

"How is that a help to you?"

"You've been strolling around town like a man who has come into his fortune. Everyone knows you as a temperate and frugal fellow. If ye are spending money, the thinking goes, ye must have plenty. If ye have plenty, it could only come from sailing with me. My reputation has soared, thanks to you. I have three hundred men begging for a berth on the *Egyptian Queen*, the next time she sails, including three journeyman carpenters."

"No more pressing, then?"

"Nay and I have something to give ye." He pulled a folded piece of paper from his jerkin and handed it to him. "It's an official letter. States that ye served the last eleven months in her majesty's navy, as an officer. If ye do encounter a press gang, this should be enough to secure your release — as long as they get the impression that ye're still in active service. As for the *Egyptian Queen*, we won't be pressing anyone — doesn't look like I'll have to. We'll be back at sea soon enough, I'm told — there's a war on, or so they say!" Foxe slapped the table and laughed loudly and was joined by the crowd of men surrounding John's table.

Foxe leaned forward. "I'll always have a place for you, Carpenter, on any ship I command. Good luck, ye are. Good luck. Everyone says so."

"I think my good fortune has mostly to do with your wisdom and skill, Captain. Any man who sails with you is lucky." John spoke loudly so that everyone nearby could hear. He didn't really put much stock in luck, but he knew that many sailors did. The compliment was not insincere, but if he could deflect some of the admiration directed at himself to Foxe, well, that might ease the burden of other men's expectations. He was hoping to leave the legends and yarns of his exploits behind when he left Harwich, to gain control of his life again. Being treated as some kind of luck charm was just another way that other men sought to use him for their own purposes — he would leave that behind, too, if he could.

Foxe was touched by John's remark but was at a loss for words. "Thank ye," he said, finally. The men standing nearby murmured in agreement. Someone patted Foxe on his back. The silence was awkward.

John sensed that he was at a moment of portent, a point of separation, of tearing his own life from the fabric of the lives around him. *These men do not know me as I truly am*, he thought, *they only know who they think I am, who they wish me to be*. And yet, he had to admit that he didn't know any of them as they truly were either, except Foxe, perhaps. And Foxe was still full of surprises. *So, if all we know of each other is in our own imagination, what is it that binds us to each other? Why do men fight together, die for each other, weave their lives together in such a way?* It was the sea, perhaps. Faced with the heedless power and utter unpredictability of the sea, what could men do, but look to each other for survival? They might go to sea for greed, ambition, or simple desperation, but those are things which divide men. The bonds of affection and loyalty must come from some other place. Call it community — a community of the desperate and superstitious, a community of illogical hope and imaginary heroes, but also a community of duty, faithfulness, and fortitude. And he was leaving this behind. The ties were stronger than he wanted to admit. It was a moment that called for a recognition.

John addressed Foxe, but loudly enough that everyone could hear. "It was not my desire to sail with you, as you well know. But there are unexpected blessings in unforeseen circumstances, and I have been blessed. I have reason to be grateful to you, Captain Foxe. Not so much for the money in my purse, as for the comrades that I have sailed with." He stood and raised his tankard of ale, "I salute you! Brothers of the sea!"

The salute was returned by nearly every man in the *Galleon*, with a cheer. A good speech, he thought, surprised that it had come from his own mouth. Foxe was smiling and looked teary-eyed.

John remained standing and moved toward the door. "I will stop by tomorrow morning, and bid farewell to you, and to Roger," he said, and stepped out into the street. There was one more farewell to say, he realized.

There were many other pubs near the waterfront, some of which catered to men of foreign origin. In one of these, he would find Dick Benby, or so he hoped. He visited more than one, asking for Benby by name. "Ah, you mean the blackamoor? Just down the street — that way."

As John approached the place, he heard the sound of drumming. A sign outside identified it as *The Two Kingdoms*. Once inside, he saw a crowd of men standing in a circle. He recognized the drummer and the two men in the middle as the Ndongans they had rescued from Santo Domingo — they were dancing, or fighting — engola, Benby had called it — as they had on board the *Egyptian Queen*. The rest of the crowd was clapping and cheering them on. It appeared that bets were being placed, though John had no idea how they could determine who the winner of such a match would be.

"Carpenter! What brings you to this part of town?" It was the voice of Dick Benby, behind him. He turned, to see Benby smiling at him. "Do you wish to join the competition?"

One of the contestants launched a kick at his opponent's head, just grazing him. The crowd oohed and cheered. John smiled and shook his head. "I was looking for you."

"Well, you have found me. Come, sit."

"Caroline! Ale for me friend, here! And some stew!"

A dark-skinned woman appeared, with two tankards of ale, and a steaming bowl of something aromatic. She set them on the table with a smile for John and a wink at Benby.

"I already had my dinner . . ." John began.

"Aye, but you've never had a stew like this one, and won't again, from what I hear. Try it."

John tasted it and had to admit it was different. He had some more.

"You see? My Caroline is a cook like no other in Harwich."

"What is in this?"

"Lots of things, some secret things. The meat is from an unlucky goat."

John nodded, his mouth full. He could believe it was goat or practically anything else.

"It reminds me of the stew my mother used to cook," said Benby. "When I discovered Caroline could cook like this, I had to have her for my own," Benby chuckled.

"Your own? Are you . . . married?"

"Of course! What did you think, I owned her?"

John shook his head. "I didn't think anything. I never guessed you were married."

"Married, with three children," said Benby.

"And you board here when you are not at sea?"

"I stay here, when I am not at sea, because I own this place. Caroline runs it when I am away."

"I had no inkling. I guess I never thought about what seamen do when they're not at sea. I suppose many of them must have other occupations."

"So, how do you like my place?"

John looked around the dimly lit interior. Not as large as the *Galleon*, but full of customers. Business was booming.

"It appears that most of your customers are . . . foreigners?"

"You could say so," Benby replied. "Most of us were not born in England. We are English enough to serve in Her Majesty's navy, but not English enough to own land, if that is what you mean by 'foreigners'."

"I am sorry. I did not know what words to use."

"The government does not know what words to use, either. It makes our presence here a precarious thing. We are free, but not free to go back to the lands of our birth. Our past is lost, and we must make our own future, wherever we find ourselves. My tavern is a place where a man can have a drink and a meal, without being gawked at, maybe find someone with whom he can speak the language of his homeland. A place where he is more than the object of curiosity, or fear."

They talked until John was nearly finished with the stew. That and the ale was making him drowsy. "I came to say farewell and thank you for what you have taught me. I might very well be dead but for your training."

Benby nodded. "That is true." He looked directly into John's eyes. "You are not quite finished with the business that came with your training. But your understanding grows. Someday, may you find peace. Innocence lost cannot be recovered, but wisdom is a healer."

John was uncomfortable and changed the subject. "I also want to bid farewell to Homer," he said. "Do you know where I can find him?"

"Omar is not much of a drinker. He eats here, sometimes. I can fetch him for you. Caroline! send one of the servants to ask Omar to join us!" He turned back to John. "Tell me, where are you bound?"

"I am planning to visit my family. I have not seen them for more than five years."

"Ah, the hero returns!"

"It's not like that." (although it was like that, at least a little. He looked forward to proving to his family — especially his grandfather, his father, and his uncles — that he was making his way in the world. A horse a cart, and a purse full of money would attest to his success). "I don't even know how many of them are still living."

Benby nodded, "Aye, you must go then. A pity, you will miss our next voyage."

John started to say that he wouldn't sail on their next voyage if his life depended on it, but remembered that he was speaking to a man who had dedicated his life to the sea — no reason to insult him by suggesting that seafaring was somehow a thing to be avoided. Just then, Homer approached them and greeted John.

"Carpenter! Has Mr. Benby signed you up for our next voyage, yet?"

"I only just heard that you are putting to sea again. Is it soon?"

"A matter of weeks, or so I hear. The *Queen* is shipshape, it only remains to provision her."

"Where are you bound? The Spanish Main, again?"

Homer shook his head. "No one seems to know, but I doubt we'll venture so far this time out. The king of Spain has assembled a fleet and intends to attack us sooner, rather than later. England will need all the ships she can muster if they are to be stopped; we will be the first line of defense, I think."

A sobering thought. Spanish soldiers in England! John determined that he must see his family again before the blow could fall. "If things are as perilous as you say, I must see my mother, again, and soon," he said.

"Ah," said Homer, "so you should. "The war may come to your birthplace sooner than anyone thinks. Still, we would welcome you to fight at our side," he nodded at Benby, and Benby nodded back.

Odd, to think that these two men, born in Africa, would so matter-of-factly presume that the English cause was their own. Then again, both of them had bitter experience of what a Spanish rule could mean. Maybe it was self-interest, or pragmatism — precarious though their lives were in Harwich, the Spanish could only offer them a worse condition. He remembered the brands that the African mates carried on their chests. How many of the other men in this place were branded, as well? Many, probably; perhaps all of them.

"If it comes to that, I will fight alongside my family, and the men of my parish," he said. He thought of the Baron's offer. "I came to bid you farewell," said John, "though I did not have in mind the possibility that one or more of us might fall in the coming battle. All the more reason to express my gratitude, now. Both of you have been mates to me, and what I have learned from you will stay with me till the end of my days. 'Thank You' is not enough; you are part of who I have become. Whatever success is mine, you own a share."

"That is the way of shipmates," said Homer, as Benby nodded slowly.

There wasn't much more to say. John stood and shook both men's hands. "God willing, we will meet again," said John, and turned out into the street.

The next morning he rose early, packed his personal chest, and moved it into the storage room of the *Galleon*. He walked southward through town to the stable, and harnessed Gordon to the cart, then drove back through town to the rear of the *Galleon*.

Danny Cornwall was up and about by now, so John settled his bill and had breakfast. They spoke as he ate.

"That's an ugly horse you have behind my pub," observed Cornwall.

"Got a good price for him," retorted John.

"Aye, so Hector says. You'll do well enough if you keep to your frugal habits."

John nodded. "Frugality has served me well, so far."

"You've been making the rounds with your farewells, so I hear," said Cornwall.

John nodded again. "And I want to wish you the best, as well. You've been a good landlord to me, watched out for my interests, always dealt fair and square. If I had listened to you more carefully, I might have avoided some of my troubles."

"Yet those troubles have been profitable enough, or so it appears," Danny replied with a twinkle in his one good eye.

"I won't deny it."

"It's a funny thing," said Cornwall, "many a ship has returned to this port from a successful voyage, and the sailors come in here, boasting of their good fortune — all except for one. The crew of the *Egyptian Queen* has been in and out of here, and they always pay their bill without protest, but nary one has blurted out how much they made. Seems to me, the voyage just managed to pay their wages. Either that or they all have something that they've agreed not to talk about. Never seen anything like it. Has Foxe got their tongues tied? What's the word?"

John looked at him. "Mum's the word."

"Agreed. You can count on my discretion. How much did you take? You can tell me."

"You asked me what the word was, and I told you. Mum's the word."

Cornwall stared at him for a moment, then whistled softly. "That much, then?"

John smiled. "Thank you for this delicious meal. I'll have my things out of your storeroom in just a few minutes."

John was as good as his word. There was ample room in the cart for his tool chest, his clothing, and the barrow. He stowed the Jack, the morion, the cutlass, and the snaphance near the front, along with the pistol case. One pistol he tucked into his belt, and then lashed everything down. As an afterthought, he found room for the basket of patatas. He covered the bed of the cart with the canvas, and tied that down, as well.

It was still early morning. John directed Gordon and the cart eastward, to Harriet's new residence, and called out to Roger. Harriet herself came out to the street. "Roger and the Captain are down at the docks," she said. She appeared younger than she had just days before — less careworn and anxious, probably. Knowing Foxe, she was probably eating better, too.

"Thank You, ma'am," said John, and turned Gordon toward the waterfront. The *Queen* looked splendid, he thought. He still had a sense of proprietorship when he looked at her — freshly painted, aswarm with men fitting her for her next voyage. He spotted Captain Foxe, and Roger on the dock, near the gangplank. He waved, and they walked to meet him. "I'm on my way," he said, "and I see that you nearly are, as well."

"Aye," said Foxe. "Last chance to join us, Carpenter!"

John smiled and shook his head. "I wish you good luck, for England's sake as much as your own. Roger, I believe we have business to conclude."

"Sir?"

"I don't think I paid you your penny a week since we sailed, did I?"

"No sir." Roger chuckled.

"I think this is the end of your employment with me. I calculate forty-eight weeks' back pay, which comes to four shillings. Do you agree?"

Roger smiled and nodded.

"Here they are then!" John tossed him four silver coins. "God Bless You, Roger. You have served me well." With that, he turned Gordon back through town, and then southwest, to the countryside beyond.

Part 12: The Road Home

August 1586: Gordon

They made good progress that day, toward Chelmsford. The road was dry and traffic was light. Once the road left the estuary and leveled off, Gordon raised his head, as if impatient to leave Harwich behind. John let him have his head for a while, as Gordon broke into a trot. In truth, the load that John's cart comprised was not very heavy for a draft animal like Gordon. John could have bought a lighter, more stylish, and prettier horse for the job. But John had other tasks in mind, tasks that only a draft horse was suited for. In the meantime, Gordon tossed his head, and high-stepped down the road for at least two miles, before slowing down. As traffic on the road became heavier, they had to adjust their pace to the other vehicles in front. John paused at the top of a low rise, to let him blow. From there, he had a view of fields and woodlands in every direction — steeples pointing skyward wherever a village lay hidden in the trees. It was a fine August morning.

John reckoned that they would make it to Colchester easily enough by that evening, and didn't push Gordon. He was enjoying the view from the road, evaluating the vigor of the crops in the fields as they passed one farm after another. Much more interesting than looking at the sea all day, he thought. Gordon seemed content with their measured pace. John had a farmer's eye, gauging the probable quality of the soil or the industriousness of the farmer in each field he passed. The wheat was still soft green, though it would be ripening to gold very soon. The oats were pale, the barley was already ripening. He began to relax. This was where he belonged, on solid ground, out of sight or scent of the ocean.

They stopped near midday in a small village on the main road. John hadn't packed anything for his lunch, but he was reminded once again that he had the money to buy whatever he needed — in this case, some cheese, a loaf of bread, an apple, and some ale. He found a spot just out of town, to eat his supper, and let Gordon browse on the grass at the roadside for most of an hour.

By late afternoon, they were in sight of the city proper. Colchester was a thriving city; the capital of Roman Britain, so it was, before London.

Lately, its streets were swarming with Huguenots and Flemings — refugees from the wars and persecutions of Spain and France. Skilled and educated men — weavers and cloth makers. The local economy was thriving. It would be a promising place for an English carpenter to establish himself, John realized. But other matters would have to come first. He found an inn with a stable, and he and Gordon lodged there for the night — a good meal for him, extra grain for Gordon.

Colchester had another legacy. No less than nineteen of its citizens had been burned at the stake during the reign of Bloody Mary. Ironic then, that it became a haven of refuge for Protestants during the reign of her half-sister Elizabeth, and that it prospered by harboring the very sort of people it would have executed without hesitation only a few decades before. *It is a strange world we live in*, thought John, *everything is changing, faster than a man can keep up with it. What is left to rely on?*

In the morning they were on their way again. There was traffic on the road, and they found their place in a long line of carts, wagons, and the occasional carriage. Plenty of people were walking, as well. Once or twice a post rider galloped by them, with some important message or other. John was content to let Gordon set the pace. Gordon plodded steadily down the road, and John let his attention wander a bit.

Gordon stopped suddenly. They were at a fork in the road. Gordon turned his head to look back at John as if to ask which fork to take. The branch to the right led mostly due west, the one on the left more southwesterly. It took John a moment to get his bearings; the right-hand road led to Braintree, near Felsted. The left-hand road would take him to Chelmsford. He realized with a start that it was the same one he had taken to Colchester four years ago when he left little Baddow. He took a moment to sort through the flood of memories that swept into his mind. The traffic behind them flowed past, choosing one fork or the other.

In truth, he had been retracing a familiar route since he had left Harwich yesterday. It was not obvious at first, because he was traveling in the opposite direction this time, and his mind was on Felsted and his family. But when he looked backward from his seat on the cart, the familiarity of the view was very apparent. Four years. Not that much had changed, and yet so much had changed! He considered the fact that a stop in Little Baddow would not put him more than a day's journey out of his way to Felsted. But was it safe for him to return there? No question but that he should avoid Chelmsford, but he was curious about the Widow Smith, and the Vessey family. There was still the tuppence that Sybil

Vessey owed him, and he had promised to return one day and give her the chance to settle the debt . . . he remembered their last parting. He had offended her, somehow. Too forward, perhaps . . . No, better to stay the homeward course. Felsted, then "Haw!" he cried, directing Gordon to the right-hand road.

Gordon looked back at him and shook his mane vigorously. John flicked the reins and pulled rightward; Gordon shifted his substantial weight to the left. John stood up and cried "Haw!" again. Gordon turned his head and shook his mane. A passing pedestrian laughed at the sight. "Looks like your horse has a mind of his own!"

"Ugly horse, though," said another voice. "Ugly and stubborn. A bad combination." More laughter. John let them pass on their way. He didn't understand what was suddenly wrong with Gordon. He sighed. Couldn't just sit here in the middle of the road. Alright, then, "Gee!" Gordon lowered his head and pushed to the left, gathering speed as he surged forward. Not quite a canter, but a quick trot, for a hundred yards or so, until the fork in the road was out of sight. Then Gordon settled back into his steady gait. John was bewildered. Had Gordon been on this road before? Was there something on the road to Braintree that he wanted to avoid? He knew that horses had a keen sense of smell; perhaps there was something objectionable down that way. At any rate, they were headed for Little Baddow now. John hoped Gordon wasn't trying to take him all the way to Chelmsford, back to a part of his past he wanted to forget.

Meantime, assuming they were bound for Little Baddow, John needed to plan how to present his sudden reappearance, how to explain his absence, and who to talk to. Asking after the Widow Smith might arouse suspicions; better to start with the vicar at St. Mary's, who would be able to fill him in on any current developments. Sybil Vessey could be his last stop, assuming the coast was clear. Maybe she would put Gordon up in her barn for the night, as a way to pay off her debt. He was pleased with the thought — better to offer her a chance to settle the debt without dipping into her purse; no need to pressure the poor woman for hard money.

They stopped for supper near a village called Rivenhall, just off the main road. John had the leftovers from yesterday's supper, and there was plenty of browse for Gordon on the roadside. When he had eaten, John climbed back onto the seat of the cart and flicked the reins, to get Gordon moving. Gordon just stood there. What could be wrong now?

John climbed down and inspected the harness, and each of Gordon's shoes. Nothing seemed amiss. Gordon was staring westward, down a narrow lane. Something down that way was holding his interest. John followed his gaze, and saw a small human figure, walking in his direction, approaching the highway. As the figure approached, he saw it was a woman, carrying a bundle of some sort. Gordon continued to stare at her as if fascinated. When she got closer, he raised his head and whinnied at her, as if he recognized her. John was puzzled.

The woman, hearing Gordon's whinny, approached more rapidly. She was young, John saw. She was carrying a baby.

"Oh sir!" she said to John, a little breathlessly, "How considerate of you to wait for us! When I saw you waiting at the end of the lane, I knew my prayers were being answered!"

"Prayers? What Prayers?"

"I am desperately weary, Sir, and I must be in Little Baddow by nightfall. Surely God has sent you to help me on my way?"

"If God has sent me, I am surprised to hear it. My horse seems unwilling to go any further down this road."

"Then God must have spoken to the horse, don't you think? Will you take me to Little Baddow, or not?

"I am headed that way if Gordon here will cooperate. You are welcome to ride in the cart, though it will be bumpy."

"They say it is foolish to look a gift horse in the mouth. The more so, if the giver is the Lord himself, I should think. I shall be happy for the help." With that, she handed him the baby (who might have been six weeks old, he thought), and climbed up onto the seat of the cart.

Gordon's gaze was down the road, now, and he tossed his head impatiently. John passed the baby back to the woman and climbed aboard, and Gordon started down the road immediately, without urging.

"Tell me something," John said, "have you ever seen this horse before?"

"No, I think I would remember a face like that one. No offense intended Sir, but you must admit that he is a remarkable looking animal. God often uses the homeliest and humblest among his creatures, or so I have been told."

"No offense taken," John replied. "I do not know your name."

"It is Rachel, Rachel Johnson."

"Do you have family in Little Baddow?"

"Indeed, I do. We are the Carters, and we have lived there for many generations."

"Your name was Rachel Carter?" John looked at her more carefully. Yes, he remembered her.

"It was, before I married William Johnson," she replied. "You have not told me your name."

"My name is John Porter, I lived in Little Baddow a few years ago. I believe I had supper at your house, on a Sunday."

She gasped a little in surprise and looked at him closely. "Indeed, you did. I am sorry I did not recognize you, at first." Then, "You disappeared quite suddenly, as I recall. There was a lot of talk about it. Your appearance is changed. Not many in Little Baddow would recognize you, now."

John wondered if that were true. Perhaps he could finish his business in Little Baddow without having to answer too many questions about his whereabouts since he left. It was worth a try. He would definitely find the vicar before speaking to anyone else.

"Are you visiting your family in Little Baddow, then?"

"Yes, certainly." she sounded a little tense. "I need a suitable home for our son."

"Where is your husband, then?"

"He is away on business. His mother is impossible to live with. I shall wait for his return at my own mother's home."

This was more information than John really wanted to hear. Domestic discord was not something he wanted to discuss.

"I think I remember where your family home is," he said, "If Gordon is willing, I will deliver you to your mother's front door."

She nodded. "I am sure the horse — his name is Gordon? — will do as he is asked." Then, "Where did you find this Gordon?"

"I bought him in Harwich, not a week ago."

"Just in time, then to answer my prayers." This seemed to explain the purpose of the events in the last week of John's life, as far as she was concerned. John could think of nothing to add to her view of the world, and her place in it. If, indeed, God was arranging the life of a stranger weeks in advance, just so that she could ride instead of walk, he could hardly deny it. And Gordon's behavior had certainly been strange to him, and convenient to her. Maybe God did talk to animals.

It was no more than eight miles from Rivenhall to the junction with the road to Little Baddow, and Gordon seemed to be in a hurry. John did not try to hold him back; if he truly was on a mission from God, as Rachel and Gordon appeared to believe, it would be foolhardy, if not dangerous, to get in the way. They made it to the junction in little more than two hours.

They turned south, then. Little Baddow should be just three miles ahead. The road was not as well maintained as the old Roman road they had left, but there was much less traffic. Gordon was energized, impatient to reach whatever destination God had assigned to him. John held him back just enough to avoid a collision with the few other vehicles on the road. At this rate, they would be in the village in less than an hour.

"Mr. Porter," Rachel began, "I would appreciate it if you would say nothing to anyone in the village about the circumstances of my return. This may come as a surprise to my family, and I see no need to provide grist for the rumor mills."

"Agreed," said John, "if you will do me the same courtesy. If my appearance is altered as much as you say, I may be able to conduct my business there, without answering too many questions about the last four years of my life. As you say, no reason to feed the rumor mills." She smiled at this and nodded.

Soon enough the spire of the parish church became visible, and soon they were rolling down the main street of Little Baddow. People on the street recognized Rachel and greeted her by name. No one appeared to recognize John. John's memory was good enough to find the Carter's house without difficulty, and Rachel and her son were soon inside the house. At this point, Gordon turned and looked at John, as if to say, "Now what?"

"The church, if you please," said John, and indicated the direction with a motion of his head. Gordon turned forward and began pulling in the direction indicated. They pulled up next to the churchyard, at the rear of the church, where some tall grass grew. Gordon gave the grass his attention, and John walked round to the main doors on the West side.

It was dark inside, even with the light from the windows on the south side of the nave. He stopped to inhale the familiar smell of the place, and let his eyes adjust.

"How can I help you?" A voice to his left. A man in clerical garb. Not the vicar he remembered, yet — "Samuel Vessey!"

"The same," replied Samuel. "And you are . . . John Porter?"

"I am. I was looking for the vicar."

"And you have found him."

"The old vicar is gone?"

"More than a year ago. What brings you back to us?"

"That is a story long in the telling. As of this morning, I had no intention of visiting Little Baddow, today. Yet here I am. My horse was determined to visit this place, or maybe it was God's will. I cannot be certain."

"That sounds like a story that should be told around a dinner table. Will you not dine with us tonight?"

"I do not think I dare refuse. Thank you. It would be helpful to me if you could tell me something of the events of the last four years in the village. Is the Widow Smith still living?"

"Indeed she is, in the same house as always. Do you intend to visit her while you are here?"

"Only if it is safe to do so. I am told that my appearance has changed since I last lived here — if I truly can move about the village without being recognized, I should like to see her."

"I do not think that the risk is great, even if you are recognized. There was a time shortly after you left, that strangers came round, asking questions. One even tried to pass himself off as a carpenter. But that is all over now."

"In that case, I will visit the widow on my way out to your place. Or . . . wait! Are you living in the village, now?"

"There is a rectory, I often sleep there. But I have my dinners with the rest of the family, out at the farm. I will send a message to Sybil to warn her we will be having company." He walked John out and to the rear of the church. "This is how you travel now?" he asked, at the sight of the cart. "It appears that you have prospered, these past years. And this is the horse that brought you to Little Baddow?" At this, Gordon turned to face the two of them. Samuel was startled at Gordon's appearance. "Well, there's no arguing with a face like that, is there?" he said with a chuckle.

John drove the rig out on to the main street, and round to the rear of the Widow Smith's building. He kept his broad-brimmed hat on and knocked at the front door.

Meanwhile, Samuel Vessey had summoned a servant, to get the message to Sybil about their dinner guest. The servant, named Janet, was full of news of her own: "Rachel Carter rode into town today, in the company of a strange man."

"Strange, how?"

"Well, not her husband, that's for sure. A grim looking figure. And he was driving a hideous-looking horse, the kind of animal that could only come from hell itself."

"Is that all?"

"No, sir. Rachel has a baby with her. Most likely not her husband's child, so they are saying."

"Whose baby do they think it is?"

"No one knows! Maybe the devil's child! It makes sense, a horse like that, a grim stranger."

"Did you know that the horse and the cart were parked right behind the churchyard, not an hour ago?"

Wide eyes, fear, "No, I never! Right here in the church?"

"No, not in the church, just outside the yard. This is sanctified ground, after all."

"Aye, so it is, vicar, so it is. Makes you shiver just to think about it."

Samuel gave Janet a message for Sybil. He didn't mention John's name: given the reputation that the "Grim Man" had already acquired, the rumors would run wild in her mind and be spread far and wide before Sybil heard anything about it. John was right to keep a low profile, though not for the reasons he thought.

John spoke with the Widow Smith just long enough to determine that she was safe. "We still need a carpenter in Little Baddow," she pointed out.

"I cannot stay long. I am bound for Felsted, where the rest of my family is, or so I hope. I just wanted to satisfy myself that no harm has come to you, on account of me."

"Harm there is, and harm there will be. But none of it is on your account, John Porter. Our government is frightened of every shadow and blink of an eye, and our people will suffer, as long as the government is terrified. I do not think I will live to see better days, but perhaps you, or your children will."

"I have no children."

"It is time you did something about that. Without children, there can be no better days. There is no hope for the future unless we make a future."

John wished her well and excused himself. He drove Gordon and the cart back out onto the road and headed southwest, toward the Vessey farm. He had no idea what he was going to say to Sybil Vessey. It was suddenly very important to him that he greet her with the right words; his mind was blank; he had no idea what he was going to say. He remembered his first encounter with her — too bad he couldn't just start over, from the beginning . . .

Part 13: A Debt Paid

August 1586: Knowing What to Say

Sybil was working in her vegetable garden that afternoon when Janet arrived with Samuel's message. "He wants you to know he has invited a guest for dinner this evening."

"A guest? Does the guest have a name?"

"No, I don't think so. Or maybe he mentioned it, and I forgot. I don't know."

Some associate from among his clerical friends, probably. At least Samuel would contribute to the cost of the extra seat at the table. It was easier to feed everyone since Samuel had become the vicar in Little Baddow. They could afford some extras, now. She would have something special for the mystery guest.

"Mistress, I know I should have gotten a name, but with all the excitement this afternoon, I'm just not myself!"

Sybil reflected that Janet seemed completely herself, excited and scatterbrained. "What excitement is that?"

"It's about Rachel Carter. She just appeared in the village, this afternoon, with a baby. She rode in on a blue wagon, just as cool as ye please, driven by a strange, grim-looking man — not her husband, mind you, but a stranger, dark and hairy. And the horse! You should have seen the horse! An evil eye, if ever I saw one!" (here Janet stopped to cross herself). "They say it could be the devil himself, with a horse like that. And who knows who the father of the baby might be?"

"The devil himself?"

"Exactly! Could be the father, who can say?"

Sybil sighed. "Thank you for delivering the message, Janet. Please tell my brother that we will make room for his friend."

Janet curtseyed and headed back to town. Sybil returned to her gardening. Over the years, she had learned to cultivate more and more varieties of vegetables, and her family was eating better for it. She grew more spices, as well, which meant less monotony. Things were getting better, from one year to the next. Her sister Mary was twenty, now, and able to care for the inside of the house on her own. Susan was eighteen — both of them were at the age of marriage for most women. Mary had a beau that seemed serious, and Susan had at least three young men hovering around her at church. Perhaps something would come of it. Or perhaps all the Vessey women would die as old maids — there simply wasn't any dowry to offer. Her brothers were prospering, and that boded well for the future of the family. Her father, Thomas, was still living, though clearly in decline.

There was the sound of horseshoes on the road — she looked up to see a blue cart stop in front of the house. And there on the seat was the "Grim Man" that Janet had described. She glanced at the horse. Ugly to the point of gruesome. She felt sorry for the animal.

The stranger tipped his hat, and spoke: "Goodwife," he said, "I am a master carpenter. I believe I can do you service."

Sybil recognized the voice, immediately. She struggled to find the words and felt short of breath. Then, "I do not know you sir, nor you me. If you did, you would not call me 'wife' and perhaps not 'good', either."

John laughed and took off his hat. She could recognize him now, older, browner (weatherbeaten, perhaps), but the same man she knew, nonetheless. She was still a little flustered, and she blushed. "What service do you propose to do me, carpenter?

"Why, to sit at your table, and eat your food, this very night. And if you can find a place in your barn for this excellent animal, I believe we might settle an ancient debt."

She giggled and felt giddy. "Excellent animal! That is the perfect word to describe the beast!"

"Please be careful what you say. Gordon is a sensitive creature." As if to agree, Gordon shook his mane and whinnied. John laughed, and so did Sybil. For a moment, the laughter enveloped both of them, as if the world around them was distant, faded. Sybil felt transported to a strange place, far from Little Baddow, far from anything she knew. Then, Sybil collected herself, and said, "Well, let's find a place in the barn for Gordon and get your wagon off the road. You have created an impression in Little Baddow today."

"Eh, how's that?"

"There is a man driving the streets of the village with a blue cart, so I have been told, drawn by the devil's own horse. Some say that only the devil himself could tame such a beast, others say he might be just a man bound to the devil's service. In either case, it's very suspicious that Rachel Carter was traveling with him, and she with a newborn babe." She grinned as she said this, and John realized she was having some fun at his expense.

Apparently, his plan to slip in and out of Little Baddow unnoticed had already failed. "If things are as you say, you might not want me around your dinner table."

"Oh, we will feed you. Best to hide you in the barn, along with your noble steed, until then." Sybil was unaccustomed to this sort of banter, and she was surprised at how easily it came from her mouth. John was thinking pretty much the same thing: was he flirting with this woman? . . . Was it working? First things first — get Gordon and the cart into the barn.

He got the cart into the barn, and Gordon unharnessed, watered, and put in a stall. There was hay, which Gordon approached with a businesslike attitude. This done, he turned to Sybil. He was suddenly at a loss for words.

There was an awkward silence. Finally, she spoke: "Shall we settle my debt, then?"

John nodded. "I think it stands at two pence. If you allow Gordon and I to spend the night in this barn, I will consider the debt paid."

"Done!" she said, spat into her hand, and offered it to him. "Done!" he replied and did the same. That business concluded John was still at a loss for words.

Sybil began to feel restless. Was it really so difficult for the man to make some small talk? Apparently, it was up to her to create some sort of conversation. "I should tell you, John, that I have spoken with my brother and his friend, Edward Chase. I know what happened in Chelmsford, the day the priest was executed, and I know the part you played there. There is no need for you to conceal these matters from me." John relaxed visibly, and nodded, with a faint smile. *That was part of his reluctance*, she thought, *he isn't sure what I can safely be told. Silly man — as if I could not keep a confidence!*

"Then I suppose it is safe to tell you something of my travels these past years, and I suppose I owe you some accounting, given the way we parted, and my delay in returning here to finish our business."

She nodded, "Yes, I believe you do."

"When I left Little Baddow, I journeyed to Harwich, which is a few day's walk from here. I thought it was far enough from here, and a large enough town, that I could easily disappear. Not as easy as I supposed, but it served the purpose. There was plenty of work in Harwich, in the shipyards, and I am now a member of the Carpenter's guild, a Master Carpenter, as I said. I have prospered in Harwich, and I am now in a position to establish myself in some village large enough to support a Master Carpenter and his apprentices. I am headed first to Felsted, to visit my family, and then I will look for a suitable place to settle."

"If there is plenty of work in Harwich, why did you not stay there?" (She caught his implication that Little Baddow was not large enough for his ambitions.)

"Things in Harwich had come to such a pass, that it was prudent for me to leave, and quickly."

"What? Another hanging? Are you in some sort of trouble, again?"

John laughed. "No, not that kind of trouble. Not as much as I am right here in Little Baddow, anyway." He walked to his cart and untied the tarp, rolling it back. "Some things I can show you," he said. He climbed into the back of the cart and invited her to join him. She sat on the side of the wagon bed, while he rummaged through the cargo.

He found the morion and put it on his head, then turned to face her.

She gasped. "Where did you come by that?"

"Spoils of war, you could say."

Sybil was skeptical. "You're telling me that you have been soldiering, these four years?"

He shook his head. "Not soldiering, sailing. And only since last September. I was pressed into the Navy, under circumstances I would rather not talk about. I was at sea for eleven months and arrived at our home port just a week or so ago. I decided it was best to leave the seacoast before I could be forced aboard another ship."

This was a far more interesting story than she had expected to hear. "Have you been to France, then, or the Low Countries?"

"No, we didn't reach either of those places."

"So, you just sailed up and down the coastline for eleven months?" That sounded like a boring way to spend a man's time.

"Actually, we sailed to the Americas (I think that is no longer a secret). England is at war with Spain, you know. We attacked as many Spanish ports and vessels as we could, before sailing for home.

"America!" (This was turning into a great story, though she wondered if he might be embellishing it) "Are the people there as strange as they say? Did you see any exotic animals?"

"I brought these back," he dragged the basket of *patatas* out where she could see them. Not so impressive, like small turnips, maybe. Still, she had to admit they were exotic — she hadn't seen anything exactly like them before.

"The people of those lands grow these," John explained, "they roast them, bake them, fry them. We ate them on board ship, as well. They keep for many months if the place is dark, and they seem to prevent scurvy. All of the green parts are poisonous, but the roots themselves are tasty enough."

"And that is your plunder? Some roots and a helmet?"

"I have these, as well," said John, as he pulled out his cutlass and the snaphance, "Plus a few other weapons, and some armor."

Sybil was impressed with the array of weapons. "Armor? Are you telling me that you are some sort of war hero?" She was mocking him, in a good-natured way.

John's face grew sober. "No, not a hero. But I would not have survived without these. Many of my comrades were not so fortunate."

She saw some sadness in his eyes, just then. Maybe a hint of guilt, because he survived, and others had not? "If I have spoken too lightly, I apologize," she said.

"No, no. Someday I may tell you an amusing story about how a clumsy man fell down in the middle of a battle and was a hero by the time he got back on his feet." He shook his head and chuckled. He had not really spoken of his battles on the seas to anyone; somehow, it felt lighter now he had done so. Maybe it was part of what Dick Benby had been talking about, the evening before he left Harwich.

"Tell me the truth. Are you a fugitive from a press gang?"

John chuckled again. "Not unless they can catch up with me." Sybil's eyes widened. "I am teasing you," said John. "I have my discharge papers with me. I am a free man."

Sybil appeared relieved. "You still have not explained how you came rolling into the village today, and with Rachel Carter, of all people, and her baby!" (*And for that matter, if you were headed to Felsted from Harwich, Little Baddow is out of your way, isn't it?*)

She sounded more interested in this part of his story than the others, he thought. Something in the intensity of her gaze was a warning that he should answer carefully, but he wasn't sure what to say. As little as possible, he supposed. "We met her on the road, and she asked for a ride into little Baddow. We were going that way anyway, so I delivered her to her mother's house."

"We?"

"Gordon and I."

"Ah. And did Rachel explain why she was at the roadside, just then?"

"She said a little but asked me not to tell anyone what she had to say."

"Ah." Just like a man to be discreet, when it was least agreeable. Sybil gazed intently at him, silently prompting him to say more. He seemed impervious to the suggestion.

"How long do you suppose she had been waiting, before you happened along?" Maybe another line of questioning would open his mouth.

"It was we who were waiting for her, I suppose," he said. Sybil gave him a strange look; more information would be required. "I will tell you how it happened," John began, "but I really cannot explain it."

"Please, speak."

"First of all, to be truthful, I was not planning to be in Little Baddow today." Sybil's eyes seemed to cloud over. This conversation was not going the way John had planned, He hastened to add, "I was planning to visit you, but after I saw my mother and father in Felsted." There. That should be clear enough. What man wouldn't want to see his mother? He continued, "It wasn't until we reached the fork in the road west of Colchester, that I was forced to change my plans."

"Forced? Forced to come to Little Baddow?"

John realized that it sounded all wrong, as if he was somehow speaking with Sybil against his will — not what he meant, at all. "It was Gordon . . ." that sounded lame, even to him.

"Gordon!? Pray tell!" She was chuckling, now, on the verge of laughter. That could only be a good thing.

"Gordon balked at the crossroads and wouldn't take the road to Braintree. It was embarrassing. Everyone walking by was laughing at me, and my horse. But as soon as I directed him toward Chelmsford, he trotted down the road like it was suppertime. I can't explain it, but it's true!"

Sybil was laughing silently now, at the image of John trying to get an ugly horse to move out of a crossroads, amid jeering and cursing throngs.

"That's not the end of it. We stopped for supper near Rivenhall. When I had finished eating, Gordon refused to move again. I could not get him to take a step, until Rachel Carter walked up, and asked for a ride."

"So, you think Gordon was waiting for her?"

"She certainly thought so, said it was the answer to her prayers, and whether I knew it or not, Gordon must have been taking instructions from God Almighty."

Sybil shook her head slightly. How like Rachel to believe that God, if not every other person in her life, would move heaven and earth (or a horse!) to attend to her personal needs. Improbable as John's story was, that detail alone had a ring of truth.

"Believe it or not, as soon as Rachel and her son were aboard, Gordon was eager to go. He pulled at the harness all the way to Little Baddow. I meant to speak with the vicar, who turns out to be your brother, just to get the lay of the land here, so to speak. He invited me to dinner and said it would be safe for me to pay a visit to the Widow Smith if I was discreet about it. Not many people in the village recognize me, anyway, I guess . . ."

Sybil sat back and clapped her hands. "You tell a good story, John Porter. I do not think most people would believe it, but I would like it to be true, so I will accept it as it is told."

This conversation was not going as hoped. Simple storytelling was getting him nowhere. "I think I have left out an important detail."

"And that is?"

"Whatever Gordon's reasons may have been, the person in Little Baddow that I most wished to see, was you."

Sybil felt herself blushing. "Yet you visited my brother and the Widow Smith before you came here."

Awkward, but true. He couldn't seem to get the conversation going in the right direction. One more try. "I saved the best for last." There. That should help. Or was he being too glib?

"You're a smooth one, John Porter, though I wouldn't have guessed it. I must be about our dinner." She waited for him to take her hand and help her down from the wagon bed. Before she went into the house, she turned to Gordon's stall and addressed him: "Gordon, your master is a smooth one!" Gordon stuck his head out of the stall, threw his head back, and opened his mouth wide, exposing his front teeth. Sybil smiled and walked to the house.

It was late afternoon, now. Samuel Vessey appeared at the barn and greeted John. "There was quite a stir in the village this afternoon. Rachel Johnson, of the Carter family appeared with an infant she claims is her son. No sign of Mr. Johnson, her husband. Could be a domestic dispute; I married the couple myself at St. Mary's, almost a year ago, and I met the groom's mother. Anyway, they say Rachel was in the company of a mysterious stranger, driving a cart pulled by a hideous animal. Some say the stranger is the father of Rachel's child, some say he is a demon in human guise, or maybe it's the horse who is the demon; opinions vary on that point. I visited Rachel at her mother's home, and she insists that Mr. Johnson is the father of the child — but says very little else about her business. She has nothing to say about the stranger with the cart, either. The stranger seems to have disappeared, and most people say it's good riddance, and that Rachel must have had a narrow escape!" He had been struggling to suppress a grin throughout this monologue, but at the end, a smile burst across his face, and he began to laugh.

John was embarrassed by the whole business but tried to find a bright side. "I guess I shouldn't travel back through the village on my way home, then?"

"I should advise against it." Samuel was still grinning. "It is the most exciting thing that has happened in Little Baddow since William Jackson's heifer gave birth to a calf with three eyes, but we've had enough excitement today, to last us a good while."

John nodded. There was more than one way to head homeward, and the fewer the people in the village knew who he was, the better. "Come into the house, we'll talk before dinner," said Samuel.

They sat down at the table, while Sybil and her sisters finished preparing the meal. Thomas Vessey joined them shortly. The aroma from the fireplace suggested to John that the quality of the cooking had improved somewhat in the Vessey household, over the last four years.

"So, you are now the vicar at St. Mary the Virgin," John began.

"Aye, it has been nigh on about a year, now. Fortunate for me, and the rest of my family." Edward replied. "The priest you knew has been promoted to a larger parish, and I was selected to replace him."

"Thanks to his friend, Edward Chase," interjected Sybil, from the other side of the room.

Samuel nodded. "Thanks to Edward, yes."

"Is Mr. Chase still about his mysterious travels, then?"

Samuel nodded again. "Mysterious. Yes, that is an apt description." Then he changed the subject. "You must tell us something of your travels, these past four years."

John took a breath. How to summarize those years? He had to be mindful of which details were pertinent, which tasteful, which best kept secret. It was all a jumble in his head. "I spent most of those years working in the shipyards at Harwich," he began. "I found plenty of work, and I prospered. You meet all sorts of people in a seaport, an interesting place to live."

"And what brings you back here?" Sybil again. No doubt she wanted to see how Samuel would react to the story about Gordon's behavior on the road. John thought maybe this was his chance to start the conversation over.

"I needed to leave Harwich, and I had thought much about all of you since I left. I guess I just wanted to see how the years had treated you." Sounded weak, and vague, but at least he had left an opening.

"Did you have to leave in a hurry, then?" Samuel asked before John could gauge Sybil's reaction.

"Not in a great hurry. I had several days to prepare for my departure, time to buy that cart, and Gordon, of course."

"You are not telling us all that there is to this story."

John took a breath. "True enough. I have been at sea for most of the past year. I was pressed into service by a certain sea captain, who was preparing to set sail again. I thought it prudent to remove myself from his purview, lest he choose me again."

"What duty were you pressed to?"

"I was the ship's carpenter. The Captain I spoke of admired the work I did outfitting his ship and contrived to have me taken aboard to serve in his crew."

"Was it a hard and dangerous voyage?"

"Going to sea is always dangerous, I suppose. I was an officer on the *Egyptian Queen*, so I had it easier than most of the crew. Most of the fighting was done by other men; some of them did not make it home — that is danger enough."

"Wait! Are you telling me that you were with Drake, in the Caribbean?"

"I'm not sure what you have heard, but yes."

"Everyone has heard of Drake's Raid. They talked of nothing else in town — until you appeared with Rachel Johnson, and that horse. Is it true that you sacked three cities, and sank fifty ships?"

"I cannot say exactly how many ships, but we did capture Santiago, Santo Domingo, and Cartagena."

"And you are now an officer in Her Majesty's Navy? You must have met Drake himself!"

John shook his head. "I sailed on a privateer. I got no closer to the Admiral than the sight of his flagship."

"A privateer?"

John nodded. "An interesting coincidence, there. Do you remember who presided at William Payne's execution, in Chelmsford?"

"I do. It was Robert Rich, the 3rd Baron of Leez."

"Well, it turned out that our ship was financed by Baron Rich, and his uncle Sir Richard. I met them at the end of our voyage, when they came to collect their share of the profits."

"Were you recognized?"

"I don't think so. I was introduced as a man from Felsted. I made a point of the fact that I attended the same parish church as they, in my childhood. He recognized my family name; if I seem somehow familiar to him, I hope he will think it is from Felsted, not Chelmsford."

Thomas Vessey had listened to this conversation with unusual (for him) attentiveness, chuckling or nodding as the tale unfolded. Sybil noted this with interest. What was happening with Papa?

Sybil interrupted the conversation, to announce that dinner was ready. The food was placed on the table, the ale was served, and Thomas said a blessing. Thomas sat at the head of the table, with Samuel at the foot. Sybil and Mary sat on the side facing the fireplace, and Susan sat next to John. All of the women, of course, had heard John's tale, as they all worked in the same room. Both of Sybil's sisters were clearly impressed with John's exotic adventures and peppered him with questions about the Americas. What did the people look like? Did he see any strange animals or plants? What did he eat on board the ship?

"You did well to get far away from that hateful captain," Susan ventured. "I don't know how you could stand the sight of such a man, after he did you that way!"

"I will not say that I hate him. He put me in harm's way, to be sure. But he also took care to protect me from danger when he could, as with all the men under his command. He is courageous, and able, and sometimes even generous. I admire him more than I resent him. But it is safer to keep some distance from him."

As dinner progressed, John told more stories of his seagoing adventures. He left out the details that still troubled him or gave him nightmares. He did not mention their encounter with the *Vengeur*, of course, nor anything about the silver ballast, or the Spanish Captain's treasure chest. The storm off the Virginia coast made an exciting tale — without the "devils teeth" (which still troubled his dreams). The appearance of St. Elmo's fire provoked a good deal of disbelief — but Thomas insisted he had seen the same thing during a thunderstorm in Little Baddow, in his youth. John waited until the meal was over to tell the story of how Dr. Lopez treated Lieutenant Cooper's knee with maggots. The women at the table were shocked at the story or pretended to be.

Thomas and Samuel laughed uproariously. Telling the stories unburdened him, somehow, as if it placed a little more distance between himself and his memories.

"How much plunder did you take?" was Samuel's question. "Was there Spanish gold and silver ?"

John demurred. "Most of our cargo on our return was the artillery we took from the prizes and the fortresses we captured. The crew's share came to about nine pounds per man."

"Nine pounds! No wonder you have your own horse and wagon. What will you do with all that money?"

"With that money, plus my wages from the voyage, and what I saved before I sailed, I should be able to buy the freehold rights to a small farm, somewhere near Felsted. I'll have Gordon to help me in the fields, and I'll also be able to start my own carpentry business. The carpentry work will fill in the slow times on the farm, or so I hope. If the business grows, and I take on apprentices, I can rent the farmland out to a tenant, probably one of my relatives. At least, that is what I hope to do."

Thomas spoke. "A sensible plan. Farming is a risky business; crops can fail. If the carpentry business fails, you could still grow your own food. Better not to have all your eggs in one basket."

This was the most Thomas had said to John in any of his previous visits. It was more than Samuel or Sybil had heard him say to anyone outside the family for several years. John thought perhaps he was making a good impression — on Thomas, at least. He wondered what Sybil thought.

Sybil was distracted. Preparing the evening meal had given her something to focus on, but now that dinner was over, the unexpected events of the day came tumbling to the front of her mind. She tried to order her thoughts. The two-penny debt to John Porter was settled, after six years. A trivial thing, to be sure, but it had bound her to him, and him to her in a peculiar way. She was free of an obligation, but the sense of relief she had expected was absent. Something should be finished, but it did not feel like anything was finished. Here he was, telling stories at her dinner table. Susan was sitting awfully close to him, for some reason, hanging on his every word. Wait, why did it matter what Susan was doing? Why should she care?

And then Papa was part of the conversation, too, as if he had come home after a long absence. It wasn't like him; another big part of her ordered life was defying expectations. It left her adrift, not knowing what to say, or what to expect next. She sat and listened. Samuel was speaking now, relating the appearance of Rachel Johnson in the village that afternoon, and her mysterious companion. John seemed a little embarrassed to be the source of all the uproar, but he laughed and shook his head as Thomas, Susan, and Mary heard the story for the first time — especially the interpretation that Janet had put on the events. Sybil chimed in with the report that Janet had made to her earlier in the afternoon. More laughter.

"I don't suppose it would be prudent of me to leave Little Baddow by going through the village, then," added John with a chuckle. "No matter, there are other roads I can take to Felsted."

"Are you leaving soon then?," asked Susan.

"First thing in the morning," replied John. "If Gordon is feeling frisky, we might make it to Felsted by nightfall tomorrow." Sybil felt a pang of disappointment, without knowing why. Perhaps it was that sense of some business left unfinished. Given another day, maybe she could sort it all out. Maybe not. Sybil recalled John's account of Gordon's strange behavior on the road, and Rachel's glib claim that it was an obvious case of divine intervention. Sybil could not dismiss the claim out of hand — she was certain that divine interventions had occurred before and would again. But what if Rachel's situation were not the only one that God was interested in? What if God's purpose was to touch other lives, as well? What if she was somehow involved? She brushed the thought away; mere speculation was silly. If God had sent John to her house, it could be nothing more than the settling of an old debt. Best to assume so, at any rate. Rachel claimed that it was an answer to prayer; Sybil had prayed for no such disruption in her life.

It was getting dark outside. Thomas spoke, "Carpenter, I'd like to see this hideous horse of yours."

"A sight not to be missed!" said Samuel. "I am off to the rectory, I will see you tomorrow."

Thomas and John went out to the barn, where Gordon was browsing on some hay in his stall. Even in the twilight, his distinctive face was plainly visible. "He's not badly formed," observed Thomas, "it's just the patterning on his face that jolts you. Otherwise, he's a fine animal. I have something that could help with that." He rummaged around and came up with an old piece of fabric. "The headgear from an old caparison," he said. "No use for it anymore."

The 'headgear' was a kind of mask that fitted over a horse's head. There were cutouts for the eyes and the nose — the horse could see and eat with it on. In ancient times, it would have served as part of a decorative garment that covered the horse's head and body. Wealthy people put them on their horses in formal situations. Now, only the headpiece was left. It fit Gordon well, and it concealed most of the bizarre blotchiness of his face. John nodded. "This will do," he said, "how much do I owe you?"

Thomas waved the idea away. "I wouldn't charge you for something of no value to me. Take it with my blessing."

John thanked him.

"I'm gratified to see that you have prospered," Thomas continued. "I remember the day you first arrived here. I don't mind admitting that I was skeptical of your skill. But the barn still stands, as you see. Work well done. You'll go far John Porter, or I miss my guess."

John saw an opening. He took a breath."Since you estimate my prospects so highly, I wonder if I might pay court to your daughter. I am at an age where a man should think of marriage, and I have the means to support someone like her. I have not said anything to her about this; I thought it best to acquire your consent, first."

Thomas looked at him with surprise. "Well, you're a fast worker, I'll give you that." He paused for a moment. "Nay, I cannot consent to such a thing. I have no objection to you personally lad, but my daughter is not for the likes of you. A man like yourself, with a bright future, should wed a woman with a substantial dowry, a foundation for the prosperity of your children. We live in a land where the few are wealthy, and the poor grow poorer and more numerous every year. A poor farmer's daughter would be like a dead weight pulling you down into poverty. I speak from experience; my life, and my children's, would have been much easier if I had married well. I did not have many choices, but you (and my sons) will do better, if you are wise."

"But . . ." John began.

"Nay, lad. You'll not change my mind in this matter. Do not speak of it again. Leave for your home in the morning and may God's blessings be with you." With that, he turned and walked to the house.

John was confused. He had been rejected, even as he was being complimented. He could think of nothing to say, nothing to do. Following Thomas into the house was out of the question; there was a clear dismissal in Thomas's tone. It was not yet dark, so he unloaded a few things from his cart, and moved some others around, to make room for sleeping. He would find some hay to make his bed softer. He thought about his

conversation with Thomas and decided he had approached it all wrong —
too sudden, caught Thomas by surprise, probably. Still, he wasn't planning
to be in Little Baddow another day, whatever he was going to say had to be
said sooner, rather than later. He was not a rash man. What had compelled
him to blurt out such a thing? What had just happened would have been
unimaginable just twelve hours ago. Gordon. It was all caused by Gordon.
He turned, and Gordon nickered from the stall. John walked over to
remove the fragment of the old caparison from his head.

"All of this is your fault!" he said. "All of this could have been avoided,
if you would just go where I say to go."

"He might be more cooperative if you didn't blame him for your
problems." It was Sybil's voice. She stood in the doorway of the barn, with
a pillow and some bedding in her arms, and a smirk on her face. "What
did you say to Papa? He just walked past me without a civil word!"

John sighed. Now his humiliation was complete. "I don't know what
got into me. I asked your father for his consent to court you."

"Me? Whatever gave you the idea that I would want to be courted by
you?" She felt a tightening in her throat.

John looked directly at her. "I can't say that anything you have said or
done would give me that idea. I don't know why it came into my head."
He knew this was the wrong thing to say the moment it left his mouth; it
was the best he could come up with, as well as the worst. Sybil looked
shocked but said nothing. He tried to recover. "I suppose it is because I
admire your character. I know you to be an honorable, hard-working
woman. You are thrifty, brave, and clever. You are kind, and loyal to your
family. You would make some man a good wife, I think." Lame, he
thought. Lame.

Sybil was looking at him with a sardonic expression. "It is well that
Papa refused you, I think. Your wooing is of a very poor sort. What reason
did he give?"

"He said that I should seek a bride with a large dowry, that his
daughter is not for the likes of me."

"Ah, so it was about a dowry then?" She felt her insides clench.

"I did not raise the issue. He did."

Yes, that sounded like Papa. "Papa is right, I have no dowry. I could
not marry a man that needed a dowry. I could have saved you the trouble;
did it occur to you that I might prefer that you speak to me, first?"

John was startled at her remark. "It seemed proper to speak to him
first, and it seemed like an opportune moment. I don't think of myself as a

man who needs a dowry; I am able to support a wife. But if that is not enough for you or your father, suppose I were a rich man, with a hundred pounds to my name, could I court you then?"

"A man with a hundred pounds who would marry a woman without a dowry is a fool. I will not marry a fool." She might as well put a brave face on a humiliating situation.

"So, if I were a pauper . . ."

"A woman without a dowry would be a fool to marry a pauper. I am not that sort of fool." She would salvage some of her pride, after all.

"Of all the reasons not to marry, I cannot imagine why a dowry is so important. If the man has enough wealth for the both of them, why is that an obstacle?"

"The problem is not with the man's wealth. It is the bride's poverty. A marriage should be a partnership. A woman who brings nothing to marriage but her womb and her appetite is like a prize heifer. I had rather be a spinster, than some man's heifer."

"And if the woman has a dowry, and the man marries her for it, by your reasoning we might as well regard her as a goose that lays golden eggs."

Exasperating man. Can't grasp the simplest concepts. "A woman's dowry is her share of her new family's wealth. If the marriage dissolves, she may expect to get it back. Her husband may use it while he lives, but if he dies before she does, she will have it to fall back on. The dowry is her contribution to their joint prosperity. She has a moral claim, if not always a legal one, to a say in how the family home and business are run. Without that claim, she is little more than a servant. Why would I give up running my own household, to be a mere servant in someone else's?"

John chuckled. "I cannot imagine you as a 'mere servant' in any household; anyone who tried to assign you such a role would be in for a rude awakening." She smiled slightly and nodded; John sensed that maybe he was on to something. He added, "And I would never court any woman who I thought would be satisfied with such a role. Marriage, as you say, should be a partnership." *As long as it is agreed that the man is head of the house,* he thought but did not say it — no reason to send the conversation off in some unpredictable direction.

That's settled, then," she said. "Here is bedding for you. I will send a breakfast to you in the morning. And with that, she turned and walked back to the house.

John was stumped. It seemed like he finally got the conversation going in a positive direction, and then she ended it. He didn't expect Sybil to defy her father, but he would have liked her to acknowledge that the whole idea wasn't completely silly. Was he really such a poor prospect? She could have refused him politely as if to avoid hurting his feelings, but instead, she launched into a lecture about dowries. And then she said it was settled. What was settled?

"Settled" for Sybil, meant that she had recovered a bit of her dignity. John's agreement that marriage should be a partnership was a moot point, but she took it for an implicit admission that he should have spoken to her, before approaching her father. He had at least acknowledged that any decisions to be made on such matters were rightfully hers. Other women might be bartered or sold like livestock, but she would not be. Ironically, the lack of a dowry took the commercial aspect of marriage completely out of the picture — there was no money for men to haggle over, so she was free — or worthless, depending on a man's perspective.

She was well aware that for women from wealthier families, financial considerations were intimately woven into the fabric of their marriages. Such women could expect a life more comfortable than hers would ever be, but at a price — a price negotiated by men.

In her teenage years, she had imagined such a life for herself. With each succeeding year, she saw how her family's financial straits pushed those dreams to the far edge of likelihood. She transferred those hopes to her sisters, at first, then gradually saw them fade. Such was the destiny of a woman without the means to attract a husband. And now a would-be suitor appears, and praises her character? Fair enough. The wages of a life devoted to hard work and love — character.

By this time, she was back at the house. She wasn't ready to go in; she walked round to the front, facing the road, out of sight of the barn. She was touched, somehow by the carpenter's clumsy gestures of courtship. He had said nothing whatsoever about his feelings in the matter — just like a man.

Not that feelings would make a difference. The practical realities would not yield to feelings, and if they were expressed, it would just make things more awkward. Perhaps she should be grateful that he spared her the embarrassment? She wasn't the sort of woman who would welcome some love-struck swain throwing himself at her feet or mooning around like a helpless puppy.

Tell the truth, said a voice inside her head, *you'd enjoy every minute of it, at least for a while.* The thought startled her — she wasn't like those silly flirts in the village! She never hung on any man the way Rachel Carter used to do with John Porter. *But it annoyed you to see her do it — anyone who didn't know you would think you were jealous, back then.* Jealous? Jealous of what?

There was nothing to be jealous about. Her only tie to the man was an unpaid debt. It had taken too long to settle, but now it was settled, and both of them were free of it. *Tied to a man for four years, for a tuppence? That's a lot of your life, for such a princely sum. And it fell to him to settle it. A penny-pincher, for sure, that one. Except that, he said he came this way because he wanted to <u>see</u> you, not for the money. Come to mention it, you're not offering him any money, and he's not asking for it. Can't imagine why he came unless it has something to do with feelings. Oh, never mind, blame it on the horse, if you'd rather.*

Sybil sighed audibly and went into the house. It was full dark, now. Papa had already gone to bed; summer nights were short enough that there was no point in staying up much past sunset. It would be time to start work again soon enough. Susan and Mary were finishing up something near the fireplace, by candlelight. "What is bothering Papa?" asked Susan. "And what is that look on your face? Has something happened?"

"Why, did Papa say something, when he came indoors?"

"No, but that's not unusual. What is strange is his decision to take the carpenter out to the barn to 'look at a horse', if you can believe that. Then he comes in, looking — I don't know, strange — not a word to say, then up to bed. Then you come in just now, looking like you just found a hog rooting around in your vegetable garden. What is going on?"

Sybil sighed, "John Porter showed him the horse, then asked him for permission to court me."

Susan and Mary both gasped, then squealed with excitement. "Did he really! Oh, this is choice! I didn't think the man could be so bold!" said Mary.

"Papa refused, of course. And I'll admit that I wish John had spoken to me first about it. It could have saved us all a lot of embarrassment."

"Embarrassment? What embarrassment? Papa always says 'no', the first time we ask. Susan and I will talk to him, and we'll get Samuel to put in a good word — we can bring him around, you'll see," said Mary.

Sybil shook her head. "Marriage is impossible for me. I do not seek it. Papa is right — without a dowry, I can never be wed."

"If what you say is true, then Mary and I are condemned to spinsterhood, as well," said Susan. "I, for one, do not accept that destiny."

"Nor I," added Mary.

Sybil looked at them. Both of them had set their jaw. They seemed quite determined, even stubborn, on the point. No reason to disillusion them. "Someone has to take care of Papa . . ." she began.

"And someone will, do not doubt it. We are all grown, now. We can take care of Papa. But he <u>will</u> have to give up some of his old-fashioned ideas." Mary nodded. Evidently, the two of them had discussed all of this before.

"Courtship is not for me. I have no knack for small talk and flirtation. And I shrink at the thought of some eager man filling my ears with flattery and praise."

"It is not as unpleasant as you make it out to be," said Susan. Mary nodded and giggled. "In truth, I think you could come to enjoy it. I suppose it does get tiresome, eventually, but I have not reached that point yet." Mary snickered.

Mary recovered, and then added, "And think of us! Even if you don't wish to marry, you could at least make it easier for us to do so. If you can open the door in Papa's mind, only a crack, it will make our path to matrimony that much easier."

Just like Mary, thought Sybil. Thinking three steps ahead. Pity the man who tries to woo her — she'll have a wedding date in mind before he asks to hold her hand. It was a point, though, that Sybil hadn't considered. Maybe she should put their interests ahead of her own, once again.

"This is our chance to talk to Papa," Susan was looking at Mary, not Sybil. Sybil realized they were up to something, but was not sure what it could be. She realized that the two of them had been waiting for some opportunity, and evidently, it had arrived.

Susan and Mary took their candles and climbed the stairs to the bedroom where Thomas Vessey slept. Sybil followed — this should be interesting. Susan knocked on the door. "Papa? Are you still awake? We need to speak with you."

A muffled answer was audible, and Susan, Mary, and Sybil all entered the room. Thomas was sitting up in his bed, dressed in a nightshirt, a candle at the bedside. "I was just about to put out the light," he said. There was a look of surprise on his face as all three of his daughters crowded around him. *He's outnumbered,* thought Sybil.

"Papa, is it true that John Porter spoke to you of courtship this evening?"

"Aye, I warned him off. Told him that Susan would bring no dowry. Seems like a decent chap; has a future, I reckon. A man like that will find a willing young woman from a family with a healthy dowry, or maybe a wealthy widow."

"<u>Susan</u>? He asked for your permission to court Susan?" Mary interjected.

"Not by name, I didn't let him get that far. But I noticed how close he was sitting to Susan at dinner; it doesn't take a lot of cleverness to figure these things out if you pay attention to the signs."

Sybil struggled to suppress a laugh. Fortunately, the dim light didn't give her away. She took a breath to speak but felt Susan's hand clamp down on her forearm — hard. Susan's glance said *say nothing, nothing at all.*

"But Papa, it could have been me he wanted to court!" Mary spoke now and sat on the edge of his bed. Sybil saw that she was giving her father the look of a child about to collapse in tears, the Baby Mary look, the one he could never refuse. "What if this was my only chance for happiness?" Her voice was quavering, just a bit.

Thomas was off guard, as well as outnumbered. He struggled a bit for an answer. "The sad fact, my dear, is that we have no dowry — for any of you," here he looked at each of his daughters in turn.

"Other young women have married without a dowry," said Susan. "I could name three in just the past two years. They seem to be happily married."

"Eh? How's that?"

"Papa, these are hard times, especially for poor folk. How would any of them marry, if a dowry was always required?" There. Susan had scored a point. Sybil could see where this was going. Her sisters had been preparing for this moment for some time, no doubt.

Mary followed up, quickly. "Papa, promise me that if a proper young man asks to woo me, you will not refuse him out of hand, simply for lack of a dowry."

Thomas nodded, as if grudgingly. "I cannot imagine a proper man being willing to wed without a dowry, but if such a thing exists, I will not reject him out of hand, when the time comes. However, I will not be overruled on my decision about the carpenter. John Porter is forbidden to pay court to Susan, and I will hear no more about it!"

"Quite so, Papa," said Susan, in her submissive voice. "Besides, I have been speaking to another man, and I quite fancy him." Her smile was visible even by candlelight.

Bold, thought Sybil. *Straight for the kill. She may have overplayed her hand.*

"Another man? What other man? Where did you meet such a man? At least the carpenter had the manners to speak to me first!" Papa was roused now. How would Susan finesse this one?

"A young man, a man I met at church. I will not name him unless you assure me that you will not humiliate him publicly. I will invite him to supper on Sunday if you would like to meet him."

Sybil was shocked at her brazenness. Surely she had gone too far, too fast!

Thomas was surprised as well and stared at her for a moment. Then, "I will give it some thought. I make no promises."

"Thank you, Papa!" Susan and Mary spoke in unison and swept out of the room before he could change his mind.

Sybil was left behind. It was her turn, now. "Papa, I know this is hard for you, but Susan and Mary deserve a chance to have their own family, do they not?"

Thomas nodded. "Aye, I have dreaded this day, hoping that somehow we could come up with the means for dowries for them. I wished to spare them the shame of having our family's poverty exposed to the whole world. But time has caught up with me — soon they will be too old to wed. They are right — it is time for them to find suitors if they can."

"Oh, Papa! You have worked so hard to raise us all, there is no shame in that!"

"And you have worked at least as hard. I suppose they are our legacy. One day, it will be just you and I, if your sisters have their way. An old man, and his spinster daughter."

Sybil felt herself wince, a little. Probably not visible in the light of just one candle. The spinster daughter, that was her destiny. "Good night, Papa," she said and went back downstairs.

Susan and Mary were waiting for her, in a triumphant mood. "This is better than we could have hoped!" they exulted in whispers.

Sybil nodded. Yes, they had played it very well. She could well imagine that both of them would be wedded ere long.

"Now, it's your turn," said Susan.

"What?"

"Silly, don't you see? Papa forbade John Porter from courting Susan. He said nothing about courting <u>you</u>. The way is open, you should speak with him before he leaves tomorrow."

Sybil shook her head. "And what would I say? That it has all been a mistake, that he can woo me if he likes, but for just one night?"

"Why say any of that? Let him think he is going behind Papa's back if he likes. Let him think you are going behind Papa's back, as well. Makes it more exciting."

"No, that would be self-indulgent and cruel. Whatever the man's deficiencies, he deserves better than to be led on."

"Deficiencies? What deficiencies, exactly? Is he ugly? Brutish? Cowardly or cruel; selfish, perhaps, or just weak and corrupt?" asked Susan.

"You know that he is none of those things, which is why it would be cruel to encourage him to hope for things that can never be. He deserves better than that."

"Better than you, do you mean?"

"No, not better than me, just different. I really can't explain it to you."

"You don't need to explain it to me or yourself, just to him."

"He is leaving in the morning, and I do not expect to see him again. I cannot marry him, or anyone else."

"So why not let the man try his hand at wooing you? A story to tell yourself about what could have been, in your spinsterhood? A little excitement would do you good," said Susan. "You do not have to make any promises, just talk."

Sybil was in turmoil. What sort of man woos a woman by praising her character, but says nothing about her appearance? Was it because he did not find her attractive? Or says nothing about his feelings? Did he have no feelings in the matter at all? Perhaps it was just a financial arrangement to him — a merger of fortunes (what fortunes?), to the building of a family business devoted to prosperity and the production of offspring? Bad enough that he blurted out some half-baked proposal to her father, but then he sounded apologetic about it!

She was not sleepy, and would not be, she realized, as long as she was tormented by such questions. "I suppose he owes me an explanation," she ventured, "for his strange behavior."

"He might say the same about you," Mary retorted. "The two of you should talk."

August nights could be cool in Little Baddow. Sybil wrapped a shawl around her shoulders and walked out to the barn with just a candle for light. The place was full of the aromas of hay, and animals, punctuated with the inevitable odor of manure. She found him asleep in the back of his cart. It took a good hard poke to waken him — how anyone could sleep soundly amid all the drama was a mystery. Perhaps the man simply had no emotions at all.

John woke and needed a moment to recall where he was, and determine why a woman with a candle was standing over him. He recognized Sybil, at last, and sat up. He was sleeping in his shirt and breeches — no shoes or stockings. He put on his doublet, to ward off the chill, then put on stockings and shoes. Finally, he spoke: "Can I be of service to you?"

"We have business to finish," said Sybil.

John was puzzled. "What sort of business?"

"Explanations are in order. Such as why you chose to speak to my father — in a barn, of all places."

John cleared his throat. "Well, as I said, I admire your character . . ."

"Yes, I remember — hard-working, brave, kind, loyal to the family — these are the qualities a man seeks in a dog, but no man marries his dog. What makes you <u>want</u> to marry <u>me</u>? And I will not believe you if you tell me it was an impulse — I know that you are not an impulsive man."

Well, John thought, *I have one more chance to say the right thing, but I have no idea what she wants to hear.*

"You say I should have spoken to you first," he said. "Very well, but if I am to open my heart and mind to you, I think our conversation might be long. Do you really want to hear all that I would say on the matter?"

"We have until daybreak if need be." Sybil looked for a place to sit. Found a milking stool.

"But, in fairness, you must agree that you will be as open and honest with me as I am with you, otherwise it is a waste of a good night's sleep." He smiled.

Sybil did not smile back. "I agree on the condition that you do not ridicule me, or laugh at what I have to say."

"Agreed." He sat down on the edge of the cart. He took a breath. "If I had spoken to you first, I would have said that I have admired you since the day we first met. I might have approached your father back then, but our financial entanglements seemed to block that path — more for you, than for me, I think."

Sybil had to agree. The debt had hung over every conversation that she had had with John, for years. She nodded.

"And then, when I had to leave so suddenly, it seemed inconsiderate to speak to you or your father about a future, when I had none to offer. I apologize to you if I offended you at our parting; the hug was impulsive, I suppose, but I wanted something to remember you by."

Sybil colored a little at the memory. She hoped he couldn't see in the dim light. Susan was right — this wasn't all that unpleasant. "And did you remember me? Through all those years in the shipyards, and away at sea?" She was fishing for something, she realized, but this was going in an interesting direction.

"Especially at sea," he said. "Though, to tell the truth, men at sea think about women often." He chuckled. Then he was serious: "I prayed for your safety, and the safety of your family, and this whole village. I prayed I had not put you in peril. I prayed for you more than the others, perhaps that was a sin. But I wanted to see you again, more than anyone else in this village."

A sin? To favor one person above the others in your prayers? If so, it was a sin she herself was guilty of — never mind, get on with it.

John continued. "I am not very good at this sort of thing, but when I first saw you in your garden today, it felt as though my heart was dancing, for just a few moments. And it seemed that when we laughed, our hearts were dancing together, just for a brief while. Perhaps I was presuming, but that moment felt like the end of a pilgrimage, to me. And that moment, more than any other, compelled me to speak to your father."

Something inside her felt released, or relaxed. Yes, Susan was right. Sybil wanted to hear more.

The candle was nearly burnt out. John had no idea whether his words were making any difference with Sybil, but she hadn't protested, yet. Might as well finish the course. "I knew that I could not stay long; I took the best opportunity that I could see. I am sorry to discover that he is so opposed to me."

"Did he give you no reason?"

"Aye, he said that I should seek a wife with a large dowry, that it would lead to my success and prosperity. I suppose I shall have to do something of the sort, but I would rather marry for the joy of it, than the prosperity."

Oh. Sybil was moved again. "Why can you not have both?"

"God willing, I shall. Although after today's events, I was half-persuaded that it was God himself who had directed me here, and for the purpose of finding a wife. It is easy to misread His intentions, I suppose."

Or maybe not, Sybil thought. *Or maybe not.* "John," she said, "come hither. Sit nearer to me, so that we can speak more freely." He approached her and sat on the floor just a few feet away. "I will explain something to you, but you must not tell anyone else about it. Agreed?"

John nodded. Sybil began, "You should know that Papa misunderstood your intentions when you spoke to him. He thought that you wanted to court my sister, Susan. You should also know that Susan has a beau, though Papa only found out about it this evening. Strictly speaking, he has forbidden you to court my sister, but that does not apply to me. I am telling you this because we agreed to be honest with each other. I would not want you to imagine that I am here in defiance of my father, or because I want you to shower me with flattery in vain, just for my pleasure, without hope of anything more."

"Please, tell me why you are here, then." He leaned closer.

Sybil blew out the candle. "Until you appeared today, I had no particular hope of seeing you again, and no hope of being courted by anyone. I was resigned to spinsterhood, and it pleased me to think I was taking care of my family, even at the cost of my own future. I see now how that pleasure was self-serving, a form of pride, the greatest of all the deadly sins, so they say."

"Ah." John's voice came out of the darkness. "We shoulder the great burdens and flatter ourselves that we are martyrs, holier than the rest, even as we wallow in pride or self-pity. I know that condition. Or we shun recognition for our labors and fancy that we are humble, and therefore virtuous when our hearts tell us we are unworthy sinners; we hope to save our pride by concealing it from everyone else with false modesty. It is all the same."

Sybil was startled at his remark. There was something more to this man, some depth of self-reflection, after all. She continued, "I confess that I do not know how to live any other way than the way I am living. But I know that my circumstances certainly must change, if only because both my sisters intend to marry, with or without a dowry, and my service to them will no longer be needed. My life will change, whether I like it or not. I want to embrace something new. I need a friend to help me with the change that I know is coming."

"Go on." He was closer, now.

"I felt what you felt, this afternoon — dancing in my heart. I am willing to believe that God is behind your appearance and willing to see where it might lead."

"So, is this a courtship?"

"Yes, I suppose it is. But don't tell Papa. Not yet."

John chuckled. "I almost feel sorry for your father. But I agree that we should keep this between us. I have much yet to do before I can be wed."

"Much to do?" It sounded as if he was getting ahead of himself.

"Much. I will need to establish my business and find a place to live. Somehow, I need to ingratiate myself with your father. That will take some time."

"Yes, especially the last part."

"I will have to find reasons to visit you. Something business-related, I suppose. Wait, I have it!" She could hear the excitement in his voice. "How would you like to plant some of my *patatas*?

"What? Those apple-root things?"

"Yes. I'm curious about whether they will grow in England, and I need a bit of land, to find out. If they grow here, they could be a valuable crop. Can you find some room in your vegetable garden?"

"I'm sure I can."

"That's it then. I will have to come by every month or so, to see how the *patatas* are coming along."

Sybil chuckled. "Of course you will."

"And I will have to stay overnight in your barn."

"Yes, in the barn."

Their mood was lighter, now, and they spoke long into the night — stories from childhood, from John's adventures at sea, stories of crop failures and bountiful harvests. Too soon, it began to get light in the East. "Time for me to go," said Sybil. Then "hug me, John, hug me tight."

He did as requested and Sybil relaxed into his embrace, savoring the moment. Then, he kissed her — longer than was really proper, she thought, and she extricated herself from his embrace. "I must go before I am missed!" and she ran to the house.

She was only partly successful. Susan and Mary both woke when she entered their room, their eyes bugged out in mock horror. "You'd better change your clothes," whispered Mary, "or Papa will think you've been out all night!" She was right, of course. By the time she had changed, Susan and Mary were both dressed, as well, and they started their workday in the morning twilight. Thomas came into the kitchen for his breakfast, and then prepared for a day in the fields "I am thinking I was a little short with the carpenter, last night," he said to Susan. "I don't think he meant any disrespect. Perhaps you could say a word on my behalf?"

"I think Sybil should speak to him about it," Susan replied. "I think he respects her and would accept her explanation." She caught Sybil's eye and winked.

"I can take care of the milking this morning, Papa," said Sybil. "And I will convey your intentions to him."

"Thank you, daughter. Wish him good fortune on my behalf." With that, he was gone. Susan and Mary were both grinning at her. She shook her head, but couldn't help smiling herself. She walked to the barn with a couple of milk pails, and the breakfast she had promised. She found John toward the rear of the barn, looking to Gordon's feeding. "Papa wishes you good fortune and says I should apologize, if he was too short with you, last night. He thinks you have a bright future."

John chuckled, then turned to look her in the eyes. "I am sure he is right."

He was rather good-looking, in the morning light, she thought. Then she wondered about her own appearance. Too late to do anything about it, now; she reflexively tried to straighten her hair, but before she finished, he put his arms around her waist and pulled her to him. She kissed him, and then said, "You have the advantage of me, Sir, as my hands are full of your breakfast, and my milking pails. I am helpless to resist you!"

He smiled, kissed her back, then said, "God forbid I should miss my breakfast over a pretty face!" Then released her. She blushed, a little.

He was half-serious, she realized: his attention was now focused entirely on the food — or was he teasing her? She left him to eat and walked over to the milking stanchion. If he could ignore her over breakfast she could pretend that milking a cow was the most important thing in her life.

Before she had finished the first cow, he had finished eating and picked up the second pail. He found a stool and began milking the second cow. It seemed like he knew what he was doing — of course, he would, he grew up on a farm. Milking was a chore that everyone had to be minimally competent at. "I haven't done this in many years," he admitted, "but it's coming back to me." The cows, of course, expected to be milked from their right sides, so Sybil could see only his back from where she sat. They chatted to the rhythm of the "squirt-squirt-squirt" of the milk into their pails.

He wasn't that fast at it, but he was thorough. Sybil finished the third cow by the time he was finished with the second. Good to know the man could do something useful if required, she thought, even if he was a bit slow. She smiled. She knew so little about this man. No doubt there would be more surprises.

Milking the cow gave John something to preoccupy his hands while he sorted through conflicting thoughts. He really didn't want to leave Little Baddow, right now, but couldn't think of any excuse to stay that would satisfy Thomas Vessey. Best to be discreet, however torn he felt. This was not what he had imagined a courtship would be like — moments of excitement, punctuated by long periods of separation. And how long would this go on? He had heard of engagements that lasted for years — and he was not actually engaged to Sybil, yet. He remembered something. He fumbled through the pocket of his doublet and found what he was looking for.

"Sybil, I want you to have this, as a token of our bond. If you accept it, it will ease my heart while we are apart." He handed her the small silver chain with the garnet that he had taken from the Spanish treasure in Scarlatti's office.

Sybil looked at it. Deep red stone on a delicate silver chain. "It's very fine. Italian work, I think?" She gave him a questioning look.

"It came from a Spanish prize, but may well have been made in Italy," he conceded.

"I will wear it every day until you come to me again," she said solemnly. There were tears in her eyes. John didn't know what to think of the tears but decided he had probably done the right thing. It was hard to say. Then she hugged him, and he realized that she was pleased.

"I have to take the milk back to the kitchen," she said, "and it is time you hitched Gordon to the cart. Wait for me." Then she was gone. John sighed and led Gordon out of his stall. Gordon was in a good mood, prancing as John put him in harness, and impatient to get moving.

When Sybil finally came out of the house to say goodbye, her appearance was altered, a bit. Her hair was arranged differently, and she was wearing a different kirtle — her best, probably. This, apparently, was how she wanted him to remember her. He was touched and fixed the image in his memory. He would remember her just this way, on an August morning, with the rising sun behind her, sunlight streaking her hair. He smiled, and she smiled back, pulling the garnet necklace from beneath her blouse, to show him that she was wearing it. Someone in the house was watching them, he realized. Let them get an eyeful; he embraced her for a long while, then kissed her thoroughly before climbing onto the cart.

"Wait!," she said, "What about my patatos, or whatever you call them?"

Of course. He had forgotten. He climbed down and pulled the basket of *patatas* from the rear of the cart. She pulled up her apron to make a bowl, and he put three dozen or so into it. "You can cut each of these up into several pieces," he explained. Each piece with an 'eye' — see these — will grow a whole plant. Be careful not to eat any of the green leaves, or other green parts, they can make you sick."

She nodded. Odd plants to put in a vegetable garden. Just as long as he kept his promise to check on them every month or so.

Then, it was time for him to leave. An awkward embrace, with the *patatas* between them, but they managed another kiss, and — too soon, she thought — he was back on the seat of the cart. Gordon snorted as if impatient to be going, and soon he was, with John and the cart following him. Sybil watched and waved until they were out of sight beyond a bend in the road. Then she turned and took the 'patatos' into the house.

Her sisters were waiting inside and could barely contain their glee. They also couldn't help but tease her: "The man is smitten, no doubt about it. A pile of dirty root vegetables — truly, the man is besotted with you!"

Sybil smirked at them and showed them the garnet pendant. That shut them up for a while.

John and Gordon moved briskly down the road to Chelmsford, the morning sun at their backs. In a little over a mile, they took a road to the north, in the direction of the Great Road. John intended to bypass Chelmsford, not only because it was out of his way, but because he didn't want to risk an awkward encounter. Clouds were rising to the west. It looked like rain.

August 1586: Felsted

John and Gordon reached the Great Road by noon, that day, just as a line of clouds began to shower them with a warm, soaking rain. It did not last long, but it was enough to slow the traffic on the road to a crawl. John pulled his hat down over his head and made the best of it. Gordon seemed less perturbed. At least the rain wasn't cold. Puddles filled. The road became miry. John looked in vain for some shelter. Soon the rain passed, and the sun came out. They turned off the road after just a mile or so, onto a lane that John thought would lead to Felsted. If the Great Road was miry, the lane was downright boggy in places. Gordon had to work to keep the cart moving. Eventually, the road followed higher ground, but mud was splattered all over Gordon, the cart, and John. He realized that they wouldn't make it to Felsted until evening. For whatever reason, the passing shower had aroused a host of songbirds along their route, who flitted and sang with renewed energy, as the afternoon wore on. It was pleasant, and they had the lane pretty much to themselves. Once, they had to wait while a flock of sheep crossed the road. John noted that the fields of grain and hay were looking like a good harvest, this year. Several times John had to ask directions at a crossroads. By late afternoon, they were heading northwestward past Leez Priory, the manor of the Rich family. John knew the way home from here, but he stopped to look at the place, in the distance. Odd how his life had intersected with this family over the years. The world was somehow smaller than he had expected, and yet vastly larger than he could imagine only years ago. It was testimony to the ingenuity of men, that they could travel thousands of miles in less than a year; testimony to the power of God that they would come at last to the place that they started: *"Whither shall I goe from thy Spirite? or whither shall I flee from thy presence? If I ascende into heauen, thou art there: if I lye downe in hell, thou art there.Let mee take the winges of the morning, and dwell in the vttermost parts of the sea:Yet thither shall thine hand leade me, and thy right hand holde me."* It was comforting and terrifying at the same time, thought John. Still, he had seen the uttermost parts of the sea, and God had certainly held him by his hand . . . and led him home.

Gordon shook his mane. Time to move on. Shadows were growing longer.

They pulled up to the house just as the sun was setting. A familiar cottage, with a thatched roof, a barn, and some other outbuildings in the back. The fading glow of the sun illuminated the Western exposure of everything he saw — including the figure of a woman who was walking toward the house. At first, he thought it was his mother, but no, she was too young. Perhaps she was a servant — then a chilling thought struck him, that maybe his family no longer lived here. Who knew what might have happened to them in six years?

He got the attention of the strange woman with a wave, and a shout, "Can you tell me if the Porters still live here?"

"And who might be asking such a question?" There was something familiar in the cadence of her voice that John could not quite identify.

"John. John Porter. I was born in this place."

The woman gasped. "Is it really you, John?" She leaned toward him, peering intently, then broke into a run. "It *is* you, gone these many years!" Then, "Don't just stand there, hug me! Hug me tight!"

She was in his arms before he could collect his thoughts and squeezed him hard. Then she backed away half a step, and shouted, "Mama! Come see who it is!"

John was still bewildered. "I am sorry, but I cannot recall your name . . ." he thought she must be some cousin or other relative.

"What! You've forgotten your only sister?"

"Ellen?" He remembered Ellen, a child of thirteen, sharp-tongued and bossy, not this woman . . . but of course. Ellen would be twenty by now.

"Ah! You've got some of your wits back, then." She was smirking at him, as she used to do. It was Ellen, no doubt.

A woman appeared at the door — his mother, recognizable enough. John strode to the door and embraced her. She said nothing at first but held him a long time. Then, standing back, she wiped tears from her face, and said, "Welcome home, son. Are you hungry?"

John chuckled. "Always." Then, "Let me take care of my horse, and I'll come straight in."

Ellen stuck with him as he led Gordon and the cart toward the barn. "What airs are you putting on, now?" she asked, as she looked at the fragment of caparison that covered Gordon's face. "Let me guess: you are traveling in disguise, and the horse's identity must be concealed, as well. Did you steal the animal?"

"You can take the mask off if you dare," said John, knowing that she could not pass up a challenge.

"This can't be difficult," she said, then "Oh," as she saw Gordon's natural demeanor revealed. "Still, he's more comfortable without it, don't you think?"

John nodded. "Probably so. His name, by the way, is Gordon." By now, they were in the barn, and John unhitched Gordon and led him to a stall. John found him some feed, then headed back to the house.

"Papa will be home soon," predicted Ellen. "If we see him first, don't say anything about that horse. I want to be there when Papa meets Gordon face to face."

John shook his head. Always looking for a little fun — that was Ellen.

Inside the house, his mother was bustling about the kitchen area. The aromas were all familiar, and John felt a pang of nostalgia. It had been far too long since he had tasted his mother's cooking.

Shortly, as predicted, John's father appeared — Thomas Porter, or Tom as he preferred to be called. He was leaner, more weary-looking than John had remembered him, a little bent with the years, perhaps. He brightened with surprise and pleasure when he saw John — no difficulty in recognizing his son, even after all these years. He greeted him warmly, and hugged him, "Welcome home, son" he murmured. Then, "Let me look at you." There was a hint of a tear in the corner of his eye as he took two steps back. Evidently, he was satisfied with what he saw, because he laughed, and said, "Well, sit ye down, and account for yourself!"

That was no small task. He began by relating the places he had been living the past six or seven years and the work that he had done there. He mentioned the voyage on the *Egyptian Queen* without detailing much about his experiences. Still, his family regarded that part of the story in the most glamorous light: "A thousand miles at sea! Can you imagine such a thing, Ann?" remarked his father.

"I can only imagine the perils of such a thing." his mother replied, "John, promise me that you will never go to sea again!" Ellen said nothing but looked at him intently — probably with some sibling jealousy, John thought.

"Mama, I will never go to sea again, if it can be helped," he said.

"Ann, he has survived. That is enough," said Tom. "And, by the look of your clothes, you haven't starved, either."

John was aware that his father was referring to his new shirt. He nodded. "Aye, I have prospered these years — more than I expected to. I am now in a position to establish myself in a business of my own and take on some apprentices."

"Is that so?" Tom raised his eyebrows.

"Papa," Ellen interjected. "John has his own cart and a horse. They're in the barn."

Tom nodded with approval. "A man of substance, then. I should like to see this horse."

Ellen was grinning, anticipating some fun. John stood. "I think you should take a look at him. You're a good judge of horseflesh, as I recall."

They all walked out to the barn. Gordon looked up, his ears forward, when John called his name.

"Oh, my!" said Ann. Ellen giggled. "Ah," said Tom.

You should see him in the light," offered John, as he put a lead on Gordon, and led him outside into the twilight. Tom looked the horse over, felt his legs, and inspected his teeth. "Paid a fair price for him, did ye?"

"I believe I did. He's strong, with a good temperament. Takes to the harness. About eight years old, is my guess."

"I'd say your guess is about right. Strong, you say?"

John nodded.

"I suppose you haggled for a proper price, given his . . . appearance?"

John laughed. "Gordon is a sensitive beast. Best to speak kindly about his appearance or avoid mentioning it at all. But the cart, the horse, and the harness cost me a pound. I think I got a good deal."

"Cart? This cart? What do ye call this?"

"I suppose it's a traveling workshop until I can find a more permanent location. Big enough for me, my tools, and my things."

Ellen was already inspecting the contents of the cart. "How do I look?" she exclaimed. She had the morion on her head and brandished the cutlass.

"John, you didn't tell us you had been soldiering!" His mother's voice was a little reproachful, with a strong undertone of anxiety.

"Not soldiering, mama, just sailing. Those are just plunder."

"Plundering!" exclaimed Ellen. "That's the carpenter's life!" She waved the cutlass in what she supposed was a threatening manner, mockingly.

John's mother was not amused. Tom put his hand on her shoulder. "There's naught more to worry about, Ann. John is home now. Still, I should like to hear more about where this plunder is from."

John sighed. "That is a long story, but to be brief, I sailed on a privateer. We captured some Spanish ships, and those are part of my share of the plunder. We are at war with Spain, you know."

"Part of your share? Was there money, as well?" Tom was eying him keenly.

"Aye," replied John. "Most of our plunder was in the form of cannons that we took from the prizes we captured. We sold them right off the dock in Harwich — it came to a little more than nine pounds, for me. These other items were the personal property of a Spanish captain."

"Nine pounds, you say?" Tom seemed impressed. "Ye're a man of substance now, son!"

"I also earned about twelve pounds as my wages for the voyage. So yes, I am a man of substance, as you say. I intend to put the money to productive use, somewhere hereabouts."

"How's that?" his mother asked.

"I hope to establish my business in Felsted, or nearby."

"So, you'll be staying, then?" He could see the ache and hope in her eyes — parting had been hard on her, he realized.

"Yes, that is my plan. I also am courting a young maid in Little Baddow, and if my hopes are fulfilled, we shall make a home here and have many children."

Ann gasped. Tom chuckled, "Ye should not be surprised, my dear. I am sure that we have changed, after nearly seven years. Why should not our son make a life for himself, in all that time?" To John, he said, "You always were a quick one, I always said. A little dull on the feeling side, but quick enough to make plans and pursue them. I suppose congratulations are in order. When do we get to meet this maid and her family?"

John realized that he had gotten ahead of himself. "In good time, in good time. I must establish myself in my business before her father will consent to our marriage."

"That's sensible," said Tom with a nod. "Sounds like a very sensible fellow."

"Still, I should like to meet the sweet, young girl," insisted Ann, "if she is to be the mother of my grandchildren. Is she pretty? Can she cook? Has her mother raised her to take care of a house properly?"

"And does she have a name?" asked Ellen.

"Her name is Sybil," replied John. And then he realized that he had turned the conversation in a direction that he was not prepared for. *Sweet, young girl* — not exactly an apt description for Sybil. Sweet, when she wanted to be, but not what his mother would call young. As for how her mother had raised her — Sybil had pretty much raised herself. And yes, she could cook, and take care of a house, but . . . "I think she is very pretty," he said, and it sounded lame when he said it. They were waiting to hear more, but he thought better of it.

There was a moment of awkward silence. "Well!" said Ellen, "There's that, at least."

Tom intervened. "It's time for dinner, mother. Let's talk more while we eat." They all returned to the house.

The food was familiar and reminded him that he was home at last. It was also a bit dull — John realized he had become accustomed to a wider variety of herbs and seasonings during his years away. No matter, his mother's cooking was nourishing enough, and comforting. She bit her lip nervously, as she watched him eat. He kept his mouth full during the meal so that he could avoid a lot of questions, and collect his thoughts.

"Did you get enough to eat, son?"

"Yes," he nodded, as he pushed back from the table. The other three were looking at him. Questions could no longer be avoided.

"I believe that you have questions for me. I will try to answer them, but one at a time, please." Into the lion's den.

His mother went first. "I want to know more about this lass of yours."

That was to the point. John cleared his throat. "I met Sybil nearly six years ago — my first job in Little Baddow was on her barn. She is not what you imagine as a 'young lass', she is twenty-five years old, just a year younger than myself . . ."

"What do you mean, *her* barn? Is she a woman of property?" Tom was keen on this point.

For Ann, the point was different — "As old as that? How is it that she is not already married?"

"Perhaps she is a widow, then? A woman of experience and property could make a fine wife," Tom suggested hopefully.

Ellen looked at John with an expression of calculation — no way to guess what she was thinking.

"Please let me finish. Sybil's mother died when she was eight years old. She has learned to keep a house and raise children — she has four brothers and two sisters. I said it was *her* barn because her father has entrusted the management of the family farm to her — she hires the help and pays them off." Ann's face bore an expression of skepticism, matched only by the look on Tom's face. Ellen looked uncharacteristically serious — no smirks.

John continued. "The family is not wealthy and owns no large amount of land. Sybil's oldest brother is a vicar; the others are all tradesmen or apprentices. Sybil and her father run the farm. Sybil has never married; she has dedicated her life to the care of her father, and her siblings. So yes, she knows well how to cook, to keep a house, and to raise children."

They all just looked at him for a moment. Then Ellen spoke, "You have told us nothing about why you would court a woman such as you have described. Her dowry cannot be large."

John smiled. "No. Not large. Sybil is a strong and courageous woman. I admired her when I first met her. I think you would like her — she has a sense of humor much like yours, though she controls it better than you." Ellen smiled back and nodded.

"As for the dowry, I do not need a large dowry, for reasons that you already know. I will be happy with a woman of virtue, whom I can trust, or so I hope. *'Who shall finde a vertuous woman? For her price is farre aboue the pearles. The heart of her husband trusteth in her, and he shall haue no neede of spoyle. She will doe him good, and not euill all the dayes of her life.'* — or so it says in the Book of Proverbs," he finished, gamely.

Tom nodded. *"And she riseth, whiles it is yet night: and giueth the portion to her houshold, and the ordinarie to her maides. She considereth a field, and getteth it: and with the fruite of her handes she planteth a vineyarde. She girdeth her loynes with strength, and strengtheneth her armes."* He looked fondly at Ann, and she blushed a little.

So, at least he had won over his father. His mother seemed unconvinced but said nothing. Ellen shot him a smile and a nod. She was impressed, as well.

"You still have not told us when we can meet this — Sybil," said his mother.

"Not until after harvest, perhaps in the Spring, just before the planting. Little Baddow is a full day's journey from here, and the weather in the Winter is hard to predict." Hopefully, that would give him enough time to get Thomas Vessey comfortable with the whole idea.

That seemed to satisfy his mother. Farmers understand the imperatives of seasons and weather. He stood up from the table. "Time to get my things out of the barn, I think."

"I'll help you," offered Ellen. Tom stayed in the house with Ann, whose brow was furrowing with unasked questions, or perhaps unexpressed fears.

"You gave a good account of yourself, in there," offered Ellen. "But you left our mother with the notion that her future daughter-in-law is some sort of brawny giantess. How tall is Sybil, really?"

John realized that she was teasing him. "A few inches shorter than me. And I think mother will agree that she is pretty."

"There is more to this than you have told us — doesn't her father insist on meeting our family?"

"Ah. I will tell you something, but you must keep it in confidence. Sybil and I have pledged ourselves to a courtship, but her father doesn't know it, yet."

"How many suitors has she had?"

"None, that I know of. The Vesseys are not wealthy. Thomas assumes that his daughters will not marry, for want of a dowry. Sybil, in his mind, is destined to be a spinster, caring for him in his old age. Sybil was resigned to that fate herself, until . . .

"Until you came along and stole the treasure of his aging heart. How do you propose to break the news to him?"

John shook his head. "I don't know. Somehow, I need to ingratiate myself with him, not the sort of thing I'm good at. How would you do it?"

"Are you sure that this is what Sybil wants? Maybe one of her sisters can take her place?"

John shook his head. "No, all three of them are determined to marry, dowry or no dowry. They're working to change his mind."

"Then leave them to it. They'll do most of the work; you must be ready when the time is right."

John had never considered what the whole business of finding a spouse was like from a woman's point of view. "Do you really think that they can bring him around?"

"What? Three young women, against one old man? They'll manage it, all right. You just have to be ready. If the family is poor, the dowry might be the sticking point. You should be flexible on that point."

"I already explained that I don't need a dowry. Sybil was offended at the suggestion. Something about marriage as a partnership." He shook his head.

"Offended? Well she might be. I like Sybil, already. Why would you say such a thoughtless thing to her?"

"I guess I was trying to be flexible."

Ellen scoffed. "You should add forgiveness and tolerance to her list of virtues, after a blunder like that. She must be fond of you. I do like her, even without meeting her."

"What about you? Have you any suitors?" It seemed a silly question when he remembered her at age thirteen, but she stood before him now as a woman. It would take a while to adjust to the fact, he supposed.

"Nothing serious, but yes, some young men seem to find me quite appealing," she said with a smirk, and a little toss of her head.

"Does Father know?"

"Why should he? Like I said, nothing serious." She gave him a sober look. "You should know that our family's fortunes are at a low ebb. We are barely scraping by; I'm not sure how we'll manage the rent, this year. Perhaps your return will ease our distress. Mother, you know has said more than once over the years, that she was sure you were dead; she has mourned you. It will take her a while to adjust to having you around."

Then she turned her attention to the contents of the cart. "Tell me how you came by these things." she insisted.

Part 14: Home

September 1586: North Sea

The *Egyptian Queen* slipped her moorings as the tide turned, in the wee hours of the morning, without fanfare, and was well out to sea before most of her crew knew anything of it. Once out of sight from land, she turned north and east, toward the Low Countries. Captain Foxe summoned his officers to the chart room at three bells into the second watch. "Gentlemen," he addressed his officers," Ye well know that the weather in these waters can be unpredictable and treacherous. With Winter coming on, we'd be fools to stay at sea for long. I expect we will back in port by Saint Andrew's Day. We are not bound on any long voyage, and we will be sailing alone. I intend to take what prizes we can for the next ten weeks or so, and spend our winter in a snug berth, with our families."

There were nods, and murmurs of agreement. "Where do we hunt, Captain?" asked VanDoorn.

"From the Rhine estuary, down to Dunkirk. We're looking for Spanish or French vessels; any Turks or Dunkirkers are also fair game; any vessel that might be supplying the Spanish Armies in the Netherlands is our particular prey. We'll avoid fighting with the Sea Beggars unless they force the issue. We'll be sailing under whatever flag suits the moment. I don't expect we'll find any treasure ships, but any prize with a full hold of cargo will pay our investors, with enough left over to keep the rest of us fed and cozy for the Winter."

He continued, "I expect many vessels, especially small ones, will seek to escape us in the shallow waters near the shore. We will have to use our best seamanship to avoid running aground. As captain, I will decide when a particular pursuit is too risky, and I'll brook no insubordination. Remember that we have no friends on these shores — we are on our own. We may well have to let some fat prizes slip through our fingers; that's the luck of our trade." The officers nodded.

"One thing I have learned from our voyage of last year," he added, "Our gunnery is a match for anything afloat. We have more guns, larger guns, and better gunners than any vessel I expect to meet. We have more range than most, as well. In a fight, I will avoid grappling and boarding —

we can stand off and pummel any who will stand against us into surrender." Several officers voiced their approval, the rest nodded. "That is all, gentlemen. Good hunting!"

As the officers dispersed, Foxe called two of them aside. "Mr. Benby, Omar, a few words. Roger, you too."

"Roger, here," he put a hand on Roger's shoulder, "is now a seasoned man of the sea. He needs to be schooled in the arts of war. Mr. Benby, you will include Roger when you drill your gunners until he is fit for service." Dick Benby nodded and smiled. Roger smiled also. "When that training is complete, he must learn to handle smaller arms, including the cutlass." Benby nodded again.

Turning to Omar, Foxe said," He also needs to learn navigation. I can think of no better teacher than you. Roger will be at your side through every watch you stand on this voyage, and you will explain what you do, and why."

Omar nodded and turned to Roger. "How is your Arithmetic?"

Roger's smile vanished. "Never had much use for Arithmetic, sir."

Omar smiled. "Then I guess it is time you learned how to use it."

"Aye," said Foxe. "Time for the pup to learn some new tricks."

September 1586: Felsted

It took a while for John Porter to get his footing in Felsted, after so many years away. This became apparent on the first full day after his return, which was a Saturday. He woke in a familiar bed and was surprised at first to recall where he was. He had breakfast, then went to the barn to tend to Gordon. Tom Porter was already up, seeing after the other livestock. In the daylight, John could see that the farm was, indeed, struggling. The pigsty, which once held a dozen animals, now had just one pig. There was a milk cow, but only one. She was due to calf in the spring, and if it was a heifer, she would probably replace her mother as the family's source of cheese and butter — but that would be two years away, at best. In the meantime, they had to get by with what "Mayflower" could produce. They had a plow horse, "Old Bob," who was approaching the end of his work life, as well. A ram and three ewes — another source of lambs, wool, milk, and cheese, but not nearly the number of animals that he remembered from his youth. Tom had already fed Gordon; "You're right about his nature," he said, "takes some getting used to from the front end, though."

John nodded. "That's why I usually stay behind him."

"How is he before a plow?"

"I don't really know. Perhaps we should try him?"

Tom nodded. "Next week, then. I'm headed into the village to a meeting, today. Time to apportion the commons for next year."

"I'll come with you, if I may," said John. "We'll hitch Gordon to the cart, and you can see how he handles."

Tom smiled. "I was thinking the same thing."

Gordon seemed glad to get out of his stall, and happy to be in harness, again. He was frisky, as they turned out of the farmyard, and onto the road. Tom chuckled. "A bit of fun in this one, eh?"

John nodded. "More than you would think, for a cold-blooded animal."

"He's got some hot-blooded ancestor, I think," replied Tom.

The meeting that they headed to was an annual affair. In a village like Felsted at this time, most of the farmers owned little or no land outright. Most of the land was the property of the landlord — the Baron of Leez, in this case. Land was leased from the landlord, usually for the lifetime of the leaseholder. The rent was fixed, and could only be raised when the lease was renewed — upon the leaseholder's death. Prosperous families, like John's uncle (also named John) might own some land in freehold, though not necessarily enough to become prosperous. Thus, even freeholders might lease some additional land, to supplement their own, and manage a farm large enough to turn a profit. The system provided dependable income for the landlord, and predictable expense for the farmer — economic stability for both, which led to social and political stability, as well. Unless something upset the system, like inflation, or a bad crop year.

A large part of the arable farmland surrounding the village was held in common. It was divided into parcels, so that each family could have some land to till the following year. Some parcels were more fertile than others, so the parcels were rotated from family to family each year. The size of the parcels might vary, but large families could handle more land than small ones; the whole thing was negotiated each year, so that each family got a fair portion, and no one starved. That was the theory, anyway. Each farmer would make decisions about which crops were suitable in his allotted parcels, according to the quality of the soil, what crops had been raised on the parcel previously, and so forth. Plowing and sowing could not begin until everyone knew which parcels he would till the following year. August or September, just prior to the harvest, was a good time to apportion the parcels for next year. Principles of crop rotation were widely accepted, but not necessarily followed — if a farmer calculated that he could get one more good crop of a high-priced commodity in the coming year, he might be tempted to ignore the fact that a cover crop was actually better for the long-term fertility of that parcel. Everyone watched what everyone else was planting — who knew which field would be theirs to till the following year? Knowing the history of the parcel was key to making a wise choice of what to plant when your turn came round.

The parish church was the only building large enough to enclose all the farmers. If the weather was inclement, they could all crowd in. But the weather was fine today, so they met on the village green, opposite the church. It was a social event; men were generally in a good mood, supplemented with some ale from the local pub. Indications were that the harvest would be good this year, and there was always the chance that some particularly productive parcel of land would be allotted. John and Tom greeted several people that he remembered from years ago.

"So, Tom, are ye looking for a bigger allotment, this year?"

"I suppose I am, now that our family has four members again."

"Hold on there," said a large man in a brown coat. "Ye don't get a larger allotment unless he's actually living with you, and farming the land."

"What makes you think he isn't farming with me?"

"Why should I believe he is? He's a carpenter, isn't he?"

"That I am," John interjected. "But I am also planning to farm this year. I brought a draft horse with me." He nodded in the direction of Gordon, who was tethered on the edge of the green, with all the other horses.

"What? That hideous creature?" The man in the brown coat laughed and was joined by several others. "I hardly think he's much use on a farm, with a face like that!" More laughter.

John was a little annoyed, though he knew it was mostly just jesting. Still, he would like to prove the man wrong . . .

"What would it take to change your mind, then?"

The man turned and looked at Gordon again. "I'd have to see him pull a load."

"Do you have a horse, sir?" John saw a chance to vindicate himself.

"Aye, Old Jasper, there." He pointed to a tall bay horse, big-boned.

"And does Old Jasper pull?"

"Aye, as well as any horse in the village. Better than any, I'd say."

"What would you wager on Old Jasper, against my Gordon, there, a shilling?"

"Five shillings, more like." The man laughed again and was joined by the crowd which was gathering around.

"Done." John spat in his palm and stretched it out. The man in the brown coat looked a little surprised. He really had no choice but to take the wager.

"Sledges, then?" John pressed the point.

"Sledges it is." The crowd moved to the edge of the green, and someone went to fetch a sledge.

"Son," said Tom, "It's fortunate ye have money to spare in your pocket. You should know that Old Jasper is the champion puller in this village."

John smiled. "We'll see. Pulling is the one task I put Gordon to before I bought him. I don't know if he can handle a plow, but I've seen him pull a sledge."

They set up a course in the dirt street in front of the church. The sledge was made of heavy timbers — two thick rails, topped by a deck, with sidewalls on three sides. Men began to load it with stones, and sacks of grain. "Wait," said John. "I want to know how much weight you're putting on."

The man in the brown coat laughed. "Having second thoughts, are ye?"

"No," said John, "but the horse is new. I'd like to know how much weight he's going to pull."

"The sledge itself is about three hundred pounds," said the man who apparently owned it. "We're putting on another three hundred pounds or so, so it comes to six hundred pounds, in all."

"Just for fun, add another two hundred pounds," suggested John. There were murmurs from the crowd all around him. "If that's alright with you, of course," he said to the man in the brown coat.

"It's your horse," he replied. There were more murmurs of pleasure from the crowd. This was getting interesting. The man who seemed to be in charge of the whole demonstration said. "Who wants to go first?"

"We will," said the man in the brown coat, with a hint of impatience. He was a little rattled, John thought. Good. He was sure Gordon could pull the load; his opponent wasn't quite as confident.

In the event, Old Jasper lived up to his reputation. His muscles bulged, and he breathed heavily, but he pulled the eight-hundred-pound sledge for thirty yards down the road, men cheering and urging him on, all the way. It was an impressive performance.

Now it was Gordon's turn. The sledge was facing the wrong way, of course, so the men unloaded it, and six of them turned the empty sledge around, before reloading it, while John hitched Gordon up.

At John's command, Gordon pricked up his ears and looked at him. Men started to laugh. "The horse is no fool, give him that," someone said, loudly enough to get more laughter. John turned to the crowd and addressed them. "Sirs, please quiet yourselves. Gordon is a sensitive fellow. I do not wish to see his feelings hurt." More laughter, then quiet. John walked forward, then turned to face Gordon. "Now, Gordon!" he exclaimed. Gordon put his head down and lurched forward. John stepped aside, as Gordon and the sledge passed him, picking up speed as they went. John followed, forced to trot, just to keep up. "Whoa, there, Gordon! Whoa!" Gordon stopped, just before plowing into the crowd at the other end of the course. Men were cheering now, and laughing at the same time. Gordon looked back at John as if to question why he had to stop when things were going so well.

"It's not a fair course," said the man in the brown coat. "It looks to me like it's uphill at that end. Your horse pulled the load downhill." There were groans from the crowd. No one else thought it was downhill.

"If that's true, it's no fault of mine," said John. "But that can be remedied. This time Gordon will draw the sledge back 'uphill', as you say, and your horse can have the 'downhill' pull. Let's make it more challenging. That sledge is large enough to carry a horse, wouldn't you say?"

The man in the brown coat nodded, unsure of what John's point was.

"So, let's do this. Unload the sledge, turn it around, and your horse can ride the sledge, while Gordon pulls. Assuming he makes it to the other end, your horse will pull Gordon back. What do ye say?"

"It's clear that Old Jasper is the heavier horse," observed someone in the crowd. John turned in that direction, and with mock seriousness said, "Please don't tell Gordon. You might discourage him!" Men laughed again.

"Done!" said the man in the brown coat, "and I'll raise the wager to ten shillings!"

John was tempted but decided to take the high road. "I'm sorry, but I cannot put up more than five. It is my policy never to wager more than I can afford to lose." More murmurs of approval from the crowd.

The sledge was unloaded, then turned around. Gordon was hitched up. They led Old Jasper onto the sledge and tethered him. "You may walk alongside if you wish," John said to the man in the brown coat, "But please don't get onto the sledge with him." The man smiled, despite himself.

Once again, John gave the command, "Now, Gordon!" and the sledge crept forward. It was clear that the load was giving him more trouble — no acceleration, just steady progress. Men were shouting encouragement all along the way. When John said, "Whoa, Gordon." Gordon took a deep breath and looked relieved. The crowd cheered again. John unhitched Gordon, and whispered, "Extra oats, tonight, I promise."

Now it was Old Jasper's turn. The man in the brown coat hesitated. "I guess I'm out five shillings," he said. "I'm not saying that Old Jasper can't do it, but I can't risk a horse like this, on a five-shilling wager. You've proved your point, John Porter." It was a gracious concession, and John bowed his head. Men were gathering around Gordon, now, to take a closer look. "Fine animal," they said, "except for that face. Would you be interested in renting him out?"

"I might, depends on the season," replied John. Tom whispered to him: "You should be prepared to demand stud fees, mark my word."

They returned home at the end of the day with their allotments for the next growing season — a bit larger than last year, since the family had one more mouth to feed. "Next season could be a good one," said Tom, "We got some good cropland, and a fair-sized piece of hay meadow, down by the river. With your help, we could turn a profit."

"What about the rent?"

"Aye, that's a challenge. I don't have the money for this year, yet."

"How much do we owe?"

"It's about fifteen shillings. I don't suppose you know where to find that sort of money?"

"I have a pretty good idea where I can get five shillings."

Tom chuckled. "I apologize for doubting your judgment. And your capabilities, Gordon!" he said, as Gordon cocked his ears back.

Tom reported the day's events with some relish, over dinner. "You should have seen the look on Jed Bone's face when Gordon pulled his horse all the way down the street!" he chortled. He turned to John, "Son, it's good fortune that you have returned to us. I think things will be easier, now."

"Amen," said Ann and Ellen, in unison.

The following day was a Sunday. The Porters dressed in the best that they had and waited for the bells at Holy Cross Church to summon them. John noticed that Ellen had done something with her hair, though most of it was covered by a cap. Of course: a young woman with admirers had to keep her appearance up. The church was well within walking distance, on a mild August morning, but Tom decided they would ride in John's cart, Tom and John on the seat in front, the women in the back, facing rearward. "Mind you, don't go too fast," Ann said, "This is no fancy lady's carriage."

Tom smiled and nodded, but Gordon was in a mood to prance, and Ann and Ellen got the worst of the bumpy ride. Mercifully, it was less than a mile to the church — their discomfort did not last long.

The green in front of the church was fringed with other wagons and carts of various sorts, as well as saddled horses, though most of the congregation arrived on foot. Tom let the women off in front of the church and parked the cart on the edge of the green.

John noticed people pointing at him — no, pointing at Gordon — among the steady stream that was arriving from various directions. This, he realized, was why his father had insisted on bringing the cart to church — Gordon was famous, at least for a while, and Tom wanted to make the most of it.

Several members of the Rich family, including Robert, the 3rd Baron of Leez, arrived just before service was to begin, and took their places in the front pews. They were splendidly dressed, according to their social rank. Everyone else stood and greeted them with bows and curtseys as they passed through to the front; when they sat down, it was a cue for everyone else to sit, as well. The Porters sat well back, near the rear of the church, with John on the aisle.

The service itself was entirely conventional. The vicar John remembered from his youth was gone; his replacement was younger and more energetic. He tucked a brief sermon into the liturgy, on the text from I Samuel 17, 45: "*Then sayd Dauid to the Philistim, Thou commest to me with a sword, and with a speare, and with a shield, but I come to thee in the Name of the Lord of hostes, the God of the hoste of Israel, whom thou hast rayled vpon. This day shall the Lord close thee in mine hand, and I shall smite thee, and take thine head from thee, and I wil giue the carkeises of the hoste of the Philistims this daye vnto the foules of the heauen, and to the beasts of the earth, that all the world may know that Israel hath a God."*

It was a stirring and timely message, with Spain's might arrayed like Goliath, against little England's David. The congregation was relieved to be assured that the God of Israel was on their side, and Spain would fall, just as Goliath had. An especially welcome message to the Baron and his family, no doubt. John wondered if the vicar had them particularly in mind when he planned the sermon.

At the end of the service, everyone stood and waited for the Riches to leave. The bows and curtsies were repeated, row by row, and acknowledged by nods from the Baron and his family. The Baron stopped when he reached the Porter's row as John bowed, and addressed him: "John Porter is your name, is it not?"

"Yes, my Lord."

"How long have you been in Felsted?"

"Only since Friday evening, my Lord."

"Ah. I shall expect a visit from you on tomorrow, then. We have business to speak of." With that, he turned and left the church.

A mistake to sit on the aisle, John chided himself. *Nothing for it now, but to call on the Baron tomorrow.* He sighed. He felt his mother grip his arm. She looked at him with wide-open eyes. "How are you known to the Baron?" she whispered. "Is it about the rent?"

John nodded. "Perhaps. I will find out tomorrow." Other people stood nearby, straining to eavesdrop on the conversation, as people filed out of the church. The vicar stood outside, greeting the congregation as they passed. When John and his family approached, he gripped John's hand with unaccustomed firmness: "Please linger awhile," he murmured, "there is a matter I would speak with thee about."

John's family heard the vicar, and each of them gave John a sharp, questioning look. *As if I understood any of this,* he thought.

Once out of the church, he noticed a crowd gathered around his cart — or rather, around Gordon, who was something of a celebrity, now. Tom had anticipated that much, and he engaged them with comments and observations about the true qualities of a good horse. Ann was chatting with some friends, and Ellen stood apart, watching the hubbub. Tom winked at John, and said, "A fine day when an ugly horse gets more attention from young men than a pretty girl, don't you think?" John had to chuckle.

After the last parishioners had left the church, and begun heading homeward, John strolled back to where the vicar still stood. "What can I do for you, Father?"

"First, let me say that I am pleased you have returned home, John. I believe your family is in need of your strength, just now." John nodded. Nothing to disagree about, there.

"Also, now that you are returned, I think I should get to know you better." John was unprepared for that remark. He thought to explain that he wasn't necessarily planning on staying in Felsted for very long, but thought better of it.

"There is a meeting this afternoon, at the church. Some other men and women from the village will be there, to discuss matters of mutual interest. I thought you might be interested."

The man gazed at him, meaningfully, it seemed. It was hard to refuse an invitation so specific as to time and place, yet so vague in its purpose. "What time should I come?" asked John.

"Three o'clock will be best. After your mid-day meal."

John bowed and excused himself. The crowd around Gordon was dissipating. "John Porter!" The voice came from behind him. He turned to see the man in the brown coat. "Jed Bones," the man said and extended his hand. John shook it. "I owe ye five shillings, and here it is," said Bones. "I pay my debts. That's a strong horse you have there."

John took the money and thanked him. Bones turned and walked away. John turned back to his family, gathered near the cart. "Ready to go home?" he asked.

The return trip was not far, and he sensed that the rest of them were waiting for him to offer some explanation of the morning's events. He said nothing — didn't really know what to say.

"Well, I will ask a question, if no one else will," said Ellen. "What did the vicar want?"

That was the easier question to answer. "He invited me to a meeting at the church this afternoon, didn't say what it was about."

"Are you going to go?"

"I'm not sure I really have a choice. He made it sound more like a summons, than a request."

"Nay, a summons is what you got from the Baron this morning. What was that about?" asked Tom.

"I'm not sure. But I think I should have at least fifteen shillings in my purse when next I see him."

"Agreed," said Tom. "And you will want to have your Bible with you this afternoon, I think."

"My Bible? Why my Bible?"

Tom cleared his throat. "I remarked the vicar yesterday, about how you read it so regularly, and memorize it so easily. I was boasting, I suppose, and that is a sin, I know. I also mentioned how you served the crew on that ship when they had no priest. I'm thinking the vicar has singled you out for some special task."

Well that, at least, made some sense, thought John. And it was good to have a plausible reason to satisfy his mother's worried approach to nearly everything. Still, his life was suddenly crowded with obligations and expectations. He thought he had put that behind him when he left the *Egyptian Queen.* He was most annoyed at the presumption of the Baron, to summon him in front of nearly the whole village. It was the Baron's prerogative to do so, but it rankled. The irony was that his status in the village had probably risen, in most people's eyes, precisely because the Baron had shown him such particular attention, thus reminding everyone of John's inferior rank. It was also, by analogy, a reminder of their own subordinate rank.

They arrived home, and John put Gordon back in his stall. At supper, Ellen's mood was noticeably subdued.

"Wasn't the sermon fine, today?" asked Tom.

"It was stirring, that much I would agree," replied John.

"Aye," said Ann, "The vicar has a way with words. I do not think of wars with such enthusiasm. I would rather think of peace."

"It was a story from the Bible, and a war has come. How else should he parse the text?"

"But the meaning was plain enough. He looks forward to a battle because he expects to be victorious — though other men must fight the battle." Ann shook her head and formed her mouth into a thin line — one more thing to worry about, thought John.

"What did you think of it?" John looked at Ellen.

"I can't say I recall much of it. Not his best effort, if you ask me."

"Don't mind her," said Ann. "She's not accustomed to being ignored by the young men, like that. That ugly horse has stolen their affections, or so it appears."

"It is a winnowing," said Tom. "Any lad who would prefer the company of a horse, to a pretty woman like yourself, is unworthy of your affections. It makes things simpler if you look at it that way."

Ellen gave him a cool look. "I know you are teasing me," she said, "and I refuse to laugh at your japes."

John tried to hold it in, but snickered, anyway. It occurred to him that his father must know more about Ellen's admirers than she realized.

Ellen tried to change the subject. "There is something you haven't told us. How does the Baron know your name, if you have only been in the village two days?"

"Perhaps he has heard about the pulling contest yesterday, and recognized that you were my son," suggested Tom.

"That still doesn't explain why he said you have 'business' with him," insisted Ellen. "What sort of business could it be? If it was about the rent, why didn't he speak to Papa?"

John sighed. "I spoke to the Baron just over a week ago." They were all clearly surprised at this admission. "It was in Harwich. The Baron and his uncle financed the privateer I sailed on, and quite naturally, they met her when we docked. My Captain introduced me to them — as a man from a village on their manor, that is all."

Of course, that was not nearly all — but John could not risk giving away any details that might suggest the business that they transacted that night. Barely a week ago — it seemed much longer than that.

"So, he recognized you?" Tom asked.

"Apparently, he did."

"And what business could it be?"

John shook his head, "I will find out tomorrow, I reckon. But I don't think it's about the rent. I'll take money with me, and settle the account if I can, while I'm at the manor house."

"Ah. About the money . . ."

"Don't worry about the money. You forget, I am five shillings richer today than I was just the day before. Hold on to your money, until we decide what we'll need for next year's planting."

Tom nodded. He had forgotten, for the moment, that they would soon have new land to till — new seed, or new livestock, perhaps new tools.

In the afternoon, John decided to walk back to the church; hitching Gordon up again just to have him seen, seemed excessive, perhaps prideful. Also, since he really didn't know what awaited him at the church, it seemed prudent to travel with as little notice as possible.

As he approached the west entrance, he encountered several other people who appeared to have the same destination — a man and a woman together (man and wife?), an older woman alone, three other men, who might have been farmers or laborers, and one man whose dress said he was a successful businessman — or who dressed like one, anyway. A few other people were in the sanctuary when they got inside. John moved to take a seat near the rear, where he and his family normally sat. "No, John," said the vicar from the front," sit up here with the rest of us." As he walked forward, John saw that several people were seated in the front row. "Don't worry," chuckled the priest, "If the Rich family attend this conventicle, we shall let them have their accustomed seats." Several of the others laughed; It echoed a bit, in the nearly empty nave. More people joined them until there were nearly thirty people seated near the front of the nave. Each time the door opened, light from the afternoon sun spilled in, casting long shadows down the aisle. The vicar seated himself in a chair, below the altar and the pulpit, and next to him sat a woman, whom John supposed was his wife. The vicar made a point of introducing John by name, and several people nodded to welcome him. He recognized many of them, and could have called their names if asked — Felsted was not a large village, and their appearances were not greatly altered, even after so many years.

The vicar stood and began praying — extemporaneously. This was a little shocking. Street preachers were known to do this sort of thing, of course, but John had never encountered a vicar who dared to do so in a church. But then, the Book of Common Prayer didn't have anything similar to this prayer, so the priest's options were limited . . .

When everyone said, "Amen!" John realized that this meeting had officially started. The purpose of this "conventicle" became apparent as one person, and then another addressed the whole group with a scripture reading, a testimony, or a question. John had attended "lectures" of a Sunday afternoon before, but here there was no featured speaker; everyone seemed to think their experience, or interpretation was worthy of the group's attention. There seemed to be an informal structure to nearly every contribution: even the longer testimonies were peppered with scriptural references, and concluded with some affirmation, to which the congregation responded in unison, with a chorus of "Amen!"

It was interesting, occasionally even thought-provoking. John wondered why he had been invited. And then the vicar turned to him and said, "Brother Porter, perhaps you have some experience or wisdom to share with us?" and all eyes were on him.

John hesitated. "I can testify to God's Providence," he began, as he stood up. "Not a year ago, I was kidnapped and pressed into service aboard a ship bound for the Americas." Several people murmured sympathetically. He continued, "There was danger of every sort, from diseases, from tempests, and from battle. Through it all my shipmates and I were sustained by the promise of the Holy Bible, as in Psalm 121 *'The Lord is thy keeper: the Lord is thy shadow at thy right hand. The sun shall not smite thee by day, nor the moon by night. The Lord shall preserve thee from all evil: he shall keep thy soul. The Lord shall preserve thy going out, and thy coming in from henceforth and forever.'* This was our comfort, in all our perils. I stand before you as a witness to the faithfulness of God."

That should do it, he thought. But no, the vicar had other ideas: "Speak on, Brother Porter, tell us more of the faithfulness of Our Heavenly Father."

More scripture, then. He gave them the account of the *hurricano*, with its winds, lightning, and the "devils teeth." He quoted Psalm 107 *"They that go down to the sea in ships, and occupy by the great waters, They see the works of the Lord, and his wonders in the deep. For he commandeth and raiseth the stormy wind, and it lifteth up the waves thereof. They mount up to the heaven, and descend to the deep, so that their soul melteth for trouble. They are tossed to and fro, and stagger like a drunken man, and all their cunning is gone. Then they cry unto the Lord in their trouble, and he bringeth them out of their distress. He turneth the storm to calm, so that the waves thereof are still. When they are quieted, they are glad, and he bringeth them unto the haven, where they would be. Let them therefore confess before the Lord his loving kindness, and his wonderful works before the sons of men."* He had quoted this passage often enough on the *Egyptian Queen*, and it came out of his mouth easily. It made quite an impression on the members of the conventicle; not only was there a chorus of "Amen!"s, but a few shrill "Hallelujah"s as well, from some women in the group. John sat down, before the vicar could press him for anything more.

Eventually, the conventicle was closed with a long extemporaneous prayer from the vicar. The sun was low in the West, and John headed for home, but the vicar caught him at the door. "An inspiring testimony," he said, as he shook John's hand vigorously. "I believe you have an anointing for the Word of God. You should be exercising your gift, so that it may increase."

John wasn't sure exactly what he meant. "How so, vicar?"

The vicar quoted Matthew: *"Surely the harvest is great, but the laborers are few. Wherefore pray the Lord of the harvest, that he would send forth laborers into his harvest."*

"Vicar, I am no priest."

"England has priests aplenty. What we lack is godly men, who will labor in the fields of the Lord. You could be such a man, I think."

Ah. A man with a plan, then, the vicar. First the Baron, and now the priest. "What labor do you need, vicar? I am a carpenter, nothing more." He turned to look at the ceiling of the church, with its curving trusses. Not at all dissimilar to the ribs of a ship's hull, he thought. Maybe an inspection was in order? He would need some scaffolding to be sure. On a building this old, there was probably always something to repair, but he couldn't see any major issues at this distance . . .

"You miss my meaning. It is not the building that needs your attention. It is the body of believers that worship in this place, especially those who attend infrequently, who need your help."

"What sort of help would that be?"

"They need to learn how to live a righteous life, a life that honors God. Many of my flock attend services because they must, because they will be fined if they do not attend a minimum number of times a year. Others attend because they wish to gossip, or to pursue some business or other. Too few come for the sheer joy of worship, or out of reverence for God almighty. There are precious few who can stand as examples of Christian manhood. You could be such a man."

"Surely, you are an example to them?"

"I am a priest; they expect nothing less from me. But most men in this parish see my work here as just that — work. I have my work, they have theirs. My work is to speak for God, theirs is to plow, plant, and harvest. They expect me to be concerned about the things of God, while they keep an eye on the weather. The Church will not truly be reformed until every man and woman thinks of God first, in all things. Men like you can lead the way."

This was flattery of an unfamiliar sort, thought John. The vicar appeared to be dead serious; it wasn't clear exactly what he was asking John to do.

"Vicar, I am only here for two days. I hardly think I am a leader in this place."

"But you have earned respect in this village, even in such a short time. Apparently, you are on personal terms with the Baron himself. You are a student of the Holy Scriptures, a man of upright conduct (This last point, thought John, was unlikely to carry as much weight with most of the village, as with the priest). Even your business dealings are talked about — how you could easily have goaded Jed Bones to double or triple his wager to his harm, or taunted him, but chose mercy and temperance."

Mercy and temperance? Rather the reluctance to make an enemy of someone whose assistance I may someday need, thought John to himself. *Or perhaps that is the same thing as temperance. Who can say?* "Other men would have done the same," he replied, "it is just good business to avoid making an enemy."

"To that I will add prudence and wisdom," said the vicar.

"What would you have me do, vicar?"

"I hope you will continue to meet with our little conventicle," he replied, "and I will call on you to assist me, as the need arises. Can I count on you?"

It was not a request that he could simply refuse. "I will attend next week, if I am not engaged in some pressing matter." There; that gave him an out for Sunday afternoons; as for being called to assist the priest, that would only arise if he could be found in the moment of need — he could make himself scarce, if need be. "If you call upon me, I may be able to assist you, or not. I am courting a wife, which will take me away from the village from time to time."

"And where does this fortunate lady live?" the vicars eyes twinkled with curiosity, and good will.

"In Little Baddow, a village over east of Chelmsford."

"Ah. You will be traveling, then. But will you join us next Sunday afternoon?"

"I will do my best, Father. That is all I can promise."

The vicar seemed satisfied with this. "Bless you then, brother Porter. Bless you."

John shook his hand and extricated himself. On the way home, he reflected on the experience. There were three parts to his religious experience, he thought, like the three legs of a stool. One was the liturgy, the rites and the sacraments — for Sundays, and other occasions. The second was in the community of believers that came together in the sanctuary on Sundays, but also lived together throughout the week. The third part was personal, and mostly private — his prayers, his Bible reading, his daily struggle with temptation and sin. These three things were not always in alignment — the words of the liturgy did not always reflect the life of the community, the public relations of the village did not necessarily conform to the doctrine of the liturgy, and the private experience of the members might be at odds with either their public or liturgical expressions of their faith. The people at the conventicle seemed to be trying to bring those three parts into agreement: they wanted to make their private experience public, by testimony and public prayer, and they wanted their social relations to conform to their doctrine and their private experience. When they prayed extemporaneously in public, they were, in effect, making up their own liturgy — and it didn't always agree with the Book of Common Prayer. John doubted that this could be successful — the three pieces were probably incompatible.

That was a disturbing thought, but he could see no other way to understand it. Any effort to reshape the social life of the village along more "godly" lines would upset the social balance, and lead to resistance and conflict. Any attempt to reshape the liturgy would provoke ridicule, and even outright hostility from the church hierarchy — and persecution from the government.

It was easier to let things continue as they were. Safer, too. The conventicles were playing with fire. And yet, something was happening there that he had not experienced before; something that clung to him as he walked home. A touch of fire, perhaps — a holy fire? Was such a thing possible? Could such a fire be contained, or would it consume anyone who encountered it?

When he arrived at home, dinner was nearly ready. Ellen looked at him and asked, "Tell us about your church meeting. Has the vicar made a Puritan of you yet?"

John smiled and shook his head. "Not yet, but I think he intends to do so." Yes, that was the nub of it, he realized. Everything that the vicar and his conventicle were about was to "purify" the church, to complete the reformation that had started — how long ago? Fifty years? A hundred? More than that, if Foxe's Book of Martyrs was to be believed. Strange how the past was not content to remain the past, but kept barging its way into the present. If Foxe's book proved anything, it was that reforming or purifying the Church was a dangerous occupation. Sometimes, the cause of the martyrs was triumphant — but the martyrs themselves never lived to see it. John resolved to be very careful in his religious associations.

Over dinner, he and Tom discussed the work of the coming week. "I will visit the Baron first thing, just to get that out of the way," said John. Tom agreed. "Can't plan much until we know what the Baron wants."

September 1586: Leez Manor

On Monday, John walked the two miles or so through the village of Cobler's Green, to the Baron's manor. It was an imposing edifice of brick, with a gate house flanked by crenellated towers — a nod to the fortifications of an earlier age; not much use against modern artillery, but still impressive. The house itself appeared to sit on either side of the gateway, with most of it on the west side. Large windows looked out to the west and south. There was an abundance of chimneys. The rear entries, if there were any, must be beyond the gate, somewhere. John was stopped at the gate by a doorman and stated his business. The man gave him a skeptical look and told him to wait.

It was several minutes before the doorman returned, with another man, finely dressed, who must have been the butler, or something. He was dressed like a nobleman — Black velvet doublet, a white starched ruff around his neck. His hose were green and bulged above the knee, to reveal pleats of contrasting color. A peacock, thought John, or a popinjay. The Baron was busy at the moment and could not be disturbed. Was there someone else that could help him?

"Is the steward in? I have an account to settle with him."

A raised eyebrow. "Yes, if you will follow me, I believe you may speak with him."

John followed the popinjay into the house and down a hallway. "Your name?" asked the man. "How shall I announce you?"

"John Porter, at your service."

"You may address me as Mr. Popham."

Popham. Popinjay. Of course.

"You know that the Baron does not concern himself with matters like rents, don't you?"

"I wouldn't have expected him to. I asked for him on a different matter."

"What matter would that be?"

"I am not certain. Yesterday, at church, he told me that I should call upon him today. He was quite clear about it. I am here at his invitation."

Mr. Popham's attitude shifted. "Do not leave until you have spoken to me. I will make sure the Baron knows that you have obeyed his summons. Ah, here we are!" They stopped before a door, and Popham knocked. He opened it and announced. "John Porter, here to settle an account."

John stepped into a small office, with a man seated behind a desk. A slim man, with a closely trimmed goatee, dressed in black. "How may I help you, John Porter?"

"I believe my family is in arrears on the rent?"

"You must be Tom Porter's son. I see a resemblance." The steward rose and shook his hand. "Please be seated." He walked back behind his desk and took out a ledger, which he opened. "You owe fifteen shillings, I believe."

John nodded. "Will the rent be the same for the coming year?"

"I was just calculating the assessments today. I believe your family received a larger allotment from the commons this year?" John nodded.

The steward consulted another book and made some quick calculations. "Next year's rent should come to eighteen shillings."

"I should like to pay for both years if that is satisfactory."

The steward smiled. "That will be satisfactory."

John reached into his purse and drew out the payment, which included a few gold coins with the silver. The steward looked them over, gave the gold ones a small bite, and nodded, "Most satisfactory. Is there anything else I can help you with?"

"I was told to wait until Mr. Popinjay — er, Popham came back."

The steward looked at him with merriment, suppressing a laugh. "Popinjay, you say? Best not to let him hear you call him that — he is a man easily offended." The steward chuckled, despite himself. "You should know," he added confidentially, "that you are not the first to call him by that name — but it amuses me, nonetheless."

It was not long after, that there was a knock on the door. Mr. Popham was back, "The Baron can see you, now. Please follow me."

More hallways, more turns, then the double doors to a large room. A library, perhaps. Inside, the Baron was seated, along with another, older man. "John Porter," Mr. Popham announced. The Baron did not stand, but John bowed deeply, as expected. "Please be seated." The Baron gestured to an empty chair. John sat.

"This is John Porter," Baron Rich said to his companion, "a tenant of mine, also a man of some military reputation. And this is Sir Walter Clive, veteran of Her Majesty's wars."

"Also of <u>his</u> majesty's wars," interjected the older man. That dated him, thought John. There hadn't been a '<u>his</u> majesty' on the throne for more than thirty years. But now he understood why he had been summoned. The Baron remembered the offer he had made on the beach in Harwich and was evidently determined to follow it up. John scrambled in his mind, to think of a way to refuse the offer, without making trouble for himself.

"So, tell me of your military experience," said Clive, as if interviewing him for some job or other. That was it — if Clive was convinced he was unqualified, the Baron would probably let him off the hook. John would answer with that in mind.

"Very little, of what you would call military experience," he replied. "I served on a privateer for most of the last year. We raided Spanish ports and took some prizes. I was the ship's carpenter."

"The carpenter? That's hardly a military occupation. Whence this reputation that the Baron speaks of?"

"I am not certain what the Baron may have told you. All the crew on a warship must have some training in the use of weapons; you never know when you may have to fill the shoes of a wounded comrade."

"What weapons, then?"

"Culverins, swivel guns, arquebuses, pistols, the cutlass. That sort of thing."

"The pike?"

"I drilled a little with the pikemen — which is not an easy thing, on the deck of a ship."

Clive turned to the Baron. "You see? It is as I said. These days, everyone is enamored of firearms. But the real battles are won with steel. Infantry wins the day. With the sorts of men you are recruiting, pikemen are the most you should try to make of them."

"What say you, Carpenter?" asked the Baron, "could the men of this parish be made into pikemen?"

So that was it. Clive was the military advisor, and Rich proposed to use John to turn the men of the parish into a company of pikemen. He imagined his cousins and childhood friends, his father and uncles as well, standing in formation on a battlefield, waiting to receive the charge of Spanish *tercio* pikemen. Not a pleasant picture. "I would not vouch for the success of such a company of pikemen against the Spanish army, without much training, and a large complement of modern firearms." That much was the truth; he did not say he could give the men enough training, nor any firearms.

Clive shook his head and looked at the Baron as if to say *I told you so. This carpenter is not the man you need.*

The Baron was not ready to give up, just yet: "Please explain how the firearms would be employed."

"When the column of pikemen is on the march, the arquebusiers form a "sleeve" — a file of men on either side of the column, to protect its flanks. If they are attacked by cavalry, the pikemen form a square, facing outward, to fend off the horsemen, and the arquebusiers retreat to the center of the square, to pick off the horsemen from a position of safety. If the attack is from an enemy line of pikes, then the arquebusiers move to the front to fire upon the enemy, then retreat behind the wall of pikes to reload. At push of pike, they can still fire upon the enemy, from behind their own pikemen."

"Cowards, then," muttered Clive, with a tone of disdain. "Shoot, then hide. Have you ever fought like this?"

"No," said John," This is the way it was explained to me when we drilled. The ship's captain insisted that I train mostly with the arquebus — said it was more likely to be useful on board ship."

"And was it?"

"Aye. We were boarded by a buccaneer's crew. We had thirty pikemen aboard, and thirty arquebusiers. The pikemen hemmed them in on the starboard side, and the arquebusiers shot them down. Two out of three of the buccaneers died on that spot; the rest surrendered. We lost two men."

"A right bloody victory, then," said Clive, chuckling. Then, "You don't look happy to tell the tale. Are ye squeamish?"

"I suppose I am. I have no appetite for blood and gore. I had to shoot a man, but his death does not rest easy with me."

Clive turned to the Baron. "Squeamish men make poor officers. Their squeamishness encourages the same in the men they lead."

The Baron nodded. John thought he had succeeded in disqualifying himself until the Baron spoke again: "Still, we have to start somewhere. We need to start drilling the men of the parish soon. Until a seasoned officer can be found, would it not be wise to start the training?"

John's heart sank, a little.

"A drill instructor, then? He could be useful in that capacity," said Clive, nodding in John's direction. John's heart sank some more. He waited for the Baron to close the door on his liberty.

"I will require your services, John Porter, to train the men of our parish in the ways of modern warfare. For this service, I will pay you four shillings a month. I trust that will be agreeable?" *As if I have any choice in the matter,* thought John.

"What weapons have we to train them with?"

"Pikes, of course. What would you expect?"

"We will need the services of a blacksmith, then, unless there is some arsenal in the parish that I do not know of. Also, if this unit is expected to stand their ground against Spanish infantry, they must have some arquebusiers among them."

Clive shook his head, as if exasperated.

"Agreed," said the Baron. "Forty arquebuses, with powder and shot. Anything else?" It occurred to John that he might still be able to talk his way out of this duty if his demands were deemed excessive . . .

"The arquebuses should be of a modern type, like a snaphance, so that they can be fired in wet weather, and reloaded quickly. Also, a couple of small artillery pieces — three inches, no more — would make the men bold for the battle."

Clive looked amazed at his presumption.

"Assuming such guns could be found," began the Baron, "how would you employ them on a battlefield?"

"We would build field carriages for them, so that they could be maneuvered on the battlefield, and quickly moved to a favorable position. They could also be towed by horses or donkeys when the unit was on the march. I have seen for myself how a few such guns can intimidate a foe, and fortify the resolve of the men who have them." (This was not strictly true, John was repeating something he had heard in a pub, from a reliable source; if Clive called his bluff, he would be caught in a lie — which might just be enough to get him dismissed.) "You would also need a caisson, to carry the shot and powder for the artillery."

"And where would we get such a 'caisson'?" demanded Clive.

"I am a carpenter. Building the caisson and the carriages would not be difficult — I built all the gun carriages for the ship I served on."

The Baron appeared to be amused at the exchange between Clive and John. But there was no indication that John's demands would be enough to get him off the hook. The Baron nodded "I will see about the artillery. In the meantime, when will you begin the training?"

John was resigned. "It is harvest time, My Lord, as you well know. I would recommend that the men assemble on the green in front of the church, on the first Saturday after the grain harvest is finished. Many of them are in the habit of being in the village on Saturdays, anyway. Two Saturdays a month for a few hours should be enough to begin with; waiting until after harvest will make it easier for them to attend. It will also allow more time to acquire the weapons that you have so generously promised." John was still hoping that some detail of the plan would be so daunting as to change the Baron's mind about the whole business. No such luck.

"I will issue a proclamation at the proper time. Also, I will provide two roast pigs at that first assembly — that will draw more men in and make it easier to enroll them." *The Baron is determined to make this work, then. Too bad,* John said to himself. He had to admit that the pig roast was a clever idea.

"I will begin your pay this month if you will see to the acquiring of one hundred poles suitable for pikes, and one hundred steel points to fit the poles. I will give you a letter that will promise payment for those materials, and any labor required to make them into weapons."

"Where shall the armory be — or do you propose that each man keep his pike at home?"

"Let each keep his pike with him. But we will need an armory for the firearms and ammunition — can't let them take *those* home. I will find a secure place for them. Please see the steward on your way out — he will give you the letter I spoke of."

Just like that, John was dismissed. He stood and bowed deeply to the Baron, less so to Clive, and excused himself. Popinjay was waiting for him in the hall and led him back to the Steward. The Steward had the letter ready, which meant that there had never been any chance of talking the Baron out of his plan, however persuasive John might have been, (or how dismissive Clive may have been, for that matter).

Once again, John found himself in the employ of someone with the power to compel his service — it was better than being aboard the *Egyptian Queen*, only because he was able to see his family, and was not under imminent danger from violent conflict (though how much longer that would be true was impossible to say). Oh, and one other thing — he had hope of being able to see Sybil Vessey again — the sooner the better.

That afternoon, he helped his father with the haying. Next morning, he visited the local blacksmith, to negotiate for the pike points. The Smith had plenty of scrap iron, but John insisted on steel. "A hundred steel pike points, will cost a fair bit, and take a month to forge, at least," said the Smith. John showed him the letter from the Baron's steward. The Smith smiled and said he could provide fifty, no more, in just a month. The price was steeper than John expected, but, *If all of us are to be put in harm's way, the least they can do is put a bit of steel between us and our enemies,* he told himself. Besides the Baron had not placed a limit on how much he could pay. If the

Baron (or his steward, more likely) believed he was overpaying, they could always dismiss him — the thought of that possibility lifted his spirits.

He found a woodman to supply him with one hundred pike poles, as well — "Stout, seasoned ash, sixteen feet long, nothing less." John found that the letter from the steward made every transaction go smoothly. It was a new experience to buy things with only a piece of paper. He recalled his nocturnal visit to Scarlatti. Perhaps there was something to this credit business, after all.

Most of his attention during all this negotiation was elsewhere. His thoughts were full of Sybil — recalling how she looked, wondering what she was doing at the moment — was she thinking of him? How was he going to approach her father? His thoughts went in circles and spirals, twisting and turning . . . He reminded himself that this was unproductive idleness, and then found himself returning to it. Nothing else seemed quite as important, or as satisfying.

There was another matter, that he had not raised with the Baron. The standard kit for a pikeman included armor — helmets, breastplates, and tassets (armor to cover the upper thighs) at minimum, sometimes protection for the shoulders and lower legs as well. The men of Felsted would have no such protection — it was simply too expensive. No doubt some men would show up for muster with a piece of armor here or there, but nothing like a complete kit. They would also bring long knives, and maybe even some old swords. The contrast with professional troops would be obvious — and demoralizing. Even if swords were provided, these men were farmers and tradesmen — not skilled swordsmen. They would not survive a hand-to-hand battle with professional soldiers. It would be much the same with the militias in every village in England.

John tried to imagine a tactical approach that would give the village men a better chance of survival. He couldn't think of one.

Part 15: Courting

September 1586: A Frog, he would a-wooing go . . .

It was mid-September before John knew it, and he was eager to get back to Little Baddow. It wasn't easy to get away. Gordon was much in demand, as the harvest proceeded. On days that Tom and John didn't need him, they loaned or rented him out. The revenue made a difference in their finances. John was careful not to let them overwork the horse, but Gordon seemed to thrive on nearly everything he was asked to do. John found time to plant the rest of his *patatas* in a bit of fallow land behind the house, where a manure pile had once been. He explained them to his family, who appreciated the exotic quality of the tubers but seemed unimpressed with them.

John arranged a mutual exchange with a local farmer who owned a saddle horse — two days of Gordon, to help with the haying, in exchange for two days of the saddle horse, named Baxter. Baxter was not the sort of horse that a wealthy man would ride, but John was certain that he was faster than Gordon and would get him to Little Baddow and back in plenty of time — not to mention the fact that he thought he would look like a better suitor to Thomas Vessey, on horseback. He dug up the sea boots he had captured in Santo Domingo (better fit in the stirrups), and tucked a pistol into his belt, just in case. Ellen giggled as she saw him off, and sang the verses of a popular song:

> "A Frog, he would a-wooing go,
> Heigh Ho! says Roley,
> A Frog, he would a-wooing go,
> Whether his mother would let him or no,
> Heigh Ho! says Roley, Poley, Gammon, and Spinach . . ."

It was an ancient ditty, modified a few years back to satirize a French prince's ("Frog") courtship of Queen Elizabeth ("Mouse"). The original lyrics were lost in the misty past, but the song was recycled from time to time to serve a contemporary purpose — in this case, to ridicule the queen's ministers who publicly urged her to marry a French catholic prince. Ellen had found a different use for it — to tease her brother, and maybe her mother, as well.

They made good time, as John had hoped. Once they had passed Leez Priory, and left the Baron's domain, John felt a sense of relief. The weather was pleasant, and the fields he passed were full of men and women, gathering in the Summer's bounty. It appeared that no one would be starving, this winter, at least in this part of the kingdom. That was a blessing not to be taken for granted.

By mid-afternoon, they were approaching Little Baddow. John realized that once again he had no idea what he was going to say to Thomas Vessey. Or to Sybil either, for that matter. He was assuming that she would be so glad to see him, that it wouldn't really matter what he said to her. A dawning realization told him he should know better by now than to make such an assumption. He rehearsed some of their past conversations, not just to linger on her memory, which was a habit by now, but from the point of view of the misunderstandings that he had been part of. And after six weeks or so, her feelings for him might well have changed, mightn't they?

He halted Baxter and dismounted. Needed to clear his head, catch his breath, and think of what he was going to say. He mustn't presume too much about her feelings for him; better to be polite, and figure out which way the wind was blowing, so to speak. And if he met Thomas Vessey first, he would have to explain his presence by something more than the *patatas* that Sybil had planted. In fact, he shouldn't assume that she had planted them, should he? No point in stalling; time to face the issue. Better to know than to wonder. Still, no idea how he would explain his sudden appearance to the man he wished to be his father-in-law. He mounted Baxter and urged him into a trot.

As the Vessey house appeared, John slowed Baxter to a walk and turned off the road and toward the barn. He saw no one, at first. Then Susan appeared at the doorway of the house. He started to greet her, but she ducked back inside, without saying anything. Puzzling. Had she recognized him? Then Sybil emerged from the house and approached him. She looked him up and down with a long, appraising look. "Well, John, you have returned at last. What is your business with us, today?"

The question, and the formal tone, took him by surprise. "Why, I am here to check on the *patatas,*" he replied, a little put off by her coolness.

"In that case," she said, "you had better get down from your high horse, and look at them. Careful where you step — wouldn't want those fancy boots to get soiled."

John was confused. Was she teasing him, or was she put out, for some reason? "Thank you, Sybil," he said, as he dismounted.

"You're welcome," she replied, "Best we get your horse into the barn," She led him into the barn, and stood with her arms folded, while he took Baxter's saddle and bridle off, and put him into a stall.

Then, without warning, she rushed to him and threw her arms around him. "I looked for thee every day until I feared thee would not come at all." Her voice was muffled as she buried her face in his chest, but her emotion was unmistakable. She squeezed him emphatically, as the words came out: "Every day. Every day." A strong woman, John realized; it took some effort to separate himself enough to bend to kiss her. Her eyes were a little moist with the emotion. She looked lovely — lovelier than he had remembered her. "I think of thee every day, as well," he said.

At length, she let go of him, stepped back, and straightened her sleeves and her bodice. She took a breath and wiped her eyes. "I have missed thee sorely."

"And I have thought of thee with every waking hour," he replied. She began weeping, a little, but John thought he had said the right thing, nonetheless.

"The patatos have begun to sprout," she said, "would you like to see them?"

"I would rather look at you, for the moment." She smiled and blushed.

"And I would rather look at you," she said, "despite this ridiculous costume you are wearing. Where did you ever get those boots?"

"Spoils of war," he replied. "I thought to make a favorable impression on your father," he added, lamely.

Sybil laughed out loud: "Aye, an impression! That they surely will do! A gentleman's boot on a carpenter's bony leg? Beware the sumptuary laws!" She giggled.

"These are no gentleman's boots. They are sea boots, something entirely different. I do not think the sumptuary laws are enforced at sea."

Sybil smiled and shook her head. It was hard to tease a man who treated every jest as a serious statement. "As far as making an impression on Papa, you should know that things have changed, since your last visit."

John gave her a questioning look.

Sybil continued, "The week after you left, Susan's beau came to Sunday dinner. Papa accepted him, and their courtship is more or less official, now. Mary is agitating for an invitation to one of her admirers, but I have told her she must wait awhile. We mustn't overwhelm Papa."

John digested what she had said. "So, I should probably not approach him for permission to court you? Assuming, of course, that I have your permission to court you?" A quick recovery, he told himself.

"You have my permission to ask him," replied Sybil, "but it would be wiser to wait awhile."

John nodded. "Well then, I must see those *patatas*."

She took his arm, as they walked out to the vegetable garden. Sure enough, he could see little green sprouts emerging from a patch in the corner of the garden. "So, they will grow in England. That much is clear," he said with a nod. She smiled, and leaned against him, a little. "So, now what?" she asked.

"I really hadn't planned that far ahead," he admitted. She stood up straight and looked him in the eye. "No plans? Really?" She sounded annoyed. Then he realized she was teasing him . . .

"Well, since you don't want me to talk to your father, I reckon my business here is finished. Time to go home, then, I guess."

She stiffened, furrowing her brows. Then he smiled, and she relaxed. He was teasing her, now. *At least he's not a complete dullard,* she thought to herself with some relief, *Life could be very tedious, with a humorless man.*

"Come, sit down and rest a bit before you go, I can get you something to drink."

John agreed and sat down on a low step at the front door. When she returned, she had a mug of ale and a slice of bread. "Now, you must tell me what you have been doing, since last I saw you."

He could tell from her tone that she was serious. "Not that much to tell. I was thinking of you, most of the time."

She scoffed as if she thought he was flattering her, but blushed a little, anyway. "I want to hear all of it — everything that happened, each day since you left me here."

John sipped his ale. "I will tell what I remember — please consider that I was distracted most of the time, with thoughts of you." She shook her head. The man was a shameless flatterer.

"I arrived in Felsted on Friday, had dinner with my parents, and my sister Ellen. Gordon created a bit of a stir. On Saturday, my father and I went into the village, it was time for the annual apportionment of the commons. Gordon created a stir there, as well."

"Is this your story you are telling, or Gordon's?" she asked.

"Well, Gordon can hardly speak for himself; it seems proper to speak for him — unless that annoys you."

"Go on. What happened in Felsted?"

Since I had come home, our family got a larger allotment for the coming year, so I will be helping my father to work it. Then a man said something insulting about Gordon . . ."

"Gordon, again!" She gave him a look of mock exasperation.

"Do you want to hear the story, or not?"

She bowed her head, as if in resignation. "Please, tell me about the man who insulted Gordon."

"Well, I had to stick up for Gordon, naturally, and I challenged the man to a pulling contest — not man to man, mind you, but his horse against Gordon."

"A pulling contest."

"Aye, turns out his horse is the strongest in the parish — or used to be."

"Gordon won the contest, then?"

"Aye. And I won five shillings on the bet."

"Five shillings? That's a week's wages for a carpenter!"

"Aye, so it is. I've been considering whether I should change my profession. A man could do very well for himself, wagering on horses. A gentleman's occupation."

Sybil had to laugh. The man had a sense of humor, after all. She was enjoying the teasing, she had to admit.

"And Sunday? What happened on Sunday?"

"Ah. On Sunday, we all went to church. Had Gordon hitched up to the cart, so everyone could see him after the service. He's a celebrated horse now, is Gordon. He got so much attention from the young men, that my sister, Ellen was put out about it."

"Put out?"

"Aye, she felt that Gordon had stolen the affections of all her admirers."

Sybil chuckled. "And did they?"

"It appeared so. Also, I was accosted by the Baron in front of the whole congregation."

"The Baron." She was suddenly very serious.

"Baron Rich, of Leez. His family attends the same parish church as mine. He recognized me from Harwich, and he summoned me to his manor house for the following day."

"And?"

"He has employed me as a drillmaster for the parish men. After harvest, I am to begin training them as pikemen. He will pay me four shillings per month until an officer can be found to command them. He has also given me letters of credit, to purchase weapons for them."

"So, you are now in the service of the Baron? That's a far cry from being a village carpenter and sometime farmer. Are you moving up in the world, or down?"

A fair question. One that had been on his mind, as well. "I am employed by the Baron, but it is only temporary. I farm to support my family. I still intend to have my own carpentry business. It is all more complicated than I hoped it would be. I thought to regain some of my liberty, once I was off the ship, and out from under the command of its captain, but it is not so — the Baron, my family, even the land itself has staked a claim upon my freedom. I do not think that any 'rise' in my station will make me any more free. Indeed, I do not think that the noblest among us are any less constrained by duty and necessity than the rest of us, but it is a discovery that I was not expecting."

Sybil was taken aback by his musing. "Don't forget about me. If you truly wish to marry me, you must be prepared to lose even more of this 'liberty' of which you speak. It is a fine thing for a man to yearn for 'liberty', but a woman cannot hope to claim it for herself. A woman's life is all obligation and necessity — she serves her parents until she is old enough to serve a husband, and children — what are children, after all, but needs which duty must answer to, until they are old enough to shoulder the duties that life requires? I doubt much whether any man or woman has true liberty — unless it be the liberty to choose between God and the devil!"

John looked at her gently. "Do not mistake me. I surrender my liberty to you out of love, not compulsion. The one surrender is sweet, the others are tiresome, or even bitter. As for the choice between God and the devil," he smiled, "I count you among the angels."

Sybil was not entirely satisfied with this answer. "Angel or no, I will not be your wife, unless you are sure that you can be a father to our children, and a husband to me, without mourning the loss of your liberty!"

"Then love must be enough for both of us," said John. "I do not wish to let you go, whatever the cost to my liberty. And if there be children, then I must embrace them, even as I embrace you."

There was a moment of silence. The conversation had veered in a direction that neither of them anticipated. A voice came from behind them: "If the two of you are quite finished with your billing and cooing, I must know if we are expecting an extra guest for dinner. And if we are, I should like some help." It was Susan, standing just inside the front door. How long had she been standing there?

John looked sheepish. Sybil stood, smoothed her kirtle, and went inside.

"How long were you eavesdropping on us?" she hissed at Susan.

"It's not eavesdropping when you conduct your business in public," replied Susan, in a low voice. "And you can thank me for interrupting you when I did."

"Thank you for what?"

Susan was whispering, but her tone was emphatic. "Thank me for preventing you from saying something foolish to a man who clearly loves you. You should never tell a man you won't marry him 'unless' he can make a promise that no man can keep . . . Unless, of course, you don't want to marry him at all. A woman like yourself is in no position to issue ultimatums, especially ultimatums about how someone must feel tomorrow, or years from now."

"A woman in my position?" Sybil's voice rose to just above a whisper.

"Aye. And my position, as well. Neither of us is a noblewoman, whose pedigree draws a swarm of suitors, nor an heiress, whose fortune beckons her admirers. Our future, as you said just moments ago, is 'all obligation and necessity'. Whether men can have true 'liberty' or merely imagine that they can, is a moot question for the likes of us. We do have freedom to choose who we love, and if we are lucky, who we marry. If that is the only 'liberty' that we can hope to have, it is still more than most will ever know. Overweening demands will not be met, but they can cost you your best chance at happiness. By the way, is he staying for dinner?"

Sybil nodded and began to busy herself in preparing the meal. Susan's remarks were sensible, yet something was unresolved in her mind. She had framed the question to John as a question of whether he might become dissatisfied with the duties of husband and father. More truthfully, the point was whether she would become dissatisfied with him — should his longing for 'liberty' come into conflict with her needs or desires. Only if the latter were true, would his own hunger for 'liberty' be her problem. And she could not be sure how she would feel about him at any point in the future, any more than he could be sure of his feelings for her.

"So, you would have me trust his professions of fidelity, and forbear the questions?"

"Not entirely," said Susan. "But you have known the man for some years, now. Is he the sort to make rash promises? Is he a fickle man, or a flatterer? Does he regard you as a bit of property to acquire, like some prized cow?

Sybil shook her head. "No, he is none of those things."

"Count yourself fortunate, Sister. I wish my William had thought to say that 'love must be enough for both of us.' Your man has a way with words."

They heard loud voices coming from the front of the house. "Samuel is here," said Susan. "Also Papa, by the sound of it."

Sybil recalled that she and John had not had time to prepare an explanation for his unexpected arrival. Too late now. She hoped John wouldn't say something completely preposterous.

The three men came into the house, Samuel had his hand on John's shoulder — delighted to see him, or so it appeared. Thomas was smiling, too, then caught Sybil's eye with a long, penetrating stare. Things were spinning out of control. What was Papa thinking?

Susan had had the meal ready before she interrupted Sybil and John. Time to seat everyone and get started. Thomas sat at the head, Samuel at the opposite end. Susan and Mary sat across from Sybil and John. Samuel blessed the meal, and the serving began. John shared some stories from Felsted — especially the account of Gordon's triumph in the pulling contest. Everybody laughed at that story. He said a little about his family, as well. The business with the Baron he avoided. Samuel had news of the village, and even of the wider world: Mary, Queen of Scots had been indicted for treason, the war in the Low Countries was dragging on, a Spanish invasion appeared to be inevitable, the government was now arresting not only Catholics, but reform-minded protestants, as well: no one could be sure where it would all end.

Thomas Vessey was silent during most of the meal, and then addressed John directly: "So, John Porter, are you satisfied with the condition of our 'potatos', or should I call them patatas ? I'm never sure what to call them."

"As long as they're growing on your land, you can call them what you like," replied John lightly. Samuel, Susan, and Mary smirked, Sybil nudged him with her elbow — not a time for frivolous banter, then. John continued, "I am well satisfied with what I see here. I planted others near my father's house, in different soil. In a few months, it will be interesting to see how they compare with the plants here."

"I still do not understand why you are so interested in these plants," said Thomas, "perhaps you can explain why you have traveled all this way to look at them."

John nodded. "I think there might be some money in them. They appear to have some medicinal value — the Spanish feed them to their slaves and sailors, to prevent scurvy. They are also used as animal feed. If they can be grown in England, we might be able to sell them to the navy, or merchants, or other farmers, for that matter."

"Sybil tells me the leaves of these 'potatos' are poisonous. Why would anyone grow them instead of beets or turnips — whose greens can be fed to our animals?"

"I have heard," said John, "that in France, a family can live for a year on just one acre of the *patatas*. I cannot say that will be the case in England, but I am curious to find out. Turnips and beets are not nearly so prolific as that, so far as I know."

Thomas conceded the point, with a nod. "But you don't know for certain that the 'potatos' are that productive, either."

"No, I do not," John admitted.

"And there's no way to know, until next summer, is there?"

"No, I think not."

"So, please explain to me, why you are visiting the 'potatos' now. It seems to me that you must have some other reason for being here, unless you intend to stay with us through the winter, to watch them grow."

Susan and Mary opened their eyes wide, staring at John, with their lips pursed, as if to suppress some outburst. John could feel Sybil tensing next to him. Samuel for some reason, was grinning. He winked at John.

John cleared his throat. "It is true that I have other reasons," he began. "I have known your family for a number of years. All of you have a place in my affections." Sybil looked at him sharply — *where was he going with this?* Samuel smiled more broadly and folded his arms across his chest.

John continued, "I suppose you could say I am a victim . . ." Samuel raised both eyebrows and looked ready to laugh; Susan and Mary opened their eyes wider, if that were possible. "My heart has been stolen by your daughter, Sybil, and I am helplessly drawn to this place, without hope of getting it back."

Samuel lowered his head and covered his mouth with his hand. Susan and Mary were struggling to hold their breath. Sybil refused to look at him. Only Thomas would meet his gaze. He nodded soberly, as if John had said something deep and profound. "I suspected as much. I suppose we'll have to get used to having you around."

Sybil sat upright and stared at her father. "Thank you, Papa," she blurted out. Susan and Mary were giggling silently, and Samuel stood, and held out his hand to John. "We hold you in our affections, as well," he said with a chuckle.

John felt a little light-headed, but he stood and shook Samuel's hand. Sybil was wiping some tears away.

And that was it. Thomas never said more about it than that, but everyone understood that John had received his permission to court Sybil.

After dinner, Thomas and Samuel invited John outside. Evidently there was more to say — men's business. They walked to the barn, out of earshot of the house.

"Let me say first," Samuel began, "that I approve of your suit to marry my sister, with but one caveat."

"What is that?" John was puzzled, wary.

"Why, only that if my sister is to be married, I must preach the sermon at the wedding," he replied with a chuckle.

John was relieved. Thomas spoke next: "The decision is up to Sybil, as you will understand, given our financial circumstance — and Sybil's mind would not have it any other way. But I will be well pleased if she accepts you. It will ease my heart to have her married to the likes of you."

This was quite a mouthful, thought John, especially considering what Thomas Vessey had said to him less than two months before. But a welcome change in tone. "Thank you, I shall do my best to win her," he said, with a slight bow.

"I shall speak to her, in your favor," said Samuel, "though I doubt she will need much persuading."

"Where will ye live, if ye are married?" asked Thomas.

"I do not know. She hasn't actually agreed that we will be married."

Thomas nodded. "Quite so, getting ahead of ourselves." He was still barely getting used to the idea that Sybil might be leaving his household for a life of her own.

Inside the house, a different conversation was underway. Susan and Mary were jubilant — once Sybil was married, their path to matrimony would be wide open, of that they were certain. "It's not as though he has actually proposed marriage, and I certainly have not decided whether I will accept him, even if he does," Sybil reminded them.

"You can be certain that he will propose, unless you do something completely foolish. Only look at the man, and you can see he is yours for the plucking. As for your decision, that is yours and yours alone. Papa has removed any barriers, for all of us. That is what counts," said Susan.

Mary nodded. "All of us are free, now. Please don't do anything to set us back!"

Set them back? Sybil was a little annoyed with them, for viewing the situation simply from the view of their own marital prospects. Things were moving much faster than she had expected. She had assumed that it would take months, or even years for John to bring Papa around to accepting him as a suitor. Instead, he somehow managed to ingratiate himself on the first visit. How he did so was a mystery: John was hardly an eloquent man. The bit about having his heart "stolen" was touching enough, but it was hard to believe that her father's mind could be changed with a single phrase like that. Men were hard to understand. She heard faint laughter from outside — evidently, they were enjoying each other's company.

Mary was looking at her, as if waiting for a response. "I will do my best to avoid harming your prospects," she said. "But I have my own life to think of. The two of you have managed your futures quite well, I think. I must find my own way, in my own time."

Susan smiled. "The way looks pretty clear to me! Look no further than the barn. And there is no time like right now!" Mary nodded and giggled.

Sybil shook her head. "I will not be rushed into marriage. John and I have much to talk about before I am persuaded that our marriage could be a fruitful and happy one."

"Then I reckon you'll be talking to him tonight, in the barn," said Susan, winking at Mary.

"Just so long as you keep his mind on the subject of your conversation," said Mary. "Men are easily distracted. Especially in a barn, especially at night. Or so I have been told." She giggled again.

Sybil did not bother to reply. They would indeed be talking in the barn — all night, if his last visit was any indication. She tried to think of how she could guide the conversation past the inevitable distractions, to the answers she needed to hear.

As the sun went down, the men returned from the barn. "John has agreed to carry a letter to our brother Thomas in Braintree, upon his return to Felsted," said Samuel. "It's only five or six miles from his family's farm. I'm going back to the rectory to write the letter."

Sybil gathered some bedding and handed some of it to John: "Let's see about a place for you to sleep," she said. The haying was done for the season, and the barn was full. Sybil found a place large enough that she could clear away enough space for John to sleep, and piled fresh, clean hay over it, then put a blanket over it. The bedding went on top of that "mattress."

That done, she turned to John and said, "I warned you not to rush Papa. Things might have gone badly at dinner."

"It's not what we planned," admitted John, "but we really didn't have a plan. And I think your father may have already guessed more than we thought he knew about our intentions."

Sybil had to agree. Papa seemed to have forced the issue, for some reason. She sighed. "What's done is done, I suppose."

"Are you not pleased?" John stepped toward her and put his arms around her waist.

"Of course, I'm pleased," she said, as he kissed her. Then she leaned away from him and looked at him intently. "Something in the way it was done discontents me." She untangled herself from his arms and found a place to sit.

John found a seat next to her. "I admit that I spoke hastily. It seemed that haste was justified. Making up another silly excuse for my presence at your table wasn't likely to satisfy your father any more than the *patatas* did. It seemed to me that he was determined to get to the bottom of things, sooner or later. Sooner seemed to me the better choice. Timidity and deception are unworthy of us and do not serve our cause. I think my judgment in this matter is vindicated by your father's response."

Sybil shook her head. "I agree that boldness serves better than timidity. But you spoke before I was ready. Yes, Papa was going to worry you with questions, like a dog with an old bone. But if you had given me just a few more moments, I could have diverted his attention. You took a risk and got away with it. It could have ended badly. It would have been wiser to plan some way for us to speak with him together."

"But you will agree that the question should have come from me?"

"I agree it is customary for the suitor to speak to the woman's father, yes. But I had rather we agree on the time and the place, rather than jump at an unexpected opportunity. I feel that my voice was silenced, somehow."

"Ah. So, is the customary approach not to your liking, or is it just that it all happened in front of your brother and sisters?"

Sybil paused. "I would have preferred that you not speak to my father in such a public way, but the presence of Samuel, Susan, and Mary may have made it harder for Papa to say 'no'. That much I will grant you. But I am not a customary woman, and you and I do not have a customary life ahead of us. I had rather we started our life together with a recognition of those facts, and a plan to overcome the inevitable obstacles together."

John ran his fingers across his head. He looked bewildered. "How is it that we are not 'customary'?"

"You," she began, "are not a typical carpenter. We live in a world where a carpenter's path is laid out clearly enough, by custom and law, yet you constantly stray from that path — you mix with men who are not of your class, you take risks that no sensible man would take, you leave your homeland for exotic places . . ."

"In my defense, I must point out that that last bit was no choice of mine," he interjected with a smile.

"Choice or no, you are smiling about it, as we speak. You are a man who tests the limits of custom, who has an appetite for liberties that most men of your station would not desire. Her voice became gentle. I know this about thee; it is one of the things I love about thee. And it may be that only a man like thee would woo a woman like me. . . "

"A woman like thee?"

"A woman who is unaccustomed to doing customary things. Of necessity, when I was young; but now that I am older, I am accustomed to finding my own path, solving my own problems, making my own decisions. I am not one of these soft-eyed, compliant women who will be content to follow a husband's whims and fancies. Neither am I the sort that pretends to surrender her will to a man because she calculates that she can bend him to her purposes with wiles and flattery."

"And that is one of the things I love about thee," John interjected.

"Why? Why do you love that about me?

"Because I know that when you speak, you speak truly. Because when you make a promise, I know that you will keep it. Because when you love someone, you dedicate yourself to that person's weal, even to your disadvantage." He looked directly into her eyes as he spoke until she had to look away.

"That's a pretty speech," she said, with a self-reflective smile. "But can two such as we truly be married, on such a love?"

John paused a moment. "We are kindred spirits, I think. Both of us have a little liberty to choose our paths and would have more liberty if we could. But the world we live in, and our circumstance would overrule us, and force us onto the path chosen for us by others. If it is possible to salvage some portion of our freedom, we shall have to fight for it and take risks that others would not take. Surely, it is better to have a partner in the fight, than to go it alone. Don't you think we would make good partners, you and I?"

Sybil looked at him. "You are asking me to make a wager, with my life, on a future that neither of us can be certain of."

"And I am prepared to match your wager, with my own life."

"But that wager does not cost a man as dearly as a woman, should they lose the bet."

John nodded. "If that is true, it is no fault of mine. The laws and customs we live under favor men over women, I suppose. Some say that is the natural way of things, some say God has ordained it so. Whatever the reason, people like us must find a way to live, survive, and — God willing — prosper. That is as much as I can offer you. That is why I want to marry you."

"And there is this," he added. "Consider the circumstances of our first meeting, and the ones that followed. Recall that I might never have come to Little Baddow, but for the advice of a recusant priest. Consider that I returned to this place only after surviving a dangerous sojourn at sea. Consider that my return was forced by a stubborn, ugly horse, who has never shown such stubbornness since. Consider that, without the *patatas* that I brought back with me, I might never have gotten your father's consent. It is not a customary sequence of events; it is most unlikely. Can we not suppose that God's hand is in all of this? And if we suppose so much, can we not believe that He will bless our lives if we wed them together?"

Sybil was quiet for some time. She believed he was sincere. His observations about their situation were truthful. Until quite recently, she had not considered these matters much — there were always chores, to do, a father to care for, sisters to keep an eye on. Ironic that a taste of freedom would unleash such a torrent of doubts and questions. She had not dared think about what marriage would mean, simply because she knew that marriage was not possible. And now this man had upset everything predictable about her life . . . Or maybe God was behind all of this; maybe this was God's will for her life, despite her doubts . . .

At length, she spoke. "Come, thou. Hold me, kiss me. Hold me tight." Naturally, he did everything that she told him to do.

They did fall asleep, at some point that night, though most of their time was spent talking. Just before dawn, Sybil woke, brushed the hay from her clothing, and went back to the house.

Samuel appeared in time for breakfast, with a letter he had written to his brother in Braintree. John calculated that he and Baxter could make it to Braintree, find Tom Vessey, and still arrive in Felsted in time for dinner if they left early enough. Sybil provided him with some bread and cheese for his midday meal, and he was on the road before either of them was really ready to part.

Braintree was a proper town, with nearly a thousand inhabitants. Nothing like so large as Chelmsford, or even Harwich, but a bustling place, nonetheless — a far cry from sleepy Felsted, only five miles away. John had visited the place in years past, and it had grown a little since his last visit. Still, it wasn't hard to find the forge where Tom Vessey was employed.

The smith stood at the forge, clad in a large leather apron, arms bare, sweating in the heat from the glowing iron in the tongs he held. He was as tall as his brother Samuel, but burlier — an imposing figure. John stood by while the smith struck sparks from his work upon the anvil. Only after the glowing metal was plunged into a vat of water with a loud hiss, did John venture to speak: "I am looking for Thomas Vessey," he said.

"And who would ye be, now that ye have found him?"

"John Porter, at your service."

"That name is familiar. Are you the man that my sister owes money to?"

"I was. I am no longer. I saw her in Little Baddow only this morning. I have a letter for you."

The Smith put down his tongs and took the letter from Edward, and read the outside of it. "How is it that you are a deliveryman for my brother? Do you owe him some favor?"

"I suppose I do since I intend to marry his eldest sister."

"Does my father know of this?"

"Indeed, he has approved me."

Tom thought for a moment. "Did ye say eldest? Sybil is the the eldest. A woman with a sharp wit, and a saucy tongue. A woman who does not tolerate fools."

John laughed. "Well, perhaps she makes an exception, in my case. But yes, Sybil is the woman I hope to marry."

Tom chuckled and extended his hand. "A brave fellow, then. Good luck to ye."

Introductions made, John began to look around the smithy.

"Is there something special, that yer needin'?"

John nodded. "Steel. I need steel pike points."

"I know what pike points are, so I won't ask what you want them for. How many are ye lookin' for?"

"I need fifty," said John, "and I need them soon. Everywhere I ask, I'm told that iron is cheaper, and steel is scarce."

"Aye, so it is. It's the war. Why do ye need fifty?"

"I've been charged with arming the men of my village as pikemen. The Baron is paying, so I don't care about the cost. But, since these men are my kin and my neighbors, I want to do right by them."

"The Baron? Which Baron?"

"The Third Baron of Leez, Robert Rich. He is landlord to my family; we dwell in Felsted."

Tom the Smith nodded. "And the Baron is paying, ye say?"

John pulled the steward's letter from inside his doublet and handed it to Tom. He half doubted that the Baron's credit was any good outside his own lands, but Tom grunted and nodded. "For the Baron, I could find the steel — assuming the price is right."

"Name it. The need is urgent."

The deal was done. Tom Vessey would deliver the fifty points in two weeks, to be paid upon delivery, by the Baron's steward. "Where will I find ye?"

"Our farmstead is on the road East of the village. You can ask for me as John Porter, son of Thomas Porter. There are other John Porters in the area, so be sure to mention my father's name." John decided he should report to the Baron's steward on Monday, to advise him of the obligations he had made in the Baron's name.

He pushed Baxter a bit, on the way back to Felsted; the road was broad and firm, and evening fell earlier than it had just a month ago. He made it back to Felsted just before sundown, returned Baxter to his owner, and walked home with Gordon. He barely had time to savor the successes of the past two days; too many other events and obligations filled his thoughts.

The next few weeks were a blur. Harvest time was always busy, long days, short sleep — when the grain was ripe, it was ripe; leaving it in the field any longer than necessary was to invite some calamitous storm or pestilence. Gordon's labor was particularly in demand, and John had to refuse to loan him out more than once. On top of that, the harvest was a good one — barely enough room in the barns and granaries to hold it all, but that much more to cut, bind, and thresh.

At the end of the second week, Tom Vessey showed up, mid-morning, with the fifty steel points that John had ordered. He was pushing a hand cart.

John happened to be at the house when he arrived and inspected the work. "Looks good," said John, "Come with me to the manor, and get your payment." It took the better part of an hour to walk through the village, and on to Leez Manor. When John knocked at the gate, he was greeted by a familiar face — Mr. Popham. Popham was dressed as a gentleman, with a dark green doublet, matching hose, and a starched ruff about his neck. His greeting was formal, but friendly enough — "What brings you here today, John Porter?"

"I need to see the steward. The blacksmith here has provided fifty pike points, as ordered, for the village company. I wish to see him paid, today."

Popinjay moved to the cart and inspected its contents. "Steel?" he noted with a raised eyebrow.

"Aye, steel. It seemed a good investment to me. If the steward thinks it extravagant, I will apologize, but I think that steel will answer in the heat of battle."

Popinjay nodded. "I agree. Let me fetch the steward."

It was but a few minutes before Popham returned with the steward. He insisted, of course, on unloading the handcart, so that an exact count could be verified. Satisfied, he paid Tom Vessey the agreed amount. "Iron would have been cheaper, I think," said the steward to John.

"Cheaper, but not better," interjected Popinjay. "These will do. Are there more coming?"

"I contracted with our local Smith for the other fifty," said John, "He was unable to promise the full one hundred."

"It will be interesting to compare the quality of the work, between the two smiths," said Popham. He looked directly at Tom. "These are well made."

Popham turned to a doorman. "We will store these in the armory until the rest arrive. Well done, John Porter." He turned, and went back inside.

John and Tom were left with the steward. "Mr. Popham is a man well acquainted with weapons," said the Steward. "His opinion will carry much weight with the Baron."

John turned to Tom Vessey. "It is nearly midday. You must have supper with us." They headed back to the village, the handcart empty.

When they reached the house, supper was nearly ready. John introduced Tom Vessey to his mother in the kitchen. Ellen stood outside the door and beckoned to John. Aside, she asked, "Who's the stout, burly fellow?"

"He will be your brother-in-law, if I have anything to say about it. Name is Tom Vessey. Sybil's brother." Tom smiled broadly and offered Ellen his hand. "Pleased to make yer acquaintance Miss Porter," he said. Ellen curtseyed and lowered her eyes shyly. What was *that* about, wondered John.

Tom Porter came home for supper, as well. Tom Vessey was the center of attention, especially for Ellen, John noticed. Conversation was congenial, and could have gone on longer, but for the work that awaited them in the fields. John's mother, Ann, was asking all sorts of questions about the Vesseys — digging for clues about Sybil, more than likely. At the end of the meal, John felt that things had gone as well as could be expected — two families getting acquainted; part of every marriage, he supposed.

November 1586: Drilling on the Green

The Baron was as good as his word. One Saturday in early October, he announced a pig roast, on the green across from Holy Cross church. Men showed up in large numbers and were informed about their martial obligations. As they stood in line to have their names entered in a book by the Baron's steward, John tried to size them up.

The Baron had kept his promise about the firearms, as well. Forty relatively modern arquebuses were displayed in the back of a cart. John needed to identify at least forty men who could be trained as arquebusiers. Should be agile men, men with skilled hands, quick hands, sure hands. It might take some time to identify them. Meanwhile, everyone could do with some drilling. He had them line up — one hundred forty seven, by his count. Various ages, heights, and builds. Would it make more sense to group them by height, or by age?

"You could start by assigning them to groups of ten." The suggestion came from none other than Master Popham, who had just appeared at John's side. Popham was dressed soberly enough, for him, with a steel breastplate over his doublet, and a rapier in a scabbard at his side. He looked quite imposing, in this crowd, which was probably his intention. The suggestion made sense, though. John had them count off by tens and lined up one group behind the other. They formed an organized-looking mass, fourteen ranks of ten men each, with a few stragglers left in the rear. Sir Walter Clive appeared, wearing not only a breast plate, but a helmet, tassets, and greaves. Very impressive. Clive proceeded to address the men, with a speech that was intended to rouse them to enthusiasm. It didn't appear to John that they were particularly roused.

"There's a boy here, who has a drum, and the Baron has provided us with a standard." Popham, again, barely more than a whisper. Of course. John had neglected to recruit a drummer. And if there was a standard, then there must be a standard bearer . . .

Clive was still speaking, beginning to get hoarse. When he finished, the men gave him a "Hurrah!"; desultory, John thought, but polite. Clive appeared to be satisfied and found a place to sit down. John spoke to the drummer. "What's your name, Lad?"

"Brian," came the reply.

John stepped forward to address the men, with his hand on Brian's shoulder. "Brian here is our drummer. I expect every man will learn to keep time with his drum, whenever we are ordered to move. We will also need a guidon bearer, to carry our standard." He made a show of scanning the formation with his gaze. A tall man in the third rank. Jed Bones, in his brown coat. Perfect. "Jed Bones! Will you do us the honor?" Bones came forward and took the flagpole from his hand. "Someone from the rear rank must fill in for Jed," said John. "This is a rule for all our company. If there is a gap in the ranks, someone must step up to fill it. Lives may depend on it." There. That remark met a sober reception.

Meantime, Popham had fitted Jed with a guidon harness, so he could carry the standard comfortably. The banner was decorated with the Baron's coat of arms. Naturally.

John ordered Brian to start a steady beat, not too fast, and he, Brian, and Jed led the men, rank by rank around the perimeter of the green. John stepped to the side as they reached the corner, and ordered each rank to wheel, as they passed. Some of the men had done this before, others were having difficulty staying in step. John had to scramble to catch up with the head of the column, in order to turn them on the far side. Halfway across the backstretch, he ordered Brian to beat a faster cadence — not a run, but a double-time trot. It was ugly — the rear ranks began to break apart, and the whole formation became a mob. John ordered a halt, and then dressed ranks. The men looked a little sheepish.

"You can see," John said, "that moving a company in formation is not as easy as it looks." Some murmurs and chuckles. "It is necessary that each of you heed the orders, to respond in a timely fashion. Each rank must choose one of your members to be a 'Corporal'. That man will be responsible to repeat my orders and ensure that every man in his rank follows them. Understood?"

They muttered their assent.

"The man on the left hand of every rank will be your corporal. At the end of today, you may choose another man, if you like. Let's begin again."

Brian started the cadence again, an easy walk. At the next turn, John ordered the first rank to wheel, and the corporal of the second rank, slow to respond, nevertheless wheeled his rank at exactly the right moment. The corporal of the third rank had done this before, so his rank wheeled at just the right moment, as well. Now three ranks had made the wheel, in perfect formation, and so it went — until the eighth rank, which overran the turn, and confused the ninth rank . . . John ordered a halt, to let the rear of the column sort itself out.

After an hour, he had them stand at ease and rest. They were getting the hang of marching and wheeling. Then more difficult maneuvers, like splitting a rank of ten, and collapsing it to ranks of five, while on the move — most of the roads in England were too narrow to allow men to march ten abreast, even five would be a tight squeeze. After that, learning to advance in a column of five or ten, then halt and deploy in three ranks of forty men, as if facing a line of enemy pikemen. Finally, the most important maneuver — to shift from a column five abreast, to a hollow square two ranks deep, with the men facing outward in each direction. The outer "face" of the square would have fifteen men, including the four at the "corners": the inner rank would comprise twelve men on each face since it was nested inside the outer rank. The square was hollow, and the guidon bearer and the drummer would form inside the square, along with the arquebusiers. Which meant that it was time to pick the arquebusiers. He asked first for volunteers who may have used firearms before. Six men claimed that experience. Then, he picked out thirty-four more, younger men, none too short, two were cousins of his. Time would tell if he had chosen wisely. The forty men stood aside, and the ranks filled with men from the rear. "Let each 'Corporal' walk to that wagon there" — he pointed to his cart — under the tarp, you will find the pike poles. Choose ten and distribute them to your rank."

From the ten ranks, three of the corporals took a man or two from his rank with him to fetch the poles; two men could carry ten poles easily enough. The other seven corporals discovered that carrying ten sixteen-foot poles by themselves was awkward, and necessitated two trips. John made a mental note of the three that had sized up the job ahead of time; thinking ahead was a sign of leadership potential, maybe.

The men in the ranks had some difficulty handling the poles but figured out that for the unit to maneuver, the poles had to be held vertically. There were some unwelcome prods and pokes, with the expected protests, before everyone was settled. Some of the men looked annoyed, others confused.

"You will notice that your pikes have no points," announced John. Murmurs from the men. "The reason for that will become clear, as you march around the green." He marched them around the green again, this time in the opposite direction, in ranks of ten, at first. When he ordered them to shift to five abreast, poles began to clash and entangle. Once they sorted that out, he ordered them into a square — more clashing, and entangling, and three or four men were tripped up, which led to more tripping, as the poles fell to the horizontal, and blocked the maneuver. To their credit, the corporals took charge of their ranks and got the formation back in order.

As the last few men got to their feet and tried to recover their fallen poles, John spoke again: "Now you know why there are no points on your pikes. Imagine how many we would have wounded, if those poles were tipped with steel!" They looked at him for a moment, and then he smiled. They chuckled and murmured their recognition. Point taken.

"I think we have drilled enough, for one day," John continued, "each of you must take his pike home, and bring it back at our next drill. We will not mount the steel tips until you have learned to handle them without skewering each other. Speaking of skewers, I believe that the Baron's hogs are ready to eat." Someone in the back ranks shouted "Hurrah!" and was raggedly echoed by most of the rest. The company was dismissed.

"A good beginning, I think." It was Popham, at his elbow again.

John sighed. "A beginning, anyway. We have a long way ahead of us."

Sir Walter approached and seemed in a good mood. "They're raw, but I've seen worse. Wise of you not to let them play with steel, just yet."

John nodded his acknowledgment. He approached the forty arquebusiers, who looked a little lost. He explained that they would be trained in due time, but he needed to be sure the pikemen were "safe to stand near to," before adding any loaded firearms to the mix. They nodded, and some smiled — all of them had witnessed the chaos just minutes before.

Popham stood nearby. "Master Popham, I thank you for your presence, today. You have been very helpful."

"You are welcome," said Popham. "I stand ready to offer any assistance that I can."

"I did not take you for a man with military experience."

Popham nodded. "Not many do. I am the third son of a noble family, which means my education included rudiments of the military arts, among others. Of course, the education does not come with property or title, so I entered the Baron's service."

A minor nobleman, then, Popham, thought John. "Why then did not the Baron choose you to lead this company?"

Popham smiled wryly. "He thought my style would not suit. Some call me 'Popinjay' behind my back, you know. It seemed unlikely that men such as these would take orders from a 'Popinjay' in the heat of battle."

John started to reply but held his tongue. He nodded. More going on here than he really wanted to know about, perhaps.

Popham continued, "I have observed you, John Porter, and I do not think you are a man of mockery. I am well aware of what others call me, and I do not always like it, but I do not let it trouble me. What I would have you understand, is that I dress the way I do, to honor my family's rank, and to serve my master, the Baron, the more effectively. Men like you may think me sumptuous, but I am intimately familiar with the sumptuary laws, and I do not violate them. I wear the Baron's livery, and when I am called upon to represent him at court (which happens more often than you might suppose), the way I am dressed commands the respect that my master's rank demands. Even when I am at the manor, my clothing speaks for me — that I represent a powerful man, and must be respected, as he is respected."

"I admit I had not thought of it like that," said John. "I suppose your job would be more difficult if you dressed as I do."

"It would be impossible unless I wished to travel incognito," he chuckled. "You should think about the way you dress when you are drilling the men. Military clothing helps identify who is in charge, and whose orders must be obeyed. You should consider some sort of garment that will identify you as the drill master."

"That had not occurred to me. I shall take your advice. Have you, by chance, any experience with firearms, especially modern ones, like the snaphance?"

"A little," replied Popham.

"Then I shall ask you to work with the arquebusiers until I have the pikemen ready. Can you help me?"

Popham looked a little surprised. "If I am not away on the Baron's business, I will be present at the drills."

"Good enough. Thank You, Master Popham."

Two weeks later, they assembled on the green again. John was relieved to see that nearly everyone from the first drill had returned. They had also picked up five or six newcomers.

At Popham's suggestion, John was wearing his Jack of Plates, with his cutlass at his side. He wore his felt hat — the morion was a bit of overkill, he thought. Other men had shown up with bits of armament, as well — some old breastplates, even three or four small, round shields, called targets. Nearly everyone had some sort of long knife in his belt, a few dozen had some sort of iron or steel helmet on their heads.

They were already a bit rusty but improved rapidly. By the end of the first hour, they had performed all the maneuvers that he asked them to. He introduced them to the rudiments of the pike — planting the butt ends in the ground, with the right foot holding it down, in the front rank, holding the pike horizontally overhead in the second rank (without skewering the man in front, if you please). Still no points on the pikes — not quite ready. He did set pairs of ranks against each other, to get used to the orders for retreating or advancing, without breaking ranks. It was here that John saw the futility of it all — these men, he was sure, were brave enough. Brave enough to die, but not skilled enough to triumph in a battle with professional troops. It didn't help that their faces were all familiar to him.

It was late October before John would be able to get back to Little Baddow. This time, Sybil made a bed for him on the floor before the fireplace. "Too chilly to sleep in the barn," she insisted. John did not protest.

In November, they drilled again. Someone complained that it was getting cold outside. John addressed the company: "I have noticed, indeed, that the weather is unpleasant. I shall send a message to the King of Spain, informing him that he must choose only pleasant days for his invasion, else we shall be very put out with him." There was loud laughter from the men. Time for steel.

November 1586: Harwich

The *Egyptian Queen* returned to Harwich on November 30 — St. Andrew's Day, just as Billy Foxe had planned. She was a little worse for wear — various scuffles with other ships had left their mark. She had pursued more than a dozen prizes, but most had escaped into shallow waters, or even been run aground, to avoid capture. Spiteful captains, those. One or two had simply outrun the Queen, which annoyed Captain Foxe even more than the ones that grounded themselves. In the end, they had seized only two prizes: a small Italian merchantman bound for Antwerp, and a large, fat Portuguese carrack.

They captured the Italian vessel with deception, under a Spanish flag. When the *Queen* pulled alongside the crew of the merchantman did not resist — the captain produced his bill of lading, which showed that his cargo was intended for the Spanish army in the Netherlands — all the reason Foxe needed to justify its seizure. A large part of the cargo was Italian wine. Foxe locked the Italian crew up in the brig on the *Queen*, put his own prize crew, under the command of Piet VanDoorn, aboard her, and sent her back to Harwich — the wine, at least, would find eager buyers in England.

The carrack gave them more trouble. She couldn't flee to the shallows like the smaller ships, but she was heavily armed and fought back. Foxe's tactic of standing off and pummeling his prey into submission worked, eventually, but not until the *Queen* had suffered some damage, as well. The carrack's cargo turned out to be mostly lumber. There were also some fine porcelains and other ceramics, most of which were broken in the gun battle to capture the carrack. Foxe fumed at the result. "What's the point of fighting a sea battle, if yer plunder is destroyed?" The captain of the carrack was unrepentant — another spiteful man, a Spaniard. There were also some Spanish soldiers aboard — reinforcements or replacements. The carrack had a large crew of sailors aboard, as well. Many were dead, more were injured. The numerous unharmed captives could barely be confined in the *Queen's* hold — more mouths to feed. The carrack itself was so badly damaged, as to be barely seaworthy. Another prize crew was required to sail the carrack back to Harwich, with a large number of wounded men from the carrack — her guns were transferred to the *Queen* so that the crew had at least that much to show for their efforts. Foxe helped himself to the Spanish captain's charts. It was mid-November by then, so after another week of chasing smaller vessels, the Queen turned homeward.

Incredibly, no one from the crew had died on this voyage, which boded well for another try in the Spring. When they arrived in port, they discovered that Grimes and Fairchild had already taken possession of the Italian merchantman, and sold her, and her cargo.

The carrack and her prize crew had not arrived.

Foxe paid off the crew of the *Egyptian Queen*, including the prize crew on the Italian ship, with the proceeds of the sale of her cargo, and the guns they had taken from the carrack — it came to about four pounds per seaman, more for the officers. No great fortune, but enough to see everyone through the winter. The *Queen* would need some work before heading to sea again, and a handful of men would be paid to stay aboard her to stand watch for a few months, once the repairs were complete.

Captain Foxe and Roger were home by evening, that day. Harriet was thrilled to see them both; she clung to Roger and wept for quite a while. Then, wiping her eyes, she curtsied to Billy Foxe, and said, "You brought my boy home safe. Thank ye, Sir."

"Never occurred to me not to bring him back safe," he replied. "Yer boy's to be a navigator, or so I'm told — has a knack for it, they say."

Roger smiled. The truth was that he had struggled mightily with Arithmetic and the rudiments of Geometry, but by the end of the voyage, Homer was allowing him to take the sightings and do his own dead reckoning. Usually, his calculations agreed with Homer's

It was a week later that they got news of the carrack. Sea Beggars had intercepted her on the way back to Harwich. There wasn't much of a fight — all the carrack's guns were in the hold of the *Egyptian Queen*. The Beggars ignored the English flag on her masthead — the ship was clearly not built in an English shipyard, and anyone might fly the English flag, in time of war. The Beggars claimed the carrack and her cargo for their own but thoughtfully transferred the English prize crew to a small pinnace, and put them ashore in Yarmouth. The Beggars were more or less allies of England, after all, but business was business. They could use the lumber, though they were particularly disappointed that the carrack was unarmed. "That serves them right for takin' another man's prize," snorted Foxe, "Sea Buzzards, I call 'em!"

In any case, the *Queen*'s prize crew found their way back to Harwich, in due time, and collected their pay.

The prisoners in the *Queen*'s hold were a different problem. Foxe turned them all over to the local authorities, though the local jail wasn't big enough to hold them all. The Italians were released almost immediately, along with many of the seamen from the carrack — none of them had any value as hostages; no one would be willing to pay a ransom to get them home. More than a few found work down at the waterfront — ships came and went, crews were constantly adding or subtracting members.

The officers and soldiers aboard the carrack were a different matter. The captain, at minimum, had some value, either as ransom, or in exchange for English seamen held by the Spanish. The Crown's agents took custody of the whole lot: The Captain, in particular, might be a source of valuable information about the state of affairs in the Spanish navy, some of the soldiers might know something about the Spanish army's affairs, as well. One detail they missed: Foxe did not mention that he had seized all the charts from the captain of the carrack, some of which were very up-to-date, and very detailed. It was the kind of information that could lead to success on his next voyage. He added those to his collection aboard the *Queen*.

Getting the *Queen* ready for another foray would take some time, but Foxe was in no hurry, for a change. December, January, and February were particularly dangerous on the North Sea, though that had never deterred him before. He seemed content to spend his days in the *Galleon*, catching up on the news, or reminiscing with old friends. Evenings, he dined with Roger and his family in the house they now owned and tussled with Roger's younger brothers on the floor in front of a warm fire. He laughed more often, now, and with gusto. His friends in the pub commented on the change in his manner: "It's as if the edge has been taken off the man," confided Danny Cornwall to one of his customers. "Billy Foxe could never be at ease ashore, always had to have some project or scheme afoot, to get him back to sea, again."

"Maybe it's the home cookin'," someone suggested, with a wink.

"Aye," Danny laughed, "Maybe it is."

February 8, 1587: Fotheringhay Castle

S imon Bull was feeling a little on edge: ironic, for a man whose career was so dependent on the keenness of edges — edges of knives, swords, and most especially the edge on the great axe that was the hallmark of his trade. He wasn't supposed to know, officially, why he was sent to this place, but it was an open secret — the Queen's cousin Mary, a queen in her own right, was appointed to die today; Simon was the chosen instrument of the government's justice.

Nonetheless, it was important that he perform well. He took some pride in his work, and this was the highest-ranking head that he had ever been ordered to remove. It was a matter of some political import that the deed be done quickly and cleanly — to show honor to the rank of the condemned woman, to demonstrate the efficiency of the government, to establish in everyone's mind that there could be only one Tudor queen in England: God save the Queen!

Simon's axe had been honed again and again — almost compulsively since it was one of the few things that Simon himself could control. He noted with some satisfaction that the execution would be conducted in the Great Hall of the castle, out of public view. The witnesses to the event were all gentry of one sort or another, dressed in black, with their fancy hose and their tall hats — no riffraff, then, to pull some stunt like that crowd in Chelmsford a few years back. That whole affair still rankled him — an embarrassment to the government, and even to himself. His reputation, after all, was pretty much all he had. So yes, he was anxious that things should go smoothly today.

A platform had been constructed in the middle of the Great Hall, and a chopping block placed near the center. Simon stood with a few other officials and waited. They did not have to wait long. Queen Mary and a procession of her attendants appeared and mounted the steps to the platform. The customary routines were observed; The warrant for her execution was read aloud, Mary prayed her last prayer, Bull and his companions knelt before Mary and asked for her forgiveness, which she granted. Then, her servants helped her remove her black outer garments to reveal a red sleeveless bodice and petticoat. Her hair was unbound, and red tresses spilled across her shoulders. Her servants attached red sleeves to the bodice and tied a white blindfold about her head. She stepped to the block, and knelt — with some difficulty, Bull noticed: evidently she suffered from rheumatism. Mary placed her head upon the block, and waited for the stroke. The whole spectacle was dazzling, Simon thought. Never had he plied his trade amid such glamour. Death was somehow glorified, elevated to something transcendent.

Simon Bull took a breath and, determined to finish the business in one clean blow, swung the axe with extra force — and missed his aim. It took a second blow to sever her neck, and then a third. Embarrassing. Nothing left, now, but to lift the severed head for all to see and proclaim "God save the Queen!" — however ironic it might sound. As he did so, the Mary's head pulled free from his grasp and landed with a thud on the platform. Simon was left holding a red wig — everyone could see that Queen Mary wore her hair short, and it was grey, not red. The overall effect was anticlimactic. Simon felt ridiculous. The body before him was that of a prematurely aged woman — no more the elegant figure that had stood before him only moments before. Whatever grandeur and nobility there had been in the ceremony was gone. What remained was a botched execution, the only victor was death itself. *And death, when it comes, looks much the same for all men and women*, thought Simon.

Simon Bull's humiliation did not last long. When the news of Mary's death reached her cousin Elizabeth, the Queen expressed outrage — she had indeed signed the death warrant, but had specifically ordered that it not be carried out. She blamed her privy council for going behind her back, and sent the man entrusted with possession of the warrant, one William Davison, to the tower for neglecting his duty. Thus, Elizabeth deflected the blame for Mary's death from herself. Simon's less-than-stellar performance was simply more evidence that the whole business had been conducted in a slipshod fashion.

With Mary dead, the struggle with Spain became a simpler contest, with fewer diplomatic components. Spain was gathering a large invasion fleet — larger than anything seen before in Europe. When the blow fell, it would be a head-to-head contest of military power — no more risings, rebellions, or revolts, just one large army against a smaller one. The only difficulty was getting the Spanish army across the English Channel. The decisive conflict would be at sea.

March 14, 1587: Harwich

Captain Billy Foxe appeared that morning at *The Galleon* a bit late. He was in a good mood and greeted Danny Cornwall and a few others he knew. He sat at his usual table, with a view of the entrance, and ordered his usual ale. Danny walked over and sat down.

"Ye're late," observed Cornwall. "Something keeping ye in bed, today?"

"Chores," replied Foxe, "had some chores about the house."

"So the seamstress has ye workin' for her, now?" Cornwall shook his head and chuckled. "A far cry from commanding a ship now, isn't it?"

"Not as far as you might suppose. The house is mine, it's made of wood, like a ship. Has to be maintained, just like a ship."

"And ye have a rowdy crew, or so I'm told," Danny added with a smile.

Foxe's eyes narrowed. "What's yer point, Danny? If ye've something to say, spit it out."

"Point?" Danny shrugged. "Why does there have to be a point?"

"So far, ye've mentioned my sleeping situation, my housekeeper, and her children, and I've barely started on my first ale. Is there a problem?"

Danny shook his head. "I've no problem with where you sleep, or how much, or who you live with. Other people might question it, but live and let live, is my policy."

"What other people?"

"People who wonder if ye've gotten soft, in yer new situation. People who wonder if ye'll ever go to sea again; whether there's any point in waiting to serve with ye on the *Egyptian Queen*, or whether they should find a berth with some other captain."

Ah. that was it. Men were getting restless; now that the weather was improving, the sea was calling . . .

"How many people are wondering?"

"Oh, men come in here nearly every day now, asking if there's a berth on Captain Foxe's ship — ye have a reputation as a lucky captain, ye know."

They were fair questions, Foxe had to admit. Well, they would have answers to some of them soon enough. As for the question about him getting "soft," he wondered about that himself. It was comfortable to live in a house, sleep as long as he liked, eat home-cooked food. He had to admit that the old yearning to be at sea was muted now. Age, probably. He was getting old . . .

His reflections were interrupted. "Captain Foxe?" A man stood near the table, vaguely familiar, not a seaman, though . . . of course, one of Fairchild's servants.

"Master Fairchild requests your presence, at your earliest convenience," said the man.

This was the summons that Foxe had been waiting for. He finished his ale with a gulp, and stood. "Now is convenient," he said, and followed the man out of the pub. Danny Cornwall noticed the briskness of the encounter. Something was about to change, he realized, and not just for Captain Billy Foxe.

It was a damp day and the cobblestones were wet, but it was not really raining; the temperature was mild — Spring was definitely in the air. It was not far to their destination. Fairchild was waiting in an inner room, an office, really, attached to a warehouse by the waterfront. "Captain Foxe! Please be seated!" he pointed to a chair.

"I will be direct," said Fairchild. "I have news from London. Our investors want the *Egyptian Queen* to be in Plymouth no later than April 8 of this year, fully outfitted for a voyage of several months."

"Where is this voyage headed?" asked Foxe.

"That I have not been told," replied Fairchild. "I believe the government wishes to keep that a secret."

"It is no small matter to prepare for a voyage on such short notice, even if the destination is known."

"I think we can draw some conclusions from the instructions I have received, and from news from abroad," said Fairchild. "The King of Spain is collecting a large fleet of ships, intending to invade our realm. Therefore, it would be foolish for the government to send its warships to the Americas, or anywhere away from the battle that is surely coming. The *Queen* will be lading extra powder and shot, ample foodstuffs, and a complement of soldiers. It will be up to you to hire a crew and get her ready to go to war."

"And where am I to find all these provisions?"

"You won't have to. They are already on the way here. I expect that some may arrive on Monday."

"Your masters have made all the arrangements, then?"

"Yes, you could say so. The owners of the *Queen* have entered into an agreement with other 'Merchant Adventurers' to share profits from this voyage. And the supply of all the ships is now in the hands of the government.”

“You seem to know a great deal about this 'secret' voyage.”

“I have told you as much as you need to know, in order to prepare your ship.”

Foxe sat for a moment. Evidently, more information would not be forthcoming. He stood and excused himself.

Once outside, he found the *Two Kingdoms*. He stepped inside, and was immediately greeted by several men, including Dick Benby: “Welcome Captain! The first drink is on the house!”

“And the second one is one me!” added a seaman.

“Nay, I haven't the time, today. Mr. Benby, I must speak with you.”

Benby directed him to a table in the back, with a jerk of his head. They huddled together. “We going to sea then, Captain?”

Foxe nodded. “This voyage is a bit different. More fighting, less booty, maybe. I'd be glad to have ye sail with me, but ye should know about the danger. I will not blame ye if ye stay ashore for this one.”

“Where will we be going, then?” Benby did not appear to be intimidated by Foxe's somber assessment of their prospects.

“I don't truly know. Our owners have not said. But we will have to sail no later than the first of April.”

Benby nodded, then smiled. “I can guess then, can't I?”

Foxe looked at him with some surprise. “Perhaps you know more than I do?”

“Perhaps. I know that the King of Spain is assembling a fleet of more than one hundred ships in Lisbon. It is no secret where he plans to send those ships. He will bring tens of thousands of soldiers to England, where he intends to make himself our king; that much he has stated openly. Our Queen does not have tens of thousands of soldiers, so it stands to reason that she must meet him on the sea if she hopes to defeat him. It falls to men like us to protect her throne.”

“We do not have a hundred ships,” noted Foxe.

“Nay, but we will not have to protect a convoy of cargo vessels and troop ships, either. Most of the Spanish ships will be merchantmen, slow and overloaded. If we defeat their warships, the rest of the fleet will flee from us.”

“It sounds as if you have been preparing for this day.”

“And why would I not? Is there any better warship in England than the *Egyptian Queen*, or any luckier captain than Billy Foxe? What sailor would not volunteer for such a voyage? We'll have no difficulty finding a full crew. And if there's a way to make a profit, you will find it, no doubt."

Foxe smiled. Benby's optimism was contagious. "I need to talk to Homer."

"I'll find him. When do you need us to report?"

"Meet me on board the *Queen* on Monday morning. Do you know where Piet Van Doorn is?"

"I heard he was back in the Low Countries, but I'll ask around. Paolo and Reuben are in town somewhere. We'll have no trouble locating the officers that you want. And once the word is out, you'll have plenty of seamen looking to sail with you. It is like old times, eh?"

"Yes. Like old times." Foxe nodded.

Benby looked into his eyes, held his gaze for a moment. "No, not exactly like old times. The man has changed, I think. What has changed in you, Captain?"

"I think I must be getting old, Dick. I find myself wondering how long a man can cheat death."

"I have survived many perils, some of them with you. I do not consider it 'cheating' that both of us are still alive. Why should this voyage be different from others?"

"I really can't say. The thought of going to sea would have delighted me two years ago. Now it feels like separating myself from something precious, something that feeds my heart . . ."

"Ah," said Benby, "Something is healing in your heart, I think. Now your life seems more precious, even as you put it at risk. I know that feeling. The same thing happened to me when I found my Caroline. Is there a woman in your life?"

"No, no woman. A family maybe. I have a sort of family, now." He was silent for a moment. Then, he stood and spoke: "Monday then, Mr. Benby?"

Benby smiled, "Monday then, Captain!"

Foxe found his steps leading him homeward. He stopped. No, something else had to be done first. He turned toward the rectory. Time to talk with a priest.

When Billy Foxe arrived at home, it was not yet dusk — the days were getting noticeably longer. He entered the shop and found Harriet and her eldest daughter working on their current orders. "Where's Roger?"

Harriet looked up and smiled. "Upstairs with the boys. He makes them attend to their studies, now that they're in school."

"I must speak with him, and you, about a matter of importance. Will ye join me upstairs?"

"Of course, Captain. Just let me finish this seam, and I'll be right up."

Foxe went upstairs and found Roger and the boys, as Harriet had said. The youngsters rushed him when he appeared, and hung on him, with their arms around him. "Lessons are over for today," said Roger with a smile.

"Lads, I need to talk to yer brother and yer mum for a bit. Don't ye have chores to attend?

The boys expressed disappointment but dutifully tramped downstairs. Harriet arrived soon after. Harriet and Roger looked at him with a questioning look. He sat in a chair and gestured for them to do the same.

"I have learned this day," he began, "that the *Egyptian Queen* is ordered to sea again. I am to be her Captain, and we must sail no later than the first of next month."

Roger was clearly pleased at the news; Harriet was reticent.

"Mama, it will mean more money for our family," Roger pointed out, "about time I earned some more."

Harriet nodded. "Aye, more money. Also more risk. We're doing well enough as it is. I fear that one of you may not come back from this voyage."

"Yer mum is right," said Foxe. "There is much at risk. This voyage will be more hazardous than our last one. In fact, ye should consider whether to remain here in Harwich and care for yer family, whilst I am at sea. I will certainly go; I would not willingly put the *Queen* in any other man's care. But you can stay behind if you wish."

"Not if you paid me," said Roger. "I won't be left behind if I have to stowaway!"

Foxe was not surprised at his reaction. Still, it was worth a try . . . "In that case, we must make arrangements to take care of yer mum . . . just in case." He reached into his doublet and pulled out some papers. "I consulted a man of the law today and had these drawn up. They say that in the event of my death, you, Harriet Frye, will inherit my property including my share of this house, and any money or other possessions that I own."

Harriet gasped. "That's very kind of you Captain Foxe, though I'm sure it won't come to that!"

"We can be sure of nothing. There is one other matter that is too delicate to discuss with a lawyer." He pulled more papers from his doublet.

"There are other funds, that the lawyer is unaware of, and that is how things must be. This letter proves that there are certain funds that I have entrusted to a Mr. Scarlatti — a very discreet man who lives in this town. If something happens to me, you can show him proof of my death, and this will, and Mr. Scarlatti will make those funds available to you."

"Forgive me, Captain. What 'funds' would these be? I don't understand what you are talking about."

"Roger understands. Mr. Scarlatti is also holding certain funds for him."

Roger nodded and reached out to touch his mother's arm. "I can take care of that part if it becomes necessary," he said.

"That assumes that ye will return from this voyage, even if I do not," said Foxe. "Are ye still determined to sail with me?"

"More than ever," Roger replied. "And yes, I catch your drift. I should be putting my affairs in order, as well."

"Smart lad. There is no need for you to have a will since you are still a minor. But you could write a letter to Scarlatti and leave it with yer mum."

Harriet was looking at her son with a mixture of shock and dread. She said nothing.

"There is one more painful thing to discuss," said Foxe. "If ye are to inherit my estate, your legal status must be clear. There is no kinder way to say this: Mrs. Frye, do you believe that yer husband still lives? I only ask because it matters somewhat whether you are to be known as Mrs. Frye, or the Widow Frye. As a widow, your rights to inherit and own property are clear. If your husband is still alive, there could be some claim from others in his family to act on his behalf and claim part of the inheritance."

Harriet nodded slowly. "I see. Yes, James Frye has some living siblings. They want nothing to do with us, poor as we are, but might change their attitude if I came into some property. I gave James up for dead several years ago, but I can't prove that he isn't alive . . ."

"You don't need to prove it," said Foxe. "Under the laws of the realm, a man that has 'deserted' his wife may be declared dead, for legal purposes, after seven years. It is a routine process, and I have drawn up papers," here he pulled more from his doublet, "that would give you complete control of any property that you inherit. Roger, I include you in this conversation because you are the man of this family, and the decision will affect yer future, as well as that of yer mum and yer siblings."

Roger nodded soberly. "Mama and I will have to discuss this more," he said.

473

"Aye, and so ye should. For my part, I have done what I could to dispose of my affairs in the best way that I can imagine. My heart is at rest. I have a mind to eat my dinner in a pub this evening." With that, he rose, went downstairs, and out into the street.

The promised provisions appeared on time, including a complement of soldiers — an indication that someone in the government was taking this enterprise seriously. Gratefully, the company of pikemen was commanded by none other than Alexander Cooper — Captain Cooper, now, in recognition of his gallant service at Cartagena — or maybe just because they couldn't find anyone else trustworthy for the command. *At least they put a seasoned officer in charge*, thought Foxe. That would count for something, maybe a great deal, in the battle to come. All of the officers from the Caribbean raid were now aboard the *Queen* (other than the carpenter), with one exception — Piet Van Doorn, the first mate, was nowhere to be found. Foxe puzzled over who should replace him. All the officers had served together, fought together, and trusted one another. Placing them under a new first mate made no sense. He should promote one of the junior officers to fill the spot — but who? Dick Benby was probably the best choice for a ship going to war, but Foxe needed his gunnery officer below decks; no other man would do as well as Benby. Foxe settled on the boatswain, Reuben Cox, who at least had worked with every man on the ship during the last voyage. A new boatswain could be found among the crew. By the end of March, the *Egyptian Queen* was ready to sail.

April 1, 1587: Cadiz

The *Egyptian Queen* slipped out of the estuary with the turning of the tide, six bells into the first watch. Billy Foxe stood on the quarterdeck and watched as the shoreline slid away astern, and the open sea embraced her. Not much wind, barely enough for steerage. Once clear of the estuary, the *Queen* turned to starboard — first east, then south by southeast, bound for the Channel, and thence westward to Plymouth. He wasn't really needed on deck now, yet he put off sleep and scanned the sea as if looking for something. The wind picked up; the clouds dispersed, and the stars came out. A good omen, maybe. He continued to scan the horizon in every direction.

At eight bells, the watch changed. Homer came on deck to gauge her speed. "Six knots," he said in passing. Foxe grunted and nodded. This voyage was almost a reprise of their raid on the Caribbean, barely eighteen months ago. But it felt different. Partly, that was a matter of their mission — he expected a head-to-head confrontation with the great warships of the Spanish fleet. Partly, the difference was in his mood. He felt none of the relief that once accompanied every foray into the deep. Some part of him longed to be ashore, sleeping in his comfortable bed. Was it cowardice, or just softness? Maybe this was a job for a younger, hungrier man.

⁂

The harbor at Plymouth was full of ships. Drake's fleet was easy enough to identify — Four of the Queen's new galleons, moored together were unmistakable. Surrounding them were a few large carracks, and a host of smaller vessels: the *Egyptian Queen* would sail in good company.

On April 12, the entire squadron of thirty-one ships slipped out to sea, and passed out of sight of land, heading south.

Captain Foxe convened a meeting of his officers and Captain Cooper, in the chart room:

"Lads, I will be frank with ye. This voyage may not be as profitable as our last. Our purpose is to find the enemy and fight him; plunder will be a secondary concern. We have been assured of a fair portion of any plunder that is taken — unusually fair, I should say. But when we meet the enemy, we will be fighting, and likely in battle formation. Turning aside from the heat of the battle to take a prize will not be tolerated."

"Where are we bound?"

"Lisbon. They say that the invasion fleet is assembling there. They say that the King of Spain has more than three hundred ships, with more coming."

"We will be outnumbered, then."

"Aye, we will be outnumbered. But if we sink enough Spanish ships, the King will have to wait another year to invade our home. We are buying time, that is all."

"And paying in blood."

"Aye, paying in blood. Spanish blood, God willing."

"And we take no plunder? Drake will not abide by such a rule, even if he himself made it!" Chuckles and nods among the officers.

"Aye," said Foxe, "Our commander will always have an eye for profit. But we must be sure to destroy anything that we cannot carry away with us — our purpose is to cripple the Spanish army for lack of supplies. Also, the manner of dividing any spoil is laid out in this document." Here, he picked up a sheet of paper and began to read:

"whatsoever commodity in goods, money, treasure, merchandise or other benefit . . . shall happen to be taken by all or any of the aforesaid ships or their company either by land or sea, shall be equally proportioned, man for man and ton for ton, [and will] be divided at sea . . . as soon as wind and weather will permit . . ."

"Which means," Foxe explained, "that every man aboard this ship will get the same share as every man on any other ship. There is no advantage for any captain to pursue a prize on his own because he will have to share it equally with everyone else. It is the same for us — we can hope for no financial benefit by taking some initiative on our own — we are under orders, and will remain so until released from service." No one voiced any complaints. There were a few nods.

They saw no land for more than a week. Roger was assigned to assist Homer with the navigation, which he was still getting the hang of. He noticed one thing, though. "We're not bound for Lisbon," he said.

"How's that?" asked Homer.

"Our latitude is all wrong. Lisbon is at latitude 38 degrees, according to this chart. We're already south of that unless my navigation — and yours — is completely wrong."

Homer looked surprised. "The Captain must hear of this! Ask him to come hither at once!"

When Foxe arrived, Homer let Roger explain what he had found. Roger showed the charts with their latitude. Homer stood back, his arms folded, with a look of pride. "He's found us out, Captain. I told you he wouldn't be fooled for long."

Roger looked at both of them. "Fooled? Why? How long have you known? Where are we actually headed?"

"Homer informed me just days ago," replied Foxe. "I told him not to mention it to anyone, and he predicted that the secret could not get by ye. He was right. As for where we are bound, neither of us knows — we follow the Admiral's flagship. Yer guess as to our destination is as good as anyone's. We could be approaching Lisbon roundabout, from the south. Or maybe the Admiral's navigator is giving him bad information."

Roger shook his head. "If Lisbon is our destination, the quicker we get there, the better. Admiral Drake must surely realize that. And all the navigators on all the ships in this squadron would have to be wrong, in order for him not to be aware of this discrepancy. We must be heading for some destination south of Lisbon, and secretly."

Foxe nodded. Homer laughed, "I told you! The lad is sharp, and pays attention to the details."

"So, clever lad," said Foxe, "where might we be headed?"

"When does the treasure fleet from America arrive in Spain? Could we be trying to intercept it?"

"A good idea, but we're too early, by months."

"Some port further south then. Attack a smaller force, instead of all three hundred ships that the King of Spain is supposed to have gathered in Lisbon?"

"I like the sound of that," replied Foxe. "We'll know when we get there. Meanwhile, not a word of this to anyone, understand?"

Roger nodded, more than a little pleased with himself for seeing through the deception before the rest of the crew.

"Report to the first mate," ordered Foxe. "Tell him to conduct an inspection of the whole ship with the new boatswain, and you. Tell him that I want you to become familiar with the duties that a boatswain must perform — in detail." Roger excused himself.

"I told you the lad was nearly ready," said Homer. "By the end of this voyage, he could serve as navigator on this ship, or any other."

"He's not yet fifteen. Needs more seasoning."

"That's as may be. Giving him a different assignment right now won't season him any faster. Why the boatswain?"

Foxe looked at Homer. "Because I have bigger things in mind for him. A man of eighteen, who knows navigation, and how a ship must be maintained, Who knows how to drive a bargain, and recognize an opportunity, who knows gunnery, and can command the respect of other men? That man . . ."

". . . can be master of a ship like this, one day," Homer finished his sentence. He nodded. "You are thinking of his future. And maybe your own, as well?"

"How's that?"

"Giving up a command like this is a hard thing. Easier maybe, to leave her in the hands of someone that you trust?"

"And why would ye suppose that I want to give up command?"

"It is in your eyes, your speech, and your manner. Men who have sailed with you before see a different man. I think you may be on your last voyage. I am not the only one aboard who thinks so."

Foxe grunted. *Last voyage? Ye'd better hope not!* "If that is true, ye should be looking to yer own lives, then. Perhaps ye have made a mistake, to sail with me for the last time?"

"Mistake or not, we would not sail under another man's command. Not this time."

Foxe shook his head. "No more of this prattle, then. What will be, will be." He knew that Homer was right — his mood was different on this voyage. Perhaps it *would* be his last. Perhaps it was foreboding . . .

Their course turned eastward the next morning. Two days later, the lookout sighted land. Roger identified their location as "Spain. Cadiz, from our latitude." The squadron hove to, and Captain Foxe was summoned to the Admiral's flagship, along with the other commanders. There was a sharp discussion about the next course, but Drake overruled his dissenters and ordered an immediate attack. It was April 29, 1587.

Cadiz was a major seaport on Spain's Atlantic coast. The city itself perched on a peninsula that projected into the Atlantic. The harbor was "behind" the city proper to the east. The harbor mouth opened to the north and west and tapered to a narrow "throat," beyond which lay a shallower inner harbor. "Looks a bit like Cartagena, only backward," said Roger.

"Aye," agreed Homer. "But the city is surrounded by strong walls, and there's no way to get into the outer harbor without passing under those guns." As if on cue, puffs of smoke appeared at the city walls, as Drake's galleons led the line of English ships into the harbor.

Upon entering the outer harbor, Foxe saw some sixty ships at anchor. "I like these odds better," he declared. The odds improved as some twenty ships, flying French flags, weighed anchor, and fled to the open sea. Half a dozen Dutchmen followed them. The harbor mouth was congested by ships entering and fleeing, all the while braving the bombardment from the shore batteries. Foxe grunted with satisfaction, "Better and better!" The Spanish vessels sought the protection of the guns of the shore fortifications, or fled to the inner harbor, to the southeast. Then the battle began in earnest.

Drake anchored the bulk of his ships in the outer harbor, just out of range of the guns on the city wall, where they could prevent any escape by the Spanish vessels. Then, he ordered lines of his ships to swoop forward, singling out one Spanish ship at a time, to bombard them into surrender. The darkness made the English ships harder to target from the shore — the cannons on the wall scored very few hits.

The *Egyptian Queen's* turn came soon enough. Foxe ordered all of Cooper's soldiers up on deck, sheltered under the gunwales. "We can't let them board us," explained Foxe, "that's the only thing that could save them." As he prepared a raking broadside, the lookout cried out — "galley on the starboard!"

Roger peered into the darkness. A flash of light from the shore batteries, and there she was, off the starboard side, and closing fast, her oars glinting in the light from shore, a faint gleam of the foam from every stroke.

"She's trying to ram us!" cried Foxe, "Hard to starboard! Mr. Benby! Let me hear those ladies speak!"

The *Queen* made the turn with seventy yards to spare; she was now approaching the galley on a parallel course. The galley began to veer toward the port side as if preparing to "cross the T," and deliver a broadside to the *Queen's* bow. She didn't quite make it, before Mary and Martha belched, and sent their 8-inch cannon balls smashing into the galley. A taller vessel might have overshot the galley at this range, but Benby had wedged his gun carriages to aim low — and the *Queen's* guns were mounted lower than a galleon's, anyway. Roger saw wood splinters flung into the air, even as the two vessels continued to close the distance. Evidently, the oarsmen on the galley's port side took the most punishment, because the galley now began to pivot to her port, as the rowers on her starboard were now rowing more strongly. Now it was the *Queen's* turn to "cross the T": "Mr Benby! Hard to port! Broadside on the starboard!" shouted Foxe. And it was so; all ten of the starboard culverins found their target, one after the other. The galley was dead in the water now, flames visible.

The *Queen* was now out of position to continue the attack on her original target — and vulnerable, as it turned out. A cannonball (either from shore or from another vessel — impossible to say, in the dark and smoke), struck the quarter-deck and sent chunks of wood flying. Captain Billy Foxe went down, in a twisted heap. Roger scrambled over to him — he wasn't conscious. "Help me with the Captain!" He cried. Two seamen joined him and carried Foxe to his cabin. Reuben Cox, now in command, ordered the *Queen* to fire another broadside in the direction of the Spanish ships, and retired to the safety of the anchorage, to the east.

Throughout the night, the English attacked the ships at anchor, setting several of them afire, and boarding a few others. Once captured, the Spanish ships were sailed or towed to the safety of the outer harbor, where their cargoes were transferred to Drake's ships, or simply destroyed. The Spanish defenders were not idle while this was happening, but their counterattack with the armed galleys did little more than annoy the English, although they did recapture one of their vessels, and take the English prize crew captive.

In the morning, Captain Foxe regained consciousness. He had a gash on the side of his head and a headache. He insisted on taking back command of his ship.

As the tide ebbed, the English backed into deeper water, then renewed the attack with smaller vessels through the next day. The *Egyptian Queen*, with her shallow draft, was ordered to lead the rest into the mass of Spanish vessels in the inner harbor. The major risk was that she would run aground; none of the smaller vessels had gunnery to match hers. Foxe contented himself with standing off and battering the Spanish from a distance, and let the smaller English vessels board the prizes, and dispose of their cargoes. There was a small, fortified island in the inner harbor, that kept up a troublesome fire on all the English ships, but that did not prevent them from seizing or sinking everything they found. Once a ship was boarded, they took what they could of the cargo and set the ship afire. The fight continued throughout the day.

In the afternoon, the Spanish asked for a truce, to exchange prisoners. The prize crew captured during the night was returned, along with several English galley slaves.

When the truce was concluded, the fighting was renewed. The second night was much like the first — continuous attacks and counterattacks, persistent, but ineffective bombardment from the shore batteries.

When the squadron put to sea on May 1st, Drake claimed to have sunk or captured nearly forty Spanish ships of various sizes; he added four of them to his flotilla, just to handle the loot. Once at sea, they lurked off the West coast of Portugal for the next two months, seizing any ship that they could. By the time his ships returned to England, as many as one hundred vessels had been sunk or captured.

The core of Spain's invasion fleet had not been touched, but the disruption of war supplies was sufficient to delay the invasion for a year. English losses were small.

Aboard the *Egyptian Queen*, the damage turned out to be surprisingly minor. Captain Foxe was the most seriously injured member of the crew. True to their agreement, Drake's squadron hove to on a calm day, out of sight of land, to divide the plunder. The *Queen's* share came to twelve pounds per man — no great fortune, but enough to satisfy anyone. The more surprising fact was that so few had lost their lives. The *Egyptian Queen* was not the only ship in the flotilla without a single loss of life.

June 15, 1587: Parade Day

The training of the Felsted pikemen had proceeded more or less as planned. They missed a session or two when the weather on a Saturday afternoon was particularly foul, but the drilling continued, and the company improved dramatically. John Porter began to feel some pride in how the men performed. He no longer feared that they would accidentally skewer one another, as they performed their intricate maneuvers. Even Sir Walter Clive complimented his work: "You've done a fair enough job with this lot," he allowed. "We'll hold a Grand Parade next month, so you can put them through their paces. They're ready for the command of a real officer, I think."

A real officer. Well, that's to be expected, I suppose, thought John. It wasn't bad news, exactly — he had been looking for a way out of his drillmaster job since the first day. Still, he had some sort of proprietary feeling about these men; it was hard to think of turning them over to some stranger, who might spend their lives carelessly or even mistreat them . . .

Christopher Popham had kept his word about the training of the arquebusiers. He drilled them until they could shoot, reload, shoot again, reload, and shoot a third volley in the space of a minute — good enough for mercenaries — and the best hope these men had of standing up to a Spanish attack. All this shooting, of course, could not be done on the village green without hazard to the villagers, so Popham had set up a shooting range on a remote part of the Baron's estate, where errant bullets would not be a problem. His men still called him "Popinjay" behind his back, but they followed his orders and John could tell that they felt some pride in their accomplishments.

Near the end of May, the Baron sent a welcome gift to his militia company — two small cannons with 3-inch muzzles. John was excited. "This will make them think twice before they take us on," he confided to Popham. Clive was not impressed: "Big guns, that can only be fired once every two minutes, or so. On the battlefield, you'll get off one round, no more."

"Then we'll have to make it a good one," said John. He spent the following week building field carriages for the guns, and a small caisson for the shot and powder. At their last drill before the Grand Parade, he presented the field guns to the company. The men were curious; he detailed six of them to learn to load and fire the guns. They decided to name the guns "Baron" and "Baroness," in honor of their donors. John had the "Baron" hitched behind Gordon, and the "Baroness" behind Old Bob — towing them was no great burden for either horse. The caisson was towed by the gun crews.

John ordered the arquebusiers to form up — four ranks of ten each. "Each of you will surrender his shot to me," he said, "We'll have no live fire on the village green, under any circumstances. Understood?"

"Aye, Sir!" was the reply. That done, he formed the pikemen in ranks of five, and arranged a single file of arquebusiers on either side. He then marched them through the village, the drum beating and their guidon flying, down the road toward the Baron's Manor, and the artillery in the rear. When they got in sight of the Manor House, he had them countermarch and return to the village. It was a pleasant afternoon, not hot; the men were in a good mood. At the green, he gave the order to form a square — this was the trickiest maneuver he had taught them, and this was the first time they had attempted it with the arquebusiers, and the artillery. He hoped they could handle it.

It went as smoothly as he could have hoped. In less than a minute, they had formed a hollow square, pikes pointed outward, with the artillery and the arquebusiers inside the hollow, also facing outward on each side. They were pleased with themselves, so much so that they roared in mock ferocity.

Then the arquebusiers fired over the heads of the men in front — and men flinched, ducked and crouched in surprise. John ordered them to attention. "You'll have to get used to the sound of firearms, if you expect to prevail in a real battle," he said. "Master Popham, another volley, please!"

At the second volley, the pikemen stood their ground. "Imagine that the arquebusier behind you is mowing down the enemy in front of you," suggested John. "It's less alarming."

Sir Walter had been observing the maneuver at a distance, and rode up on his horse: "A good idea, to get them used to the noise," he said, "that's often the hardest thing for green troops to tolerate." John bowed slightly, to acknowledge the compliment.

He dismissed them early, except for the field gun crews. He enlisted Popham to help him walk thru the loading drill. This was something that John felt confident about — he had trained with the best, on board the *Egyptian Queen*. The drill was a little different, because the guns did not have to be run in and run out again. That would make the loading quicker. At each firing, of course, there would be recoil — but not so very much with a 3-inch gun. When he was satisfied that they had the hang of it, he had them actually fire each one — without any shot in the chamber. The noise was enough to draw men out of the pub, to see what was happening. Through the smoke, he saw the wadding fly halfway across the green; he sent a crewman to fetch it — waste not, want not.

The guns were cleaned, and sent back to the armory at the manor, along with the artillery; once delivered, John brought Gordon and Old Bob home with him. Tomorrow was Sunday. Another week was beginning.

His status in the village had changed over the past several months. Once the native son returned, now he was mostly recognized as the village drill master — a respected man in the community. His carpentry business had prospered over the winter, but now he needed to spend more time in the fields with his father. He still had his eye out for some small farm that he could buy, with a barn or shed that he could run his carpentry business out of.

Mostly, his thoughts were with Sybil Vessey. He had gotten away to visit her at least once a month, and the wedding date was set, just before harvest. If responsibility for the company was indeed passing to another, the timing couldn't have been better . . .

And then there were the Sunday afternoon conventicles. He was not always in attendance, but that did not seem to matter. More frequently than not, he found his way there. It was hard to explain what drew him; something about the simplicity of the group made his faith feel more authentic, more vital. Something was here that the liturgy could not replicate. And so he was drawn back again and again. He felt close to these people, in a way different from his feeling for his family. It was a closeness, he decided, that had to do with the fact that everyone in attendance was there voluntarily — no law or tie of blood required them to be there; it was purely a matter of a calling, or a yearning for the things of God. It felt freer than almost anything else he did in a week — and more satisfying, more purposeful. Maybe, he decided, this is how things would feel in heaven . . .

The day of the parade was overcast and breezy. That was fine with John, as he was dressed in all the weaponry that he had — the morion, the Jack, his cutlass, two pistols and the snaphance. None of his firearms were loaded. He met Sir Walter on the green, before the assembly; Christopher Popham was there as well, a plume atop his helmet.

"There's a change in plan," announced Sir Walter. "We're to form on either side of the road from the Manor, so that His Lordship may ride past us in review and take his seat on the platform. We'll follow his train onto the green and perform our maneuvers there. I'm told we'll have some special guests in attendance."

"Best we look sharp, then," said Popham. "How many volleys should we fire?"

"Three volleys will show how rapidly you can fire," said John. "No shot — only wadding and powder, understood?"

Popham smiled and nodded. "That will make the loading faster — one less step in the drill — maybe we could try for four?

"Alright, four then. Enough powder and wadding for three loads, plus the load already in the gun."

At mid-morning, they assembled the company on the green, dressed ranks, and began their march down the road toward the manor. John put the pikemen in a column two abreast, with the arquebusiers to the outside, forming a "sleeve." When he calculated that they had gone far enough down the road, he halted them and ordered them to stand beside the road, facing it on either side. The color guard and the drummer formed as the "front" of the column. Sir Walter, who had been riding his horse in full armor, stood in the road, as if in review. He nodded his satisfaction, then blew a horn.

Moments later, the Baron appeared with his entourage. He was accompanied by his wife, the Baroness, his uncle, Sir Richard Rich, and a handful of other servants, all mounted. The Baron and his wife nodded acknowledgement to the pikemen and arquebusiers as they passed. Once the cavalcade was well down the road, John ordered the color guard to wheel back behind them down the road, between the ranks on either side. Sir Walter led the procession, looking splendid in his ancient, but polished armor.

The column was halfway back down its length, now. John could see the artillery and the caissons just ahead. There was a commotion in the rear; he ordered a halt. A dozen or more horsemen were pushing down the road in their direction, cursing and shouting at the pikemen to "Make way! Make way for the cavalry!" John stepped to one side; Sir Walter did the same, opposite.

The horsemen were on them now, their horses were lathered. The leader of the group appeared to be a young man on a white horse, armored in the modern style: a cuirass (breast plate) with tassets and a plumed helmet, and swinging a sword as if he intended to strike the pikemen with the flat of the blade. John resented him, immediately. The young man halted long enough to address Sir Walter: "I am Cedric, son of Sir Edward Pike. I demand that you clear this rabble from the road, so that my men may pass!"

Sir Walter was deferential. "I know your father, Cedric. We were not expecting you. Give us a moment to clear the way. Looking to John, he said, "Drillmaster! Dress your ranks!"

John bit his tongue and ordered the pikemen off the road. The rest of the cavalry thundered by, in a whirl of dust and horse manure. As the last horseman passed, John overheard Sir Walter mutter: "Young jackass!"

It took a moment to form ranks again and get underway. The resentment in the ranks was palpable, and it didn't help that the road ahead was littered with steaming, fresh "road apples." John felt that the morale of his men had taken a beating — and this on the day that was supposed to be their showcase! His face must have shown his mood, because Christopher Popham stepped up alongside, and said, "Do not trouble yourself with that fool. Concentrate on leading the men, and they will follow you, as you have trained them." John nodded, grimly.

He halted the company just outside the village and reformed them into a column five men abreast, not counting the "sleeve" of arquebusiers. Then it was into the village, and onto the green across from the church.

He ordered the column to split into two, both five abreast, and then joined them into a single square, ten ranks, ten abreast, with the color guard in front, and the artillery and the arquebusiers behind. Sir Walter left the column and joined the dignitaries on a reviewing platform just built for the purpose. As the square passed the reviewing platform, each rank turned their faces to the right, as a salute to the Baron and his companions. The salute was returned. John began to feel more confident and relaxed a little.

When they reached the edge of the green, he wheeled them left, still in a square, along the northern edge. When they reached the next corner, he simply ordered them to left face, and march back southward: they did it perfectly — each column became a rank, each rank a column. The arquebusiers and the artillery had to scramble to take up the rear, but John thought the Baron should be impressed.

Halfway across the far edge of the green, John ordered another left face, followed by a maneuver to form two ranks, fifty men wide, with the arquebusiers posted front and rear, as in a battle line. At his command, the front rank planted their pikes in the ground, facing forward, and the second rank hoisted theirs overhead. It was all done smoothly and quickly. John was satisfied. Just for punctuation, he ordered the four volleys from Popham's arquebusiers, which was reassuringly crisp and rapid. He wondered if anyone on the platform realized just how important that part of the demonstration was . . .

Sir Walter stood on the platform and waved them forward. John ordered the company to advance, steadily, with pikes forward. An intimidating sight, or so he hoped.

They were just short of the middle of the green, when John noticed a flash of steel on his right. Young Cedric and his companions were there, waving their swords in his direction, as if they would charge. Very well, the men were trained for this scenario, too. As the horsemen surged forward, the ranks became a hollow square, pikes facing outward, artillery and arquebusiers in the center. It happened more quickly than Cedric and his lads expected, and the range of a sixteen-foot pike was longer than they anticipated. Their horses barely avoided a collision with a pincushion of steel; several riders nearly lost their seats in the confusion. The cavalry tried again, from a different direction, then from a different angle, with the same result. John began to smile. He could feel the confidence in the men. "I wish to God I'd held back just one round for every arquebus," said Popham; "That would give 'em a surprise!" The men murmured their assent, and a few laughed.

After a dozen sorties, the cavalry paused, their horses snorting. Young Cedric rode to the reviewing stand and appeared to be speaking to the Baron. After a while, Sir Walter left the stand, mounted his horse, and rode over to the pike square, followed by Young Cedric. "The Baron requests that your men hold their pikes at stand, the next time the cavalry charges, so that Cedric's men can approach closely, without peril."

"How closely?" asked John. "I fear that if they get too close, some injury to my men may result."

Cedric snorted. "These are gentlemen, accomplished in the saddle. We won't be trampling any of these farmers. Even if we do, that is a small matter. What matters is that my men get the training that they need, before we go to war!"

"It would be easier for us if we knew from which direction this 'attack' is going to come," said John, in an even tone. "It is hard for so many riders to approach a formation as tight as this one." His sarcasm was lost on Cedric; Sir Walter raised an eyebrow.

"Excellent point," said Cedric. "You should array yourselves in a battle line. We will attack from the south." He rode back to join his companions at the south end of the green.

Sir Walter was looking curiously at John: "Cedric's father is a friend of the Baron, and the Baron owes him a favor. Cedric just called it in. I must say, you're being mighty sporting about all this," he said, "I thought you might resist the Baron's request."

"The Baron's requests are the Baron's requests," replied John. "What choice do we have?"

"Quite so," replied Sir Walter, and trotted his horse back to the viewing platform.

Every man in the square had overheard the conversation; there was no need to explain what was going to happen next. The pikemen formed two ranks, fifty men abreast, facing southward. John posted half his arquebusiers in front, with orders to retreat back into the cover of the pikes, when the cavalry got close enough. Except that there would be no cover from the pikes, this time. A test of discipline, perhaps; that was the best face he could put on it . . .

A trumpet blared, and the line of cavalry moved forward, at a gallop. The arquebusiers waited for Popham's command to "fire," pretended to do so, and then stepped back into the ranks of pikemen, who stood their ground. John heard Popham order the arquebusiers in the rear to "fire" as well — might as well go through the motions . . .

And then there was an explosion of sound. The horses in front of him bolted and bucked, at least five riders were on the ground. Smoke rolled in, obscuring his view, for a moment. He realized that someone had fired both cannons directly at the gentlemen. When the smoke cleared, the riders that were still mounted were heading helter-skelter to the south end of the green; some didn't stop there but kept on going. The five gentlemen on the ground slowly got to their feet. Among them was Young Cedric, and, once he collected himself, he appeared to be angry. He stalked toward John, with a red face — a little smudged with soot, but still recognizably red.

"You should be ashamed of yourselves!" he shouted. "Cowards, all of you! Can't stand your ground, without stooping to some low-born trick! I'd challenge you to a duel of honor, but there isn't a gentleman among you worthy of the killing!"

"There is one." John heard the voice from behind him, calm, steady.

"Who dares?" demanded Cedric.

Christopher Popham stepped out from between the ranks. "I am the third son of Sir Francis Popham," he said. "Does that bloodline meet your requirement?"

"It does, sir!" exclaimed Cedric, and pulled the glove from his right hand, throwing it at Popham's feet. "Name the place, the time, and your weapons!"

Popham drew the rapier from his side and picked up the glove with the point of it. "Here," he said. "Now. With this weapon." There was murmuring from the pikemen, more from the arquebusiers.

Cedric was clearly surprised by this turn of events, but he threw off his other gauntlet, and peeled off his tassets and cuirass, with some help from one of his companions. John stepped forward to help Popham do the same. "A rapier!" demanded Cedric, and one of his party supplied it for him. Both men faced off, clad in their breeches and shirts. This would be a gentleman's fight.

The company stood in silence as the whole scene unfolded. The party on the viewing stand was silent, as well. John thought the Baron might intervene and forbid them from fighting, but no . . .

The two circled each other for a bit, then crossed swords a few times, each testing his opponent. John got a sense fairly quickly that Cedric had bitten off more than he bargained for. Popham appeared to be quicker, smoother, more confident. *He has done this before*, John realized, *a gentleman's third son with no inheritance, but trained in combat, nonetheless.* He wondered if

Popham had ever killed a man, this way. Cedric was probably wondering the same thing . . .

It was clear with every thrust and parry that Popham was the more skilled. Cedric's lunges became more awkward, his parries more desperate. Before long, he was slashing his blade from side to side, as he retreated — might have worked with a cutlass, but useless against the narrow steel blade of Popham's rapier. There was a certain terrifying beauty in the focused precision of Popham's attack. In the end, Cedric got his feet crossed and tripped himself. He tried to roll out of the way, but Popham was on him like a bird of prey, pinning Cedric's blade to the ground with his foot, and resting his rapier's point on Cedric's throat. "Sir! Are you satisfied?" demanded Popham.

"Yes, I am satisfied," he replied.

"I don't think they can hear you on the viewing platform," said Popham, just tickling Cedric's throat with the tip of the blade.

"Yes! I am satisfied!" Cedric shouted. Popham stepped back and sheathed his sword. "Then allow me to help you to your feet, Sir," he said and offered his hand. Cedric stood, looking sullen, and walked back to his companions.

It was Jed Bones, holding the Baron's banner, who shouted "Popinjay!" at the top of his lungs. "Hurrah!" responded the company, in unison, then "Popinjay! Hurrah! Popinjay! Hurrah!" A moment of triumph for the whole company of men — his men, John thought, his men. Vindicated and from an unexpected source. Whatever the Baron might think of their parade, he was satisfied that they had done their duty.

"Company dismissed!" he ordered. The men cheered again and then, incredibly, seized Christopher Popham and carried him on their shoulders in the direction of the pub. Popham appeared to be more surprised than anyone. John looked at the viewing platform. Let the Baron chew on that for a while. A man on a horse blocked his view — it was Sir Walter Clive.

"Well, Drillmaster, you've had your fun today."

John couldn't help smiling. "Aye, great fun."

"I will admit that you were right about one thing, and I was wrong," said Sir Walter. "The artillery. Very effective. We need more such guns."

"Does the Baron agree, do you think?"

"Hard to say what the Baron's opinion is, on any matter. But he certainly got an eyeful today."

"I half thought the Baron might put a stop to that duel just now, especially since his servant was put at risk."

"The Baron employs many servants, with many diverse skills. He did not fear for Mr. Popham's life, and he trusted that Mr. Popham would know better than to kill young Cedric. And now that the Baron's debt to Cedric's father is paid, his Lordship has reason to be well pleased with the outcome. The Baron would like to have a word with you."

Ah. Here it comes. John took off his morion and held it under his arm, as he approached the viewing platform. The Baron was still seated there, with his wife, his uncle, and their attendants. John bowed, as he approached them.

"Mr Porter, you have proved yourself a drillmaster. The men performed well today. Unfortunate business about the artillery though, wouldn't you agree?"

John bowed again. "It was a regrettable misunderstanding, Your Lordship. I did not train them for a situation like that. I authorized Mr. Popham to fire imaginary volleys at the cavalry — imaginary because I knew they had no ammunition — just to get the timing down, in case they ever have to face a real cavalry charge. It did not occur to me that the cannons were still loaded — although we took care that none of the firearms in the parade had any shot in their breeches. The only thing that was 'fired' at the gentlemen was the wadding. The fault is mine."

The Baron's uncle chuckled. The Baron himself struggled to keep a straight face. John realized he was trying to suppress a laugh. "Do not be troubled, Mr. Porter. Some entertainments cannot be planned in advance."

John was half hoping that the Baron would be angry and dismiss him from his service immediately. Apparently, this would not be the case. "I think my service to you is completed, this day," he offered hopefully.

"I agree that you have trained them, as requested. However, they still need an officer to command them and lead them into battle."

John nodded. "Yes. It should be a gentleman; a doughty man; someone they respect and will follow into danger." John turned to where the men of the company were still celebrating Popham's victory. "I think," said John, "that such a man is already in your service."

The Baron raised both eyebrows and looked across the green. "You may be correct. If I release you from your duties, what will you do?"

"I intend to be married this year, to a maid in Little Baddow, over near Chelmsford. I hope to make our home here in Felsted."

"And if the war comes to us, here in Felsted?"

"Then I will take my place in the ranks, along with my countrymen."

The Baron nodded. "Consider yourself released, then."

John bowed and excused himself before Lord Rich could change his mind. He hoped his delight was not obvious. By tomorrow, he intended to be on the road to Little Baddow.

July, 1587: Harwich

The *Egyptian Queen* sailed into Harwich in mid-July. Foxe summoned Fairchild and paid off the crew for three months' wages the same afternoon. Then they were gone — the men's share of the plunder had already been paid out, and Fairchild and Grimes would haggle over what was in the hold. "A very lucky voyage, Captain," said Benby.

Foxe grunted and nodded. "Aye. Very lucky."

"And yet, I see in your eyes that something has shifted in you. That reminder of your mortality that you got in Cadiz, perhaps?"

Foxe pursed his lips and looked at Benby. "It is not death I fear, Dick. But something on this voyage has made me think about my life, my purpose. It does not please me, to think my life might end on the deck of a ship. It feels hollow, somehow unfinished. It makes me restless."

"You have been a restless man, as long as I have known you."

"That's true, Dick. That's true." Roger approached, "Captain! Shall we go home, now?"

Foxe started, just a little. Home. He had a home to go to. "Aye, lad. Home it is!"

Harriet Frye greeted them both with excitement and relief. She hugged Roger as if she wouldn't let go, and when he pried himself loose, she curtsied to Foxe. "Welcome home, Captain!" Then it was the boys's turn, to throw their arms around him, attempting to wrestle him to the ground.

Foxe laughed. "Easy there, lads! I'm a wounded veteran of the war!"

Harriet's face wore a look of concern. "Wounded?"

"It's no great matter. Struck by some splintered railing. I'm recovered, now."

"Lucky, I say," said Roger. "Could have taken his head off!"

Harriet's expression turned to horror. Foxe shot Roger a look of annoyance. "No need to trouble yer mum, that way." Turning to Harriet, he said, "It was no closer to my head than many others. We lost no men in any of the battles we fought. So yes, we were lucky — all of us."

Harriet wiped away a tear. "I'm grateful to have ye both home in one piece," she said. "I'll get some dinner ready." She bustled out of the room.

Foxe turned to Roger: "It's cruel to frighten yer mum that way. Some things she doesn't need to know about."

"Some things she deserves to know, even if they frighten her. This is not our last battle. The Spanish will be coming, sooner or later, and both of us will be in harm's way!"

"Both of us? You presume too much, lad."

"I'll either be sailing with you, or with someone else. The nation requires that every man do his duty."

Every man? Thought Foxe. *Ye're a man, then are ye?* He decided not to ask that question out loud. Roger had proved himself, no reason to question it. "I only wanted to spare yer mum the worry," he said.

"She is stronger than you imagine," said Roger. "She needs the truth, more than false hope, especially when it comes to people she cares for."

"I have never suggested to her that sailing with me was without risk. I merely promised to take care of you as best I can."

"It's not only my safety she was fearing for."

"She knows I am an old sea dog, with few enough years left to me. Ye're the focus of her worry, not me."

"If you truly believe that, you've not been paying attention."

"What? What do ye mean?"

Roger shook his head. "I've said all I have to say."

It was evening, two days later, that Harriet Frye approached Billy Foxe as he sat before the fireplace, warming his feet. It was summer, yet he found it harder to keep warm enough these days. His extremities, especially his feet, were prone to chill. *Next thing you know, ye'll be needin' a lap robe, old dog*, he told himself.

"Are ye feeling ill, Captain?"

"Nay, just a little chilly. No reason to worry over me."

Harriet looked at his eyes. "But I do worry. I worry that ye may be going to sea, again."

Foxe smiled. "It's no great matter. I have arranged for yer needs to be taken care of, should any misfortune befall me."

"I know that, and I am grateful — more than I can put into words. But we would miss ye, more than I want to think about, if ye should fail to return."

"We?"

"Aye. Roger regards ye as a son does his father. The girls adore ye, and the other two want nothing more than to be around ye."

Foxe nodded. He had found a new life, with these children; his heart was eased when he was among them. He had not much considered what his presence felt like to them.

"And I," added Harriet, "I have become more than fond of ye. Ye have no idea how my life has changed, since we moved into this house. It is not just that the struggle to feed and clothe my children is eased by yer generosity; I feel that I have a partner now, in preparing them for a life of their own. I have hope for more than just the present day, now; I see a future for my family." She looked as if she were about to cry.

Foxe was touched by her sentiment. "There now, Mrs. Frye. Don't be cryin' over me. I won't be going to sea, until I am summoned."

"But you will be summoned. Is there no way that you can be spared?"

Her plaintive tone touched and alarmed him a little. Women and their feelings had always seemed like an insoluble mystery, to him. That was true with his wife, so many years ago. It was a relief to be at sea, really, which was probably why . . . He collected himself. What had Roger said? '*She needs the truth, rather than false hope*' . . . "The nation's need is very great. I do not think she can spare me, or any other man of the sea, in her hour of need."

Harriet nodded, sniffled a bit. "God protect ye then, for my sake, and my children's."

Foxe was about to remind her that Roger would be in as much peril as he but realized that that would not be a comfort to her, just now. Women. Feelings. Too much.

He tried to change the subject. "Now that ye are a widow in the eyes of the law, have ye thought that ye might remarry?"

Harriet shook her head. "Have you?"

"Have I what?"

"Have you considered that ye might remarry?"

Foxe snorted. "What, an old dog like me? Learn to live like an honest man again, with a wife and responsibilities? Who would have me?"

Harriet looked him in the eye. "I would."

It was an offer, Foxe realized, and it had caught him unprepared. It lay there between them as if there were a log of wood on the floor between them, waiting to be fed to the fire in the fireplace. Careful; a man could get burned.

Foxe cleared his throat. "Harriet, I am not a young man. I have not may years left on this earth."

"Nor have I," said Harriet, "In case you haven't noticed."

"Nay, say not so! Ye're a lively, handsome woman, as I have often noticed. What would ye gain by marrying the likes of me?"

"Gain? I would gain nothing, I suppose, unless the companionship and care of a man counts for something. Or maybe a yokefellow, to share the load. Does it have to be about gain?"

Foxe was nonplussed. This was not where he had intended the conversation to go. But suddenly, marrying Harriet Frye seemed like a very sensible thing to do. He realized that his life in this house had all the features of married life — except one. She was indeed a handsome, lively woman — no question about that. "You have given me reason to reflect," he said. "My feet are warm now. I shall take a walk." He rose, excused himself. Harriet sat where she was and sighed. Perhaps she had spoken out of turn.

Billy Foxe was in the street before he had decided where he was going. *The Galleon*, perhaps. No, he didn't feel like bantering with Danny Cornwall. *The Two Kingdoms*, then. Some of that stew that Caroline Benby sometimes made.

The pub was full. It took him a moment to find a place to sit. He was greeted by several men he knew, but Dick Benby was not to be seen. Might as well eat, then. By the time the stew was served, a handful of seamen had stopped at his table to greet him, ask questions, and offer to pay for his ale. He didn't have much news to offer them: the raid on Cadiz was a success — no secret, there. As to when he would be putting to sea again, that would depend on his investors, whose decisions would be influenced by the priorities of the government in London . . . Foxe did not add that he was in no hurry to be at sea again.

He was nearly finished eating, when Dick Benby found him. The *Two Kingdoms* was still packed with customers, but Benby pulled up a chair. "Something is on your mind, Captain," he said, looking hard at him.

"Aye, Dick, ye're a man of insight. Not much gets past ye."

"Do you want to talk about it?"

"Not sure that would help. I've a decision to make; one that affects a number of folk besides myself."

"You make decisions like that all the time when you're at sea. Why is this different?"

"This would be like taking command of a new ship, in strange waters, without a navigator, or even a chart. Not sure I've got the seamanship to bring her safe to port."

"Ah. A woman, then. I thought as much before we sailed." Benby grinned and shook his head. "Are you afraid the lady will refuse you?"

"Nay, that's the devil in it. She's made her position quite clear. Pressed the point, ye might say."

"So, she's willing to back this voyage? Is the cargo a problem?"

"Aye, she's willing, even eager, ye might say. And nay, the cargo is no problem — the sweetest part of the voyage, ye might say."

"What is holding you back? No crew?"

"Oh, there's a crew, alright. A fine lot. Happy to sail with them. I'm thinking they might deserve a better captain — one not so near the end of his rope, so to speak."

"Captains are hard enough to find, good ones harder. Is there another you would recommend for the job?"

Foxe shook his head. "None that I know of."

"If this doubt is because you think you may not return from your next voyage, answer me this: If you do die at sea, will these folk be better off, or worse off if you marry the woman?"

Foxe paused. "No worse off, I guess. Nor better, I suppose."

"And if you live another twenty years? Better off, or worse off?"

"Better, I think."

"In that case, I think you know everything you need to know to make your decision." Benby leaned back in his chair, arms folded across his chest. Smiling, maybe even smug, Foxe thought.

"Look at it this way, Captain. If things turn sour with your new wife, ye can always find somewhere else to be."

Foxe nodded and chuckled. A seaman's haven from domestic strife, the sea.

They were married two weeks later, in St. Nicholas' Church, near the waterfront. Harriet would have preferred a small service, but Captain Billy Foxe was a man with lots of friends, and a great many showed up; the sanctuary was full. Roger gave his mother away. Afterward, there was a reception, of sorts, in *The Galleon*, which was barely large enough to contain the crowd. The more prominent guests stayed just long enough to pay their respects to the bride and groom, then left. The remainder, mostly seamen, stayed longer and got a bit rowdy. The newlyweds slipped out the back before things got completely out of hand.

August 1587: Felsted

In the nick of time, John Porter had found a place that would be home for himself and Sybil. It was not quite what he had in mind, but it had the two things that he required — a small cottage, and a long, if narrow barn. It wasn't for sale: he had to rent it, for a pound per year, and it was in serious disrepair. There wasn't much land to go with the place either, but John needed to put a roof over his new family, as well as his growing business. The repairs he could manage himself — patched the roof, painted the inside of the house, replaced some missing siding on the barn. His sister Ellen helped him tidy the inside of the place, as well. It wasn't in Felsted proper, but only two miles from his parent's place — near a crossroads called Cobler's Green. This land was still part of the Rich family estate, and its availability had been mentioned to John by none other than Christopher Popham, the Baron's personal secretary. At one time, the farm had included forty acres of cropland with enough pasture to keep a few cows and sheep. When the previous tenant died, the Baron decided to "enclose" most of the acreage, turning it to pasture for sheep — more income than rent from farming would provide. That left the house, the barn, and enough land for a garden — they wouldn't be able to keep a cow unless they bought the fodder from someone else. Sybil said she wouldn't miss the milking; she could keep a flock of chickens for — well, chicken feed — and buy the milk and meat they would need, assuming that the carpentry business prospered. So far, it had.

Then there was the matter of furniture. John could build the most basic things — a bed frame, a dining table, and benches. Kitchen cabinetry was another matter — shelves would have to do, for a while. Sybil would be bringing an old chest of drawers, as part of her trousseau. John moved his clothing and other personal items into the cottage in mid-July. There was room in the barn for Gordon if need be, but it made more sense to stable him at John's parent's house, which was closer to the fields that he and his father were farming that year.

So, on many evenings, as well as occasional days, John worked alone, preparing the house for his bride or working on a carpentry job. He got some unexpected help from his future brother-in-law, Tom Vessey, who appeared one Saturday morning with some hardware for the cottage — new hinges for the front door, and a lock, a few other useful bits of ironmongery. John was glad for the help and invited him for dinner at his parent's farm. Tom stayed overnight there and went to church in the morning with the rest of the Porters. Fortunately, he had thought to bring a change of clothes, suitable for church attendance with him. John lost track of him after the service for a while; Ellen went missing at about the same time. They both showed up for Sunday Supper back at the house. John gave Ellen a quizzical look, but she ignored him. After supper, Tom Vessey headed back to Braintree.

John confronted Ellen outside after Tom Vessey left: "Is there something I should know about you and Tom?"

"I can't think of anything," she replied dismissively.

"I mean, is he courting you? Flirting?"

"What if he is? I can't see how that's any business of yours."

"If someone is courting you, I think I should know."

"If a man wished to court me, he would speak to Papa about it, not you."

Fair point. Still, "But Tom is about to become my brother-in-law. Don't you think I should know about something like this?"

"No, not really. You're not marrying him, are you?"

John said nothing. He liked Tom Vessey. Ellen could do worse than marry a successful blacksmith. It would be a good match, actually, from a financial point of view. He wasn't sure that Tom, or any man, for that matter, could be happily married to a woman like his sister — merciless wit, sharp tongue, always the last word. He wouldn't get anywhere talking to Ellen about this; he would have to talk with Tom Vessey.

The opportunity came a few weeks later. Tom showed up at the new place with some more ironmongery for the new house, and the barn — on a Saturday, as it happened, so naturally he was invited to dinner, and to stay over and go to church with the Porters.

"Tom, I'm grateful for your help with this place," said John, not sure how to broach the subject that was on his mind.

"No trouble. It fell upon my sister to raise me, my brothers, and sisters. Giving her a comfortable home is the least I can do — not repayment in full, just a down payment on a new life."

"I suppose she'll be missed by your family, when she comes to live with me."

"I suppose. Better that she should have a life with you though, than die a spinster. Susan and Mary can take care of the place, now."

"Better for me, that is certain. I hope to be a good husband."

"You will find Sybil to be a good wife, I think, if you can learn to live with the strength of her will and her opinions."

John nodded and smiled. "I am learning. I have great admiration for her strength; it is one of the things I love most about her."

"You are a good match, I think. Not every man could say that, without lying. Not many would even pretend to prefer a woman with a mind of her own. A strong woman may wear a mask of meekness, to seem more appealing. Sybil is not that sort."

"No more than my sister, Ellen," John offered.

Tom looked surprised for a moment, then smiled and nodded. "Aye, no more than Ellen."

The conventicle at Holy Cross church continued to meet on Sunday afternoons, and John joined them more often than not. John found a sort of comfort there. He was not the only person in Felsted with doubts about the outcome of the war, he discovered. And many people faced poverty, loss, and fear in ways that he had no experience of. Yet there was hope as well, and courage, and genuine affection. Week by week, in a hundred small ways, there were testimonies to God's faithfulness as the day-to-day challenges of the people were solved, or remedied. The consensus was that Grace was active in their lives — an assertion that would have seemed hopelessly, rustically naive to better-educated men. But John found the idea comforting — his own experience was full of such testimonies.

There was another, darker side to this sense of God's oversight. A God who sent special blessings his way might well be a God who expected some unusual response from him as well — some task or purpose for his life, something difficult or costly, some sacrifice of his happiness — for the good of others, or even some unfathomable purpose that God alone understood. That possibility lurked in the back of his mind, and in the minds of others, as well.

For some, this tension produced a zeal to work harder, to excel, to improve in every way — to become more worthy of the blessings, better prepared for the sacrifices to come. For others, it led to despair.

Like many, John lived somewhere between the two extremes; sometimes dwelling upon the depth of his spiritual depravity(sound theology, that, though it left him vulnerable to the prideful notion that his discernment was deeper or purer than that of ordinary men), at other times absorbed in reflection upon the quality of his spiritual condition (which could lead to pride of a different sort). He exhorted himself to the pursuit of holiness in every detail of his life, in hope that he might be found worthy of the greater sacrifices — even as he feared what such sacrifice might entail.

On Mondays, and through the rest of the week, there was work to do. He was, after all, a carpenter — a man who could touch the fruit of his labors every day. Whether it be good or ill was simply a matter of skill and effort. On Sundays, and in the quiet of the night, in bed or at his prayers, John strove with the invisible and immaterial — to fear God, yet to trust him; to love life, but to love God above all; to receive grace, but never to presume upon it.

It did not help to be surrounded on every side by men and women, institutions and customs that regarded these matters as trivial or impractical. Thus, the comfort of the conventicle. Their government had declared them to be unlawful; the world was full of enemies who sought their extermination; temptations to frivolity and vice were everywhere. Their very souls were under siege:

"Loue not this world, neither the things that are in this world. If any man loue this world, the loue of the Father is not in him. For all that is in this world (as the lust of the flesh, the lust of the eyes, and the pride of life) is not of the Father, but is of this world. And this world passeth away, & the lust thereof: but he that fulfilleth the will of God, abideth euer." — so said the Apostle John.

It should have come as no surprise that the people who met on Sunday afternoons began to feel that they were living in a different reality than their fellow countrymen, or even that their religion was somehow more authentic than that of their neighbors; that they out of all people had been specially chosen for some holy purpose. They were the Elect, in the language of their minister; people chosen by God to serve him, through no merit of their own. God was sovereign in choosing some and rejecting others — there was no other explanation for it. Indeed, a man could not be certain that he or anyone else was truly chosen: it was the task of every believer to "make his election sure" by a life of devotion and discipline. They called themselves "visible saints" — members of the true, invisible church, called to make their election known to the wider world. Here and in places all over England, the "visible saints" "covenanted" with one another — in writing — to live godly and fruitful lives, to stand together in resisting the established church.

John's suggestion to the Baron about command of the Felsted company was apparently persuasive. The next time they assembled, Christopher Popham was identified as their 'Captain'. Drills were now held once a month, instead of twice. This gave John one less duty to perform, though Popham pressed him to take command of the crews on the two field guns. This was not an onerous duty, though firing the guns, even without shot, was forbidden on the village green. Drilling consisted of hitching and unhitching the guns, and positioning them as needed, while the pikemen and arquebusiers maneuvered. After a few months, the field guns were no longer dragged to the green for the drills, and Popham put John in charge of the arquebusiers. It was a reversal of roles for the two men but somehow seemed to restore a sense of balance — the commander of a company *ought* to be a gentleman, of some sort — that was their traditional function in time of war. Something about the whole notion of mercenary soldiers, led by men whose qualification consisted mostly of surviving disease and brutality, seemed to coarsen the whole business. A war waged by the whole community, with every man in a position befitting his social class, seemed more patriotic, more Christian, more English.

"Perhaps you feel I have taken the position that you earned for yourself," commented Popham to John. "I want you to know that the Baron appreciates the service you have rendered to him, in this matter. Your reputation stands high with him; this can only be to your advantage, in future."

John smiled and shook his head. "I am not jealous of your command, nor do I seek advantage with the Baron. If it were up to me, I'd be at home right now, preparing the house for my bride."

"Still, you must have had some hope of advancement, when you entered the Baron's service."

"The Baron summoned me to this duty on a Sunday morning in church. I did not seek him out."

"Nay, but you served on one of his ships, or so I have heard. There must have been some hope of reward when you volunteered for such a dangerous duty. One thing leads to another, so they say. There is no reason to pretend that you have no ambitions, with me. Such expectations are reasonable and respectable — I have done the same."

John shook his head. "I did not volunteer to serve aboard that ship. I was pressed into duty."

"Pressed? How?"

"Someone put a sack over my head, on the way from the privy. They bound me with ropes until the ship was out to sea — farther than I could hope to swim. That is how I entered the Baron's 'service', as you call it."

Popham was genuinely surprised at this revelation. "I had a better impression of your service, than that."

"The captain of the vessel made a point of introducing me to the Baron when we returned. You could say he went out of his way to tout my contributions to the success of the voyage — at any rate, he made sure that the Baron knew I was raised in Felsted, on the Baron's manor."

"So, you owe your success to the captain, then?"

"And by extension, to the Baron who employed him, I suppose," admitted John. "If success it is. I thought I was doing well enough on my own before I found myself at sea — but I am not bitter; I bear no ill will toward the captain, or anyone else. By God's grace, I am home. If God's grace be sufficient, I shall survive this war also."

"But you admit that you are better off now than then?"

John nodded. "Yes, in many ways." *Few of them have anything to do with the Baron,* he thought to himself, but he said no more about it.

"So, you take my point. You and I are from different levels of society, but we are bound together by similar circumstance. Men must either rise, or fall. Our social betters have the power to reward our work, so it makes sense that we should seek to please them, to show ourselves worthy of their trust. If they wield their power benignly, we shall receive the recognition that we justly deserve and reap the benefits thereof."

John simply nodded. *What power is wielded benignly? Is such a thing even possible? Surely only God is righteous; whether He is benign or not — who can say? Human power must always fall short of God's standard; whosoever would rule us should be humble. Failing that, they should not rule, at all . . .*

September 12, 1587: Little Baddow

The Reverend Samuel Vessey had some very definite ideas about the nature of a Christian marriage, and the wedding ceremonies that were appropriate to the establishment of such. They were not entirely his own — he had appropriated them from his teachers, notably John Calvin, who had a great deal to say on the matter. As a priest in the Church of England, Rev. Vessey was expected to follow the liturgy in the Book of Common Prayer. In practice, he deviated from this somewhat, when he could get away with it. The laws of the kingdom required that a wedding be "performed" or "solemnized" by a priest, and registered with a local magistrate, for legal purposes. Samuel Vessey and others of his persuasion rejected the quasi-sacramental sense of a wedding, choosing instead to regard a marriage as a "covenant" between a man and a woman, by their "agreement"; no priestly function was required. Of course, the covenant had to be registered by the government, because there were innumerable legal obligations that both parties assumed, when they "agreed." But a covenant, by implication, could be terminated, if one or both parties failed to abide by its terms. And the parties themselves were best able to determine whether such was the case. The Book of Common Prayer prescribed the exchange of rings, but Samuel regarded such things as "Popish" remnants of a dark past and discouraged them. The most obvious difference in a Puritan wedding was the absence of a feast, or reception for the bride and groom, after the ceremony. Feasting (gluttony), drinking (dissipation), and especially dancing, were crass contradictions of the sober and holy nature of a marriage covenant. On this matter, Samuel was at some extremity to enforce his beliefs — he didn't have to attend such a feast, of course, but the in-laws frequently wanted an excuse to party, whether to assert their family's status and importance, or merely to satisfy (some of) the lusts of the flesh. The village pub was always available.

In the case of his sister, Sybil, he had more than the usual amount of leverage. Neither the Porters nor the Vesseys had the kind of money to host a big celebration, anyway. There would be no wedding ring, and no wedding gown — the expense of making a dress that would be worn only once was an unimaginable extravagance for the Vessey family. Sybil's sisters would go to some trouble to arrange her hair, and she would wear a small, pretty cap, with a bit of lace, on her head. She would carry a bouquet of asters, picked from her garden.

Samuel planned to perform a small, evening ceremony — John Porter's parents and sister, Sybil's father and siblings. But of course, in a small village, such a thing could not be kept secret. The villagers simply showed up at the church to witness the wedding. There wasn't much Samuel could do about it. He did have a captive audience, so he preached to them about the significance of marriage, and of covenants more generally. Sybil caught his eye, as he was just catching his second wind — the message was clear enough — this was her wedding, her day; no need to make a long-winded oration of it. He nodded and finished after only about an hour.

And then it was time for Mr. and Mrs. John Porter to greet all the people who wanted to congratulate them. Fortunately, most of the greetings were brief and formal — the guests were thirsty, and the pub was just down the street. Before long, it was just the members of their immediate family, plus the Widow Smith, who informed John that she wished to present the couple with a wedding gift: "I have a lathe," she said, "that no one is using. Please take it off my hands." John couldn't stop smiling. "With that, I can make us some fine furniture," he assured Sybil.

The family shared a dinner together, outside, at the Vessey farm — not enough room for everybody, inside. The evening was cool, but not chilly. It was harvest time, time to reflect on the blessings of another year. John was reminded of the supper he had eaten in the same circumstance, more than five years earlier — the day he repaired the Vessey barn. Many of the same faces were there, and he knew the names that went with them. He thought of William — no — John Payne, and the circumstances that had brought him to this village, this farm, this woman, now his wife. He imagined that the martyred priest would be pleased to know how his brief encounter on the road had led to all of this — the families, the bounty, the hope. He wished that Payne could be here, and that he could thank him once again. Sybil noticed the look on his face.

"What is it, John? Is something amiss?"

John smiled and shook his head. "I was just thinking how pleasant this is, how fortunate we are to be here. I was thinking of the priest who sent me here, so many years ago."

"The one who was executed in Chelmsford? Why now?"

"I wish that he could be here, to see the goodness that has come from his act of kindness, that is all."

Sybil said nothing more, clearly a little puzzled. John turned to Samuel, and asked, "What ever happened to your friend, Edward Chase?"

Samuel shook his head slowly. "I haven't heard from him in some time. He seems to have disappeared. Probably on some mission, or other. He has a way of turning up at unexpected times . . ."

Sybil interrupted. "You must explain to me what Mr. Chase's mission might be, but not today. This is our wedding day, please try to remember where you are, and who you are with."

John nodded. Point taken. Odd that Chase had just disappeared, though. He would talk to Samuel about it later.

There were a few traditions that the Rev. Vessey could not object to: after the dinner, Sybil's sisters, Susan and Mary, took her aside to prepare her for her wedding night. It was traditional that they escort her to the bedroom, undress her, and place her in the wedding bed. This was not the elaborate affair that a wealthy woman would go through — there was no elaborate wedding gown to help her out of, no corsets, or jewelry in her hair. This was just as well — the couple were eager enough to consummate their marriage.

Then it was John's turn to be escorted into the chamber by Sybil's brothers, including the Reverend. In a more prosperous family, the couple would have been serenaded with ribald songs by an entire wedding party, or even an entire village. Acts of humiliation or vandalism were not unheard of. But these were families of modest means, and temperate behavior. They sang one song and left the couple alone. John locked the door behind them when they left. He stood with his back to the door, and caught his breath, exasperated.

Sybil laughed at his expression. *"Come hither, thou weary and heavy laden,"* she said, *"Take my yoke on you, and learn of me that I am meek and lowly in heart: and ye shall find rest unto your soul."*

He was growing accustomed to following her suggestions.

1587: A Year of Respite

The news of the raid on Cadiz was slow to filter its way to the general public. Even when it did, its strategic significance was not universally recognized. For the government, and for most of the population in the seaports, the meaning was clear — the Spanish would not be coming, this year. Next year, probably; sooner or later, certainly; but one could never tell how things would play out, so far into the future. A victory was a victory.

Elsewhere, the news was not so good. The Queen had sent a small army to the Netherlands in 1586, to help the Dutch revolt. Elizabeth did so with reluctance because the establishment of an independent republic on the shores of the North Sea might give some Englishmen, especially Puritan ones, some dangerous ideas. The English troops were commanded by Robert Dudley, Earl of Leicester, who was ordered to avoid decisive engagements with Spanish forces. Leicester had other ideas, especially after the Dutch offered him the title of "Governor-General" of their territories — a king, in all but name, though not a hereditary position. Leicester accepted the office and began to move directly against the Spanish. In open battle, his troops did not have much success. A couple of fortresses were captured — the only real success that he could claim. When his hand-picked commanders of the fortresses defected to the Spanish in 1587, Leicester was disgraced. He was recalled to England, and the Dutch offered the position of Governor-General to Maurice, the son of William the Silent, who had been assassinated by agents of the King of Spain, just three years prior.

Maurice was young, and no one expected much of him; the situation in Holland was a stalemate, at best.

In France, the civil war continued. The Huguenots, numerically inferior, nonetheless seemed to be holding their own against the Catholic League. The King of France, Henri III, although Catholic himself, was not as ruthless as the Duke of Guise, leader of the Catholic League demanded he be, perhaps because the leader of the Huguenot faction was his first cousin, also named Henri, King of the province of Navarre, in southern France.

Henri III was the last survivor of four brothers, none of whom had sons of their own. In the event of his death, the nearest claimant to the throne of France would be his cousin, the Huguenot. The Duke of Guise and his allies, of course, were determined to prevent this at any cost, and bullied Henry III relentlessly, to name a Catholic heir. This would prove to be a serious mistake. For now, the war raged on. For England, it meant that a united France would not be allied to Philip, the King of Spain — for now.

For Philip, the invasion of England was all the more urgent. The raid on Cadiz was an embarrassment, but a successful landing on the English coast would turn things in his favor. Once England submitted, affairs in

France and the Netherlands would fall into place. The logistical challenge was greater than any that his armed forces had ever faced; his servants would have to figure it out as they went along . . .

Volume 3: The Garden of the Lord

Part 16: The Conventicles

August 1586: Norwich

Edward Chase needed his shoes re-soled, again. He knew this because his stockings were wet. The light rain was just enough to create some shallow puddles on the road, and each time he stepped in one, he felt a fresh squirt of cool water on the soles of his feet. He tried stepping around the puddles at first, but eventually, it was just too much trouble to walk around all of them — he dodged the ankle-deep ones and just trudged ahead as best he could. He was bound for Norwich, on the Great Road from Ipswich, as he had so often been before. He was in a hurry — more so than usual. There was news to deliver, and news to gather, and the dreary weather fit his mood.

The cause of reform had suffered setback after setback in the last few years, and Chase had begun to expect the news to be bad, more often than good. Archbishop Grindal was dead. His replacement as Archbishop of Canterbury was John Whitgift, a firm supporter of the status quo. Bishops and priests sympathetic to the cause of reform were being removed, one by one, from positions of influence in England. The universities were being purged of reform-minded scholars, as well. In their place were men who favored a church ruled from the top of a hierarchy. The Queen, whose position was at the very top of that hierarchy, supported them, naturally enough.

The weight of ecclesiastical discipline fell on men of lesser status as well — nowhere near the numbers that had faced the flames during Mary's bloody reign, just enough to set the tone of the times. Norwich, where Edward Chase was headed on this day, was a place where the weight fell particularly hard. Norwich was a battleground.

The battleground was messy. Edmund Freke, the Bishop of Norwich, had the full support of his Archbishop, and the weight of the government on his side. That should have been enough to carry the day. But Freke had other contestants to deal with.

Recusant Catholics were still present in Norwich, and priests were known to be serving them. Locating such priests was not easy, and it required a fair amount of the bishop's time and energy to hunt them down. When a priest was apprehended, any laymen found in his company were suspected of treason, as well, and executions followed.

More numerous and public were the Puritan reformers. They had deep roots in Norwich — many local officials were sympathetic to them if not outright Puritans themselves. (Norwich had been a haven for heretics and troublemakers since the days of the Lollards). In the countryside, it was even worse — more than a few of the landed gentry were elected to Parliament as men of Puritan sympathies and protected both Puritan preachers and their followers. Whole districts were dominated by Puritan teaching and practice. It was an open secret that the Puritans hoped to gain enough influence in Parliament to change the laws of the realm in favor of their opinions — the Queen herself was the last line of defense against their agenda.

More exasperating was the emergence of more radical preachers, like Robert Browne, whose teachings had already incited so much disorder. Browne had left England with a band of his followers two years back, to establish a new "purified" church in the Low Countries. He returned to England just months ago, and it was anyone's guess what sort of trouble would result. Browne and his ilk threatened to undo years of patient work that Edward and his colleagues had labored over; careful placement of godly men in parish churches everywhere, teaching and leading the people to the truth, laying the foundation for a purified and renewed church. It was a bitter irony that these patiently nurtured flocks could be so easily led astray into extremism and even separatism by a handful of rash and articulate preachers, most of whom were too narcissistic to foresee the consequences of their behavior.

These and other reflections dominated Edward Chase's mind, as he trudged northward. The rain eased, then the sun came out. Soon the road would be dry, and even his stockings. It was August, after all. Nothing like the chill that winter would bring.

By the following day, he had reached his destination. Norwich was the largest city in England, after London. It was no great difficulty to lose himself in the bustling streets and find his way to the servant's entrance of a substantial house. Here he would rest for a few days, before setting off on his next journey. He arranged to have his shoes re-soled and was served a meal in his room. Soon afterward, a servant summoned him downstairs, to a large room, where his host and a couple of other men were already seated. Chase took off his doublet and began loosening the seams of the lining.

"Ah, you have a message to deliver, of course," said his host. "That can wait. I invited you here to speak with these men, about some matters of concern."

Edward bowed slightly, stopped what he was doing, and took a seat.

"Gentlemen, I believe you know our guest, Edward Chase, by reputation, if not by introduction. He has been an indispensable part of our mission, and I thought it well to include him in our conversation, not least because he may add some valuable insights. He is . . . well-traveled, I would say, and observes things that men like ourselves might miss."

Edward looked around the room. John More, priest and preacher at St. Andrew's church was well known, and recognizable for his exceptionally long and full beard, if by nothing else. His host was a prominent magistrate of the city — Chase had lodged here on many occasions. The third man looked familiar, but Edward couldn't recall the name . . .

"William Burton, priest and minister of the gospel," offered the man, noting Chase's look.

Chase nodded. Yes, that was it. "I am sorry that I could not recall your name, I am weary from my journey, I suppose."

Burton smiled. "As well you should be. No offense is taken." Edward thanked him.

"Our topic of concern," began The Magistrate, "is the condition of our mission, in the face of such strong opposition, and dare I say, persecution. The Archbishop and his minions are determined to suppress true preaching and sound teaching. Hardly a week goes by without the news that one of our member has been forbidden to preach or even removed from his position. The question is, how are we to prevail in such a hostile circumstance?"

Good question thought Chase, and nodded slightly. If anyone had an answer, one of these men was likely to offer it.

More spoke first. "It should not astonish us if the road ahead appears steep and stony. We should expect that our faith will be tested, as gold in the fire. Most of all we must be patient and diligent, and resist the temptation to despair, or turn to extreme measures. We can find ways to get our message to the people that the bishops are powerless to stop, God willing. My own case will make the point. Ten years ago, I was prohibited from preaching at my own church, by Bishop Freke's orders. It grieved me to be silenced in that way, but I persevered, and with reasonable compromise, recovered my ministry. Reasonable, I say, because it is my habit to preach no less than three sermons each Sunday, and I can see the Word of God at work in the hearts of my hearers. This is the way forward for us — patience, faithfulness, diligence. In the words of the Epistle to the Hebrews, *'Consider therefore him that endured such speaking against of sinners, lest ye should be wearied and faint in your minds. Ye have not yet resisted unto blood . . .'"*

And what if it comes to blood? Thought Chase, *what is a reasonable compromise?*

The Magistrate read Edward's face. "Mister Chase, do you have something to add?"

"I do not disagree with the esteemed preacher about the approach we should take. But I fear it may indeed come to bloodshed nonetheless, before our mission truly succeeds. I am not sure I am ready for that test."

There was an uncomfortable silence in the room.

The Magistrate spoke: "Do you think such testing is imminent?"

Edward replied carefully. "I do not think we need to fear such intense persecution from our government, just yet. As long as the threat of invasion from Spain hangs over our heads, the government will try to avoid any domestic tumult whatsoever. I have heard that Robert Browne has returned from Scotland; I suppose he thinks he is safe, for the same reason. If we were recusants, we would have reason to fear the government. If Spain conquers our kingdom," — all his companions frowned at the thought — "if I say, then all of us in this room will be in danger of our lives. If Spain is defeated, the government may well move against us when the threat recedes."

He continued. "In a way, our best hope is for a long war with Spain. As long as the government fears the recusants more than it fears us, we will have some breathing room."

"You seem to have a very low opinion of our government," said Burton. "Do not forget, we have strong friends, in very high places. They have protected us thus far, from government oppression. It is the church hierarchy that threatens us, not the civil government."

"I also remember that the head of that government is also the head of the church." Chase noticed some fidgeting among his companions. "Do not misunderstand me. I am the Queen's man, through and through. If Elizabeth's throne were in the hands of her sister, we all would have gone to the stake years ago. (*Unless we could come to some 'reasonable compromise',*

Edward said to himself). If the government were not effective and strong, the Spanish would be ruling us now. But the Queen will always put the security of her throne first, and men like us are expendable if our beliefs seem to weaken her. It cannot be otherwise; the Queen is obligated to defend her realm against any and every threat."

"But we are no threat to the kingdom! We are loyal to our Queen, however many times we are challenged to prove it." Burton sounded a little annoyed.

"I pray that our loyalty will be enough. For now, the recusants seem the greater threat, and they are the victims of the bishop's attentions."

Victims? Surely, we need not feel any sympathy for traitors and heretics. Their words and deeds are their damnation," replied Burton.

"I suppose it is easier to watch a man be tortured to death if we are certain he is going straight to hell anyway," said Chase with a wry smile. "But nothing we can do to him will compare to the agonies of that place. It's a wonder that we go to so much trouble, just to inflict suffering on a man or woman whose eternal condition is — suffering!"

"Mr. Chase, you are being flippant, on a topic that requires gravity," interrupted the Magistrate. "You have digressed from our original topic. Have you anything to add?"

"I apologize, sir. You are right, I digress. Please ascribe it to my fatigue. I will add this: If the Spanish threat recedes, I am convinced that the Archbishop will become more vigorous in removing our leaders than he already is. If we lose our positions in the universities, who will train the next generation of parish priests and scholars? That is what I fear — not a sudden violent attack on our mission, but a slow strangulation of our message. I think that the Archbishop has already decided on this strategy; it is the same as the one he employs against the papists — without priests, there can be no sacraments; without sacraments, there will eventually be no Catholics."

"Our guest is correct on this point, I think," said More. "Whitgift thinks to defeat us with the same methods that he uses against the papists. He won't be able to accuse us of treason, so he won't be able to hang us, like so many Catholic priests. He will attack the most prominent of our leaders directly, wherever they defy him, and remove them from office, but will be content to deny positions or advancement to those among us who conform outwardly to his authority. He hopes that ambition or flattery will induce our men to drift away from the true faith and join his party."

"Your own career would be a case in point, then?" asked Burton.

"My case will illustrate the point," replied More. "I have been offered many preferments and promotions, as you know, but I have accepted none. All the offers came with an unspoken expectation that I would cease preaching, to take on other duties. For me, preaching is too important to give up. It is the main thing — too valuable for compromise."

An unreasonable compromise thought Chase. *Good to know that John More recognizes the thing when it comes his way. But he knows that many others would take the bait.*

Chase continued, "We have time to plan our response to this threat, but I do not think we will be rescued by friends in the government. We will have to find other ways to train more young men to lead us and maintain their fidelity to the cause."

"But it will be hard to recruit men if it is understood that their financial security will be in doubt," added Burton. "'*The spirit in deede is readie, but the flesh is weake.*'"

"We have two advantages that the hierarchy cannot take from us. One is the fact that so many laymen have become enlightened by our message. They are like creatures released from a dark dungeon into the light of day. They will not willingly return to the darkness they have known. The other is that so many of them can and do read their Bibles. It will not be easy to persuade them to abandon the truth, once they have found it in the Holy Scriptures. This means that they are able to read such books and sermons that are available in printed form. Even if we are prohibited from preaching to a congregation, there is nothing to prevent us from publishing a written sermon. Bishops have tried to suppress the written word before and have always failed."

"That still does not assure that we can recruit and keep men in the parish pulpits," the Magistrate pointed out.

"No, but if the congregation is faithful, they may strengthen the faith of their priests, even to the point of keeping the faith in the face of ecclesiastical pressure."

"Ah. So you would turn the church upside down, to purify it? Make the laymen the stewards of the true faith, and use them to keep the clergy in the path of righteousness?" More raised his eyebrows.

"Surely, it is the Lord's task to lead us all in his paths," replied Chase. "but the Lord may speak from the pew, as much as the pulpit, when the situation requires it, may He not?"

"Like Balaam's ass, you mean?" asked Burton.

Before you dismiss the laity as 'asses', thought Chase, *you would do well to remember that the ass saw the Lord's angel, when Balaam did not, and Balaam's pride nearly cost him his life!*

"In extremity, yes," said Chase, "and we may find ourselves in such extremity, in divers places, ere long. I have visited parishes where the support of the congregants has strengthened the resolve of the vicar to hold to the truth, even in the face of a reprimand from his bishop."

"How would you fit them for such a task?" asked The Magistrate.

"Conventicles," Chase replied. "Conventicles for the laity, in every parish. And everyone must be able to read their Bible — men, women, and children."

"This we have done, wherever we could. Our conventicles must be held in secret because the bishops will arrest any they can catch in attendance. Our prophesying meetings are forbidden; we don't have enough trained men to serve all the parishes that might tolerate such conventicles, anyway, much less the parishes that would reject them altogether."

"Is not the Spirit of God on our side? What of the promise of the prophet Joel, *'your sonnes, and your daughters shall prophecie, and your yong men shal see visions, and your old men shall dreame dreames.'*? Are we to suppose that the Archbishop and his underlings are mightier than the Spirit of God? In the words of the apostles, *'We ought rather to obey God than men'*!" Edward Chase realized he was preaching, now, to men who were his social betters, and of higher religious rank. From the looks on their faces, it was apparent that they were not accustomed to being addressed in this manner. "I sometimes get carried away with preaching, when I should be conversing as a scholar. It is a defect of character; I pray the Lord may apply the remedy, as it pleases him."

His companions nodded, some chuckled.

"To your point," said More, "I see some pitfalls. As the Magistrate noted, we don't have enough ordained men to meet the need in every parish. And without the supervision of ordained ministers, the conventicles and prophesying of which you speak can all too easily lead to error — such as the error of Robert Browne, which you are familiar with."

Chase nodded. "You are right, there is risk of error. Browne led a whole congregation out of the church, and then out of England altogether (for all the good it did him). Browne has done our cause much harm, but mostly because of his writings. Men and women are led astray by men like Robert Browne because their knowledge of the scriptures is too meager, not because it is too much. The errors of his teaching would be exposed in the open discussion of a conventicle, in the presence of godly men and women, well-versed in the scriptures."

"I wish I was as certain as you are, on that last point," said Burton, "but you are right about the writings doing the most harm. If Browne or others like him lead a few people into error, and then out of the country altogether, our problem is largely solved. It is the writings that persist and lead even more into error."

"That is true." agreed More. "I have heard that other separatist groups are forming all over the kingdom, now. Even with Browne gone, there are plenty of preachers and plenty of local magistrates who tolerate or even support them."

"Which argues for the other advantage that I mentioned," said Chase. "The best weapon we have to refute the errors of men like Browne, or the Archbishop, is our writing. The more of our people who read the truth, the stronger our cause becomes. If the Archbishop condemns our writing, it will only whet the appetite of men to read what we have written. The written word will live on, long after the Archbishop has passed from this life into whatever his eternal destiny may be."

All three of his companions nodded.

"So. Conventicles for the laity, more instruction in reading and writing, wider publication of our message. Have you any more recommendations?" the Magistrate asked.

"I would only add that our writing should use words with plain meaning. The debates of scholars do not address the concerns of the common folk, however they may fascinate the well-schooled among us. We should speak to the people in their own language," Chase replied. "Time is in our favor if we hold our ground against these assaults. Our strength must now be in the parishes since the universities are under the control of our enemies."

"God willing, we will not have to wait forever," ventured Burton, hopefully.

"What do you mean?"

"Delicately as I may say it, Her Majesty is now fifty-three years old. It is unlikely that she will produce an heir to succeed her. Her cousin Mary is virtually Elizabeth's prisoner, as long as Elizabeth reigns, and a Catholic — she cannot succeed to the throne, as proclaimed by the Bond of Association. Mary's son, James, has the clearest claim to the throne, and he is a sound Protestant. This may sound like idle conjecture, but I am informed that Elizabeth and the Privy Council are thinking along these same lines," said Burton.

"How does that possibility favor our cause?" asked Chase.

"James is not only a firm Protestant; he is well acquainted with a church that is organized along the lines that we are seeking for the Church of England. Surely he would look favorably on our appeal for church reform!"

Edward Chase reflected on Burton's optimism. He had heard about King James's relations with the Presbyterian organization of the Kirk of Scotland — by all accounts, it was tempestuous and acrimonious. James fancied himself a theologian of the first order and published lengthy dissertations on the Divine Right of Kings (in Latin, no less!) to exercise absolute rule over their subjects. Given the opportunity, James was more likely to impose Elizabeth's system on the Scottish church, than to bring Presbyterianism to England. Nonetheless, "There is that to hope for," he said with a nod and a smile.

"We are speaking of possibilities that may be decades away," interjected More. "Who can say if any of us will live to see that day? In the meantime, we must strengthen our cause in any way that we can. Master Chase, your recommendations are well made. We shall give them serious consideration."

Chase nodded. It sounded like a dismissal, and he rose to leave. The Magistrate held out his hand, "I believe you have a message for me?"

Edward remembered the sealed letter in his doublet. It took him a moment to pull out enough of the stitching on the lining to pull out the letter and hand it to the Magistrate. "Wait just a moment, all of you, while I look at this," he said. Edward put his doublet back on and returned to his seat.

The Magistrate skimmed the letter, then reread parts of it, while his companions waited. Edward was aware that he hadn't eaten in some time, Burton began to fidget. The Magistrate looked up. "There are some things here, that may be of interest to you. This message is from someone high up in the government; I will not give you his name, but he is in a position to know of what he speaks. As of three days ago, the Queen's cousin, Mary, has been arrested and charged with treason."

"Yet another plot to place her on the throne has been uncovered, no doubt," said More.

"But she was not charged in the others; the government must have some strong evidence, to charge her directly."

"Either that or the Spanish threat has moved them to take more decisive action. If she is found guilty and loses her head, the King of Spain's plans for England are disrupted. Without Mary, who would he put on the throne to replace Elizabeth?"

"Disrupted or not," said Edward Chase, "I doubt that Mary's death would deter Philip from his invasion. Having her out of the way could actually serve his purpose."

"Perhaps Elizabeth intends to use Mary as some sort of hostage, to prevent Mary's son James from making trouble for England, while we are preoccupied with the threat from Spain?" offered Burton.

Not impossible, thought Chase, *but James will probably be content to wait for things to play out — if Phillip succeeds in removing Elizabeth, the Protestants would look to him as their champion; if Elizabeth survives the war (long odds, those), he would most likely succeed her, anyway. The greatest threat to his own reign is — his mother! Should Phillip succeed in placing Mary on the throne of England, Mary's most obvious move would be to reclaim the throne of Scotland for herself, with Philip's assistance. James is probably praying that Elizabeth will somehow survive, and pass the throne of England to him; in good time, all in good time.*

"Nothing in this letter explains the government's reasons for Mary's arrest. We shall have to wait, like everyone else, to understand what is going on. Something has changed. These are turbulent times." The Magistrate continued, "There is another matter in this letter, more to the point of our earlier conversation. It seems that Robert Browne's followers are becoming bolder and more numerous in London and throughout the kingdom. We are urged to be watchful, to identify any such groups here in Norwich."

"Identify?" More looked surprised. "Are we now to work for Archbishop Whitgift, to help him hunt down his prey?"

The Magistrate shook his head. "We will not be helping the Archbishop, in any way. But we must know where the separatists are gathering if we are to reach them with sound teaching."

"If Browne has returned to England, why has he not been arrested?" asked Burton. "Surely, we have the means to detain him and stop the spread of his errors!"

The Magistrate shook his head and chuckled. "Browne has returned, but he is not spreading his errors. He has renounced his earlier writing and published refutations of them. He has made — what did you call it? (here he looked at More) — a reasonable compromise. He speaks for the Archbishop, now."

"And yet the problem grows? How can that be?"

"Browne is denounced as a traitor by his followers. They continue to preach and publish in the vein of his earlier writings. Some of the leaders are more persuasive, and less annoying than Browne himself ever was. Browne put the cat among the pigeons, but it is up to us to catch the cat and save such pigeons as we can — Browne declares himself enlightened, now."

Burton shook his head and snorted, "Who are the greater fools, the ones that promote error, or the ones that follow the error after it has been exposed? How have we come to such a pass, that one fool's excess becomes the credo of fools everywhere?"

"Mr. Chase. I see your brow is furrowed. Can you shed light on this matter?" The Magistrate was looking at him as he spoke.

"It is not the babbling of just one fool that bedevils us, I am afraid. The roots of it are everywhere, and none are blameless."

"Please, say more." All three of his companions were looking at him, now.

"The roots of this spirit of separatism are everywhere. You might say it began when the King decided to separate our church from the control of the Pope. You could say that it is the spirit of Lollardry — long present in Norwich, despite the church's best efforts to burn it out. You can find it in the witness of martyrs — burned outside these very walls — who proclaimed that every man should read the Holy Scriptures in his own language and seek his own understanding. You might consider that our conventicles and prophesying meetings are a model for separatists everywhere. You can certainly find its roots in Lutheranism, and the teachings of John Calvin, as well — who are the elect, after all, if not a people separated from the rest of humanity, according to God's sovereign will? If men are free to choose, then they will choose differently, and the differences will lead to separation of one kind or another. The problem for the Brownists is that they cannot come to a 'reasonable compromise' on the question of spiritual authority — though the Archbishop would say the same thing about us, no doubt."

The Magistrate nodded. "Robert Browne would agree with you, I think. They say that soon after he led his band of followers into exile in the Low Countries, they came to irreconcilable disagreement — and they expelled him from the very church he had established." Burton and More both chuckled and shook their heads.

"I have heard the same," said Burton. "It is a wonder the Brownists exist at all, with their constant splitting into factions. They can feed discontent and turmoil among the rest of us, but can establish no enduring institutions of their own."

"That may be true," conceded Chase, "but while they continue to agitate and dissent, our cause is tainted by their excesses, and it gives the government more cause to mistrust us. Their ideas have taken root in the civil government, as well. You mentioned the Bond of Association, that so many of our leaders have signed. It purports to prohibit any Catholic monarch from succeeding Queen Elizabeth, but it also states that Parliament may choose her successor! If Parliament is competent to choose the sovereign, then those who choose the Parliament must be competent, as well. If legitimate authority comes from men's choices, whence the notion of divine anointing?"

The Magistrate stroked his beard, "I suppose God's anointing must come through the choices of godly men. Calvin certainly thought so. He said that a Republic was the preferred form of civil government, just as a church governed by presbyters was the preferred form of church governance."

"We have embraced the latter idea, without formally endorsing the former," Chase pointed out, "though I can think of many among us who secretly would like to see England become a godly republic. The Queen's advisors understand what we prefer not to admit — organizing the church along the lines we seek, would lead to demands for a different form of civil government. Archbishop Whitgift and his servants are the means by which they think to forestall those demands."

"But we are the most loyal of the Queen's subjects!" protested Burton. "There are Papists that would overthrow her for religious reasons, and no lack of Protestant aristocrats who think they would make a better King than she, but we have no political ambitions, whatsoever. We simply seek to worship God in a way that seems godly to us."

Burton continued, "And for all that, they accuse us of hypocrisy and opportunism. We support the Queen now, they say, because she stands between us and the King of Spain. We make a 'reasonable compromise', in the interest of self-preservation. In other circumstances, they say, we might well try to seize power for ourselves. In this, they say, we are no more godly than they and less honest about our motives."

"And what, exactly, do you say, Master Chase?" The question came from John More.

"I say that the contradictions in our position must be faced one day, but not today, and not soon. I say that the 'reasonable compromise' must suffice for us, for now. The day may come, God forbid, when we face a Papist government that seeks to wipe us from the face of the earth. If that day comes, we will need to fight — just as the Huguenots are fighting now — for our survival. We will need an army, an army of the godly. And we will need our own civil government as well. May none of us live to see that day!"

"In the meantime," he continued, "we should continue to teach and preach the truth to any who will listen to us. The instruction of our children must be given the greatest attention. We must build up our strength in every parish in the kingdom, and debate our opponents as skillfully as we can, wherever we can."

His companions were silent for a moment. Then The Magistrate nodded and smiled, followed by the other two men. "You have given us something to think about. You must be hungry. Go to the kitchen and ask the cook to serve you something. Tell her that you are running some errand for me. We will speak more after you have eaten."

That was definitely a dismissal. Edward stood and bowed to each of his companions in turn. Each acknowledged him with a nod and a smile. He *was* hungry. He left to find the kitchen. His joints ached a little — from sitting so long, he supposed. It came to him that this vagabond life would have to come to an end, someday. He needed to find a less demanding employment. Something that would let him sleep in the same bed, every night.

Later that evening, he was summoned back to the room where he had met his host and the others before. This time, it was just him and The Magistrate. "Please take a seat, Edward," his host gestured to a chair. Edward sat.

"So, Edward," his host continued, "You have had a taxing trip, by the look of you."

Chase nodded. "I was trying to hurry, and it fatigued me. I honestly don't know how much longer I can continue this life on the road. I am thinking I should be looking for some other employment, something less arduous."

The Magistrate raised his eyebrows and nodded. "I shall keep that in mind; perhaps we will find something for you here in Norwich. You are a preacher, so I'm told. There are places that we could use a man with your gifts. I *will* say that you have been invaluable to our cause as a courier, but

I suppose it is only a matter of time before the authorities grow suspicious of your constant travels. You have never been arrested and searched, is that right?

Chase nodded. "Often watched, sometimes followed, but never arrested, never searched."

"A spotless record, then, of protecting our most sensitive communications." The magistrate smiled and nodded. "You have served well, better than most. I have one more journey for you, one more message to deliver. Once you have completed this, come back to Norwich. We shall find a suitable position for you, one commensurate to your abilities."

"This," he held up a sealed letter, "will be your last delivery. You will have to handle this one a bit differently."

"How so?" asked Edward.

"This will not be concealed within your garments. You will carry it openly — that is, in your pack, or some other place where it might be seen. If you are arrested and searched, as I think you may be, they will not have to tear the lining from your doublet to find it (though they may do so, anyway)."

"Am I to serve as — a decoy?"

His host smiled and nodded. "I have not said so. You are simply delivering some personal correspondence from myself, and certain others here in Norwich, to their friends or relatives in Ipswich, Colchester, Chelmsford, and London. I have several such letters for you, but this one — he held up the first letter — this one must be delivered to each in turn. Do you understand?"

"I think so. But will it not seem odd that I am delivering the letter to someone other than to whom it is addressed?"

"Quite so. See here, the letter is addressed to someone in Ipswich. Once they have read it, they will return it to you, resealed, but addressed to someone in Colchester, and so on, do you understand?"

Edward nodded. "I understand that much, I still do not understand why I am taking the same letter to so many, unconcealed."

"I will be frank. We have heard (from friendly sources) that Archbishop Whitgift's agents are looking to make an arrest. They hope to intercept some communication that will embarrass us or even lead to indictments of some sort. We have also heard that you are a person of interest to them. As you admit, you are often followed on these journeys that you take. This letter" — here he held it up again — "contains nothing incriminating, any more than the others. Certain phrases in it will have meaning only to the recipients, but are otherwise innocuous."

"And the other letters?"

"Merely personal communications — some dealing with business, or family news, whatever. Nothing to embarrass us."

Edward nodded. "My shoes need resoling. Once that is done, I can slip out of here unnoticed — perhaps as early as tonight."

"I am sure you could, but we want you to be noticed — better to leave in daylight, I think. It would be a shame if you eluded them altogether."

"Yet if they have been watching me, it will seem suspicious if my mode of travel changes suddenly. If this is to work, I must still appear to be traveling in secrecy. I will move about in darkness, until I think I am being followed, and then depart."

"I will defer to your experience in these matters," said The Magistrate.

It took the next day for Edward's shoes to be sent to the cobbler for new soles and returned to him. He rested, ate, and stayed indoors. The stitches on the lining of his doublet were repaired by one of the household servants — using old thread, to match the color and wear of the rest of the seams. Edward was comfortable with the plain dark doublet, and hoped no one would be ripping it apart, but putting new thread in part of the lining was an invitation to investigate.

By evening, he was ready to leave. He went first to a public house and had a leisurely meal. He chatted up a serving maid, told a joke, eavesdropped on some conversations. He rose to leave and scanned the room. He exited to the street, walked several paces, then stretched his arms, as if he were stiff from sitting. He looked back at the pub, and sure enough, someone was exiting from the same door: drab clothing, and a nondescript hat. He cleared his throat loudly and spat on the street, then turned to his right, and began walking. He turned right at the next corner, then left onto a smaller street. He emerged onto a wider avenue and slowed down. Shortly, a figure emerged from where he had just come — same person, same hat. Good. Now to lose them, but just for a while . . . wait, another figure emerged from the same narrow street, taller, maybe thinner . . . made sense to use two, if they thought he might elude one of them. He wished he were younger, more vigorous; he could make a game of this. Now, however, he would walk at a more deliberate pace; a dance in slow motion, for three.

A row of modest houses was across the street. He crossed and ducked into a breezeway between two of them. He was followed by the nondescript hat. Moments later, he emerged from the same breezeway and headed to his left. The nondescript hat was somewhere in the cluttered rear of the row of houses, among the privies, chicken coops, and other structures. Edward allowed himself just a glimpse to confirm that the taller, thinner figure was waiting for him to emerge, before heading to his left, and out the nearest city gate.

Once on the open road, he picked up the pace for a while. It was a pleasant summer evening, with few people on the road. Night insects were chirping, there were animal sounds from the farms that he passed. He slowed to a more comfortable pace. Might as well enjoy the August night; Lord knows it would not be so pleasant out here come November. Perhaps by then, he would have a more comfortable occupation. Something indoors, with a warm fire.

He was tempted to walk through the whole night — he was well rested, after all, but took pity on his pursuers, for some reason. Maybe because they had no way of knowing that this was all a bit of cheap theater. He would rest somewhere, in some village or other, or maybe a barn. Of course, that would mean that his pursuers would have to wait in the dark somewhere . . . He chuckled. No way to make it easier on them; they were fated to suffer some discomfort, whatever he did. Poor sods.

In the event, he found a barn near the road, slept in the hayloft for a few hours, and was on his way before dawn. Shortly after sunup, he passed through a village and found a public house that would serve him breakfast. Halfway through his meal, he was surprised at the entry of a familiar figure — the man in the nondescript hat! The newcomer took a seat at the other end of the room and ordered something to eat. Edward resisted the urge to finish his meal quickly and force the other man to cut his breakfast short. He took his time. He determined that weather permitting, he would try to cover another twenty or so miles this day, and stay the evening in a village called Stoke Ash, where he had friends that he trusted. His pace would be brisk — might as well let his companion eat a hearty breakfast; he intended to give him a good run, today.

When it appeared that Nondescript Hat had had enough to eat, Edward stood, paid his tab at the bar, and strode out of the pub and onto the Great Road. He didn't look back for a few miles. There was plenty of traffic on the road that morning, and he found an agreeable farmer driving a hay wain who would let him ride for several more miles, for a penny. Chase wondered where the other taller/thinner man might be — had he been lurking about outside the pub this morning? In that case, he probably missed his breakfast — too bad!

Edward reflected that he was enjoying the prospect of his pursuer's discomfort more than was proper for a Christian man, and resolved to pray about the matter.

The farmer was delivering his hay to Pulham Market, a village just off the Great Road. Edward parted ways with him here. It was still a good ten miles or so to Stoke Ash, but he knew from experience that the next village with a good meal was at least a two-hour walk unless he ventured off the Great Road. It was just possible that he would lose his pursuers if he walked the backroads, so he resolved to have an early supper, and wait for some indication of their whereabouts.

He indulged himself with a serving of beef stew, at a local public house, with ale, of course, and some rye bread. The proprietor's wife had baked a pie, and he tried some of that, too. Just as he was finishing, the taller/thinner man walked in, looking tired, and hungry. No doubt his companion was outside in the street, somewhere. They had made a smart choice to send the taller/thinner man in since Edward might have been alarmed if his breakfast companion just happened to appear at his supper. Besides, taller/thinner had probably missed his breakfast. Out of mercy, or perhaps wickedness, Edward nodded to the man as he passed his table and said, "The beef stew is very good today."

The man stopped, looked surprised, then recovered. "Thank you for the recommendation. May I sit down?" he seated himself before Edward could answer him. He caught the attention of a serving maid, and ordered the beef stew, then turned and gazed directly at Edward. Blue eyes, long, narrow nose, beard trimmed short. "Charles Bedford, at your service," he said.

"Edward Chase," was the reply. Edward was surprised at the boldness of the man and then realized that his companion's best chance of a full meal was to detain Edward long enough to finish it. Desperation, maybe. Still, there was nothing to prevent Edward from leaving the pub immediately and leaving his companion with the painful choice of following him and going hungry, or eating a meal and losing him. No doubt the other man was waiting just outside, in case Edward decided to do just that . . . Edward decided to sit awhile and see the game out.

"What brings you to Pulham Market, Master Chase?" *A direct approach then* thought Edward; his move. "I am on my way to Ipswich, on some personal business." Vague enough, but entirely truthful.

"I am on my way to Ipswich, myself. I believe I saw you on the road from Norwich, this morning, did I not?"

No point in denying what they both knew to be true, but . . . Edward tried to feign surprise, as if he had not seen the man before — "You may well have done since I left Norwich only yesterday. What is your business on the road, today?"

"I am bound for Ipswich, as I said, on some personal business . . . for the Archbishop of Canterbury."

Chase was surprised at the name-dropping. Charles Bedford (*probably not his real name*, thought Edward) wanted to impress him with the gravity of this encounter, for some reason. Given the fact that both of them knew Bedford had been following him, it was a bold or even brazen admission that Edward had attracted the attention of the Archbishop, with all that that implied. It was a confirmation of what Edward had long suspected, yet hearing that fact admitted publicly was a little alarming. Then he recalled that all the letters he carried (as far as he had been told), were innocuous — he was, in his own words, a 'decoy' on this trip. Somehow, someone in the reform movement was still a step ahead of the Archbishop's men. He relaxed. "And how is the Archbishop, these days?"

Chase saw surprise in the man's eyes. "Do you know the Archbishop?"

"Not well. I have met him once or twice, in London. He would not remember me, I think. I was on better terms with the old Archbishop."

"The old Archbishop?"

"Archbishop Grindal, that was before Archbishop Whitgift." There. The battle line was drawn: Edward Chase from the old regime, and Charles Bedford from the new. It did not put Edward on equal footing with his companion, but it suggested that Edward was no mere errand boy, either. If anything, it made him a more attractive 'decoy'; in the worst case, (if he were arrested), his examiners would be reluctant to handle him too roughly — hard to know if he had powerful friends somewhere in London. *I am getting too old to play this game*, thought Edward to himself, *but not too old to enjoy it.*

The beef stew arrived, and his companion turned his attention to it, needing to collect his thoughts, no doubt. "You are right. This is very tasty," his companion remarked.

"You should try the pie before you leave," added Edward, in a helpful tone.

"Master Chase, I have a suggestion. Since we are traveling the same road to the same destination, why not travel together? I think you must have some interesting stories to tell of the old Archbishop, and I have some that I could tell you about the new one."

Another bold move. Edward could hardly refuse, without implicitly admitting that his journey was more than it appeared to be. Traveling together would allow both of them to maintain the fictions they had adopted — fictions that were of no relevance to any but themselves. Silly. But maintaining the fictions allowed each of them the hope, however slim, that they could outmaneuver the other, in the end. *Bedford knows, surely, that I am on to him — else he is a fool or thinks that I am a fool, which is the same thing. And that can only mean that he is on to me and that I am aware of that. Yet I am obliged to play along if only to lead him and his fellows on a wild goose chase. If I agree to travel with him, it should cause him to suspect the deception, but it will be difficult for him to change his mind and let me go on my way alone. It should create some doubt in his mind, in any case, and that suits my purpose.* "I would not wish to tell any stories that would be embarrassing to the memory of the Archbishop — God rest his soul . . ." Edward paused. ". . . but I would be glad for the companionship. I am in no particular hurry. Have some pie, if you like."

Bedford nodded and looked to his stew. *Thinking of his next move? Should have planned that before he spoke.*

Bedford finished his meal, including the pie, and they left together. Chase spotted the man in the nondescript hat outside, but Bedford did not acknowledge him. It was a warm day, but not hot. Bedford did, indeed, have stories to tell. Chase decided to make the best of it; he had done this sort of thing many times before — he could tell stories all day and not give away any compromising information about himself.

Bedford admitted that he worked for the Archbishop in an investigative capacity, focused mainly on identifying recusant Catholics and their priests — a matter of keen interest to the Crown, in these perilous days. He had some information about the arrest of Queen Mary — apparently, the government had documents that proved she was plotting the assassination of Queen Elizabeth. He also was interested in identifying Brownists — the business in Bury St. Edmunds was still remembered, especially in London.

Chase took the opportunity to ask questions: Had Bedford heard that Browne had renounced his own books? Was it possible that Mary would be put to death? He had no reason to believe that Bedford was particularly well-informed, but men who have much to say can be flattered by questions about their opinions about nearly everything; as long as Bedford was talking, Chase would not have to answer any questions.

Bedford's take on Queen Mary's situation was actually informative. Mary was Queen of Scotland or claimed to be (her son James begged to differ), and as such, was not truly a subject of Elizabeth, the Queen of England. Many charges that a true subject could face would not necessarily apply to her. As a sovereign (so she claimed) of a foreign state, an attempt to assassinate Elizabeth would be a hostile act, an act of statecraft or of war, but it was a stretch to indict her for treason — she owed no particular loyalty to England or its queen. Exile was out of the question; it would free her to do more mischief and strengthen the hand of the King of Spain. Imprisonment did not serve any better; what had the last eighteen years been, but a kind of house arrest, with retainers? "In the end, said Bedford, "I think it is the Bond of Association that will be her death — the Aristocracy and the Parliament are sworn to kill anyone who seeks to kill the Queen — simple as that." Edward had to agree with him.

Inevitably, Bedford began to ask questions of his own. Edward was careful to tell the truth, without giving away awkward details: He had traveled this road often and was familiar with many of the villages in the surrounding countryside. He was a Cambridge man — not an ordained priest, yet, but in time, he might be. He was acquainted with many parish priests, and civil officials in the eastern shires, and had mentored many others who served in parishes all over the country.

"Mentored, you say? How mentored?"

"Mentored in developing their ministry of preaching. It is not something that the universities place a great deal of importance in, but in the parishes, it is the most important way that the people hear the truth."

"More important than the sacraments?" A careful answer was required here, thought Chase.

"The sacraments feed the soul. It is preaching that shapes the mind."

"Are you licensed to preach, then?"

"I am. Archbishop Grindal licensed me to do so. I have preached in many places, sometimes at the urging of a bishop, sometimes not." Usually not, actually, but not to split hairs . . .

"What are the matters that merit the attention of your sermons, then — in the village parishes, I mean?"

"There is a great deal of Papist superstition in the villages. I do not mean that the people are Papists; it's just that they are confused about the true religion. They get things mixed up in their minds; they do not understand why the rituals of their grandmothers must be abandoned. The Book of Common Prayer does not always speak to them; a priest who is not 'diuiding the worde of trueth aright' is not serving them as he should."

"Ah. So, you agree then, that Papists and recusants are the greatest threat to our church."

Edward took a breath. Honesty was the only prudent answer, he thought. "No, I do not."

Bedford looked honestly surprised. "But you just said . . ."

"I said that Papist superstitions are the most common problem I encounter. But most of the threat from Papism fades over time. Foreign Papists, of course, are a grave threat, but the government must face that one. I was speaking of the false ideas that many of our people are still bound by. These ideas are of very little political consequence, but they befog the minds of believers. Good preaching can remedy that."

"You do not fear the King of Spain, then?" Bedford looked askance.

"We all should fear him. But any Englishmen who dream of restoring Papism in this country, with all its foolish excesses, are fools. Apart from some ambitious Aristocrats, who think they would reign in such a world, or some merchants who think they might become wealthier, there is no appetite for such a restoration in the countryside. Many miss the old rituals, the vestments, the images, and the candles. But few indeed would welcome the Pope into their homes, if he was knocking on the door. There is no going back."

"So, if this is not the greatest threat, what is?" Bedford was genuinely curious. He found Chase's analysis insightful and compelling. There was more to the man than he had been led to expect.

"Brownists. Separatists. Men who teach that every congregation but their own small one is corrupt beyond redemption, men who would splinter the body of Christ over petty disputes. They teach that any and every man can discern the truth for themselves, yet condemn any who discern differently than they, as hypocrites or heretics," Chase said.

"But with Browne now recanting his views, that movement has no leader. The Pope still lives, and conspires against us, as we speak. If that threat is no longer potent, as you say, why should we strive so hard to catch and execute their priests? Why is the jail in Norwich full of recusants this very day?"

"Why indeed?" asked Chase. "Perhaps the government believes that they will rise to rebellion when the Spanish land on our shores. If that is what they think, they are mistaken, but that is the only reason I can think of. Have you seen the wretches in the jail? Do they look to you like an army of rebellion? Nay, the recusants cling to a past long gone, as if remembering something they dreamed. The separatists follow a light that they fancy to be the Sun of Righteousness, though it is naught but a will-o'-the-wisp. I leave it to you which will appeal the more — the fading dream, or the light in the darkness?"

"I suppose the will-o'-the-wisp may outlive us all," said Bedford.

Chase added, "And if you suppose that Browne's repudiation will discourage those who have followed his teaching, you are mistaken. They repudiate Browne, now, and are more convinced than ever that he had it right at first. It is only a few years past the foolishness in Bury St. Edmund's, not more than a day's journey from here — you may have heard of it?"

Bedford nodded. "Indeed, I was there."

Chase shot him a surprised look.

"I was there assisting Richard Bancroft, in sorting the whole business out," Bedford elaborated.

"Ah," said Chase. That was a bit of pertinent information. His companion worked for Bancroft, who worked for Archbishop Whitgift, then. Not good news, really. Bancroft had a well-earned reputation for punishing those that the Archbishop considered dangerous. Still, better to know what he was up against . . . "And have you spoken with Master Bancroft since?"

Bedford was a little startled at the question. "Yes, not a week ago."

"And does he still wear that hound-dog look?"

Bradford was at a loss for words. "Hound-dog" was not the term that a servant used when describing his master.

Chase chuckled. "You are wise not to answer that question. All of us at Cambridge used to call him "Old Basset" behind his back. Not something you should remember though, lest you blurt something out at the worst possible moment. He was a fine preacher and trained many like me. Also a scholar of the ancient languages. Nowadays, of course, his reputation is built on the 'stirs' in Bury St. Edmund's."

"We thought we had put that infernal fire out for good," recovered Bedford. "If you are to be believed, it has broken out elsewhere. What can you tell me about these other flare-ups?"

Here it comes, thought Chase, *If I tell him everything I know (which isn't much), it will only lead to more questions. If I tell him less than he thinks I know, he will conclude that I am hiding something, which will lead to more questions. No way out, now. Careful, though, careful* . . . "I have heard only rumors," said Chase.

"I have heard that as many as a thousand separatists reside in London, and meet to worship secretly (this would not be news to Bedford or his Archbishop, surely). And I believe there are such in Norwich, as well. It stands to reason that they reside in any sizable town that you could name. Browne's books are illegal to own, of course, but they are still in circulation. Burning books does nothing but make them more attractive."

"You own Browne's books, then?"

Nice try, thought Chase. "No," he chuckled, "look at me. All my worldly possessions I carry on my back. I cannot be burdened with books, much less contraband books. I admit to having read Browne's books, but that was years ago before they were banned. I am familiar with his ideas, and I have preached often enough to refute them. But the fact that they need refuting is proof that they are still buzzing in men's minds, like so many bees." *You won't catch me on so trivial a matter as that*, Chase thought to himself; which meant only that some weightier matter was still to come.

They were closing in, he realized; from here on, it was just a matter of putting off the inevitable. He was sure he would be arrested, sooner or later, and examined by someone of higher rank than Charles Bedford. He braced himself, with the thought that the longer he could delay, the more chances he had to warn his friends that he had been found out. He tried to think of a way to be sure that his arrest was public. It seemed probable that Bedford still thought he was carrying something important; best to keep that deception up as long as possible — maybe he could stall his arrest until they reached Ipswich, tomorrow. Eluding Bedford, just to deliver a meaningless letter was pointless. *Of course*, he thought, *if I never arrive in Ipswich, or that letter is never delivered, everyone will know that I have been detained.* That would be his plan. Time to ask some questions of his own.

"Are you familiar with Browne's books?" Chase asked Bedford.

"Only by reputation," he replied and looked uncomfortable with his answer. Probably a lie. Chase pressed further.

"What have you heard, then?"

Bedford cleared his throat. "That he would do away with bishops, and presbyters, and let every congregation choose its priest or vicar. That he holds the sacraments in low esteem, and — most to the point — he rejects the authority of the crown over all ecclesiastical matters."

"That is a fair summary," said Chase, "But see what follows from such ideas . . ." Edward launched into a long and detailed analysis of the separatist credo, its biblical foundations, its errors and over-simplifications. He compared it to the Calvinist, Lutheran, and Catholic doctrines as well.

It was no great difficulty for him to do so, he had preached many a sermon on just this topic, sometimes for up to three hours in one session.

Bedford appeared interested for a while but then was visibly overwhelmed, and eventually bored by the whole dissertation. But as long as Edward Chase was talking, it was Bedford's business to keep him talking and listen as carefully as his weary attention would let him — the man was bound to make a slip eventually, some phrase or admission that would warrant his arrest. Still, it was hard to keep track of so much speaking, so many technical terms . . .

Chase noted Bedford's waning attention with satisfaction. A bored man was an unwary one. There might be one more opportunity to send a warning before he was behind bars . . .

Before he knew it, they had arrived at Stoke Ash. Chase explained that he intended to find lodging for the night there, and Bedford quite naturally decided to do the same. They entered a public house, and Chase approached the bar at the rear. "Ale for me and my friend, if you please! We must drink a toast! When the drinks were poured, he lifted his mug and proclaimed, in a voice loud enough to be heard by everyone, "To the Queen who defends our faith, to the Archbishop of Canterbury, who serves our queen, and to Richard Bancroft, who serves our beloved Archbishop!" He heard some murmurs of assent from the crowd, none were enthusiastic.

Bedford excused himself, "Personal business, a long walk, today," He exited the rear of the pub, where presumably, the privy was located. He did not reappear for several minutes. Chase looked around the room. There were at least three men in the place that he had met before. None of them greeted him. His toast had been noted; the name Richard Bancroft was well enough known. Good.

Just then, three men entered the pub. One of them was none other than the man with the nondescript hat — shorter than Chase had supposed from a distance, young. He approached Chase directly, and spoke: "Edward Chase, you are under arrest, under suspicion of conspiracy to disturb the peace of the realm."

"Have you a warrant for this arrest?" Chase looked down at him. The man was taken aback but pulled some paper from inside his jerkin. "Indeed, I do."

Edward snatched it from his hand before he could be stopped. It was indeed a warrant, dated four days prior, signed by none other than Richard Bancroft, officer of the Court of High Commission. Chase gave it back to the shorter man — "You have me at a disadvantage; you know my name, I do not know yours."

"You may call me Mr. Hightower," said the man, "though that is more than you need to know about me. These men will assist me in transporting you to a secure place, where you will face these charges." The pitch of his voice got higher, as he spoke. He looked nervous. *This is probably the first arrest he has made,* thought Chase, and almost pitied the fellow. They had the full attention of everyone in the pub. That was as good as could be hoped for — word of his arrest would soon be widespread. He had achieved his aim; no reason to put up a fuss. "We should be going, then, shouldn't we?" He walked briskly toward the door, his captors trailing behind him.

There was no sign of Charles Bedford outside — which made sense; Bedford's usefulness to his employers would diminish if he were associated with an arrest. Likely he would appear in the pub soon, profess astonishment at news of Edward's arrest, and commiserate with anyone who expressed sympathy with Edward's situation. Hopefully, the toast would warn any of Edward's friends to stay well away from Charles Bedford.

An open cart was waiting in the street, drawn by a team of horses. Hightower insisted on shackling Edward's legs inside the cart, and they set off, at a good clip. It was a rough ride at any pace; the speed they were making would be bruising. Edward hoped it would not be a long one. He tried not to think much about his possible destination, or what sort of treatment awaited him there. The fact that his arrest warrant was several days old confirmed that the information that Norwich received was accurate — there was comfort in that, he supposed. He might consider it a compliment that his activities had attracted the attention of the Court of High Commission — the supreme English legal authority in religious matters, or civil matters as well, when it pleased them to be. He was traveling in rarefied circles, indeed. He wondered if Richard Bancroft would remember him from their Cambridge days — possibly not; his mind must be full of weighty matters, these days. He hoped that maybe Bancroft would be in charge of his questioning. Too bad they couldn't get him a more comfortable ride to his destination.

September 1586: London

They arrived in Ipswich well before midnight, and Edward Chase was transferred to a cell in the local jail. He was offered nothing to eat, but at least there was a sort of latrine in the place. Edward's ankles were bruised and bleeding a little from the shackles, and he was glad to have them off. All his personal effects, of course, were taken from him — and his doublet as well. Fortunately, it was a warm night. The next morning, his doublet was returned, with his breakfast, which he forced himself to eat. No sign of his pack or his other possessions. It was dark, humid, and reeked of urine, feces, and a dozen other unidentifiable odors. There was noise, as well, muffled through the door, but continuous. Apart from that, he was comfortable enough. He made a point of counting the days, and saying his prayers, lest he lose track of himself.

As the days went by, he had ample opportunity to reflect on his life and his probable fate. The Court of High Commission could keep him here as long as they wished of course, or just as likely leave him to rot here. There was always the chance of a general amnesty if the Queen died — assuming, of course, that she didn't die at the hands of the Spanish: In that case, he might well wind up tied to a stake, surrounded by a pile of burning faggots.

After a few weeks, the uncertainties began to gnaw at him. He had succeeded in his role as a 'decoy', of that much he was certain. And he did not expect any of his friends to visit him in jail, not so long as his case was pending. But the decision to send him on his last mission in this way seemed to make less sense. He was a pawn, really, in a great chess match — he accepted that. But why sacrifice this particular pawn in this way, (if that is what they were doing)? His captors could be forgiven for supposing that he harbored some deep secrets from them (indeed, that was the very deception he was trying to maintain), but surely his friends could get some message to him, through bribery or whatever means, to encourage or even instruct him. It seemed that they had abandoned him altogether.

It was thirty days by his count, before he actually saw another human face. On the day the door opened, two men stood there. "You must come with us," they said. That was all.

He complied, not knowing or caring where he was going — it was a relief just to get out of that stinking cell. He was led, one in front, the other behind, to a larger room, with a window, a prominent drain, and a bucket of water. "Take off your clothes," he was ordered. No choice but to comply, but what was going on?

"You must wash yourself," said one of the guards, and handed him a grimy-looking bar of soap. Edward did as he was instructed, and washed out his hair, as well. The water was cold, but somehow a relief. When he was finished, the guard handed him a bundle, and said, "Now, put these on."

'These' he recognized as his own clothing; a change of clothes that could only have come from the pack he carried on his journeys. They were clean enough, and he put them on as instructed. His shoes were the same that he had just taken off, but when he reached for his doublet, the guard prevented him, saying, "We are keeping that. Come with me."

Once again, it was one guard in front, another behind. They climbed a flight of stairs, and then Edward found himself blinking in the sunlight. He was confused and looked around for a clue to what was happening. "There." One of his captors pointed to a richly decorated horse-drawn coach that stood nearby. Standing next to it was none other than Charles Bedford!

Edward walked slowly in the direction of the coach. "Edward!" Bedford greeted him, "You look well!"

The improbability of the whole situation touched Edward's sense of humor. "If I look well to you, perhaps I should have tried incarceration sooner. I must admit that I do not feel very well."

"A good meal will remedy that, I trust. Get in." Bedford gestured to the coach.

Edward did as instructed. The seats were soft and comfortable. He eased into them tentatively. Bedford climbed in also and sat opposite. He ordered the driver to move, and off they went.

"You should understand that you are in my custody," said Bedford. "I have shackles for you, but I hope they won't be necessary. There are also two coachmen riding outside, who will not hesitate to shoot you if you try to escape. Not that escaping would do you any good. You are a marked man, now. I doubt your friends would welcome you into their company, after your so public arrest. More sensible to enjoy the ride, don't you think?"

By now the horses were proceeding at a quick trot down a main thoroughfare of the city, Edward could tell by the angle of the sun that they were headed westward, out of the city. The ride was bumpy, but nowhere near as rough as it should be, given their speed. "This is more comfortable than I would have thought," admitted Edward.

"Aye, the coach has special springs above the axles, to soften the ride. It's the latest thing in coach building. Only the very rich get to ride this way. You should enjoy it while you can."

Edward's head was spinning at this turn of events. At length, he spoke: "So, if I am, as you say, in your custody, why am I riding in a rich man's coach?"

"Because you are with me, and I prefer to travel in comfort," Bedford replied. "And if your next question is why I am riding in a rich man's coach, the answer is I have borrowed it, and the owner wants to see you in London, without delay."

None of this made any sense to Edward. By now, they were out of the city proper, and onto the Great Road. The driver whipped the horses into a full gallop. One of the coachmen blew a trumpet to warn the other traffic on the road to get out of their way. Edward watched the scene whiz by from the coach window — Farmers harvesting their fields, villagers stopping to admire the coach as it passed. It was a little like sailing, he decided. After a couple of hours, they stopped at an inn, to change horses. Bedford bought supper for both of them: "The beef stew is very good, today," said Bedford.

He was right about the stew — though almost anything would seem delicious after thirty days of prison food, Edward thought. Still, he was grateful. What was the saying about a condemned man eating a hearty meal? There had to be more to it than that. Someone in London wanted to see him and wanted to see him clean and well-fed. That was something to be grateful for.

"I suppose I have you to thank, for the bathing, and the clean clothing?" he stated, more than asked.

"Yes. I have found that incarcerated men acquire fleas, lice, and other vermin, not to mention unpleasant aromas. Since we are traveling together for at least a day, I wanted to spare myself that experience. Also, if I return this coach to its owner with — shall we say 'passengers'? — I will probably not be able to use it again — ever."

Humor. Self-deprecating, but a clear reminder of which man was in charge. Edward worked on his stew.

A fresh team of horses was in harness, and they were soon galloping down the road again. They stopped for dinner, changed horses again, and pressed on through the night. Edward fell asleep at some point — not the most comfortable bed, but compared to a prison cot, not so bad either.

When he woke, it was daylight. They were stopped somewhere, to change horses again. Edward asked to use the privy, and one of the coachmen accompanied him. An hour later, they stopped for breakfast. "Where are we?" he asked.

"Romford," Bedford replied. "London, in two hours or less; depends on how much traffic is on the road."

It scarcely seemed possible that they had covered such a distance. Edward thought of all the shoe leather he had worn away on these very same roads. This would be a story to tell his grandchildren — if he lived that long.

It was not yet midmorning when the coach stopped in front of a substantial house in the city of London. Bedford got out first, then he and a coachman escorted Edward Chase to the front door. Servants let them in, and they were led to a room in the lower levels of the house, with a couple of chairs, and a small writing desk. "May as well be seated," said Bedford, "while you wait." Bedford left, and Edward heard him bolt the lock from the outside. Nothing to do but wait.

In a few hours, the door opened and a servant brought in something to eat. Edward caught just enough glimpse outside the room to see one of the coachmen standing guard outside. The servant left, and he heard the door lock.

The servant returned in less than half an hour with a chamberpot and took away the utensils that had come with the midday meal. Several minutes later, Bedford was back. "Time to face your accusers," he said, and led him out of the room, and upstairs to a larger room, behind tall double doors. Inside the room, behind a large desk, sat Richard Bancroft, of the Court of High Commission. He wore the same doggy look that Edward remembered from school. He looked up and said, "Good afternoon, Mr. Chase. Please be seated." Edward heard Bedford pull up a chair behind him, in the corner.

Edward returned the greeting. "Good to see you again Dr. Bancroft, though I wish the circumstances were different." He sat down in a chair facing Bancroft.

"I am sure that you do," replied Bancroft. "Have we met before?"

"We were at Cambridge together," said Edward. "You probably don't remember. I attended some of your lectures on preaching."

Bancroft's face showed a flash of recognition. "Ah, I thought your voice was familiar. You were a preacher of some ability, as I recall. A worthy student."

He paused. "This is not a trial; it is an investigation of certain accusations made against you. I am here to determine whether there is enough evidence to support the accusations, that is all. You are charged with conspiring to disturb the peace. Specifically, you are accused of aiding a network of malcontents who regularly undermine the authority of the bishops of the Church of England, who plot to replace loyal officials with men sympathetic to their peculiar beliefs and encourage the laity to ignore the lawful requirements of our Queen, and her servants, in matters of religious conformity. Is this true?"

"On what evidence are these accusations based?" asked Edward.

Bancroft shuffled through a pile of papers on the desk. "We have innumerable accounts of your movements, between certain cities of this realm, over several years. You have been seen in the company of prominent Puritans, and Papists. You have no permanent home, as far as anyone can tell, but seem to appear at random all over the eastern shires. How can you make an honest living? You appear to be guilty of vagrancy, at the very least."

Edward nodded. "I freely admit that I am a well-traveled man. It is how I make my living. I travel from town to town, and people pay me to deliver documents of one sort or another to the places that I visit. I deny that I have been involved in breaking any law, or seeking to undermine the authority of our Queen, or any of her servants."

"You make a living from delivering letters and other papers? How is that possible?"

"Wealthy men have servants they can send to deliver their correspondence. The less affluent have to hire someone, like me. I also preach at divers places, and I receive some income from that. It is not a career for old men, but I manage to get by."

"Preach? Where do you preach? And under whose authority?"

Edward replied carefully. "I am a licensed preacher and have been for many years. I am invited to preach occasionally at well-known places such as St. Andrew's church in Norwich; more often to smaller congregations, in the villages. There is a hunger for good preaching in the villages, not all parish priests are trained in the rhetorical arts."

"So, you take the priest's place, and preach a sermon? What about the liturgy?"

"I do not perform the sacraments, nor lead the liturgy. I do not preach on a Sunday morning unless invited to by the local vicar. I may be invited to preach on a topic on a Sunday afternoon, in the sanctuary or some other location."

"Who decides what matters you preach about?"

"Most often the vicar asks me to address certain matters that he feels his flock needs to be instructed about, it varies from one parish to another, naturally." (Best not to dwell on the parishes where the vicar was not happy to see him).

"What matters?"

"Matters of the true faith. There is still a lot of Papist superstition in the remote villages — purgatory, images, praying to saints — that sort of thing."

"And you persuade them of the truth, do you?"

"I hope to. It is not always easy to tell who has accepted the truth, and who has not. I try to follow my sermon with a time of questions and discussion. Sometimes a layman will speak about my message; in that case, I can tell whether it has been heard aright. Sometimes a layman is inspired to expand on some point — when that happens, I know that the truth has reached his heart. That is the most gratifying part of the sermon, for me — knowing that the light of truth has dawned in the hearts of the people."

Bancroft stared at him for a moment. "And do you not call these events 'conventicles'? And do you not call these extemporaneous outbursts, whether from men, or even women, 'prophesyings'?"

Edward realized then that the real target of this examination was not what he had thought. *They aren't worried about the letters,* he said to himself, *they're worried about the conventicles! They're worried what may happen if laymen, and — God forbid, women, begin to trust their own understanding of scripture!* He decided he needed to shift his defense strategy. The most obvious approach was to emphasize his disdain for Brownists. Fortunately, he had already laid the foundation for that argument, with Bedford. Bedford could be called as his witness!

"They are indeed called 'conventicles'. 'Prophesyings' is a term that is usually applied to the words of scholars, but I suppose it could also describe the testimony of a lay person if the Spirit has so inspired them." (This was splitting hairs; Edward knew very well that the laymen believed they were speaking inspired messages, quite often).

Bancroft looked at him sternly. "I am surprised at you, Mr. Chase. You are an educated man. And yet, do you not see how perilous this business of yours is? Do you not see how your conventicles feed the errors of the separatists, and undermine the unity of our church, just at the time that we are most under threat of the papists?"

"I deny that my preaching undermines any church unless it be the Catholic church, and I deny that my preaching strengthens the cause of the separatists, in any way. Mr Bedford can testify that I am no friend of separatists — indeed, I denounce their error at every opportunity." He turned in his chair to look directly at Bedford, who nodded laconically. Edward avoided mention of the conventicles; the enthusiasms of such events could foster some very odd ideas, including, possibly, ideas so extreme as to lead to separatist sentiments. Which was why it was important to have a sound Minister of the Word in charge of them . . .

Bancroft shook his head. "Name the parishes you have preached at, over the last five years."

Edward was surprised at the question; needed to divert the direction of the examination long enough to collect his thoughts. "I cannot possibly remember them all. But it appears that you must have reports of most of them, in that pile of papers on your desk!" That put the focus back on what evidence Bancroft actually had in front of him, at least for a moment. "May I read one of them?"

It was Bancroft's turn to be surprised. He drew a piece of paper from the pile and handed it to Edward. Edward skimmed it and read it aloud, "June 14, anno domini 1581, Stoke Ash: Chase attended parish church, and was heard preaching in a barn that afternoon, to fifty or so local subjects; preached on the 'Excellence of God's grace, and the futility of Praying to Saints, also the Sufficiency of Christ's Mediation for Sin', preached overlong . . ." he stopped, and heard a snicker from the corner where Bedford was sitting. "This appears to be a true account of my actions that day, I cannot contradict it." He felt that he had won a point.

"Here is another," said Bancroft. "March 31, anno domini 1582, Chelmsford: Chase visited condemned heretic John Payne. Showed a note to the jailer, which he said was to be delivered to a friend of Payne's. It seems that you carry correspondence for Papists, as well as Puritans, Mr. Chase. So, if you are not a Papist, are you a Puritan? Or are your affiliations promiscuous?"

That was a blow. He should have seen it coming. Was this Bancroft's trump card, or did he have another yet to play? Edward's mind was racing. He could concoct some story that might account for the visit to the jail, but if Bancroft had evidence of his journey to Little Baddow, leaving that detail out of his story would only look like he was covering something up. At any cost, he wanted the carpenter to be left out of the story; he would protect the Vessey family, as well, if he could. The question was, what did Bancroft know? Was there a report on that pile that he had been followed from Chelmsford to Little Baddow, and disappeared? *First, take back the initiative by pretending to be offended,* he decided.

"The name of 'Puritan' is an insult in most places," he began. "But if I understand your meaning, then you may well call me a Puritan. I am of that persuasion which hopes to see the reformation of our church complete, and I could explain what that means at some great length if it please you."

Bancroft put up his hands. "Spare me that, it would not please me. Answer my question."

Edward was still collecting his thoughts. *I shall wager that the person who followed me from Chelmsford to Little Baddow that morning preferred not to admit in writing that he lost track of me. If I am wrong, I will say that I was visiting my colleague Samuel Vessey that day. God, help me!*

"If I understand your question, I think I have already answered it. I have no sympathy for Papist teaching, as my preaching will attest. John Payne was a friend of mine . . ."

Bancroft raised his eyebrows with surprise at the admission.

". . . not for his religion, but for his character. I met him some years before, under the name of William Payne. I did not know he was a Papist, much less a Catholic priest. I was not certain that the condemned man was the same man that I knew as William Payne, until the night I saw him in the Chelmsford jail — though I will say that his appearance was much altered by his harsh treatment. I expressed my sympathy for his plight, and yes, he asked me to accept a note from him."

"It does not help your case, to admit that you sympathized with a man convicted of plotting to assassinate the Queen," said Bancroft.

"I am certain that John Payne was guilty of no such thing," retorted Edward, with some heat rising in his voice. "He should not have died, simply because the Pope is at war with our Queen. He was no threat at all."

"Do you often feel such sympathy for papists?" It was an attempt at entrapment, Edward realized. Bancroft must certainly be aware of everything he had said to Charles Bedford, on the road from Norwich. Yet Edward was content to let the examination go in any direction but Little Baddow. "I think that Mr. Bedford will attest that I have protested the treatment that recusants receive in the Norwich jail, and you could easily find others who have heard me express similar sentiments. Catholic Priests may reasonably be suspect as agents of the Pope (if the evidence is strong) and treated as such (Though I think that imprisonment would serve our cause better), but torturing and starving ordinary Catholics is pointlessly cruel, and serves no purpose at all." He was carrying this a bit far, perhaps, but if Bancroft pursued this line of questioning, the whole business of the note might be forgotten . . . the important thing was to convince Bancroft that this line of questioning could lead to something incriminating.

Bancroft appeared to take the bait. "What say you, Bedford? Has Mr. Chase expressed such sentiments in your hearing?"

"Indeed, he did," replied Bedford, "on the road from Norwich, the day he was arrested."

"And did he speak of other matters, relevant to this inquiry?"

"He spoke at greater length about the dangers of separatism. I cannot relate everything he said, in less than two hours, for that is how long it took him to say it. He did say that he counted the Brownists as a greater danger than the recusants."

"What say you to this, Mr. Chase?"

"Mr. Bedford has fairly summarized my remarks to him." *Go on now, Edward* thought to himself, *ask me more questions about separatists. Let me explain myself for as many hours as you can stay awake . . .*

It was not to be. Bancroft plucked another piece of paper from the pile on the desk, "I would hear more of this note that you took from John Payne," he said. "Who was it intended for? What was the message?"

Edward hoped his face did not show his disappointment at this turn. *Here it comes, no avoiding it. Time for some creative — what did the Jesuits call it? Prevarication — concealing the truth without actually lying.* He needed some creative prevarication. "Payne did not name the person to which I was to deliver the message. When he gave it to me, I did not read it. I folded it and tucked it into my belt. I delivered it to the jailer when I left, and he read it."

"So you have no idea what Payne wrote?"

"I think you have an idea; unless I miss my guess, the paper you are holding contains the jailer's report, including details about my visit that I have probably forgotten, and the contents of the note, as well. I was told that Payne sent many messages during his last days. If that is true, then you must know the contents of all of them — but that is only what the jailer told me." Bancroft smiled, just a little. Chase felt that he had scored another point.

"And where was the note delivered?"

"To the fire," replied Chase.

"You burned it?"

"Technically, the fire <u>burned</u> it, but I was the agent for the burning."

"If you intended to burn it, why agree to take the note in the first place?"

This is my opening, thought Edward, *Time for a story. Make it a good one.* "I suppose that it caught me by surprise, the note. I thought I was there to say farewell to a friend. I was shocked to see his condition, to tell the truth — I think he was cruelly treated. I pitied him; it seemed the least I could do for him. When I was outside the jail, I realized that there could be some peril in carrying a note that he had written, so I did what I thought was prudent. William — I mean John — would have no way of knowing what I did with it, under the circumstances."

"And you have no idea what the note said?"

"How could I? Oh, I suppose he named the intended recipient, and it seems most likely the destination was in it too. But I cannot say for certain that it is so. Surely, the jailer's report has that information?"

"I will tell you what the jailer recorded. The note began 'Dear Friend', and thanked the recipient for unnamed favors and considerations — that is all. No mention of whom the note is intended for, or where to deliver it. How do you account for that?"

In a flash, Edward saw his escape. The realization must have appeared on his face, because Bancroft said, "Well? How do you account for it?" again.

Edward buried his face in his hands. *Don't overplay this,* he told himself. When he raised his face, there was the hint of a tear in his eyes. "I account for it thus. He intended the note for me. It was the only way he could say thank you and goodbye, from inside that cell, and he knew he didn't have much time. If I had known it was intended for me, I would have kept it as a keepsake of our friendship — but now it is gone." He sighed. "Cowardice, I suppose; fear of being tainted by association with a condemned man." He straightened himself, as if unburdened from some guilt or regret. Bancroft was looking at him intently.

"There is the matter of other letters," Bancroft said and produced the several letters that Edward had been carrying on the day of his arrest. Edward was relieved and tried not to show it.

"They were sealed when I received them, so I know nothing of their contents."

"And their intended recipients?"

"I'm pretty sure all of them have the recipient's name written on the outside. If memory serves, they should have been delivered to people in Ipswich, Chelmsford, and London, and — oh yes, I think there was one for Colchester."

"There were two for Colchester."

"Ah. Two then, for Colchester." Edward nodded.

"I cannot help but recognize that each of these letters is addressed to a known Puritan. What do you say to that?"

Edward tried to look miffed. "If, as you say, I am 'Puritan', then it stands to reason that the people I associate with would be 'Puritans', too, I suppose."

"It stands to reason," agreed Bancroft. "But I would know more of these letter's contents."

"I assumed that you had already read them," replied Edward, "in that case, you know more of their contents than I do." Bancroft smiled again. Edward thought he had scored another point.

There was silence in the room, for several minutes. Then Bancroft spoke: "Mr. Chase, I will speak plainly. I believe that you and your friends, and many others, are engaged in some sort of secret conspiracy to change the very character of our beloved church. I believe that you intend to do it slowly, all the while conforming outwardly to the law. I am determined that you will not succeed in this effort. I cannot charge you with a crime, at least not yet, but laws can be changed. I think you have served as a trusted courier of secret communications by these conspirators, though I do not have proof. Your arrest will at least deny them your services, because once they know you have been jailed and then released, they would be fools to ever entrust you with anything important. You have been a weapon in their hands, and I think I have taken that weapon from them. I am determined to crush these 'conventicles', and put an end to their 'prophesying'. I have the full power of the government behind me, and I will succeed."

Edward had to admit that Bancroft's analysis was on the mark — no one would want him to deliver any sensitive message for them, for fear it would be intercepted, or even betrayed by the courier. Crushing the conventicles would not be as simple as Bancroft imagined, but he was certainly in a position to make things very unpleasant.

Bancroft continued, "To that I add the fact that you express sympathy for recusants, and admit to befriending the traitor and heretic John Payne — you are under a cloud of suspicion. You are going to have to find some other employment, Mr. Chase. I do not think you will find it easy to do so."

Right again, thought Edward, *there's not much else I'm qualified for.*

"It seems to me a shame to waste your gifts and your education. I have an offer for you to consider: There is a parish in the North that needs a priest. I think you would be a suitable candidate for that position. The job is yours, if you want it."

"A parish priest? But I am not ordained to the priesthood!"

"It is no great matter to ordain you; a ceremony, an oath. You will have to wear the vestments, of course. And you will be under the authority of your bishop, subject to discipline if you try to lead your flock astray. On the other hand, you will know financial security, a comfortable income, and a parsonage to live in. You could do worse."

Edward was caught entirely off-guard. "And the terms of this offer are?"

"As I said, you will serve under the authority of your bishop, you will no longer serve the Puritan cause. The place I have in mind is quite remote; you won't easily get into trouble there. It is a pretty place, I am told."

"And why am I suited to this position?"

It is remote, as I said. The people of that parish are inclined to cling to the old ways — or maybe some of the new ways, as well. Anything other than what their government requires. A history of risings and rebellions . . ."

Edward imagined a small, poor village inhabited by savage men, with wild beards and unkempt hair, women devoted to sorcery, and hordes of dirty children. Still, he might be helpful in such a place. He shifted his weight because his left leg was getting stiff. He remembered what life on the road was like. He needed a change. Perhaps this was it? "You said there is a parsonage?"

"Indeed there is," said Bedford from behind him. "Well-kept, large enough for a family with children. A housekeeper comes with the place."

Edward took a moment to think it over. Not a very long one. This was at least a chance for a better life. If he turned the offer down, the Court of High Commission could keep him in jail for the rest of his life if it chose to. He was no use to his 'Puritan' employers now, and they would not pay him for rendering no service at all. If the place was as remote as Bancroft said, he would not be bothered much by the bishop, who most likely spent most of his days in London, near the center of power and promotion. He could still find ways to preach and teach the truth, whether the laymen would receive it or not. Perhaps, in time, he would make 'Puritans' of them; that would be his revenge. "I accept your offer," he said.

Bancroft nodded and smiled. "I did not think you were a fool, to refuse a chance at redemption. Come, let us have some supper."

Three days later, Edward Chase was on the road, again. This time, his route was more westerly, away from the seacoast. It would take him at least ten days to reach his new home on foot, but this would be the last time his feet would have to carry him so far. A hearth with a warm fire, and a roof over his head; that was his destiny.

Part 17: The Peaks

Edward Chase did not make his northward journey alone. The paraphernalia of his new profession was more than a man could carry on his back for any distance, so he had been provided with a traveling companion, named Bruce. Bruce was not much for conversation, but with four legs and a strong back, he was well able to carry the load and keep up with Edward.

They stopped every night in some village along the way, and Edward had to remember to attend to Bruce's care, as well as his own. Generally, Bruce was an amiable companion, braying only when excited, or missing his supper. The days were noticeably shorter and cooler now, but still pleasant for walking. Many of the fields they passed were ripe, bronzed by the long summer days, now bracing for what was to come. Harvest was underway, and as far as Edward could tell, it was a good one.

There were plenty of others on the road, of course, and Edward noticed a difference in how strangers approached him. Perhaps it was the presence of Bruce ("Sturdy donkey, that. Is he tractable?") that made him seem more approachable. Or perhaps it was the perception that Edward was a man of some substance or importance — after all, most people couldn't afford a donkey of their own — maybe he was a man worth knowing. Perhaps it was that his demeanor was different — he was no longer trying to avoid notice and may have seemed more approachable.

At any rate, this pace was not as demanding, and he was much more relaxed. It was easy to strike up conversations with others on the road, and he did not worry about revealing too much about his business.

About three days out, he heard more news about Queen Mary, of Scotland. After eighteen years as Elizabeth's "guest" (confined in various manors and castles in the north of England), and despairing of getting her throne back, Mary had been caught up in a conspiracy to escape from Elizabeth's control, and flee the country, with the intent of replacing Elizabeth, should the Spanish invasion succeed. She was charged with treason — a charge which she rejected since she was not an English subject, but a sovereign in her own right. There was little doubt of the outcome of her trial: The political liability of letting her live was simply unacceptable. If Mary was dead, Phillip of Spain would have one less weapon in his diplomatic arsenal, one less reason for English Catholics or ambitious Protestant aristocrats to join the Spanish cause.

Edward reflected on his own recent incarceration. Only thirty days, and he was ready to doubt whether he would ever see the sun again. Mary's confinement was certainly more pleasant — but eighteen years! No surprise that she would grasp at any straw that was offered to her, however flimsy.

As he journeyed north, the landscape changed — first, some gentle hills, with broad, shallow valleys between them, then some undulating uplands, where sheep grazed — the soil was probably too thin for wheat or barley, he thought, but good enough for pasture.

On the evening of the seventh day he arrived at Chesterfield, an ancient free town on the River Rother. Here, as per his instructions, he was to turn westward, into the high moors and dales where his assigned parish lay. It was raining and misty; he was chilled. He sought out the rector of the local church, who offered him accommodations. It was a relief to hand Bruce over to a stable hand and change into dry clothing.

The rector was married, with three children. The rectory was large enough to house them all comfortably, with room for Edward, as well. At dinner, Edward was seated across from two of the children, with the third one at his side, and the rector and his wife at either end. A servant brought the meal in from the kitchen. Over dinner, his host offered some perspective on his destination: "'Tis a bit rough over there. Farmers don't do well in that country, most make their living as lead miners or sheepherders. Things are a bit primitive, you could say."

Edward was not encouraged by this, though it was more or less what he had been expecting. "What do you know of Derwent?"

"Derwent? Ah. Well, I've never been to the place, but it has a reputation, you could say."

"Reputation?"

"It is very remote. People there still cleave to the ancient ways."

"You mean they harbor catholic sentiments?" This was something he felt he was well equipped to deal with — all his training was preparation for the task of redeeming recusants.

"No, I mean ancient ways — traditions and lore that are far older than St. Augustine, ways that were here when the Romans arrived. They practice old ways of healing and knowing that are lost to the modern age."

"You mean that they are sorcerers and pagans?" This pretty much confirmed Edward's worst expectations of his new position — it sounded like a hazardous place, indeed. Bancroft had placed him in a kind of exile, apparently. Clever, ruthless man.

"There may be a few such among them, though that is rumor only. But these people have been shielded, you might say, from the wider world for a very long time. Their remoteness has protected them from wars and tumult, and they prefer their traditions to new and unfamiliar ones. One man's sorcery may be another's medicine, in a place like that."

Edward was a little put out at the whole prospect, and his face must have shown it.

"It's not all bad, you know. Most of the parish priests in the Peaks receive a tithe of the proceeds from the mines in their parish each year. It's a steady source of income. The miners build stout houses of stone — wood is scarce — which can be quite snug in the winter. There's plenty of peat up on the moors to heat the houses. Summers are not as hot up among the peaks, either. I once traveled as far as the village of Hope, in the Peaks. It was very pretty, and the people were pleasant."

"How far did that journey take you?"

"I'd guess it was a little more than twenty miles. The roads are not wide or well-maintained, as you can imagine, but we covered the distance in a day and spent a pleasant night in an inn there."

"And how far would Derwent be?"

"I think it would be about the same distance. You would take a turn toward Derwent before you reach Hope, I believe. There is but one road into Derwent from the south, and I hear that it is a narrow one."

"The way you make it sound, I'm surprised that there is a road at all."

"Oh, of course, there has to be a road. They have to have a way to move the wool and the lead to market!"

At this point, one of the rector's children, who had been maintaining a respectful silence, piped up: "Papa, tell him about the wolves!"

Wolves and Witches!? Thought Edward to himself. *Has Bancroft sent me to my death?*

The rector chuckled, and shook his head, "Nay, that is only a tale to tell in the dead of winter." He leaned toward Edward and said, "There used to be wolves on the moors around the peaks — no doubt about it. But that was a hundred years ago. The wolves are long gone."

"But what about the beasts on the moors? The ones that eat the sheep?" The boy was insistent.

"Yes, please," said Edward, as his stomach knotted a little. "Tell me about the beasts that eat the sheep."

"It is only a story," replied the rector, with a dismissive wave of his hand. "A complaint that the shepherds make when taxes are due. They want to claim compensation for the loss of some animals."

"And do they get it? The compensation, I mean."

"Not without some proof that a sheep was actually killed by a wild animal. There never seems to be enough left to prove that a wild beast actually attacked a sheep — or even enough left to prove that it was a sheep that was attacked."

Edward Chase was speechless, for the first time in his memory. The rector's son helpfully added his own information: "They say the beast prowls the moors only at night when the moon is full, and especially in winter. They say the beast roams over all of the Dark Peak and runs so fast that none can catch it. They say that when it howls, you can hear it for miles . . ."

"William, that's enough," the boy's mother said.

The rector chuckled. "It does make quite a story!"

Edward had a mental image of Bruce and himself on a narrow, muddy track in deep woods, surrounded by — wolves!? Something more terrifying? He thought of his walking staff and his knife. Would it be enough to defend them? Would it be kinder to let Bruce loose, to escape if he could? His imagining was interrupted . . .

"Do not be frightened of a few tales, Mr. Chase. I'm sure you will find your new home agreeable enough."

"What is the Dark Peak?"

"Ah. I will explain. The country you are about to visit is high ground, which separates this side of England from the western counties — places like Lancashire and Cheshire. We call it the Peaks. There is a river valley that divides the Peaks north and south. South of the river is called the White Peak, north is called the Dark Peak. The Dark Peak is the larger, higher, and wilder part of the Peaks."

"And why is it called dark?"

"From the valleys below, it looks darker. Although it is sometimes covered with snow in the winter, in which case the Dark Peak looks whiter than the White Peak. Both are used to graze sheep and cattle, both are covered with heather in the summer. Both can be inhospitable in the winter."

"And I suppose Derwent is somewhere on those moors."

"Nay, the village is in a valley, on the banks of the river. Only the wildest folk try to live up on the moors. Like I said, you will find the place agreeable enough — though isolated. I'm curious as to why you were assigned to that parish. You seem like a man more suited to the wider world."

Edward nodded. "You are right. All of this is new to me. All that I was told was that the parish needs a priest. I suppose the previous one was promoted to a larger parish, or perhaps he died?"

"Died."

"God rest his soul. He must have been old, then?"

"No. Not old."

Edward hesitated a moment. Then, "Are you saying that he died a young man, through some mischance or mischief?"

"He was about your age, I believe. The circumstances of his passing are uncertain. By the time that the bishop heard of his passing, and sent someone to investigate, the fellow had been in the ground for more than a week."

There was something sad about the idea of a priest dying alone, in some remote place, buried in a churchyard, before his family even knew he was gone, thought Edward. Then he realized, with a start, that that was exactly the fate that Richard Bancroft had planned for him.

"Who performed the funeral service?"

"Who, indeed? There was no priest there, of that I am certain."

This would be a terrifying prospect for a sacramentalist, Edward reflected — a soul sent to the afterlife without absolution. For a Puritan like himself, who believed in only two sacraments — baptism and communion — it was less problematic. Still, to die without family to mourn him — that was a hard thing. He wondered about the man's mother. Was she mourning him? Or had Bancroft contrived to so separate him from his family, that he was lost to them forever? "I suppose that they held some sort of ceremony for him after his fate was known."

"Yes, I am sure they did."

On that note, Edward excused himself and went to bed — it was full dark outside, and he was weary. He did not sleep particularly well that night; the revelations about Derwent and the Dark Peak were a jumble in his thoughts and dreams.

In the morning, the weather was clear and fine. He enjoyed a hearty breakfast, and the servants provided him with a midday meal for the journey. The rector joined him near the front door, to see him off; Bruce was waiting for him in the street, packed and bridled. Across the street was the Church of Mary and All Saints. Something was wrong with the church spire. The rector noticed him staring up at it.

"You didn't see our church last night, what with the mist and all?"

Edward shook his head, "No, what has happened to the spire? Was it lightning?"

"That's as good an explanation as any. Most say the Devil himself caused it, twisting and bending it like that. Personally, I think it is some defect in the workmanship. It has been that way for a hundred years."

Edward decided that whatever awaited him among the peaks, it couldn't be as intimidating as a city where the Devil himself had license to alter the architecture of a parish church. "I thank you for your hospitality," he said, "May God reward you for your kindness to me."

The rector nodded. "And may God bless you on your journey, and in your new home," he replied.

Edward and Bruce left the city behind them, and headed west. As they left the river valley, the road began to rise slightly, then fall and rise again, more steeply. They passed farmsteads and fields, then pastures of sheep, and some shaggy cattle with large horns. Farther along, trees grew more thickly beside the road, until their branches formed an archway overhead. They met few others on the road, fewer the farther they traveled. Progress was slow — there were many muddy places where yesterday's rain had not yet drained away. The upward climb was more than he was accustomed to, as well — He had to stop to catch his breath once or twice. Stopping in a clearing was pleasant enough; birds sang, and the sun was bright. He caught a glimpse here and there of the hills that rose on either side of the road — steep at their crests.

Stopping in the woods was a different matter. There were still a few bird calls, but it was dark. The trees seemed to be crowding the road as if to gradually close it off altogether. And there were sounds — just out of sight in the undergrowth, some faint, others heavier, as if from the footfalls of someone, or something large. Edward urged Bruce forward. They came out into open country near the village of Grindleford. It was already after noon; they had traveled nine miles, less than half the distance to Derwent. Edward was hungry, so they stopped to eat beside the road.

Grindleford lay at the foot of a hill with a prominent scarp, or "edge" of exposed rock atop its crest. The village overlooked the River Derwent, with a fine view of the broad river valley, and its fields and pastures. It was a lovely sight, thought Edward — none of the ominous gloom he had experienced just a mile or so behind him. Bright sunshine, the woodlands bronzed in Autumn's garb. Harvest was underway. The road ahead led down to the river; there must be a bridge, or maybe just a ford, across the river and into the village. He would ask for directions there.

It was a bridge, not a ford. The river was not too deep, but Edward didn't feel like getting his feet wet, so the bridge was a welcome sight. He found a public house and went in to ask for directions, while he refreshed himself.

"Derwent, ye say?" The barkeep looked a bit skeptical. "That'll be straight upriver from here, past Hathersage and Bamford.

"How is the road?" asked Edward.

"Which way did ye come, this morning?"

"Over the moors from Chesterfield. It was slow going."

"Aye, it would be. From here to Bamford, the road follows the river — not much climbing, There's a ford at Hathersage, where the lead packers cross the river. It's about three or so miles to Hathersage, and another three or so to Bamford. From there, the road to Derwent follows the river, but it's no better than the one ye traveled this morning. Another three, maybe four miles to Derwent."

Edward felt weary. He wouldn't be able to make it to Derwent in what was left of his day. He thanked the barkeep and headed north with Bruce.

The river passed through a narrow gorge for the next hour or so. But the road hugged the river and didn't climb much, just as the barkeep had said. There was a fair bit of traffic on this stretch, as well, and the shoulders of the road were cleared of trees. On either side, the hills loomed, with their rocky edges exposed to the sky. Beyond them, lay the moors, with thin soil good for heather, or perhaps pasture. The slopes were forested in the places that were too steep for pasture. Just before they reached Hathersage, the road turned to cross the river at a ford. The valley was more open here. Pack trains of mules and horses could be seen wading their way across the river, laden with lead from the mines, or whatnot.

Edward paused at the river's edge, to pick a pathway across. A voice spoke from behind him: "If ye're thinkin' ye'd rather not wet yer feet, ye can tie yer ass to the back of me wagon, and ride across."

Edward turned to see a man seated on the seat of a freight wagon, drawn by a team of sturdy horses. "I'll be grateful for your kindness, Sir," he replied. He tied Bruce to the back and climbed up on the seat. "Amos. Amos Watkins," the man introduced himself.

"Edward. Edward Chase." It took but a few moments to ford the river, but Amos kept his team moving. Edward didn't mind riding a while longer. He tried to make conversation. "So what is your business, Amos Watkins? I see that your wagon is empty."

"Aye, so it is. No point in hauling grindstones to the Dark Peak."

"How's that?"

"It's all uphill from here. Easier to haul 'em downhill, than up!" He chuckled at his own humor.

"So you haul grindstones down from the Dark Peak?"

"Of course I do. Best grindstone in the kingdom comes from the Dark Peak. Everybody knows that!"

"I am a stranger here, I did not know that," offered Edward.

"Yer accent gives ye away," Amos nodded, then explained: "It's how the Dark Peak got its name, I reckon. The dark gritstone that lies on the high moor. Quarries all over the place, up there."

"I thought that lead mining was the thing, hereabouts."

"The lead is mined lower down. The gritstone comes from the heights. I'll haul either one, given the chance, and I usually haul some foodstuffs back upcountry on my return trips, but none this time."

Edward chewed on this thought for a moment. It sounded like the moors weren't so desolate, after all. If there were quarries, there had to be people living there, as well.

"Where are ye bound, then, stranger?"

"I'm headed for Derwent. I was hoping to make it by nightfall, but the roads are slower than I expected."

"Derwent? Now, there's a pretty place. Don't go there often — that road is a mess. Wouldn't try to walk it in the dark — too much chance of gettin' lost."

"Thank you for your advice," replied Edward. "I suppose I'll spend the night somewhere else — maybe Bamford?

Amos nodded. "If I were ye, that's what I'd do. Ye can ride with me for a mile or two. I'll show ye the way to Bamford."

And so it went. The two miles to Hathersage were across the valley in plain sight of the surrounding hills, with their distinctive, stony "edges." Tilled fields and pastures spread up the slopes until it was too steep to cultivate- from there to the top, heather and moorland grasses clung to the slopes. Here and there, Edward could see a few higher points, or "Tors," as Amos called them.

In less than two hours, Amos stopped at a fork in the road. "Bamford is to yer right," he nodded in that direction. "I'm bound for Hope, on the left. I wish ye good fortune in Derwent."

Edward thanked him and untied Bruce from the rear of the wagon. Then Amos was off, on the road to Hope. *Hope seems like a good destination*, Edward said to himself. But he had to put Hope behind him and turn his face to the Dark Peak; his destiny lay in that direction.

Bamford was about a mile further on, at the mouth of a narrowing valley, with prominent "edges" on either side. It was fortunate that the distance was short because just as he arrived, the weather turned. Clouds formed over the Dark Peak and moved down the valley toward him. In the event, he made it to a public house with a stable and got Bruce inside before the rain arrived. His decision to wait another day for Derwent was vindicated.

The rain stopped just before sundown, and the westering sun cast rainbows on the remnants of the storm to the east. Edward dined in the pub, on barley bread and a mutton stew — simple fare, but filling. The Innkeeper explained how to get to Derwent — "Just follow the river, keep it on your left. It's four or five miles, no more." He determined to face whatever was in Derwent with optimism and faith — he slept soundly that night.

In the morning, he rose to another bright Autumn day. Streets were still wet from the previous day's rain, but the sky was clear. Edward and Bruce set out, up the river.

The road rose as they followed it, but it followed the river closely. The riverbed rose as well, riffles and currents were rushing by. The valley was narrowing, too; he could see the "edges" closing in overhead until the trees cut off his view. He was back in deep woods again, dim light, and the road was muddy and narrow — a "mess" as Amos had said. Still, it was apparent that it knew traffic — lots of hoof prints in the mud, a hint of wheel ruts. Progress was slow.

Edward would have preferred to push on through to Derwent without stopping, but there were streams to ford, rushing more than usual with yesterday's rain, and he took off his shoes and stockings to wade across them. The road was turning gradually to his left, and then he found himself looking straight at a ford in the river itself. Had he missed a turn? What had the innkeeper said? "Keep the river on your left?"

He looked to his right, and there it was, a narrow gap in the trees. Must be the road to Derwent. How far could it be? No more than three miles, by his calculation. Into the wood they went.

Once they got into the trees, the path was easy enough to follow — muddy, but wide enough for a wagon. It followed the river, gradually upwards. It was dark, and the leaves of the trees were dripping. Soon, the valley was so narrow that the roadway was cut into the side of a hill — an upward slope on his right, and a gentle slope down to the river on his left. He could hear the river, even if he could not always see it. It was difficult to know how far they had come, or how far they still had to go. He looked for a clearing where they could stop to catch their breath, but none appeared. Finally, he just had to halt in the road, for his own sake, as much as Bruce's. He chose a spot where the road was a little higher and less muddy. He tried to scrape some of the mud off his shoes. Bruce looked at him. "Sorry, old fellow. I'll clean up your feet when we get to the village."

It was quiet. Even the dripping of the trees seemed to have stopped. He could hear nothing but the rushing of the river, until — what was that? Something upslope, something in the undergrowth. Something large. Bruce cocked his ears and looked in the direction of the sound. Edward held his breath. There it was again, a thrashing sound, then a moan!

Edward remembered to breathe. It had to be some sort of beast. He looked at Bruce, who appeared to be curious, but not frightened. Probably not a wolf then, or a sheep-killing moor monster. He thought of running up the road until he reached the village, where he could find help. But what if it was a human, in distress? He was reminded of the parable about the Samaritan man who rescued a wounded man on the road from Jericho. "Wait here, Bruce," he said. Not that Bruce would have obeyed his instructions unless it suited him to do so. He took a firm grip on his staff, and pulled his long knife from under his doublet, then stepped off the road, into the trees.

It took him a few minutes to locate the sound and to climb to where it was coming from. It was half-hidden behind some kind of woodland shrub. Shaggy — not human, then; lying on the ground, moaning and panting. It was a sheep.

When he got close, he saw that its foot was tangled in something, and appeared to be bleeding. He knelt to see what it was. It was a rabbit snare, he realized. He looked around and suddenly saw the woods in a new light. There were small pathways everywhere, he saw — the familiar paths that small animals used every day. Someone had placed the snare across the path, hoping to catch a rabbit — and snared this sheep instead.

He cut the snare off the sheep's leg with his knife, then stuck it into his belt. The sheep's leg was bleeding, where the snare had chafed its way into it, but he didn't think the leg was broken. He tried to get the sheep on its feet, but it was unsteady — probably exhausted from struggling with the snare. It tumbled over and rolled down the slope toward the road. The sheep's wool was waterlogged, from lying in the rain all night — or perhaps longer — who knew?

Edward followed the sheep down slope, and tried once again — no luck, the sheep stumbled and rolled down to the road, where it lay panting. Edward followed it down. He didn't know what else to do — the sheep was too heavy to carry. The wool was surprisingly thick and matted — probably padded the sheep pretty well, as it rolled down the hill. He knelt by it once again, to see if he could get it to stand, and maybe steady it.

"And what, pray tell, are ye doin' with that ewe?" A woman's voice, from behind him. Bruce turned to look, and Edward rose and turned. A youngish woman, in a crimson cloak, her hair unbound, black and shiny, like the feathers on a raven. She looked at Edward with an accusatory expression, as if he might be a poacher or something.

"I found her up there. Caught in a snare. I'm trying to get her on her feet."

The woman glanced up the slope, then looked back at Edward. Green eyes, suspicious. "By rollin' her down the hill? And with that whoppin' big knife?"

Edward looked down, pulled the knife from his belt, and tucked it away inside his doublet. "I used it to cut the snare off her leg."

"That yer donkey?" She nodded at Bruce.

"Indeed he is. Bruce, meet er . . . I don't know your name, miss."

"My christening name is Margaret. What is yours?"

"I am Edward. Edward Chase, at your service." He bowed slightly and smiled.

She was not impressed. She did not smile. "And what do ye propose to do, if the ewe gets to her feet?"

"If she can walk, I think she may recover. There's not much else I can do for her."

Margaret approached the ewe and looked closely at the bleeding leg. "She won't walk far on that leg, without some doctorin'."

"Is there someone in Derwent who could help her?"

"Derwent? What do you know of Derwent?"

"Practically nothing. I am headed there now. Do you think that the ewe can walk as far as Derwent, and is there someone who could help her there? Her owner, perhaps?"

"Perhaps. This sheep hasn't had an owner for nigh on two years — look at the wool. She wasn't shorn this spring, maybe not last spring, either. Been lost to her owner a long time, I reckon."

"Still, every sheep must belong to someone."

Margaret looked at him, with her green eyes. "Aye. One way or another. What did ye say yer business was in Derwent?"

"I am to be the vicar in the parish church, there."

She laughed. "A vicar! Aye, of course! Who better to find a lost sheep than a man of God?" Her laugh was a little sarcastic, he thought, or maybe just ironic. But her suspicious mood seemed to be eased. Edward relaxed.

"Can you help me with her?" Edward asked. "I don't know anything about caring for sheep."

"Anyone can see that. If you take this load off the donkey, we could tie her over his back and carry her that way."

Edward hesitated. Leaving his possessions on the side of the road for any stranger to claim seemed risky. But the ewe was there, and in pain . . . "I'm guessing she weighs about two hundred pounds. That's more than I can lift, I think."

"I didn't say that ye could. I said *we* could. I'll hold up my end if you'll hold up yours." It was a challenge; he could see it in her eyes.

"Let's try it, then," he said.

He unburdened Bruce and set his load at the side of the road. Then, the two of them tried to get a grip on the ewe and lift her onto Bruce's back. It took three tries, but they did it. Edward could tell that Margaret had, indeed, held up her end — maybe more than her share, he thought.

Once the ewe was on Bruce's back, they tied her down. Edward selected a few of the items that Bruce had been burdened with, and carried them under his arms, as they started down the road to Derwent.

It was in fact, not far at all to the edge of the village — a few hundred yards around a bend, and the houses came into view. People greeted them as they passed: "What's that ye got there, Meg? Another sheep for the shearin'?" People laughed. Margaret, or Meg, just smiled and waved. They turned left, toward the church, once they reached the center of the village. "Rectory's this way," said Meg. Sure enough, they came to a good-sized stone house, with a second story, windows in the second-story gables, and on either side of the door. Edward paused to look at the place. This would be home, now, and quite possibly for the rest of his life . . .

His reflection was interrupted by Meg: "There's a shed around back, with a couple of stalls." She looked at him with a hint of impatience.

Quite so. They took Bruce around the back and lifted the ewe off, and down onto the straw on the floor of a stall. She lay there, looking a little confused.

"Who's there?" another woman appeared, from the direction of the house. "Oh, it's you, Meg. What have you brought us this time? And who" — here she looked at Edward — "is this man?"

"This is your new vicar," replied Meg. "Found him on the road."

"Edward Chase, at your service," said Edward.

"Oh." The other woman curtseyed. "Welcome to Derwent, Father Chase. I am the housekeeper at the vicarage. Elizabeth. Or, Bess, if you prefer."

She appeared to be of middle age, her hair tucked under a cap, neatly dressed in clothing appropriate to her class — a stark contrast to Meg, with her wild hair and her crimson cloak. Village life: always the unexpected.

"Ye'd better see to your things on the road," said Meg. "I'll doctor the ewe." Edward looked at Bess, who nodded. So back he went with Bruce, to fetch the rest of his things. People stared at him as he passed back down the street. Clearly, they didn't know who he was — yet.

It didn't take long for him to find his things in the woods, and return to the village. This time, he walked to the front door and knocked. Bess answered the door with "Welcome to your new home, vicar!"

It was a startling thing to hear. His new home. His. Home. He had not lived anywhere that he could call "home" since he left his uncle's house to attend the university. What was he? Thirteen years old? Almost fourteen. Years ago, at any rate. The place was generous in size, with a separate parlor for sitting, and a dining area near a large kitchen. There was a fireplace in the parlor, another in the dining room, and the kitchen had its own brick oven, with a chimney. There was a large bedroom on the main floor, with its own fireplace and chimney, and two more rooms upstairs. The whole house was built of finely cut stone, solid and strong.

"I'll just get these for you," said Bess, and began hauling his gear to the bed chamber. He watched for a moment, then remembered that Bruce was still standing outside. He led Bruce to the shed around back and put him in a stall. There was some hay in back, which he fed to Bruce. The ewe was lying in another stall, with some sort of bandage on her leg — no sign of Meg.

He went back to the house, where Bess was busy in the kitchen. "I'll have supper for you ere long," she called out, "rest yourself awhile. From the aroma, he judged that supper was another mutton stew. Edward wondered if this was what folks always ate in this part of the world. It might get tedious, but he was eating the food in the jail at Ipswich, less than a month ago. Mutton stew would do just fine, thank you very much.

The stew was tasty enough, served with some bread and cheese, and a tankard of pretty good ale. Bess stood by as if waiting for his approval, until Edward said, "Bess, why don't you sit down and have some supper?"

"With your permission, sir. Thank ye." She stepped back into the kitchen, and returned with her own portions, seating herself near the opposite end of the table.

"This is quite tasty, Bess." She nodded and blushed a little. "I'm going to need your help, Bess, to learn about this village, and how best to serve them. Can I count on your assistance?"

Her eyes widened a little. "Of course, vicar. What do you need to know?"

"To begin with, how many live in this village? How many should I expect in church on a Sunday morning?"

Bess had plenty to say. It spilled out of her in a torrent that Edward struggled to keep up with: About one hundred ten people were living in the village proper, including a carpenter, a blacksmith, a butcher, an innkeeper, and several shopkeepers. There were also people living in farmsteads up and down the valley — mostly sheepherders, but a few farmers — also, miners who might live in the village, or the outlying areas, depending on how far from the village their mines were. There could be as many as two hundred at a Sunday service, but not usually so many.

The men of the village made their livings from two principal sources — wool and lead. Men of the one sort did not always get on well with men of the other: Miners dug pits and shafts in the moors that could be hazardous to livestock; whenever an animal disappeared, accusations followed that the miners were filling their bellies with someone else's property. On the other hand, some of the long-horned cattle that ranged the moors had gored a miner from time to time: Edward's predecessor, one Father Jacobs, had been called to mediate a conflict more than once.

"What can you tell me about Father Jacobs?"

"A good man. A brave one. Saved my Jack's life, I reckon, though it cost him his own."

"Jack?"

"Jack Clegg, me husband. There was a collapse in a mine pit up on the moors, and Jack was trapped. Father Jacobs and some other men went to get him out, then there was another collapse, and Father Jacobs was struck about his head. He seemed alright at first — went to bed with a headache; but in the morning, I found him in his bed. Died in his sleep, poor man."

"You are a widow, then?"

"By God's grace, no! They got Jack out before the second collapse. His mining days are over, and he can't walk, but it's a mercy I still have him with me."

"Where is Jack, now?"

"Why, upstairs of course. That's where they brought him after the collapse. They put Jack in one of the upstairs rooms, so's I could care for him, and keep an eye on Father Jacobs, ye see. When the Father died, I still needed to look after the rectory. It was easier to keep Jack here, don't ye see."

Edward nodded. "Yes. I understand your reasoning."

"But do not fret yerself; now that you have arrived, we can move Jack back to our little cottage. It's not far from here — though I will admit it's easier to care for Jack in this place than to be runnin' back and forth all day."

"I think I need to meet Jack. Will you introduce me?"

"Of course, Father! I'll take you right to him now! She walked to the stairs, and called out, "Jack, dear! We have company!"

Jack Clegg was a man with a rugged, weatherbeaten, but pale face. He sat up in his bed and greeted Edward cordially enough. His injuries appeared to be in his legs — one had been broken, the other had no feeling.

"So, you haven't been out of this room since the accident?" asked Edward. The air in the room was worse than stale; Bess hurriedly snatched up a chamberpot and took it downstairs. Edward opened the casement, to let in some fresh air.

"Nay, vicar. Can't manage the stairs. I'm lucky to be alive, though, no complaints."

"How long have you been here?"

"A few months, I'd say. It was June when the mine pit collapsed — too much rain, softened the ground, and the next thing I know, I'm up to my neck in mud and stones. I'd be there yet, if not for Father Jacobs."

Bess returned. "Bess," said Edward, "We need to get Jack some fresh air and sunshine before the weather turns. He's pale, and will only get weaker if he stays in this bed."

"How can we move him, Father?"

"The two of us can manage, I think. He's not the man he was before his injury. He can sit in the parlor. Or on the front stoop for a while."

"He's right, Bess. Time for me to get out of this bed."

In the event, it was simplest for Edward to carry Jack on his back down the stairs. The man was lighter than that ewe, by a fair bit. He sat Jack up in a chair in the parlor. Bess stood by, looking anxious. "It's fine, Bessie, really, it is," said Jack, "The fresh air will do me good."

"Let me look at your legs," said Edward. Jack's right leg was encased in pieces of wood, and strips of fabric. "How long has this been on your leg?"

"Since the day I broke it. Meg set it for me, then wrapped it up like that."

"Meg?"

"Aye, Meg o' the Moors, we call her. She's a healer, is Meg — we've no other physician hereabouts. Lives on the moor with her kinfolk. Knows about herbs and poultices, and such. Also knows how to set broken bones. You'll meet her, one of these days."

"I think I already have." Then, "Bess, do you know where Meg is?"

"I suppose I can find her if she's still in the village."

"Please go look for her. I think it may be time to remove these splints from Jack's leg."

Bess scurried out the door, and down the street.

"Now, let's have a look at the other leg. You say you have no feeling?"

"Only a kind of tingling. Like a funny bone, ye know."

"Can you move it?"

"I'm not sure." Jack's foot began to wiggle, as he looked at it with some surprise. "Don't think I could have done that, a week ago," he said. "Meg's poultices must be working!"

"Can you bend your knee, and straighten it again?"

"I'll try. Look at that! It moves!"

The movement was none too vigorous, thought Edward, but it did move. "But you still have no feeling in the limb?"

Jack shook his head. "Nay, just a tingling. Can't tell whether the knee is bent or straight unless I look at it."

"Jack, I believe you could walk, with the help of crutches, if the break is healed, and the splints come off. Let's see what Meg o' the Moors has to say."

It was several more minutes before Bess returned, slightly out of breath. "Meg is on the way," she reported.

It was a few minutes more before Meg appeared at the door. She entered the house and looked at Edward and Jack. "Bess, did I not tell ye two weeks ago, that it was time for Jack's splints to come off?" she asked.

"Aye, but I thought a few more weeks might be better. Did I do wrong?"

Meg pursed her lips. "Let's see about the splints, Jack." She knelt, drew a large knife from beneath her cloak ("*whopping big one,*" thought Edward), and began cutting away at the bindings, until the splints came away, exposing Jack's leg. Edward could see some inflamed patches on his pale skin, and one spot that was oozing pus. "This," Meg pointed to the oozing patch, "is why splints must come off at the right time. I will prepare a salve for this wound. Jack, it's time to see if the break is mended. Stand up!"

Edward found his walking staff and handed it to Jack. "Here. Use this."

Jack pulled himself to a standing position, leaning all the while on the staff. Tentatively, he put weight on this right leg, until most of his weight was on it. He smiled, "I believe it's mended!" he said. Bess clapped her hands together and began to cry.

Meg turned to Edward. "I suppose he'll be staying with you in the rectory, then?"

"Apparently so," Edward replied, "for a little while longer, at least."

Meg smiled. To herself, she said, *longer than you imagine, I'd wager.* "In that case, he should be getting more exercise. His muscles are weak from lying abed for so long."

Edward nodded. "I'll have him walk up and down the room with my staff, for a while, until he gets stronger. Hopefully, he'll be able to walk outside in a few days."

Meg nodded. To Bess, she said, "Are you still applying the poultices, like I said?"

"Yes, of course. But it seems like they should go on his other leg . . ."

"No, on his back, on the left side of his lower back. That's where the injury is."

Bess nodded meekly. "Yes, Meg. On his back."

Meg turned and walked out the door. Edward went after her: "Wait, there's one more thing!"

Meg stopped in the street and waited for him. "What thing?"

"The ewe, in the shed. What should we do about her?"

"Let's go see," said Meg. When they got to the shed, the ewe was standing, and bleating. "It looks to me like you should feed her," said Meg. with a wry smile.

"That we will," said Edward. "I must say I am impressed with your skill as a healer — not just the ewe, but also with Jack."

Meg looked him in the eye. "It is well you arrived in Derwent, today. Bess did not do the things that I advised her to do, with Jack. She is the sort of woman who prefers to keep the things she prizes near to her, and under her control — even when that is not the best for them."

"Do you mean that she would rather keep him an invalid in an upstairs room, just so that she will know where he is at all times?"

"You said it as well as I could. But that is just my opinion. Jack will wander, if he gets his legs under him, again. That is also just my opinion."

Edward had to chuckle. "Thank you for your opinion."

"Why thank me?"

"I am to be these people's priest. I cannot know how best to serve them unless I know something about them. Opinions like yours are all I have to go on — until I can form opinions of my own."

"Remind me to be more sparing in my opinions, when next we speak," she said with a crooked smile. And then she was gone.

Edward took a walk through the village, just to get a sense of the place. Thirty or fewer stone buildings — a few with shops at street level, and living space above, the rest mostly cottages. A couple of women waved a greeting, then looked at each other and giggled. Edward wondered if the way he was dressed seemed amusing to them. He came to what looked to be a carpenter's workshop. He went inside and introduced himself. He described an idea he had for a crutch that Jack Clegg could use to begin walking again. The carpenter agreed to make something. Edward continued his tour of the main street in town, visiting the butcher, the blacksmith, and a shoemaker. Everyone seemed friendly enough but seemed to find something about him quite funny. It was the blacksmith that offered an explanation: "Some folk think it quite amusing that a shepherd of the spiritual flock should have to bring his own sheep with him. It's funnier when Meg tells the story."

"Ah." So Meg o' the Moors had been spreading the news all over the village. No doubt she added some details to make the telling more entertaining. This could work to his advantage: he knew enough of rhetoric and oratory to recall that telling a joke on himself was often an effective way to connect with an audience — warmed the room up, so to speak. He would use the sheep story in his sermon on Sunday. That there would be a sermon, he did not doubt. It wasn't required by the liturgy, but he was licensed to preach, and preaching was key to what he hoped to accomplish in Derwent.

By the time he got back to the rectory, Jack had hobbled back and forth from the parlor to the dining room several times and professed to be tired. "Bess," said Edward, "I think we need to make some changes. I think you and Jack should sleep in the bedchamber here on the main floor, and I will take one of the rooms upstairs. Also, the linens will need to be changed, and the room where Jack has been staying should be thoroughly scrubbed. That way, Jack can take his meals with us, in the dining room."

Bess was surprised at the suggestion, and curtseyed. "As you say, Vicar. That is very generous of you." She got busy. Edward took his personal baggage upstairs to the other bedchamber. It appeared to be clean, and comfortably large — larger than any of the rooms in the inns he had been staying at. Too bad there wasn't a fireplace. There was some sort of armoire, or wardrobe, and a chest of drawers for his spare clothing — adequate for his needs, at least until Winter arrived.

Dinner was a lighter meal than supper, as was the custom for a farm family — some boiled carrots and turnips, with a chicken broth, more bread, cheese, and some apples. Jack hobbled over to the table on his own and seated himself — he was getting the hang of walking with the staff. Bess set out plates and silverware — evidently, the vicarage came with such things. It looked a bit elegant, Edward thought. *Welcome home, Vicar.* Had a nice ring to it. After dinner, Edward helped Bess clear away the table, and wash the dishes. Jack hobbled his way back to the sitting room.

"Bess, how have you been paying for this food, since Father Jacobs died?"

"I grow most of the vegetables myself; the flour, butter, and meat I buy on credit."

"Credit? The account must be substantial, by now."

"Aye, it is. But I didn't think it proper to dip into any of the church funds, without a priest approving it."

"That's an honorable position. Have you been paid, since Father Jacobs passed?"

"Nay, I have not."

"First thing tomorrow, we'll figure out how to pay your back wages and settle accounts with our creditors."

"Yes, Father." Bess looked a little relieved, he thought.

He awoke in the morning feeling refreshed, and optimistic. The sky was a little overcast, and mist clung to the edges that loomed above the village, but it was not cold. Jack rose of his own accord and joined them for breakfast. Edward remembered that he had neglected to feed Bruce the evening before. "I took care of Bruce, and the ewe too," said Bess. Edward reflected that having a servant was very convenient, indeed.

After breakfast, Bess produced a set of keys — "This one's for the church doors on the West end, this one's for the rector's office, this one for the offering box, and this one for the rector's strongbox."

"Has no one opened the offering box for three months?"

"Nay, vicar, I think not."

"Then that is our first order of business. I will fetch the offering from the church if you will tot up what we owe."

He took several minutes to look the sanctuary over. It was nothing fancy, but there were ample pews in the nave, a small chancel, a pulpit. There was a small lectern on the north side, in the front, with a large book chained to it. This, of course, was the Bible that was legally required to be made available since the days of Henry VIII. He couldn't tell whether anyone had been reading it since then, or not. The rector's office, or vestry, was on the south side of the chancel. He found the strongbox easily enough, and it appeared to be undisturbed. Also, a ledger, with entries that ended in June of the current year. On his way out, he opened the offering box that stood near the West entrance. There was a good handful of coins in it. All this he brought back to the rectory with him.

Bess was waiting for him at the dining room table. "We'll start with you," said Edward. "If I read this ledger correctly, you are to be paid a shilling a week. Is that correct?"

"Aye, sir, it is."

It says here that you were last paid on June 14. That would be . . . fifteen weeks, as of the day after tomorrow. Do you agree?"

Bess nodded. "There. Fifteen shillings it is." Edward handed the coins to her and wrote an entry in the ledger. "Now, who else do we owe money to?"

Bess went down the list, and Edward set aside the payment amounts for each creditor. After the ledger was updated, he locked up the strongbox and walked into the village with each creditor's payment. All of them were glad to see him, once they understood what he was about, and he talked with each of them at some length, learning their names, the size of their families, their relations to other families. The family trees of all these folk were deeply entangled with one another. By the time he reached the last creditor, it was apparent that they knew why he was coming; they had a bit of biscuit to offer him, and a tankard of ale. Edward had planned to visit the public house on his way back to the rectory, and buy a round for everyone in the place, just to announce his presence in the village, but thought better of it. He could do that another time.

All of this was intended to create some goodwill in the village for his ministry, and he was satisfied that he had made a good start. Two days from tomorrow was a Sunday. That would be the measure of his success.

September 27, 1586: A Sermon

Friday, the carpenter delivered a newly made walking stick to the rectory. Bess was about to send him away, but Edward intervened, to explain that it was for Jack. "I need my walking staff back," Edward explained.

The walking stick was shorter than Edward's staff, but had two short, horizontal projections — one was waist high, so that Jack could grip it in his hand, the other just high enough to allow Jack to fit it under his arm and rest his weight on it. Jack was outside most of that afternoon, hobbling up and down the street, greeting anyone who passed by, resting when he got weary.

By Saturday, Jack said he was ready to venture into town — as far as the pub, at least. "Now Jack, ye mustn't overdo it. Remember Dear, ye're not a well man," Bess said, wistfully.

This warning was not sufficient to deter him. Saturday was the busiest day of the week at the pub, and he expected to see a lot of old friends there. So, after dinner, he was off — one good leg, the left one dragging along, with the stick on his left side.

"Can you move the left leg at all, Jack?" asked Edward.

"Only if I look at it," he replied.

"Use your eyes, then. Use your eyes!"

Jack nodded and laughed. "Why not come along, vicar? It could be a merry time!"

Edward decided Jack was right — should have thought of it himself. He turned to Bess, who was looking distressed. "Don't worry, Bess, I'll look after him."

"Father," she said in a low voice," ye should know that Jack may be apt to overdo it a bit, in the pub."

"Ah," Edward nodded, "I'll be on my guard, then." He winked at Bess, who looked back at him with an expression of exasperation. Before she could think of anything else to say, Edward had caught up with Jack, and they were both on their way to the pub.

There were indeed, a great many men in the pub who greeted Jack like a long-lost comrade — which in a sense, he was — at least in the society of the ale house. More than one insisted on buying a drink for Jack, and listening to the tale of his injury, and recovery. There were also general expressions of loss over the death of Father Jacobs.

Each new encounter, of course, involved an introduction of Father Edward Chase, the new vicar. For Edward, this was serendipity — he was meeting many of the men in his parish, without the expense of paying for the rounds himself.

In the course of the conversation, someone asked, "Father Chase, does this mean that Jack will be assisting ye like he did Father Jacobs?"

Edward was surprised by the question. "How's that? What assistance?"

"Jack used to read the text on Sunday mornings. Father Jacobs often entrusted him with that job. Some said it was favoritism, but the vicar trusted Jack, and they were friends . . ."

. . . "which is why Father Jacobs rushed up to the pit, when he heard it had collapsed on Jack," Another man chimed in.

"Nay," said Jack. "Father Jacobs was the sort of man who would have rushed to the aid of any man in this pub. That's just who he was — no favorites, there."

"Amen," said several men, all at once.

"So, Father, will Jack be helping ye tomorrow?"

"I hadn't considered it," replied Edward. (This personal history was precisely the sort of information he needed, and might only hear about in a pub, he thought). "It sounds like a good idea to me. What do you say, Jack?"

Jack, now well into his fourth tankard of ale, replied with a dignified air, "Father, it would be an honor to read for you." There were murmurs of approval from the other men. Edward felt he had scored a point.

"Of course," Edward continued, peering closely at Jack, "You'll have to be on your best form — it won't do if you're hungover." The men laughed: "That's right, Jack — no hangovers."

Jack nodded soberly (though sober did not quite describe his condition).

"In fact," said Edward, "Jack and I need to plan tomorrow's service." He looked at Jack. "Time to go, I think."

Jack looked reluctant to leave the pub, but the idea that he had important business to attend to was enough to get him on his (unsteady) feet, and moving toward the door.

Once in the street, Edward offered an arm to Jack — who was a bit wobbly. Jack had an odd expression on his face. "I can feel my foot," he said.

"That's good, Jack. I guess that's one way to tell that you haven't overdone it with the ale." Edward chuckled.

"No," said Jack. "I'm talkin' about the left foot. I can feel both my feet, where they touch the ground."

Edward was startled. "Are you sure?"

"Sure I'm sure. Hold this." He thrust the walking stick into Edward's hand and began walking in the direction of the rectory. Wobbling, rather than walking, but he managed to stay on his feet. To an observer, it must have appeared that he was a drunk reeling and staggering on his way home from a night at the pub. Bess certainly saw it that way, because she gave Edward an indignant look, and began scolding Jack when they reached the front door.

Edward interrupted her with a raised hand. "Bess, please find a place for this." He handed Jack's walking stick to her. It took her a moment to grasp what was going on. She looked at Jack, then at the stick, then back at Jack. "Father, how much has he had to drink?"

"About four, I think."

"Ales?"

Edward nodded.

"That's not enough to put my Jack in his cups!"

"He says he has feeling in his left leg, now."

"Does he now? Here, Jack, can you feel this?" She gave him a good swat with the walking stick on his left leg, above the knee.

"Ow!" said Jack, "Woman, watch what yer doin' there!"

Bess's expression changed from annoyance to surprise. Then, "Glory be! It's a miracle!"

All of this happened too quickly for Edward to intervene. But before Bess could test the "miracle" again, he took hold of the stick: "I'll take care of this; you should see to Jack," he said. Jack, meanwhile, was still rubbing his leg where Bess had struck him.

"How does it feel, Jack?" Edward asked.

"Hurts."

"Try rubbing your leg below the knee."

"Why would I do that? It hurts up here!" He was rubbing the outside of his thigh.

"I mean, do you have any feeling in your lower leg?"

"Ah. Right." Jack rubbed his lower leg. "I do feel something, but it still tingles. Like a funny bone, ye know. Maybe I need another drink?"

Bess snorted. "Nay, ye've hit yer limit for today, Jack Clegg. Tomorrow is Sunday. Ye need to be at yer best, by morning." She shot Edward an annoyed look.

"She's right Jack," added Edward, "remember, you offered to read for me at tomorrow's service."

"Aye, so I did. What will ye have me read, Father?"

"A Psalm. The twenty-third one. It's about sheep."

"Aye, so it is. Learned it by memory, from my mother. I can recite it tomorrow, whenever you ask me to." With that, he limped into the bed chamber and closed the door.

In the morning, Edward rose early. Bess was up even earlier and had breakfast ready. Jack joined him moments after he sat down; hobbling, but appearing none the worse for last evening's adventure. "Good Morning Jack. How's the left leg this morning?"

"About the same as last night. I can drag along without the walking stick if I have to, but it's easier with the stick."

"Any feeling in the left leg?"

"Some. Sore where the missus hit me. I wonder if a little more ale would make me right?"

"More likely it's the poultices, I think," offered Edward.

"Or a miracle," interjected Bess.

"Or, a miracle," Edward agreed. "Jack, I'd like you to sit on a front pew near the lectern on the north side, where the Great Bible is kept, and read the psalm from there. I will tell you when it's time to read."

Jack nodded. "Wouldn't do it any other way, Father. Though I won't need to read it from that Bible. Got it memorized, ye know."

Edward nodded. "Still, I often like to have the Bible open before me, when I read it out loud — just in case my memory stumbles."

"As you say, Father. I'll open it before the service starts, so there won't be any delay.

"Father, the sexton is here," said Bess.

"Eh?"

"He wants to know when you'll be ready to ring the church bells, this morning."

Of course. The bells. Come to think of it, he hadn't heard any bells rung since he arrived in the village — should have noticed that. Regular ringing of the bells was ordinarily the pulse of a small village, yet the bells had been silent, for — how long?

"Bess, how long since the bells have been rung?"

"Not since the day we buried Father Jacobs, rest his soul."

"Hasn't the sexton had any reason to ring them since?"

"Aye, I suppose so. But the church is locked. He can't get to the bell tower without a key."

"But, don't you have a key? Didn't he ask you for it?"

"I did, but now you have it. And yes, he asked for it, but I thought it better to keep it safe with me." She caught Edward's skeptical look, and added a little stiffly, "I thought I was doing right, Father. If I have been mistaken, please credit it to my reverence for the things of the church."

"I must speak with the sexton," Edward said.

The sexton was a small man, perhaps sixty years old, mild-mannered, and seemed eager to please. The sort of man that Bess could easily bully, Edward thought. No doubt she had bullied him. He was glad to see Edward but shrank a little when Bess spoke to him. "Bess, the sexton and I will go across to the church, and prepare for the service, now.

"And what about your vestments, Father?"

Right. The vestments. One of the very specific requirements of the job. He turned to the sexton and said, "Wait for me by the West door. I'll only be a few minutes."

The sexton smiled with relief, bowed slightly, and excused himself. It took a bit longer than Edward had expected to get the garments on, over his ordinary clothing. Bess fussed over it quite a bit, til everything met her approval. At least she seemed to know how everything was supposed to look, which was more than Edward could truthfully claim for himself. He gathered up his Bible, his prayer book, and his sermon notes, and headed toward the door.

"Wait, Father! Ye can't go without this!" She handed him a parcel, wrapped in cloth. It's the bread for communion," she explained. The chalice and the wine are in the vestry. They have to be locked up," she explained, with a sidelong glance at Jack.

"I'll be along shortly, vicar," Jack added helpfully. Edward got out the door as briskly as he could and walked to the church. He hadn't actually decided on whether to perform the rite of the Eucharist on his very first Sunday, but now his hand was forced. There was no particularly technical problem with this — the Book of Common Prayer included a complete liturgy for a Eucharistic service, and he had attended such services more times than he could count. If it came down to it, he could probably do the whole thing from memory. But the service took a bit of extra time, and he didn't want his congregation to feel overwhelmed on his first Sunday. He would have to cut down his sermon, a bit more — disappointing, because he had already pared a good two-hour sermon down to just one hour, by sacrificing so much of what they needed to hear. So much for eloquence and inspiration; that would have to wait for another week. He would stick to his illustrations, and just one or two critical points of doctrine . . .

The sexton was waiting for him at the West door of the church. His name, it turned out, was Benjamin. Another man was there also and identified himself as Peter. Peter was a lay deacon, or so he said, and Benjamin confirmed that it was so. "Peter, here will fill the chalice, and lay everything out for you, if you give him the key to the vestry," suggested Benjamin. Edward was grateful for the help, grateful also to realize that at least a few people in the village were looking forward to resuming Sunday service. It seemed reason for optimism. He reflected that all this preparation was the part of a service that he had never really seen. Just took it for granted, really, but without a few people like Bess, Benjamin, and Peter, the whole thing would never come off . . .

Another man appeared at the doorway and introduced himself as Bertram, or just Bert — "the beadle," he said. Of course, there had to be a beadle — someone to manage the crowd, discipline the unruly, rouse the drowsy from their slumbers.

Peter had the altar ready in just minutes. "Ben's about ready to ring the bells, Father. Why don't ye wait in the vestry until everyone arrives? More dramatic, if ye make yer entrance, don't ye see?"

The thought would not have occurred to Edward, and he wasn't sure he wanted to make a dramatic entrance, but the vestments seemed to recommend it if nothing else.

"There's a peephole in the door," said Peter. "You can watch the congregation come in. When Ben stops ringin' the bells, that's your cue to appear." Apparently, this was just part of the routine, thought Edward. Oh, well, routine would do, until he had a chance to come up with a routine of his own. The bells began to ring. He retreated into the vestry.

People began to appear in the doorway and find their seats. Jack took a seat in front, on the right, with Bess at his side. Soon there were at least one hundred people in the sanctuary, with more coming in. Before long, he guessed the crowd at two hundred, at least. He caught a glimpse of a woman in a crimson cloak. Suddenly the bells stopped ringing. He realized, with a start, that it was time for him to make an appearance.

As he emerged from the vestry and walked to the pulpit, the entire congregation rose to their feet. He turned to face them. He recognized a dozen or so faces, but as for the rest, *I don't even know their names. God, help me learn their names. And help me remember them!* "Please, be seated," he said. There was a rustling sound, as they all sat, all eyes on him.

He opened the Prayer-book, and began the litany:
"God, the father of heaven, have mercy on us miserable sinners . . ."

In unison the congregation replied,
"God, the father of heaven, have mercy on us miserable sinners . . ."

And so it went. The congregation was well-versed in the litany and fell easily into a familiar rhythm. When they were finished, Edward felt a sense of relief, and almost elation, at the power of a worshipping people, speaking in unison, agreeing in their hearts and minds. He let silence rest in the room for a moment, before nodding at Jack.

Jack rose from his seat, made a show of placing his walking stick on the pew, and walked to the lectern with a noticeable limp. The Bible was already open, and Jack looked at the congregation. "The word of the Lord . . ." he began, and then, he chanted or almost sang:

" The Lord gouerneth me, and no thing schal faile to me;

This was not quite right, thought Edward. Close, but . . . was Jack paraphrasing? Jack was not looking at the Bible before him, working from memory, no doubt. This was awkward . . .

And then, as Jack continued, the congregation joined him:

"in the place of pasture there he hath set me.
He nurschide me on the watir of refreischyng;
he conuertide my soule. He ledde me forth on the pathis of riytfulnesse; for his name.
For whi thouy Y schal go in the myddis of schadewe of deeth;
Y schal not drede yuels, for thou art with me.
Thi yerde and thi staf; tho han coumfortid me.
Thou hast maad redi a boord in my siyt; ayens hem that troblen me.
Thou hast maad fat myn heed with oyle; and my cuppe, fillinge greetli, is ful cleer.
And thi merci schal sue me; in alle the daies of my lijf.
And that Y dwelle in the hows of the Lord; in to the lengthe of daies."

It wasn't plainsong, exactly, more tuneful; harmonies in at least four parts. Beautiful, really.

Edward Chase was astonished and confused. He was sure that nothing quite like this could be found in the Book of Common Prayer, and he knew the Psalms very well, in more than one language. Where did they learn this version of the Psalm? For Psalm 23 it certainly was, but in a language ancient, not foreign, but not familiar, either. Jack returned to his seat. All eyes were on Edward.

His mind was still in turmoil. "Peace be with you," he said.

"And also with you," the congregation replied, in unison. There. That much at least he could understand.

"I shall read from the Gospel of Saint Matthew," he said:

" How think ye? If a man have an hundred sheep, and one of them be gone astray, doth he not leave ninety and nine, and go into the mountains, and seek that which is gone astray?
And if so be that he find it, verily I say unto you, he rejoiceth more of that sheep, than of the ninety and nine which went not astray."

He looked up from his text. "As many of you know," he began, "I am not a man much acquainted with the care of animals." Here and there a titter or chuckle from the congregation.

"But I have learned a few things since I arrived in this village. For one, I can testify that sheep are round enough to roll down a hillside . . ." Outright laughter, now . . . "And that sheep are too heavy for a man like myself to carry on his own." More nods, chuckles, and a few "Amens." He had them now, he could feel it.

"There are also spiritual lessons that we can learn from sheep." Some men were leaning forward, now, he noticed. Good, very good.

He went on to describe the snare that had trapped the leg of the ewe in the woods, how men were like that ewe — snared in their sins, or the sins of others, helpless to help themselves — until a deliverer appears with the means to set them free. How sheep need to be watched and cared for, lest they all become ensnared, just like the ewe in the woods. How men need watching and care, lest they lose their souls to the snares of the Devil. The "Amens" from the congregation continued. Jesus was the deliverer that men need, the Spirit of God watches over us and guards our hearts, the Father is full of grace and mercy, the church is a place of safety and healing, like a stall for an injured ewe.

He finished his parable with: "If anyone here is missing a ewe, I invite you to join me after the service, behind the rectory. I would rejoice to see her returned to her rightful owner, just as our Heavenly Father rejoices when a repentant sinner returns to Him." More "Amens," more chuckles, and murmurs of approval.

Then he began to read his sermon, which was a careful exposition of the witness of the Holy Scriptures on the topic of Grace, by which sinners receive benefits that no man can earn, and Mercy, by which we receive less than the punishment we deserve. Also, weighty questions, such as how it can be that God's mercy is sufficient for all men, yet some are damned, anyway; how the atoning sacrifice of Jesus can cover every sin, yet all are not forgiven. These were topics that he was well-versed in, through innumerable debates and conventicles. It was the core, really, of what was distinctive about his "Puritan" theology.

Not quite so fascinating to his congregation. He sensed that he was losing them, a few at a time. Before he finished, Bert the Beadle had walked up the aisles to tickle the noses of several sleepy people, with a feathery plume attached to a long stick. It would take some time, Edward realized, to accustom these people to theological discourse. But time he had.

When the sermon was finished, he turned his attention to the communion service. The Prayer book specified everything he needed, right down to descriptions of how the elements were to be distributed. Peter was at his side from the beginning, so it ran smoothly enough. The congregation lined up, row by row, to receive the bread and wine. Edward noted that some knelt to receive communion, but others did not. Curious. Strictly speaking, everyone was supposed to kneel. In practice, Puritans opposed kneeling, as a leftover Papist practice. These people appeared to be of two minds on the topic. Maybe this could be a starting point in the process of thoroughly reforming this parish.

When the last congregant was seated again, It was time for the benediction. He asked the congregation to stand:

"The peace of God, which passeth all understanding, keep your hearts, and minds in the knowledge and love of God, and of his Son Jesus Christ, our Lord.
And the blessing of God almighty, the Father, the Son, and the Holy Ghost, be among you and remain with you alway. Amen."

"Amen!" The congregation replied.

He stood for a moment. No one moved, everyone was looking at him. He smiled. They smiled back. Then he remembered what he had to do: He walked down the main aisle to the West Door, where he would greet his flock on their way out. Sure enough, they followed him out. He began shaking hands as they passed him. So many strangers; it became a bit of a blur. Many stopped to speak to him; mostly they spoke of their appreciation at having a priest again — the names, he was sure, he would not be able to remember. After the last member passed out of the church, there were still people milling about outside, chatting and laughing.

Jack appeared at his side and said. "There's some here that would like to look at that ewe, Father."

Edward led a fair-sized crowd — some shepherds, some just curious — out of the church, and across to the vicarage, then behind it, to the shed where the ewe was kept. Meg was among them, and she led the ewe out into the yard, where everyone could see it. She took the dressings off the ewe's leg, so everyone could see that the wound was healing.

"Hard to say what she looks like, with all that wool," said one observer. Murmurs of agreement.

"I think that's Bluebell, my ewe that disappeared, two years ago," said one man.

"Jake, you accused the miners up on Back Tor of eatin' Bluebell. You were pretty certain about it, as I recall. Besides, I think she looks more like my Daisy, who disappeared around the same time."

Jake shrugged. "Maybe I was wrong about the miners. Looks like Bluebell, to me. Your Daisy had a lazy eye, as I recall." Someone in the crowd tittered, and others murmured.

"Nay, she did not! This here ewe could be her twin, and the more I look at her, the more I think this *is* Daisy!"

"Nay, it's Bluebell. Vicar, I thank ye for bringin' my Bluebell back to me. I'll take her off yer hands now."

"Nay, ye won't! That's Daisy, and she's mine!"

The men were growing heated; if this went on, they might come to blows. Edward noticed that the rest of the crowd was looking at him, as if he could resolve the dispute, somehow. He looked closely at the ewe, who stared back placidly. Could be Bluebell, or Daisy, or Daffodil, as far as he could see.

"Let the vicar decide. It was he that rescued the sheep, after all." Someone spoke from the back of the crowd; he couldn't identify the voice. There was a murmur of support for the idea. "Aye, let the vicar decide."

Edward sighed, and stroked his beard, for dramatic effect. "I suppose we could use King Solomon's method," he said. The crowd looked at him with interest, but no hint on anyone's faces that they recognized the biblical reference. "King Solomon decided a case like this, by dividing the disputed creature and giving each claimant half. Would that be satisfactory to you?" He looked at Jake and the other shepherd, whose name apparently, was Bob.

"We'd have to shear her first, and weigh the wool, to make it fair," said Jake.

Bob nodded. "And we'd have to weigh the halves of the carcass, as well, to make it completely fair," added Bob.

Edward was flummoxed. The whole point of the story about Solomon was that the true owner would surrender his claim, to spare the ewe's life, and thus prove who the true owner was. By that standard, neither of these men had a right to the ewe. Neither man was familiar with the biblical text. What now?

"I have another suggestion," he said. "Why doesn't one of you sell his claim to the other? How much would you take for a sheep like this? A shilling?"

"Aye, that's about right," said Bob. Jake nodded.

"So, if Jake gives Bob sixpence, and Jake keeps the ewe, that would be fair, wouldn't it?"

"Nay vicar," said Bob. "If the ewe is worth a shilling, I'd be a fool to sell her for sixpence, even if he has sixpence, which he doesn't."

Edward turned to Jake. "How about it Jake, will you sell your claim to Bob?"

Jake shook his head. "Bob is right about one thing. It's a fool that sells a ewe worth a shilling for only sixpence. And *he* doesn't have the money, in any case!"

Edward sighed. "Here's a shilling, Jake. Will you sell your claim to me?"

Jake snatched the shilling out of Edward's hand. "Done!" he said.

Edward turned to Bob. "Will you sell me your claim, Bob?"

"I will, for a shilling." Edward offered him a coin. "Thank ye, vicar. A pleasure doin' business with ye." There was chortling from the crowd. Both men turned to leave.

"Wait!" said Edward. "I have a sheep for sale, a healthy ewe, with a fine wool coat. Worth a shilling, or so I am told. Which of you will buy her? And don't tell me that you haven't the money; I know for a fact that each of you has a shilling in his purse." At this, there was a roar of laughter from the crowd.

"That's a fair price, vicar, but I'll be spending my money on other things," said Bob.

"Aye, that goes for me, too," said Jake. "A fine animal, though. You drive a hard bargain." More laughter. The crowd dispersed, leaving Edward and the ewe, looking at each other. Oh, well, he could probably find a buyer somewhere . . .

"That was well done, vicar," Meg spoke from behind him. "Those two would have made a life-long feud over that ewe. Not to mention that one or the other would have considered you to be his enemy. Well worth a shilling or two, wouldn't ye say?"

Edward smiled and nodded a little ruefully. "Well worth a shilling or two, as long as it doesn't happen very often."

Meg chuckled. "Aye, be wary of the precedent. If two men come to ye tomorrow, or next week, with some sheep that they both claim as theirs, I'd be careful about offering them money to settle the dispute — it could get to be an expensive habit, for ye."

It took Edward a second to grasp her meaning: "Do you mean to say that there are men in this village who would pretend to have a dispute over the ownership of some animal, just to put a few coins in their purses?"

"Ye'll find plenty of such men in the pub — some because they need the money for their ale, others just as a prank. Ye wouldn't have to look too far to find women who would do such a thing, either. Best be careful with your money."

A question popped into Edward's head: "How can I be certain that Bob and Jake did not invent this dispute, just to get into my purse?"

"Ye can't be certain. Few things in life are certain. But there is this: they *are* rivals and seldom agree on anything. Also, they could not have guessed that you would offer to buy them out, ahead of time. They might possibly have conspired to get each of them half a mutton, but the money was your idea, not theirs. I think it more likely that each hoped to get a live sheep out of the deal, and failing at that, determined that the other would not have what they themselves wanted."

She continued, "A shilling goes a long way, in a village like this. Both of them are probably in the pub right now buying a round for everyone in the place" (That, Edward realized, explained the merry mood of the crowd, and the speed with which they followed Jack and Bob — in the direction of the pub, of course — after they had been paid). Meg read the look on his face: "I've no doubt they're toasting yer health at this very moment. As I said, it's well done — ye've burnished yer reputation in the village, and eased the hearts of a multitude, even if only for a moment."

Edward shook his head. "I did not think they were such rascals, here." He began to feel he had been taken advantage of. Just as it had seemed that things were going well for him in Derwent . . . the expression on his face must have shown it.

"Nay, Father," Meg's tone was gentler. "Do not say 'rascals'. Everyone here would rush to your aid without a second thought if they thought ye were in trouble. But ye are a stranger here, and ye seem to be well-provided with the necessities of life. Some would consider it only justice if a little of your bounty spilled over into a poor man's pocket. There is no malice in it; but we have learned that to survive in this place, the poor must be clever. We do not treat outsiders any worse than they treat us."

An outsider? Well, of course I am, thought Edward. "And if the poor man is not clever?"

"Then we help him when we can, as we can. None shall perish of want until all of us are in want, and if that day comes, then God help us."

Edward felt the wisdom in her words. The world that he had spent his life in was more affluent than this village, more strict in its definition of honor, and its standards of proper conduct, more concerned with protecting a man's property — but not particularly successful when it came to meeting the needs of the majority of its people, who often clung desperately to the edge of stark poverty. *God help us, indeed.*

There was something to learn from this place, he realized. It was a bit of a shock to admit that these people might have something to teach him, as he tried to teach them. This was going to be more complicated than he had thought. *No hurry,* he thought to himself, *you have a lifetime to figure it all out.*

"How many 'outsiders' have become accepted in this village, then?"

"Many pass through, only a few have left a permanent mark. Father Jacobs was well-loved and is fondly remembered, but he was not with us long enough to be truly part of us. It is more common for some among us, especially young men, to leave us, in search of some distant destiny. Some return to us in time. Most do not."

"Can you think of no one from the outside who has made a permanent home, here?"

"Not in my lifetime. There are tales of the ancient days; the prophets, the preachers from olden times. I know them only by reputation."

"Tell me about the prophets."

"There was a prophet that came to this place many years ago. His predictions, they say, were always fulfilled. He was a healer, too. He had a vision that this valley was filled with water, and the whole village drowned."

"When is this supposed to happen?"

"No one knows. But some people, like my father, would not live in the village, but made their homes up on the hillsides, or even on the moors above the edges."

"What happened to the prophet?"

"He died, as all men do. He is buried on high ground, overlooking the valley; so that when his vision is fulfilled, men may still visit his resting place out of respect — even if the churchyard is underwater."

"You said there were preachers who left their mark on this place?" This was more pertinent to Edward's purpose. Perhaps there was something he could learn that would lead to success . . .

"Aye, but ye have already heard the evidence of that."

"How so?"

"Why, in the scriptures, of course! Did ye think that Jack was actually reading? And did the words not ring with the ancient tongue?"

"The words did sound ancient in my ears. I was surprised by the singing, more than anything."

"The song helps the remembering. We were taught that way by our mothers, who learned it from theirs, all the way back to the preachers who brought the scriptures to our village."

"When was this?"

"Oh, long before I was born. Nigh on two hundred years, I suppose. The preachers knew the scriptures in English, ye see. Since most could not read, they taught it by memory, with a song, to help the remembering."

"And how much remembering can you recall?"

"Father, I am surprised that you seem so unfamiliar with these things. There are one hundred fifty songs that I have memorized, each with its own tune."

One hundred fifty. *Of course, it's the Psalter — one hundred fifty Psalms, in some ancient dialect . . .* Lollards. The ancient preachers were Lollards. *And these folk are their legacy, a century or more after their passing!* Edward was familiar enough with Lollard doctrine, of course, in an academic sense. Most of their "heretical" beliefs had since become widely accepted in the church. In a few cases, their teachings were more radical than his — they not only denied transubstantiation but even went so far as to deny the real presence, for instance — much like the Brownists, and other separatist factions. But on most points — rejection of purgatory and prayers for the dead, rejection of confession, priestly celibacy, pilgrimages, veneration of saints, excessive decoration of church buildings — his Puritan beliefs were in full agreement. His only real quarrel with their beliefs was their insistence that Christians should avoid violence and warfare, especially crusades against infidels and heathens. That particular teaching had not served them well — they did not fight back against their persecutors and were burned for heresy . . . except a few, who managed to hide in villages just like this one. Exactly like this one — so remote, that hardly anyone bothered to search for heretics in such a place. And they taught what they knew to people who could not read, and somehow the teaching survived . . .

"Vicar?" Meg was staring at him, with her green eyes, a look of concern.

"Forgive me. My mind wandered there, a bit. I understand about the singing, now. It is a beautiful story, really. An inspiring example of how

God preserves his people and his message, even in the face of persecution."

Meg cocked her head as she looked at him, and then changed the subject: "So, Father Chase, what are yer plans for this animal, now that ye are a shepherd twice over?"

"I thought I'd try to sell her to someone else. Perhaps I can get at least one shilling of my investment back."

Meg shook her head. "That's not likely. Jake and Bob both told ye the truth when they said that the other didn't have sixpence to spare. If you sell this ewe, ye'll get less than sixpence for her, and if you sell her so cheaply — after payin' two shillings for her — you'll look like a right fool. If there are any rascals in the village, they'll beat a path to yer door like a swarm of pesky wasps."

She continued, "It's no trivial expense to feed a sheep through the winter. Not many can afford to take on an extra animal at this time of year. Ye'll have better luck in the spring, after the lambing and the shearing, when the animals can graze up on the moors."

"Lambing? Could this ewe be carrying a lamb?"

"It's too soon to tell, but more than likely. A randy old ewe like this could certainly find a willing companion. There's always 'a ram in the bush', as they say."

Edward was startled at the biblical reference in this context and started to explain that 'a ram in the bush' meant something else entirely, but thought better of it. Instead, he said: "So, there's a good chance I'll have two sheep by Spring. If I sell both, I can get more of my investment back?"

"Now yer thinkin' like a proper shepherd. Ye'll have to pay something for her feed, but ye can cover most of that cost by selling that extra wool on her back." Meg pointed to the ewe. "Then in the spring, ye'll have two sheep to sell, just in time to graze them up on the moors. Anyone who loses a sheep over the winter will be looking to expand his flock. Ye'll get the best price then, especially if mother and lamb are both healthy."

"How do I get her sheared, then?"

"That requires some skill. It won't do to shear her like it was Spring; ye have to leave her enough to warm her through the cold months. It's also matted and dirty. Still, there's a lot of wool she can spare; once it's washed and combed, it'll make a good bit of yarn."

"I should have said, how do I get the ewe sheared, without taking a shearing myself?"

Meg chuckled. "Aye, ye're a quick fellow, vicar. I'll give ye that! The best parts of that sermon were the witty ones. Do not fear that everyone in the village will take advantage of ye; yer reputation is rising, people esteem ye now, more than they did a few days ago. We're not the sort to fleece our own priest. I can recommend someone to shear the ewe, and I know a woman who will take the wool off yer hands for a fair price. I can also tell ye where to buy hay for the winter, and how much to pay." She was still chuckling. "What name are ye givin' to this woolly lady?"

Edward thought a moment. "I'll call her Mary. And about my sermon . . ."

"Mary. That's a fine name for a lady gone astray." Meg nodded, with a twinkle in her green eyes. "Like Mary Magdalene, you mean?"

"About the sermon. You said you enjoyed the witty bits — most of which were jokes I told on myself. Is there anything else that you remember?"

Meg's eyes narrowed a bit as if thinking."Not much. I enjoyed the singing, and I laughed at your illustrations. All the talk about the grace and damnation was a little hard to follow."

Edward nodded, ruefully. He had sensed the same thing. He would have to find another way to reach these people. He prayed that God would show him the way.

September 28, 1586: Schooling

Benjamin the sexton was back on Monday morning. He asked to speak with the vicar, but Bess tried to put him off. She might have done so but for his persistence. Edward came downstairs to the sound of their arguing.

"Father, I'm sorry ye had to be bothered with this," said Bess, "but he won't go away!"

"What's the problem?" asked Edward.

"I need to open the church if I'm to ring the bells," explained Benjamin.

"Quite so. How is it that the church is locked?"

"I did so yesterday," Bess admitted. "Better to control the comings and goings."

"Is it not customary for the doors to the sanctuary to be open at all times?"

"Not since Father Jacobs died. I thought it best to secure the church and its valuables."

"Aren't the altar goods kept locked up in the vestry?"

"Aye, but two locks are better than one, I'd say."

"Bess, a sanctuary locked is no sanctuary at all. Either we leave the church doors open, or we must make duplicate keys so that our sexton can gain access when he needs to ring the bells." Benjamin smiled at this remark, Bess looked a little putout.

Edward turned to Benjamin. "I will have a duplicate key made for you. Bess, can you take care of that today?"

"Won't be necessary," she said, with a hint of a pout. "Here's a copy." She handed a key to Edward. He wondered how many keys and copies of keys Bess had in her possession.

"Thank you," said Edward. Then, turning to Benjamin, he asked, "What's the occasion for ringing the bells?"

"It's time for the school to start again. Need to let the children know."

"School? At the church?"

"Aye, just for the young 'uns out of the Dame school. Father Jacobs started it, I helped him. Now that the harvest is over, they'll be coming back, I reckon."

Edward thought back to the "Dame school" of his childhood; a dozen or so boys, aged five to seven, drilled in reading and arithmetic. The woman who taught him was strict but gentler than the masters of the grammar school that would follow. Some woman in the village was teaching the youngsters to read and do sums. It made sense — how else would Bess be able to keep a ledger of the church's expenses? And Father Jacobs had decided to offer schooling for the slightly older boys. Nothing like a real grammar school, probably, but . . .

"What was Father Jacobs teaching the boys? Latin? Philosophy?"

"Nay, Father none of that. What use is Latin to the likes of us? He taught the Bible, and sound doctrine, penmanship, some practical Arithmetic — things a working man could use to his profit."

Sound doctrine. Edward saw it in a flash. The children. Of course. Young minds, eager to learn, ready to be molded. He would continue to preach sermons to their parents, and some might find their way to deeper truth, but the children would be the fertile field of his labors. He would forge them, in time, into a weapon of righteousness; soldiers in an army of the Lord, fit to inherit the promised land. *Thank you, Lord God, for showing me the pathway through this wilderness,* he prayed. His heart was lifted. This was why he had been sent to this place, this was his destiny. Bancroft and his ilk would ultimately be defeated, whether Edward lived to see it or not.

"I will walk with you to the church," said Edward to Benjamin. Soon after the bells had rung, children began appearing at the west door. There were barely a dozen, with their hornbooks, and slates. A few had books with them. And four of them were girls. Edward was unprepared for this. Benjamin intuited his surprise, and said, "Father Jacobs said that girls grow up to be women, and women become mothers, and mothers are the first teachers. He didn't expect them to do well at arithmetic, but he said that they should study the Bible, anyway. Actually," he lowered his voice, "he was surprised to learn that the girls make attentive students. Some of the boys require discipline." He gave Edward a knowing wink.

Edward had to agree. Godly men, and godly women. A double-edged sword, in the Lord's hand: *Amen. Euen so, come Lord Iesus.*

December 1586: Advent

Edward Chase's life settled into a routine in Derwent. His weekday mornings were occupied with teaching his young students. This became the most rewarding part of a typical day for him. They were attentive, most of them quite bright, he found. More so the girls, to his surprise. They seemed to pick up the Arithmetic quickly, and all of them could recite the catechism from memory before the end of November. More to the point, they could answer his questions about the meaning of each question and answer. He sometimes asked them tricky questions, just to trip them up, but they rose to the challenge and weren't afraid to tell him if a question was silly. One of the boys in the class was at least as sharp as any of the girls — Edward thought he might make a priest, if he could continue his education, somehow. The rest of the boys could get bored rather easily, but he got them interested in reading selections from Foxe's 'Book of Martyrs': lurid, sometimes gruesome, but the boys found it fascinating. The greatest need was for books — not all the children had any books at home. Edward decided that he would make sure every family represented in his class had a Bible at home and undertook to obtain some. He was able to get a passing merchant to agree to bring some Bibles with him, on his next visit. He also contrived to get a message to a certain man in Norwich, requesting any new writings that might have been recently published. When they came, they gave him a small window into the world where he had spent his life for the last decade or so. Most of it was too dry for children.

Sundays were more challenging. Attendance at the morning services was nearly two hundred people, most weeks. But his sermons seemed to put people to sleep if they lasted for more than an hour. He tried to spice them up a little, with humorous anecdotes and illustrations, but he discovered that people remembered the illustrations more than the doctrines that they were intended to illuminate. The offering box was well supplied — in fact, he was able to pay for the Bibles that way. People were friendly and often warm, but their interest seemed mainly to be in the sacramental events, and the rites of their daily lives. He performed one wedding, several baptisms, and two funerals in the first three months.

Jack Clegg had recovered most of his mobility; he still carried the cane, but it was mostly for dramatic effect. When he wasn't at the pub, he hung around the rectory, getting underfoot of Bess. Edward spent a lot of his time at the church, but it was clear that Jack needed something to do. Going back to mining seemed the obvious choice, but Bess insisted that it was too dangerous. What then? It wasn't exactly Edward's problem, and yet it was — as long as Jack lived at the rectory, at least.

Christmas was coming. He dreaded it, a little; he wasn't sure how this village celebrated Christmas, and he feared it might be something that smacked of papism, or even paganism. Their celebration of All Hallows Eve had been close to riotous, but he was not obligated to recognize that event with a church service. He did hold a special All Saints service the following day, which was well-attended by the village; not a few of them appeared particularly repentant, some seemed hungover. His sermon that day focused primarily on Luther's ninety-five theses. And now Christmas. His own beliefs, of course, were influenced by those of John Calvin, who agreed that an annual day to celebrate Christ's birth was appropriate, as long as everyone understood that Jesus was not actually born on December 25, but firmly rejected any feasts, festivals, or other celebration on that day. Edward was pretty sure that the villagers of Derwent would not find this approach agreeable.

Christmas, as it happened, fell on a Monday this year. He debated whether it was even necessary to hold a Christmas service so close to Sunday. He wondered whom he could ask on this point: he didn't entirely trust the judgment of Bess or Jack on this matter; they might give him conflicting advice, anyway. Maybe he would ask Peter or Benjamin.

He was surprised and a little dismayed at what they told him. "Don't worry about it, Father. The village already has it well in hand," Peter assured him.

"How in hand?"

"Well, we already chose our Lord of Misrule for the Christmastide. It's Jack — on account of his recovery, don't ye see? I'm sure he'll do a fine job."

Edward nodded. Jack Clegg. Of course. Who else? Jack would be the very epitome of misrule, given enough ale. And there would be plenty of ale. He could almost hear Bess scolding him, now. Edward asked, "What other arrangements have been made?"

"Well, Christmas in Derwent isn't such a grand affair as ye'd find in Chesterfield or another big town. But we do the best we can. There's a flock of geese that will be finding a home on our tables, I can tell ye that. We've no wealthy families here that would feast us all, but we'll go wassailing, anyway. There's no place for dancing, apart from the pub, but we make do."

Edward felt a little relieved. Wassailing he was familiar with, and as long as the dancing stayed in the pub, it shouldn't do too much harm . . .

"We'll have mummers, too, of course," added Benjamin helpfully. Noting Edward's worried look, he added. "It'll be no great burden for ye, Father. Peter and I will take care of the decorations in the sanctuary."

"Decorations?"

"Aye, the greens — the ivy and the holly, maybe some boughs of yew. It's the fragrance I love, more than anything, at this time of year."

So. Greens in the sanctuary he could handle. "Anything else to do in the church?"

"Nay. Not unless ye want to have a statue of the infant on the altar. Father Jacobs forbade it, when he was with us — couldn't tolerate images of any kind in church, he said. An educated man, he was, and we had to make allowances for him."

"If it was good enough for Father Jacobs, it's good enough for me," said Edward. He decided he would be keeping indoors, for most of the twelve days of Christmas. Still, he could hardly avoid holding a service on

Christmas day, could he? Something short, maybe some carols. The following Sunday would be New Year's Eve. Maybe the celebrations would have run their course by then . . .

By now it was apparent that the village was preparing to celebrate. A stream of traveling merchants passed through, selling all manner of spices and condiments for the season — raisins, figs, even exotic things like cinnamon and sugar. Bess had apparently placed her own order for many of these things — the peddlers showed up at the rectory almost daily. Among them was a merchant with a dozen Bibles that Edward had ordered — not cheap, but essential to his purpose. He intended to present them to his pupils on the Feast of Epiphany. Then, as soon as classes resumed, they could begin their studies in earnest.

A week before Christmas, a young boy appeared at the rectory door, limping. He might have been eight or nine years old, Edward decided. He did not recognize the boy: "My gramps needs to see the priest," said the boy.

Bess explained: "This lad is from the moors — his name is Ethan, his family has a croft up near Back Tor. None of that family attends church in the village — they say it's too far to travel. Seems that the old man is dying."

Church attendance or not, the man was entitled to the ministrations of a priest. "How will I find the place?"

"They sent Ethan to lead you there. He must have injured himself on his way into the village." The boy nodded in agreement.

"Then I'll take Bruce," said Edward. "The boy can ride, and I can walk. Ethan smiled at the thought.

"Better take some food and drink, and warm clothes, then," said Bess. "It's an overcast afternoon, as ye can see."

Edward packed his prayer book, his Bible, a small communion set, and his staff. Bess handed him a bundle with his provisions. They set out through the village, across the valley, and up the slopes toward the edge, which was lurking somewhere above them, hidden in the clouds. The path zig-zagged across the slope. Before they had gone far, Edward could see that they would be walking straight into the base of the clouds that hung above the valley. Soon enough they were in the clouds, or rather in a fog. The path was barely visible now, but Ethan pointed the way.

As they climbed, the air became brighter, until they emerged near the edge itself, into sunlight. Once above the rim, Edward looked back from whence they had come. The sun was lowering in the West, but the skies were clear. Behind them, the valley was filled with cloud, or fog, as far as he could see. Somewhere down there, he knew, were snug houses, and people heading home for the afternoon in the gloom and gathering darkness. Up here, the sky was blue, the winter sun still shone, the air cool and crisp.

He recalled the story of the prophet who had "seen" the whole valley flooded, and the village submerged. You could almost believe it, up here. If the village, with all its people, disappeared beneath some lake, the people up here would see pretty much what he was seeing — beautiful, clean, invigorating. It gave the prophecy a different tone, somehow. He could understand why a man might wish to be buried up here, rather than in the churchyard below.

"It's miles yet," said Ethan. "We should make it before dark." They pressed on. Once above the edge, the path was straighter — winding around knolls, and straight across the shallow valleys. At one place where the path was narrow, Ethan pointed to a pothole, rocky and rough: "Took a misstep right there," he said, "sprained me ankle." Edward was surprised he had made it to the village — tougher than he looked, was Ethan.

It was nearly dark when they arrived at the small, stone cottage, tucked into a swale below a hillock. The landscape was dissected into fields separated by stone walls (evidently stones were plentiful here). Near the house was a large pen, with a few dozen sheep. Shepherds, then. It *was* a long way from the village.

Ethan's arrival was greeted by a woman, evidently his mother, who embraced and scolded him at once — they had begun to worry about him and expected him back much sooner. He explained that he had fallen and injured his leg, which had slowed him down.

Edward was invited into the cottage, which was crowded with people — relatives of the old man who lay in bed in a back room, propped up with pillows, and a pair of candles for light. Edward was surprised to see Meg standing there, alongside a couple of weepy women who might have been the old man's daughters.

The man in the bed was named Alfred, he was told. He looked frail, his breathing was labored, but his eyes were clear, and he fixed them on Edward. "Father, if ye've come to offer me absolution, ye've made the journey for nothing," Alfred said firmly.

"I am come because I was summoned. I have no absolution to offer you," Edward replied, "only God can do that."

"That's well, then. It can't hurt for you to pray for me." He looked at the women at his bedside. "Which of you summoned the priest?"

"I did," said Meg. "I've done all I could for ye. It's time for ye to see a priest."

Alfred nodded. "I feel it, too Meg. Bless ye for comforting an old man in his last hours."

Meg nodded and struggled to hold back her tears.

"There now, Meg. No tears for me. I've drunk my fill of the cup of life. It's time to move on." He turned to Edward. "One thing I ask, Father . . ."

Edward nodded. "If I can, I surely will."

"Don't let them bury me down in the churchyard. Let me find a resting place up here, where I can lie under the stars, with the wind and the weather. Let sheep graze over the place I am buried. Let the sun scorch me, and the snow freeze me, but never in a churchyard."

Edward thought a moment. How many others were buried up on the moor, outside the confines of the hallowed ground of the churchyard? Did it matter? "Do you have a place in mind?"

"Aye." Alfred smiled, "I do. My daughters know the place. Their mother lies there. Please explain to them that I will not burn in Hell if I am laid to rest outside a churchyard."

Two of the other women in the room were looking directly at Edward now as if his opinion on the topic would matter. "I think a Christian man is entitled to rest where he chooses," said Edward. "Especially if it is near those that he loves."

One of the women began to sob, the other nodded in assent. *Theological dispute solved*, Edward thought.

Alfred smiled and seemed to relax a bit. "I would see my children and grandchildren. Bring them to me." The summons was given, and more than a dozen people from outside crowded into the room — various sizes of children, and their parents.

Edward stepped out into the main hall, to make room for all of them. Meg joined him. There were still plenty of neighbors and other kinfolk in the room, some had brought food and drink, some were cooking by the fire. Edward looked for a corner to stand, where he might be out of the way. The only place he could spot was occupied — by a long-haired, spotted dog, who lay there watching the whole scene with some anxiety, in some sort of shallow wooden box. As Edward approached, the dog raised its head as if warning him to keep his distance. "That's Queenie," said Meg. "She's friendly enough, once she knows ye. Look," Meg knelt and extended her hand. Queenie sniffed it, then licked it, and wagged her tail. "See why she's a bit nervous?" Meg reached into the box and pulled out a squirming mass of fur. "She's a mum, is Queenie. "Isn't he lovely?" she said as a small, pink tongue emerged from the fur ball. She held the pup up, and let it snuggle under her chin. "Aye, laddie, go for the throat," she chuckled. "Here." She handed the pup to Edward.

The incongruity of the whole scene was bewildering. In the back room, a man was bidding his final farewell to those he loved most in the world. Out here, people were eating, and drinking, coming and going — and he was holding a puppy, with a small, pink tongue and — ouch — small sharp teeth. He smiled and handed the puppy back to Meg, then stepped outside. It was dark. It was also foggy.

Meg followed him out, wrapped in her crimson cloak. "Is there a problem, Father?"

"No, I just need to clear my thoughts. Perhaps you can explain some things to me."

"Aye, if I can."

"It is a solemn thing, or so I believe, when a man must meet his maker."

"Aye, so it is."

"And yet, it is as if the people in that house are of two different worlds. In the bedroom, Alfred is setting his affairs in order in a sober and dignified way, while outside in the hall, you might suppose they are just entertaining a few close friends."

"Ah. That is our way, here on the moor. A small house must fit all the pieces of a life under one roof. Sometimes, it gets a bit crowded." She smiled.

"And what is my part in all of this? Is there to be a funeral, do you think?"

"I am sure that Alfred will die tonight. I am seldom wrong about these things. Alfred is ready, and that makes it ever so much easier. I have known men and women to fight it to their last breath — and it is a fight that they do not win. The family will expect you to perform a funeral service, tomorrow. And, since you have agreed that Alfred can be buried up here, it will be easier for folk to attend. Your presence is welcome here."

"Why did you call for me?"

"Because these are a Christian people, and you are their priest. Not all of them believe as you do, including Alfred, but a funeral is for the living, not the departed."

That was true enough, thought Edward. "I don't suppose I'll be going home tonight, then." Edward peered into the fog and darkness.

"It wouldn't be safe to try, even if ye knew the way, which ye don't. Bess won't be expecting you tonight — she sent along some food, did she not?"

Edward had forgotten about the dinner Bess had given him. "Where is Bruce, by the way?

"No doubt someone put him in a stall and fed him. The barn is this way." She led him to a ramshackle building behind the house. "This is where ye'll be sleeping tonight, along with most of the men and boys. The women will bed down in the house."

That made sense if the crowd inside intended to stay over. All indications were that they intended just that. "Tell me what you know of Alfred."

"He is my father's uncle. Our family name is Moorcroft — or that is the name we have taken, over the years — it fits us, don't you think?"

Edward nodded. "And all these people are your kinfolk?"

Meg nodded, "One way or another. We have lived up here for many generations."

"So, Alfred is your grandfather's brother, or . . ."

"Aye. My grandfather's brother, the last of that generation."

"Will your father be at the funeral, then?"

"Nay. Papa died four years ago. My mum two years before that."

"Any brothers or sisters?"

"Nay. I have plenty of cousins, though."

They found Bruce in a stall, just as Meg had predicted. He seemed contented enough.

"It's chilly," said Meg, as she drew her cloak around herself. She found a seat on a pile of hay. "Sit with me, awhile."

Edward sat down beside her. She shifted up next to him, snuggled a little. "The chill is eased, if ye sit closer to me," she said with a grin.

Edward could feel the difference, right away. "You live alone, then?"

"Aye," she smiled and arched an eyebrow.

"Wouldn't it be safer to live in the village?"

"Not necessarily. Besides, I have a croft to manage."

"A croft? Up here on the moor?"

"Aye, the name is 'Moorcroft'; do ye remember?"

Edward shook his head. "I'm sorry. For some reason, I supposed that you made your living from herbs and medicines. It did not occur to me that you might be a landed gentlewoman."

She chuckled. "Aye, a right lady, that's me. I help people when I can, and sometimes they pay for my help. But it's not a lucrative business. I have a house, a garden, a flock of sheep."

"You learned to do this from your parents, then?"

"The shepherding from my Pa, the medicines from my Mum. She was a village lass, but Pa would not live in the valley. Said it was the prophecy about the flood, but I think it was more a matter of too many people. Some men are not made for society."

More than a few, thought Edward, given the number of people in the house, none of whom he had ever seen in the village before. "Tell me about your mother, was she a woman of . . . special abilities?"

"Was she a witch, ye mean? Nay, my mum was not a witch. She had knowledge of minerals and plants, which she received from her mum, and passed on to me. Some call women like us 'Wise Women', by which they seek to make us objects of superstition or fear. Sometimes they use us as a scapegoat for their misfortunes. All we do is try to help people, with the natural things that God has made for people's help."

There was a note of weariness in her voice — evidently, she had found it necessary to explain that she did not dabble in witchcraft more than once. Edward nodded, as if satisfied with her answer. Not likely that a witch would admit to it, if it were true, anyway.

"Ye have told me nothing about yer parents," said Meg, leaning closer in the chill.

Ah. "Not much to tell. My father was a scholar, among the many men who had to flee England when Mary was queen. He died in Geneva, or so they say. My mother stayed behind because she was pregnant — with me. She died when I was just three years old. I was raised by my aunt and uncle, so no inheritance. My uncle did pay for my schooling, out of respect to my father's reputation. I did well enough at University — might have made a career as a scholar, like my father. But the circumstances were not favorable. I made a fair reputation as a wandering preacher, but that door was closed to me, as well. So, here I am in Derwent."

She looked closely at him. Her eyes were green — not that he could see their color in the dark, but they burned green in his memory. "Ye have left something unsaid. A scholar does not come to Derwent of his own accord. Someone sent ye here or compelled ye to come. Which is it?"

Edward sighed. It would come out, sooner or later. "I was compelled to come. It was either Derwent or a lifetime in prison."

She surprised him, by gasping, and blurting out, "I knew it! I took ye for a dangerous man when I first saw ye!" She whispered, "Tell me what crime ye have committed!" with a tone of eagerness.

Edward was bewildered. Not at all the reaction he expected. "I committed no crime, at least none that I could be convicted of. My 'crimes' are crimes of conscience. I dared to challenge the Archbishop and his minions, and now I pay the price."

Meg's voice was subdued. "And Derwent is yer punishment?"

"Derwent is a place where they hope that no one will pay any attention to anything I say. They intend for me to stay here for the remainder of my natural life."

"Who'd have thought that Derwent was such a special place." There was irony in her voice.

"When they sent me here, they told me that Derwent was a troublesome place. I see now what they meant."

"So, you are a spy for the Archbishop? Do ye hope to get back into his good graces, by betraying us in some way?" She sounded disappointed.

"I have made a career out of keeping secrets, even when threatened with torture," (the torture bit was not strictly true, but for some reason, he felt the need to cast himself in a more heroic light) "I will not betray anyone to please the Archbishop — not that there is anything to betray here."

"But you could leave Derwent, one day if ye decided to do so?"

"If I leave, they will pursue me. If they catch me, I will die in prison."

Meg shivered a little and snuggled closer. Edward caught a whiff of — lavender? "It is like a prison for you here, then."

"There are worse places to live, and I have lived in some of them. I have a warm place to live, a comfortable bed, and good food. I have the open sky and sunshine. I do not pity myself if that is what you think."

Meg spoke in mock disappointment. "Ye started a good story, but now ye've made it boring."

"Would you rather I were a highwayman or a thief?"

She rested her head on his shoulder. "No, I think ye'd make a poor thief. A highwayman who gets lost on the road is no highwayman, at all. Better to stick with the priesthood." She giggled to herself — he felt, rather than heard it. Just then, two men stumbled into the barn — a little too much ale. They groped around in the dark for a place to sleep. More would be coming out from the house, soon. Meg stood and brushed the straw from her cloak. "Good night, Father," she said, "See you in the morning."

Edward stretched out on the hay. There was a little warmth remaining, where Meg had been sitting. He covered himself with more hay — too chilly for one to sleep alone, he thought.

Alfred died during the night, as Meg had predicted. At dawn, Edward woke, along with nearly a dozen men and boys, who emerged from the hay like so many hibernating animals in the Spring. Breakfast was served, and men were sent to dig a grave for the departed patriarch. It was a bit foggy, but the sun came out eventually. By noon, the arrangements had been made. They ate first, and then Alfred's casket (where had that come from?) was carried from the house, and out across the moor. Edward put on his vestments over his coat — it was a chilly day, sun or no sun.

The site that Alfred had chosen was a fair distance from the house, on a high knoll with a fine view of the White Peak to the south. There was a small graveyard, surrounded by a stone wall. Alfred would not be the first to be buried in this place. The fresh-dug grave was not too deep; the bedrock was near the surface, here. Edward began reading from the prayer book, as the procession approached:

"I am the resurrection and the life (saith the Lord) he that beleveth in me: yea, thoughe he were dead, yet shall he live. And whosoever liveth, and beleveth in me, shall not dye for ever . . ."

There were more than thirty people present. Apart from Meg, none of them had ever attended a Sunday service, as far as he could tell. Somehow, the "Order for the Buriall of the Dead" seemed familiar to them all. Had he only known this was going to happen, he could have prepared a suitable sermon for all these unchurched people — no, it was just too chilly, he decided. Pity. When he finished the last prayer in the service, he started to turn away. But the rest of the crowd stood, and Meg began to sing:

> *"The Lord is my lightening, and mine health; whom shall I dread?*
> *The Lord is defender of my life; for whom shall I tremble?*
>
> *The while noisome men nigh on me; for to eat my fleshes.*
> *Mine enemies, that troubled me; they were made sick and felled down.*
>
> *Though castles stand together against me; mine heart shall not dread.*
> *Though battle riseth against me; in this thing I shall have hope.*

I asked of the Lord one thing; I shall seek this thing;
that I dwell in the house of the Lord all the days of my life.
That I see the will of the Lord; and that I visit his temple.

For he hid me in his tabernacle in the day of evils;

he defended me in the hid place of his tabernacle. He enhanced me in a stone;
and now he enhanced mine head over mine enemies.

I compassed, and offered in his tabernacle a sacrifice of crying;
I shall sing, and I shall say psalm to the Lord.

Lord, hear thou my voice, by which I cried to thee; have thou mercy on me, and
hear me.
Mine heart said to thee, My face sought thee; Lord, I shall seek again thy face.

Turn thou not away thy face from me; bow thou not away in wrath from thy
servant.

Lord, be thou mine helper, forsake thou, not me; and, God, mine health, despise
thou not me.

For my father and my mother have forsaken me, but the Lord hath taken me.

Lord, set thou a law to me in thy way; and dress thou me in a rightful path, for
mine enemies.

Betake thou not me into the souls of them, that trouble me;
for wicked witnesses have risen against me, and wickedness lied to itself.

I believe to see the goods of the Lord; in the land of living men.

Abide thou the Lord, do thou manly; and thine heart be comforted, and suffer
thou the Lord."

By the second verse, all the adults, and most of the children were singing along. Unchurched they might be, but something of the ancient faith was still in them. It was a little humbling to think that the words of some ancient teacher were still alive in the hearts and minds of these people. He wondered if any of his sermons would live on, like this, for centuries. He knew the answer to that question. It was also humbling.

After the singing, they walked back to Alfred's house. Edward stayed long enough to drink some ale and then got Bruce ready to return to the village. "It's about three miles back to the edge," said Meg. "Stay on the path, and ye'll be safe. When you get to the edge, ye'll be able to see the village, unless the valley is filled with fog. In any case, you can find yer way home from there. Be careful." The sound of music was coming from the house — evidently, the family had some celebrating to do. Strange customs, these.

The path was clear enough, for the first mile or so. Then, mist rolled in from in front of him, and things got murkier. He had to peer along the ground in places, to find the path. Progress was painfully slow. At length, he realized he had missed a turn somewhere. Nothing to do but backtrack and find the path again. As he turned, his foot slipped. He was falling headfirst, sliding down a slope of gravel — until his head struck something large and hard. He sat up. Dizzy, ears ringing, headache. He felt around for his footing. He felt loose gravel in his hands, rolled over onto his stomach, and began to crawl back up the slope. Shooting pain in his left ankle. Head throbbing. He would have to crawl on three limbs, not four. First, he would rest . . .

When Edward got back to Derwent, it was night. The street was wet — no, it was not just wet, water was standing in the street. No, the water was <u>rising</u> in the street. He realized that something was wrong. Time to get to higher ground. He struggled to run toward the slopes above the village — it seemed as though the mud on his shoes was holding him back. The water rose. The slope got steeper; he was climbing on his hands and knees, now. He looked up. The edge loomed there — how could he hope to scale it? He looked down — He saw only the church steeple; all the village was under water. And yet the water was still rising, as if pursuing him . . . A voice called out "Father! Take the rope!" It was Meg, good Meg, kind Meg. The rope. Of course. He seized the rope, and Meg pulled . . . he was rising, above the water, rising, rising . . . He giggled. The water couldn't get him, now. And then he was flying, soaring over the edge, and landing on the grass. He laughed out loud and tried to stand. Mistake. Pain. Headache. Everything got dark.

December 1586: Lady Lavender and the Raven Queen

Edward Chase woke groggily, with a headache. It was dark. The air was smoky. There was another aroma in the air — lavender maybe? He was facing a stone wall. It occurred to him that he might be back in the jail at Ipswich. Or maybe he had never left? Maybe he had been dreaming? He rolled over. A woman was lying there, the faint aroma was stronger, definitely lavender. This was not the Ipswich jail, then. The woman and the lavender were all the proof he needed. So, not a jail cell. He tried to sit up. His head was swimming; he flopped back down on the bed. The woman stirred, turned to him, and spoke: "Good Morning, Father. How are you?"

The face seemed familiar. He struggled to recall the name. She had called him "Father," which meant — what exactly? "Good morning," he replied, stalling for time for his memory to come back. Lavender. Lady Lavender. Lady Lavender, of the green eyes and raven hair — that would be her proper name.

Lady Lavender rose and crossed the room. He could see more, now: a fireplace, a table and chairs, windows, a door. A cottage. He was in a cottage. A flood of memories (or dreams?) filled his mind. "Do they call you — Margaret?" he asked.

She turned and smiled. "You may call me Margaret if you like. Most people just call me Meg."

He managed to sit up, still dizzy. "Take it easy, Father. The potion will addle your mind for a while, but you'll recover it, ere long."

"Potion?" Edward's mind skipped a beat. What potion? Was he under the influence of some sorceress?

"For the pain," she explained. "Your ankle. You were grateful for it, last night."

"Last night?" His mind skipped again.

She laughed. "No fear, Father. You've lost nothing but your memory from spending the night here. Your reputation is safe with me."

His head was beginning to clear. This must be Meg's cottage. In Derwent. He was the parish priest. The Ipswich jail was a thing of the past. He got lost on the moor. Fell into a hole . . . Bruce. "Where's Bruce?" he blurted out.

"Bruce is outside, where he belongs. How much do you remember of last night? Why were you on the moor?"

Why, indeed. Edward tried to remember. "I was visiting the miners up on Back Tor. I was headed home. The fog closed in. I guess we lost the path, Bruce and I . . ."

"Do you know where I found you?"

Edward shook his head. "I don't recall being found, though I think I must be lucky that you did."

"Lucky indeed, Father. You can thank Bruce, as well."

"How's that?"

"I would never have looked for you in the fog, much less found you, but for Bruce's braying. I wasn't looking for you at all. I thought I was aiding an animal in distress. When I did find him, he refused to come with me; and then I heard you moaning. Bruce helped me drag you out of that hole and carried you here on his back. That's as good a friend as a man will find, in this part of the world."

Edward nodded and took a deep breath. "What was it that you gave me last night?"

"Something to ease the pain in your ankle and your head. And before you ask, I lay next to you because I have only one bed, and you were chilled — I have not taken advantage of you."

Edward felt a pang of . . . disappointment? Missed opportunity? He caught another whiff of lavender. Best not to dwell on that, think about it later. Time to get back to the village; Bess would be asking everybody about his whereabouts. He tried to stand. Pain. He winced as he sat down.

"Aye," said Meg, "you'll be needing to take it easy, for a while. I'll fit the ankle with a brace so that ye can hobble about some. Ye won't be walkin' much for a week or two — lucky you've got a friend like Bruce."

"I need to get back to the village."

"Aye, ye do. We'll eat first, then I'll lead you back through Derwent on Bruce's back, like a hunter's trophy. Here's a crutch — the privy is outside, to your right."

He made it, with some difficulty. He stepped outside into a misty morning and found himself looking out over a deep valley. The fog was lifting enough to see the edge on the opposite side of the valley, though wisps obscured the view here and there. The sun broke through from behind him in places, illuminating fields and pastures on the opposite slope. It was a dazzling sight: the colors of the landscape glowed as if aflame. He turned to look behind him, at the small stone cottage where he had spent the night. It was perched near the base of a stony outcrop that loomed above, on a small natural terrace. Behind the cottage was the opening to a tall, shallow cave, open to the Western sky, but sheltering the cottage to the East. He found the privy where she said it would be — a flimsy wooden structure perched over a deep crack in the bedrock; adequate for the purpose. He sensed that the crack was very deep. How long before someone would have to move the privy to another crack? Maybe never, if the crack was deep enough; maybe it would take a century to fill it. Maybe people had been using it for centuries, already, maybe . . . He realized his speculation was getting out of control. Must be whatever was in that potion that Meg gave him.

His business finished, he stepped out of the privy and found himself staring a large bird in the face, or rather the bird was staring at him. It was a raven, perched on the top of the privy, leaning slightly toward him, examining him closely. Up close, the bird seemed enormous. Edward felt that he was intruding, somehow. He stepped out and hobbled back toward the cottage. His head was still throbbing, but clearer now. He heard the rustle of wings. The raven was following him as he hobbled forward, perching here and there along the path, or walking behind him, as he approached the cottage. Just before he reached the front door, the bird flew to the roof edge ahead of him and opened its beak to emit a harsh, screeching sound. Edward stepped inside as quickly as he could and shut the door firmly behind him. Meg looked up at him when he entered, and saw the look on his face. "Ye've met my Johnny, by the sound of it."

"Johnny? The raven has a name?"

"Of course! Had to give him a name, he always shows up for breakfast." she chuckled.

Breakfast was porridge, with some rye bread and a boiled egg. They drank water, which Edward was skeptical of, but there was a spring just outside Meg's door. "Been drinking from this spring all my life," she said. He realized he was thirsty. Then he realized he was hungry, too. The flavor of the porridge was intense, the water felt like a cold fire as he swallowed it,

After breakfast, Lady Lavender bound up his ankle, which made it easier to hobble about. Edward felt his strength returning. "How far back to the village?"

"Well, if ye're in a hurry, ye can throw yourself off the edge, and roll into town. Less than a mile that way. But if ye can wait till I feed the animals, we can take the gentler path, with Bruce — more like two miles, I'd say." She was showing that lopsided smile again — teasing him, in her own way, reminding him of just how unfamiliar he was with this land and its ways.

"I'll wait," he said with a smile. "Couldn't leave Bruce behind." She nodded and smiled more broadly. She had a pretty smile when she wasn't trying to tease him, he decided.

Meg went to the back of the cottage and filled a basket with some grain from a large barrel. "Got to feed the chickens," she said. Edward followed her outside and to the rear of the cottage. Johnny was still perched on the roof. There was a chicken coop there, with a small enclosed hen yard. The hen yard was surrounded by low fencing, the sticks close enough together that a fox couldn't (hopefully) squeeze between them. Meg unlatched the door, and called out "Here, my biddies, come get it!" Five hens and a rooster trotted out into the yard. Meg tossed the grain on the ground, and the chickens scampered around, scratching and pecking at it. Meg fetched four eggs from the coop, before closing the gateway to the hen yard.

"I'd be grateful if ye'd wait here, and keep an eye out for vermin," she said. Edward waited while she took the eggs back into the cottage. He wasn't exactly sure what "vermin" would look like — foxes, maybe, or weasels? He noticed a large cauldron with a fire under it. Whatever it held, it was hot — he could see wisps of steam rising from it. He began to see a worrisome pattern: familiarity with wild animals, potions, mysterious cauldrons . . .

She was back with the remnants of a loaf of bread. "Johnny, Dear," she called, "Here's yer breakfast!" Johnny swooped down from the rooftop and landed on her shoulder. She broke off a piece of the bread and held it between her teeth. Johnny leaned over and snatched it from her mouth. "That's a good boy. Who's my pretty, pretty boy?" Johnny responded with a hoarse, screeching caw. "That's it, Johnny; Call the lads!"

Edward was speechless. He wasn't sure what he was witnessing. The woman had a familiarity with animals that could easily be explained as witchcraft. He wondered again what she was brewing in that cauldron. He edged over to get a whiff of it . . .

"I wouldn't taste that if I were you," said Meg. "It's the laundry."

Just then, the 'Lads' arrived, swooping down onto the roof, the hen yard fence, fluttering and squawking as they contended for a favorite perch. Some landed on the ground around Meg and began walking toward her. All eyes were on Meg. They formed a rough circle around her, like so many courtiers around the throne of a queen. Edward counted nine ravens, including Johnny, who rested on Meg's shoulder, like the first among equals. No longer Lady Lavender, she was the Raven Queen. It all made sense, now. A great sorceress, disguised as the beautiful Lady Lavender.

Edward felt a chill. He also felt an urge to bow before the Raven Queen. He hesitated. What could it be, other than sorcery, for a woman to command the ravens to assemble, and pay court to her? He decided that he liked her better in the guise of Lady Lavender.

Then Meg began to tear pieces of the bread and toss them on the ground. The ravens abandoned their orderly formation and set to tussling and flapping for every crumb. The winners tried to escape with their prizes or swallow them on the spot, while the losers pursued them, with loud protests. Meg laughed out loud, for the sheer chaos of the scene, or maybe just for the enthusiasm that the 'Lads' demonstrated for nothing but a few bits of stale bread. The Raven Queen was cruel, Edward realized.

Edward was torn between fear and admiration. He reminded himself that he was still under the influence of whatever 'potion' Meg had given him. Still, he could not shake the feeling that something eldritch was happening. How could she summon ravens at will, if not through some occult power?

"Whatever is the matter, Father? You look like you have seen something fearful?" Meg approached him, and looked closely into his eyes. Green eyes, had the Lady Lavender. Green eyes and raven hair — as befit the Raven Queen . . .

"It's the mandrake root," said Meg. "I gave you more than I should. Some require more, some less. It'll wear off, Father, in due time. Just don't do anything rash, until it does."

"Rash?"

"Don't imagine things that cannot be. Don't imagine that ye can fly, or that animals are speaking to you, or any such nonsense. Wait for the potion to wear off."

"But I saw you speaking to the animals, just now. Or did I? Is it sorcery, or is it the mandrakes?"

Ye did indeed see me talking to the animals. It isn't sorcery unless the animals talk back. If you think the animals, or the plants, or the stones are talking to you — it's the mandrakes."

Ah. The mandrakes. What was it about the mandrakes . . . Then, "Did someone die?"

"Aye. Someone died. Do you not remember the funeral?"

Funeral. Funeral? "I remember some singing," he volunteered. "Was there singing?"

"Aye. There was singing."

By the time they entered the village, plenty of people were up and about. There was some laughter, and a great deal of curiosity about Edward on Bruce's back, being led through town by Meg. She waved off the silly remarks and pushed on to the rectory. The fewer people talked to the vicar in his present condition, the better.

Bess was relieved to see them and then alarmed when she realized that the vicar was injured. "Found him in a collapsed mine pit, last night," explained Meg. "Patched him up at my place. He needs to be put to bed."

Bess nodded and helped Meg pull Edward inside. "No stairs for this one, until he recovers," said Meg, "put him in the first-floor chamber. "

"Let's set him in a chair, then, until I can change the bed linens," said Bess. Jack had heard the news, somehow, and appeared at just the right moment. "Jack!" said Bess, "we're swapping rooms with Father Chase. Help Meg move our things upstairs, and his things down here."

Edward sat in the chair and looked around curiously as if seeing the room for the first time. Bess and Jack noticed this and asked Meg: "Is he addled or drunk?"

"Not drunk. Addled, certainly. Bashed his head on a rock, I reckon. I think he'll be better in the morning."

"But what if . . ."

"There's nothing we can do about 'if'. He survived the night, so I think he'll still be with us tomorrow." She avoided any mention of mandrakes — no reason to feed gossip, especially gossip about the effects of mandrakes.

They had the contents of the bed chambers changed in just a few moments and put Edward to bed in the hall chamber. Meg lit a fire in the fireplace, to warm the place up.

"Meg?" His voice was a little dreamy . . .

"Yes, Father?"

"My name is Edward. Did you know that?"

"Yes, I did know that. Do you want me to call you Edward?"

"Not sure. Just wanted to be sure that you know my Christian name. I think you should call me 'Father' unless we are alone together."

"We are alone together now, Father. Shall I call you Edward?" He did not answer. He was asleep.

December 25, 1586: Twelve days and a Night.

Edward Chase's mind was much clearer on the morning after his return to the rectory. His ankle was another matter; swollen and purplish. Meg came to check on him that afternoon and prescribed some hot plasters for the swelling. "You'll need a crutch or a cane, to get around for the next month," she predicted, "nothing is broken, as far as I can tell. What do ye remember from two days ago ?"

"I remember there was a funeral. The man was your great uncle, a man named Alfred. Alfred Moorcock, I think. I conducted the funeral, which was outside. I remember being cold. I remember the singing of a Psalm, in the ancient style. I remember getting lost in the fog and falling."

Meg nodded. "Yer memory is returning. That's a good thing."

"I also remember the evening before, and the scent of lavender in the dark. I also remember . . ."

Meg placed a finger across his lips. "Hush, Father, that's enough remembering for one day. Don't tire yourself."

Why do I always smell lavender, when I'm around you?"

She smiled. "It's probably because I carry a small bag of lavender around my neck. It's called a *sachet*. Helps me sleep at night."

Then she was gone. Bess announced that it was suppertime. He wondered who was supervising the schoolchildren, remembered that he had to finish his sermon. And with all that, he felt distracted, unfocused. There was a trace of lavender in the room. How was that possible? Bess called him to supper.

The following day, Edward felt strong enough to hobble over to the church to lead his class. At the end of the lessons, he declared that they would be suspending classes, until after Christmastide. "I expect you all back here, the day after Epiphany," he said.

Christmas Eve fell on a Sunday, and Peter and Benjamin had recruited a whole committee to decorate the sanctuary in the week prior. They twined greens around the pillars in the nave and around the base of the altar. Edward drew the line at decorating the pulpit, which surprised them. "Not like the old days, then, vicar. One year, the Lord of Misrule decreed that there should be a kissing bough hung just over the West doors — took a long time to get folks in and out of service that year, let me tell ye!"

Edward tried to imagine the chaos that would cause. He decided the greens would be acceptable. He made a mental note to inspect the sanctuary regularly, just in case some irreverent character slipped in and hung a kissing bough somewhere.

He felt a guilty pleasure at sleeping in the Hall chamber, instead of upstairs. It was larger than the upstairs rooms, for one thing, and most of all, it had its own fireplace. The upstairs rooms were chilly, at this time of year. Evidently, Jack and Bess found it so, because Bess approached him the day before Christmas Eve, and said, "Father, Jack and I will be moving back to our cottage, now. I'll still be here every morning, to make your breakfast, supper, and dinner, and I'll still do the housekeeping. But Jack is well able to fend for himself during the day, now."

Just as well, thought Edward. *Whatever the Lord of Misrule is plotting, best he do his work somewhere other than the rectory!*

That evening, he built a fire and crawled into bed with a sense of satisfaction. This was the life he had planned on when he first arrived in Derwent. He would sleep soundly at night, his dreams would be pleasant. Somehow, the faint aroma of lavender persisted in the room, reminding him of Meg Moorcroft. He reflected that if she hadn't found him on the moor, he would most likely have died up there. He hadn't thanked her properly — maybe he would speak to her Sunday, after the service. Yes, after the service . . .

In the morning, he was awakened by the sound of Bess making his breakfast. He dressed, ate, and hobbled over to the church, to see how things were going. The decorators were already busy.

"How long do these adornments stay up?" he asked Benjamin.

"We'll take them down right after Twelfth Night, Father. No worries."

"Are people expecting an evening service this Sunday? On account of Christmas Eve, I mean?

"It's traditional if that's what ye mean. Usually, there's more singing and less preaching — but that is up to you, of course."

Of course. Edward decided that he would focus on the sermon for the morning service, and . . . well, he did enjoy the singing. Maybe they would sing some carols, maybe some that he remembered from his childhood . . .

He was not disappointed. The morning service was packed, which helped mitigate the chill in the sanctuary. He thought his sermon particularly fine on that morning, and the congregation did not give him any indication that he was mistaken. In the evening, the attendance was lighter — folk that lived outside the village were less likely to travel after dark — but the singing was beautiful. Edward was touched by the music as he had not been for many years. The service was not long — hearty singing eased the chill, but not indefinitely. Afterward, Edward came home to an empty house, set a fire in the chamber fireplace, and went to bed. The songs were still echoing in his head, and there was the faintest scent of lavender . . .

Christmas Day was another service. Not so well attended as the Christmas Eve service, but still a full congregation huddled together for warmth. They celebrated the Eucharist, so Edward shortened his remarks, lest their feet get numb before they could approach the altar.

On the Tuesday after Christmas, Bess announced it was time to change the bed linens, and shooed Edward out of his room, right after breakfast. It was brisk outside, but sunny. There had been some rain the night before, and mist hung to the edges above the valley, but the sky above was clear and blue. From where he stood on the street, Edward could see the heights of the Dark Peak, looming to the north, dusted with snow. He remembered what the teamster had told him on the road, about the Dark Peak looking whiter than the White Peak. That seemed like a very long time ago . . .

His ankle was improving, and he took a stroll through the village. People were in a festive mood, in the middle of celebrating all Twelve Days of Christmas, and he was greeted warmly. He was asked about his injury, and his rescue on the moor time after time. "Ye really should have a guide, Father, before ye venture up there. Better men than you have gotten lost." Everyone agreed that his rescue by Meg was an act of divine providence — and Edward did not disagree with them.

Somehow, that event had severed some ties with his past; it felt like a fresh start to his life, to be in this place, with these people — injured, but still very much alive. He felt exhilarated — and might have danced, if his ankle would let him — though dancing had never been his habit, even before he was schooled in the moral perils of such foolishness. Perhaps he was getting carried away with the mood of the season.

He stepped into the pub on his way back to the rectory. He was offered some mulled wine, which was welcome — warm going down, warm in the afterglow. Jack Clegg was there, seated on a chair that was set on a platform, like some throne: the Lord of Misrule. He was accompanied by six other men, who were acting as his attendants. Their job was to carry Jack around in his chair, visiting various houses in the village to demand food, drink, or the performance of some ridiculous, or possibly humiliating deed.

"Come hither, priest, and bow before yer Lord!" exclaimed Jack. The attendants laughed. Edward played along, and limped forward, making a slight bow.

"What is yer request?" demanded the Lord.

Edward tried to think of something clever to say. "Only, my Lord, if it be in your power, to restore my injured limb."

"<u>If</u> it be in my power? Do ye doubt my power?" More laughter

"Nay, Lord, I only doubt your sobriety." Louder laughter.

"Yer request will not be granted, until the end of Twelfth Night. 'Til then ye must suffer the consequences of your foolishness."

"Foolishness, my Lord?"

"Aye, foolishness. Everyone knows that it is the hero who must rescue the damsel. You have turned it backward so that the damsel has to rescue you. If that is not foolishness, it is the definition of misrule. There can only be one Lord of Misrule; you are poaching in my domain. The next time you wish to catch the notice of a fair maiden, offer her money!" Loud, long laughter, men pounding on the tables and hooting. Edward felt himself blushing — why, he could not explain.

"Thank You, My Lord, for these words of wisdom. And for your patience with such a fool as I." Edward bowed again, and limped backward, out of the Lord's purview, then turned to leave. Laughter followed him out the door.

Bess had nearly finished changing the linens — only the pillowcase needed changing. It was a fine pillow, stuffed with goose down. As she pulled off the old pillowcase, something fell to the floor. She stooped to pick it up — small, nearly flat. She rubbed it between her finger and thumb: the scent of lavender rose to her nose. It was a sachet, she realized. Why would the vicar keep such a thing inside his pillowcase? Where would he get such a thing? She thought to toss it away, and then a smile spread across her face. It made sense, now. She put the clean pillowcase back on the pillow, and tucked the little sachet inside, where no one would find it — unless they knew to look for it . . .

On the street, Edward caught a breath of fresh air. He considered his duty done — no more visits to the pub, until Twelfth Night was past.

It wasn't to be quite that easy; the revelers brought their celebration to him. Though he stayed inside in the evenings, there were plenty of visitors to the rectory. Bess had anticipated this and kept a large pot of "wassail," and some baked morsels ("soul cakes") at the ready for every evening. Since Jack was attending his duties as Lord of Misrule in the streets every evening, she would have been home alone, so it made sense for her to stay in the rectory during the evenings, until Lord Jack was finished with his day — or night, most properly. Edward was glad to have her take responsibility for refreshing the "wassailers," who appeared at the door of the rectory, as well as all the houses in the village. He recognized nearly all the wassailers, and they were in a merry mood — most of them, he thought, were passably sober.

As Benjamin had promised, there were also mummers. A troupe of them appeared one evening at the rectory and demanded an audience. "It's bad luck to ignore them," explained Bess, "A little money is all they want." Edward wrapped himself in his coat and stood just outside the front door. Several of his neighbors stood round the troupe of a dozen or so young men — a few he recognized, the rest were in some disguise or other. The starring role in this drama was "The Tup," a man dressed in a sheep's costume. The Tup's head was a ram's skull, mounted on a pole. The man carrying this was wrapped in a costume that appeared more or less wooly, to create a 'beast' more than six feet tall, on two legs. Other players were a butcher, a boy, and a demon. The rest of the troop sang, while the actors danced and acted out the drama:

"As I was going to Derwent, all on a market day
I spied the biggest ram, sir, that ever was fed on hay . . . "

The Tup pranced around the rough circle of spectators, as the singers sang verse after verse, each punctuated by a nonsensical chorus — or maybe, thought Edward, a coded one. There was something in the skull and the costume that echoed of the distant past, something pagan, perhaps. He had been warned that the people in Derwent held to — what was it? — ancient ways. Yes, that was what the rector in Chesterfield had said . . .

This tup was fat behind, sir, this tup was fat before
This tup was nine feet round, sir, if not a little more.

And the horns upon this tup they grew, well they reached up to the sky
The eagles made their nests within, you could hear the young ones cry.

Yes the horns that on this tup they grew, well they reached up to the moon
A little boy went up in January and he never got back till June . . .

At this point in the drama, the "butcher" made his appearance, and began to chase the Tup around the circle — until the Tup turned on him, and chased him for a while. The crowd hooted and laughed. Ultimately, of course, the "butcher" won the battle:

The man that killed the ram, sir, he was up to his knees in blood,
But the poor boy that held the basin, he was carried away in the flood . . .

And indeed, the "boy" rolled out of the circle, and out of the story. The Tup collapsed, and lay on the ground:

And all the men of Derwent come begging for his tail
To ring St George's passing bell from the top of Derby Gaol.

And all the women of Derwent come begging for his ears
To make 'em leather aprons to last 'em forty years.

And all the boys of Derwent come begging for his eyes
To make themselves some footballs cause they were of football size.

Took all the men of Derwent to carry away his bones
Took all the women of Derwent to roll away his stones.

And now my story is over, and I have no more to say
Please give us all a New Year's gift and we will go away . . ."

The crowd gave them a round of applause and laughter, then the "demon" addressed them, and demanded payment, threatening to "sweep ye all to hell" if they did not pay. The sound of coins dropping in his cup rang, as he walked around the circle. When the "demon" got to Edward, he reached into his purse and dropped a shilling into the cup. The "demon" bowed deeply, and said: "A special blessing on you, sir, for generosity is a virtue that will be paid, in prosperity and fecundity, more than you can imagine." with that, the troupe was off down the street — in the direction of the pub, Edward noticed.

As Edward turned to enter the rectory, he noticed that Bess gave him an odd look. "Is something wrong?" he asked.

Bess tilted her head. "Whatever moved you to give them a whole shilling, when a pence would have done?

"I don't know," Edward replied. "The shilling was the first coin that came to hand, I suppose. Somehow, sorting out coins in my hand didn't seem proper. Carried away in the moment, maybe."

Bess nodded, "Aye, I think you must have been. What's done is done, I suppose."

Edward was puzzled at her remark. "Do you mean that they'll be up to some mischief with the money? They seemed like young men out for a lark, to me."

Bess shook her head. "The money will be spent tonight — you gave them enough for two rounds at the pub, and they'll probably drink your health. But not everything in Derwent is what it seems. The play is an ancient tradition, and folk hereabouts still respect the blessing or cursing that comes of it."

Edward couldn't tell if she was serious. "Well, I suppose I should be grateful that he did not curse me!"

"Do not mock the mummer's blessing, Father. There are things in the world that your books know nothing of. Many in this village could tell you stories about the blessing, and the way it manifested in their lives. You do not have to take their word for it, but we have found a way to honor God and respect the power of the earth, at the same time. That balance has allowed us to survive in this place."

Edward thought that this was the clearest expression of superstition that he had heard since coming to Derwent — and from Bess, of all people. He bit his tongue and nodded as if he understood what she was saying. "I don't know what prosperity and — fecundity was it? — could come to a man in my position," he remarked, with a smile.

"Time will tell," said Bess, "What's done is done."

The following Sunday was New Year's Eve. The attendance was a little lighter than usual, and Edward thought he could see evidence of a week's revelries on some of the congregant's faces. A good time for soul-searching and repentance, he thought, and his sermon stressed those themes. A few seemed moved to repent and reform, as he hoped. The Beadle was busier than usual, too — some of the people appeared half-asleep when they first arrived. He toyed with the idea of calling out the superstitions of the season but realized he needed to know more about them if he wanted to change anyone's minds. His work was cut out for him.

The goose that Bess had acquired for Christmas tide lasted until New Year's Day — that is, it lived long enough to appear on a spit in the kitchen fireplace on that day. The brick oven in the kitchen was full of something aromatic, as well. It would be a feast, something that Edward had experienced often enough, but this time in his own home. Something about that fact pleased him very much. "This will be more than we three can eat," Edward remarked.

"Aye," said Bess. "Don't worry, I've invited some guests."

"Anyone I know?"

"Aye. The Widow Jackson and her three young ones, and an old bachelor that lives on the other end of the village. It's Christmas time, Father. We must show kindness to the poor in this season."

"I quite agree," said Edward, already beginning to feel like a benefactor. "Thank you for attending to this for me. I don't know how I would manage without your help."

Bess nodded and smiled. "There could be one or two others, at the last minute, so to speak."

"Splendid!" said Edward. This was the sort of Christmas he could enjoy celebrating — a warm house, hospitality for the most deserving, thanks to the generosity of the village priest . . . Or more properly the generosity of God, he reminded himself. Pride was always lurking about somewhere, eager to turn every blessing into a sin, every kindness into self-congratulation, every act of love into conceit. He resolved to be more humble . . .

The widow Jackson appeared at the front door just before noon, with three children, Tim, aged ten, Agnes, aged eight, and Titus, aged six. Jack put aside his duties as Lord of Misrule long enough to help Edward add a bench to one side of the table and shift the chairs so that everyone could be seated. Another knock at the door, and Edward answered it. A small, white-haired man stood there, and introduced himself as "Henry — miner" or was it "Henry Miner?" Maybe his family name, maybe his profession, maybe both. "Here for supper," said Henry.

The house was beginning to feel full — Edward decided he liked it. Bess called them to the table and told Jack to help her bring the supper out of the kitchen. They seated the Widow Jackson and her three children on one side, with Jack at one end, and Bess and Henry on the opposite side.

Edward's place was at the "head" of the table, and Bess handed him a long carving knife. "Do the honors for us, if you would, Father," she said.

Edward realized at the last moment that he was expected to pray a blessing over the meal and put the knife down. Should be a short one, he decided, looking at the children . . . there was another knock at the door. He excused himself and answered it. Meg Moorcroft stood there, her crimson cloak and hood framing her face. He looked at her for a moment, tongue-tied. . .

"Am I to come in, or not?"

"Please. Please do. We're just about to eat, will you join us?"

"Isn't that why you invited me?"

Ah. One or two others, at the last minute. Edward looked toward Bess, who had her back to him. She might have said she was inviting Meg . . .

Edward took Meg's cloak and found a place to hang it. Jack had risen, and pulled an extra chair up to the table, between Henry's seat, and Edward's.

"Meg," said Edward, "I have neglected to thank you for saving my life. It was thoughtless of me . . ."

Meg nodded. "That's true." Her eyes turned to the ceiling and scanned both rooms. "Since ye have no kissing bough, ye'll have to tell me all about it, after supper." She smiled at him and then winked.

Everyone at the table overheard the conversation and laughed.

"Then, let's eat before it gets cold," said Edward. He seated her. and gave a sincere, if abbreviated blessing. He had truly never carved a goose before. He had seen it done, as a child, but wished he had paid closer attention. Meg saw his bewilderment and offered him some gestured hints on where to begin. Bess nudged Jack, who stood and said. "Father, I think it proper that I should do the honors (as Lord of Misrule, mind you)."

Edward surrendered the knife and sat down. He could tell that Meg was giggling, silently. At least she was smiling.

Edward did his best to be a good host through the meal. He asked questions and learned a little about everyone seated around his table. Henry was indeed, a miner, with a bell pit he was working up above the valley edge. The Widow Jackson actually had inherited a bit of land from her husband and rented the pasture out; her older son found employment as a shepherd. Mrs. Jackson was a spinster in the literal sense of the word — she made a living spinning wool into yarn, and her daughter helped her.

Jack, of course, was famous in Derwent — and shared a few stories about his deeds as Lord of Misrule; Bess was known to everyone and was praised for her cooking triumph. Meg was well-known too; in fact, everyone at the table had been treated by her for some malady or other. All of the adults at the table had known her for most of her life and known her parents also.

There was plenty of food — turnips and cabbage, some baked apples, a meat pie. At the end of the meal, Bess brought out her *piece de resistance*, a bread pudding, with figs, raisins, nuts, and a bewildering chorus of spices, sweetened with honey. The children clapped at its appearance. Everyone did their duty; a glorious victory was won — the ruins of their foes were scattered from one end of the table to the other.

Edward was full, as he had seldom been. And in an unusual mood — he couldn't stop smiling. Meg gave him a bemused smirk. Bess, Meg, and Mrs. Jackson cleared the table, Henry excused himself. The Jackson children said little but kept glancing between Jack and Edward, at the opposite ends of the table. Edward supposed that as the host, he should entertain them somehow, but he couldn't think what children would be interested in. Catechism, maybe? He remembered a pastime from his university days. Tim sat nearest him, and he leaned over as if inspecting the boy's head.

"Do you wash your neck regularly, lad?" The boy nodded.

Edward glimpsed Meg standing in the doorway, looking askance.

"Behind your ears, as well?"

The boy looked a little uncomfortable. "Yes, sir!"

"I think you missed a spot," said Edward, and reached behind the boy's ear, to pull out a tuppence. "I think this must belong to you."

The boy's eyes widened. "Mama! Come see what the vicar found!"

Mrs. Jackson stepped out of the kitchen, with a look of concern. When she saw the coin, she looked bewildered.

"What about you, miss?" Edward turned to Agnes, the eight-year-old. "Shall I look behind your ears?"

The girl stiffened. "You won't find anything. I washed just this morning."

Edward reached back and found another tuppence. He shook his head in mock seriousness. "You've been saving this, have you?"

Mrs. Jackson was smiling, now. Meg had her hand over her mouth. "Me! Check me!" Titus, the youngest child insisted. Edward looked, and sure enough, another tuppence appeared.

Meg had turned back into the kitchen. Mrs. Jackson looked at Edward and bowed her head slightly.

Jack shook his head. "I never saw the like, vicar. Ye'll be in the running for Lord of Misrule, next Christmas." Meg laughed, from the kitchen.

The Widow Jackson declared that it was time for her family to leave, and they bundled up — the afternoon was sunny, but chilly. Jack announced that he had "duties" to perform, down at the pub. Bess remembered something she had left at her cottage and went to fetch it. Suddenly, Edward was alone, with Meg. She gave him a questioning look.

"As I was saying," he began, "or, rather, as I neglected to say, I owe my life to you."

"And to Bruce," she added.

"Aye, and to Bruce. Though nothing that Bruce could do would have been enough if you had not found me."

Meg nodded.

"So, thank you. Thank you for my life."

She smiled and nodded.

Edward took a deep breath. "My life is not the same, since that day — or that night, I should say. There is something I need to know about that potion you gave me."

"What do you need to know?" She sat down at the table in the seat she had occupied during supper.

"Do the effects of the potion last long? As long as two weeks?'

"I have never heard of them lasting so long. What effects are you talking about?"

"I feel my life has changed, as if I am living a different life altogether, from the one I knew. There is more pleasure, more laughter for me, now. There is a faint aroma, like lavender, that seems to follow me around. I sense it most strongly when you are around — as I do now, but it is with me even when you are far away, especially when it is quiet, and I am in my prayers, or falling asleep. Is this because of that potion?

Meg looked at him with an inscrutable expression. She reached into her bodice and pulled out a sachet. "Is this the aroma you refer to?"

"Yes. That's it."

"It's plain to me then, where the scent comes from. Sometimes people associate a smell with a person or a place so that they are reminded of the person or place whenever they catch a whiff of whatever it is. Sometimes the thought of the person or place reminds them of the scent. As for the sense of a new life, did you not tell me that your old way of life was closed to you? Maybe you really do have a new life, or at least the chance of a new one. Maybe your heart was changed by that night on the moor. Tell me, do you miss the friends from your old life, would you see them again, if you could?"

Edward shook his head. "It was not like that. It was dangerous to be close to me. The people that I loved and trusted had to be avoided, to keep them safe. Conversely, I was required to spend most of my time with people that I dared not trust, and dared not open my heart to; indeed, I had to conceal my purpose from them, and deceive them whenever I could."

Meg stared at him for a moment. "You were a lonely man, Father."

"I think I would like you to call me 'Edward' when it is just the two of us."

Something in her eyes said he had hit a nerve, quite by accident. She composed herself and said: "You were a lonely man, Edward. I did not suspect that about you. You seem confident, and able to face any challenge — except carving a goose." She chuckled. "I have misunderstood you, and I think I gave you more of that potion than I should have. But what you are feeling now is not because of the mandrakes. None of these people that you ate with today means you any harm — nor are any of them in danger of their lives because they know you, respect you, and wish to be your friends. Derwent is a prison for you, as you once told me, but it is a safe prison, a prison where you may find love and honor if you wish."

Edward was moved by what she said; it rang true. Navigating a world of deadly peril had been his career, and he was proud — proud to have done it so well, for so long. But only in a place of safety could he lower his vigilance enough to see, taste, and breathe the world in its fullness; it was indeed a new life. "And the lavender, will it be with me always?"

"Perhaps," she said, with a faint smile. "Would it displease you, if it stayed with you — always?"

"Nay. A small price to pay, for a new life."

"Edward, I must go," she said as she stood up. "The day is short, and I must get home in time to feed my animals."

"And the 'Lads'?"

She laughed. "Aye, and the 'Lads'."

He helped her into her cloak, the aroma of lavender all the stronger. Then she was gone before it occurred to him that he should have come up with some excuse to make her stay awhile longer. He suddenly wanted to know more about her life . . . but that would have to wait for another day . . .

Meg strode briskly through the village, the shadows lengthening on the western side of the valley. Fortunately, she did not have far to go — a mile or two, maybe, and it was all uphill, but she had made this climb so many times before. Unburdened, she could do it in less than an hour. She was greeted of course, on her way through town, and she smiled and waved, but did not stop. She needed to think, to make sense of her feelings. The conversation with the vicar — Edward, she corrected herself, had forced some things into the open. She needed to sort them out. At first, she had enjoyed sparring with the new vicar — flirting, really, but all in fun. In time, he had earned her respect, and he seemed to respect her, as well. She liked him, and wanted him to like her, but she really couldn't say that she had intentions for him. That night on the moor cast things in a different light — she genuinely feared that he might die, and she was surprised at how much that distressed her — a sense of personal loss. The truth was, her life was a lonely one — all her cousins and patients notwithstanding. She had known her share of admirers — lovely lads, some of them — but she was not moved by lads. The sight of Edward with the Jackson children opened a sort of window in her heart, and feelings rushed in — he was more real to her than those eager lads had ever been, a man acquainted with loneliness, not unlike her. She wished she had the chance to tell him about her life, the loss, the loneliness — would he understand? Would he? It mattered a great deal, now . . .

Edward tried to avoid appearing in public for the next several days — he wanted to minimize involvement with the revelries and mischief that seemed to be more outrageous with each passing day. Friday would be Twelfth Night, the last day of Christmas. By all accounts, it was the rowdiest day of the feast, and the threat of some embarrassing confrontation with a drunken parishioner was enough to keep him indoors.

It almost worked. It was just after dinner, on Friday evening that he heard a knock on the door: "Father, ye are needed in the pub, right away. It's urgent!" The messenger was gone before Edward could question him more closely. It sounded suspicious, like something that Jack Clegg could've cooked up. On the other hand, what if there was a brawl in the pub? What if someone was breathing their last? Nothing to do, but to go see.

As he approached the pub, he heard music and laughter. Probably not a brawl, then. Oh well, having come this far, he might as well see it through. If he went home now, they would only send someone else to fetch him.

He stepped through the doorway. The place was packed. People greeted him with drunken roars and applause. He stepped forward, and suddenly Meg was there. She put her hands to his face and kissed him. He was stunned. More laughter, this time from a group of young women seated to his left. "Father," said Meg, loudly enough to be overheard, "If ye stand in this spot, every woman in the place will have a go at ye!" Hooting and laughter from the crowd of young women.

"How's that?" It sounded like a very indecent suggestion.

"Ye're standing under the kissing bough," she said with a grin.

He looked up. It was true. He tried to move, but she held him there, until he kissed her back. "The Lord of Misrule has summoned ye," she said softly. "Best ye answer, and quickly."

Edward stepped out from under the kissing bough and located Jack Clegg. He was seated on his "throne," holding what must have been intended as a scepter. He saw Edward from across the room and extended the scepter toward him. Edward approached and bowed in mock obeisance. "Come sit here," said Jack Clegg. "I must have a man with your craft by my side." He indicated a chair to the right of the "throne." Edward sat where indicated.

Jack stood, and waved his scepter, until the hubbub died down a bit. "I have commissioned a performance for this, the last day of Christmas," he declared. "The mummers have never presented this play before . . . and may never do so again."

There was a roar of acclaim, with stomping of feet, pounding on tables, and whistling. Jack waved his scepter again, until the tumult died down. "Let the play begin," said Jack.

They moved some tables and cleared a space in the middle of the room for the mummers to perform. Edward had a good view from where he sat; Meg and her companions were seated opposite, facing him. He caught her smiling at him, once.

First, the beat of a small drum. Then the first mummer appeared, dressed in what appeared to be vestments. They were an uncannily accurate reproduction of his own vestments, he thought, then realized that they <u>were</u> his vestments. How in the world did they lay hands on his vestments? This was irreverent, if not sacreligious. He was no fan of vestments himself, of course, but if the bishop heard of this, there would be trouble . . . He should probably call a halt to the whole, scandalous business — and lecture everyone within earshot about the importance of treating holy things with respect . . . the very definition of hypocrisy, since he had spent most of his adult life denying that vestments, or any other material things could be holy things, at all. Ironic that he would consider repeating the very lies that Bancroft had sent him to Derwent to tell — because he didn't want trouble with his bishop . . . *how easily we become tools of our persecutors,* he thought to himself. Someone pressed a warm drink into his hand: mulled wine. He took a long drink . . . He bit his tongue and hoped it would be over soon.

The first mummer announced himself:

> "I am The Priest, though you may call me vicar,
> I walk upon the moor, though other men move quicker,
> You may see me in the daytime, wind and weather tossed,
> If you see me in the nighttime, know that I am lost . . ."

Roars of laughter. The man sitting next to Edward gave him an elbow in the ribs, and a wink, as he laughed. So, Edward was the butt of the joke. That explained the vestments: it was a personal, rather than theological satire. Edward laughed along with everyone else. The next player, wrapped in a brown costume, entered the circle:

> "I am Ass, the vicar's faithful steed,
> Bearer of his burdens, I serve his every need,
> Despise me not, though humble is my station,
> I am not the fool, here . . . that is his vocation."

More laughter, another dig in the ribs, a hard slap on the back from somebody behind him. Someone filled his cup with more wine. The priest and his ass wandered around the circle, looking lost. Edward was reminded of similar skits he had performed in his university days . . . A third actor made his appearance:

> "I am Mist, the clouding of man's vision,
> I am death to any fool who makes a bad decision,

Here comes one now, lost upon the moor,
To sleep, to sleep, and wake no more . . ."

Now the action of the play began in earnest. Mist approached The Priest from behind and dangled a strip of gauzy fabric in front of his face. The Priest tried to brush it away with his hand, but Mist was persistent. Some of the audience hissed their disapproval of Mist, some shouted warnings to The Priest. But every time he turned around, Mist avoided his grasp. Ass was also braying and stomping, but Mist would not be denied. Finally, turning, and spinning, The Priest fell to the floor. "I die!" he exclaimed. There was a chorus of sympathetic moans from the crowd. Edward caught Meg's gaze from across the room — she appeared to be laughing silently. He had to admit that the young men were bringing enthusiasm to their performance — and enthusiasm was the key to success, in performances of this kind.

As The Priest lay upon the "ground," another mummer appeared, wrapped in a crimson cloak. It looked like Meg's cloak. It <u>was</u> Meg's cloak. Edward glanced at Meg — she appeared to be as surprised as he was. The crimson mummer spoke:

"Doctor Quack am I, healer of men's woes, . . .

Howls of laughter from the crowd, squeals from the young women. Meg shook her head, and bowed it, in mock humiliation. "Dr. Quack" was a familiar character in Christmas plays like this one. Whenever a character died (such as Saint George), Dr. Quack was expected to produce some elixir to "revive" him. Edward now knew how the play would end. Clever of the lads to incorporate a current tale into the familiar form of the play . . .

There was one more plot twist. Dr. Quack's elixir revived The Priest, sure enough. But The Priest was unable to stand — he was crippled! Dr. Quack could think of nothing but to put The Priest on the back of Ass. Easier said than done. Finally, Dr. Quack found a method. He picked up a strip of fabric that just happened to be lying on the "ground," wrapped it around The Priest's neck, and dragged him onto the back of Ass. The Priest waved his arms, he appeared to be choking — but Dr. Quack would not be deflected from his purpose. Finally, The Priest was on the back of Ass, where he exclaimed again, "I die!" and Dr. Quack, Ass, and The

Priest made their exit, to the shouts of "More elixir! More elixir" from the spectators.

"More elixir?" someone refilled Edwards wine cup. Shouts of "More elixir!" were repeated all over the pub, and refills were forthcoming. The mummers reappeared to take a bow and receive the applause of their audience — along with a pelt of pennies and other small coins.

A fiddler struck up a tune, and people began to dance. Meg and her companions formed a rough circle in the center of the room and began whirling and stomping to the music. There was a sort of organization to it, Edward realized, but he couldn't quite make it out. The women lifted the hems of their skirts just enough to show their shoes — the footwork was intricate — round and round they danced. Meg would smile his way, and toss her head, when she whirled past him. He began to feel dizzy. Too much wine, he realized. He was an ale man; wine was a bit too strong for his head. But for his ankle, he might have stood and tried to dance, but no, he was no dancer. He was offered more wine, but refused. The dance ended with cheers from the crowd.

"I must beg your leave to go, Lord," he addressed Jack. "A most edifying play — your servants have done you proud." Jack nodded, and he moved toward the door, unsteadily.

"Father, are ye leaving us so soon?" Meg was standing next to him. "Is there no other hospitality that we can offer?" The young women behind her laughed and hooted.

"Nay," said Edward, "I've had too much hospitality already, I think . . ." He looked up at the rafters, to locate the kissing bough. There it was. Several steps away.

Meg caught his glance and giggled. "Ye're a rogue, Father, that's for sure. A girl's not safe, when ye've had a few too many." She curtseyed. "A merry Twelfth Night to ye." And with that, she rejoined her companions.

Edward found his way out into the street. One more kiss. A kiss would have been a perfect end to the evening. He turned and looked back at the pub. Maybe if he made another entrance . . . The cold air was clearing his head. No, wouldn't do to push his luck. He thought of something else he needed to check on.

He entered the church at the West doors and walked down the south aisle toward the vestry. Someone else was there; he stood back in the shadows, and waited to see what would happen. In just moments, a figure emerged from the vestry, locked the door, and hurried down the center aisle, then outside. Edward glimpsed the figure only in silhouette, but he was pretty sure it was Benjamin, the sexton. He entered the vestry and checked the closet. The vestments hung there, just as he had left them the previous Sunday. There was the faintest scent of stale ale and wine about them. Edward locked the vestry, returned to the rectory, and crawled into bed. The faint aroma of lavender embraced him. A kiss, just one more kiss . . .

Part 18: In the Garden

March 29, 1587: Lambing

As January passed, the weather became milder. The snow gradually retreated from the Dark Peak, and rainy days became the norm. The students in the school had all received their Bibles with excitement, and Edward devoted much of every class to recitations — students stood, one at a time, and read some passage that he had assigned them. For the younger ones, he assigned stories like David's battle with Goliath — he even encouraged them to dramatize it a bit. The older ones got passages from the Epistles and were expected to explain the doctrines that those passages supported. Edward was pleased to think that he was making progress in the formation of these young minds.

February 11 was the beginning of Lent this year. Edward held the prescribed service on that Wednesday, which was lightly attended. The following Sunday, his sermon focused on fasting — particularly the tradition of fasting during Lent. As a committed Calvinist, he cautioned the congregation on the perils of superstition — of imagining that self-denial was somehow pleasing to God or could earn God's favor. Instead, he urged them to meditate on their own fallen nature, and their sinful deeds. Lent was a time for reflection and repentance, not fasting or "giving up" simple pleasures. This message was received with sober attention, but no particular enthusiasm, with the notable exception of the local butcher — who beamed at the pulpit from the fourth row, as happy as Edward had ever seen him . . .

As Winter faded, Edward was also summoned to the moorlands above the edge, either to visit the sick or (once) to console the dying. He was careful to arrange for a guide to escort him both to and from his destination, on each foray.

The river at the village ran high after the rains, and when the summons came from the west side of the valley, he had to ford it. On more than one occasion, he crossed on Bruce's back, his feet held high out of the water. It was a ridiculous sight, and people would stand on the riverbank, and tease him when they caught him at it. It was all good-natured, and he found it oddly reassuring that they felt comfortable enough with him to ridicule him . . . a new life, indeed.

He also began to get a sense of the land above the edge — some pathways looked familiar, now. Maybe, he thought, he would be able to find his own way, one day . . .

On the Saturday afternoon after Good Friday, in March, Meg Moorcroft knocked at the door of the rectory. Bess answered and welcomed her inside. "What brings you here, on such a chilly afternoon?"

"Just passing by," said Meg. "Thought I might trouble ye for some refreshment . . ." she appeared to be looking around for something.

"Father Edward has been called away," said Bess, with a knowing glance. She handed Meg a small cup of ale and a bit of bread and cheese. "If that is what you're looking for."

Meg gave her a disinterested look. "Ah. Is that so?" She took a sip from her cup.

There was a moment of silence. Then Bess spoke: "Meg, I've known you since you were a wee child. You've something on your mind; if you want to talk about it, you might as well say it. If it's about Father Edward, you can count on my discretion."

Meg looked surprised. "What would I have to say about Father Edward?"

"Everyone in the village knows that you fancy him, except possibly the man himself. And he will catch on, sooner or later — although some men are slow about these things. Everyone can see that he fancies you, as well, and even he recognizes that. It bothers him a good deal, for some reason."

"I admit that I admire him, and respect him, and I hope that we are friends," she said, "I would not go so far as to say I fancy him more than any other man."

"Meg! Are you telling me that you plant your lavender sachets in the beds of other men? I am shocked to hear of it!" Bess said in mock dismay.

Meg's eyes widened. "Does he know?"

"Nay, I do the laundry in this house. I was confused at first, but I see the cunning in it. You've done your mother proud."

Meg shook her head. "At first I thought it would help his headache," she said, "But after he kept remarking on how the scent of lavender was following him everywhere, and reminded him of me . . . It pleased me to think that he would remember me when he lay down at night, and while he slept. I suppose it was cunning; I have taken advantage of him, I reckon . . ."

Bess shook her head. "A woman uses the means that come to hand. There is no shame in that. But it will take more than a few dried flowers to open his heart to you if that is what you seek."

"In truth, I am not sure what it is that I seek," Meg admitted. "I had fun flirting and bantering with him, but there is more to it, now . . ."

"Come to supper," said Bess.

"Eh?"

"Tomorrow is Sunday. Come to supper, after church. It will be Jack, the Jacksons, the vicar, myself — and you. Jack and I will have business elsewhere in the afternoon so that the two of you can talk."

Edward Chase arrived home that afternoon, just before dusk. A farmer up the valley had fallen suddenly ill, and the vicar was summoned to anoint and pray for him. By the time Edward arrived, the man had improved, and before Edward left, he was sitting up in bed and able to eat a little. Hard to say for sure that the prayers had made a difference, but the farmer's family believed it had. They thanked Edward with a live chicken, which he tied up and loaded onto Bruce's back, where it hung upside down, all the way home. As he put Bruce into his stall, he noticed that the ewe was lying on her side, panting. He called Bess out to the shed to look at the ewe and presented her with the chicken.

"I'd say she's about to lamb," said Bess, with a nod to the ewe. Inspecting the chicken, she added, "This looks like tomorrow's supper."

Edward nodded and turned toward the rectory. "Someone came by today, looking for you," offered Bess.

Another emergency, thought Edward, "Am I needed somewhere tonight? Is it far?"

Bess shook her head and smiled. "It was a social call, nothing amiss. Dinner will be ready soon."

"Well then, I am weary. I will sleep well tonight," he went into the house. He had a sermon to preach tomorrow; it was Easter Sunday.

That morning the sanctuary was crowded. It was a lovely day — a warm breeze from the south fulfilled the promise of Spring. He thought his sermon was particularly impactful, and the congregation seemed to confirm this, by fidgeting less than usual. Or perhaps it was just because the sanctuary was warmer . . . He scanned the crowd for a distinctive, crimson cloak (as he did every Sunday), but was disappointed. Perhaps she was lost in the crowd.

He finally spotted Meg after the service, as he walked to the rectory. She was carrying something in her arms. She greeted him and offered him a bundle with something squirming inside it. It was a dog, or more properly, a puppy. "He's the pup you held up at my uncle Alfred's last winter. Look how he's grown! The pup was an armful — licking Edward's face and nibbling at his hands.

"He has grown indeed," admitted Edward . . . "Can I put him down?"

"He's yer dog, ye can do what ye like," said Meg. "But I'd put a leash on him before I put him down if I were you."

"My dog?"

"Aye, payment for yer service to the family. We're a bit short on cash at this time of year."

Just then the Jackson children appeared, and began making a fuss over the pup: "What's his name? Can I pet him? Where did you get him?"

"Better put him in the shed," said Edward, "until I figure out what to do with him . . ."

Inside the shed, Edward could put the pup down, and the children crowded around to pet him.

"What's this?" exclaimed Meg. She was looking at the ewe, Mary in the stall. "I see lambs!"

The children rushed up to see what was going on. The ewe still lay on the straw, but the two squirming forms of newborn lambs wriggled near her, as she nuzzled and licked them.

"Twins!" said Meg. "A fair day's work, for a lady like this!"

"Shouldn't she be on her feet?" asked Edward. "So that she can nurse them?"

Meg shot him a reproving glance. "It's harder work than ye imagine." Then she looked again. "Something else is up, though." She took off her cloak and draped it over the stall divider, then climbed into the stall, and rolled up the sleeves of her blouse. She knelt by the ewe and ran her hands over the ewe's belly. "There's another," she said. "There's one more lamb waitin' to be born."

The Jackson children were joined now by their mother and Jack Clegg. They all lined up just outside the stall.

"I might be able to help her," said Meg. "I'll need some water." Jack went to get some.

It took nearly a quarter of an hour to deliver the third lamb, and when he was delivered, he was lifeless. The ewe stood, then licked and nuzzled her last born, while the other two lambs found their feet, and began to nurse. The children looked distressed. Meg picked up the third lamb and began to wipe and massage it. "Poor little fella," she said, "just took too long getting out, I guess . . . and then there was a twitch and a sneeze.

"Well, I never," said Jack. "Meg, ye have a healer's touch, no doubt! Look at that, Father! Ye have yer own flock now!"

Edward was too surprised at the whole business to say anything. From one sheep to four, and a dog in the bargain. And he knew nothing about caring for sheep, or dogs either, for that matter . . .

Meg set the last born down on the straw, where he struggled to his feet, and joined his siblings at their mother's side.

"I hear Bess calling us to supper," said Jack. They nearly had to drag the children out of the shed; Meg found a bit of rope and left the pup tied inside while they went into the rectory. Mrs. Jackson helped Bess set food on the table, while Meg washed up.

Edward realized they were waiting for him to bless the meal; he was still a little dazed by what had just passed. As the meal progressed, the children were full of questions about the pup and the lambs: "What will ye name them?"

"I really hadn't thought that far ahead," admitted Edward. "Do you have any suggestions?"

"Well, are they girls, or boys?" asked Agnes.

"The first two lambs are 'girls', the last born is a 'boy'," said Meg. Edward wondered how she could tell . . .

"I think the boy lamb should be named 'Jesus'," said Agnes, "on account of he was dead and came back alive."

Edward detected a teaching moment. "Why not 'Lazarus'? He was resurrected too, you know."

"But this is Easter. Jesus came back on Easter."

Chortles and nods from the adults around the table. Oh well, no point in explaining the pitfalls of sacrilege to an eight-year-old . . .

"And the two ewe lambs could be named Mary and Martha," Tim chimed in.

But their mother is named Mary," said Edward. "That could be confusing . . ."

"Then Magdalen and Martha," suggested Agnes. "Because they were the first to see Jesus when he came alive again."

Edward had no argument to make. It probably wouldn't matter what names they were called by, in the long run.

"And what about that pup, Father?" asked Jack. "He has the bloodlines to be a famous sheepdog."

"How can you tell?"

"I recognize the breeding. The Moorcroft shepherds are famous hereabouts. Very valuable animal, if he's trained properly."

Of course, Edward had no clue what proper training would involve . . . "I suppose we'll have to call him 'David', then." The children all nodded their sober approval. David, it would be.

"I confess that I did not expect such a bounty of animals," said Edward. "I can't explain it!"

"Fecundity," said Bess, looking him straight in the eyes. "It's fecundity."

After supper was cleared, the Jacksons left for home; the children wanted one more peek at Jesus, Mary, and Magdalen, and wanted to pet David, too. They waved goodbye, as their mother led them homeward. Jack and Bess both agreed that they had business elsewhere, which left Meg and Edward with the animals.

"I have no idea how to care for these lambs," admitted Edward.

"Not much to it, at this age. You keep the ewe fed, and she feeds them," said Meg.

"And I have no idea how to raise a sheep dog, or any dog, for that matter."

Meg nodded. "That requires some skill and patience. Jack was right about the bloodlines — David could be a famous dog, one day."

"Can you take him back? Find him an owner who knows how to train him?"

Meg shook her head. "Not without insulting the family. Ye earned a lot of goodwill with them, and they heard about yer injury on the moor — they reckon one of them should have guided ye home that day. They thought it the least they could do, to repay ye. Besides, ye're a sheepman now. A dog could be a big help."

"Then what am I to do?"

"I'll make ye an offer. I'll train young David, there. He can live with me until he's ready to go to work in a couple of years. When yer lambs are old enough to go up to pasture on the moor this summer, ye can run them in with my flock, until Autumn. In return, ye will split the proceeds from the wool with me — That's Mary's wool in the shearing later this spring, and half the wool from shearing of those three, the following year. If ye decide to sell any of them, we'd split the proceeds from that, as well."

"Or I could sell them now?"

"Aye, ye could. And all four, plus Mary's wool, would cover the cost of yer original investment. Then ye'll just have the dog to care for."

Edward was silent for a moment. "What if I sell the sheep to you in return for training the dog, and a share of the wool, for the next three years? You can pay me in wool — no money need change hands."

Meg looked thoughtful. "I accept your terms. If everything goes well, ye'll get a trained shepherd at the end of it, worth more than yer investment in old Mary, there."

"And if everything doesn't go well?"

"That's the risk that both of us take, I reckon." They shook hands on it.

Meg untied David as if preparing to leave. "Are you leaving so soon?" asked Edward.

"Is there a reason to linger?"

Of course, there's a reason to linger, he thought, *I just have to come up with one . . .*

"You have been on my mind," he began. *That's true enough.* "Much on my mind."

"And what does yer mind say?" She fixed those green eyes on him . . .

"It tells me that I should have drawn you under the kissing bough on Twelfth Night before I left the pub, and kissed you at least once more . . ."

"I doubt that's yer mind talkin'. Some other part of ye, maybe." She smirked; he thought he saw her blush as well, just a little.

"Perhaps it is my heart, then." He could see that she was touched, a little.

"What else does yer 'heart' say?" Her look was a little skeptical, he thought, but not mocking.

"It says I do not know you well enough to love you the way I should want to. It says that I might not be able to love you the way you deserve. It says that I must find the answer to such questions, or spend the rest of my natural life wondering . . ."

She caught her breath suddenly. "Ye have a way with words, Father, no doubt."

"Please, call me Edward."

She bit her lip, then smiled. "I have asked myself questions about thee, Edward. They frighten me, and I am not a woman easily frightened. My heart is stirred when I think of thee, and I think of thee more often than I intend to. I do not know if I can be with any man, the way I should like to be with thee. And if I cannot be with thee, I doubt that any other man will do. I fear that to be with thee might be to lose thee — not to death; I know how to live with loss and grief. But to lose thee due to some defect in myself — that would be a mortal blow. I suppose that is my pride talking, but there it is . . . I have said more than I intended."

Edward realized he had been holding his breath. She had said more than he expected, more than he could digest. "What are we to do then, Meg?"

"I think we should be practical. What are the chances that you will ever have cause to leave Derwent?"

"Small chances. If I do something truly outrageous, they could come for me and take me away, or simply deprive me of my living. Far more likely that I will die in this village."

"What is it you have done, to make them fear you so?"

Edward sighed. "That is a long story. Best we sit down, somewhere."

"In the rectory, then," she motioned with a jerk of her head.

Once inside, They sat down at the table, and Edward explained himself. "I was employed by men who intended to overthrow the governance of the Church, to reform it . . ." he began.

"No small plans, then," Meg remarked with a sardonic tone.

"The men who I worked for — or rather worked with, since I was as much a part of the planning as they — included the Archbishop of Canterbury, and other bishops, University professors, and members of the Queen's Privy Council, not to mention many thousands of other like-minded people.

Meg's eyes focused on him. "A great conspiracy, then! What prevented yer success?"

"Mostly, it was the Queen herself. She prefers that the Church remain under her personal control."

"And this conspiracy has been crushed, then? I never heard of such a thing!"

Edward shook his head. "The struggle continues. Our cause still has many powerful advocates. In time, we may prevail. God willing, we shall prevail."

"And yet yer friends cannot rescue ye from this 'exile'." It was a statement, rather than a question.

"My friends, as you call them, imagine that I may have betrayed them. My enemies, including the current Archbishop, have arranged it that way. I am a pawn in a great chess game — sacrificed for the greater purpose."

"Are ye bitter?"

Edward shook his head. "Nay, as I told you, I feel that I have been transformed into a different man, with a different life. I do not miss my old one. I would not go back to it, even if the opportunity came my way."

"Still, it is a hard thing to give up your life's mission. Is there no trace remaining of yer old loyalties?"

"I have not given it up entirely. I believe that God has placed me here to continue the struggle, even without the help of my old friends. You have heard me preach; you know that I am trying every Sunday to turn the hearts of these people to the truth, to a truly reformed faith that will one day shake the foundations of the Church of England and purify her. It is the same with the children I teach. I prepare them for a spiritual war that will not be won until I am long dead. But it will be won, of that I am certain."

"That's a great burden to place on the backs of children," Meg observed. "What makes ye think these little ones can win a war that ye appear to be losing?"

"It is this place. It is this small village, that has kept faith for more than two hundred years, with the truth that was entrusted to them by the ancient preachers. Through all the attempts to stamp it out, the Faith has been nurtured and kept — not pure exactly, but purer than that which the Archbishop and his minions would impose. What I do here is happening in thousands of other villages, all across this kingdom. God is trying us as with fire, just now. But I am certain that he will act, in His good time. We must prepare the children for that day."

Meg was silent for a moment. Edward wondered if she felt overwhelmed by his life's mission.

"When I said we should be practical, I wasn't thinking of anything so ambitious," she said at length. "I was thinking more of how two people like us could co-exist in such a small village, given the feelings that both of us profess to have for one another."

"Ah." Edward realized that he had gotten carried away.

"If you are to remain here, as it seems you must, and I remain here, as I certainly must, I think it will be a hard life unless we can be together."

Edward nodded. "It's all I can do to keep from embracing thee and kissing thee, right now. A lifetime of such yearning, unfulfilled, would be torture. And yet, I cannot leave."

Meg cocked her head and looked at him with a rueful smile. "Ye have such a way with words, Edward. Torture, that's a good one." She shook her head.

"Derwent is my home," she continued, rising to her feet. It is not a battleground or a nest of conspiracy. It is where I live, and likely the only place that I can live. The people here understand that the world outside is complicated and perilous, but we do not seek to rule it. Rather we take it as it comes. There is no great wealth in this place, nor power, nor great learning. We survive without those things because we do not yearn for them. We have our people, the land, and the God that made us both. What more do we require?"

She had more to say: "Ye are an outsider here. The difference between ye and us is the difference of two hundred years, as ye have said. I do not think you will become as we are in a single lifetime. In truth, we will not be able to remain as we are in my lifetime; the influence of the outside world — your world — encroaches like a looming storm that sweeps down from the Dark Peaks. Perhaps the prophet's vision of a great flood that drowns our village is just an image of something that is happening already . . ."

"Surely, there is something that could be saved, if such a flood is coming. Perhaps there are things that I could teach these folk, to spare them the worst," Edward's tone was somber, yet hopeful.

"Perhaps. But that would depend on whether ye are prepared to learn from us," she replied. "Not all wisdom comes from your world." Her tone was challenging.

"How well I know that. How much I am reminded of my ignorance, every time I get a whiff of lavender."

She looked at him, with her green eyes. "Aye. The lavender may be the road to yer salvation, Edward."

"As a practical matter . . ." she was insistent, and stood up, folding her arms across her chest, ". . . Would ye give up a chance to go back to the outside world, to marry a lass from a village like this one?" A fair question. Direct, but fair.

Edward sighed. *Choose your words,* he told himself. "The question," he said slowly, "Is not whether I would give up a chance to leave this place in order to marry, here. That chance is practically zero. A better question is whether I would marry a woman in this place and agree to stay with her, even if such a chance were to happen at some point in the future."

"And how would ye answer that question?"

Edward stood and looked her directly in the eyes. "For the right woman, the answer would be yes."

She colored, just a little. "And how can a man predict what he will do in the future?"

"He cannot predict; he can only promise. And the promise is only as good as the man's character."

She smiled slightly, but pressed her questions: "And what makes the woman 'right'?"

"She is lovely, fearless, honest to a fault," he began, "she does not suffer fools gladly; she sees into the hearts of men, but does not condemn them. She is kind and sensible, she cares for others, even in her loneliness."

She drew another breath. *More points,* said Edward to himself.

"It is my turn to ask a practical question," said Edward. Before she could demur he asked, "Would you have a man who comes from the outside? Who does not understand all your ways? A priest, perhaps, whose duty it is to answer the call from others at any time, day or night? A man whose learning makes you drowsy, whose ignorance of all things agricultural makes him useless for any other work?"

Meg giggled, then shook her head. "That's a great burden for a young woman to bear. Part of me says it is altogether impractical to consider such a thing. Part of me says that this is what I want, more than anything in the world."

Edward stepped forward and put his arms around her waist. "Ye're making mighty free, vicar, considering there's no kissing bough in this place!" She was smiling, as she said it.

"It's there, right over your head," he said. "You have to close your eyes, and see it, in your imagination."

"Imagination?"

"Aye, you have to close your eyes, to see it clearly." And then he kissed her, and she said, "Ah, I see it now," as she pressed against him, strong arms enclosing him. A bond not easily broken. At length, she said, "This answers none of my questions, nor any of yours, ye understand?"

"Aye, but it gives us something to do, as we wait for the answers we seek . . ." he smiled.

She chuckled. "Ye're a right rascal, vicar — I mean Edward. Takin' liberties with a helpless woman like this." Her eyes were bright, her face flushed. Edward thought he had scored another point. Maybe two points, maybe more . . .

Someone knocked at the door. "Father? Are ye within?" It was Benjamin, the sexton. "There's men here to pay the tithes, Father," he explained, as Edward opened the door.

"Tithes?"

"Aye, the yearly tithe on the mines. They're about to haul the year's production down to Bamford. It's traditional to pay the tithe before they haul the rest away."

"Traditional? On Easter?"

"Well not usually on a Sunday, but there's a few who don't get into the village often, because their mines are so far out. They were here this morning for the Easter service and had their supper in the pub. They'd like to settle accounts today so that they can get an early start in the morning."

"Very well, ask them to meet me in the vestry. I assume this transaction needs to be entered in some ledger?"

"Indeed it does, vicar. They are bound by ancient custom to pay a tithe of their minings each year. It is the greater part of your 'living', I believe."

Edward nodded. "I'll meet you at the church." This had been mentioned when he accepted this appointment. Slipped his mind. Lead. They would be paying him in lead. He stepped back inside to get his keys. Meg was standing there with an amused look on her face.

"I'll check on the ewe and her lambs before I go home," she offered. "I'll fetch young David, too.

"I think we have more to talk about."

"Aye, we do. But it won't be happenin' today."

"I could visit you in your home if I knew the way."

"So ye could, but ye don't. We'll have to remedy that." She smiled and gave him a quick kiss, and sent him on his way.

March 30, 1587: Tithing

Edward met Benjamin, and two other vaguely familiar-looking men at the West door of the church. There was also a string of pack horses and donkeys standing by, laden with some heavy burdens — almost certainly lead ingots, Edward realized. What was he supposed to do, weigh the whole lot, and claim his ten percent?

"You'll have to pardon my ignorance about this business," he began. "How is the tithe determined?"

"You have some discretion in the matter," replied Benjamin. "The miners are required to show you all of the metal that they are taking to market in Bamford."

They're selling all this in Bamford?"

"Aye, the buyers come to Bamford in the Spring, to buy whatever the miners have dug up and smelted over the Winter. Once they get paid, they settle accounts with their creditors and buy more of what they need for the year to come."

"Assuming I claim a tithe of what they have here, I would have to sell it somehow as well wouldn't I?"

"Aye," Benjamin nodded. "Father Jacobs used to send his share along with them and receive his payment when they returned."

"That seems simpler than selling the lead myself. But if I'm going to do that, why not simply wait for the miners to sell all their lead, and simply pay me the tithe from the money that they get?"

"By tradition, you are expected to agree on the weight of the lead before it is sold and record it. What you do with it afterward is not specified."

Maybe someone didn't trust the miners to contribute the full tithe? Edward wondered. "I see," he nodded. "How would I weigh all this, then?"

Benjamin scratched his ear."Well, sometimes, the miners unload the animals, and make ten equal piles of the ingots, and then the priest gets to pick the one he wants — that way the miners are sure to make the piles as equal as they can, you see; If one of the piles is clearly heavier, the priest would pick that one . . ."

"So you don't necessarily know exactly what the weight of the metal is?"

"Doesn't matter, as long as the priest gets his share."

"But don't they weigh it when they sell it in Bamford?"

"Aye, of course, they do. The buyers bring scales with them for that purpose."

"How do you know if the buyers are using honest scales?"

"It's largely a matter of trust; some miners bring a standard weight of their own with them. The process is not without contention."

I'll bet, thought Edward. "I have business in Bamford myself. What time are you men leaving in the morning?"

"At sunup, or soon after," one replied. "We hope to be the first to arrive — get a better price, that way."

"Very well, I'll meet you right here at Sunup tomorrow. I'll go to Bamford with you, and we'll see it weighed there. I'll bring a ledger with me, and I'll give you a written letter that specifies the amount you will pay me — in money, not lead. Is that acceptable?"

Both men nodded and smiled. They understood that a precise valuation of their goods was impossible without an accurate weight, and had grown accustomed to the idea that the priest probably claimed a little more than a strict tenth each year; this could work to their advantage.

Edward walked back to the rectory, followed by Benjamin. "Father," he said, "you do understand that more miners will be coming?"

"Coming where?"

"Down from the moors. They'll be stopping to pay their tithe, on their way to Bamford, don't you see?"

Of course, they would. Silly of him not to figure that out. "Are there any more in the village?"

"Aye. At least three more pack trains; the men are in the pub. Probably planning to see you tomorrow."

"Ben, do something for me. If the miners are still in the pub, explain to them what I agreed to do with the first group, and tell them that I will be going to Bamford, tomorrow. If they want to join me there, we can settle the tithes that way. And, please let the pupils know that there will be no school, tomorrow."

"Very good, Father." Ben turned and headed off in the direction of the pub.

Early next morning, Edward led Bruce out to the West door of the church, where a crowd of nearly fifty pack animals had gathered. He briefly explained what he intended to do in Bamford, and the men nodded and murmured in agreement. He had enough presence of mind to anticipate how much animal waste would be on the road that day and managed to get himself and Bruce at the head of the line.

The road down to Bamford was the same one that he had taken only months before, but it felt like a different trip, altogether. Being in the company of a dozen other men, not to mention fifty beasts of burden, was part of the reason — Edward was pretty sure all the others in the party were armed; not much fear of a highwayman demanding that they surrender tons of lead, but on the return, they would all be carrying money.

Also, the appearance of the forest on either side of the road was different — leaves were freshly green, flowers bloomed all through the woods, birds sang in chorus. The condition of the road was the same — worse if anything, but the two miles down to the main road passed in less than an hour. Once they were in open country, the last three miles or so were very pleasant.

The buyers were waiting in the village square, as predicted. They were a little put off by the way Edward wrote every transaction down. In one case, he caught an error in their calculation — inadvertent, perhaps, but the miner in question was entitled to three shillings more than the buyer offered. Edward realized that most of these men had only the roughest familiarity with multiplication and division; there was general suspicion of the honesty of the buyers, but double-checking their calculations was beyond the skill of most of them. The miner who was nearly short-changed insisted on buying Edward a drink in the local pub. His story was widely circulated; Edward felt that his reputation had been elevated, just a little.

Once paid, the miners gave him his tithe, and he provided each with a written note indicating the amount, and date of payment. It was a more official acknowledgment than they were accustomed to, but several men took it very seriously, carefully folding their note and slipping it into their purses. Once everyone was paid, they invited Edward to join them for supper, but he deferred, saying, "I have some other business to attend. I will see you back in Derwent." He left Bruce tied among the other pack animals at the edge of the square and paid a lad to give him some grain in a feed bag.

The business led him to the rectory of the local parish, where he found the priest, one Father Hooper, a full-bodied, round-faced man. Edward introduced himself.

"Pleased to meet you," said Hooper. "I heard that they had a new vicar up in Derwent. Shame about poor Father Jacobs."

They exchanged some small talk; Edward tried to get the measure of the man. Hooper said nothing that would indicate whether his personal views would align with any particular ecclesiastical faction. He was a local man, so probably not an exile like Edward. Married, four children, a conventional village vicar. Edward got around to the reason for his visit. "I hope to marry. I cannot perform the ceremony for myself, and I thought you might be willing to do the honors. Your parish is the nearest to Derwent, I believe."

Father Hooper smiled broadly. "Good news, then! Who is the lucky lady?"

"She hasn't agreed to marry me, yet," admitted Edward. "But I hope to win her hand shortly. Perhaps we can wed over the summer."

"Have you spoken to her father?"

"No, she is an orphan, sadly."

"That is sad. What is the family name?"

"Moorcroft. Although she has not yet agreed to be my wife, you understand."

At the name "Moorcroft," Hooper's eyebrows raised. "I know that family. Tight-knit clan. Are you on good terms with all of them?"

"I believe so. They presented me with a gift just yesterday."

"A gift?"

"A dog, actually. A sheepherding dog. I've heard that he is a very valuable animal."

Hooper nodded. "A gift like that is a clear indication that you a worthy sort of fellow, in their estimation. Are you aware that marrying a woman from a family like that one might not be the best match for a man who hopes for promotion?"

Edward shrugged. "I am not a man who hopes for promotion. I expect to be in Derwent for many years to come."

"Ah. Well, in that case, you can count on me to officiate at a wedding service, should the time come. I will keep this confidential, of course, until you tell me that the engagement is public. Will you sup with us?"

"I would be delighted to," Edward replied.

The supper was not lavish, but entirely satisfying. The vicar set an ample table, with a good mutton stew, and good ale. Plenty of bread, and a pie of dried apples for dessert. Edward enjoyed every bite. Hooper's wife was a gracious hostess, and his children well-behaved. A model of domestic bliss.

"I see that you are a man who relishes a good meal," observed Hooper. "How is the food in your home?"

"I've never had reason to complain. I have a housekeeper who cooks my meals for me."

There was a knock at the door. Someone was looking for "that vicar, from Derwent."

"More miners have come down from Derwent. They need to pay their tithes so that they can sell their lead."

Edward explained briefly what had brought him down to Bamford on this day, and the arrangements that he had made for calculating the tithes.

"Generous of you, I'd say," said Hooper. "The less precise calculation would be more to your advantage." Edward smiled and excused himself. Father Hooper turned to his office. He had a letter to write.

When Edward got back to the village square, sure enough, two more pack trains were waiting for him. One was quite long — must have been a big mine, or maybe a family with more than one mine. By the time the transactions were finished, Edward had a little more than fifteen pounds worth of coins in his purse — which meant that the miners, together, had received one hundred thirty-five pounds, at least. This was not a small business, he realized. It was, indeed, the greater part of his living. Already, the pack trains were lining up, the animals now burdened with the day's purchases — barrels of flour or salted fish, maybe. Bolts of fabric, tools — lots of tools. Bundles with clothing, from doublets to shoes — most anything that the miners could not raise or make for themselves.

As the pack trains headed out of Bamford, and back to Derwent, Edward realized that he should travel with one of them. He had just enough of his old sensibilities about him to notice several men around the square who had been observing the business all day — no doubt these men could tell you exactly how much money he and the miners had in their purses. Safer to travel in company.

He attached himself to a train of eight ponies, accompanied by three miners. With Edward, that made four men — probably enough to deter any small-time thief. His senses were on alert all the way back to Derwent.

They arrived in Derwent before dark, and Edward stopped at the church, to safely lock up the tithes. Two pack trains were waiting for him. Benjamin appeared, moments later.

"I suppose that they are here to pay their tithes?"

"Of course, Father."

"Ben, how many other miners should I expect to see?"

"I think you should expect to receive tithes from at least a dozen . . . that's including the five groups you were with today . . . plus, these two . . . probably at least five more payments, over the next week or so."

Five more? That could come to another fifteen or twenty pounds, at least. Edward sighed. Another walk to Bamford? More like two or three more trips. "Ben, come with me," he said. Benjamin followed him into the church office. Edward locked the door and spread the contents of his purse out on a table. "Please count this for me," said Edward.

Benjamin did so. "Fifteen pounds, four shillings, five pence," He reported.

Edward opened the ledger to show him the day's entries. "Do you see, I received fifteen pounds, two shillings, and five pence in Bamford?

"Aye, Father," said Benjamin.

"Can you tell me how much was in my purse, before I put the tithes in? I mean, how much of the money was mine, personally?"

"No, I can't, Father." Benjamin replied, "Unless you can tell me how much you spent on this trip."

Right answer! Thought Edward. "So, how much of this money should we be locking up?"

"Why, the fifteen, two, and five. It says so right here in the ledger."

Edward smiled and nodded. "Very good, Ben. I want you to travel with the miners to Bamford tomorrow and accept the tithes on my behalf. Make entries in the ledger, just like these, so we'll know exactly how much to put into the lockbox when you return."

"I'm not sure, Father. Some people might accuse me of helping myself to the proceeds, so to speak. What if I write a lesser amount in the ledger than I collect, and keep the difference? Besides, I have my shop to mind. Taking a day off will cost me. Even if I did go, it might be dangerous to walk that road with money in my purse."

"Good point. I'll send another man with you. I'll pay you each a shilling to make the trip, and you will have to give the miners receipts for the tithe you collect. When they come back this way, I can read their receipts and be sure that the church is receiving what she is owed."

"A shilling, you say? Who's my companion?"

"I was thinking of Jack Clegg."

"Jack! Why Jack?"

"He's not busy. He could use the shilling. He's honest, wouldn't you say?"

"Honest enough. But it's a long walk for a man with a gimpy leg. Or a pair of old ones, like mine, for that matter."

"You can take Bruce. Take turns riding him, or both ride him, for that matter. As for safety, you should take care to travel the road back with one of the groups of miners. Do you see any problem with that?"

"Jack could do it alone, I think. Why spend a shilling on me?"

"I fear that Jack might forget his business, especially if he visits the pub at Bamford. I'm not sure he would understand the fine points about accurate records and receipts, either. And I'm not completely confident in his arithmetic. It will be safer for the two of you to travel together."

Benjamin nodded. "Ye're a wise man, vicar. I'll do it."

"Thank you, Ben. I'll have Jack meet you at Sunup by the West door."

"Ye're sure he'll do it?"

"Bess will make sure he does it."

Benjamin chuckled. "Aye, so she will."

At dinner, Edward explained his plan to Bess and Jack.

"Seems like a job you'd rather handle yourself," commented Bess.

"I need to be here, to teach the pupils. Ere long, some of them will be staying home to work for their families, now that Spring is here. I imagine that the school will be on recess through the summer months."

"Quite right, Father," Bess agreed, "Soon, they'll puttin' the sheep back up on the moor — the boys will be expected to help with that."

The new procedure for payment of the tithes worked as well as could be expected. Ben and Jack made three trips all told, and the total for the four trips came to forty pounds, two shillings, nine pence. It was a great deal of money, in a village like Derwent.

April, 1587: Shearing

Within two weeks, it was clear that there would be no more tithes coming down from the Peaks. Also, attendance at the school was waning. Two or three of the older boys were missing the first week, and by the following week, the girls were missing too. By the third week, he had only two students — children of the Butcher and the Blacksmith. Edward sent them home and told them that school would resume after Harvest.

His days were less busy now, as he was called to fewer emergencies as the weather improved. On the other hand, he had his animals to take care of. Meg dropped by one morning and explained that Mary really should have been sheared just before she lambed, but that now was better than later. She had some shears with her and showed Edward how to hold the ewe in a sitting position from behind, with her rear legs splayed out in front of her. "Hold her in that position with yer left arm," she said, handing the shears to him, "Then trim away the wool with these."

"She's squirming," Edward observed.

"Aye, she's a bit wild, and she can tell that ye don't really know what ye're doin'. She can't stand though, as long as ye hold on to her. She'll settle down, once ye get started."

That much was true. Edward worked the shears slowly down her belly, then sideways, until the wool came free in one tangled, smelly mass. The ewe's neck and legs took a second try to shear. The three lambs looked at him accusingly from the other side of the sheep pen. When it was more or less over, Edward released Mary and stood up. "Does wool always smell like this?" There was a heavy smell clinging to his clothes, with a greasy film of something on his hands, shirt, and hose.

"Aye, it's a rank business," said Meg. "Better you than me — you're a sheepman, now."

Edward felt a touch of pride in his work. Then he looked at the ewe. Strands of wool he had somehow missed were clinging to her. Not the neatest job.

Meg chuckled. "Ye'll do better next time, I reckon."

Next time? Of course, there would be a next time. He was a sheepman. "How soon should these sheep be put out to pasture?"

"Not for another month or two, With three lambs, you have to allow more time before weaning them. Give Mary some grain, and let them into the churchyard, if you like — good for the little ones to run about for a while."

"How do I do that?"

"You need to get the ewe to follow ye, and the lambs will follow. Get some grain from the bin."

There was a wooden scoop in the grain bin, and Edward filled it.

"Now offer some to Mary, there."

Edward did as instructed. Mary seemed to understand what was happening and approached him with a look of interest. "Don't let her eat too much," cautioned Meg, "Ye still have to lead her. If she eats it all before you reach her destination, she'll wander off on her own."

Meg opened the stall and Edward let Mary have a mouthful of grain, then walked out of the shed and headed for the churchyard across the street. Mary followed, and then Magdalen and Martha followed her. Jesus stood at the door of the shed and bleated. Meg chuckled and scooped him up in her arms. "This one's going to be trouble, mark my words."

The procession made its way to the churchyard, without incident. Once inside, Edward gave Mary the rest of the grain; Meg put Jesus down.

"Best check the fence, to make sure Mary can't escape," said Meg. "She's a rover, that we know." Edward walked the perimeter and didn't see any obvious gaps or holes. The lambs began showing off their acrobatic skills, running, leaping, and chasing around the headstones. Meg laughed. It was a lovely day in the graveyard.

"Ye should use a little grain to lead them to and from the churchyard every day," said Meg. "In a week or so, they'll be accustomed to following you anywhere — and you can lead them where you will — even up onto the moor. Up there, they'll have to get by on grass, so the lambs need to stay here, and Mary needs to eat enough grain to keep all three thriving."

"Thank you for being here, today. I have been wanting to talk with you about some personal matters . . ."

"We're not done with business, yet, vicar. You will recall that we have a business agreement?

"I do, indeed. I'm selling these sheep to you, and you will pay me in wool, over the next three years . . ."

"Good Mornin' to ye!" exclaimed Meg, looking past Edward, over his shoulder.

Edward turned, to see Jack, Benjamin, and another man leaning against the churchyard fence (well within earshot, he realized).

"Father! There's been a cave-in up at the mines. They're asking for a priest," volunteered Jack.

"I can go with ye," said Meg. "Fetch Bruce, and yer things. I'll be along in just a few minutes. "Jack," she said, "These sheep are mine, now. I'd appreciate it if ye could get them back in their stall for the evening." Jack made a face but nodded his head.

A few minutes later, Edward and Bruce were out front of the rectory, where Meg and the miner were waiting. Their path lay through the village, and up to the edge along the East side of the valley — a familiar enough path, by now. Edward made a point of looking backward as they progressed, trying to commit the view to memory; this was the way his return journey would appear.

The sight of the collapse was about three miles beyond the edge, to the east. They came to a cluster of buildings that comprised a smelter — a large shed to dry the peat, a few small shacks where the workers slept. A crowd of men were clustered around a spot a hundred yards downhill — evidently the site of the collapse.

As he approached, Edward could see that there was a depression in the ground, and men were digging busily at its edges, and hauling the diggings away to the side. They had created a pit about twelve feet deep, and at the bottom three or four men were scooping up stones and earth, filling buckets with it. Men at the top were hauling the buckets up with rope and dumping it into barrows, to be wheeled away.

His arrival was welcomed. "We're nearly there, Father. Won't be long, now."

Nearly *where?* He gave Meg a quizzical look.

"They call this a bell pit," explained Meg. "It starts with a vertical shaft, like a well. When they strike a deposit of ore, they cut away at the sides of the shaft, until the bottom of the shaft is wider than the top — like the inside of a great bell."

Edward pictured it in his mind. "So, the ground around the shaft at the top is actually hanging over the miner's heads?"

Meg nodded. "It takes too long to widen the top of the shaft — no money in that. Sometimes, the upper part collapses into the void below."

Edward turned to look at the collapse. "And it becomes a grave for the unlucky."

"Not always. Sometimes, there is a space below that does not fill with rubble. Sometimes men can survive down there, for days."

"Listen!" said one of the diggers. "I can hear a voice!"

He was right. Someone was still alive down there. Shortly, a scoop of rubble revealed a dark hole near the bottom of the shaft. It took another half hour to remove enough of the loose rubble to pull two men from the pit. Both were muddy and bleeding, but Meg found no broken limbs. "Probably broke ribs," Meg suggested, "but I can't do much about those. One of them took a stone to the head."

The miner with the head injury lost consciousness, soon after. The men were taken to one of the shacks and laid on their cots. Edward anointed both with oil, and prayed a prayer for their healing.

"I've done all I can for them," said Meg. "I think the one with the head injury may not last long." Then she was gone — home, he supposed. Edward agreed that the unconscious man seemed to be getting weaker. He decided to stay awhile. If the man died, he would be called upon to officiate anyway, either up here on the moor, or down in the valley.

In two more hours, the man was dead. He had no family, that anyone knew of. His comrades asked that he be buried that very day. There was a spot not far from the smelter, where two other gravesites were visible. There were two rough headstones, with the names of the deceased, and the dates of their deaths. Edward looked into the faces of the men and decided it would do no good to demand that he be buried in the churchyard, so he agreed to officiate. By mid-afternoon, the ceremony was over. Men were already returning to their work. Edward felt a chill, to see how the earth commanded these men's devotion with the promise of riches, or maybe only the suggestion of the possibility of mere survival. It was lead, not gold, that they scraped for, and no alchemy would deliver them from their harsh fate.

Edward asked for a guide back to Derwent; a man agreed to take him only as far as the edge above the village — "Ye can find yer way back from there," he said.

It was less than an hour's journey to where his guide stopped at the top of a rise and pointed westward: "Ye see that knob? The pathway runs along the left side, and from there, ye can see the gap that leads down into the valley."

Edward did not argue. He had recognized several landmarks on his way back and could visualize what the pathway ahead would look like. Besides, there were ample horse prints and donkey prints on the pathway. It was no more than half a mile to the edge, he calculated.

"I suppose you think us a cold lot, for burying our comrade in such haste," said his guide. "But he had no family to grieve him, and no friends to speak of, neither. From childhood, he worked in the smelters, until his deafness and forgetfulness made it unsafe to work around molten metal. His moods became dangerous, too. After that, he was only good for the pits — and not a good man, even there. There are more than a few who get that way in the lead mines. A decent burial is the best they can hope for." With that, the guide turned back and started for his home.

"May God deliver you from such a fate, Sir," said Edward. The man said nothing and kept walking.

Edward had just made it past the knob and was in sight of the gap where the path descended into the valley when a harsh sound assaulted his ears. A raven swooped down and lit on a stone outcrop near the path. It cocked its head and stared intently at him. Something stirred in Edward's memory: "Johnny? Is that you?"

At the mention of the name, the raven fluttered off to the south of the path and settled on another outcrop of stone. Edward noticed that a side path branched off the main route there. Curious, he led Bruce down the side path a ways. Johnny, if that's who it was, moved again, further down the path. Edward looked backward, fixing the location of the main path in his memory, then followed the raven farther still, southward, up a slight rise . . . and there it was, below him; Meg Moorcroft's cottage — smoke trailing from the chimney — in the shadow of a stony prominence, with a shallow cave on one side. Memories came flooding back, half-remembered, but now suddenly all too vivid — pain, fear, the Raven Queen; also the haunting scent of lavender, warmth, laughter — the Lady Lavender. Mandrakes. She said it was the mandrakes.

Johnny — for so it surely was, he decided, flew to the roof just above the front door and let out a loud screech. Shortly, the door opened and Meg stepped out. She looked up at the raven, and then noticed Bruce and Edward, picking their way toward the house. She was surprised but moved to meet them.

"So, thee found thy way here, at last?"

"I had some help," said Edward, "from Johnny, there."

"Is that so?" she turned to look at the raven, who rose from the roof and flapped away across the valley. "Animals can sense more than we suppose. I have had thee on my mind, this afternoon. Johnny must have been aware of it somehow."

"So, you did not send him to fetch me?"

"Not in so many words. But Johnny is a clever fellow. We are well acquainted. Thee said this morning that thee would speak of something personal. Perhaps Johnny knew thy thoughts, as well."

Edward nodded. "Perhaps. But I most desire that my thoughts be known to thee."

She smiled. "Come in then. We shall sit by the fire."

Edward tied Bruce up behind the cottage and entered it. Meg was waiting, just inside the door. She embraced him and buried her face in his chest. He caught the scent of Lavender. She kissed him and then released him. "Come, sit with me."

He sat, and she snuggled up against him. "What matters would thee speak of?" she murmured.

"I wish to marry." That was plain enough.

"Do you mean, you wish that I should marry thee? That is a different thing."

"I wish to marry thee, and I wish thee to marry me. I do not think one can be true without the other."

She sat up and looked him in the eyes. "Edward, there is no other man that I would be married to, if I were to marry. But thy choice and mine are different."

"How so?"

"For you, marriage is an expected thing. A wife will make your work easier by sharing some of the load and make you an example of the respectability that a priest should exhibit. Children, should they come, will be another part of a respectable life — a parish priest as an example of domestic stability and prosperity."

Edward tried to grasp what she was saying. *What respectability could she be talking about? An exile in a tiny village in the wilderness? A lone voice of reason in a sea of ignorance?*

Meg continued, "For me, to be your wife would mean giving up this life" — she gestured around her cottage — "and all that goes with it. I would be a woman of the village, but no longer a woman of the moors. It would mean bidding farewell to half the life I live now, or perhaps more. Can a vicar's wife be a 'wise woman'? Can she roam the woods and meadows in search of herbs and medicines? Can she keep ravens chickens, and sheep? Can she doctor the sick? Can she dance in the pub on Twelfth Night? I think, rather, that you would expect me to cook, clean house, and be at home all day — especially if there should be children, to raise them to be respectable, like their father."

Ah. "I had not thought that far ahead," admitted Edward. "As for children, I suppose I would expect thee to care for them. I'm not so particular about the housekeeping and cooking — my living (as I have just discovered) is adequate to employ someone like Bess Clegg to take care of the house." He sighed, while he chose his words: "As for thee being a 'wise woman', I admit that it is not what most people expect a vicar's wife to be, but I am not what most people think a vicar should be, either. If I thought that was a problem, I would not be asking for thy hand."

She was a little surprised at his words, he thought. "As for Twelfth Night, I would very much like to see thee dance — as long as it is not with some other fellow. And I would not have thee stand under the kissing bough with anyone but me."

Meg giggled. "What, jealous already?"

"The thought of thee in the arms of another man tears at my heart."

She looked at him seriously. "I feel the same about thee. But that does not mean that we should be wed. I will think and pray on it. Give me time to find my answer." She stood up, and the warmth of her was gone as if a chill had entered the cottage.

His disappointment must have shown on his face. "Do not look that way," she said, with a furrowed brow, "know that I love thee."

There was silence for a moment. Nothing left to say, for now.

"Come," she said, "I will show thee where my sheep are pastured."

Edward wasn't sure what she meant, but her words were not euphemism. They went outside, and she led him to the top of the rise just south of the cottage. From there, he could see a wide vista across the moor. A gridwork of low stone fences divided the expanse. In one of them, a dozen and a half sheep could be seen. "The sheep can stay up here from March to November," she said, "They have to be moved from pasture to pasture every week or so. There are springs of water in each enclosure so that I don't have to bring them to water unless the weather has been very dry. I have to check on them every day, rain or shine. When David is a bit older, I can train him to move them from one place to another at my command — which will make it even easier, until I have to give him back to you."

"If you will marry me, I will make a wedding present of David," offered Edward with a smile, "he could be yours for as long as he lives."

"Father, ye should know better than to trifle with the affections of a young maid, by promises of lavish gifts. If ye turn her head, ye must pay the piper!" She grinned.

"I wanted thee to see this, to understand how I spend my days," she explained. "I want thee to understand what is at stake for me. Some say this is a hard life, but it is the life I know — wind and weather, sun and rain, moor and woodland — all of it alive, all of it fruitful, all of it beautiful. I am not sure I can live any other way."

Edward nodded. Of course. It occurred to him that his arrival in this village was a disruption to the lives of many; in fact, he had made a career of planning and abetting disruptions in the lives of unsuspecting others. He could claim no great success in his previous life, nor yet in this one. A wiser, kinder man might set his affections on a woman more suited to his situation; the heart is a treacherous thing — no respecter of common sense, nor reason . . . He realized that Meg had just said something to him, but he had missed it. She was giving him a querulous look, waiting for an answer . . .

"Edward? Did ye hear what I just said?"

"I was thinking how beautiful this place is, how rich your life must be," he said lamely.

She smiled and shook her head. "It will be dark, soon. Let's fetch Bruce, and I'll show thee the way home."

Edward arrived in the village just before sunset. He fed Bruce, washed up, and sat down to dinner. He told Jack and Bess about the man who had died up in the mine pit. He said nothing about his visit to Meg Moorcroft's cottage.

July, 1587: David

Summer in the Peaks had arrived in full force. The days were long, and the nights were mild in the valley. Up above the edges, it was cooler, especially at night, but bracing rather than chilling. Edward felt comfortable on the moors now, mostly due to the trips he had been making up to Meg Moorcroft's cottage — twice a week, at least. He learned to see the landscape with a traveler's eye; to note which landmarks could be spotted from miles away and used to approximate his location with respect to the village. Fog was much less common at this season, as well. Bruce also seemed to find his bearings, and Edward sometimes gave him his head, when returning from some visit or other. Bruce could usually be counted on to find his way back to his stall behind the rectory, or failing that, Meg's cottage. Edward suspected that Bruce actually preferred Meg's place because she often had some sort of treat for him — a dried apple, or some such. This did not conflict with Edward's preferences, in any way.

He still did not have the answer he sought to his proposal of marriage; he didn't press the point. He knew that if he forced her to a firm 'no', being around her would only become more awkward — business partnership, or no. For now, he wanted to enjoy her company as long as he could. *This summer will be ours*, he told himself, *whatever else may come*. Many of his visits were short — on the way to or from some other destination. Meg usually introduced him to some aspect of her life on the moor that she thought he should be aware of — how to tell when an area was getting overgrazed, how to recognize certain poisonous plants, how to recognize certain healing plants, how to repair a stone wall between two pastures. There was plenty to talk about.

The heather had just begun to bloom when Meg appeared at the rectory and announced that it was time for the ewe Mary, and her three lambs to join the rest of her flock for the summer. Edward had done as she advised him, and Mary and the lambs would follow him just about anywhere, by habit. Whether they would follow all the way up above the valley edge, remained to be seen. They formed a procession through the village, Meg and Edward in front, with Mary and the lambs following. Young Jesus lagged, curious about everything they passed. People pointed and laughed at his antics. By now the village was well aware of the business agreement between Meg and Edward (most said Meg had the better of the bargain), and there was general speculation that their partnership was more than financial, though no one said anything publicly about it.

It went better than Edward expected. Mary must have recalled what delights awaited her up on the moor, after a winter eating dry hay, and followed them willingly enough, sampling what she could from either side of the path. Martha and Magdalen followed her example. Which left Young Jesus, with a mind of his own. "Don't worry about him," said Meg, as Edward kept looking back to see what the lamb was getting into. "He's a stubborn rascal, with a mind of his own, but he'll come round."

They made it to the cottage and stopped long enough to introduce the sheep to David, who was tied near the door. Meg untied him so that he could sniff the newcomers and they him. Edward got a cursory lick as well — they were well acquainted. From there, they led the four newcomers over the rise to where the rest of the flock was grazing. "We'll put these four in the adjoining field for a day so that the others can get used to them," explained Meg. The arrival of Mary and her lambs attracted the interest of the other sheep, who crowded up to the stone wall to get a better look — or smell, as the case might be. Mary was attentive but continued to snatch mouthfuls of fresh grass from the turf. Edward noticed that there were several lambs among the larger flock, as well — these were generally larger (older, probably) than Mary's lambs.

Meg unleashed David and ordered him to "sit!" which he did, though wriggling with excitement. Then, at her command, he jumped over the wall into the next pasture and began circling the larger flock. As he did so, they bunched up and moved away from David, first in one direction, then another. Meg shouted commands to him to move to the right or left, and he obeyed, more or less. Edward thought he did pretty well, but Meg shook her head. "He still has a lot to learn."

"He has an intention, but not a purpose," she explained. "He is bred to be a shepherd; he is determined to gather as many as he can into one flock and keep them there. He would protect them from danger and prevent any other from taking them from him. But he does not know what to do with them. For that, he needs a Master. Until David learns to follow the commands of a good Master, he is just a dog, tirelessly running about the pasture. Left alone, he could even harm his flock. He is no true shepherd until he understands his Master's will."

Edward looked at her closely. A rebuke? No, a parable perhaps. Still, she was talking about him, as much as the dog . . .

"How long before he needs no more training, do you suppose?"

"It's a lifetime task. No matter how well the shepherd performs today, he will forget all he knows if the training lapses. To own a dog like this is to assume the task of training him for as long as he lives."

"Lucky dog, to have such a dedicated Master," said Edward. "Lucky Master, to have such a dog?"

Meg chuckled and nodded. "Aye, lucky. That's the word for it."

She caught him by surprise, then. "I will marry thee Edward, but only if thee can make certain promises. I cannot be confined to thy house, or the duties of a housemaid. I cannot give up this life" — here she gestured with her arm — "to wither away in some darkened rectory. I will gladly share thy bed, but I must also share my life with those who need me."

"I have gifts, skills, learning. I cannot enter into a covenant that does not honor those things; it would be a wrong — as wrong as wasting a dog like David here, by letting him be idle, by not using him every week of his life for the work that is his destiny."

Edward was at a loss for words. His mind scrambled to come up with an answer . . . "I agree that your gifts and learning must not go to waste," he began, "and I would not keep thee withering — in a rectory, or anywhere else." *So far, so good . . .*

He continued, "My vocation requires me to live near the church, where the parishioners may find me, at need. I do not think the parish priest can reside up here for practical reasons, even if the ones who sent me to this place would allow it. If I must live in the village, and you must live on the moor, where shall this bed that we share abide? On the hillside, betwixt the valley and the moor?"

She giggled. "That could make for fine sport. But nay, I would share your bed, wherever you would have it be. It is our lives that I am speaking of. And yes, I suppose that betwixt the valley and the moor is how I would have it. Can you promise me that I will not lose everything I have up here when I am married to a man of the valley?"

"I cannot make promises about what either of us might lose, by marrying. But I can vow that I will not try to prevent you from caring for these sheep or ministering to the sick. I will not try to separate you from your family, or any of the others in the village below who depend upon you. I will not demand that you leave this place if I am compelled to do so, by some events that I cannot predict."

"Compelled?"

"I have already explained to you why I am here, and why my remaining here depends on the whims of others. This place was supposed to be my prison; it has become for me like the Garden of Eden because you are here; if we are truly meant for each other, I would never wish to leave it. I cannot promise you that others will not compel me. I am not a free man — not in the way that you are free. Binding yourself to me and my fate will be a sacrifice."

"That is a sacrifice that I choose to make," she said and took him in her arms. "Yes, I will wed thee, Edward Chase. I will be thy wife, thy bedmate, the mother of your children. And when both of us are too old to climb the path to the moors — should we live so long — I will sit before the fire with thee, in whatever house you choose." She sealed her vow with a kiss.

Edward felt a rising sense of elation, as he headed home. His feet were light and he may have skipped, a little, down the narrow path — until he took a misstep and twisted his ankle — the same one he had injured last December, as luck would have it. He tried to shake it off — not completely successfully, but it wasn't as bad as the earlier injury, and he hobbled on down the path to the village.

As he was passing the pub, he met Jack Clegg. "Father, there's a stranger in the pub. Seems to be asking about yer business."

"How's that? Did he ask for me by name?"

"Nay, he's the sly sort. Asks the question, while pretending to be interested in something else. He's been in there all day. The barkeep warned me about him; the lads won't have much to do with him."

Edward felt a knot in his stomach. "Describe him to me."

"Not much to tell. Yer age, I suppose. About yer height. Narrow face and, a short beard. Blue eyes."

Familiar. All too familiar. "Is he still in the pub?"

Jack nodded.

"I shall speak with him."

"Careful, Father. He's a slippery one. Don't give him a chance to trip ye up."

Quite so. A slippery one. A serpent in the Garden of the Lord. Edward walked into the pub, and stood for a moment, while his eyes adjusted to the dark, then walked to the bar, and ordered an ale.

"There's a stranger here, today," said the barkeep in a confidential tone. "Seems to be interested in our vicar." He nodded to his right, where a figure sat near the far wall.

Edward turned to look. Couldn't see the man's face. Ale in hand, he walked over to where the stranger was seated. "Welcome to Derwent, stranger."

The man looked up. Blue eyes; none other than Charles Bedford.

"Mr. Bedford, I thought it might be you! How come ye to Derwent?"

Bedford gestured for him to sit down. "I travel widely, in my trade. You should not be surprised to see me here, since it was I who told you of this place, not a year ago."

"Aye, and I admit that it is all that you said it would be. I owe you a debt of gratitude, I think, for directing me to this place." He took a sip of his ale.

Bedford looked at him, sizing him up. "It appears that this place agrees with you."

Edward cocked his head and nodded. "It does. Although when last I saw you, I was not at my best. I'm eating better, now," he said, laying a hand across his belly. "Sleeping better, too. Fresh air, you know."

Bedford was still eyeing him, warily.

This means he is alone, thought Edward, *if he were going to arrest me, he would have brought some help. This must be some sort of spying mission, for him.* "You still haven't answered my question. What business brings you to Derwent?"

"I'll tell you plainly. The Court of High Commission makes a point of keeping track of the progress of men that they . . . place; men like yourself.

"So, you'll be filing a report on me, then?"

Bedford nodded. "Something like that."

And what will your report say ?"

"What should my report say?"

"That I am serving this parish as its priest. That I wear the vestments, as required, that my sermons are not overlong, and I follow the liturgy to the letter. You might add that I anoint the sick, baptize the young, and bury the dead. Not much more to say, I think."

"That is accurate, as far as I can tell," allowed Bedford. "There is also the matter of your marriage, is there not?"

"Marriage? I am not married!" *How could Bedford possibly have heard about my betrothal to Meg? Did he have spies lurking about up on the moor? I've spoken of this to no one . . . except . . .* Except, of course, Reverend Hooper, the priest in Bamford, a few months ago, and Hooper had promised to keep it confidential. But inevitably, Hooper would divulge any bits of information that the Court of High Commission asked for. More likely, he was under orders to report on things in Derwent on a regular basis; maybe they even paid him for information . . .

"Perhaps I was misinformed. I could swear that someone hereabouts mentioned that you are intending to marry a young woman in Derwent."

Swear all you like, thought Edward, *you have revealed one of your sources to me, and I thank you for that. I shall be careful to avoid Rev. Hooper, whenever possible.* No, that wasn't the best strategy. Better to feed Hooper any tidbits of misinformation that would be to his benefit . . . with a chill, Edward realized that he was thinking and planning as he had in the old life, where staying one step ahead of his enemies was a high-stakes game. He realized immediately afterward that he did not want Meg Moorcroft to be touched in any way by that life, that he wanted to protect her, if at all possible; keep her safe in the Garden of the Lord, for as long as he could.

"I hold a particular woman in my affections," he allowed, "but I have not discussed it with anyone — except her, of course. I can only imagine that you have been listening to some local gossip."

"Either that, or the woman has been talking to her friends, about you," suggested Bedford.

"Perhaps you are right," said Edward. *I'll let you slide out of that one, weasel. I'll pretend that I believe you. Get out of my garden, now!* he thought. But, of course, Bedford would not be leaving until he was ready to go. Edward took another gulp of his ale. "You were right about one thing," he said. "The rectory is very comfortable. And the living is ample."

"How ample?"

"I would not speak of it in public, but I can show you the ledger if you like. Perhaps you will dine with me this evening? I have two spare rooms in the rectory, you can take your pick." It tested his self-discipline to extend hospitality to this man, but it was the best way he could think of to shorten his unwelcome visitor's stay. Pray he wouldn't get too comfortable.

"I accept your gracious offer," said Bedford. *No doubt he feels entitled to my hospitality. No doubt people try to curry his favor everywhere he goes,* thought Edward, *No doubt most of them are hoping to kill him with kindness, or at least rid their homes of him!*

Bedford expressed surprise at the size of the lead tithes. "This is by far the largest tithe this parish has produced in many years!" he stated.

"I guess the miners had a prosperous year, then."

Bedford shrugged. "Did you value their ingots any differently, this year?"

Edward explained how he had claimed the tithe in Bamford, as the ingots were weighed by the buyers, and how in past years, the valuation had been made by estimation.

"Your predecessors were lazy, then," said Bedford.

"How is that?"

"The old system presumed that the priest was shown the full amount of the miner's ingots before they were separated into piles. Who's to say that the miners weren't holding back part of their lead when they let the priest choose his 'tithe'?

"Surely, they would have unloaded their pack animals in full view of the priest?"

"More likely they hid some of their animals in the woods, and only showed part of their minings to the priest. Easy enough to fetch those animals out of hiding, once they were on their way to Bamford. The priest need never know."

Edward decided Bedford was on to something. *A weasel has its uses, after all,* he thought. "It didn't occur to me that the miners might not be completely honest. I just didn't trust that my eyes would take an accurate measurement."

"And the church is better off for it. I'll mention that in my report."

The offering income was a bit better than average, Bedford noted. "Attendance must be up, a little."

"I think it was a good harvest year," volunteered Edward.

"Probably so, probably so," nodded Bedford. "A lot of parishes did well this year. You should expect a visit from the Archdeacon, over in Sheffield — he'll be claiming a portion of your income, on behalf of the bishop — the living is yours to keep, though. Don't let him get his hands on that."

Edward's estimation of Charles Bedford improved, a little. At least there was some advantage in his visit.

Then it was time to arrange for dinner. They walked to the rectory, where Edward introduced his guest: "Bess, this is Charles Bedford. He'll be staying in one of the guest rooms this evening."

Bess froze, for a moment, and then recovered. "Certainly. Mr. Bedford, you may choose either of the rooms upstairs." And then she turned to leave: "We'll need a few more things, for dinner, then," she explained, and she was gone.

An awkward silence. Then, "Why don't you move your things upstairs?" Edward suggested. Bedford nodded and ascended the staircase.

Moments later, Jack appeared at the door. He motioned Edward outside. "What's this I hear about the stranger? He's coming to dinner? He's a friend of yours?" — all of this said in a low voice.

Edward shook his head and put a finger to his lips. "Not a friend, more likely an enemy," he murmured, "I must keep an eye on him, and entertain him."

Jack looked surprised, then gave Edward a conspiratorial wink, and a smile: "I'll go let Bess know," he said. "We'll be five for dinner."

"Five?"

"Aye, Bess invited Meg for dinner. Didn't she say?"

Edward shook his head. Things were going from bad to worse. Meg was the last person he wanted Bedford to meet. "Best find them both, then," he said. "Tell them we have a guest from outside."

Jack winked again, and headed back into the village, with his characteristic limp. Edward sighed and stepped back into the rectory. Not only was there a serpent in the Garden of the Lord, it seemed inevitable that Meg would meet him. He wished he could warn her off, but leaving Bedford alone seemed like a very bad idea — not to mention that it would arouse his suspicions. His only hope was that Jack would warn her off. *It has come to this. Jack is my best hope. Jack. Lord, don't let him get diverted into the pub . . .*

He heard Charles Bedford descending the stairs and stepped back inside. Bedford had more questions: Was there evidence of recusancy in the parish? Separatism? Anabaptism? Puritanism? Any other heresy? Was everyone attending church every week, as required by law?

Edward decided that truthfulness was the best policy, not only to protect his position in the parish (a too-rosy assessment would not be believed), nor merely to protect the village from a harsher rector (should Bedford recommend that Edward be replaced), but because, if Bedford had one spy in the area, he probably had others.

"No recusancy that I can see," he began, "These people are rooted in this place, no separation from it would appeal to them. As far as Puritans go, I am the only reformer here that I know of. There have been three births in the village since I arrived, and I have baptized all of them — none of their parents have objected; I do not know what other evidence could determine whether there be Anabaptists among us."

"You have not answered my questions about attendance, and other heresies."

Edward sighed and nodded. "As far as the village goes, attendance is nearly perfect. I can vouch that everyone receives the eucharist three times per year, as required. This applies to the farms in the valley, as well. There are miners and crofters who dwell up on the moors — I am not sure how many, exactly — who may not come into the village but once a year — or maybe never in their lives, as far as I know. Offering has been increasing, as you noticed, and I think that means that attendance is more consistent, since I arrived."

"And other heresies? Witchcraft? Superstition?"

"As you must be aware, this place has a certain . . . reputation, for adherence to 'ancient ways', as the vicar in Chesterfield put it to me. I do what I can to dispel such superstitions when I encounter them. I've seen no evidence of witchcraft, though (*except for when I was under the influence of mandrakes, or some such,* he reminded himself)."

"What sort of superstitions?"

"Oh, such things as mummery, and Christmastide. Many seem to believe that a blessing from the mummer confers good fortune, for the coming year."

"And what do you believe?"

"I believe that mummery feasting, and dissipation during the Christmas season should be done away with, altogether. I believe that sobriety and good cheer would serve better. I avoid all such celebrations when I can, but I cannot control what goes on in the pub, or the street. Someday, perhaps, my stature in this village may be high enough to persuade them to give these things up, but I have not been here long enough to have such influence with them." (This was a good point, Edward realized; it argued in favor of his staying on in Derwent until the process of reform could be completed — might take a lifetime, such a task . . .)

Bedford scoffed, then chuckled, "And after that, you can eliminate the yuletide celebrations in the whole kingdom, I suppose. You truly are a Puritan, Father Chase!"

Just then, Bess bustled in. "I got some extra mutton for our dinner," she explained, "need to stretch the stew, a bit, with company coming." Then she curtseyed to Edward, and said, "If that will please ye, Father. If not, please tell me, now."

Edward nodded "That will be fine, Bess." *What was going on with Bess? Why the curtseying, and groveling? Bess always cooked what she wanted, and expected people to eat it — any man foolish enough to turn up his nose would simply go hungry . . .*

Jack appeared, with Meg, moments later. "Jack Clegg, at yer service, Sir." Jack bowed awkwardly to Bedford. "And this is Meg, our . . . village midwife." Meg curtseyed as well, looked a little shy, and scurried into the kitchen. *Village midwife?* Well, that was true, but why emphasize that? The three of them had cooked something up, he realized, and it was going to be served to Charles Bedford. There was some risk that the whole thing, whatever it was, would be exposed as a fraud — they probably didn't appreciate how clever Bedford was. Foolish. Foolish to take such a chance. And why was Meg here, at all? Why couldn't they come up with some excuse for her absence? *No choice but to play along,* he told himself, *If only I knew what game they are playing.*

Jack was telling Bedford a yarn about his experiences in the lead mines. A good first move, Edward thought; boredom was the best way to lull him into inattention. Meg appeared moments later, with three goblets of wine for the men. *Wine? I never serve wine in my house!* He took a sip — it was mostly water, he decided. That did not seem to put Jack off — he gulped the whole thing down at once. Bedford took a swallow of his and pronounced it tasty. "One of those wines from Portugal, isn't it?" he asked.

Edward nodded. Jack looked hopefully at Meg, who demurred shyly: "I think you should wait for dinner, Jack."

Bedford and Edward had just enough time to finish their wine before Bess had dinner on the table. They seated Charles Bedford at the opposite end of the table from Edward. Meg refilled all the wine goblets. Edward looked at his — it was only half full if that. He was certain that Bedford's would be filled to the brim. "Jack," said Bess, "Ye'll do better with ale, I'm thinkin'. Let the gentlemen have the wine — remember Twelfth Night." Jack looked a little disappointed, but Edward wondered if it was genuine; *it looks like a plan to get Bedford drunk! What then?*

Jack leaned toward Bedford and began to speak in a conspiratorial tone: "The missus fears I may overdo things," he winked. He then began to regale their guest with tales of Twelfthnight, and his reign as Lord of Misrule. Bedford laughed out loud, at some of the antics that Jack described. *So far, so good,* thought Edward. *Maybe we'll get through this meal without any questions for Meg. Maybe this will work . . .*

Bedford praised Bess for her cooking and raised his cup as if to say something. Meg stood and poured more wine into it. "That'll do, Miss, that'll do." He took a sip, then. "If I am not much mistaken, our rector here intends to wed you. I think he is a fortunate fellow if you will have him. What do you say?"

Meg smiled, looked at Edward, and giggled. "I say, I am fortunate, indeed, to have the affections of a priest. It is a wonder he should cast his eye on a simple shepherd girl, like myself. I am highly favored, to be sure!"

"A shepherdess? I thought you were a midwife."

"That I am, but there are not enough babies born in this village to occupy a midwife full-time. I make my living from my sheep."

"You mean, your family makes its living from your father's sheep," he corrected her.

"Alas, my father and mother are both dead. I am an only child, an orphan. *Don't lay it on too thick*, thought Edward. Then, "So the sheep, and the farm are mine." she smiled.

Bedford shot Edward a meaningful look. "But if you marry, your property falls under the control of your husband, does it not?"

Meg looked thoughtful. "Yes. Yes, I suppose it does."

"And it passes, then to your heirs, thereafter."

"You mean children? Oh, I hope we have lots and lots of children!" Her face lit up like she had seen a heavenly vision. *How can Bedford not recognize that she is putting him on*, wondered Edward.

He didn't. Maybe it was the wine.

"A toast to the betrothed," said Bedford, raising his goblet. "May God bless you with lots and lots of children." He noticed his goblet was empty. Meg noticed, too, and quickly filled it. "And many prosperous generations of them! May they be blessed with prosperity, and . . . and . . ." Bedford was having difficulty finding his words.

"Fecundity," Bess volunteered. She looked hard at Edward.

"Aye! Blessed with fecundity!"

"Amen!" replied everyone else at the table.

Dinner was over, more or less. Meg and Bess rose and cleared the table. Edward, Jack, and Bedford 'retired' to the sitting room, Jack limping, and Bedford a little unsteady on his feet. *What was in that wine?* Edward wondered.

Bedford leaned over and spoke in a low tone: "She's a lovely lass; you're a lucky man. And about to become a man of property — very clever." He leaned back and exhaled. His eyes began to close. Soon he would be asleep, by the look of things. Jack looked drowsy, too. *What was in that wine?*

Edward waited until Bedford was snoring softly, then rose and went to the kitchen.

"Time for you to walk Meg home, I suppose?" suggested Bess.

Edward nodded. "Yes, I think so."

Meg smiled and offered her hand, "Lead me home, Father."

A full moon illuminated the streets and the edges above the valley. "Where did that wine come from, and what was in it?" demanded Edward.

"Why do ye ask? Did it put thee under the weather?" She was grinning.

Edward shook his head. "No, I was drinking mostly water, I think. But I also think that Charles Bedford was drinking something else. And another thing. I sent Jack to warn both you and Bess about how dangerous that man is. Did he not explain that to you?"

"Aye, he did. It gave us enough time to make our plans for the evening — though Bess gets more credit for the plan than Jack."

"I was hoping that you would not have to meet that man, that Jack's warning would keep you away."

"Why?"

"Because he is dangerous. Because he is my enemy. Because he has the power to harm me, and anyone dear to me. I wanted to protect you from what he still may do to me — and to you if he knows that I love you."

Meg was touched, and her face showed it, even in the moonlight. She kissed him, right there in the street. Then her face took a serious expression. "Edward," she said, "we are betrothed. Thy enemies are my enemies, thy danger is mine. Once Jack explained that thy guest was thine enemy, there was no place for me, but by thy side. Nothing would have persuaded me to be anywhere else."

"But you do not understand all the ways he could ruin us — he is like the serpent in the Garden of the Lord!"

Meg shook her head, slowly. "Ye are not the only one who has learned to survive by dissimulation. The people of this village know how to recognize a 'serpent' when they see one — especially one from outside. We are still here because we have learned how to deal with them. They continue to come, and yet we survive. God willing, we will survive this one as well. Running or hiding are of no use — we face them with what we have."

"This was to be our Eden. Only this morning, I had hope that my life here would be different, that our life would be different. I thought I had found a place of safety for us, a refuge from all the corruption of the world I came from. And now I fear that we will never be at rest from the corruption that lurks outside . . ."

"There are always enemies waiting to enter," she replied. "We must cultivate our garden — remove the weeds, drive the serpents away, or capture and confine them. This place can be a garden of refuge — for those willing to till it. Vigilance and labor are required — that is our task. Adam and Eve made this our destiny, long, long ago."

He started to respond, but she placed her fingers over his lips. "Take me home," she said, "It is dark, but the moon will be light enough for thee to find the path."

This was mostly true. The steepest part of the slope, under the edge, was still in shade, because the moon had not risen high enough in the east, yet. The opposite slope was brightly illuminated, and Meg took his hand and led him up the last bit in the dark. Once on the moor, everything was bright; almost daylight it seemed, and the stars burned like a thousand distant suns. "This," said Meg, "is where our lives must be rooted. The outsiders have no power over this. Nothing they can do, even to the destruction of our bodies can overwhelm us; if we remember where we come from. We know who we are — nothing can take that away from us."

There was a glint of green in her eyes, and Edward caught a whiff of lavender. The power of the moment rolled over him. She was right. They had nothing to fear. It was their enemies who should be trembling.

"Come," she said. "I have to feed the livestock." David greeted them with a bark, as they approached the house. She wasn't jesting about the animals — they took David out to the pastures and brought the sheep into the pen for the night — Mary and her lambs mixed with all the others. Edward helped her water them, and feed David. By the time that was done, the moon was higher — it must be nearly midnight.

"Ye'll have light enough to find yer way home, now," said Meg.

Edward put his arms around her waist and drew her to him. "It grieves me to part from thee."

She kissed him again. "Then find us a priest, so that parting will not be necessary. And do it quickly, please." she chuckled. "I'll walk thee back to the edge."

When Edward got back to the rectory, he found Bess and Jack waiting for him. "Didn't want to leave Mr. Bedford alone in a strange house, in his condition," explained Bess.

"Where is he?"

"We helped him upstairs. He's asleep."

"I owe you both a debt of gratitude . . . "Edward began.

"Nay, Father. It is we who owe you. This matter is not yet settled. We helped as best we could." With that, they left, and Edward found his own bed.

It was late when he awoke to the sounds of Bess in the kitchen. He rose and dressed. Bedford was still in bed, apparently. Edward had finished his breakfast when Bedford appeared, dressed and groomed, ready to leave, by all appearances. "Will you have breakfast?" asked Bess.

"Gladly," Bedford replied. "And I must thank you for last night's repast. I slept better than I have for many a day." With that, he tipped her a sixpence. Bess was speechless for a moment, then curtseyed, and put the coin away.

"It looks as though you plan to leave us, this morning," Edward observed.

"Aye. I have other places I must be. *Others, like me, that you must report on?* Edward realized that there must indeed, be others — perhaps many others, in his situation. How many other men of Puritan persuasion had been exiled to remote villages like this one? It would be interesting to know how many, what their names were, their places of exile . . . but he had no way to find out. Such was the power of the government . . .

"Mr. Chase," Bedford began, as he ate, "I have enjoyed this visit, as I enjoy few others. I will not pretend that we are friends, our history belies that possibility. But you have done well here, for the church and for yourself. You are well housed and fed, and shortly, it appears, to be wed to a woman of rare beauty. You might at least thank me for that."

"I am grateful for that," agreed Edward. "I only hope that God will allow me to continue to enjoy these blessings."

"You've no worry about that, on my account. My report will say that you are making slow progress among these people and that it may take years to achieve what we are seeking."

Edward hoped that he was telling the truth. He hoped, as well, that the report would be accepted by Bedford's superiors.

The wedding was just over three weeks later. Edward announced their intent to marry for three weeks in a row, at Sunday service — a wedding "bann," as required by law. Rev. Hooper made the trip up from Bamford on a Thursday. The Moorcrofts escorted Meg down from the moors, about fifty strong. They formed a procession down the eastern side of the valley, and through the village, to the church. Meg was wearing a new gown — new to Edward, at least — with a full skirt and a garland of flowers in her hair. Everyone in the village was there as well, plus plenty of farm families; more than could be seated in the sanctuary — so people stood. The village blacksmith had presented them both with silver rings (made from some silver coins that Edward had provided), which was everything that the liturgy required. Bess had organized the village women to prepare a feast, which had to be eaten outdoors; the pub master provided a large keg of ale. Rev. Hooper was suitably brief in his remarks and had time to eat before saddling his donkey and heading homeward. Afterward, there was music, toasting, and dancing — everything that Edward's Puritan sensibilities told him to avoid. He refused to listen to his sensibilities; he thought of the stars and the moonlight on the moor. He looked at Meg, with the flowers in her hair, and her green eyes. Here, he was rooted. Here he would stand. God be praised. God willing, he would cultivate this garden.

The Moorcrofts had their own wedding tradition, which required another procession — back up the slope to the moor. Meg and Edward were carried up, which seemed precarious, amid singing, chanting, and the noise of clanging metal pots, and anything else that came to hand. Once they were delivered to Meg's cottage, the crowd stood outside, shouting, cheering, and singing ribald songs, for at least an hour. Edward was in a daze, or maybe drunk. By this time it was full dark. Suddenly, it got quiet. Edward walked to the door and peeked out.

"They're all gone, I guess," he reported.

"Then lock the door, and come hither," she said. "If thee cannot help me out of this gown, I'll have to tear it off."

"Tear it? Why tear it?"

"Because I intend to have my way with thee, drunk or sober," she smirked, "and I am not a patient woman! This gown can only hinder my purpose!"

Edward felt suddenly very sober, indeed. Well, sober enough to remember what he was about, at any rate . . .

Part 19: Armada

May, 1588: Harwich

Captain Billy Foxe was restless: in the kind of mood that would once have driven him to sea. Except in the present circumstance, he could not put to sea. He was also troubled with a brooding premonition that his next voyage would be his last — and yet this would be the one voyage that he could not refuse. He rattled around in his house, once his haven of contentment, content with nothing — until his wife ordered him to take a walk. He hung around the pubs until they told him to go home, and around the waterfront, looking for — what, exactly?

Harriet Foxe, now his wife, understood his discontent well enough, but she had learned not to trouble herself over things she could not control (and there were a great many such things, in her life). Her example was no help to the Captain. If anything, her condition — she was four months pregnant, and beginning to show it — made his distress more acute. If he survived long enough, he would be a father again, in more than name (a fact which served to remind him of the death of his first family). If he survived: if, if, if . . . If he could just get on with it, get past it, one way or another. It was the not knowing that tormented him, the waiting . . .

In mid-May, the orders came that he had both dreaded and longed for. "The fleet will assemble in Plymouth, just as last year," he informed Harriet. "They couldn't decide, for the longest time, whether to assemble the whole fleet in one place, or multiple places where the Spanish might appear. At least they have a plan! The *Queen* must sail tomorrow or the following day, at the latest."

Harriet nodded, trying not to show her worry. "God protect thee then, Captain, and come ye home, whatever else may happen." It was all she could think to say to him. Later, she said her goodbyes to Roger. "I'll be back, Mum, and I'll bring the Captain with me," he promised. Harriet nodded and smiled. But she knew very well what promises were worth when men went to sea.

Foxe's mood improved with the news. "We've loaded extra powder and shot," he said to Roger, who knew very well that it was so. "No soldiers, this time. We'll avoid grappling and pound those Spanish ships to splinters;

that's the best strategy. If we sink enough war galleons, the rest will flee, mark my words. No point in landing their army, if they have our fleet in their rear, cutting off their supplies." Roger nodded. Foxe had explained this to him countless times before. It remained to be seen, whether the other captains in the fleet would follow this strategy or prefer to fill their purses with prize money.

Roger had seen enough of sea battles to know that his stepfather was right; the raid on Cadiz had demonstrated that the English ships could inflict enormous loss on a Spanish fleet by avoiding boarding altogether, with minimal losses to themselves. This was what it would take to prevent the Spanish armies from reaching England. He hoped that the senior commanders understood this.

They reached Plymouth at the beginning of June and found the harbor full of ships — more than two hundred, it was said. Foxe was impressed: "Even if they bring three hundred ships, they'll have a hard time matching us," he said.

Word came the following week that the Spanish fleet had left Lisbon at the end of May: "Took two days for all of them to get out of the harbor," said the news. Foxe snorted, "That tells me that they're slow. The fleet can't go any faster than their slowest ship. Don't look for them here for three weeks, at the earliest."

Foxe's assessment was more accurate than he knew. The Admiral of the Spanish fleet, one Alonso Guzman, Duke of Medina-Sidonia, had been called into service at the last moment. The man intended for the task had died, only in February. Admiral Guzman was not an experienced seaman, and he knew it. The King of Spain gave him very specific orders, in part to prevent him from making a bad choice in the heat of battle. This lack of flexibility, appropriate perhaps for a soldier unaccustomed to naval tactics, would mean that unexpected opportunities would be bypassed, in favor of following a script. Getting his fleet out of Lisbon in two days was just the first hurdle in a long race. Once at sea, he assembled his ships in a tight formation, warships on the outside, transports protected inside. There were in fact, one hundred thirty ships under the Admiral's command: twenty war galleons, four Neapolitan galleasses and four galleys, and one hundred two armed merchantmen of various sizes. The galleons would bear the brunt of the fighting; the merchantmen were crammed with provisions for the 25,000 soldiers and sailors, as well as some for the 30,000-strong Spanish army that waited in the Netherlands to be ferried across the English Channel.

Speed would not be the Spanish advantage in the coming battles. They learned from the raid on Cadiz that the English ships would be faster and guessed that the English would prefer to stand off and bombard from a distance, rather than grapple and board. The armada's strength was precisely here — seventeen thousand soldiers, ready to board any English ship, and overwhelm its crew. A tight formation would make it difficult for the English to maneuver within it, without risk of grappling and boarding. The galleons would form a protective shell around the rest of the vessels. The Admiral's main responsibility was to bring his armada, intact, to a port in Flanders where the rest of the Spanish army could join his ships, then protect the troop transports as they crossed the English Channel and landed that army in England, somewhere close enough to London to fight a decisive battle on shore. Other considerations were of minor importance.

Less than a week out of Lisbon, the Duke of Medina-Sidonia got his first hard lesson in naval warfare. A fierce storm struck the armada from the west, and damaged so many ships that he was forced to put them into port for repairs. His galleys had proved unsuited to the weather of the Atlantic and could not continue. One of the war galleons was also permanently disabled. Repairs to the rest of the fleet took more than a month. His fleet was not ready for sea again until the 1st of July — and now he had one hundred twenty-four ships under his command.

In Plymouth, the English fleet waited. Billy Foxe was not a man who liked to wait under any circumstances; he liked it even less, in the present situation. "We'd be better off putting to sea, and catching them before they sight land," he complained to Roger.

More news from the south trickled in. The Spanish fleet was at Finisterre, at the northwest "corner" of Spain. They were fewer in number than expected but still had an advantage in firepower — more guns, of larger bore. "Doesn't matter, unless their gunners are accurate," said Foxe. He was itching for the fight, now. His conferences with the English admirals were not encouraging: "They don't see the advantage in striking first," he lamented, "They won't move until they know exactly where the Spanish are, and by the time they find out, it may be too late! They have agreed that we won't grapple with them, but they have ordered us to stand off at least two hundred yards. That's out of range of their biggest guns, but not close enough for ours to do the most damage. We should be closing to a hundred yards or less, if we hope to sink them!"

And so it went. Roger listened, but did not express opinions of his own — Foxe wasn't in a listening mood. Roger knew his stepfather well enough to realize that his bravado was largely a mask for the uncertainties that lay ahead. The prospect of not returning from battle, and never seeing the child that Harriet was carrying frightened him, no less than the possibility of a Spanish victory. The stakes were too high to do anything but fight, and he wanted the fight to be over.

On the evening of July 19, signal fires were spotted to the west — the Spanish fleet had appeared somewhere in that direction and was assumed to be moving eastward. Still, the English fleet did not move. Billy Foxe was beside himself. By the following evening, the Armada appeared off Plymouth, heading eastward. By now, the winds were onshore, and the tide was against them. The English were trapped in their harbor, helpless to do anything until the tide changed. Billy Foxe cursed the situation bitterly: "We could've put to sea this morning and been waiting for 'em. Now, we'll have to chase 'em!"

He was half right, again. The Armada could have bypassed them altogether, but hove to, for a council of war. Some of Guzman's captains wanted to attack the English fleet in Plymouth harbor and start the invasion from there. But Guzman had his orders and overruled them. As the tide turned, the English fleet made it out to sea. "We're downwind," Foxe complained, "we have to get behind them if we want the weather gauge. As soon as we do that, the way eastward is open to them." It took hours for the English to tack westward and re-assemble. By that time the Armada had passed further eastward.

Each vessel in the English fleet hung a lantern near the stern so that their location could be verified. "Without those, any ship could wander off on its own," explained Foxe. "Our job is to keep up with the lanterns in front of us and keep an eye out for any behind that may be lagging. We can't sail faster than the vessel in front of us without scattering all our firepower across the English Channel. Lucky for us, the Spanish have the same problem."

At four bells into the second watch, it began to get light in the east. Foxe summoned all the officers to the chart room. "Lads, I expect we'll be in the thick of it soon. We're to follow in formation. It's important that we keep our position, and attack only when ordered to. Our strategy is to avoid boarding at any cost. We'll stand off and let Mr. Benby's gunners smash them to splinters. There will be no stopping for prizes. If a Spanish ship is dead in the water, we will pass it by and go on to the next one. The whole point of this strategy is to disable so many Spanish warships, that there won't be enough left to protect their troop transports. Without that protection, the troop transports dare not try to land anywhere in England.”

“I have heard that we are outgunned,” said Reuben Cox.

“Aye, I have heard the same. But their biggest bores don’t have the range that ours do, and in Cadiz, we learned that they’re not very accurate. Also, it takes them a long time to reload. Some Spanish captains will fire only one broadside, then close to grapple and board. If we’re nimble, we can stand off until they fire their first volley, then swoop in close, and give them a broadside or two, before they can reload, and then slip away, out of range.”

“How close?”

“A hundred yards or less.”

“As close as seventy-five yards? Fifty?”

“If opportunity permits.”

There were murmurs from the men. Fifty yards was well within the range of the largest Spanish guns.

“Like I said, we’ll have to be nimble. If the wind is right, we’ll be firing at their hulls at the water line. If they heel over in a strong breeze, we’ll hole their hulls below the line, so they’ll flounder if they dare to tack or come about. If not, we’ll try to dismast them — leave them adrift upon the sea. Anything that delays that fleet, or disperses them, serves our purpose.”

At sunup, with the wind astern, the English moved to the attack. The Armada’s tight formation meant that the attackers were forced to engage them at the periphery, where the heaviest warships were located. The English avoided being boarded, but no ships were sunk on either side, after a day of fighting. “We have to get closer,” Foxe said, “two hundred yards is too far out to hole their hulls.”

The Spanish held their formation for the most part. They took some punishment from the faster English ships, and one of the Spanish galleons collided with a large carrack, disabling both, but the bulk of the Armada was not diverted from their course. That night, Vice Admiral Drake extinguished the lamp on his stern that was guiding the rest of his squadron and turned back to take possession of the damaged Spanish ships. Without the lamp to lead them, the rest of the squadron became dispersed and disorganized — the Armada escaped to the east.

Foxe was livid when he heard the news: “Curse that man, for choosing plunder over his duty!” was the mildest thing he had to say on the subject. At daybreak, Drake was back, but the hunt for the Armada had to start all over again. In the chartroom aboard the *Egyptian Queen,* Roger and Homer plotted the position of the English fleet, and speculated about where the Spanish might be.

"It's a chase now," said Foxe. "We're faster, but we have to keep the weather gauge. That means we have to be south and west of them when we find them."

"Unless the wind shifts," said Roger.

"Aye. Unless the wind shifts. We have to find them first, then maneuver to get upwind of them."

"If the wind turns to the north, and they tack to shoreward, what do we do, then?"

"We stand back, and try to lure them out, where we can attack them."

The pursuit continued through the night.

They did not sight the Armada before sunset the following day. Sometime in the night, the lookouts reported faint lights to the east, and by sunup, a great mass of sails could be seen ahead of them. The winds turned northerly, and the Spanish tacked toward the coastline, so that the English could not squeeze by upwind of them and thus acquire the weather gauge that their strategy required. As the English fleet formed to their south and west, it was the Armada's turn to attack. It became a disordered affair — the English avoided all attempts to grapple and board by superior speed and maneuver, but couldn't concentrate their fire on any single ship, to sink it. At the end of the day, the Armada continued on its slow and steady course.

In the chartroom, Roger and Homer speculated on where the Spanish might be headed. "They might land on the Isle of Wight," suggested Roger. "They could turn it into a fortress, just offshore."

Homer nodded. "If they do, we'll have to fight them in that narrow channel — less room for us to maneuver, more chances for them to grapple and board us. But it's a long way from London. It might be better to fight there than somewhere farther east."

In fact, some of Admiral Guzman's officers were recommending just that strategy. "Our losses have been small," they pointed out. "It doesn't seem likely that the English can break our formation. Men are getting sick from so long at sea. We could land and resupply. Let the English throw themselves against us. Once the reinforcements from France arrive, we'll cross to the main island, and march on London." Admiral Guzman overruled them. He had his orders.

In the event, The English caught up with the Armada just where Roger and Homer had guessed. Another day of fighting, without decisive result. The *Egyptian* Queen threw broadside after broadside at larger and slower vessels, and Foxe's tactics proved successful — wait for the Spaniard to fire a broadside, then swoop in and deliver their own at close range, and pull away, out of range, before the Spaniards could reload. The Spanish ships took more damage, but neither side lost a ship. From the Isle of Wight eastward, all the English ports were fortified. Admiral Guzman had no intention of seeing his fleet trapped between the English fleet and shore batteries. By July 27, his Armada was in France.

June 1588: Fecundity

Edward Chase was in the vestry, updating his registry of baptisms, weddings and funerals, when Benjamin banged on the door. "Father Chase! Meg says her time has come!"

It was news both welcomed and dreaded. He hastily closed the registry, locked the vestry door, and rushed home. The last few weeks had been a whirl of preparations for the arrival of this baby — and now, apparently it was on the way. He rushed into the rectory, and then to the hall chamber, where Meg was pacing around, panting a little.

"Shouldn't you be lying down?"

"Nay, not yet."

"What does the midwife say? Shall I fetch her?" his voice was pitched a little high . . .

"Edward, the midwife is already here. She says not yet."

"What can I do?"

"Nothing at all, unless thee calm thyself. I have sent Bess Clegg to fetch Mrs. Jackson. The three of us will manage this delivery. Thee should wait outside. I sent Benjamin to tell thee it has begun. I wished to see thee beforehand. Give me a kiss."

He embraced her, and kissed her, then she grunted, and her body tensed.

"What's wrong?

"Nothing is wrong. It is called 'labor', and that is what it is. Now leave me to it."

Reluctantly, he stepped outside. Moments later, Bess was back with Mrs. Jackson, and a lot of linens. "Shoo now, Father. This is women's work," said Bess. "Why don't you go find Jack? Look for him down at the pub."

Jack wouldn't be at the pub; Edward had assigned him another job just this morning. He was supposed to be mending the fence around the churchyard — any sheep they put in there always seemed to find a way out — and into someone's vegetable garden. Especially that lamb that the children insisted on calling Baby Jesus — though he wasn't a 'baby' anymore: he was a bold and energetic young ram now, always challenging older sheep, butting heads with the old rams, generally creating mischief. He especially enjoyed defying David, the sheepdog. Separating him from the rest of the flock seemed necessary, and the grass in the churchyard needed to be trimmed, so isolating him there seemed like a sensible plan. He turned out to be a master of escape. The children at school had an explanation: "The graveyard can't hold Baby Jesus," they said, "the gospel says so!"

Jack Clegg was not in the churchyard. Neither was Baby Jesus. Edward sighed. The pub, then.

He found both of them in the pub. "Baby Jesus followed me in here," explained Jack. "Thought it best I keep track of 'im — until the fence is mended."

Several men were gathered around the sheep, some of them appeared to be strangers — passing through, he supposed. They were in discussion of some matter — a wager was involved, apparently. A wager involving Baby Jesus.

"I'm not sayin' he can't make the jump, I'm sayin' he won't jump on command, and if he does, he won't stay up there until Jack commands him to get down. A good dog could make him do just about anything, but sheep just don't obey people like they do dogs — and this one doesn't take orders from dogs either, or so I'm told."

Edward supposed he should say something about taking the Lord's name in vain, especially in a pub, and then compounding the offense with gambling — but his mind was on Meg and the baby. He sat down with a sigh and ordered an ale.

While he nursed his drink, he eavesdropped on the conversation. Apparently, Jack had been bragging about his rapport with Baby Jesus and claimed that the sheep would leap on top of a table in the pub, and stay there until Jack told him to get down. The barkeep should have objected to the prospect of a farm animal on top of one of his tables, but his curiosity had gotten the best of him.

The stakes had been agreed, and Jack stood up and addressed the sheep: "Now, Jesus, I only brought ye here with the understanding that ye'd mind yer manners. There'll be no leaping upon tables, else I'll never bring ye back here, again. Do ye follow?"

Baby Jesus looked at him and flared his nostrils. *He's looking for some tidbit, or other,* thought Edward, *Jack has been training him, for some purpose, somehow . . .*

"We have an understanding, then. That's fine!" said Jack and then slapped the top of the table. Jesus launched himself into the air, and landed on the tabletop, still looking at Jack, his nostrils flaring. The other men groaned and shook their heads.

"He still has to stay there, until Jack orders him down," said one man. "Looks to me like he's getting fidgety."

"He's just thirsty," said Jack. He held his tankard of ale in the sheep's face, and the sheep thrust his nose in. "There, there, that's enough."

"I agree with ye, Sir. The wager specified that the sheep must remain on the table, and only get down upon my command. We can sit round the table if ye like, for a few minutes, just to prove my point."

"Agreed," said the stranger. "In the meantime, if he gets down from the table at anyone else's command, you lose the wager, correct?"

Jack's eyes narrowed a bit. "Aye, that seems fair."

The men sat down. The sheep turned around on the tabletop, sniffing. *Hoping for more of that ale,* thought Edward.

The men began making calling noises, or saying things to the sheep that they supposed would induce him to get down — anything from "Here sheep!" to "Baaaa," to "Down, sheep, down!" Baby Jesus stared at each of them in turn but remained on the table.

After several minutes, Jack interrupted them. "The sheep has other places to be, Lads. If ye'll be silent, I'll show you the command that he obeys." They didn't look happy about the suggestion, but it would be unfair not to let him try.

Jack stood and walked toward the door. He stopped, turned to the table, and said, "Oats!" Baby Jesus leapt off the table and trotted to his side. The men groaned but paid up. *I could have gotten him to come, with "Oats,"* Edward thought to himself.

"Father, I have to get back to work now," said Jack.

"I'll come with you," said Edward. Baby Jesus followed them back to the churchyard.

"I think he must be lonely," said Jack.

"Who?"

"Why the sheep Father, the sheep. Sheep are accustomed to company. He'd be more likely to stay if he had a companion."

Jack was probably right, Edward realized. Should have thought of that himself. Sure enough, as long as Jack and Edward were in the churchyard, the sheep browsed on everything in sight. If they stepped outside, even to repair a gap in the wall, the sheep began to bleat and scrambled up on top of the wall so he could see them.

"Jack, Meg is in labor."

"Ah, that explains yer visit to the pub, then."

"It also means that I need someone to go up above the edges and feed and water our animals. I've been doing it for the last month or so, but I don't want to be that far away when the baby comes."

"Right, you are, Father. "I'll ride Bruce up there and take care of 'em."

"Take some scraps for the dog with you. He knows how to fetch the sheep into the pen for the night."

"I'm ahead of ye, Father. Bess has already put something aside for the dog. Don't have anything for the ravens, though."

"The ravens will fend for themselves."

"Aye. One way or another."

After Jack left, Edward worked on the churchyard wall, looking for gaps that Baby Jesus might slip through, or more likely, places where a fallen stone could provide him with a platform from which to vault to the top of it. He realized he was hungry — he had missed his supper — then he realized that Bess had her hands too full to cook a dinner. He could eat in the pub. First, he opened the gate to the churchyard and let Baby Jesus out. He said, "Oats!" once, and the sheep followed him back to the shed behind the rectory. He made sure to feed him a handful, in addition to some hay, as he locked him inside. He was about to head into the village when he was called from the house. It was Bess. "It's time for you to come in now."

He felt a little dazed. "So soon? Is it over so soon?"

"It's never over 'soon' enough. This delivery was 'sooner' than most. Come in and meet your offspring."

Meg was in the bed, sitting up, smiling. Looking tired, but triumphant, as well she might. "Here," said Bess, "hold this one."

This one. This tiny one, squinting, puckering — tiny face, tiny hands. He gazed at his . . . daughter or son, didn't matter . . .

"Here. Take the other."

"Other?"

"You're the father of twins, one boy, one girl. Please try to keep up, Father."

Meg giggled. She was beaming. Edward looked for a place to sit down, "Two babes?"

"Fecundity," said Bess. "Don't say I didn't warn you."

Edward sat on the edge of the bed with a bundle in each arm. He looked at Meg and struggled for words. "Was it hard?"

She nodded. "Hard as anything I've ever done. Now comes the harder part."

"The harder part?"

"Aye. I reckon your son will be like his father and your daughter like me. Or maybe the other way 'round. Can you imagine a family of four, like the two of us?" She chuckled.

He nodded. "I can. Are you hungry? I'll see about some dinner." He walked into the sitting room and called for Bess — no answer. The door was open, perhaps she was outside. He stepped out the front door into the fading afternoon, a babe cradled in each arm. It was a beautiful day.

There was a fluttering sound just overhead. A raven settled on the edge of the roof, looking at him. "Johnny?"

The raven answered with a hoarse croak followed by a long, loud, rasping series of caws. And then there were more ravens, circling down from above the edges, settling on the ground about the threshold of the front door.

"Take a good look, Lads," Edward said, "your mistress has done a great deed today."

One by one, their inspection complete, the Lads took wing. Bess saw them, as she came up the street. "Father, are you talking to the ravens now? Those babes should be kept safe inside. People will think you're dabbling in sorcery, talking to animals, like that!"

Edward shook his head. "It isn't sorcery unless the animals talk back." He turned back into the house and Bess closed the door.

July 28, 1588: Gravelines

he Armada took refuge off Calais — across the Dover strait, facing England at the narrowest point of the English Channel. The harbor at Calais was controlled by French forces unsympathetic to the Spanish cause, so they hove to just offshore, in their tight defensive formation. The waters nearest the shore were shallow and full of shoals — and controlled by scores of smaller Dutch gunboats, called "flyboats." To make matters worse for the Armada, the army that was supposed to meet them in France was nowhere to be seen. The plan had been to ferry the troops to their rendezvous with the Armada in unarmed barges. But the barges were not ready yet, and the shallow waters between Calais and the army were under the control of the Dutch flyboats.

"We've got 'em bottled up," Foxe said with satisfaction. "Word is that the Dutch flyboats are blocking the Spanish troop transports from joining their fleet here. All we need is the right wind, to fall upon them and disperse them."

Other facts that Foxe was unaware of also boded ill for Admiral Guzman. The 30,000 soldiers that were supposed to be awaiting him were fewer than promised — 13,000 or more had died or deserted over the last few months, mostly from disease. The Spanish army, if it ever reached England, would not be as strong as planned. Calais was safe enough for his fleet as long as his shield of galleons could protect the rest, but he had only eighteen such ships left. If every one of his galleons went head-to-head with an English one, it still might not be possible to get his transports across the channel, without crippling losses of men and material. He needed a decisive battle with the English fleet — one that would sweep them from the channel. But his orders were clear — he had to wait until the rest of his army was ready to embark before venturing westward.

Meantime, the provisions on board his vessels were beginning to run low — the plan had always assumed that the voyage would be a fairly short one and that he would be able to resupply in France. Neither assumption proved true. If the rest of the army arrived in a week, and if he could get them across the channel without major losses, they might still be on the brink of starvation. Perhaps they could live off the land, in England. Perhaps the English Catholics would rise in rebellion and welcome the army as liberators. Any chance of success now depended on these sorts of "perhapses."

As night fell on the evening of July 27, the Admiral conferred with his officers. They suggested attacking the Dutch flyboats with his own smaller vessels, to clear the way for the troop barges. Guzman hesitated — if too many of his own vessels, even the smaller ones, ran aground or were captured, he wouldn't have enough ships to protect the troop transports when it was time to cross the channel — galleons alone could not do the job. He deferred a decision — the troops weren't ready to move yet, anyway.

At midnight the lookouts reported some small vessels approaching, riding the wind toward the Armada. Suddenly, flames appeared — which lit up the ships in the dark. The English had launched fireships, or "hellburners" — eight of them, as it turned out. Small boats were launched to tow them out of the path of the Armada, but six of the fireships passed through into the tight formation. Spanish captains, fearing to lose their ships, broke formation and fled out to sea. In their haste, many of them simply cut their anchor cables. A southwest wind pushed them miles up the coast, into the North Sea. There was no way to return to Calais in the face of that wind, especially given the fact that the English and Dutch fleets stood in their way — with the weather gauge.

The battle began at dawn, in sight of the French town of Gravelines. The Armada organized itself as best it could, facing a westerly wind with the sandy beaches of the French coast and treacherous shallows behind them, and the English in front. The Dutch flyboats, familiar with the locations of the shoals near shore, harassed them from the flanks.

Billy Foxe was in a bellicose mood: "This is the battle we've been waiting for," he told Roger and Homer. We either scatter 'em, or drive 'em aground on the shoals and beaches. Either way, we win!"

To his officers, Foxe announced his tactics: "We have to get closer. Fifty yards, or less. With our shallow draft, we can even get behind them and attack them from the rear. I need sharp lookouts in the rigging to spot the sandbars, and I need eyes at bow, amidships, and stern, to watch their galleys and flyboats. Once we are in the midst of them, I expect they'll try to box us in so they can board us, even as we fire at them. If we have any shot and powder left at the end of the day, I'll take it as a sign that we haven't been doing our duty."

It unfolded much as Foxe expected. The Spanish tried to use the speed of their Venetian galleasses to harry the English gunships and fend them away from the troopships and cargo vessels. That worked, only as long as the galleasses stayed afloat and mobile: the *Egyptian Queen* went head-to-head with one of them. The galleass was quicker, with its banks of rowers, until a broadside from the *Queen* found the rowing benches on the port side. Without a full complement of rowers, the galleass was floundering. "A shame to kill so many of those oarsmen," Foxe commented, "They're slaves — didn't choose this battle. Some of them are probably Englishmen."

The galleass had plenty of guns of her own, but they had to be of smaller caliber, because they were mounted on the deck above the oarsmen. The wind was picking up, and the gunners had a hard time finding their targets. A second galleass approached the *Queen,* as if to ram her from the opposite side. Foxe ordered the *Queen* "Hard to starboard!" to bring her to a course parallel to the second galleass, just barely. Volleys from both the galleasses passed across the quarterdeck. There was a strange *pong* sound overhead, and Roger felt the lash of a mainmast stay across his back. Looking up he saw that several stays on the upper half of the mainmast had been severed — lucky shots, those — and the mast itself was beginning to lean toward the bow, with the wind behind it. "Captain! We're about to be dismasted!" he cried.

Foxe glanced up, and then at the galleasses. Nothing for it, but to avoid being rammed, at any cost. "Clear the deck!" he shouted, and then, "Mr. Benby! Let me hear those ladies sing!" With that, the *Queen* completed her turn — and the main mast leaned forward with a groan until it snapped, not twenty feet above the deck; the top of the mast, with all its sails and rigging, hung up on the foremast, or landed on the foredeck. It was not enough to help the galleass on their starboard side — she was out of position to ram and her oars prevented her from getting near enough to grapple. Before she could make any adjustment, the *Queen* was sliding by, broken mast and all. And then the "ladies" spoke — a devastating broadside, at a distance of only twenty yards. Smoke and splinters were all that Roger could see of the galleass, for a moment, and then flames.

By now, the *Queen* was well away from both galleasses, though losing speed, because only the foremast and mizzen were still upright. The two galleasses were in no condition to pursue. There were injured seamen among and under the rigging on the deck; there could have been more but for Foxe's warning. The crew cut away the canvas and rigging as best they could and threw it overboard. They salvaged the colors and ran them up the mizzenmast. The *Queen* continued to drift eastward, toward the French shoreline.

Foxe ordered a turn to port, so that they were paralleling the coast. The water was shallower here, and treacherous. But the large Spanish galleons dared not approach; the *Queen* had a respite, time to get herself in order. With the decks cleared, she was underway again. Homer reported that the wind was shifting — "Nearly due south, now," he said, "and it's freshening."

So it was. The *Queen* was slower now, with nearly half her sails overboard, but the rising wind made up for some of the loss. "We'll have to chase something more our speed," declared Foxe. There were plenty to choose from. The Armada, with a more southerly wind, had an escape path due north, away from the coastline. They took it. The galleons were still trying to shield the slower cargo vessels, and they were continuously engaged with their English pursuers. Foxe and the *Queen* joined the chase. It was a running fight, now.

It did not end when night fell. The night and the rising storm made for poor visibility, but the Spanish plunged forward, and the English followed. In the morning, Homer was able to get a sighting of the sun before the clouds closed in. "We're about sixty miles north of Gravelines," he guessed, "Harwich is almost due west. We could make Harwich by night maybe, with luck." Roger looked hopefully at Foxe. Surely the damage they had taken would justify a withdrawal from the battle? Foxe simply glared and shook his head. "Nay, we finish this — one way or another."

Foxe demanded an inventory of the ship's ammunition. "Enough powder and shot for three broadsides on each side, no more," he was told. "Then we'll continue the pursuit until we have no more supplies, or until there are no more Spanish ships in the North Sea," Foxe said grimly. Roger looked at Reuben Cox, who just shrugged.

They spotted a slow-moving Spanish carrack later that following morning, and Foxe was determined to engage her. This was not as easy as it should have been — the *Queen* no longer had the speed to simply run up on her, fire a volley, and scoot away. They rigged a large spar near the top of the broken mainmast, and lashed some spare canvas to it: it gave them just enough headway to close with the carrack, gradually.

As they approached from astern they could see that the carrack had taken a beating, but she was still making headway. And she had some guns at her stern, as well. Puffs of smoke appeared, followed by the whirr of cannonballs passing overhead.

"We'll hang off her port quarter," said Foxe, "until we're close enough to cross her stern to the starboard side. That way, we can bring a broadside to bear on her rudder as we cross. Once we're on her starboard quarter, we'll catch up, then cross back the other way and give her another broadside."

Roger nodded. Of course, that tactic would expose the broad side of the *Queen* to the carrack's stern guns, at close range. Seemed risky . . .

The first pass went well enough. The *Queen* crossed the carrack's stern at less than fifty yards, and unleashed a broadside that sent splinters and smoke flying. They reached the starboard quarter before the gunners on the carrack's stern had time to reload. From there, it became trickier. The turn to starboard had increased the distance between the ships, and it took several minutes to get up to speed again. Foxe kept the *Queen* to starboard of the carrack, so that she was not in the line of fire from the stern guns.

The captain of the carrack recognized what Foxe was trying to do, and changed course, cutting to starboard to "cross the T," and bring her broadside batteries to bear on the *Queen's* bow. Foxe had to turn back to port to stay out of reach. The carrack, slow as she was, was at least as agile as the *Queen* without her mainmast. As the two ships circled, Foxe had a decision to make. If he kept on his present course, he would have to yield the weather gauge to the Spaniard. He broke off and turned back to starboard. This put the *Queen* improbably ahead of the carrack, heading north while the carrack, completing her turn, was heading southward — that is, until she was headed into the wind, which brought her nearly to a dead stop. The *Queen* tacked across the carrack's stern to deliver another broadside.

The carrack's gunners were ready this time, and they had the range. The *Queen* shuddered as several large cannonballs struck her amidships and astern. One of them tore across the quarterdeck and killed Reuben Cox immediately. Captain Billy Foxe and the helmsman went down, too. Roger was knocked down by the blast and stunned, for a moment. He found his footing and knelt beside his stepfather. "The tiller," grunted Foxe, "Take the tiller!"

Roger saw that the whipstaff was wobbling on its own as the ship, rudderless, turned in the wind. He seized the whipstaff and surveyed their position. The carrack was still upwind, but turning, preparing to deliver a broadside against the *Queen's* stern. Roger pulled the whipstaff to turn to starboard, trying to maintain a position off the carrack's quarter, and put some distance between the two ships. He realized that soon he would be sailing directly into the wind and be dead in the water. Back to port, then.

Get the wind behind him, get away from those enormous guns on the carrack.

In a few minutes, the distance between the ships was more than two hundred yards. Roger breathed a sigh of relief. The carrack fired a last volley, but the cannon balls missed the *Queen*. A seaman appeared and took the whipstaff. Roger climbed to the poop deck, and looked astern. The carrack was not trying to follow; in fact it was hard to tell what she was trying to do — drifting, or so it appeared. Smoke was pouring from below her decks. Perhaps that last broadside had so damaged her rudder that she could not maneuver at all . . .

Then he remembered the Captain. He rushed to where Foxe still lay on the quarterdeck; his left leg was bleeding and appeared to be mangled. Homer knelt beside him. Foxe himself was lucid. "Where's the carrack?" he demanded.

"Three hundred yards astern. Appears to be adrift. On fire, as well."

"Good Lad. We're well rid of her. "If it's as bad as ye say, she'll run aground before nightfall. What's our damage?"

"Reuben is dead, the helmsman, too, I think. No fires. Most of the crew is still with us."

"Aye," Foxe nodded. "If Reuben's gone, ye're the first mate, now. Get us home, lad."

"First mate? There are plenty of other officers with more seniority than me."

"True enough," Foxe's voice was getting weak, "but you'll need those men at their stations, if the *Queen* is going to make it home. You and Homer can set a course. Stay out of trouble . . ."

Foxe was unconscious. "Let's get him into his cabin," said Roger.

"Nay," said Homer, "I'll get others to do that. You need to be on deck, now. You're in command of this vessel."

Roger nodded. In command. The crew had already taken Reuben's body below and were clearing the decks of debris. The damage amidships appeared manageable. Several seamen were injured by flying debris, but the greatest losses had been on the quarter deck.

Or so it seemed until the Boatswain reported. "Took a look in the bilges, where the mainmast is stepped," he said. "Found a crack, which can only get worse."

"A crack in the bottom of the mast?"

"Nay. A crack in the keel. We're alright for now, but a grounding or even a storm with strong waves will make things worse."

"And if the crack gets worse?"

"Then this ship will start coming apart."

Roger's heart sank. He called a meeting of the officers. They all took his promotion to First Mate matter-of-factly, as if he was the only logical choice. He laid out the situation. "Based on what the Boatswain says, I'm not sure we can make it back to Harwich, or any English port. What about Holland?"

"Holland is closer," Homer agreed, "though the Sea Beggars will loot this ship if they get the chance — with a broken keel, she's a salvage job, not an English warship."

"In that case, don't tell them about the keel. Aren't there shipyards in Amsterdam that could make the *Queen* seaworthy, again?"

Homer nodded. "They could if someone's paying."

"Then I think Amsterdam is our destination. I'm hoping we could find a surgeon there who can mend our captain, as well."

There were nods and murmurs from the officers. Amsterdam was their destination. "Any idea of our position?" he asked Homer.

"Haven't seen the sun in some time, though it will be getting dark soon. England is west, Holland is east. Once we get close enough to shore, we can try to fix our position with landmarks."

"In the dark?"

Homer shook his head. "The whole coast up here is mostly sand dunes and beaches — no high ground, hardly any villages, even. All the towns are behind the dunes — hard to see from seaward; there won't be many lights at night. We need to find the coast, then sail parallel to it until we spot a harbor."

"Due east then, until we spy land. Weather permitting."

Homer nodded. "Weather permitting."

The wind was westerly now and getting stronger. "Looks like a storm is brewing," observed Homer, as if everyone on board didn't know it.

Part 20: Amsterdam

July 30, 1588: Wyck op Zee

The *Queen* ran before the wind, but Roger thought he could detect a change in her movement — a little flexing, fore to aft, perhaps, as the rollers from her stern passed her by, first lifting, then dropping her. The wind was tearing the foam off the breakers now, spraying the deck with every gust. It was nearly dusk when the lookout on the mizzenmast spotted the shore. Half an hour later, Roger could see it for himself — a long expanse of beaches with the surf crashing white against them, backed by sand dunes. Roger ordered a turn to port, intending to follow the coast north and east, but the *Queen* protested, with strange creaks and groans, at being asked to take the rising waves at an angle that twisted her one direction then another.

The Boatswain rushed on deck. "She can't take much more of this," he shouted. "Find another heading!"

There were only two headings to choose — with the wind, or against it. Either one would drive her onto a sandbar, or all the way to the beach. Roger opted to ride the wind, hoping for enough steerage to choose where she landed. He ordered everything battened down, and everyone below decks. "Mr. Benby! Secure your guns! Fetch all our food stores up from the orlop deck — we're going to be getting wet!" He left the lookout atop the mizzen mast, in hopes of spotting a sandbar in the waning light, and another at the bow. Then he turned the *Egyptian Queen* directly shoreward, into the gathering dark.

The lookout on the mizzen did his job; he spotted a sand bar off the port side and directed the *Queen* to deeper water to starboard, though the hull groaned and creaked in protest. Once past the sandbar, Roger turned back to hit the beach at a slight angle, with the wind directly astern. Waves seemed to be rolling in every direction, toward shore, away, and even across it. He thought of anchoring here — between the sandbar and the beach — but the moaning from the hull told him that the waves might simply pull the ship apart if she stayed where she was. There was a shudder, then a cracking sound, as the *Queen* struck another sandbar and then slid over it, buoyed by another wave astern.

"We're taking on water!" came a cry from below. Nothing to do now, but find the beach and get everyone off, if he could. "Find some men to mind our wounded," Roger shouted at Homer. Homer rushed below and returned with half a dozen seamen.

And then they hit the beach. There was a shuddering, and then a sliding feel, as the *Queen* slid upward onto the sand. When the waves receded, her bow was high and momentarily, dry. A second, higher wave lifted her with a cracking sound and pushed her farther up the beach. "Mr. Benby!" he called out. Benby was at the quarterdeck in moments. "We could get pounded to pieces, here. Can we get a crew on the beach and use our kedge anchors to haul her up above the surf line?"

Benby smiled and saluted, "Aye, Captain!" When the waves receded, the men jumped off the bow and ran up the beach. They set the anchors and rigged the tackle. With each wave that lifted the *Queen* even a little, they pulled her a little bit higher. Soon, they had her high enough up that only the occasional large wave reached her at all. She was also nearly upright, owing to her broad beam and shallow keel. It was full dark, now. They lit some lanterns, and the men built a fire on the beach with some of the damaged wood from the ship. As far as Roger could tell, everyone had survived their rough landing.

He sent a few men up on the dunes, to see if they could spot any sign of human habitation. They reported some lights, well inland, just to the north — a village, no doubt. They would check at daylight — not sure if this part of Holland was under the control of the Dutch or the Spanish.

The orlop deck had been flooded, but the food supplies and the powder magazines were dry. They salvaged enough canvas from the hold to rig some shelter from the intermittent showers. Getting Captain Foxe and the other wounded ashore took some effort. The extent of Foxe's wounds was apparent, now. He was in and out of consciousness, and in pain. "We need to get him to a surgeon," said Roger.

Homer nodded. "In the morning we'll find a village, Spaniards or no Spaniards, and get him some help."

By daybreak, help had found them. The winds and rain had passed. People came walking down the beach from the direction of the village, to look at the wreck. (And no doubt to scavenge anything that they could, Roger supposed). One of the visitors spoke enough English to inform them that the village was called "Wyck op Zee," and was firmly part of the Dutch Republic. They had no doctor, but there was one in the town of

Beverwijk, about three miles inland. It was also possible to travel from Beverwijk to Amsterdam, another twelve or so miles beyond.

"Ahoy, the *Egyptian Queen!*" The voice came from across the water to the west. A Dutch vessel floated there. Apparently, someone aboard her recognized the *Queen*, even in her battered state. A longboat put out from the Dutchman and landed nearby. Out stepped a familiar-looking figure. It's Piet! Piet Vandoorn!" All the officers of the *Queen* recognized him and greeted him warmly.

"How came you here?" asked Homer.

"That is a question I should be asking you," Piet replied.

"Been fighting the Spanish. Gave better than we took."

Vandoorn nodded. "So I've heard. We saw some action, too. Took a prize, and sank another one. Where's the Captain?"

"It's Roger, for now," Homer nodded in Roger's direction. "Captain Foxe is wounded. Reuben Cox is dead."

Vandoorn raised an eyebrow, then said to Roger, "Looks as though you got your crew ashore. That's something."

"Aye," said Homer, "got 'em ashore with a broken keel, in a gale, past sandbars and shoals, in the dark. *That's* something."

Vandoorn extended his hand to Roger. "Congratulations, 'Captain'. I didn't mean to insult you."

"No insult taken," said Roger. "I've got two seriously wounded men who need a surgeon, the best I can find, and soon. I'm glad you found us, by the way, rather than some Spanish ship. Can you help me get a doctor for these men?"

Vandoorn nodded. "Straight to the point. I like that. Put together a shore party and carry the wounded to Wyck op Zee. There's a road from there to the town of Beverwijk. You can hire a boat from there to Amsterdam — takes a few hours. Anything is possible in Holland if you have enough money. I assume you have money aboard?"

"Aye, though that is hardly your concern."

"Oh, but it is my concern," said Vandoorn. "If, as you say, the *Egyptian Queen* has a broken keel, there's no way she'll get off this beach without help. Help costs money. That's the Dutch way."

"Thank you for your helpful advice," said Roger. "I'll set about finding that doctor." With that, he summoned the officers to the map room. "I have to get the Captain to Amsterdam," he told them. "I need Paolo and Homer to go with me, in addition to the party that will carry Captain Foxe and any other injured men. Mr. Benby, you will be in command, while I am gone. Piet Vandoorn is an old friend, but I don't propose to let him take possession of this ship, or anything on it, without our consent. And that consent will require money — something that Piet understands very well, I think."

Benby smiled and nodded. "We've provisions enough to last for two weeks, and weapons enough to stake our claim. I can't promise that all the crewmen will still be here when you get back, though."

"Paolo will take the payroll chest and his ledgers with him," said Roger. "You can tell the men that we will pay them off when we know how soon Captain Foxe will recover. I have a hunch that the *Egyptian Queen* has finished her last voyage, but there's no reason to let the Sea Beggars have her again unless they want to pay."

They picked six men to carry Foxe's litter, and six more for another wounded seaman with a broken leg, plus two more, just for extra security. Paolo brought his ledgers and the payroll, Homer bundled up all the charts. Two of the men carried arquebuses, the rest had pistols and cutlasses.

Walking on the beach was strenuous, but once they got over the dunes, the land was flat, and the footing sound. It was all farms behind the dunes, and their guide got them to the village easily enough. From there, the road to Beverwijk was plain enough to follow. Beverwijk was situated at the edge of a large, shallow estuary called the "Ij." Amsterdam was on the same estuary, so it was a fairly direct path to their destination. They hired a shallow-drafted canal boat for the next leg of their journey.

Once afloat, Roger could give more attention to Captain Foxe. He had a fever and was in and out of consciousness. The other man was more alert — but complained of a headache.

By midmorning, Amsterdam was in sight. It was a fortified city but dissected by a series of concentric canals — connected here and there by short cross channels. Few places in Amsterdam could not be reached by boat. They needed a guide. They found someone who spoke English.

"I'm looking for a doctor," Roger declared. "A Dr. Lopez. Antonio Lopez. Have you heard of him?"

"Ah. In Jodenbuurt. He is a Jew, ja?"

Roger hesitated. "Is there any other Dr. Antonio Lopez?"

The guide shook his head.

"Then he must be the one. How can I find him?"

"Like I said, in Jodenbuurt. Anyone there will know him."

Roger turned to the Captain of the canal boat. "How do I get to this 'Jodenbuurt'?

"It's not far. I'll take you."

The sight of seventeen armed men carrying two stretchers attracted some attention on the streets of the city. They drew up in front of a large house, on a prosperous-looking street. Roger knocked at the door. A servant answered and eyed the group of men in the street warily.

"Is Dr. Lopez in?" asked Roger.

The servant hesitated. "Who is calling?"

"Please tell the doctor that Captain Billy Foxe is in need of his care."

The servant withdrew inside. Moments later, Dr. Lopez appeared at the door. "Where is Captain Foxe?"

"He is here," said Roger, and gestured to the litter where Foxe lay. "Bring him in," said the doctor. Antonio Lopez looked much as Roger remembered him — a little heavier, perhaps, with a small skullcap on his head. He led them into a large room with a low table. "This is my — how do you say — surgery," said Lopez. He said something to Homer in Spanish.

"The doctor thanks you all for bringing these patients to him," said Homer, "but asks that you wait outside; he needs room to work."

The seamen were shown outside; Roger, Homer, and Paolo stayed in the surgery. Dr. Lopez cut away the bloody bandages that Foxe's leg was wrapped in. Foxe stirred, and moaned a few times, while Lopez probed and poked at his leg. Lopez straightened and spoke to Homer in Spanish: "He says that the damage is too great to repair, that removal of the lower leg is the only course of action."

"But he salvaged that soldier's leg back in Cartagena, didn't he? Cooper was his name, I think."

At the mention of the name "Cooper," Lopez nodded and looked intently at Roger. Then he spoke to Homer again: "He says he recognizes you now, as the cabin boy. He says you've changed. He also says that this case is different — Cooper's leg still had the bones intact. The Captain's leg is shattered, and missing several pieces of the bone that once was there. He says that someone did a good job of binding up the Captain's wounds, but there is no way to save the leg if the bone is missing. He says that the Captain is likely to recover if he amputates today."

Roger realized that both Homer and Paolo were looking at him as if the decision were his. Of course, they were; he was acting Captain and next of kin, more or less. He took a breath. "If there truly is no choice, then saving the Captain's life is better than nothing. What about the other man?"

Homer translated, and Lopez nodded. He turned to the other seaman and inspected the leg. "He says that the bone can be set, and the man should recover. He will do that first, so that the rest of us can then leave the surgery, to let him treat the Captain without being disturbed."

Lopez gave the seaman something to drink. "Laudanum," explained Homer, "helps with the pain." Shortly, the seaman began to look drowsy. Lopez had Homer and Roger hold the man's arms, while he set the broken bone back in place, then bandaged and splinted it. Lopez spoke to Homer as he worked.

"This man should keep the splint on for four weeks," said Homer. "After that, he should not walk without a crutch for another four weeks. From then on, he should be able to walk unassisted. His companions should carry him to wherever he is lodging."

Back to the ship then, Roger decided. He went to the front door where the rest of the party was waiting and summoned two men to fetch the seaman out. Paolo joined him. "I have some business to attend to — on behalf of our investors," said Paolo.

"Business?"

"Aye. The Rich family has an agent here in Amsterdam. I need to inform them about the condition of the *Egyptian Queen*. It is their right, as owners, to determine how to dispose of her."

Of course. Always the investor's interests thought Roger. "I suppose you'll be taking the payroll with you?"

"I can't really let it out of my sight."

Then take two men with you — those two, with the arquebuses. Can't be too careful."

Paolo nodded. "Yes, a prudent policy."

"Before you go," said Roger, "I need to send this man" — he nodded to the seaman with the broken leg — "back to the ship, with the rest of the crew. They'll need some money to hire a boat back to Beverwijk."

"I think we can manage that," said Paolo, "also, all these men should eat, I think. Appoint one of them to lead the rest back to the ship — I'll give him enough to get them all a meal somewhere in the city before they return." With that, he stepped back inside Lopez's house.

Roger explained to the rest of the men that they would be returning to the *Queen* that afternoon, but that they would eat first. They were pleased with the plan. Roger selected a man he thought trustworthy and made sure that all the men in the party knew that he was carrying the money for their meals and transportation, and how much money there was. "Don't spend it all on ale," he said, "or you'll have to walk all the way back."

Several men chuckled. Roger hoped that they took his message to heart. The last thing he needed right now was to find out that some of his crew was in a Dutch jail for brawling in a pub.

Paolo and his two companions left, in a different direction than the returnees. Roger turned and entered the house; a servant directed him to a sitting room and offered him some refreshment.

It was more than half an hour before another servant summoned him to Dr. Lopez's surgery. Captain Foxe was still lying on the table, asleep. Lopez spoke at some length, and Homer translated: "The Captain is sleeping now, the laudanum makes him drowsy and eases the pain. He has some fever, which the doctor believes will subside in a day or two. If that happens, the Captain will recover. He will need a wooden leg — there are several men in this city who specialize in these things and do excellent work. It will be a month or more until the Captain has healed enough to begin wearing his new leg. Once he has learned to walk again, he can return home. Someone will need to stay with him here in Amsterdam, until then."

"That would be me, I suppose," said Roger. "I can stay, also," said Homer. "We can find lodging nearby. The Captain will stay here, until his fever breaks. What of Paolo?"

"He had some business in the city. I expect he'll meet us here when he's finished. I sent two men with Paolo since he's carrying the payroll. The rest I sent back to the ship, with a little money for their supper and the boat fare back to Beverwijk."

"You should sup with me, then," said Lopez.

It turned out that Dr. Lopez had a large family — a wife, a mother-in-law, and four children. His house had a separate dining room, with a large table. Dr. Lopez stood and blessed the meal in some language that Roger did not recognize — Portuguese, maybe? The meal was served on silver platters or serving dishes; the utensils were also silver; the plates were colorfully decorated china. Roger had never eaten like this in his life. Servants brought the food to him — no passing of platters or serving bowls. The meal was served in courses, beginning with a chicken soup, then some roasted vegetables — peas and carrots, something called "aardappel"- followed by roast lamb. The bread was white — something Roger had heard of, but never tasted. Several varieties of cheese were offered. The "aardappel" reminded him of the *patatas he* had eaten on board the *Queen*, though this was seasoned, and coated in melted butter. There was pie for dessert.

Roger was stuffed. Dr Lopez announced that it was time to check on his patient. In the surgery, Captain Foxe was groggy but awake. The fever seemed to have abated, some. He recognized Roger and Homer. "Tell me what has happened," he demanded. "Where is the *Queen* ?"

"Captain, I am sorry to report that we are shipwrecked. Run aground on the Dutch coast." Roger could think of no way to soften the blow.

"And the crew?"

"Reuben Cox is dead. A few others, also. Several wounded, including yourself. Most are alive and well."

"Where am I?"

"In Amsterdam. At the home of Dr. Lopez. You remember him, don't you?"

"Of course I do. Excellent doctor, Lopez! If I ever needed a surgeon, I'd choose Lopez before any other."

"Then you are a fortunate man, Captain," offered Homer.

"How's that?" He tried to sit up, and almost made it, before flopping back down. "My leg," he said, "what has happened to my leg?"

"I am afraid that Dr. Lopez had to remove some of it. Your injuries were too severe to save the leg. It was the leg or your life," said Roger.

"Who said so?"

"Dr. Lopez said so, and I trust his judgment on these things."

"The decision was mine to make, not the doctor's. Why was I not informed?"

"You were feverish and delirious. There was no way to let you decide. I told the doctor to save your life, rather than your leg."

"On what authority? Because ye are my stepson? If I was incapacitated, the acting Captain should have made the decision."

"And I did. When you are on your feet again, I'll gladly surrender command of the *Egyptian Queen* back to you."

"You?! How does a pup of sixteen years seize command of my ship? This is mutiny! Get out of my sight!"

Roger was shocked for a moment, unable to move. Then he wheeled and left the surgery.

Foxe was still in a boil. "How could ye let this happen, Homer?"

"I agreed with the acting Captain's decision. I trust the doctor's opinion."

"I mean, how could ye let him take the ship?"

"He was the obvious choice. All the other officers were needed at their posts."

"The First Mate? Benby? Paolo? You?"

"Reuben was dead. We were in a battle, if you recall; Benby was needed on the gun deck. Paolo knows less of navigation and tactics than Roger. It was you who appointed him acting First Mate. The lad did well, better than you could have expected."

"Well enough to wreck her, ye mean!"

"She was dismasted in the battle. Her keel was broken. We'd never have made it to Harwich in that storm. Roger brought us safely to land. No lives were lost in the wreck. The men will attest to his judgment and skill in the matter, without exception. We owe our lives — you and I — to his seamanship."

Foxe shook his head. "Get me Dick Benby. I'll appoint him in my stead, over that young pup."

"Mr. Benby is in command of the ship now, as it happens. He's tasked with protecting the *Queen* from scavengers and Sea Beggars."

"Well, there's that at least," growled Foxe. Then he closed his eyes and was asleep.

Dick Benby's ears might have been itching at that moment, but his hands were too full to notice. Piet Vandoorn had returned to his ship briefly, but now he was back with a boatload of armed crewmen. "What's with the arms then, Piet?" he shouted. "Are you planning on taking this vessel by force?"

"I hope that won't be necessary," Vandoorn shouted back, "but I like to be prepared. Those guns on the *Queen* are valuable — especially to a government that is in a war for its very survival — like mine."

"So you'd take them by force, from your old mates? That's harsh, Piet, very harsh."

"War is harsh."

"Aye, so it is." Benby turned toward the *Queen,* resting on the beach — the tide was out.

"Ahoy, the *Queen*! Are those demi-culverins loaded?"

"Aye, Sir. As you ordered!" The reply was loud enough for Vandoorn and his men to hear it.

"The gun deck is alist, though. What is the range of those guns?"

"About fifty yards, Sir, give or take. We've wedged 'em up as high as we can. Anything we fire will hit the beach."

"So, loaded with grapeshot, then?"

"Aye, Sir. Just as you ordered."

"How about the guns on the starboard side?"

"We had to wedge them down, Sir, to get the same range. She's listing a little, ye know."

Benby turned to face Vandoorn, who was looking uncomfortable. Grapeshot, of course, turned the guns essentially into oversized shotguns. Firing all ten of the demi-culverins would turn the beach at fifty yards or so from the *Queen* into a deadly cloud of flying metal. Any man in that zone would be mowed down like ripe grain before a scythe. More men appeared at the railing of the *Queen* as well, armed with arquebuses, which they rested on the rail. The men on the beach were also showing weapons, now. A direct assault was out of the question, at least until the tide came in. He could try approaching from the opposite side, but it would take time to move his men around . . .

"I didn't come to fight," said Vandoorn. *The devil you didn't*, thought Benby, *you didn't come prepared to fight an opponent as strong as we are, more like.*

"So you brought these men to negotiate?"

"That seemed sensible, under the circumstances."

"I am not authorized to sell this vessel or its contents. The one who is, has gone to Amsterdam. I am charged with protecting this property, until his return."

"And when will that be? Can you be certain that Captain Foxe will survive his wounds? He looked nearly dead, to me."

"Nearly dead does not count for much with us," said Benby. The men behind him murmured in agreement. "We will wait for word from Amsterdam."

"You realize that I can bombard you from out there"- he pointed seaward- "until there's nothing but splinters on this beach?"

"Piet, you're a hasty man. Both of us know that this ship won't be sailing off this beach anytime soon — maybe never. And those guns are too heavy for my crew to carry away with them. The guns will be sold. All you have to do is wait for them — assuming, of course, that you can meet the price."

Vandoorn ordered his men to stand down. He could afford to wait, at least until the tide came in.

Roger was in turmoil from Foxe's harsh dismissal. The rebuke was unfair. His stepfather's words stung, not only because he craved the Captain's respect, but also because he was sure he had made the right decisions, for both the Captain and his crew. The man's ingratitude was humiliating. A carriage drew up in front of Dr. Lopez's house and out stepped Paolo with three other men that Roger did not recognize.

"Acting Captain Foxe," said Paolo, "allow me to introduce Herr Walter Klein, and his banker, Frederick Smits, and the Honorable Maurice Kettner. Herr Klein is an agent for the Rich family, here in Amsterdam. Herr Kettner is a representative of the government of the Dutch Republic. I have explained the condition of the *Egyptian Queen* to them, and they propose a sale of the assets by the Rich family, to the government. Of course, they will need to inspect the *Queen*, before concluding the deal. I told them that we could take them there this afternoon.

"I'll be happy to take you, gentlemen, though I should warn you that other parties have expressed an interest in seizing the wreck outright. Ordinarily, Captain Foxe would be involved in the negotiations, but he is . . . indisposed, you could say."

"We will see the Captain," said Herr Klein. Roger showed them to the surgery, where Billy Foxe lay asleep, with bandages where the lower part of his left leg had been. No one said anything; they had performed due diligence. On the way out, Herr Klein spoke to Roger, "Dr. Lopez is among the best physicians in the city or any other city. It is lucky for the Captain that you found him. Not all physicians are as successful as Dr. Lopez."

Roger turned to Homer. "I am told I must go with these men, to inspect the *Queen*. Someone must stay with the Captain. Will you serve here until I return?"

"It will be an honor," Homer replied.

Roger turned to the doctor. "Dr. Lopez, we will make payment for your services as soon as this business is finished, if that is acceptable."

Lopez shook his head. "For Captain Foxe and a member of his crew, there is no charge. I consider my debt to him only partially paid."

There was room in the carriage for Roger, who had never seen anything as luxurious. The two seamen who had escorted Paolo found seats at the rear of the carriage, and they were off.

"I did not realize that Captain Foxe and Dr. Lopez were previously acquainted," said Herr Klein.

Roger nodded. "Dr. Lopez served as our ship's surgeon a few years back."

"What is this debt he speaks of?"

"We found Dr. Lopez on a Spanish prize. He was virtually a slave, I guess. Captain Foxe agreed to deliver him to Amsterdam, in return for his service aboard the *Egyptian Queen*. Dr. Lopez saved many lives on that voyage. He more than earned his passage. But he did say that escaping from the Spanish was a great boon and that he would be forever grateful to the Captain."

"Captain Foxe associates himself with all sorts and classes of men," Klein explained to Smits and Kettner, "Jews, blackamoors, rascals, and lords. It is the way of the sea, I suppose."

Roger reflected that he had little idea what a "Jew" was, but apparently, Dr. Lopez was one. "Blackamoor" referred to Homer, of course, and Dick Benby, and a dozen or so other seamen he knew. As for himself, he certainly was no "lord." Perhaps Klein would call him a "rascal." Yet here he was, digesting the most expensive and elaborate meal he had ever eaten, riding in an unimaginably luxurious coach — if this was the rascal's life, it was going very well. Except that he had lost the respect of his mentor and stepfather. That was going very ill.

The carriage stopped at a dock on a canal near the edge of the city. A boat was waiting for them — large enough for the whole party, including eight oarsmen. They embarked, with the oarsmen rowing vigorously westward — toward Beverwijk. The tide was coming in, and they made good speed. Roger was surprised to see another carriage waiting for them when they landed, and a dozen mounted cavalrymen. Someone had made arrangements, he realized; someone was ready for trouble.

The carriage at Beverwijk was not as comfortable or luxurious as the one in Amsterdam, but that did not slow their progress. They reached Wyck op Zee almost before Roger had settled in his seat. From there, it was a hike across the dunes to the *Queen*, but the carriage and its escort slogged due west until they reached the shore. "The wet sand makes the smoothest ride you can imagine," Klein assured his riders — and he was right. As long as the carriage skirted the ocean, where the sand was wet and firm, the carriage felt like they were flying. Roger made a mental note to try this again somehow if he ever got home . . .

Dick Benby had his eyes on the dunes, hoping to catch sight of someone — anyone, returning from Amsterdam. The tide was coming in, and with it, the uncertainties of the standoff. If the tide rose high enough to shift the *Queen*, it was just possible that Vandoorn might try to rush them, silly as that would be. No telling how desperate he was. Benby was a man willing, sometimes eager, to fight his enemies. Shooting it out with an old mate was just a waste of blood and ammunition. He would avoid it if he could.

"Horsemen! Up the beach, to the north!" Benby's eyes followed to where the lookout pointed. Sure enough — cavalry, by the way, the sun glinted on their armor. A coach, too. They were behind Piet Vandoorn and his men, but were closing fast . . .

They were barely one hundred yards up the beach when Vandoorn's party noticed them. The sailors scrambled inland, out of the way of the horsemen and the carriage, who passed to seaward, and pulled up beside the *Queen*. No one moved for a moment, and then Benby recognized the two armed men riding at the back of the carriage — his mates. The door of the carriage opened and out hopped Roger and Paolo. Benby laughed. The lad certainly knew how to arrive in style.

Three more men emerged from the carriage — richly dressed, and well-fed. Money men. Roger had found what they needed.

Benby greeted Roger warmly. "You have a good sense of timing, Sir."

Roger shrugged. "Let me introduce you to Herr Klein, who is the Rich family's agent in Amsterdam; Herr Smits, a banker; and Herr Kettner, who represents the government of the Republic. They are here to sell the *Queen* and her contents to the Republic."

Benby shook their hands and bowed his head respectfully. "There is another here, who should be part of this business." He turned to where Vandoorn and his men still stood, "Captain Vandoorn, you'd best join us, I think!" Vandoorn walked over to be introduced. He had the look of a man who has just seen a window of opportunity slam shut — on his fingers. The Money Men stood back and looked at the *Queen*. Even as a wreck, she was impressive — longer than any ship the Money Men had ever seen.

The three Money Men wanted to inspect the *Queen*. Benby took them around to the south side of the ship, where the keel could be seen. A crack was barely visible, half-concealed by the sand and water of the incoming tide. Two of the Money Men got their feet wet because they weren't quick-footed enough. Getting inside the ship was a challenge. They rigged a kind of ladder near her bow and they all managed to climb aboard. The deck was aslant, but not impossible to walk on. The stairwells down to the hold could be managed.

"We moved everything out of the orlop deck when she began taking water," explained Roger. "Nothing down there, but bilge and ballast. The value in this ship is these," he said as he pointed to the culverins and demi-culverins. The Money Men nodded. This part of sailing they understood. They took measurements and wrote things down in small books. They whispered to each other and nodded. At last, they seemed to have come to an agreement.

Klein spoke to Roger: "I understand that the keel was damaged before she ran aground?"

"That's correct. It happened while we were in a fight with two Spanish ships. We got dismasted. It took a while before we discovered the damage."

"And how many men were lost?"

"Our first mate was killed, also two others, I believe. You've seen what happened to our Captain."

Klein nodded. "Still, the ship was handled well. No reason to blame the captain for this, I think."

Roger looked at Paolo. "Blame the Captain?"

Paolo shook his head, and beckoned Roger close, "It's part of his report to the investors, that's all. Fear not. This is going to turn out well."

"Three men are dead, several more injured, and the Captain has lost a leg. We are stranded in a foreign land. How is that turning out well?"

"Turning out well for the investors, who expect to absorb some losses. The sale of the guns will still turn a profit for them. They will not look for scapegoats, our men will be paid and returned home, and the Captain's reputation is preserved. That is what I mean by turning out well."

"About the men . . ."

"Klein has authorized me to pay them off today. He will also pay for one night's lodging for each of them in Amsterdam, and passage back to Harwich, for any who wish to return."

"Any who wish to return?"

Paolo nodded. "This ship isn't going to sail again. Sailors need to find work. Amsterdam is a good place to find work. Not all will be returning to England, at least not yet."

"And what about Captain Foxe?"

"Captain Foxe is a wounded hero. Klein will pay for his lodging in Amsterdam until his recovery is complete."

"And if he does not recover?"

"In that case, for as long as he lives. But Dr. Lopez has a very fine reputation. Klein considers the Captain's recovery a foregone conclusion. Klein will also pay for your lodging, and that of one other, to care for the Captain during his recovery."

"I suppose I must stay with him, then, though I do not think that will please him."

"If the Captain prefers someone else, Klein will pay their lodging, instead."

The arrangements were complete, Roger addressed the crew and explained them. There was general satisfaction. Paolo had them line up to collect their wages, including their living allowances. In groups of a dozen or less, they shouldered their chests or seabags and began trudging up the beach toward the village of Wyck op Zee. From there, they would take the road to Beverwijk, and thence to Amsterdam. The twelve who had carried the wounded to Amsterdam had not yet returned. Roger had their possessions removed from the wreck, and piled on the beach, under a canvas tarp, above the high-tide line. A villager passed by, and offered to haul the stuff to Wyck op Zee, and store it in a secure place, for a shilling. An outrageous price thought Roger, but probably enough to ensure that the stuff would be kept safe. He paid the man out of his own purse.

Herr Kettner left a guard to look after his new guns, and took the carriage back, along with Klein and Witt. Even Piet Vandoorn got something out of the deal: Kettner agreed to sell him the hull of the *Queen*, once the guns had been removed. "I once heard a carpenter remark that there was enough wood in this ship to build two merchantmen," said Vandoorn, "That's worth something."

"Don't forget the nails, hardware, and rigging," said Benby. "It all adds up." He walked to a place where the quarter-deck railing had been shattered by the cannonball that had killed Reuben Cox. He pulled out a two-and-a-half-foot railing spindle from the debris — untouched, or so it appeared. "This is my souvenir of the battle," he declared. Vandoorn did not protest.

The sun was getting lower in the west now. Roger was left with a handful of his officers. Paolo paid them off. His payroll box was lighter, now. All of the officers stated an intention to bid farewell to Captain Billy Foxe before they headed home. So up the beach and over the dunes they walked, first to Wyck op Zee, then to Beverwijk. It was dark by then. They walked to the docks and encountered eleven of the sailors who had carried the wounded to Amsterdam that morning — they had lingered in the pubs for longer than Roger had expected and missed their pay. Among them was also the man with the broken leg — hobbling along with his mates, drunk, by all indications. Roger told them where they could retrieve their possessions. Paolo explained what their compensation was and paid them off. "Only missed one," said Paolo with satisfaction. "That's very tidy, for a shipwreck." Roger reflected that he must be right; a truly tidy shipwreck must be a rare thing.

The voyage to Amsterdam happened in the dark. As they approached the city, the lights from thousands of candles and lanterns reflected off the dark water of the Ij, and then off the canals inside the city in a curious way. The city looked like a vast, dark ruin, speckled with tiny candle lights to Rogers's eyes — he had never seen anything like it. When they reached Dr. Lopez's house, Roger hung back. "Our last conversation was — unpleasant," he said. "The rest of you should go in first. He may not be in the best of moods."

He waited outside. The night was mild and there was traffic, even at this hour, in the street and up and down the canals. The city seemed alive. *And I'm alive, too,* Roger realized; *twenty-four hours ago, that fact was very much in doubt.* Whatever was going to come of his relationship with his stepfather, Roger was glad to be alive — glad to be alive in this place, at this moment. Billy Foxe was still alive too, and likely would be for some time, whether he wanted to be or not.

A servant came to the door. "He's asking for Roger," she said.

Roger went inside and was led into another room. Billy Foxe was in bed, sitting up. It appeared that his fever had broken. The officers stood round the bed, in a rough semicircle, like attendants around a king's throne. Foxe looked at Roger, and spoke: "Acting Captain Foxe, I hereby relieve you of your duties."

Roger felt his cheeks burning, and bowed his head.

"On account of the fact that the *Eqyptian Queen* is no more. She was the terror of the seas, the hardest-fighting ship in Her Majesty's navy. She has earned a glorious legacy, not least because of the gallantry of her crew, and her officers. And particularly I should mention the brilliance of her commander, Captain Foxe. Or rather, I should have said, the brilliance of two commanders — both of them, as it happens, named Foxe. May their names live in the history of our nation!"

"Hear, hear!" intoned the officers. Roger realized they were looking at him.

"Son," Foxe continued, "ye must forgive me, for my hasty words this morning. I was not in my right mind. I do not fault ye for anything ye have done — you saved my crew and my life. Every man in this room knows it."

Roger exhaled. "Gladly, Sir," he said.

The following morning, the officers made their arrangements to leave. It was Dick Benby who volunteered to stay in Amsterdam with Roger and the Captain. "Homer is a well-known navigator," said Benby. "He can easily find work on another ship, as can the rest of the officers. It will not be so for me. I can get employment as a seaman, but Billy Foxe is the only captain I know who would have me as an officer on his ship."

Roger and Benby got a room nearby so that one or the other could sit with the captain every day. Foxe took his meals in Lopez's house as well. His appetite faltered — some days he would only eat chicken soup. After a few weeks, Dr. Lopez declared that he was well enough to move out, so they got a second room for Foxe. Klein was as good as his word — their rooms and meals were paid for. The Captain, however, was not thriving in his recovery. He had lost weight through the ordeal. His cheeks looked hollow, his skin pale. Some of this, Roger realized, was due to being indoors all the time. He and Dick Benby sometimes helped the Captain outside, where he could sit in a chair, and watch the street traffic. They got him up on crutches, eventually. He could hobble up and down the street when the weather was fair.

As August turned to September, Dr. Lopez said it was time for the Captain to be fitted with his new leg. Foxe was not enthusiastic — "The crutches will do. A wooden leg — what is that? A home for termites, that's what it is."

Benby sighed. "A new leg will leave both hands free. You need your hands free, to command a ship."

"Ship? What ship? Who would let a one-legged man command a ship? The *Queen* was my last command. I told ye I had foreseen that, before the last time we sailed!"

Benby shook his head. "No, you told me you thought it would be your last voyage because you wouldn't come back alive. You were only half right. The *Egyptian Queen* is gone, but you are still here."

"Ye needn't remind me of my loss," mumbled Foxe.

"Would you rather the *Queen* had survived, and the sea claimed you?"

"Perhaps that would have been better."

"How could that have been better? Are you disappointed that your premonition of death proved false?"

Foxe sighed. "Not disappointed. Bewildered, ye might say. I made the necessary preparations for my death. I was not expecting this" — he nodded in the direction of his missing leg. "What sort of life is there for me now?"

"What sort of life do you want? You have a house, family, and friends in Harwich. Two months ago, you loved that life so much, that you were looking for a way to avoid this last voyage altogether — don't deny it, I could see it in your eyes."

"But I bid farewell to all of that when I determined to go to sea. Ye could say that I chose the *Egyptian Queen* over my family, the way some men choose a mistress over their wife. I truly did not expect to come home from that voyage, and now that it seems I must, I feel like some faithless husband, crawling back to his wife and family, because his mistress has thrown him over. I feel humiliated, or unworthy, somehow . . ."

Benby snorted. "It sounds to me that you are afraid to go home. If the *Queen* is your 'mistress', she is no more; mourn the loss if you will, but do not turn your back on the people who love you and the life that could be yours, just for the sake of pride. No one is demanding that you renounce this 'mistress', or apologize for your devotion to her. You have the chance for a new life now, without the *Queen*."

"If only I had a piece of her left, some memento to keep with me . . . "

"I have just the thing," said Benby, chuckling. He fetched a bundle from under his bed and unrolled it. Do you recognize this?" He held up the railing spindle from the *Queen*'s quarterdeck.

"Looks familiar." his eyes lit up."From the quarterdeck on the *Queen*! How did ye come by this?"

"I salvaged it, the day she was sold. Thought you should have a — memento, you call it. It's yours, now."

Foxe shook his head. "Nay, I'd look a silly fool carrying this around, like it was some keepsake."

"You're going to look silly, whatever you do. But if you turn this into your wooden leg, no one has to know what it was."

Foxe looked offended, for a moment, then smiled, and finally laughed. "Aye, that can be our secret!"

August 5, 1588: Felsted

John Porter was roused by the pealing of church bells, as was nearly everyone else in Felsted and Cobler's Green. The peal was distinctive; a call to assembly of the militia. He dressed in his jack, the morion, and all his weapons, as Sybil watched him — torn between the thought of losing the husband of her youth to war, and resignation to the nation's necessity. The baby woke as well. Time to feed him. Then, the chores.

The militia assembled on the green in Felsted. Christopher Popham was officially Captain of the company, now. John had been 'promoted' to 'Sergeant', in command of the arquebusiers. Popham addressed the company: "Lads, we've been called to duty. Each of you must be prepared to march within three hours. You should pack a change of clothes, a bedroll, and any coat or cloak you own that will keep you dry in the rain. Each man should bring his own eating utensils. You'll be responsible for repairing your own clothing, including your shoes. The Baron will provide tentage. Go pack your things, say goodbye to your families, and be back here in three hours, no more." He dismissed them.

John approached Popham with a question, "Are you expecting me to bring Gordon, as well?"

Popham looked at him and paused. "No, we won't be needing Gordon, on this trip. The Baron has made other arrangements."

John stopped by his parent's home first, said goodbye to his family, gave his mother an extra-long hug, then rushed home to Sybil. The packing did not take long — they had been anticipating this day. By now, the news of the appearance of the Armada off the southwest coast had been widely reported; it was known that there had been sea battles in the English Channel — only contradictory rumors of the outcome. Today's summons could mean only that a Spanish army was expected to arrive in England somewhere, and soon.

"You'll be welcome to stay in Felsted, with Ellen and my mother. Mum is always happy to have her grandson about the place."

"We'll see. I suppose your father has been called up, too?"

"Aye. And my cousins and uncles."

"How long will ye be gone?" She looked at him soberly, with her grey eyes. She knew he couldn't answer that question or any of the ones that she could not ask, such as *Who will bring in the harvest, if you are gone for two months?* Or *What becomes of us, if you do not return at all?*

"You know that that is impossible to say."

"I do, but it seemed careless not to ask the question. I will visit your parent's home this afternoon. Perhaps Francis and I, and the chickens will move to their place for a while. I still know how to work a draft horse, and we can get the hay in, next month if we have to. I suppose you'll be taking Gordon to war with you?"

"No, I specifically asked about that. I'm told that the Baron has made other plans. Apparently, we'll be sleeping in tents, thanks to the Baron's generosity."

"Well, there's that. I don't suppose you can tell me where you're going?"

"We haven't been told. I doubt that our Captain knows much more than he's telling."

Sybil sighed. "So, we've got three women, a baby, and Gordon and Old Bob — I guess we can manage, for a while. Come, kiss your son goodbye."

Francis woke as John took him in his arms and smiled at his father. John smiled back. Sybil wrapped her arms around the both of them.

They formed into ranks of five and marched out of the village to the south and east, toward Leez Manor. Captain Popham led the way, on horseback. Four long flatbed wagons, each drawn by a team of sturdy-looking horses, waited at the side of the road, where the lane to the manor house joined it. The wagons fell in behind the arquebusiers at the rear of the column. "Must be our tents and provisions," remarked a man marching beside John.

John nodded. "Must be." Something was missing. It took a second before he realized that the cannons and their caissons were not in the column. Curious. Surely the Baron would not have forgotten about them! Perhaps they had been sent on ahead. He hoped they would all arrive at their destination together.

They made good progress for the first several hours. They halted at midday near the junction with the Great Road, for a midday meal. There was bread, cheese, and ale in one of the wagons, and the mood of the company was lifted. Whatever the challenge of being separated from their families, it was reassuring to know that someone had a plan to feed them.

After their meal, they reformed and turned southward onto the Great Road. John had walked this way before; it looked familiar. His thoughts wandered to the day he had met William Payne and Edward Chase, on just this road. Three men, just walking, and talking. One of them dead now, executed on a false charge of treason. One disappeared, lost to the world. And himself, the youngest, just starting out on the road to a new life. Before he had killed a man, before he had met Sybil, before he had become a father, a man of reputation. He speculated about how different his life might have been, had he not struck up a conversation with those other two on that day. Was it fate? Was it God? Was it merely chance?

<hr>

Chelmsford lay ahead; they should make it there before sundown without difficulty. Where they would sleep was another question.

In the event, they pitched their tents in a pasture west of the city, not far from the road that night. It was more difficult than anyone had anticipated; setting up tents had never been part of their drill. Fortunately, the wagons held all the components that they needed, and before dark they had figured out how to put up the tents and assign the appropriate number of men to each. John realized that the tents would all have to be taken down and re-packed in the morning, as well. Progress would not be as fast as he had first thought.

Progress of course, had to be measured against the distance they were traveling; no one had said, as yet, exactly where they were going. John approached Popham after the men had been fed: "Looks as if we're headed to London," he observed.

Popham smiled and called him aside. "Let the men believe that, if they want to. London's no place for farm boys like these. We'll be posted about a day's march from the city proper."

"Where will we find our artillery?"

Popham made an awkward face. "The artillery is probably at our destination now, but it's not properly ours, I'm afraid."

"How so?"

"The usefulness of the guns was demonstrated on the green — you remember parade day? They made a deep impression. The Baron was persuaded to give them up several weeks ago."

"So we go into battle without our field guns?"

"As I said, they're likely to be where we're going. But other men will be firing them."

John's heart sank. There went his best chance at surviving the coming battle.

Popham noticed the expression on his face. "The Baron knows that he got the guns upon your recommendation. He credits your judgment, as well as your skill in building the carriages and the caissons. This will only enhance your reputation in his eyes."

"My reputation." *A reputation for what? For filling my friends and family with a false sense of confidence? To what purpose? So that they will make a brave stand, before the Spanish mercenaries cut them down?*

"Aye. The Baron has mentioned you with approval more than once, in my presence, and the presence of his retainers. He holds you in highest regard among his tenants. Your service will not go unrewarded."

John shook his head. "I am not concerned with rewards for my service. I am concerned with the welfare of this company — my family and friends. We have lost our best chance of surviving this war. I know of what I speak — I have seen such guns in action. I will admit that our chances were not good in any case, but those guns gave us reason to hope, however forlorn."

"Best not tell the men then," replied Popham.

John nodded. "Best not. You mentioned that the guns made a 'deep impression' on last year's parade. Am I right in thinking that Sir Walter Clive had something to do with this?"

It was Popham's turn to nod, "You are not wrong. But see here — fighting to defend our queen and our nation is not an option for any of us. We are obligated by honor, ancient tradition, and self-interest to answer the call. It is our duty to be here, with or without the artillery."

"Aye, that is the way of things. Some men will die and others will live, on the day of battle. But the Baron's decision favors certain men, to the disadvantage of the men of my village, myself, and even you. Tell the truth. Would you prefer to face the enemy on horseback, with a full suit of armor and artillery at your back, or face them on foot, as we must? And if we are to fall in battle, will not the man on a horse be celebrated for his heroic sacrifice, borne on a litter to his family's burial place, mourned with libations and flowers, while men like me and the rest of this company are simply buried in some mass grave (yourself a possible exception, I suppose)?"

Popham was put off by these last remarks, but said nothing, for a moment. Then, carefully, "If it is as you say, and a common grave awaits the men of this company, then I hope to find my resting place with them."

But your family will have other ideas, thought John to himself, *that is the way of things.* "A noble sentiment. I hope that will not be your fate, or mine. It offends me that both our lives are to be offered so cheaply."

"Pray, be not offended. You can only demoralize the men with such talk. Even your demeanor speaks discouragement. Is it not better to meet whatever peril we face with hope and good cheer? So long as God is on our side, faith and courage may win the day."

John was roused by the sound of trumpets and marching men. It was dark, or maybe misty. He fumbled with his jack and weapons; couldn't locate his morion at all for a moment. When he spotted it, it looked odd . . . oh, of course. There was a bullet hole in the front of it . . . strange that he had not noticed it before . . .

"Ye'll miss the battle, if ye do not hurry." The voice came from a shadowy figure at the entrance to his tent.

"Coming!" he replied. He stepped outside. It was chilly, foggy. Must be early in the morning, yet. Here and there, he could see the blurry silhouettes of other men — soldiers, no doubt — hurrying one way and then another in the fog, fumbling with their clothes and weapons, as he had.

"This way!" said his companion. John followed him off into the fog. He heard the clash of weapons, and men shouting somewhere off ahead. They were climbing, he could feel it underfoot. Presently, his companion stopped and turned to face him. The light was a little better, here. Good enough to see the man's face. It was familiar enough, though he had not seen that face for a few years. The hole in the man's forehead, the swarm of flies, a maggot; there was no mistaking that face . . .

"How do you come to be here? What is your purpose? Do you mean to take my life, in revenge?"

His companion shook his head. "How do any of us come to be where we are? What purpose does a dead man have? I could not take your life, even if I wanted to — I am dead, can't you see that?"

"You wish to torment me with feelings of guilt, then. I did not start that fight with you, you attacked me. I was only defending my life, you gave me no choice, but to kill you."

"Now you shall have to defend it, again," said the Dead Man. He gestured downhill, with a sweep of his arm. John saw an army there, marching up the hill toward him — a host uncountable, armor glinting in the twilight. To his left, he saw some of his own men; some lay on the ground, some were stumbling, some began to flee. "This is the choice of all men in battle," said the Dead Man, "If you flee, you may survive, but only by leaving your companions to die in your stead. If you fight, you may lose your life — as I did. You may also keep your life and honor by fighting, but only by taking the life of another."

"I chose to stand," said John. "because there was nowhere to flee to, anyway. I defended my life and the life of my comrades; I took yours. It did not please me to do so."

"And you shall defend it again, please you or not," said the Dead Man. "I am here as your witness, though you have more to lose than I do. Look at the host that approaches, look at your comrades. Do you really think you can stand against so many? Nay: the day approaches that you become as I am, as all men will be, sooner or later. Prepare to meet your God."

John awoke with a gasp and a shiver. His companions in the tent appeared to be sleeping soundly. Outside, someone was moving around, coughing. He groped around for his morion, just to check. There was no bullet hole in it — yet.

Breaking camp in the morning was a chaotic and time-consuming affair, as John had anticipated. It was midmorning before they were fully on their way. Farmers are not wont to sleep late but getting all of them up at the same time, all fed at the same time, all ready for the march at the same time — you would have supposed that they were being asked to perform some feat of sorcery.

Fortunately, the weather was fair and the road was wide. The drummer kept up a steady tempo, and some of the traffic actually moved aside as they advanced, even cheering them as they passed. Everyone knew that the Spanish were coming.

It was just midday when they passed the village of Ingatestone. Popham ordered the company off the main road, and then eastward for half a mile or so. They approached a large manor. "Ingatestone Hall," said Popham. "They have been warned to have a supper ready for us."

"Warned?" asked John.

"Aye. Recusants have lived here. Time for them to show where their loyalties lie."

The residents of the manor appeared, indeed, to have been "warned." Rough tables and benches had been set up on the grounds before the manor house. The aroma of roasting hogs filled the air. "We were told to prepare for a hundred fifty men," said the Steward of the manor. They were prepared.

The meal boosted the morale of the weary company. Bread, meat, and plenty of ale were served. Popham kept a sharp eye on the beverages: "Two servings of ale, no more," he insisted, "We can't be carrying any drunken soldiers with us."

"You said that recusants lived here?" asked John.

"Aye, the Petre family. This is their manor. Some are loyal Protestants, some Catholic. You may have heard of the traitor John Payne, who was executed in Chelmsford a few years back?"

"Yes. I believe I have heard of him." It was chilling to think of his old friend again, on such terms — better to remember him as William Payne, the journeyman.

"He was arrested at a manor owned by this same family. Turns out that they hid him here sometimes, right under the noses of the authorities. The old widow, Lady Anne, ran the place in those days. The story goes that when Payne was arrested it broke her heart — at any rate, she died within weeks of his execution. No charges could be brought against the Petre's — the nobility is nearly always protected from the consequences of their recusancy — but we're sending a message to any that doubt our government's resolve. Fitting that they should feast us, don't you think?"

John nodded and took a drink of his ale. Fitting was not the word he would have chosen. Ironic, perhaps. *To William Payne, may he rest in peace,* he said to himself and took another drink.

After their supper, Popham was eager to get underway. They had made up some time by eating a meal already prepared for them. "We may not make it to Tilbury by nightfall," he confided to John.

"You hadn't told me that Tilbury is our destination," noted John.

"It hardly matters, now. We're less than fifteen miles from there. We'll be joining the rest of her majesty's army at Tilbury. If the Spanish are attacking up the Thames, we'll try to stop them there."

"And if they're not?"

"If they attack elsewhere, we'll go wherever we're needed."

They didn't quite make it to Tilbury that evening. Popham allowed that they could have reached the encampment about dusk, but he thought a repeat of the previous evening's struggles with setting up their tents would invite the curiosity — and ridicule — of soldiers from other units. Better to march into camp in broad daylight, with the drum beating, like a company of well-trained soldiers. They stopped just east of a place called Orsett for the night. The tents went up more smoothly than they had on yesterday; Popham pronounced himself satisfied.

"There is a large parish church in this village," said Popham, "they call it St. Giles and All Saints. Tomorrow is Sunday. We will ask the priest to conduct a service for us before we march on."

The priest came to them: Apparently, adding a hundred fifty or so men to the usual Sunday morning crowd would exceed the capacity of the chapel — "The crowd is larger on first Sundays," explained the vicar. He conducted a full eucharistic service; John reflected that whatever a man's beliefs about sacraments, the eve of battle was a good time to take communion.

Once again, it was mid-morning before the company was back on the road, but the military camp was just four miles away. They marched in before noon, with the drum beating, just as Popham had planned. They were greeted by a few cheers of welcome.

The camp itself was a pungent hodgepodge of men, tents, latrines, outdoor kitchens, animals, and waste dumps. Fortunately, there was a breeze from the west, and the company from Felsted was told to pitch their tents on the upwind side.

Popham was summoned to a conference with the senior officers. He returned to announce that there would be maneuvers that very afternoon. Thankfully, the tents were put up fairly quickly, and the men marched to the mess for their midday meal.

There was news of the war at sea or at least rumors. The Spanish fleet had been defeated off Calais before they could load any of the troops from the Netherlands. The fleet was blocking them from returning to their rendezvous — or so went one of the stories. Other accounts insisted that the the Armada was just drawing the English fleet northward so that troops in the Netherlands could cross the channel unmolested. Still others insisted that the English fleet had returned and was anchored at Margate — just ten miles east of them, to prevent just such a maneuver. None of the rumors suggested that the English fleet had been anything but overwhelmingly successful — reason enough to doubt their accuracy. Still, there was hope, John thought. If the Spanish couldn't get across the Channel, the missing artillery really wouldn't matter . . .

In the afternoon the troops assembled, company by company, in the open land south of the camp. Each company formed a solid square, which emphasized that they were not equal in size, or in armaments. There were "trained bands" from London, clad in steel breastplates and tassets, with a steel helmet on every man's head, swords at their sides, pikes in hand. Other units, like the Felsted company, had hardly any armor. Some units numbered several hundred, a few were smaller than one hundred. It was up to the officers to group them into effective fighting units.

From where the Felsted men stood, the army appeared vast in size: "We'll have the Spaniards outnumbered if they dare to land," opined Jed Bones. John nodded and smiled, then did some mental estimation of what he could see. He guessed their numbers at less than five thousand men, which would be about 1/9th of the army that Spain had supposedly mustered. He said nothing to the troops about his estimate — to them, the assembly was an immense horde, larger than any crowd they had ever seen. They needed all the confidence they could get. He remembered his dream from two nights earlier. He tried to imagine what forty-five thousand soldiers would look like. Like something out of a nightmare.

The following day, the whole army was roused and ordered to form up for a march. The march was not long, less than a mile south of the camp. The company formed in a square ten ranks deep on one side of a road, with other units on either side of them, and waited. Captain Popham was summoned away, to confer with the commanders. When he returned, John could tell that he was excited. "We are to be reviewed," he said to John, "Tell the men to look sharp — dress the ranks, stand to attention." Then he was gone again.

John walked up and down, found a few instances of sloppy dress, got the doublets straightened, and the collars turned. It would have to do — these were farmers, not courtiers. If the general officers thought the company too unkempt, they could always send them home — not likely, with a Spanish army on the way.

There was some commotion down the road to the right — a group of riders was approaching, working its way down the road at a deliberate pace. Something was happening to the ranks, as the procession passed — helmets. They were lifting their helmets and bowing or maybe kneeling.

Popham rode up, looked at the company, and spoke: "Every man must be prepared to kneel," he declared. "Whatever you do, hold your pikes erect. Look like soldiers: your queen approaches!"

The Queen. Impossible. No one in the company had ever seen the Queen, or any other royal personage — except perhaps, for Christopher Popham. "Let every man kneel on his right knee," suggested John. "It will look more orderly."

"Yes, of course!" said Popham. He still seemed a little rattled.

By now, the procession was closer. John could see that a woman on a white horse was in front, led by two men on foot, who held the reins in their hands. Behind her was her escort — mounted men in armor — nobles and courtiers, no doubt. There was a broad collar, or ruff, around the Queen's neck, and she appeared to be wearing armor. John glanced at the pikemen, who were peering curiously down the road. "Eyes front!" he ordered. "Stand to attention!" This they did, to some degree or another. Curiosity got the best of some of them.

As the Queen and her party passed in front of them, they all swept off their hats (and a few helmets) and bent their knees. John held his morion under his left arm and looked up as she passed — not a young woman, reddish hair, a weariness about the eyes. Her skin was pale, nearly white. He realized that she must have applied some sort of white paste to her face. Such was the way of royalty, he supposed. It was hard to tell how old she was — but perhaps that was the way of royalty, also. Her eyes met his for an instant, then moved on. She nodded at Christopher Popham as if she recognized him and appeared to say something to him. Then the rest of her party passed on in front of them — horses, armor, plumed helmets.

After passing in review, the Queen's party turned and retraced their steps, stopping fifty or so yards to the left. The Queen dismounted and began to address the army. She walked among the ranks as she spoke; the Felsted men strained to make out the words — something about ". . . the body but of a weak and feeble woman; but I have the heart and stomach of a king, and of a king of England too . . ." here her words were drowned out by cheering. The excitement of the moment swept through the ranks, and the men shouted "God Save the Queen!"

Elizabeth promised to reward the men for their valor, and concluded with "We shall shortly have a famous victory over those enemies of my God, of my kingdom, and of my people!" More cheers from the army. The Queen remounted her horse and rode back the way she had come, while her army cheered until she was out of sight.

Popham was glowing with excitement. "She spoke to me! She remembered me! Did you see how she was dressed, in white? Like Pallas Athena, with her sword and shield!"

"Pallas Athena?" the name meant nothing to John.

"The Greek goddess of war. You know — the defender of Athens."

John shook his head.

"It is like poetry," Popham explained, "or a stage play. The Queen appears as the goddess of victory, to inspire us with memories of glorious victories of the past."

"Ah." John nodded as if Popham was making sense.

The men were excited, too. None of them had any expectation of ever seeing their Queen; it would be the stuff of stories they would tell their children and grandchildren. The entire formation was marched back to camp. John found himself wondering about the whole assembly. If the Queen was determined to fight alongside her army, as she had said, why had she left so quickly? If, indeed, they were to have a "famous" victory over the Spanish "shortly," did she mean that an attack was imminent? What, in short, did the Queen know that her army did not?

Christopher Popham had some answers by that evening. "The latest, and most reliable information is that the fleet is anchored off Margate and is well able to prevent a crossing by the Spanish army near Calais. That army is much reduced in size, at any rate — camp fever has taken nearly half of them. The rest of the Spanish fleet is dispersed, and unable to return to Spain through the English channel."

"So the 'famous victory' has already been won?"

Popham sighed. "It appears so. Glory for us will have to wait for another day. We are to be paid off tomorrow and be on our way home the following day."

"You are disappointed?"

"I am. A man in my position has few enough opportunities to burnish his reputation. A victory in battle, especially one at which the Queen herself has noted my presence, could open the door to many advancements."

"Advancements?"

"Aye, many careers at court have been built on just such a foundation. If I could get a position there, I am sure that my efficiency and ability would be noted — and rewarded. All I need is a chance to prove my worth." Popham noted the expression on John's face. "Ah, I see that this is a blow to your ambitions, too."

"Not at all. I have no such ambitions. I was merely realizing how a man of your class must see these things. I am a carpenter, well able to make my living with my hands — I need no other opportunity than employment. It is different for men like you, I see."

Popham nodded. "But it does not have to be that way. Yeomen have been known to distinguish themselves in battle, and profit from it."

"Profit was never in my imagination, on this march. I am grateful to think that we may be on our way home soon, all of us alive and well. If God allows me to embrace my wife and son again in good health, that will be 'famous victory' enough. If every man in this company arrives safely home, we all may share the 'victory'."

"But what of glory? What of fame? Surely these are part of every man's yearning."

"I have seen war as it is. There may be valor and honor, but there is also great waste of life and limb. The glory is in the telling of tales, the fame is a will o' the wisp. The best part of a war is when it ends." John paused. "Listen. Do you hear that coughing?"

"Aye. What of it?"

"I have heard that sound before. When the fever struck — and carried off hundreds of men, all brave, all honorable. Their bones rest on an island in the Caribbean Sea, or else at the bottom of the ocean. A third of the soldiers on that expedition did not return — the fever took them."

Popham looked alarmed. "And you think that fever is in our camp? How do we stop it from spreading?"

John nodded. "The sooner we leave, the better. The crew of the ship I sailed on lost fewer men to the fever because we did not mix with the other crews. It would be wise to separate the men of our company from the rest of the army."

Popham made an effort to keep the Felsted men isolated from the rest of the army, but the camp was in a very good mood — they had seen the Queen! She had spoken to them! And by now, the rumor had spread through the camp that they would be going home soon. Men insisted on celebrating and mixing.

John slept fitfully that night. It was a relief to think of heading home, with all the men in the company alive and well. He was already running through a list of chores and tasks in his mind, which jobs to tackle first. He dozed, then woke, then dozed again . . . a familiar figure stood at the entrance to his tent. *Dreaming again*, John told himself. The figure beckoned, and John rose and stepped outside. The night was clear. Stars shone brightly overhead.

"No arms or armor?" his companion asked.

"Won't be needing any," was John's reply. "You seem to me a poor prophet — I did not die two days ago, nor yesterday. Nor is it likely that I will die tomorrow. The battle you warned me of is not to be."

"You mistook my meaning," replied the Dead Man. "I am not here to name the day or place of your passing, merely to remind you of what your fate must be. The eve of battle makes the reminder more keen."

"I hardly need to be reminded of that, though you seem to think it is your business to haunt my dreams. I am mortal. I shall die one day, as you have. Am I supposed to live in guilt because my life has been a little longer than yours?"

The Dead Man smiled, gaps between his teeth. Something wriggled out of the hole in his forehead. "Guilt is pointless. Knowing that you are mortal is not enough. My 'haunting', as you call it, must continue until you understand that you and I are the same."

"The same? How are we the same?"

"Rather, how are we different? I am dead you say, and you are alive. But that is the matter of a brief moment — every man begins dying the day he is born. I was a pirate you say, a man who seeks gain by taking from other men by violence. And yet, here you are, ashamed lest any man should know how you have enriched yourself with the property of others."

"What property is that?"

"Why, the treasure you took from me and my mates. I believe your share of that booty is in your purse right now."

"You are right," said John, "but you and your mates took it from others by violence. You have no more claim to it than I."

"And the ones we took it from, did they get it honestly?"

"I really hadn't thought about it."

"Think about this. The gold and silver came out of the ground. The Spaniards did not mine it themselves — they used the labor of other men, men that they seized by violence, or paid others to do so. And the country in which they found the gold and silver was not their own — they seized it by violence as well. You are simply the last link in a chain of violence and murder; and one day soon, your property and your wealth will belong to other men, who will inherit whatever remains of your hidden riches, and the guilt that clings to them."

"By your lights, every man in the world is guilty of profiting from the sins of his ancestors — if not someone else's ancestors. What does that matter?"

"That is not my point. The point is, all men are the same. Hiding behind a veil of secrecy is futile. Everything hidden will be revealed. You and I are alike — men who fatten themselves for the day of slaughter — yet you seek to separate yourself from the rest of us . . . Because you imagine yourself to be better than other men. Because you cling to that conceit, in spite of the facts you know. Because you think it somehow unfair that your labors cannot change those facts, yet you cling to the illusion that your virtue, your labor, your character, your cleverness sets you apart. Pride is your sin — the kind of pride that hides behind a mask of humility and self-control. Until you accept me as your brother, and neither of us more worthy than another, you will be 'haunted' by the likes of me."

"Then hear my confession," John replied:

"What shall I crie? All flesh is grasse, and all the grace thereof is as the floure of the fielde.

The grasse withereth, the floure fadeth, because the Spirite of the Lorde bloweth upon it: surely the people is grasse.

The grasse withereth, the floure fadeth: but the worde of our God shall stand for euer.

"Is that what you want to hear?" The stars burned overhead. He was alone.

In the morning, the paymaster visited each company in turn and paid the men their wages. Popham had ordered his men to pack their gear already, and after a midday supper he had them on the road north. "We camp at Ingatestone Hall, tonight" he told John. "They cannot refuse us."

It was so. Servants from the manor house emerged as they were pitching their tents in a grassy area facing the manor. They did not protest the presence of the company, but explained that given such short notice, the meal would be served a bit late. It was chicken — no time to roast any larger animals; bread — probably the week's bread supply for the great house, John thought; cheese and ale. Not fancy, but the men were in no mood to complain. Popham seemed to be getting over his disappointment, as well. He recited a poem to the men:

> " Because I breathe not love to every one,
> Nor do not use set colours for to wear,
> Nor nourish special locks of vowed hair,
> Nor give each speech a full point of a groan,
> The courtly nymphs, acquainted with the moan
> Of them who in their lips Love's standard bear,
> "What, he!" say they of me, "now I dare swear
> He cannot love. No, no, let him alone."—
> And think so still, so Stella know my mind!
> Profess indeed I do not Cupid's art;
> But you, fair maids, at length this true shall find,
> That his right badge is worn but in the heart.
> Dumb swans, not chattering pies, do lovers prove:
> They love indeed who quake to say they love."

It was greeted with a respectful silence, or maybe just silence, by the company.

"It is a poem by Sir Philip Sidney," Popham explained, "He who died of battle wounds, not two years ago, fighting the Spaniards. A heroic soldier!"

"Ah," murmured the men, and nodded, as if that explained everything. There was a moment of awkward silence, then someone in the ranks began to sing:

> O God, my strength and fortitude,
> of force I must love thee;
> thou art my castle and defense
> in my necessity.
>
> When I sing praise unto the Lord,
> most worthy to be served,
> then from my foes I am right sure
> that I shall be preserved.
>
> The Lord shall light my candle so

that it shall shine full bright:
the Lord my God will make also
my darkness to be light.

Unspotted are the ways of God;
his Word is purely tried;
he is a sure defense to such
as in his faith abide.

Now blessed be the living God,
most worthy of all praise;
he is my rock and saving health:
so praised be he always.

By the second verse, the entire company had joined in. It was a bit ragged, but they sang with gusto; even Popham joined in. John could not help but smile. It aptly summarized the company's composition — a veneer of aristocratic love poetry over a foundation of Puritan devotion.

In the morning, Popham roused them at sunrise. "We can be in Felsted by nightfall, if we push hard," he said. The men were willing. Somehow, Popham had requisitioned some bread and cheese from the manor — some was breakfast, the rest they distributed to the troops; each man was now responsible for his own supper. Servants from the manor stood and waved them off — *happy to see the back of us,* thought John. The men began to sing as they marched.

By noon, they were well past Chelmsford. The column stopped beside the great road for their supper — modest as it was. The mood was jubilant — everyone was eager to get home, and all of them would get home, this time. This deployment was more of a lark than anything else — everyone survives, everyone gets to tell their children and grandchildren about the time they met the Queen herself. Next time, John reminded himself, it might be a very different matter.

He supposed that the men would interpret this day differently — some would say that God's mercy had spared them; others might conclude that the whole business was a waste of time — time better spent tilling the ground. Few would admit that they had feared for their lives; when in danger, men told themselves that death might strike their comrades but would pass them by: "*A thousand shall fall at thy side, and tenne thousand at thy right hand, but it shall not come neere thee.*" — or some such. To believe otherwise, would make it impossible to fill the ranks with enough willing men.

It was late afternoon when they reached the lane to the manor. John marched his arquebusiers to the armory where the guns would be stored. That done, he dismissed them. He took the road through Cobler's Green toward Felsted. He expected that Sybil and Francis would be at this parent's farm, but he would stop off to check on things at the cottage before showing up there — he might surprise them.

It was he that was surprised. Sybil was there, bent over her vegetable garden. He approached her as stealthily as he could, and then spoke: "Goodwife," he said, "I am a master carpenter. I believe I can do you service."

She gasped as she started, then recovered. She threw herself into his arms and squeezed him tightly. When she lifted her face, he saw tears in her eyes. "Indeed you can, master carpenter. Come into the house and rid yourself of these weapons."

He barely had time to take off his jack and stow the morion, the cutlass, and the guns, before she wrapped her arms around him again. "You offered to do me service, Sir. Are you an honest workman?"

"My wife says that I am," he smiled.

"Then come into the bedchamber and show me your work."

It was the best job offer he had received in a very long time.

They had a late dinner that evening. It wasn't anything fancy — some cheese, some ale, and some of the 'potatos', as Sybil preferred to call them, that she had dug up that afternoon.

"They're not bad," she said, "and the yield is very ample. You say that the French eat these often?"

"And the Spanish, too, I'm told."

"I like them better than turnips," she decided. "We can grow more next year."

It was late when they both remembered Francis. "We'll have to hurry. Your mother is probably worried about me," Sybil said.

"By now, she knows that the company has returned to Felsted. She'll be worrying about me as well," said John.

Fortunately, the twilight runs late in June. They walked the mile or so to the Porter farm in the gathering dusk, hand in hand. "I almost forgot. I saw the Queen the other day."

"Oh? And did she send her greetings to me? It's been so long since I heard from her — I was beginning to think she had forgotten me, altogether. Such a fickle woman . . ." Sybil sighed dramatically.

"No, it's true. I actually saw the Queen. She came to the camp to address the army."

Sybil peered at him, looking for a smirk that would give him away.

"Did all the men see her, or was this a private audience?"

John laughed. "You're jealous! I wouldn't have thought it of you!" Then, "Sooth, the Queen spoke to the whole army. All the men in the company are probably telling their families about it right now."

That was true. The news had already reached the Porter household in Felsted. "Here they come, like two stray sheep," remarked Ellen, as they entered the house. "We couldn't wait dinner for you."

"We have already dined," said John. Ellen raised her eyebrows and smirked at Sybil, who rolled her eyes and tossed her head ever so slightly.

"Come," said Ann, "sit, and tell us about your war."

On Sunday afternoon, John, Sybil, and Francis were back at Holy Cross church. The group had grown in numbers over the past few years; there were now nearly forty people present. The safe return of the Felsted men from the war was the most frequent topic of people's testimonies, the apparent defeat of the Spanish invasion only slightly less so. John had intended to say nothing — he was still digesting the dreams he had had while in camp. The vicar had other things in mind: "Brother Porter, surely you have something for our edification?"

John stood. At length, he began to speak: "I will first thank God, the almighty ruler of men's affairs, for bringing me safely home to my family. All of us must surely bear witness to the power of God, our deliverer, who has destroyed our enemies in the sea, even as he destroyed the host of Pharaoh when Moses led God's people out of Egypt."

A chorus of loud "Amen's" rose from the pews.

"Such a great deliverance can only be the work of God, and gives us cause to confess, with David, that His ways are too wonderful. It should move us to reverent silence." There. That should do it. He sat down.

The vicar was not satisfied. "Say more, brother. What has God shown you, in the travail of war?"

Travail of war? That hardly describes what we went through, John said to himself. Unless, of course, the vicar was speaking of a different war . . . He stood again. "I now see how vain my life has become, how ruled by pride and self-deception. I fancy myself a man of Christian humility, and my fancies are shown to be what they are — a self-serving tale told to myself. My 'charity' may ease my conscience, even as it feeds my pride — pride that I am not like other men. As if God's grace has fallen upon me for some virtue that sets me apart. As if God's blessings, which I enjoy . . ." Here, he looked at Sybil and Francis with a smile, ". . . are proof of some special merit, or that by receiving them, I become worthy of them." The room was silent now.

John continued, "Brothers and sisters, I have glimpsed my complete and wretched unworthiness, like a man peering into the abyss of hell — which is where I deserve to dwell (I do not speak of other men, only of myself) . . . Truly, I am a stranger in this place, without claim of any inheritance here. I am a wanderer without a home, a leper in the eyes of God, food for maggots, soon to be less than a memory."

He stopped to catch his breath. He supposed that he had gotten carried away (carried away by what, exactly?) — he certainly had not planned on saying any of those things . . . well, that was the vicar's fault. Should have left him alone. He glanced at Sybil. She seemed appalled at his words. There were tears in her eyes.

A woman cried out, "Have mercy, Lord!" and was joined by a chorus of others. The vicar stood and raised his hand as if pronouncing a blessing.

"Mercy there must be, else we all should perish," agreed John. "I beg for mercy, as all of you do. But receiving grace is the more difficult thing. For it is not truly grace until I know in my heart that it is completely unmerited. Any trace of entitlement, even the entitlement that I might presume because of God's love — turns it from grace, into something else — some merit, something that sets me apart from other men. And unless it is truly grace, it only feeds my pride: thus blessing becomes my downfall."

More "Amen"s from the assembly.

"Today, I shall return to my home, to eat, and sleep, and love . . ." — another glance at Sybil — ". . . and tomorrow, I shall return to my labors. God willing, I shall prosper. God forbid that I should fall back into the presumption that prosperity infects us with. I am no more deserving of these things than any other man — not the Spaniard whose bones rest on the bottom of the sea, or the most miserable beggar in England. Not the sick man on his deathbed, or the felon at the gallows. God willing, I shall remember this always."

Afterward, the vicar approached, and said, "The Spirit was strong in you today, brother. We were all blessed by your words of encouragement."

Encouragement? Was that what it was? "I do not know what came over me," John replied.

"I think I do. I was right about you; you have a gift. You should learn to use it," said the vicar. John felt Sybil squeeze his arm — hard. It was time to go.

"Gift?"

"And afterward will I pour out my Spirit upon all flesh: and your sons and your daughters shall prophesy, your old men shall dream dreams, and your young men shall see visions" quoted the vicar. *"Quench not the Spirit. Despise not prophecying."*

John had no answer for his remark. He bowed his head slightly, and let Sybil lead him outside.

She said nothing until they were well away from the church. Then "I know the scripture of which the vicar spoke. There is more that he did not recite."

"What's that?"

"And I will shew wonders in the heavens and in the earth, blood and fire, and pillars of smoke. The sun shall be turned into darkness, and the moon into blood, before the great and terrible day of the LORD come."

"Ah. Do you think he meant us to reflect on the portion he did not quote, then?"

"I do not know what he meant. I am not sure that even he knew what he meant. I doubt that you understood the meaning of what you said."

That surprised him. He didn't actually recall everything he had said. "In that case, it is probably nothing. I am no prophet. Do not let it worry you."

"Whatever it is, it is not nothing. I know thee well — well enough to distinguish between thy ordinary speech, and the Word of the Spirit. The vicar is right. You were prophesying."

Once again, John had no answer for her remark. It was true that half of what he had said was prompted by his dreams (did that make him an 'old man'?)

"I am not worried that thy speaking was inspired. I am worried about what it may mean for us — or our family. If God has placed his hand upon thee, it cannot be undone. But our future cannot be the same as I had imagined it. If the 'great and terrible day of the LORD' is indeed coming, what of our children?"

"I cannot say. Two weeks ago, I would have assured thee that God himself would protect us from all harm. Four days ago, I would have pointed to the defeat of the Armada as proof of God's protection. Today, I have no such assurances. Perhaps God's mercy will spare us; if it be so, then it is purely mercy — no merit of mine can claim it. If I perish, it is no more than justice; if I prosper, it is not to my credit. I am sorry that I cannot offer you any more comfort than that."

She looked into his eyes. "There is love, is there not?"

"Aye. There is love."' He smiled at her and kissed her.

"I mean, God's love," she said. *"For what man is there among you, which if his sonne aske him bread, woulde giue him a stone? Or if he aske fish, wil he giue him a serpent? If ye then, which are euill, can giue to your children good giftes, howe much more shall your Father which is in heauen, giue good thinges to them that aske him?"*

John bowed his head. "Well spoken. *Who shall finde a vertuous woman? for her price is farre aboue the pearles."* He sighed. "I cannot say why my hopes should be dimmed so; perhaps the war has grown doubts in me, about God's love."

"Perhaps that is why he has given thee into my care," she said.

October, 1588: Harwich

The crew of the *Egyptian Queen* trickled back into Harwich, starting in August, and throughout September. The wreck of the *Queen* was old news, by then — although everyone had his own version of the story to tell. It soon became apparent that nearly all of the men had survived, one way or another; their paths back to their home port were various and complicated.

For Harriet Foxe, each group of arrivals brought disappointment. Everyone agreed that Roger had been spared in the battle with the Spanish fleet, and that Captain Foxe had been wounded. No one seemed to know more than that, though some had heard that both of them were still in Amsterdam. Every new arrival was a moment of hope, and every one a disappointment.

There was also news about the Armada itself. The English fleet had continued its pursuit northward for several days after the battle of Gravelines. As ships ran out of ammunition, they turned back southward, in the face of rising southerly winds. The Spanish, struggling to reorganize, slogged northward. Admiral Guzman decided that the best course was to circumnavigate the British Isles altogether and return to Spain by sailing west, far enough to pass either through the Irish Sea, or west of Ireland altogether. It was a fateful decision: they were already short of food and water, and they were not prepared for the storms that they would encounter in the North Atlantic. Spanish ships were driven as far north as the coast of Norway and wrecked. Their effort to pass westward of Scotland and Ireland was nullified by that old bugaboo of sailors — the inability to accurately measure their longitude. Without their anchors, many of the ships were at the mercy of the wind and waves. Dozens were wrecked on the west coast of Ireland by a gale off the Atlantic; most of the sailors who made it to shore were executed. In the end, only sixty-seven ships of the Armada ever returned to Spain, and their crews were much reduced by disease and starvation. Fewer than four in ten of the men who had left Lisbon in May were alive by the end of that year.

It should have been a triumph for the English Navy. Instead, it was a fiasco nearly as complete as the defeat of the Armada. The fleet reassembled at Margate, the closest English port to Calais, where the sailors remained on board their ships until they were paid, as was customary. Parliament was in no hurry to appropriate the funds: It was anticipated that the Armada might try to force their way southward again, and the government wanted the fleet to be positioned to intercept them. While the fleet waited, typhus spread through the ships; sailors began dying in large numbers. More died from malnutrition. When it was over, the crew of the fleet that had scored such an overwhelming victory was only a memory.

A Dutch fly boat slipped into the harbor at Harwich in mid-October, and three men disembarked. One was unmistakably African, one was young and spry, the third was older, and walked with a peculiar gait — he had a wooden leg, which sounded off the cobblestones with every other stride. He held a crutch as well, to steady him.

It was a raw day, with a stiff onshore breeze. All three men were cloaked against the wind. It took a moment for people on the street to recognize them — Dick Benby, the blackamoor alehouse owner, Roger Foxe, the young man, and haggard, red-haired Captain Billy Foxe, with his wooden leg. They were greeted then, and as a crowd grew, cheered. "Billy Foxe lost a leg and a ship," people said, "but the men who sailed with him are the lucky ones — none of them are starving to death aboard some ship in the harbor at Margate."

That was the consensus on the waterfront. Captain Foxe had lost his ship — his pride and joy — but nearly all the men who had sailed with him were still alive and healthy. Losing a ship was a small price to pay for a man's life — or so they said in the pubs and alehouses. Foxe's investors were not so sanguine.

Dick Benby left them to hurry to his own family. Roger and the Captain stumped their way to their house. Harriet, who had just heard of a new arrival at the docks, was just leaving to question whoever it was about her missing family. She gasped audibly and shrieked when she recognized Roger, then her husband, and threw herself into their arms.

"Easy, woman! There's less of me than you remember," said Foxe, attempting a gruff tone. Harriet could see that there were tears in his eyes.

"I'll take all that there is," she said and smiled as she wiped her tears, then his.

Roger was grinning. "I brought him home, Mum, just like I promised."

"Aye son, so ye did." She reached out with her free arm, and caressed his face. Then "Come, I have a surprise for the both of ye."

She led them into the house. "Well, take off yer coats. Ye won't be leavin' anytime soon!" She left for a moment and came back with something in her arms. "Meet yer new brother, Roger," she said with a smile. Billy Foxe stood, as if his wooden leg was nailed to the floor. Harriet held the baby boy up for him to hold. "His name is William," she said. "I thought you wouldn't mind that name, for your son."

Foxe took the child in his arms and began to weep.

"We can call him something else if the name doesn't suit ye," said Harriet, looking flustered.

Foxe shook his head. "Nay. William is perfect. He is perfect. William it is." He was sobbing, now, and handed young William back to his mother. "Forgive me, Love, I have been away for a very long time."

"Well, ye're home now. That's the important thing."

Foxe wiped his face with his large, rough hands. "Aye. That's the important thing."

Part 21: Against the Current

1590: The Protestant Wind

Young Maurice, Prince of Nassau, had attained his position of "Stadtholder" of the Dutch Republic, more or less by default. His father had been assassinated at the behest of Philip, King of Spain, in 1584. Maurice's older brother, Philip William, was a hostage in Spain, abducted by King Philip when he was thirteen years old and groomed to become the Catholic King of the Netherlands. The Earl of Leicester had held the title briefly in 1587 until his disgraceful mishandling of his troops and the ire of his Queen had forced him to give it up. Which left Maurice, twenty-three years of age, as the man with the strongest hereditary claim to lead the revolt. Against all expectations, he rose to the challenge. 1590 would be the first of ten "Glory Years," in which Maurice's army captured city after city from the Spanish. The King of Spain was forced, at last, to ask for a truce, which did not constitute a concession of Dutch sovereignty; but for all intents and purposes, the Dutch Republic was established as an independent, permanent state.

Unexpected events in France had shifted the balance in England's favor, as well. Henri III became exasperated with the bullying of the Duke of Guise and the Catholic League (he was the King, after all), and it led him to rash acts. He invited the Duke to a private meeting in his own palace, where his guards assassinated the Duke, hoping to end his troubles with a single stroke. It did not have the effect hoped for: the Duke's followers rioted, and threatened the life of the King. Henri was forced to flee Paris, and there was only one place to go — to the army of his Huguenot cousin, the Prince of Navarre. Together, the two last male members of the royal line advanced on Paris — Henri III to reclaim his throne; Henri, Prince of Navarre, to cement his claim to the royal succession. It was a strange alliance indeed and lasted only until Henri III was himself assassinated in 1589, by an agent of the Catholic League — in revenge for the murder of the Duke of Guise. There seemed to be no way to end the long civil war in France. Henri of Navarre came up with an unexpected solution — he claimed the throne as Henri IV, a Catholic king. His religious conversion was politically significant, as it ended the civil strife. He was no friend of the Catholic League and insisted that the Protestant religion would be tolerated and protected in France. Personally,

Henri is supposed to have said, "Paris is well worth a mass," — hardly an endorsement that Phillip of Spain would welcome; but France was weary of war, and a nominally Catholic King was preferable to a Protestant one. By 1594, Paris would welcome Henri IV as their King. Spain had one less ally in her war with Protestantism in the Netherlands and England.

Philip was not ready to give up. He assembled a second Armada in 1596, and a third in 1597. After his death, a fourth one was launched in 1601. None were able to approach the success of the first; in all three years, the Spanish fleets were dispersed and damaged by fierce storms — "Protestant winds" — before the coast of England was sighted. By this time, the financial losses were becoming ruinous. There would be no peace between England and Spain while either Philip or Elizabeth lived, but no invasion of England was practical.

June 1594: Felsted

Sybil Porter's fourth child was a boy. They named him John, after his father. There were so many men of that name in the village, that they called him "Johnny," just to keep things clear. The years of poor harvests, so long dreaded, had come at last. Food was scarce, and thus expensive. But the carpentry business was thriving, so they could afford to eat well enough — unlike some of their neighbors. Sybil began to rely on her potato patch to make up the difference. Soon she was planting nearly an acre each year. She gave some to her neighbors as well and showed them how to grow their own. In a matter of a few years, many families came to rely on these strange "earth apples" (or "devil's apples," as some insisted on calling them). Sybil also sold some of her crop. You could tell something about the financial condition of a family, by whether they fed their 'potatos' to their livestock, or ate them for dinner. More than a few purchased 'potatos' from Sybil "just to feed the hogs," when Sybil knew very well that they owned no hogs at all. Sybil understood why keeping up appearances in hard times was important; she thanked God for feeding her family, every day.

More children were born: William in 1596, then Rose, four years later. John added a second story to the cottage, with rooms upstairs for the children to sleep. Business was so good that he stopped farming with his father and focused on woodworking. The lathe was his pride and joy; no other carpenters in the area had one, short of Braintree. And even as the poor were pushed to the brink of starvation, other men prospered; the sort of men whose wives had a taste for furniture with a more contemporary look — chairs and tables that featured turned spindles and other elements that the lathe could produce. The market was lucrative, and he prospered. Soon, his sons would join him in his shop. Then they would expand . . . he had visions of great success — God willing, of course.

God's will was never very far from his mind. He continued to attend the "conventicle" at Holy Cross on Sunday afternoons, with the other "visible saints." There, he testified and "prophesied," as the Spirit moved him, aside from the other congregants. But the question of where the Spirit was moving his affairs to remained a question. Some circumstances could be taken as 'signs' that he was on the right track: his family prospered through the lean years while others suffered, his children were healthy; even the plague passed them by the previous year. Surprisingly, they seemed to have escaped the notice of the government, whose agents were still making arrests, and imposing fines across the kingdom.

John came to believe that God was preparing him and his fellow believers for some great work in the uncertain future, as did many others. Waiting and watching was the task at hand. He and Sybil sought to prepare their children for whatever God had in store. They began every day with prayer for the whole household; any child old enough to speak was expected to offer some sort of prayer, however simple. Older children were taught to read and expected to recite passages from the family Bible. When they were old enough for grammar school, the expectations were more stringent — memorizing and reciting the Heidelberg catechism, praying extemporaneously, explaining the meaning of a parable.

The family conformed strictly to the laws on church attendance (the better to avoid the attention of the government), and the children were held to an even stricter standard of personal behavior — most recreations were forbidden on Sundays, coarse or crude language was punishable by corporal discipline, clothing in bright colors or fashionable styles was frowned upon.

The vicar regarded the Porters as a model family: pious, reverent, hard-working. He took their success as a validation of his own spiritual discernment, and preaching: "I recognized that God had a special purpose for the man when he first came back to the village." he would say, "He has become an example of godliness to the whole parish. He has submitted himself to the discipline of the Lord, and he has reaped the harvest of obedience. Note how obedient his children are, how submissive and mild his wife is."

John found these remarks amusing. Sybil's 'mildness' was because she had no time for gossip or banter, and could not be goaded into an exchange of insults with anyone — it annoyed her, and her children required her full attention in any social situation, lest their 'obedience' falter. As for 'submissive', she was submissive enough, just so long as John didn't infringe on her areas of responsibility — which he had learned not to do. She was the person he trusted most in this world — more than he trusted himself, at times.

Meanwhile, they watched and waited.

July 1595: Derwent

The Archdeacon was late this year. Edward Chase had been ready for his visit for more than two weeks. That was not a problem, really, but Father Chase was looking forward to putting this one annual contact with the church hierarchy behind him. The harvest had not been that good this year, and the offerings reflected that. The news was that other parts of England had suffered as well — in some places, the people were facing famine. Things were not so dire in Derwent; food prices were up for those things that had to be brought in from outside, but most people could grow the bulk of what they ate.

Father Chase and his wife were blessed with six children, now — a bountiful harvest of another kind. Only the one set of twins, thankfully, because keeping the whole brood under their parent's control was a challenge. The twins were seven years old now, which meant that they could help watch after their younger siblings, at least for part of every day. This was needed whenever Meg was called to serve as a midwife or otherwise bring her healing skills to some house or farm. Sometimes, Edward could look after them, which suited him very well. Sometimes, both of them were called to the same house.

Bess could be relied on in a pinch, but keeping house at the rectory was a bigger job than ever — children are not innately tidy creatures — and there were now eight mouths to feed, not counting her own.

They managed it. It was as different from Edward's old life as he could imagine. All of these small people, who needed to be carried, or demanded to be held, who clung, who cried, who laughed, who disrupted everything orderly and sober — all the tangle of emotions and passions in his children — was overwhelming, yet it called something out of him that he did not suspect was there — even as it absorbed his energy, he found energy that he didn't know could be found. And there was laughter, more than he had ever known. He reflected on the circumstances that had brought him to Derwent, how he had imagined that his exile to this place would be quiet, if not boring — something about warming his feet in front of a fire on a winter's evening, or some such silly thing.

It was midmorning. Edward was in the sanctuary at the church, just emerging from the vestry, when the familiar and ample figure of the archdeacon appeared; he was not alone this time. His companion was a familiar figure as well, though not expected. "Welcome to Derwent," he greeted them both, "I trust you had a pleasant journey?"

The Archdeacon shook his head, "That road from Bamford seems to get worse every year. Someone must do something, or this village will be simply unreachable one of these days!"

Edward nodded. *Someone certainly must do something. Although talk like that might suggest to some of the villagers that they'd be better off without the road, and the outsiders that used it from time to time . . .* "And what fortune brings Master Bedford to our village this day?"

Charles Bedford smiled faintly and replied, "I have other business here, so it seemed prudent that the Archdeacon and I travel together — especially in consideration of the condition of the roads."

It sounded like a mild rebuke, but Edward wasn't sure who it was directed at. Maybe Bedford was in a grumpy mood — traveling with the Archdeacon could have that effect on a person . . . "Can I offer you some refreshment?"

"I would be glad for a drink," said the Archdeacon, "But I haven't much time. I intend to return to Bamford this afternoon. The accommodations are more suitable there."

By which you mean the Rev. Hooper's house, and his ample table, thought Edward. This was good news; sending the Archdeacon on his way as soon as possible suited Edward very well. If he could prevent Charles Bedford from spending the night in the rectory, the day might well be salvaged.

"Will you be leaving with the Archdeacon, as well?" he asked Bedford.

"More than likely," was the reply. "I have some business to transact here. I do not expect it to take very long."

Edward turned back to the vestry. "I'll fetch the ledgers and the money box, and we can meet in the rectory. If we finish our business by suppertime, Bess will prepare us a meal, and you can both be on your way."

The Archdeacon agreed before Charles Bedford could say anything: "That will be satisfactory."

The three of them sat around the dining table, while Edward went through the ledgers with the Archdeacon. Bess provided each man a stein of ale, which relaxed the Archdeacon, at least. "The harvest last year was not bountiful" Edward explained, "enough to fend off starvation, but the offering was a bit smaller."

The Archdeacon nodded. "It is the same everywhere, or worse. At least you have met your quota." After Edward paid the agreed amount, the Archdeacon sighed, took a draught of his ale, and spoke: "There is another matter that I shall make you aware of. . . ."

"I am listening," Edward replied.

"Your work here in Derwent has been noticed — you have served this village well — no scandals, disorders, tumults, or controversies . . ."

That's because you're not here on Saints Eve or Christmastide, Edward thought to himself.

". . . in short, your . . . rehabilitation appears to have been successful. The bishop supposes that you might be ready for a larger parish, one less out-of-the-way. One with more opportunities for advancement. I have heard that you are an accomplished preacher, and your administration of this parish appears to be faultless. I will be making a report to my bishop about your progress here."

Edward leaned back in his chair, stunned. *Is he really saying that my exile is over? What would Bancroft have to say about this?* He resisted the impulse to glance at Charles Bedford for a hint — surely he was in on this . . .

"Father Chase," Bess stood in the doorway to the kitchen, "I must buy a few things at the market if these guests will be staying for supper."

Edward nodded. "Of course, Bess. I should have said. Thank you for taking care of this."

"The baby is asleep; the other children will be coming shortly, looking for their supper." She hurried out.

"Children?" asked the Archdeacon. "I don't recall meeting any of your children."

"If you had, you would remember," said Edward. "There are six of them, and they always make an impression."

"And what about your wife?" asked Bedford. "A lovely woman, as I recall. A shepherdess, wasn't she?"

"She still is. Also, the village midwife. She was called out this morning — another babe is on the way, it seems."

"Where are the children now?"

"The baby is sleeping yonder. We pay a local widow to look after the rest when both Meg and I must be working."

"Then you should welcome this opportunity," suggested the Archdeacon. "A larger parish, with better educational choices — school, apprenticeships. Given your own academic record, perhaps your sons could attend a university one day."

That last remark hit home. One question that Edward had been avoiding was the education of his children, especially his sons. There wasn't much future for them here in Derwent . . . The matter was out of his hands though. The Bishop and the Court of High Commission would decide. It would be hard for Meg . . . or maybe impossible, he realized with a chill . . . He began to wish that his administration of the parish had a few faults — not enough to get him removed, just enough to allow him to stay. He had no idea how many such 'faults' would do the job. There was a knot forming in his stomach.

Just then, there was a commotion in the hall chamber. The baby, Catherine, was stirring. Edward rose and went to see what the fuss was about. Just boredom, apparently. She smiled when he appeared and raised her arms. He picked her up and returned to the kitchen. His two companions smiled and cooed at her for a bit, but none offered to hold her — *Just as well*, Edward thought, *I'd rather she not learn anything about the likes of you two, until she is old enough to recognize the danger; better never at all.*

There was a commotion outside. In burst the twins, Edwin and Edwina, breathless — they had been racing each other, as they often did. That meant that the other three would not be far behind.

"Papa!" said Edwin, "Old Jesus has escaped from the graveyard, again. Shall I set the dog on him?"

"What good would that do? How many times have we committed Old Jesus to the churchyard? And how many times has he escaped? He won't stay there without some companionship. Where's his mother, Mary?"

"Up there," Edwina pointed toward the sky. "She was taken up this morning."

"And how is it that Old Jesus was left behind?"

"The shepherd said he didn't have time to bother with Old Jesus today; he always wants to fight with the other rams — thinks he's Lord of the flock."

The look on the Archdeacon's face almost made Edward laugh. Bedford was puzzled by the conversation, but the Archdeacon's expression was somewhere between outrage and terror as if he expected lightning to fall from heaven.

"Then we'll have to lock him up for the day and send him up tomorrow. Where is he?"

As if on cue a large, fat ram ambled in through the open front door and stared at his guests.

"There he is!" cried Edwina, and rushed to put her arms around the ram's neck.

Edwin addressed the two guests: "We call him Old Jesus because he was resurrected on Easter," he offered soberly, "by my mama. This was before I was born, but there are many living witnesses to his resurrection. First, we called him Baby Jesus, then Young Jesus, but now we call him Old Jesus, because he is old now — old for a sheep, that is."

There was a twinkle of recognition in Bedford's eyes, the Archdeacon was still struggling with a mix of emotions.

"This is quite nearly blasphemous!" sputtered the Archdeacon. He slapped the table loudly, for emphasis. Old Jesus, on cue, rushed toward the Archdeacon and leaped up on the table — an impressive feat, for a three-hundred-pound animal. He shoved his nose into the Archdeacon's stein and could be heard lapping up what he found there. The Archdeacon was too surprised to react, for a moment — he froze, his face barely a foot from Old Jesus's impressive set of horns; Bedford's mouth hung open, as he leaned back in his chair. "Oats!" shouted Edward, Edwin, and Edwina, almost in unison. Old Jesus turned and jumped back down onto the floor. It had all happened so quickly, that no one said anything for a moment. The Archdeacon recovered himself and exclaimed hoarsely, "Resurrected? By a woman?" An explanation was in order.

"He was stillborn," said Edward, "or so it appeared. On Easter Sunday, just after the church service. My wife, who is a shepherdess," — here he glanced at Bedford — "was able to revive him. There were several children present, and they insisted on naming him. I rather favored 'Lazarus', but they were quite insistent about it. He's a family pet really, but he isn't housebroken" — Old Jesus chose this moment to 'baaa' loudly, as if he had been insulted, and Bedford began to laugh out loud.

"I am disappointed," huffed the Archdeacon. "I expect the man of God to take a stronger hand in educating his children. This can only lead to doctrinal confusion. What do the other people in the parish call this animal?"

"Old Jesus," said Edwin, slowly. His face bore an expression of forced patience as if he were explaining some simple matter to a very dull-witted listener. Bedford tried to suppress his laughter down to a chuckle.

Just then, two more children burst into the house, followed by their mother, holding a third child by the hand.

"May I present my wife, Meg," said Edward. "Meg, you have met Master Bedford. This is the Archdeacon, whom you also know."

Meg smiled and curtseyed. "We are honored to have you in our home," she said. "Can ye stay for dinner?"

The Archdeacon appeared somewhat mollified by the suggestion of dinner; Bedford, still chuckling, nodded.

"We've no wine today, I fear. The vintages have been poor, along with all the other harvests. Wine is too dear, these days. I have difficulty even keeping an adequate supply in the vestry," John explained, with a glance at Meg.

Bedford looked a little disappointed. "The ale will do fine," said the Archdeacon. With all six Chase children in the house, things were noisy and busy. John suggested to his guests that they return the ledgers to the vestry until summoned back for dinner. The Archdeacon seemed reluctant to move — trapped amid the whirlwind that the rectory had become. "Let him stay with me while Bess and I start dinner," suggested Meg, "we'll see to his needs."

"I'll go to the vestry with you," interjected Bedford. Meg shot Edward a look that said, *Trust me to take care of this*. Something special in the Archdeacon's ale? Bedford looked determined; something was on his mind. Maybe separating his guests for a moment was a good idea . . . Edwin and Edwina appeared to have engaged the Archdeacon in a discussion about husbanding sheep — their diseases, their feeding, the best uses of their manure . . .

It was a short walk to the church. It took only a moment to lock the ledgers in the vestry.

"There is somewhat for us to discuss," said Bedford. "Better if the Archdeacon is elsewhere occupied."

That was direct. Evidently, Charles Bedford had his own reasons for visiting Derwent.

"I will put it to you plainly," said Bedford. "Things have changed in England, in the years that you have lived in this place. Perhaps you recall our conversations when first we met, on the road to Ipswich?"

"That would be the day I was arrested, as I recall."

"Quite so. Do you remember that I asked you about the threats that our church faces?"

Faces? Not 'faced', but 'faces' — as if the threat is still present . . . "I believe I do. I think I explained that the Brownists were a greater threat than the Catholics."

Bedford nodded. "So you did. I did not find your ideas particularly credible at the time, and neither did my master, Richard Bancroft. Time has given your opinions more weight."

More weight. More weight to the opinions of an exiled parish priest. This makes no sense. What is Bedford up to?

Bedford continued, "Now that the military threat from Spain has subsided, we are more troubled by domestic opponents. You have heard of the writings of 'Martin Marprelate'?"

"I have heard the name, but no more than that. Is he a Brownist?"

"It would appear so. 'Martin Marprelate' is a pseudonym; the identity of the writer is unknown to us."

"A separatist, then. Perhaps he writes from outside the kingdom?"

"We do not believe so. The writings refer to events and situations that would be of little matter to a separatist living in a foreign land. We suspect that the writer, and the press that prints his vile work are here in England, somewhere."

"And you imagine that I would know? Do you think that there is a secret printing press here in Derwent?"

Bedford chuckled. "That would be a bold thing indeed, for a place like this. Nay, the writings suggest a man well-acquainted with the affairs of the church, its bishops, scholars, and the like. Indeed, 'Martin Marprelate' claims to be a bishop, in his own right, or even a member of the privy council."

"Then I do not understand why we are speaking of this."

"Let me be plain. Martin Marprelate's tracts are widely read. All attempts to suppress them have failed. Men who would read nothing else will revel in these tracts, men who cannot read at all will cheer anyone who will read them aloud. Printing presses have been found and destroyed. Men have been hanged for writing the tracts, even as they deny authorship. But the damage is done; these ideas are whispered everywhere, even proclaimed publicly where men dare to do so."

"And you cannot hang enough men, or burn enough of them, to put out the fire," injected Edward. "Depriving priests of their livings is useless because they are not the ones spreading the message."

Bedford nodded. "You grasp the problem very well. Indeed, I suppose you predicted it."

"Predicted or not, what makes you suppose that I have anything to say about it now? Are you seeking my advice?" *Unbelievable. Ironic, but unbelievable.*

"The church needs more than advice. We need an answer that will refute these tracts and change the hearts and minds of those who have fallen under their influence. We have scholars aplenty, but their writing does not appeal to the common people. A man like yourself, who has lived among the lower sorts, might be able to speak to them in terms they would understand. (I do not discount your education and scholarship, nor your skill as a preacher, but an academic answer is not the answer we need)."

"You want me to author tracts to refute them? What could I possibly bring to a debate with an author that you admit is anonymous? Why would you imagine that I would do so? I understand that I am at the mercy of the Court of High Commission, and the whims of 'Old Basset' (How is he faring, by the way?), but you cannot imagine that any writing you would wring out of me by coercion would be more than dead words — and you have plenty of those, already!" (This last remark was a bit intemperate, but Edward was annoyed with the presumption of the man, and it just slipped out.)

"As for your last question, the Reverend Doctor Bancroft is chaplain to the Archbishop of Canterbury. He will almost certainly be elevated to a bishopric of his own, though it is said that he is already such, in all but name — the Archbishop is in declining health and relies heavily upon him. He is likely the second most powerful man in the Church hierarchy today.

Referring to him by nickname is an indulgence that most men cannot afford."

That sounded like a warning. Edward took it as such.

Bedford continued, "Doctor Bancroft, in his current position, can scarcely be concerned with matters in a small parish like this one, or a person such as yourself. He barely recognized you when you last spoke to him; I am certain that he has forgotten that encounter. I have been given wide latitude in the matter at hand, and I am here to negotiate."

Forgotten? That stung, as it was probably intended to. Not as much as the reminder that while Edward was reminded every day that his very life depended on the whims of Bancroft, Bancroft was free to forget about him altogether. That fairly summarized the balance of power between them. "Negotiate?"

"Aye," said Bedford. "I hope to obtain your willing cooperation. As you say, nothing of value could come from forcing you to write something against your will."

"Why me?"

"I have spoken with you at some length; I have taken the measure of your mind. There are a few men I know of who have the rhetorical skills for this task. You had the insight to predict this state of affairs before anyone else that I know of did. And truthfully, your condition of life is such that you may be more willing than others to offer your skills for the inducements that I can offer."

In other words, Edward said to himself, *you suppose that my miserable existence in this tiny village will make me more malleable to your purpose than other men.* "What inducements do you offer?

"I could arrange for your promotion to a larger parish, though I suspect you might not find that appealing. I could provide some monetary compensation, should your writing prove successful. You have three sons, I believe. I could arrange for them to be admitted to the university of your choice — Cambridge, for instance? — when they are of age."

That last offer hit home. Bedford knew how to play this game — identify a man's weaknesses, offer some flattery, then serve up something tempting.

"I doubt that anything I would write with a clear conscience would suit you. As you say, you know my mind. My honest opinions would hardly be a comfort to your superiors."

"That is true. Your writing would have to be anonymous."

Edward was shocked into momentary silence. What was Bedford's game?

"I see your astonishment. I will explain. 'Martin Marprelate' has attacked the Church hierarchy, as your old Puritan friends have, but his attacks are also directed against the leaders of the Puritan party. The words of this 'Marprelate' are coarse — which makes them appealing to secular readers — anyone who enjoys seeing the authorities on our realm held up to ridicule or shame. We must respond in kind — with coarseness and ridicule of our own. It does not serve our purpose if the Puritan luminaries are seen to be in league with the Queen's bishops in any matter of religious discourse. Anything you write must appear as if it comes from the common folk, in the tradition of poking fun at all figures of authority. Only then can we expect to win their approval."

"So you would expect me to advocate a Puritan view?"

"More like a yeoman with Puritan sympathies — a tradesman or a farmer, maybe. The sort of people that you know. Nothing academic, none of these debates about divine authority and church polity — and absolutely nothing that would detract from the Queen's supremacy in religious matters. You must attack the non-conformists and separatists — not directly, but by making them look silly, petty, or hypocritical. We need to discredit them, make them a laughingstock."

"But Parliament just passed an 'Act Against Puritans'; anyone who refuses to worship in the Queen's way must pay a fine for the first offense, and must leave England altogether if they persist in their error, else be put to death. Why engage them in controversy at all?"

"There aren't enough constables and magistrates in the kingdom willing to enforce the law everywhere, and not enough jail cells to hold them, even in places where the civil authorities are on our side. Once, we could harry them into leaving for Holland or some such other place; now, they refuse to leave. They meet in secret, for 'prophesyings', they attend their local parish church on Sunday morning, and secret conventicles at other times. They are too numerous to keep track of. We must find a way to change their minds."

It was all familiar to Edward Chase — too familiar. It appeared that things had gone more or less the direction he had feared, years ago. Ironic that his prescription for conventicles in every parish had succeeded so well — too well, it seemed. But that was mostly the fault of the government — by removing or coopting the leadership of the Puritan movement, they had, in effect, decapitated it — they had removed the scholars and teachers that could have kept them all on a path of sound doctrine and good order. Left to themselves, the separate groups were vulnerable to excesses of every sort — even to the point of taking the attitude that their homegrown theology, rudimentary as it was, was good enough, that the scholarly positions of both the Puritans and the Hierarchy were pointlessly arcane, and even self-serving. It was a playground for preachers with charisma, and an exaggerated sense of their own spiritual insight. No one, apparently, was alarmed yet about the other side of his prognosis — that the forces feeding the rise of religious separatism would lead, inevitably, to a demand for a larger share of political power. Time would tell.

"It is not clear to me what you would have me refute," he noted. He doubted that Bedford had actually read the tracts that he was so determined to counter.

"As it happens, I can show you some of it," said Bedford. He reached into his doublet and produced a folded sheet of paper. "This," he said, unfolding the paper and spreading it out, "first appeared in February of 1589, the year after the Armada. See here, how he ridicules the Bishops as papists, then the prayers of Puritans as 'beeble babble'."

Edward scanned the document. The phrases were there, but he understood them to be satirical — 'Martin' was not so much attacking Puritans, as repeating the attacks that the bishops had made upon them. "Are you sure that he intends to attack the Puritans?"

"Quite. He focuses most of his venom on the bishops, but he seems to regard the Puritan leaders as complicit in their errors. All of the evidence points to a non-conformist with separatist sympathies — the anonymity, the secret printing press. This writer is the enemy of every other view. The criticism he levels at the authority of Bishops could be equally applied to Presbyters in Scotland. His message is subtle, but it amounts to complete freedom of conscience for every man, without "interference" from the secular government, or any ecclesiastical authority whatsoever. He is as much your enemy, as mine."

"I could try to refute these tracts if I could read them all," suggested John.

"Nay, that is not possible; possession of these tracts is a crime. And it is not what we need. We simply need a persuasive voice to uphold the necessity of good government in the church — Episcopal or Presbyterian. We need a voice that the common folk will hear and heed. We need to hold the separatists up to ridicule. We need to show that they are rejecting the rule of the Queen herself . . ."

Which of course, is treason, thought Edward. *Of course. Hanging is the time-honored solution for the government when encountering people with troublesome ideas.* "That I cannot do," he said, shaking his head.

"How's that?"

"I cannot sustain an argument that separatists are guilty of treason, simply because of their beliefs about conscience. If they truly conspire to harm the Queen or overthrow her government, that is treason, regardless of their religion. But I will not propose that a man is a traitor simply because he reads his Bible differently than I."

"Others have done so, with great success."

"How do you measure that success? With hangings and quarterings? Where has that success gotten you other than where you are today, asking for help from the unlikeliest places? None of the 'common folk' whom you propose to persuade are impressed with your 'successes'. If you truly would speak to them, you must take a different line."

"You will not help us, then." It was a statement, not a question. "Even for advancement, or reward, or the future of your sons?"

"No advancement or reward could induce me to accuse a man of treason simply because he disagrees with me. Indeed, such things no longer hold any appeal to me whatsoever." *Careful! Don't give this man any more leverage than he already has . . .*

Edward sighed. "My son's futures are of course, important to me. But even if I were willing to denounce a man to his death, it would not serve the purpose you have described. You should take a different approach altogether."

"What approach?"

"The people you say that you wish to persuade will not be moved by more writing like this," he said, brushing the document with the back of his hand. "They will chuckle at the insults directed toward the bishops. They will laugh at hypocrisy. But if you want them to reject separatism, you must appeal on other grounds. They see hypocrisy everywhere; laughter is their antidote to bitterness and anger. In their own lives, these people look to practicality more than philosophy. They will readily agree that order, stability, and integrity are wanted in the church. They recognize that men who seek to lead a congregation without the oversight of others is likely to do so for reasons of vanity and pride, more than humility and righteousness. They understand that the church can be a source of unity in a village and recognize that self-righteous prattle and controversy can tear the fabric of their community apart. They will turn away from separatism if it can be shown to be divisive."

"You will help us, then?" Bedford looked hopeful. Edward felt strangely sympathetic for some reason.

"I will write an essay about the folly of separatism. I cannot promise that it will suit you."

"That will be a beginning. If the writing is good, I can arrange for your son — Edwin, isn't it? — to be admitted to Cambridge, when he is thirteen years old. We can also bear the expense of his education."

"What author's name shall I use for this essay?"

Bedford thought for a moment. "Something like 'Goodman Commonsense' would do, I think. You can send it to me in London, care of the Archbishop's Palace at Lambeth. Better yet, address it to 'Eager Disciple' at that location. I will have the Archbishop's servants look out for it, and make sure that I receive it."

And that was it. Edward realized that he had made a sort of bargain — a bargain with the devil himself, quite possibly. How likely was that to turn out well? *At least the serpent will be out of my garden for another year or so,* he told himself. Then another voice spoke from inside his head: *What need has the serpent to be in your garden if you are tilling it for him?*

He reassured himself. What choice did he have, really? An outright refusal could have prompted Bedford to send him to jail, or worse. He had tried to walk the fine line between resistance and collaboration. Surely a path of integrity was there if only he could find it. As for Bedford's promise to send Edwin to university, that was unlikely to be kept — in another five years, Bedford could be disgraced, or even dead. Thinking of it in that way made it seem less like accepting a bribe. And there was always the chance that his writing would be rejected — that would let both of them off the hook. Perhaps that was what he should hope for . . . In the meantime, Bedford would be leaving Derwent; that had to be a good thing.

They walked back to the rectory, where the Archdeacon was waiting for them. Dinner was ready; Bedford ate heartily, the Archdeacon appeared somewhat mollified. Then it was time for them to leave. Both men had arrived on horseback, and their mounts were saddled and ready. "I will be expecting some writing from you within the month," said Bedford.

The Archdeacon beckoned Edward aside, with a wave of his hand: "I must tell you, Reverend Chase, that I am unconvinced that another position for you is warranted at this time. You have unquestionably had success here. Indeed, this sort of rustic placement seems suited to you, and you to it. I regret that I will have to report some of the unorthodoxies I have witnessed to my superiors." In a lower tone, he murmured "You would do well to take more care with the naming of animals." With that, he bade farewell to the household, and joined Charles Bedford, with the horses. The men mounted and headed south, toward Bamford.

Meg stood next to Edward. "Tell me what just happened," she said, in an undertone.

"For one, I think we have persuaded the Archdeacon that I should remain here in Derwent for some time to come. It was fortuitous that Old Jesus chose to make an appearance, right before supper."

Meg nodded. "Fortuitous."

Edward looked at her sharply. "Did Bess tell you what the Archdeacon said to me at the dining table?"

Meg shrugged. "She may have said something."

"Wait . . . Was this some sort of plan? Did you use Old Jesus to put the Archdeacon off? Were the children in on it? They should not have been involved in this business, at all!"

Meg looked at him blandly, with her green eyes. "The children had a stake in the outcome of today's 'business', as much as you or I. You should not underestimate their capabilities."

"But a scheme to manipulate an Archdeacon? It could have gone horribly wrong!"

"I don't see how. We told him nothing but the truth. Let him see our family as it is, you could say. What did Bedford speak to you about?"

Edward explained what had transpired, along with his unease. "I did the best I could to keep our family together — here," he said apologetically. "I have bought us some time, I don't know how much."

She took his hand and pulled close to him. "Time is precious. God willing, we will find enough."

Edward realized that it was time he paid more attention to his son's education. Even if the chance of a university education was slim, it was wise to be ready. He would start tutoring Edwin next week — Latin to begin with, Greek later. He would need to find some books; maybe there was a bookseller in Bamford.

Edward Chase's sermons had changed quite a bit over the years. For one thing, he had learned to shorten them, to accommodate his congregation. More than an hour of preaching simply put them to sleep, in almost any kind of weather. Better to serve them the Word in small bites, week by week, he decided. Still, there were days when he pushed the limits of their attention a bit. He tried to include a humorous remark or a funny illustration at the forty-five-minute mark, to sharpen their attention.

Something else crept into his preaching too. It was an article of faith with him that the words he spoke should move the hearts of his hearers — this was the work of the Spirit of God. He prepared each sermon with prayer, trusting that God would give him the words that his people needed to hear. He wrote all the words down, so as not to forget a single one. But more and more often, he found the words speaking to him in unexpected ways while he preached them — not while he prayed over them or wrote them, but unexpectedly, in the middle of an argument. When that happened, he found himself deviating from his text in confusing ways.

At first, he thought perhaps he was suffering some decline in his intellectual faculties. But it was not a lapse of memory — he had the text right in front of him. Perhaps he was losing his mind? No, the digressions and elaborations were not the rantings of a madman — sometimes, he had to admit that the new words were better than the written text. It was almost as if his carefully prepared sermons were being revised by some unseen editor, just as he delivered them. This was problematic. He was all too aware that the wrong phrase or conclusion could be reported to whoever was monitoring his sermons (someone must be, he was certain), and used against him. He resisted every impulse to deviate from his carefully chosen words. But sometimes, and more and more frequently, he felt himself carried away with the power of the message. Ironically, or perhaps perversely, it was at these moments that his congregation seemed most attentive — even Meg would comment afterward that "they heard the Word of the Lord today, Edward."

It was a little humiliating, a little frightening. If it was indeed the "Word of the Lord" that intruded into his sermons, it felt like a mild rebuke of his own best efforts. Did the Spirit of God understand how precarious his position was? Did God care, or would the Spirit place him in the path of danger for reasons known only to God, heedless of the consequences to Edward and his family?

At the back of his mind was the nagging thought that God's chosen path for his life led to some sort of martyrdom. He had been headed that way when he accepted this position in Derwent; was all of this — Meg, his children, the village — just a detour in the proper course of his life? Was God prodding him back to the path prepared for him? Did that path lead to pain and loss?

He ruminated about these things for a good while, before talking them over with Meg. She listened and said nothing for a while. "Come," she said at last," Walk with me."

They walked through the village and up the path to the moors to the east — without much thought, really — it was a daily routine for one or the other of them. David came along, as was his habit. They passed Meg's cottage and went to check on the sheep.

Meg spoke: "I cannot look upon this place, and thee, without a heart full of gratitude. I cannot hold my children, or kiss them goodnight, without thanking God for the life I have. It seems to me that God would not have lavished blessings such as these upon thee and me, if our life here was just a mistake, or — what did you call it? A detour? You once said that this life we have is like the Garden of the Lord — and I agreed with thee. What has happened to change that?"

Edward sighed. "Perhaps there is something in me that expects life to be harsher, more painful. Perhaps it is a weakness of faith. Perhaps it is a lingering guilt — other men have suffered and died because they believe as I do. How is it that I should be happy, and they should be destroyed? Perhaps I feel guilty, somehow. Perhaps I am guilty — guilty of straying from the path that God set before me, to pursue my own comfort and happiness. Perhaps God will have the last word."

"Who is to say that <u>this</u> is not God's path for you? Do you really think that the painful path must always be the right one? Does not Jesus say *"Care not then for the morowe: for the morowe shall care for it selfe: the day hath ynough with his owne griefe.*"?"

"God will certainly have the last word." she continued, "But that is reason for hope, not for dread. Pain and loss there may be, but that is not the last word — unless every sermon I have heard thee preach for these many years is a lie."

Edward looked at her. "You are right. I cannot know what the future holds, whether joy or pain. It is pointless to worry about it. May God grant us courage to face it, whatever it may be." They continued walking in silence for a while. Then they began to speak of more mundane things — the children, the sheep, the foibles of their families and friends.

They arrived, as it happened, at the spot where the Old Prophet had been buried. "If I am to be buried," he said to Meg, "let it be here."

"Where you can see the valley, so that you may see the vision fulfilled? A whole village drowned?"

"I do not think it will be a drowning. A cleansing, more like."

"Cleansing from what?"

"From centuries of fear and pain, from the threats of the outside world, and the treachery of the world within. From all the scars that we inflict upon each other's souls. For peace. For rest. Cleansing."

"If I must bury thee here, then I must also rest beside thee when the time comes."

He nodded. "When the time comes."

1600: Harwich

Ironically, Captain Billy Foxe had become a respectable member of the community in the years since the wreck of the *Egyptian Queen*. He had always been well-known, well-connected, and popular (after a fashion). But his stature increased after he stopped going to sea. His wife Harriet had grown her business to the point that she employed several seamstresses now, even as she bore the old Captain three children, in addition to the six he had adopted. The Foxes were a 'solid' family, now. Church-going folk. The Captain might be seen anywhere about town, stumping about on his wooden leg, in public houses, or the public square. He was always ready to tell a yarn, or a reminiscence from his early days, always ready with a joke, or some tidbit of wisdom. People who claimed to know said that behind that jolly facade was a wealthy businessman — owner of shares in multiple shops and pubs, a landlord with dozens of properties — with a soft spot for old sailors like himself. And there were plenty of old sailors in Harwich, men who claimed to have sailed with Captain Billy Foxe in his glory days. Tales of his daring and courage were told and re-told in Danny Cornwall's *Galleon* of an evening.

Sometimes, the old Captain made an appearance at *The Galleon* in person and told a tale of his own. One tale, which never failed to amaze, was of a sailor of rare courage and prowess, who once captured a French pirate ship single-handedly by leaping aboard her with a cutlass in each hand, and defeating three pirates; a man who had mysterious spiritual powers: — "I saw him stand on the quarterdeck in a storm and calm the waves, just by sheer force of his will," recalled the Captain. "We called him 'Elmo'; Elmo Carpenter was his name."

The Captain's eldest adopted son, Roger, earned a reputation as an able sea captain in his own right — diligent, trustworthy, competent — none of the flamboyance of his stepfather. Investors seemed to prefer his style — he was always employed by someone or another. In time, everyone agreed, he would be the owner of his own ships — a man with a bright future. His brothers found work at sea as well. His sisters married and had children of their own. Billy Foxe's grandchildren were so numerous that he boasted he could crew a good-sized ship with them.

Part 22: End of an Age

1603: London

On March 24, 1603, The church bells rang to announce that the Queen had died in her sleep. She had been ill for most of the previous year — a fact known to her government, but not to the general public, for whom the Queen was as much a symbol, as a person. She was nearly seventy years old — an extraordinary accomplishment, considering that somebody or other had wished her dead almost from the day she was born. She had outlived her suitor and nemesis, King Philip of Spain, all the popes who had placed a price on her head, and most of the Englishmen of her court who had sought to win her favor, and possibly her hand in marriage.

Before noon on that day, her privy council met and arranged to declare her successor — James VI, King of Scotland and son of Mary, Queen of Scots. James had been waiting patiently for the offer for many years. In Scotland, he was known as James VI; in England, he would be James I. He was thirty-seven years old.

His family name was Stuart — his father's family name. He was a cousin of the late queen, a grandchild of Henry VII even as Elizabeth was. So, while historians would regard him as the founder of a new dynasty — one son and four of his grandchildren would sit on the English throne — he was related by blood to all of his predecessors. Patience had served him well — better than he could have anticipated. He left his palace in Edinburgh on April 5th of that year, and journeyed overland to London with a large retinue of retainers and servants, including his wife, two sons, and a daughter — there would be no crisis of succession upon the passing of this king. It took over a month to arrive in London; James and his retinue were feasted and celebrated all along the route. James was surprised by the comparative wealth of his new realm. He is supposed to have remarked that he was "swapping a stony couch for a deep feather bed." It would not take him long to become accustomed to the wealth and comfort of his new realm.

By the time James arrived in London, Elizabeth's funeral was more than a week in the past — no need to publicly mourn the woman who had executed his mother — a clean slate. Crowds greeted his arrival with enthusiasm. His coronation was held more than six weeks later, and he left London promptly thereafter — it was another plague year.

January, 1604: Hampton Court Palace

Cardinal Wolsey's old palace was not yet one hundred years old — an adolescent, really, as palaces go. The Italian architectural style that Wolsey had preferred was a little dated now, reminiscent of the splendor of Papal residences in Italy. No one really objected to the 'papist' feel of the place, except perhaps for some Puritans. King James's decision to meet with the nation's most prominent Puritans in this place was probably his way of sending a message — he would meet with them on his terms and did not have much respect, much less sympathy, for their ideas.

The Puritans presented a petition, signed by as many as 1,000 scholars and ministers — 'ministers of the gospel in this land' — asking James to complete the reformation of the English church. The list was long: They wanted to change the Book of Common Prayer, to eliminate the requirement for wedding rings, to bowing at the name of Jesus, and the practice of Confirmation; they asked that the liturgy be shortened, that preaching be required at any eucharistic service — indeed, they asked that priests unable or unwilling to preach at any service should be forced into retirement, or required to hire a preacher to do that work on their behalf; They urged that midwives no longer be allowed to baptize newborn children — a long-standing practice that hearkened back to Catholicism, and also created a "loophole" for Anabaptists.

They asked that the King take action to ensure that "the Lord's Day (Sunday) be not profaned" (in other words, outlaw certain '"profane" activities on Sundays), but that "the rest upon holy days (be) not so strictly urged" — which would mean fewer or less stringent holidays for businesses and their workers, less drinking and gambling on Sundays, fewer fast days.

They also wanted to restrict the role of secular institutions in matters of church discipline — excommunication would not occur without the explicit consent of a member's pastor (each congregation would determine who was or was not a member).

One of their requests might have been construed as a personal attack on the Hierarchy — they asked that the practice of clergymen receiving multiple incomes from various 'livings' be terminated — bishops, for instance, who had continued to receive income from parishes where they once served, would have to give up that compensation to receive pay for their current office. Many of the attendees at this conference were bishops and officials in just that position.

James did not reject all of these requests outright. Implementation of them would require an Act of Parliament or the active support of the bishops. Whether the bishops would voluntarily take a pay cut remained to be seen. James could be non-committal.

Another request from the Puritans warranted a more explicit response: they proposed to do away with bishops altogether — instituting a system of "presbyteries," similar to the way that the Church of Scotland was organized. Perhaps the Puritans thought that James would welcome the chance to impose a uniform system of church government across all his realms. They were only half right. James, as it happened, was hoping to reform the Church of Scotland along "episcopal" lines — his Scottish presbyters had been a thorn in his side for years, always hindering his right to absolute rule. A system where the king could choose his own church officials made a lot of sense, to him. He told the Puritans so, in no uncertain terms.

Most of the high hopes that the Puritans brought to Hampton Court were crushed. James was a skilled enough politician to throw them a bone or two — so long as the bone did not cost him too much. He agreed that preaching had been neglected in the liturgy and promised to "plant preachers." He also agreed to overturn the prohibition on Puritan conventicles and prophesyings that had been in place since 1593. Let the Puritan scholars convene and chatter where they will, the law was too difficult to enforce with any consistency, in any case. Archbishop Whitgift was not pleased, but his side had won more points than the other; it was political prudence to take his winnings and wait for his next opportunity. The conflict with the Puritan academics would continue, but Whitgift still held the high ground. There were other ways to harass them.

Less attention was given to the impact of suspending the provisions of the Act Against Seditious Sectaries at the level of the local parishes. Unauthorized assemblies might still be accused of plotting against the government, but on the whole, that attention would not fall on laymen who regularly attended their local parish. Separatists would continue to feel the weight of the government's mistrust, but Puritans who were willing to conform would continue to meet, and "prophesy," garnering their strength, increasing in numbers, until the time was ripe.

James had his own religious aims to pursue — he commissioned a new English translation of the Bible, which he intended would be the only authorized version in his kingdom — and thus the only one permitted to be read in a church service. He intended to eliminate the Geneva Bible that the Puritans were so fond of and replace it with a translation more to his liking: His authorized translation would have none of those troublesome and seditious glosses and margin notes. A fresh, new version of the Bible would support his claims to rule by "divine right." His opinions on this topic were explicit:

"The state of monarchy is the supremest thing upon earth; for kings are not only God's lieutenants upon earth, and sit upon God's throne, but even by God himself are called gods. . . . and to God are both souls and body due. And the like power have kings: they make and unmake their subjects, they have power of raising and casting down, of life and of death, judges over all their subjects and in all causes and yet accountable to none but God only. . . ."

Parliament, of course, would have other ideas about accountability. And the Puritans would be in no hurry to give up their Geneva Bibles.

To ensure the outcome that James expected, the committee of forty-seven scholars entrusted with preparing the new translation was selected and led by none other than the esteemed Bishop of London, Richard Bancroft. Before the committees had their first meeting, Archbishop Whitgift died. Richard Bancroft was appointed Archbishop of Canterbury, the highest-ranking cleric in England. He spent the next six years of his reign vigorously attacking the Puritan movement. He died in 1610, a year before the new translation was finished.

The first few years of James's reign saw other portentous achievements: one was a diplomatic triumph. James was determined to end England's war with Spain. Both countries were weary of the decades-long conflict and signed a treaty of peace in 1604. The consequences of this treaty were several: Privateering against Spanish ships was now illegal, but Spanish ports became more open to English trading vessels. The coasts of Virginia and New England, long claimed by England, but never successfully colonized, were now safe from Spanish raids (the French were a different matter), and two colonies were established in 1607 — one in Virginia, at a place they called Jamestown, and the other farther north, in Maine, at a place they call Fort St. George. Of the two, it was the Jamestown colony that survived, though barely.

The second event was less auspicious, though memorable. Assassination plots against James were uncovered almost as soon as his coronation. A handful of Catholic priests, Puritans, and a courtier named Sir Walter Raleigh were found to be guilty and executed. The most memorable plot was uncovered in 1605. Its scale and ambition are breathtaking, even today. The conspirators managed to place thirty-five barrels of gunpowder under the House of Lords. Their apparent intention was to detonate it while the King addressed the opening of Parliament, thus killing the King, most of his privy council (including the Archbishop of Canterbury and other high-ranking church officials), and the members of Parliament. The opening of Parliament had been delayed that year, because of the plague, and the plot was discovered in November of 1605, just days before the King was scheduled to speak. A soldier named 'Guy Fawkes' was arrested at the site, and tortured, until he gave up the names of his co-conspirators. All the major participants in the plot were arrested and executed. The audacity of the plot left a lasting impression; "Guy Fawkes Day" became a national holiday.

Part 23: Epilogue

May 30, 1623: Felsted

In the name of God, amen. The thirtieth day of May in the year of our Lord God 1623" . . . so began the document . . ."I John Porter of Felsted in the county of Essex, yeoman, being frail in body, but of perfect memory . . ."

Well, that was mostly true. The body was certainly frail, but the memory was 'perfect' enough to sign the will. It wasn't that complicated. Sybil was to be the executrix, five shillings and eight pence for Thomas, Francis, and Rose; Sybil would get the rest. Johnny, William, Margaret, and Grace would receive their inheritance when their mother passed. Forty shillings to bury him — a last testament to his legacy, something for his descendants to remember him by. He signed it.

Which left one piece of unfinished business. It was a delicate matter, requiring discretion. In the ordinary course of events, the task should have gone to his eldest son, Francis. But successful as he was, Francis was not a man to keep a secret. Thomas, then? Thomas was ill-suited for a different reason: wouldn't know what to do with it. Which left Johnny and William — this was not a job for a woman. He was tempted to just forget the whole thing, but something told him that could prove dangerous, one day — not just to his legacy, but to Sybil and the rest of his descendants. The government was becoming more desperate for money; the King's long struggle with Parliament over the limits of his authority had produced deadlock after deadlock. People were going to prison for financial irregularities. And this matter was definitely irregular.

Parliament refused to authorize the taxes that James demanded to run his government unless James would concede their traditional rights to power as defined in the Magna Carta. Parliament, now dominated by Puritans, demanded the abolition of the Court of High Commission, their long-time persecutor. There were also rising demands to restrict the issuing of monopolies (a source of revenue for the King that did not require Parliamentary approval) and a great deal of protesting that the 'rights' of Englishmen were being ignored by the King.

The King would not yield. The notion that Parliament had any role in governing the nation, apart from providing revenue through taxation, and enacting such laws as the King thought proper, was completely antithetical to his own well-articulated beliefs about the divine rights of a king. A storm was brewing; it might not break during the King's lifetime (he was fifty-five years old and in poor health), but unless his successor was prepared to be more conciliatory, there was trouble ahead.

Puritan men and women were talking about leaving the country altogether. Some separatists had already established a colony in Massachusetts Bay, just two years earlier, which they called the "Plymouth Plantation." Wealthy investors, like the Rich family, had founded "companies" for the purpose of establishing more colonies in New England and Virginia. They were recruiting colonists for their enterprise. More and more men that John knew were discussing the idea — maybe this was the only way they would ever succeed in purifying the Church of England: by transplanting it to the New World — a fresh start, a chance to build a society of righteousness from the ground up.

John was too old and frail to contemplate such a move. Of all his children, Johnny seemed the most likely to entertain such a notion — his older brothers were doing very well, thank you, in King James's England. Johnny, on the other hand, was a bit of a misfit — like his father, John reflected. He sent for his son, who now lived just outside of Felsted, a few miles to the east, near Braintree. A week later, his namesake son arrived in Felsted.

"I came as soon as I could," he offered. "Is there some family business that needs my attention?'

"In a manner of speaking. It is a private matter; it must remain known only to the two of us."

Johnny cocked his head, raised an eyebrow. "Only the two of us? Can I tell Anna or any of the children?"

"No. Especially not them, nor anyone that you care for."

Johnny gave him a skeptical look. "Is it safe for us to be speaking of it at all then?"

"Not here. We must be sure that no one overhears what I am about to say."

Johnny was intrigued; he wondered if perhaps senility had finally claimed his father's mind. Best to humor him. "The barn, then?"

John shook his head. "Someone might be in the barn or have business there. Better we speak at the far side of the pasture, where we can see in every direction, whether anyone is near enough to hear us."

Johnny nodded. "Now?"

"Now," John agreed. He stood with the help of a cane, and they stepped out the back of the cottage and walked across the pasture behind the barn. There was a low stone wall, separating the pasture from the next field. John sat down on it, with a grunt. "You have heard the stories of my youth, how I was pressed into service on a privateer, and served Her Majesty the Queen in the Caribbean, with Sir Francis Drake."

Johnny nodded. Of course, he had. Other stories, too — seeing the Queen at Tilbury, discovering potatoes. . . they had enthralled him as a child, but seemed far away now. A different sovereign, a different age . . . "The money you made from that voyage became the foundation of your business success, and indeed, the fortunes of our whole family."

John agreed. "So it did. You should know that I have drawn up a will — I do not think this body will carry me through many more winters. Your mother will inherit the bulk of my property. Francis, Thomas, and Rose will receive five shillings, eight pence — the rest of you will share whatever is left when your mother passes."

"This is your secret?"

"Nay, I am telling you now, so that you will not be taken by surprise when the day comes. You are my witness that this is my intention — your younger siblings will believe you, even if they are put out about it."

"I doubt anyone will be put out over five shillings and eight. None of us live in poverty."

John smiled. "Praise God, that is so. The matter I will divulge is ticklish — I reckon that you are better suited than any of your siblings to carry this load, and someone must shoulder it, for the good of our whole family." His voice was lower now.

"Pray tell, what is this deep secret?"

"Something happened on that voyage that I have never told to anyone — not even your mother. Only two other men know about this — after nearly forty years."

Johnny was intrigued. "Go on."

'Under the law of the sea, the sailors aboard a privateer are entitled to claim any items of personal property from the crew of the prize that they please. Neither the investors nor the crown have any claim upon it."

"Yes, I believe that you explained that to us when we were still quite young. There was a treasure aboard that Frenchman you captured, that you divided among the crew of your ship; that was the nest egg that helped you establish your business in Felsted. Also how you paid for old Gordon, I think you said. Something about how the cargo of the prize belonged mostly to the crown and the investors, but the personal things could be kept . . ."

"Do you remember why we decided to give each crewman an equal share?"

"Something about the possibility of a mutiny, if some got more than the others?"

"Aye." John nodded. "There was another treasure that we took; just the three of us. The rest of the crew did not know, could never know."

"To avoid mutiny?"

"To avoid having to share it with them," John nodded. "It was ours by right — it was the personal fortune of the vessel's captain — but under the circumstances, we couldn't have hoped to get it home if the rest of the crew found out about it."

"Unless you offered them an equal share, you mean."

John nodded again. "My share came to more than four hundred pounds sterling."

Johnny's surprise was written all over his face. He lowered his voice and leaned forward. "What happened to that fortune?"

"We secured it when we returned to port. As far as I know, it is still there."

"Have you spent any of it?"

John shook his head. "Not safe. An amount that large would be noticed by the agents of the crown. I do not doubt that they would like to get their hands on it and quite possibly levy a fine on us, in the bargain."

Johnny looked skyward for a moment. "Which is why this is a 'ticklish' matter. If the money cannot be spent, why are you telling me about it?"

"Because when I die, the matter could be exposed if no one claims it. Because I think you are better at keeping a secret than any of your brothers."

"Where is this money now?"

"If it is anywhere, it is in Harwich. In the safekeeping of a moneylender."

"A moneylender? Perhaps he has lent it all to strangers, then?"

"Perhaps. But we need to be sure. That is why I need someone to go there with me and discover the truth. If it is all gone, we have no problem. If it is still on account, we must ensure that ownership is transferred to a living heir — to avoid uncomfortable questions. It is best if the rest of our family remain ignorant of its existence — safer for everyone."

"Safer for everyone except me, that is." Johnny smiled ruefully. He wasn't offended by his father's choice — he *was* better at keeping secrets than his brothers. And out of them all, he was best disposed to hide a pile of money for as long as necessary . . . "Does this mean that we must journey to Harwich, you and I?"

John nodded. "I think that would be wise."

"We will need a reason for this journey."

"I have prepared one. I will say that I wish to travel to Harwich, to see if any of my old comrades are still alive before I go to my reward. You have in-laws in Messing, which is nearer to Harwich than Felsted. We can say that we are visiting your in-laws, the Whites, on our way. No one need know of our real purpose."

He was right, Johnny realized. It seemed strange to be conspiring with his father to hide some secret from all his siblings. Not to mention how strange to discover that this father had been hiding the same secret from all of them, for — how long? — forty years? He looked at his father closely: What other secrets did this man keep?

"If I am going to Messing, Anna will want to come along and bring the children as well — to see their grandparents."

John nodded. "That is a good plan. Anna and the children can stay in Messing for a few days until our business in Harwich is complete."

"A few days?"

"It's at least a full day's journey from Messing to Harwich. If we finish our business in one day, it would still be at least a three-day visit."

They waited to put their plan into motion for nearly a year. In the spring, after the planting was finished, John borrowed a wagon from a friend which had a new-fangled set of leaf springs above the axles, to make the ride smoother. He hitched Oswald, his draft horse, to the wagon. They left early one morning in July, just before the haying. Anna was delighted at the prospect of seeing her parents again — it had been nearly four years since the wedding, and she had three grandchildren to show for it: Thomas, age three, John, age two; and the baby, Sarah.

When they pulled up in front of John and Sybil's cottage, there was a delay while Sybil fussed over her grandchildren and kissed them goodbye. John hobbled out with his cane and tossed an old pack into the back of the wagon. He kissed Sybil goodbye but was impatient to leave: "Let Anna sit up front with the baby, I'll ride with the boys in the back," he said.

They took a roundabout route through Braintree, to take advantage of better roads — less chance of getting bogged down on some muddy lane or other. After a few hours, John traded places with Anna, so that she could nurse the baby. Sitting on the seat next to Johnny, he chuckled. "That's a familiar sight."

"What's a familiar sight?"

"The back end of your horse. Looks just like old Gordon — same dappled grey, same beam. I miss that old stallion, sometimes."

Johnny remembered Gordon, of course. "Gordon was Oswald's grandsire; I reckon that's a family resemblance."

"Aye. Didn't inherit his grandad's face, though. Never saw a horse with old Gordon's face."

"From what I remember of Gordon, that's a blessing," offered Johnny.

"That's as may be. But I never saw a horse with Gordon's heart, either. No load too heavy, no day too long for my old Gordon."

Oswald had at least a good portion of his grandsire's stamina. They arrived at the home of Anna's parents, Robert and Bridget White, by mid-afternoon. Bridget was, of course, delighted to see her grandchildren, delighted as well to learn that they would be staying for a few days. John and Johnny left early the next morning.

They made good progress. The condition of the roads had improved a little since John had traveled them with Gordon, almost forty years before. Harwich had changed, too. The town had spread southward over the years. The old part of town, down toward the waterfront, seemed more familiar. But still, there were new storefronts scattered here and there among the old ones.

John told Johnny to stop in front of a public house. The sign that hung above said *The Galleon.* "Wait here," said John, "I'll get us a room."

"I'll come in with you," said Johnny.

"Nay. You're liable to lose this rig if you leave it on the street. "I'll only be a moment."

Johnny looked around nervously. Apparently, his father had led him into a den of thieves. The people passing up and down the street were certainly strange-looking: not just their clothes, either. Some of these men could only have come from across the sea — hard to tell the honest ones from the thieves, though . . .

John entered the pub, and stood in the relative darkness, waiting for his eyes to adjust. It was smokier than he remembered, for some reason. Then he saw the cause — several men in the place had pipes in their mouths, which they puffed and sucked on — "drinking tobacco," they called it. It had become a popular pastime among the wealthy in recent years; now even men of the lower classes had taken up the practice. Behind the bar was a familiar silhouette. He found his way across the dimly lit room and greeted the man: "Hello, Danny."

The man looked back at him, without recognition. The same tall, lean frame, blue eyes — wait, the man had two eyes, not what he remembered . . . "My name is Martin," said the man, "Martin Cornwall."

John caught his breath. "I mistook you for Danny Cornwall, who used to run this place."

"That would be my father," the man nodded. "Ye're five years too late. Sorry. Is there anything I can get ye?"

"I need a room for tonight, for my son and myself. Also, a stall for my horse, and a secure place for my wagon."

"That can be arranged. Knew my father, did ye?"

"Aye. I boarded here for about three years — but that was nearly forty years ago. I am sorry I missed seeing your father — he was a good friend."

Martin nodded. "A good friend to many. Some of the old crowd still live; you might see them, if you stay awhile. And your name would be?"

"John Porter. I am not here for long. There is one I should like to see, if he still lives. Is Captain Foxe still among us?"

"Do you mean Captain Billy Foxe, or his stepson, Roger?"

"Do you mean Roger Frye? Is he a captain, now? I should be glad to see him again. But Billy Foxe is the man I should most like to speak with. Does he yet live?"

Martin looked hard at John. "Not many know that Roger's family name was Frye. How is it that ye knew him, then?"

"He worked for me, when he was a lad."

"Worked for ye, ye say?" Martin's attention was focused now, trying to figure out exactly who this stranger was.

John realized that giving away too many details of his life in Harwich could put his whole plan in jeopardy. "He helped me find work. I worked in the shipyards. We had an arrangement — your father's idea, actually. But how about Billy Foxe? Is he yet alive?"

"Alive enough — as you can see for yourself, if ye stay for dinner. The Old Captain usually shows himself here in the evening — has a sentimental attachment to the place, I reckon."

"Aye, that would be Captain Foxe. About the room and the stabling — my son is waiting outside, we'd like to take care of the horse and get settled."

Martin nodded and signaled to a servant, who showed them to a stable where Oswald and the wagon could be secured for the night. They walked back to the *Galleon* from there, with their luggage. Once in their room, John opened his pack and took out a wooden case of some sort. Inside were two pistols. While Johnny watched in surprise, he loaded both of them. "Here," he said to Johnny, "tuck one of these inside your belt, at your side — where it will be hidden by your doublet. Like this," he said, as he tucked the other away inside his own clothing. "Time for dinner, I'm thinking."

Johnny was speechless for a moment. "Are these weapons necessary? If they are, you should know I've never fired a pistol like this one."

"Ah." John nodded. Then, "It's simple enough," — he drew the pistol from beneath his doublet — "you cock the hammer like this . . . then point it at someone and pull the trigger. Simple." He gently eased the hammer back and put the gun away.

"You didn't tell me that this trip would involve firearms," Johnny said, reproachfully. "Is there more that you haven't said?"

"I doubt you'll have to use that pistol, but best we be ready. Don't even show the pistol, much less fire it, unless I say so. We'll be meeting some rough-looking characters this evening. Most of them will be our friends, but we have to be ready for anything."

Johnny didn't have time to digest this remark, before John insisted that it was time to leave. They walked downstairs and across the main room to the doorway. When they got to the street, John paused and looked around, as if trying to get his bearings. Then he was off down the street to the left.

Johnny kept up as best he could. The whole situation was unbelievable, he thought to himself. His father's stories about adventure on the high seas seemed to be coming to life — his life. The people they passed, as they walked — especially the men — were strange to Johnny's eyes — men with peculiar hats, or even strips of cloth about their heads, or no hats at all, and no hair, Others with lots of hair — hair in locks or tied behind their heads; men with dark skin, pale skin, brown skin. Clean- shaven men, and bearded men. Men with rings in their ears. It was a confusing kaleidoscope of men, to his eyes . . . "Don't stare so. You'll attract attention — or worse," John muttered. Johnny tried not to stare.

"We'll have dinner here," said John at last. They were in front of another pub, this one called *The Two Kingdoms*, according to the sign outside. Inside, it was dark. Very dark. Most of the customers were dark, as well. It took a moment for their eyes to adjust, and then John pointed to a table at the far side of the room, against a wall. "We'll sit there, for our dinner," he said.

Men looked them over briefly as they crossed the room, then returned to their food and conversations. Johnny caught bits and pieces along the way, enough to realize that multiple languages were being spoken. In some cases, one side of a conversation sounded like English, while the other was — what? Impossible to guess.

When they were seated, a serving maid approached them. Dark-skinned, young. Pretty, thought Johnny. "How is the stew today?" asked John.

"We have an excellent fish stew, Sir," she replied, "Also, a mutton stew, if you prefer."

"I once had a memorable stew in this place, with goat meat in it, I believe. Do you have anything like that?"

The serving maid looked surprised. "Aye, not many English ask for that."

"We'll have two," said John, "also, ale and bread. And I am looking for a man named Benby, who used to own this establishment. Is he here?

"You must mean my father," replied the girl. "He is out just now . . ."

John shook his head. "If your name be Benby, it's more likely that the man I seek is your grandfather — Ndikwe Mbembe? Dick Benby?"

The girl's eyes widened. "You know my grandfather? How long?"

"Nearly forty years ago. Is he still living?"

"Yes sir," she chuckled, "He is very much alive. Would you speak with him?"

"If that is possible, yes."

She whisked away, toward the kitchen. Moments later, she returned with their meal. "Grandfather will be arriving shortly," she said.

John dug into the stew with gusto. "Just as I remember it," he said. It smelled strange to Johnny's nose, but enticing, in an exotic way. There were unfamiliar flavors and texture, blended in ways that he couldn't quite identify . . . but satisfying.

Johnny looked over his father's shoulder to see an old man approach their table. White, curly hair, supported by a cane. The man had dark skin — must be the grandfather, Johnny realized. The man looked at him intently, as if trying to place him . . . "Porter? John Porter?"

At the sound of his voice, John stood and turned to look. "Mr. Benby," he said.

The old man's eyes moved from father to son, then smiled. "He looks a lot like you. Better than you, to tell the truth." He laughed out loud and embraced John.

"This is my son, Johnny," said John. "Come, sit with us!"

Old Benby sat. "I see you know what to order here," he observed with an approving nod. "It was Caroline's recipe. Our daughters make it now, just as their mother once did."

"And your son runs the place?"

"Aye. So he does. I keep an eye on him, but he takes care of the day-to-day business, now."

"And Caroline?"

"Dead. Four years ago." he sighed.

"I did not know her well, but she was a good cook."

"Aye, that she was." He sighed again. Then he straightened himself in his chair. "What brings you to Harwich, Carpenter?"

"Some personal business. I am reaching the end of my time. I wanted to see if any of my old comrades were still living — a farewell, of sorts." Johnny noted that his father said nothing about their real purpose to this man — evidently it was a secret from him, as well.

Benby stared into John's eyes for a moment. "You have journeyed far, Carpenter. I see that you are indeed near the end. You have finished the journey that was your lot, I think. It is well."

John nodded. "It is well, indeed. I have heard that Captain Foxe is still among us. Do you see him often?"

Benby chuckled. "Often enough. We have been partners in a few business ventures over the years. He is old now. Still, a force to be reckoned with."

"And Roger? Is his name Foxe now?"

"Aye. The Captain married Roger's mother and adopted all of her children. After that, they had three more of their own. A tribe of grandchildren, has the Captain. It has mellowed him a bit, they say. Or maybe he's just too preoccupied to get into trouble." John and Benby both laughed out loud.

The two men reminisced for quite some time. Johnny heard enough to conclude that his father's tales of high seas adventure were not exaggerations — the truth was even more shocking than the stories he remembered — and darker, as well: a great deal of the treachery and pain had been left out in the telling.

It was full dark when they left *The Two Kingdoms*. A light rain had begun to fall. "What was that about?" asked Johnny, "the finished journey, and such?"

"Dick Benby is a man of insight and wisdom, that is all."

"Did you fulfill your purpose, in speaking with him?"

"I learned a few important facts, and did so in a place that is out of the public eye. That much of my purpose is fulfilled. It was good to see Old Benby — not so many of us left . . ."

"But this Captain Foxe is still alive. Do you need to speak with him?"

John nodded. "Him more than anyone, if he is still alive."

"Where can we find him?"

"Unless I miss my guess, he will find us."

John was right. When they returned to *The Galleon*, the place was full. A crowd was gathered around a table near the center of the room. An old man sat there, surrounded by younger men. He was white-haired, with a full beard. The beard was mostly white, with a peppering of red. He spotted them almost as soon as they entered and stood to his feet — or rather, foot. There was a wooden peg where one of his feet should have been. "Who's that I spy?" roared the old man. "I'm a liar if it isn't John Porter, the ship's carpenter!"

John smiled and greeted him; "You're no liar, Captain. A rascal perhaps, as some may have said, but no liar!" At this, the Captain glowered for a moment. Then he burst into laughter; the crowd around him roared in laughter also.

John approached the table, embraced the Captain, and introduced Johnny. "Another carpenter, eh?" said Foxe. "I suppose we can find a berth for such a man on my next voyage." He laughed again.

They found seats at the table. "This man," Foxe pointed to John, "was with me when I sailed the Caribbean. He can attest to the truth of my tale." People looked at John with interest.

"Maybe. What tale is that?" asked John.

"Why, the tale of Elmo, of course!"

"Elmo?"

"Elmo Carpenter, we called him. You remember. Served on the *Egyptian Queen*. Captured that Frenchman nearly single handed. A man of rare heroism. "

John nodded. "Aye, so he was. Any idea what happened to him?"

"Died, more than likely. Fighting the Armada. The Spanish never had a chance against an old Sea Dog like Elmo." The Captain continued his yarn. Most of the exploits actually involved the Captain himself. "Elmo" appeared to occupy a supporting role, for the most part. He was a bit of a landlubber at the beginning of the story — "green as they come," was the Captain's assessment — but the Captain trained him to be the ablest of seamen, fearless and cunning . . .

Johnny followed the story but watched his father's face. It was hard to read. He could tell from looking at his father's expressions that some of the details were obvious exaggerations, but a great deal was close to the truth. Oddly, the parts of the story that rang true seemed to be the most uncomfortable ones for his father. He had questions — he would ask them later.

Once the tale was ended, people began to drift away. Soon, it was just the three of them. "I heard ye were lookin' fer me," said Foxe.

"So I was, Captain. I am glad to see you alive and well, after so many years."

"Alive, true enough. Leave it at that." He winced visibly, as he shifted his weight in his chair. "Ye did not come all this way just to see if I was still alive."

"Nay. There is a matter that I wish to settle before I go to my reward. Do you recall our visit with a man named Scarlatti?"

Foxe raised his eyebrows. "Aye. What of it?"

"I left something with him. As far as I know, he may still have it. I am not sure how it would be disposed of in the event of my death. I wish, most of all, to avoid — inconvenience, and unnecessary . . . exposure."

"Anything you left with Scarlatti is safe, you may be sure. I have left things with him from time to time, and he has always proved completely honest and discreet in his dealings."

"You have recovered them?"

"Aye. I have needed his assistance from time to time in my business ventures. All very honest and discreet. Perhaps you should go see him about whatever it is you left with him?"

John nodded. "I shall. I am encouraged by what you have told me."

Then the topic of conversation changed. The two men spoke of their families — children and grandchildren — and their livelihoods. Foxe explained how he had lost his leg, and the *Egyptian Queen*, both on the same day. Roger's career was of interest to John, as well. "He's away at sea now," said Foxe. "Pity ye won't be able to see him — he'll be sorry to have missed ye."

In time, others joined them at the table and John and Johnny excused themselves and went up to bed. The Captain remained where he was, bantering and toasting the night away.

In the morning, John got them up early. "Do we still need the pistols?" asked Johnny.

"Aye, today especially." They had breakfast downstairs, then stepped out into the street. It was foggy. "Ye see what I mean, about the pistols?" said John. He led Johnny down the street toward the harbor, then turned uphill to the right; a few more turns, then stopped in front of a large house. They knocked. John asked for a 'Signor Scarlatti'. They were admitted and shown to a windowless room in the lower levels of the house, with a few chairs and a desk. They were seated and asked to wait.

Moments later, a middle-aged man appeared. "How may I help you, Sirs?"

"I was asking to see Signor Scarlatti," said John.

"Scarlatti is my name. What can I do for you?"

"I was expecting an older man. A man I met here about forty years ago."

Scarlatti's eyebrows rose. "That would be my father then. Sadly, he is deceased. I will help you, if I can."

John looked disappointed. He reached into his doublet. Johnny watched with trepidation. Were they about to rob this man? John pulled out some sort of document. "I received this from your father in exchange for some valuables. I should like to know what, if anything, this paper is worth, and what, if anything, will happen when I die — as far as this paper goes."

Scarlatti took the document, unfolded it, and read it. He rose and went to the door. He spoke to someone out in the hall — in Italian maybe, Johnny couldn't really be sure. Then he returned and sat back down at the desk. "It will be just a few moments," he said. "Please be patient."

Soon, another man appeared with a stack of books — ledgers probably, Johnny guessed — and set them on the desk, then left, closing the door behind him. Scarlatti leafed through the books for several moments, then cleared his throat:

"It says here that you deposited a little over four hundred pounds with us in the year of our Lord 1586. Both your letter and our ledger confirm this. Apparently, none of that money has been withdrawn for thirty-eight years."

"That sounds right," said John with a nod. If I withdraw all the money in my account, I would receive four hundred pounds, is that right?"

"Not exactly," replied Scarlatti. "The current balance in your account comes to . . . let me see . . . eight hundred twelve pounds, fifteen shillings, and four pence."

Johnny sucked in his breath. John appeared to be confused. "How is that?"

Scarlatti cleared his throat again. "Well, someone should have explained to you back in 1586, that we loan out the funds entrusted to us. The money in your account is the same — it has been loaned to governments and merchants many times over, in the last thirty-eight years. Each time, the borrower pays back the loan with some interest, which is added to your account. Some loans are not repaid, and we deduct some for our operating expenses, but the eight hundred twelve pounds is all yours."

"And I can withdraw it today?"

Scarlatti nodded. "I would recommend that you take it in gold coins, rather than silver, because of the weight. And you should take some precautions to protect it from thieves, of course." He cleared his throat again. Johnny was suddenly mindful of the loaded pistol under his doublet.

"If I leave the money where it is, and then die, what becomes of it?"

In that case, your heirs would have to present that letter, along with a copy of your will, to claim the money for themselves."

"And if it is not mentioned in my will?"

Scarlatti sat back in his chair, and nodded. "That would make it a matter for the courts. Very messy. Inconvenient, at the least. Possibly, the government would claim the money."

"So I thought," said John. "Is there a way to transfer ownership to my son, here, without anyone else knowing of it?"

Scarlatti smiled. "There certainly is. I can draw up the paperwork for you today. At the end of it, your son will have a letter just like the one you brought me, that will entitle him, and only him, to the funds in the account. Your letter will be rendered invalid and destroyed."

"That is what I wish to do," said John. "What is the charge for this . . . service?"

"That is a service we will provide free of charge," said Scarlatti, "for a client as reliable as you have been."

An hour or so later they emerged from the house. Johnny had a letter tucked under his doublet. He was a rich man — richer than he could ever imagine. And yet, he couldn't spend any of it — not at least, while his father was alive. He realized his father must have felt the same way — for the last thirty-eight years. John, for his part, seemed a man unburdened. Curious.

They spent the rest of the afternoon walking about the town, as the fog gradually lifted. "The fog is our friend," explained John. "It is possible that no one saw us visiting Signor Scarlatti, but I cannot be certain of that. Better to be seen at numerous places today, so that any particular visit becomes lost in the crowd, so to speak. If anyone is watching us, our disappearances and re-appearances will confuse them about our true purpose."

Johnny nodded. He thought of himself as a prudent and clever fellow, but his father had taken this to a whole new level. What other secrets did this man carry? He had a hunch that not all the secrets involved treasure; something more dangerous, perhaps?

That evening they dined in *The Galleon*. They were just finishing their meal, when a stranger approached their table. "John Porter, ship's carpenter?" came the query. The stranger was taller than average, perhaps fifty years old, a trimmed beard, weathered face.

John looked up, searched the stranger's face, then "Roger? Is it you? I thought you were at sea!"

"I was, until this afternoon," he replied with a smile and a chuckle. "Father told me you might be here."

"Sit, sit," insisted John. "This is my son, Johnny."

Roger took a seat. They exchanged news about their families, and their fortunes. Roger had a wife and four children. He also commanded a merchantman now. "In the Fall and Spring, we trade up and down the Channel," he explained, "Sometimes as far as Norway. Most summers we make a run across the Atlantic to Virginia — tobacco is the big crop there, now, and folks in Amsterdam and London can't get enough of it. Some try their luck in the Spanish ports in America, but you can't always do business there — in spite of the fact that we're at peace with Spain. There's always the threat of the Dunkirkers, and the French, and even the Turks, but we've a nimble ship."

"You have visited the plantation in Virginia? Tell me, how does it prosper? I have heard that they are seeking men to emigrate there."

Roger nodded. "The Merchant Adventurers have promised land to any who will settle there. Any man who pays passage for an indentured worker is entitled to eighty acres — for each one."

"What sort of land is it? Good farmland?"

Roger chuckled. "Most of it is forest, some is swamp. It is fertile enough, once it has been cleared, but you have to do the work yourself or bring over some indentured labor. A few African slaves have been brought in — Ndongans, like Old Dick Benby; they know how to grow tobacco — been doing it for the Portuguese in Angola, you know, since . . . I don't know how long. The thing is, after seven years the indentures are up and the workers are free men. Some of them get enough money to pay for new indentures and claim their own free land. Others will work, but for wages. There's a shortage of workers, so wages are high. After a while a man can save enough to pay for a woman's passage — women are in very short supply in Virginia. Lucky for all concerned, the market for tobacco is strong — men like me can sell everything that the farmers can grow, with enough profit for everyone."

"Who profits the most?"

"Why, the stockholders, of course, like Nathaniel Rich, Merchant Adventurer and Member for Parliament for Harwich! He and his friends are financing all my voyages, plus many others — New England, the Caribbean — lots of projects, lots of new destinations for seamen. Say what you will about King James's foreign policy, peace is better than war for men like me."

You sail only to Virginia, then? I mean, in America?"

"Visited New England last year. They don't produce much cargo, except for furs — and the French and Dutch have that market pretty well sewed up. Stopped in New Amsterdam when I only had half a cargo of Virginia tobacco. Traded some for beaver pelts. Made money on that voyage, but it's not as profitable as tobacco."

"I have heard that things in New England are more . . . orderly." John gave Johnny a look that said *pay attention to this!*

"I suppose that is true. Not so many planters, but they are farmers, with families — orderly villages, churches, constables, and magistrates — a lot like England. Virginia is more turbulent — or more exciting; Many come to Virginia hoping to make a fortune, then return to England. In Plymouth Plantation, the people intend to stay — they wouldn't be welcome back here, anyway."

"Would you say that they are godly people?"

"Compared to the Virginians, they are. It's all a matter of taste, I suppose. Not that much fun in Plymouth Plantation. Are you thinking of emigrating?"

John shook his head. "Nay, I am too old for that, I think. I just wondered what success those separatists had, in their New World."

"Many died in the first few years. They had not figured out how to sustain themselves. But more come each year to join them. The climate of the place is more like Scotland, than England. People must be tough, to survive."

They left early the next morning. It was foggy at first, then less so as they moved inland. "What was that about New England?" Johnny asked.

"I have been thinking about my life, my legacy, my children, my grandchildren," replied John. "When I was a young man, or even your age, I believed that the task of reforming the Church of England would be completed in my lifetime, or certainly in yours. Now I am not so certain. I have watched sovereigns come and go, and archbishops succeed archbishops. I have concluded that things go on the way that they do because so many of our countrymen, from nobleman to peasant, prefer it that way."

"Anyone can see why the nobility resist change — they have nothing to gain. But why do not men such as we, or those poorer still, press for a more just realm?"

"Because it is easier to continue as we are, hoping that some stroke of fortune may increase our prosperity — meager as it may be — hoping that no unforeseen disaster may appear at our doorstep; hoping that our government will not single us out for persecution. I have known men from many classes, and they all resort to the same pattern. Only the most ambitious, or most desperate, are willing to challenge the powers that be. There is always some law or other that they break, and they try to escape the consequences, if they can. The powerful may hope for pardon, the poor can only run and hide . . .

"And we, who would follow God, are supposed to forbear ambition and greed to be content with God's provision. As the apostle says, *'I speake not because of want: for I haue learned in whatsoeuer state I am, therewith to bee content'*. So, we must live righteously, in a world where ambition and greed are rewarded. We have three choices — to accommodate, to revolt, or to flee. We may accommodate ourselves to the ancient order and hope to prosper among our peers, through luck or toil. If that be our choice, we must understand that we are in competition with a host of others who also toil, and hope for luck to smile upon them. Some of these will be more ruthless than we; we are at a disadvantage, if we conduct our affairs righteously . . ."

"But surely God favors us over them, if we conduct our affairs according to his laws?"

"God's favor will preserve us, but not as the world defines favor. *'I returned, and I sawe vnder the sunne that the race is not to the swift, or the battell to the strong, nor yet bread to the wise, nor also riches to men of vnderstanding, neither yet fauour to men of knowledge: but time and chance commeth to them all.'"*

"What other choices do we have?"

"We can seize control of our government by force, to institute a society of justice and establish a godly kingdom."

"We would need an army for that. An army of the righteous."

"Probably so — if indeed there is such a thing as a righteous army. Our Parliament strives mightily with the King's tyranny, but I believe that sooner or later, it must come to war."

"You agree, then, that that is not truly a path forward?"

"There are men who think it might be, but I am not among them."

"What, then, do you propose?"

"To make a new beginning, in a new place. A new world, a new realm, fit for the righteous: *'And I heard another voyce from heauen say, Goe out of her, my people, that ye be not partakers of her sinnes, and that ye receiue not of her plagues. For her sinnes are come vp into heauen, and God hath remembred her iniquities.'"*

"A new England?"

"There is such a place, I have been told."

"But you have said you are too old to make such a move."

"And so I am. But you are not."

"Me? Why should it be me?"

"You have money, for one thing — enough to pay your whole family's passage to the new world. You dare not spend it here without risking considerable inconvenience, or even peril — unless you leave the country altogether so that no one can question how you came by it. Also, you know some of the Merchant Adventurers who are looking for colonists — your reputation with them will stand you in good stead."

"Those are practical considerations. None of them make me eager to leave England."

"Nay. But of all your brothers, you are the one most likely to go, I think."

"How so?"

"Francis is prosperous and well satisfied with his lot in life. Nothing short of the apocalypse could persuade him to leave. He has made his way in the world by careful calculation and cold-eyed assessment of risk.

Thomas likes to take risks, but his luck is not that good — he is fortunate to be married to a prudent woman who can rein in his enthusiasm: on his own, he might rush carelessly into a disaster."

Johnny had to concede that his father's assessment of his older brothers was accurate. He nodded. "But I am prosperous as well, and my Anna is also a prudent woman."

John agreed. "Your Anna is very attached to her sister, Mary. And Mary is wed to Joseph Loomis, your sometime business partner. You know that Mary and Anna's father has separatist sympathies. I have heard that Joseph Loomis has been talking about moving to America, for some time now."

"Many people talk of such things, hardly any take it farther than that."

"Aye, but your brother in-law seems to be taking it further than most."

"How do you know this?"

"People talk. People ask questions. Joseph Loomis's questions seem to involve very practical matters, such as the business climate, the cost of labor, the cost of shipping textiles to the colonies, the cost of land."

"Based on what Roger told us, Virginia sounds like a place that would not suit him — everyone is preoccupied with growing tobacco."

"He wouldn't have to go to Virginia."

"Plymouth Plantation sounds worse — they're barely surviving, if Roger is to believed."

John nodded. "The colonists in Massachusetts are few in number, and poorly financed. A more ambitious effort is being planned — more ships, more people, more food. Men of skill are being recruited; not just farmers, but craftsmen — including carpenters, like yourself. The intent is to send over thousands, not mere hundreds."

"But that would require many ships, careful preparation unlike anything that has been attempted!"

John nodded. "True enough. The preparations are underway. The Merchant Adventurers are raising large sums of money. If Joseph Loomis goes, his wife Mary will go with him; If she goes, your Anna will want to go as well. And now you have the means to make that happen when the time comes . . . which is why I have put my money on you, so to speak."

"More than a figure of speech then," said Johnny, with a crooked smile. "Time will tell. But you are right about one thing: if Mary and Joseph Loomis go, Anna will be longing to go as well."

Apparently, John had nothing more to say on the topic. They rode in silence for a while, then Johnny asked: "Those stories about Elmo Carpenter — are they true?"

John chuckled. "Most of what you heard is true, I suppose. The telling of the tale is always better than the actual experience."

"Did you know Elmo? Do you remember him?"

"I knew him as well as anyone, I reckon. I would not have thought him the stuff of legend when he first came aboard, but some men are changed by the sea — it calls things out of them that no one suspects are lying there. Elmo was that sort of man."

"That tale about him boarding a pirate ship all by himself, with nothing but two cutlasses, and capturing the pirate captain — surely that's an exaggeration?"

John thought for a moment. "Elmo would not have told the story that way, but no one can control the stories that others tell about them — it's the sort of tale that men like to hear, so that is the way it's told, I suppose. The pirate captain was indeed captured, along with his ship."

"And where were you while this was going on?"

"I? I was doing my best just to survive. Some of my friends died that day."

"Did you fight? Did you kill?"

"Aye, I fought and killed. But that is a matter that I do not speak of. It is not suitable for a tale told in a public house."

He was silent for a long time, after that. Johnny tried to engage him with more questions, but he did not reply. Johnny remembered the pistol, still at his side under his doublet. Perhaps a man had been killed with that very pistol. Perhaps his father had pulled the trigger. It seemed indecent to ask, but he felt the weight of it, all the way back to Messing.

April, 1625: Felsted

King James died on March 27, 1625, and was succeeded by his son, Charles. It was another plague year. Charles and the royal court were compelled to leave London for a time, until the ferocity of the outbreak abated somewhat.

This time, the pestilence visited Felsted. Among the afflicted was old John Porter. In April, just as the planting was in full swing, he complained of a headache. This was followed by fever, then by coughing and chest pain. Sybil insisted on caring for him herself — she forbade her children from entering the house where he lay. A doctor was summoned but could do nothing other than recommend bleeding him. In two days, he was dead. They buried him quickly, without the funeral that his will had specified. Some argued that a plague victim should not be buried in the churchyard at all — isolation was believed to be the best way to contain the infection — but his reputation in the village stood so high that his family's wishes prevailed. His sons and daughters gathered for the reading of his will; the terms were not contested.

Johnny, who from now on would be called simply "John," invited his mother to come live with his family. After a few months, Sybil declared that she would prefer to spend the years of her widowhood in Little Baddow, where her brothers, sisters, nieces, and nephews still lived. There was some consternation over this among her own children, but Sybil was nothing if not strong-minded. It fell to John, her son, to help her move her few possessions. In September he loaded a wagon with her things and drove her to Little Baddow. Anna stayed home with the new baby, also named Anna, who had not been weaned yet. John realized that his father's death had been a hard blow for his mother. She was adrift, he decided, after so many years with one man.

"We knew joy and hardship," she confided to him, "as much as my heart could hold. I shall not live much longer, now he is gone. But I am at peace with that. Let me return to the place of my birth. *'I haue fought a good fight, and haue finished my course: I haue kept the faith. For hence foorth is laide vp for me the crowne of righteousnesse, which the Lord the righteous iudge shall giue me at that day'* . . . I should like to be in the place where I first met him, to smell the place again, to wait there for the day I may rejoin him." She did not have to wait long; on November 26th of that year, she died. The plague had reached Little Baddow, too.

Sybil was buried there in the churchyard of St. Mary's — her brother's long service to the parish was sufficient to overcome any objections. The plague did not subside until the following year — by that time more than thirty-five thousand were dead in London alone. Elsewhere, who can say? Some villages were hit very hard, others seem to have been passed by altogether. The records are incomplete.

For John Porter and the other survivors, it was one more reminder of the brevity of life and one more sign that God's judgment was imminent. The idea of leaving "Babylon" began to make more sense.

1631: Little Baddow

Thomas Hooker was served with a summons from the Court of High Commission in the evening, at his home. It came as a bit of a surprise, but apparently, the Court wanted to avoid unnecessary publicity. The Court's interest in Hooker was no mystery, but the timing seemed odd; Hooker had given up his position as curate and lecturer at St. Mary's Church in Chelmsford more than a year ago and sought the obscurity of a small village some miles away. He was employed as a schoolmaster in Little Baddow. The obscurity was not enough to avoid the attention of the Court, as it turned out.

The Court of High Commission had received a new infusion of power and purpose, with the rise of the new Bishop of London, William Laud. Laud's theological ideas were distinctly different from his predecessors, more aligned with the King's notions of divine right to rule his kingdom and his church as he saw fit. Laud was opposed by many in the church hierarchy, for the weakness of his Calvinist commitment. For Puritans and other dissenters, the "softening" of his theology meant no relief at all — he was more vigorous than his predecessors in persecuting them. In particular, he pursued a policy of suppressing lecturers, preachers, and conventicles — the lifeblood of the Puritan movement.

Thomas Hooker was one such lecturer — influential, even celebrated for his preaching and writing. He continued this work at Little Baddow, far from the eyes of the government — or so he supposed.

He supposed wrong. This was partly because his fame and influence were too great for the government to ignore — people traveled from significant distances to Little Baddow, just to hear him speak.

Hooker was jailed until bail was raised for his release. There was no doubt about the outcome of his impending trial; he fled to Holland, as so many Puritan leaders had done for years. This time, circumstances were different. There was now another option for men like him: a land on a distant shore, where men who believed as he did could preach without fear of interference from bishops, or courts.

Among those people who had traveled to Little Baddow to hear what Thomas Hooker had to say were John Porter, his wife Anna, and their seven children. Their reasons for making such a journey had as much to do with visiting their cousins in Little Baddow as it did with Hooker's appeal, but once there, they were eager to hear what he had to say.

John's brother-in-law, Joseph Loomis, and his wife Mary (Anna's sister) also followed Thomas Hooker's teaching with interest. Circumstances in England were becoming steadily more difficult for families like the Loomises and the Porters. The long struggle between King and Parliament that had dominated England during the reign of King James only intensified during the reign of his son Charles. Parliament demanded changes in policy from the King and withheld authorizing taxes until he agreed to cooperate. Charles, raised to believe that his rule should be absolute, was unwilling to compromise. He tried to cut expenses: signed treaties to end wars, reduced the size of his staff, declared martial law, so that soldiers and sailors could be housed in private residences — whether they were welcome or not. When the expense reductions were not enough, he borrowed money. When his creditworthiness deteriorated to the point that banks and foreign governments would loan him no more, he instituted a policy of "forced loans," by which Englishmen were required to "loan" money from their personal wealth to the King. Persons refusing to make such "loans" were imprisoned, until they could come up with the money — without trial. The loans were required of the wealthy, but also (in lesser amounts) from yeoman families like the Porters. John reflected that it was fortunate so much of his wealth was hidden from the government's sight, else the "loan" required would have been much larger (maybe even one hundred percent of his balance at the bank, considering how he came by it). The Loomis family liked it no better.

Charles also was able to increase tariffs and duties on imported goods, and raise "ship money" — a traditional means of financing the Royal Navy — though in this case, the funds went to cover the expenses of the Royal Household. Eventually, all these measures proved inadequate, and Charles was forced to call a new Parliament.

Parliament was not in a conciliatory mood. The King was denounced as a "Tyrant." They did agree to authorize new taxes, but on condition that Charles agree to a "Petition of Right," a document that declared the "forced loans', imprisonment without trial, and the billeting of soldiers and sailors in private homes to be unlawful (except in time of war). It also reaffirmed that taxation was exclusively the right of Parliament. Charles was forced to sign the petition into law — then promptly dissolved Parliament and began looking for new sources of revenue.

It was apparent, by now, that King Charles intended to rule the country without the involvement of Parliament if he could. He did this by further reducing his government's expenses (abandoning his plans for war, for instance), and finding new sources of revenue that did not require Parliament's approval. These measures alone would not have had much immediate impact on the lives of yeomen families, but the excises on imported goods made some things more expensive, and the "forced loans" would not be repaid anytime soon. More problematic was the change in attitude. Charles surrounded himself with advisors who shared his views on absolute rule. Notable among them was William Laud, soon to be Archbishop of Canterbury. If the King could rule England without regard to Parliament, it followed that he could rule the church in the same way, through his Archbishop and the rest of the hierarchy. Laud was determined to impose discipline and uniformity on the Church of England. Thomas Hooker's arrest was just one example of his policy. "Tyranny" was as likely to be used to describe Laud's rule, as Charles'. The chance for compromise slipped away, year by year. Many people began to believe that the issue would be decided by violence and bloodshed. "A storm is brewing," said John Porter, "we must find shelter."

The Porter family had continued to grow. This time a daughter, whom they christened Rebecca. There were now seven children in the family. "A number of completion," said John.

"How's that?" Anna asked.

"The Lord rested on the seventh day when he made the world. Seven days were enough for him, I have labored long; I must rest from my labors." He smiled.

Anna nodded. "'*And God sawe all that he had made, and loe, it was very good . . .and the seuenth day he rested from al his worke, which he had made.*' I think you have overlooked my labors," she said. "For you, it was the work of an evening. For me, it was nine months at a time."

"I did not overlook it. But that is no fault of mine. Whether children come from my labors and yours is a matter that God decides, is it not?"

"God or time," she said. "Our efforts also play a part."

"Efforts?"

"Aye. I do not think that the children come without our efforts."

"What can we do about it?"

"It's less about doing, than about forbearing."

"Forbearing?"

"Aye, for a season. Until the little one is weaned."

"A day of rest, then?"

"More than a day, I think. "

"I shall pray on it."

In 1633, Thomas Hooker slipped back into England briefly to liquidate some assets he had left behind. Then he was gone again, before the authorities could apprehend him. He appeared in Massachusetts later that year in the company of about two hundred other emigrants. He was called to pastor a church there, in a new settlement known today as Cambridge. From there, a year later, he led a band of a hundred or so like-minded colonists farther to the west, where they established a new colony, which they called Connecticut. The town they founded was named Hartford. Soon they would be joined by more English emigrants. Soon they would find themselves at war with the people who had lived in that place for millennia and really had not invited any Englishmen to settle among them.

1631: Derwent

Edward and Margaret Chase lived long enough to see their children grow to adulthood and prosper. Unlikely as it seemed, Edwin and his younger brother both attended Cambridge University and graduated; Charles Bedford was a man of his word if nothing else. Edward's polemical writings against the separatists were never published, but many of his arguments were incorporated into documents attributed to other writers. It was hard to say if his contributions made any difference in the end. After the death of Archbishop Bancroft, the struggle between the Puritans and the Hierarchy changed. The controversy became less about the governance of the Church, and more about governance of the Kingdom. Edward's predictions were being fulfilled in his own lifetime. Parliament was now the battleground in the long struggle to complete the reformation.

A village like Derwent was no place for educated young men, so their sons found employment in the wider world beyond. One was ordained a priest, another became a successful businessman in Liverpool, a third became a schoolmaster. Their daughters married and had families of their own. The youngest daughter married a local farmer, up the valley from the village. The other two married men who dwelt in larger, more distant towns. Edward and Meg had so many grandchildren that they could scarcely remember all their names, but they saw most of them no more often than once a year, or even less. The exception was the children of their youngest daughter, whom they saw every Sunday in church.

When Edward became too old to fulfill his duties as vicar, he was replaced by a younger man. Edward and Meg moved out of the rectory and into the cottage up above the valley, on the moor. There they lived for a number of years, receiving visitors occasionally, keeping sheep. Meg was still called upon to tend the sick or serve as midwife; Edward was occasionally asked to preach at the parish church, or fill in at the parish school if needed.

Meg was the first to finish her race. She was late for dinner one evening. Edward went to look for her and found her lying in a pasture, eyes closed, on her back, facing the sun with a smile frozen on her lips. He summoned the priest, and all the Moorcroft relatives. The priest would have buried her in the churchyard, but the Moorcrofts, informed of her wishes, overrode him. She was buried where she had wished — near the grave of the Old Prophet, overlooking the valley. Her intuition about the prophecy was confirmed, Edward thought. The road to Bamford had been improved, and more outsiders came flowing in every year. More miners, more tradesmen, more merchants. Soon the old ways would be buried by a flood of new customs, new beliefs, new traditions.

Edward lived another year, alone in the cottage, with the ravens, his dog, and his sheep — a reluctant shepherd to the end. His daughter and son-in-law were in the habit of checking in on him every day. One morning, he did not answer the knock at the door. They found him inside — he had died in his sleep. When they cleared out his things, they found something curious tucked into his pillowcase — a small packet, or sachet, with the faint scent of lavender. "Sentimental, I suppose," said his daughter, "- it must have reminded him of Mum."

Edward was buried next to Meg, near the edge overlooking the village. No one remembers exactly where they were laid; the moors may know, but they do not speak. But you can visit the place, if it please you.

In 1942, the British Government (a republic with a constitutional monarch, by then) built a dam on the river, to create a reservoir. The residents of Derwent were evacuated before the rising waters covered the village entirely. The moorlands and the valley are now part of a National Park. People climb up and across the moors for recreation. No one remembers the Old Prophet, but that does not seem to make the view less enjoyable.

1638: A Distant Shore

London had rebounded from the last severe outbreak of the plague. The thirty-five thousand or so lost in 1625, and a lesser number, in 1636 and 1637, had been replaced, and then some — the census of 1631 recorded more than 131,000 Londoners; by now there were at least 150,000 of them.

The city now sprawled beyond its ancient walls, despite the government's attempt to regulate the expansion. To the east, downriver from London Bridge, the shipyards and docks expanded, as the demand for imported goods steadily increased.

It was here that the Porter and Loomis families gathered, waiting to board the ships that would take them to their new home. Their belongings — what they still had — were loaded on handcarts and barrows, packed with bundles of clothing, and a few items of furniture. Most of what they would need in their new home — and the home itself — would have to be purchased, or more likely built at their destination. It had taken them two years to get this far. They had planned to join Thomas Hooker's community in Massachusetts — until word came that Hooker had led a hundred or so immigrants to a new town south and west of Boston. While they waited for news of this new town, called Hartford, the plague returned to London. It was unsafe to travel to a place that so many were fleeing. Their plans had to be postponed in 1636. 1637 was a plague year, too. But here they were, at last, ready to abandon "Babylon" for a Land of Promise.

The colony in Massachusetts Bay was thriving — a steady stream of ships sailed back and forth to America, with letters that described the conditions there. The planning had paid dividends. The colonists were well supplied with food and other necessities during the first few years; before long, they grew enough food to feed themselves. Mortality was low, and lessons learned by the Plymouth colony were applied. The "great corn" cultivated by the native peoples of the place produced much more grain on an acre of land than the crops that the English were accustomed to — so they adjusted; they planted less wheat, oats, and barley, and learned to make bread from cornmeal.

John and Anna Porter now had five sons and five daughters — the youngest was still an infant in her mother's arms. Seven was not the number of completion after all. Maybe ten would be. The older boys were fascinated by all the activity at the docks — the ships, the crews, the hustling stevedores. It was all that John and Anna could do, to keep them from wandering off somewhere.

"What is it we're looking for?"

"Our ship. The *Susan and Ellen*."

"Strange name for a ship."

John cocked his head. "I had two aunts named Susan and Ellen. Perhaps it is a favorable sign from God."

"Papa, tell me again where we are going," said Rose, his five-year-old daughter.

"We are going to New England."

"On a boat like these?"

"Aye. On a boat like these."

"James says it is far away, so far that I cannot see it from here. Maybe I could see it if you put me on your shoulders."

Her father laughed and placed her on his shoulders. "There," he said. "What do you see?"

"It all looks like Old England from here. Lots of boats in the water. Which way will we be traveling?"

"Well, first we have to go down the river to the Channel," he pointed to his left, "then we will turn south, and then we will turn west across the ocean."

"It seems a long way."

"Aye, it is. A long, long way."

Thomas and John, his eldest sons, returned from their explorations. "Found the *Susan and Ellen*," Thomas reported, "a hundred paces or so that way." Thomas pointed down the river.

"Tell the Loomises that you have found it," said John, "Then come straight back here and help us move our things."

They gathered beside the *Susan and Ellen*, with the Loomises and several other families. As time passed, more joined them, until more than one hundred emigrants had assembled. The loading of all their possessions took a while. Then they boarded, up a plank onto the deck. Their quarters would be below — crowded and stinking, before their voyage was over. Better to stay on deck as much as possible. In the evening, with the tide, their ship raised anchor and moved down the river, toward the sea.

"Say goodbye to England," John said, looking shoreward, "we are bound for a new land, on a distant shore. However perilous the journey, or our destination, we shall be far away when the storm breaks here. God willing, it shall not reach us in our new home."

"Amen," said Anna and the children.

Historical Note:

Some of the characters in this book are "real"; that is, they are recognizable as people who actually lived and breathed through the events that I have placed them in. In some cases, they left behind written traces of themselves, which offer hints about how they would speak or behave, in other cases, we have records of what their contemporaries thought of them, but their words and actions in this book are largely imaginary. The very famous may have had their portraits drawn or painted during their lifetimes, but it is difficult to tell how much artistic license was employed during their creation. Still, that's about as "real" a presence as any of us have, once we are deceased.

The Porter and Loomis families are also "real," in the sense that there are dated historical documents that include their names — baptisms, marriages, wills, and burials. The record says that they emigrated to Connecticut, in or about 1638, and became founding families in the town of Windsor, Connecticut. Their descendants and relations are scattered all over the United States, and indeed the world today. Little is known of them, apart from their names, so portrayals of their words or their personalities in this book are completely a product of my imagination.

Many of the minor characters are completely imaginary. They are no less important to the story, for that — this is a work of fiction. Use your imagination, as I have. Enjoy the story.

About the Author

A.L. Porter is a child of the 50's, a "boomer," etc. and a history buff and storyteller who especially likes stories that explain something about who we are and how we got here. His writing incorporates his love of history with his family genealogy - his ancestors actually lived through the events of this book.